C000061123

Where Time Winds Blow

Welcome to a planet where eerie time displacements, like winds, can dump alien artefacts from the past and future into now, or sweep things away from now into anywhen. Welcome to a world that attracts both scientists and fortune hunters, rummaging among the strangenesses, risking oblivion, to solve the mysteries of the time winds.

Earthwind

On the planet Aeran, the original colonists have undergone a drastic change: under the influence of some strange psychic force they have forgotten their identity and created a new culture – an exact reconstruction of the Stone Age society that flourished in Ireland 6,000 years ago. Has some strange racial memory been awakened? Or are both cultures the product of a social blueprint implanted throughout the cosmos by a long-vanished race?

In the Valley of the Statues and Other Stories

The stories in Robert Holdstock's first collection amply demonstrate his interest in the creative of myth against the exotic alien landscapes of far future and past, ranging in time from the prehistoric to Europe in the 40th millennium AD, and from the landscapes of post-War England to the full canvas of the inhabited galaxy.

Also by Robert Holdstock

Mythago Wood

Mythago Wood (1984)
Lavondyss (1988)
The Bone Forest (1991)
The Hollowing (1992)
Merlin's Wood (1994)
Gate of Ivory, Gate of Horn (1997)
Avilion (2009)

The Merlin Codex

Celtika (2001)
The Iron Grail (2002)
The Broken Kings (2006)

Novels

Eye Among the Blind (1976)
Earthwind (1977)
Necromancer (1978)
Where Time Winds Blow (1981)
The Emerald Forest (1985)
Ancient Echoes (1986)
The Fetch (1991)

Night Hunter (writing as Robert Faulcon)

The Stalking (1983)
The Talisman (1983)
The Ghost Dance (1983)
The Shrine (1984)
The Hexing (1984)
The Labyrinth (1987)

Raven (as Richard Kirk, with Angus Wells)

Swordsmistress of Chaos (1978)
A Time of Ghosts (1978)
The Frozen God (1978)
Lords of the Shadows (1979)
A Time of Dying (1979)

Writing as Robert Black

Legend of the Werewolf (1976)
The Satanists (1977)

Berserker Trilogy (writing as Chris Carlsen)

Shadow of the Wolf (1977)
The Bull Chief (1977)
The Horned Warrior (1979)

Collections

In the Valley of the Statues and
  Other Stories (1982)

Robert Holdstock

SF GATEWAY OMNIBUS

WHERE TIME WINDS BLOW
EARTHWIND
IN THE VALLEY OF THE STATUES
AND OTHER STORIES

GOLLANCZ

LONDON

This omnibus copyright © Robert Holdstock 2013
Where Time Winds Blow copyright © Robert Holdstock 1981
Earthwind copyright © Robert Holdstock 1977
In the Valley of the Statues and Other Stories copyright © Robert Holdstock 1982

All rights reserved

The right of Robert Holdstock to be identified as the author
of this work has been asserted by him in accordance with the
Copyright, Designs and Patents Act 1988.

First published in Great Britain in 2013 by
Gollancz
An imprint of the Orion Publishing Group
Orion House, 5 Upper St Martin's Lane,
London, WC2H 9EA

An Hachette UK Company

A CIP catalogue record for this book is
available from the British Library

ISBN 978 0 575 11880 5

1 3 5 7 9 10 8 6 4 2

Typeset by Jouve (UK), Milton Keynes

Printed and bound by CPI Group (UK) Ltd, Croydon, CR0 4YY

The Orion Publishing Group's policy is to use papers
that are natural, renewable and recyclable products and
made from wood grown in sustainable forests. The logging
and manufacturing processes are expected to conform to
the environmental regulations of the country of origin.

www.orionbooks.co.uk
www.gollancz.co.uk

CONTENTS

ENTER THE SF GATEWAY . . .

Towards the end of 2011, in conjunction with the celebration of fifty years of coherent, continuous science fiction and fantasy publishing, Gollancz launched the SF Gateway.

Over a decade after launching the landmark SF Masterworks series, we realised that the realities of commercial publishing are such that even the Masterworks could only ever scratch the surface of an author's career. Vast troves of classic SF & Fantasy were almost certainly destined never again to see print. Until very recently, this meant that anyone interested in reading any of those books would have been confined to scouring second-hand bookshops. The advent of digital publishing changed that paradigm for ever.

Embracing the future even as we honour the past, Gollancz launched the SF Gateway with a view to utilising the technology that now exists to make available, for the first time, the entire backlists of an incredibly wide range of classic and modern SF and fantasy authors. Our plan, at its simplest, was – and still is! – to use this technology to build on the success of the SF and Fantasy Masterworks series and to go even further.

The SF Gateway was designed to be the new home of classic Science Fiction & Fantasy – the most comprehensive electronic library of classic SFF titles ever assembled. The programme has been extremely well received and we've been very happy with the results. So happy, in fact, that we've decided to complete the circle and return a selection of our titles to print, in these omnibus editions.

We hope you enjoy this selection. And we hope that you'll want to explore more of the classic SF and fantasy we have available. These are wonderful books you're holding in your hand, but you'll find much, much more ... through the SF Gateway.

www.sfgateway.com

INTRODUCTION
from The Encyclopedia of Science Fiction

Robert Holdstock (1948–2009) was a British author, with an MSc in medical zoology from the London School of Hygiene and Tropical Medicine. He spent 1971–1974 in medical research before becoming a full-time writer. He published his first short story, 'Pauper's Plot' for New Worlds in 1968. He went on to write a number of pieces of short fiction before concentrating for most of his career on novels. Among the more notable stories of this period are the novelettes 'Travellers', a Time-Travel tale, and 'The Time Beyond Age: A Journey'; some others are collected in *In the Valley of the Statues* (1982) (see below). After the mid-1970s his writing broke into two superficially incompatible categories.

Under the House Names Ken Blake and Richard Kirk, and as Robert Black, Chris Carlsen, Steven Eisler and notably as Robert Faulcon, he published at least twenty novels, novelizations and works of popular sf 'nonfiction' (these under his own name), almost all of them commercial efforts and most of them infused with a black intensity of action that gave even clichéd Sword-And-Sorcery plots something of a mythic intonation. Among the most interesting of these titles was the quasi-fictional *Tour of the Universe: The Journey of a Lifetime: The Recorded Diaries of Leio Scott and Caroline Luranski* (1980) with Malcolm Edwards, which describes a 26th century tour of the local galaxy.

At the same time, under his own name, Holdstock began to publish sf novels in which he accommodated the mythologizing of his dark fantasies within the frame of 'normal' sf worlds. For example in *Eye Among the Blind* (1976) (in which he explores the interplay between Aliens and alienation), *Earthwind* (1977) and *Where Time Winds Blow* (1981) (see below). The later sf approaches fantasy in intensity.

With the publication of *Mythago Wood* (1984), Holdstock's two writing directions suddenly and fruitfully converged in a tale whose elaborate proprieties of rationale are driven by narrative energies and an exuberance of language previously most evident, crudely, in his Berserker novels, written as Chris Carlsen. Much expanded from his short 1981 fantasy with the same title, *Mythago Wood* is a central contribution to late 20th-century fantasy and is dense with fantasy tropes. It is fantasy rather than sf, perhaps because its cognitive premise – that it is possible to construct an 'engine' through which one might literally conceive racial archetypes – is much easier to convey in fantasy terms. The frame of the Mythago Cycle, which this tale initiates, is obdurately rational in tone, and the 'mythagos' discovered – and transmuted – by the contemporary protagonist are appropriate expressions of what might be called the unconscious tale of the race: they are that tale made animate, and each mythago bears a name or names – and enacts the nature – of those archetypes from whom flow the permutations of that tale. The wood from which they come – like the interior lands for which the protagonists of much British fantasy long – is a classic Little Big heartwood, huger inside than out, and more and more ancient the further one penetrates inwards. In describing this world Holdstock engages in language of a metaphoric density rarely encountered in marketable fiction, and through his language articulates a hard knotty pain of desiderium so many English people feel for an Ur-land that never existed but which seems still to pulse through what remains of the astonishingly dense world of Britain. *Mythago Wood* won the 1986 World Fantasy Award.

The next volume in the Mythago Cycle, *Lavondyss: Journey to an Unknown Region* (1988), only increases the intensity of the Chymical Marriage between rational discourse and desiderium or *Sehnsucht* (a term C. S. Lewis employed to describe the melancholy longing for 'something that has never actually appeared in our experience', and by which he meant to designate the impulse behind certain kinds of fantasy). The longing of the protagonists of *Lavondyss* to enter the 'unknown region' – Holdstock's term here for the wood within (and prior to) the world – is absolute, and it gives the book much of its obdurate potency. 'Toward the Unknown Region' (1906) is a choral work by Ralph Vaughan Williams (1872–1958), a composer whose evocations of a longed-for Britain are refreshingly muscular; Holdstock's citing of this piece of music is therefore heavily loaded (Vaughan Williams himself appears in the novel); and the obdurate *Sehnsucht* of his music conveys to most listeners what Holdstock at his best conveys: a sense that the Matter of Britain is a Story that can be told.

The title novella in *The Bone Forest* (1991), and the title novel in *Merlin's Wood: Or, The Vision of Magic* (1994), continue the Mythago Cycle in modes closer to conventional fantasy, as do *The Hollowing* (1993) and *Gate of Ivory, Gate of Horn* (1997). Holdstock's further singletons are also fantasy, as is the Merlin Codex sequence. Comprising *Celtika* (2001), *The Iron Grail* (2002) and *The Broken Kings* (2006), the Merlin Codex is a complex and hauntingly surreal reworking of some central motifs from the Mythago Wood tales into a rendering of European mythology as a whole into a kind of temporal labyrinth, with lines of story interweaving through time. The central drama whose ramifications echo through the worlds of the series is the conflict between Jason and Medea, underlier figures who shape the complex epic.

The central character, an immortal Merlin, serves as both victim and guide, whose quest for a primordial riven family – Jason's abducted children – knits the sequence together.

In his last completed book, *Avilion* (2009), Holdstock returns directly to the central knot of story of *Mythago Wood* and *Lavondyss*, continuing the Huxley family tale through deaths and resurrections that amount in the end to a grave-song for England, though the wood continues.

Of the novels reprinted here, *Earthwind* utters slow but moving hints of the powers of a 'chthonic' atavism pulsing deep in the blood of all that lives universe-wide. It is a portrait of a planet colonised by humans, who can scarcely comprehend the multifaceted nature of a world they were not born to. *Where Time Winds Blow*, the other novel in this volume, is much more complex. On a world riven by literal winds, a conflicted cast is caught up in an ornate narrative which gradually reveals to them some of the plumbings of the structure of time, through which time winds blow, depositing valuable artefacts, which are coveted by all. The stories assembled in *In the Valley of the Statues*, which is the final volume presented here, includes not only the brilliant novella that became *Mythago Wood*, but also a trove of stories whose techniques and topics range across Holdstock's entire career to that point. They are stopping points in the Holdstock geography, they are good places for us to stop.

For a more detailed version of the above, see Robert Holdstock's author entry in *The Encyclopedia of Science Fiction*: http://sf-encyclopedia.com/entry/holdstock_robert_p

Some terms above are capitalised when they would not normally be so rendered; this indicates that the terms represent discrete entries in *The Encyclopedia of Science Fiction*.

WHERE TIME WINDS BLOW

To Fellow Voyagers:

Chris, Garry, Chris, Chris and Andrew
T'ung Jên!

PART ONE

Where Time Winds Blow

CHAPTER ONE

Towards dusk, five days after they had left the city, Lena Tanoway led her small team through the rugged foothills of the Ilmoroq mountains, and out onto the narrow coastal plain that bordered the Paluberion Sea.

It had been an exhausting mission, and Leo Faulcon, the team's middle-runner, was tired, uncomfortable and very ready indeed to return to base. He could not comprehend the reluctance of the leader to turn for home; her seemingly endless enthusiasm for continuing the exploration was ununcharacteristic, and bothered Faulcon, and he could assign blame to no other than the third member of the party, Kris Dojaan.

Kris was young, and had only recently joined the team. He lay back in the deep seat of his touring byke and whistled through his mask; he was saddle-blistered and sore, but the newness and excitement of this routine expedition had been serving as a balm for his various wounds for all of five days. Whilst this unconcerned attitude to physical discomfort disturbed Faulcon he could have coped with Kris Dojaan's immunity to pain if the youth would not keep making suggestions: why don't we try this, why not explore there? And Lena, with a finely misplaced, and long overdue, sense of responsibility was quite evidently determined to conduct this mission in a proper way, and for a proper length of time, something that ought to have been unthinkable.

Thus, after more than two days exploring the high hills and lower slopes of the Ilmoroqs, where the terrain was rough and abundant in dangerous life-forms, Leo Faulcon found himself sullenly agreeing to a tour of the ocean's shore, a last ride before the long journey home.

The coastal plain was a land dominated by giant blackweed, forests of tall, branchless trees that crowded so high towards the deepening red of the sky that their tiny, flowering tops could not be seen. But it was not the plant life that fascinated the travellers so much as the crumbling, calcite towers and arches of the land-corals that huddled between the trunks of this silent forest. Built by *skarl*, a tiny, winged life-form that had adapted well to these dry, pollen-rich lands, some of the castles were half as tall as the blackweed, their arches and passageways wide enough for a shuttle to pass. It was a crowded, shadowed land, and as Faulcon watched so a flock of *skarl* rose silently above their castle and streamed towards the distant, brilliant red-sheen of the ocean.

Riding her battered rift-byke along the easiest route, Lena Tanoway led her group in the same direction. Soon, the ground beneath them softened and they entered a landscape of dunes and tangled, grey plants. Megalithic fingers of sand-scoured rock rose high above the riders; in their lengthening shadows whole flocks of *skarl* fluttered in panic as the noisy machines passed by.

They rode across a ridge-back of harder sand and the wind hit them, brisk and cold. From here they peered down a slope, and across a mile of nearly lifeless shore, to the dusk-lit sea and its gently moving waves. An object gleamed there.

At first glance Faulcon thought it was some gigantic sea beast, stranded on the shoreline of this inland ocean; dead now, its corpse half buried in the darkening sands, it seemed to reach a stiffened limb towards him, scaly skin all-shining in the light of Altuxor. It had crawled there, perhaps, from the unfathomable depths of this dark and dying sea, and had expired in the red heat of the planet's day. And yet this thing, this rounded beast, was no beast at all, but a machine, an artifact of some other age, cast adrift on more than just the shores of a moon-torn ocean.

The team approached cautiously; during the last few days a time wind must have blown across the sea, and there was always the possibility that the beach would be swept by a breeze, scurrying across the sands to reclaim the wreck and the fragile beings who were exploring it.

Faulcon climbed down from his byke a hundred yards or so from the derelict and walked across the dunes, following Lena Tanoway. It galled him a little to notice how strongly she stepped out across the heavy sand, how sure she was in every movement of her wiry body. Faulcon took no comfort from the fact that she had been on VanderZande's World – he disliked the new name, Kamelios – a good twelve-month longer than he, and was consequently more experienced than he, and far less cautious than she should have been. He found his feet dragging, his body labouring for breath; he was sure that some rudimentary element of survival within him was desperately trying to slow his pace. It was not fear, then, but survival tactics, and he shrugged as he watched Lena's shadowy figure vanish behind the machine.

Behind Faulcon young Kris Dojaan stumbled and fell face down in the sand. His swearing was muffled as grit clogged his face piece, and Lena chuckled as she realized what had happened. Faulcon watched until Kris was on his feet again, and he smiled at the youngster, though in the fading light the gesture was probably lost.

'How can you trip on sand?' Kris asked, his voice plaintive, hurt. *Sand* of all things. Faulcon laughed. A rasping sound, like the evacuation of a vacuum closet, accompanied Kris Dojaan's over-enthusiastic unclogging of the filter he wore. 'Wait for me.'

Faulcon held his ground as the new recruit floundered through the sand and clinging scrub to make up distance. He had lagged behind, perhaps dragging his feet as much with fear as with awe as he stared up at the ruined machine. If Kris was scared, Faulcon thought kindly, he could not be faulted for it. This particular discovery was very big business for a young man's first few days on this particular planet. (He had brought luck to the team, Faulcon realized!) The thought of the time winds both fascinated and terrified, and the balance between those two emotions varied, as if by some precise mathematical equation, with the distance one moved from the bubble-like security of Steel City, the mobile installation where the non-colonists lived on VanderZande's World.

Kris caught up with his team mate, grumbling about the necessity of leaving the bykes so far away. Faulcon reminded him that the bykes were filming the whole scene, just in case they all got swept up by a wind. Lena was standing in the deep shadow of the machine now, a tiny figure gleaming in stray light from the sun. Kris grimaced behind his mask, looking strangely insectile as he peered through the wide goggles, and continued to blow sand from the proboscis that was his filter and air-booster. They were ants, then, scurrying in their skin-hugging black suits across the dunes, dwarfed by the scarred hulk of the alien wreck.

It was a land machine of sorts, a fact evident from the enormous wheels and tracks. It had been blown out of time and into the ocean, and had crawled across the floor of the sea for weeks, perhaps, before emerging onto the shore and burying itself in the sand. The metal was pitted and scarred by the corrosive salts in the ocean; fragments of weed were still visible. There had been a storm raging about the Ilmoroq foothills just a day before, and the sand had blown across the dead machine and hidden it from the prying eyes of the satellites above the atmosphere; a regular prize, then, a prize for the ground team and not for the luxuriating men in the orbiting stations.

'I have a feeling we've done well,' said Kris, palpably excited, his thin body shaking more than his voice as he peered upwards.

'We've done *very* well,' said Faulcon. 'And we shall live like kings for a seven-day or more.'

'You've brought us luck, young Dojaan,' said Lena as she hoisted herself up the ridges and spars of metal to obtain a view in through one of the windows.

'I guess I have at that.'

In the deepening red dusk they stood before the metal creature and contemplated their discovery. Twelve convex windows, bulging outwards like gleaming silver blisters, gave the thing its animal appearance; sensory apparatus, extending forward like a spider's legs, gave the machine a sense of panic, as if those spindly protrusions had tried to scrabble through the sand to free it from the clinging sediment. The hull was metallic, plate upon plate of heart-shaped armour: like scales, Faulcon thought, like the skin of a reptile. And here and there he could see hatchways, and incomprehensible painted motifs; and pipes and wires, weed-clogged and bent; and the bristling finery of antennae, broken now, and useless. There were scant signs of wind and sand abrasion, which confirmed their feeling that the machine had crawled from the sea only hours before. Glancing up into the sky, where three of the world's six moons were already high and bright, they searched for the winking orbital lights. There were none, although they could tell, by the haloes around the moons, that the organic zone was deep here, which would make such lights difficult to see. Faulcon, nonetheless, laughed with triumph. 'We've beaten them!'

'They're going to be so *mad*,' said Lena, echoing Faulcon's delight. 'If I could wear you round my neck, Kris, I'd do just that.' She fingered her charm, a jagged shard of green byrilliac taken from the first piece of time-junk she had ever touched. Faulcon involuntarily touched the leathery object that was his own amulet, mummified animal flesh from the corpse of a time-blown creature he had discovered in a cave in Kriakta Valley.

Kris watched the movement of his colleague's hand, and behind his goggles he seemed wide-eyed. 'I don't have a charm yet.'

'You're a charm yourself, boy,' said Faulcon.

'But he needs a necklace,' said Lena more seriously. 'Everyone on Kamelios carries a bit of flotsam. Luck is finite, and the amulet extends it.' They looked up again, up the wall of the alien. 'A shard from this,' she said. 'It's all that will work. Get up there, Kris, and crack yourself a bit of the pre-historic.'

Pale red light gleamed on hundreds of small windows, high on the flanks of the derelict. Kris Dojaan crawled his way across it, hitting here, hitting there, cursing as the metal failed to yield. 'Are you sure this is such a good idea?'

Lena used her sand blaster to clear the ruddy grit from about the wide, salt-caked tracks. Faulcon searched for a doorway into the vehicle that would open: pressing, squeezing, coaxing, pressuring, kicking. Nothing moved.

'What can you see?' he called to Kris, and the youngster slipped a bit and polished up a window, no more than a foot across, and peered through. 'Black. All black.'

'Try another!' shouted Lena; she was across at the bykes, relaying a routine description of the discovery back to Steel City; they had registered the wreck some minutes before. Kris Dojaan reluctantly changed his position, high on the scaly roof of the machine. 'Some sort of control desk. Ridges on the floor, and a face … that's me. I'm being reflected in something on the opposite wall.'

'The floor,' Lena pointed out as she approached, and Faulcon chuckled for no reason that he could fathom. Kris sat upright on the top of the vehicle and kicked frantically at a jagged piece of the outer structure. It didn't give.

Faulcon photographed the hulk from every angle on the ground, then followed Lena Tanoway down the shore to where the sea broke almost soundlessly against the land. A line of tangled weed, and oyster-shaped shards of rock, marked the highest tide-line. Kamelios had six moons, all small and insignificant lumps of rock that skipped and danced above the world to no one's great concern, although the pink, striated bulk of Merlin, being always partially occluded by silvery Kytara, had an appreciable effect on the seas, causing small but noticeable tides. Tharoo, a pitted and ugly moon, was the largest, and drew on the waters too; but since it rose and fell with the twins, only a single tide was ever seen clearly. Aardwind, Threelight and Magrath were pretty, but fleeting; there were human bases on all the moons.

'This is a good one,' said Lena, drawing Faulcon's attention away from the indistinct discs that scattered the dusklight. She was turning a palm-sized shard over and over and touching the rippled green and yellow pattern in its matrix. She skipped the stone and Faulcon whistled approval through his proboscis as it made the eight-bounce and plopped out of sight.

Before them the huge red disc of Altuxor moved closer to the horizon; more stars shone through.

'I hate the dusk,' said Faulcon, skipping; he only got five bounces, and kicked around the tide-line looking for a better shard.

'I like it. It reminds me of a time when I was younger, happier, prettier, richer and when sunset meant beach parties on New Triton, and more fun in one night than you can have in a year in Steel City.'

If Faulcon had thought she meant it he might have wept mock tears for her. He noticed that Kris Dojaan had slipped down the alien machine and was walking slowly … the gait and posture of disbelief … towards them. His voice, as he called out to them, testified to his confusion. 'What the hell are you doing?'

'He who gets the ten-skip gets the girl,' Faulcon said, and Lena laughed.

'Unless she gets it first herself.' Her dry voice was slightly muffled through the mask, slightly distorted through the transceivers. She skipped another stone, but Faulcon had turned round and was staring at the motionless youngster.

Kris took a step forward, then changed his mind, glancing back at the alien hulk for a moment. Red light reflected brilliantly off his faceted goggles; his eyes seemed filled with fire. 'But the machine … it's alien, it's ancient, it's wonderful.'

The word 'ancient' sent an unexpected thrill through Faulcon and he found himself frowning, staring at the ruined vehicle and thinking of the whole of time, the immensity of time gone by. But Lena's cynical laugh – a peculiar rasping until he turned round towards her – broke the flash of the spell, countered that brief return to the way he had once felt about Vander-Zande's World.

She was staring up the beach and Faulcon could see that she was slightly irritated. 'But this whole world's alien, Kris. This whole world's ancient!' She swung round, skipping a shard out across the ocean, into the glare of the red sun. It went so far, the bounces becoming so low, that Faulcon lost the count. Lena wiped her hands on the tight fabric of her suit and watched the sluggish Paluberion Sea.

Kris was shaking his head as he walked back to the machine. Dwarfed by its bulk he leaned forward to rest both hands against the giant tracks. His voice was shrill as he said, 'But this was made by intelligent creatures! It's a sign of the life that once lived here ...'

'So's this ocean,' said Lena calmly, almost inaudibly. Faulcon was walking towards the youngster, picking his way carefully as the shadows lengthened and the red light confused his senses. Lena was chuckling again. 'Didn't you know that, Leo? They carved this ocean out of the crust ... they filled it up with sea, then closed it off. We're skipping stones across the biggest damned swimming pool in the Universe.'

'But the machine ...' cried Kris Dojaan.

'Is just a damned machine.'

Faulcon said, 'You've seen one, Kris, you've seen them all.'

'This is the first *I've* ever seen!'

'And in a year you'll wonder why you ever got excited about it,' said Lena. 'Go on, Kris, have fun, feel the thrills, feel the cold shivers. Why not? I did. Leo did. You have the right to that at least, to feel a certain *awe* ...' she emphasized the word with effort as she flung a shard out towards the sun, '... for something dead. But in a year, mark me and mark me well, you'll think of this as cold, hard cash. Why the hell not? To whoever built this thing it's no more than a bicycle. Would you go berserk over a bicycle if you dug one up?'

'Yes! Leo ... tell me it thrills *you.*'

'It thrills me,' said Faulcon dully. 'I'll fetch the bykes.' He walked past the youngster, trying not to think about how upset his colleague was, or of how dulled he himself had become by the cycles of change on VanderZande's World. If I could feel it, Kris, I'd scream along with you, and toss Lena out across the water head first. But I'm dying, and you'll be dying too. Don't fight it. The world is hard enough to beat.

One by one he led the rift-bykes across the barren land and into the lee of the machine, away from the ocean winds. Here, watched by the irritable figure of Kris Dojaan, he erected the survival tent, and pumped it full of sweet air. Darkness grew about them, stars shining, redness deepening to grey and a time when dusk was gone.

Lena came to the tent and they unsealed the outer lock, crawled in, crawled through. Resealing the small chamber they sat silently, for a while, and listened to the night winds. Faulcon activated the light and they all unclipped their masks; for the first time since early morning they scratched their faces and breathed air that was free of the choking organic poisons that soured the natural atmosphere of the world.

Lena was pale, her angular features drawn, her green eyes dark-rimmed with fatigue; she combed through her long fair hair and dabbed at her skin with a pad of moisturizing cream. She watched neither Faulcon nor the young Dojaan, but Kris watched her intently, almost studying her. He looked every bit as youthful as his speech and action indicated; his beard was hardly in evidence, and he was flushed and angry. He had tied his dark hair into a single, short pigtail, and a gleaming green jewel sparkled in the lobe of his left ear.

'Do you want to talk or eat?' asked Faulcon, reaching for the small case of food supplies. He shook the box and it rattled ominously. Opening it he peered in some dismay at the remnants of their mission supplies. 'We have beef chews, three, halka chews, four, some nutrient paste still untouched – and who can blame us – and ...' he held up a shrivelled red object. 'I believe this is a carrot.'

Lena smiled. 'Kris here's the vegetarian.'

Kris eyed the ancient vegetable with some distaste; carrots were an imported vegetable and very expensive. Faulcon had made up the food pack, and had included fresh vegetables for the new recruit as a special treat; but the items had, for the most part, not survived. Kris asked, 'What's halka, did you say?'

'A local animal; the soft organs are very tasty; the chew is a concentrate of various bits and pieces—'

'I'm not hungry.'

'You'll have to eat something. We shan't find edible plants until we get back beyond the Ilmoroqs.'

Kris shook his head. 'Fasting's good for the soul. I'm really not hungry.'

Faulcon, on the contrary, was ravenous. He carved himself a slice of meat compress and settled back as it expanded in his mouth, chewing and swallowing and letting the day's aches dissipate into his extremities. Lena ate sparingly of the same compress. She had exhausted her anger at the way Faulcon had packed the box two days ago. In the mountains they could shoot olgoi, perhaps even halka, and feed better. The carrot was consigned to night's oblivion, through the small disposal chute next to the air-lock entrance.

For half an hour they relaxed in silence, listening to the wind, Kris apprehensive despite Faulcon's calm assurance that the chances of the wind being a time wind were reasonably remote ... well, unlikely, at least. Kris grinned humourlessly, eyeing the older man. 'How many times have you been out this far?'

'Four,' said Faulcon. 'This machine is the first thing I've found. I had more luck to the north; it's colder up there, but at least the world looks like a world; it's richly vegetated,' he explained as Kris frowned. 'The southern hemisphere is mostly ocean, a few islands …'

'Thousands of islands,' said Lena, without opening her eyes, or moving any part of her supine body other than her lips.

'Thousands of islands,' Faulcon echoed. 'There are six other rift valleys, or canyons, like Kriakta Rift. Kriakta is the biggest, and the only one with a mobile city unit. It's also the most spectacular. Everything's watched from the satellite stations, of course. Have you been on one yet?'

'I've been here seven days,' said Kris irritably. 'I've hardly had the chance.'

'That's odd, though. Most new arrivals spend a two-to six-week on the sat-stations, getting primed, learning the boring facts of the world's climate and geography.'

'I obviously got missed out.'

'You've missed nothing,' said Lena, her eyes still closed. 'Pollen week can be counted among the greatest moments of near-nausea in the history of the human race.'

'Pollen week?' Unsure whether he was being teased or not, Kris had relaxed, smiling, yet looking from Lena to Faulcon with almost frantic regularity. As if a light dawned: 'Oh, you mean learning about the organic atmosphere.' He picked up his mask, put it down again, stared at it thoughtfully. 'Without the chemicals we could use Kamelios like another Earth, isn't that right?'

'If it didn't have a habit of transporting you instantly into times gone by. Yes. I think you could.'

'Or times to come,' Lena pointed out.

'Indeed. Time, not being the simplest thing on Kamelios, it's hard to tell.'

'There really is no future in it.' Lena and Faulcon laughed at their shared joke. Irked, by missing the humour, Kris said, 'Anyway, I think I'd like a look from orbit.'

'You will, you will.' Faulcon's gaze took on a distance; his face slackened. 'I shall be up there in a six-month or so, and there I shall stay, unless I quit. Which I'm thinking of doing. It's the job I came to do, orbit-watch. I was adapted to artificial-weight living.'

'I thought you looked thin.'

Faulcon pinched his flesh through the tight suit. 'I've been thinner. Lena was supposed to be sat-personnel as well. We got overlooked – it happens a lot. Steel City is run by the rules of Chaos. After the introductory period in orbit, everyone has to do a six-month on the planet. We came down, Lena first, me later, and somehow we didn't get recalled. I've been here a year, now – Lena's been here two.'

'But you've been called back up ...'

'Indeed we have. It's going to hurt. I don't think I could ever enjoy life up there ...'

'It'll never happen, Leo,' said Lena tiredly. 'The only thing anyone cares about around here is the valley. As long as we keep working, we'll stay down.'

'They'll be keener, now, since we struck lucky.'

And Lena said, 'We've made it rich. Well, quite rich.'

'There'll be a big bonus coming our way,' said Faulcon. 'And furlough; a few days off. Time to go upland, time to go hunting.'

Kris shook his head in despair, saying, 'Why this money fixation? My God, Leo, I hope I keep my sense of wonder.'

'You won't,' said Lena, and then more kindly, as she sat up and wrapped her arms about her knees. 'But I hope it lingers for a while, Kris. I really do.' She lowered her gaze to the food box in the middle of the tent. She was silently thoughtful for a moment, then laughed at some private joke. 'You're right, you know. You're right, we've lost something very precious, something intrinsically human. I don't worry about it, it doesn't hurt, or ache ... but it's gone, and I wish I could remember how it felt.'

Faulcon said, 'We get over-exposed, I suppose. On a world where so many millions of years of past and future surround us, it's hard to stay interested. We're jaded.'

'It's not over-exposure,' said Lena solemnly, 'I'm sure of that. It's the world. VanderZande's World. It gets in through the ears and eyes and nose and mouth and every time it changes it changes you, every time a wind blows through time it blows through your skull, and upsets things, changes things; like the *fiersig*, but worse.'

'*Fiersig*? What's that?'

Faulcon said, 'You'll see one soon enough, Kris.'

'It's a dehumanizing world, Kris,' Lena went on, 'and if you had any sense you'd recognize that now and get the hell off. Except I think it's probably too late. You've got sand under your nails, VanderZande's World has got you, and I think you'll find it won't let you go.'

Kris looked slightly apprehensive, glancing at Faulcon, his face creased into a frown; when the ocean-wind whipped about the fabric of the tent he seemed startled, hugging his knees tighter and nodding soberly as he ran thoughts and facts and advice through his head.

Faulcon, intrigued by the moody youngster, prompted him: 'Why did you come here?'

'Why do people usually come to Kamelios?'

Faulcon glanced at Lena, then shrugged. 'Curiosity, perhaps?'

'Not curiosity,' said Kris quietly.

'Seeking ... searching ... chasing, chasing a dream.'

'Chasing a dream,' echoed Kris, and Faulcon saw the boy's eyes mist up, even though just the hint of a smile had touched the pale, mask-marked lips. 'I'm certainly doing that. Chasing a dream – seeking.' His gaze hardened on Faulcon. Lena was propped on her elbows, her long legs crossed at the ankles, between the two men. 'Are you going to tell us what you're seeking?' As she spoke she exchanged an almost quizzical look with Faulcon.

Kris Dojaan shook his head. 'I'm not ready to talk about it, yet. Will I really change?' he said more brightly, altering the subject. Lena smiled kindly, perhaps angry with herself for having been so blunt.

'Maybe you won't change as much as me,' she said. She fingered her amulet. 'And with your lucky shard maybe the world will treat you respectfully.' She looked at Faulcon. 'I think it's prayer time.' She lifted the leather necklace over her head and placed the strangely patterned metal on the ground before her. Faulcon unslung his own piece of VanderZande's pre-history and placed it next to Lena's. Kris made no move and Faulcon said, 'Where's your shard?'

'What shard?' The boy looked blankly from one to the other of them for a second, then, quite clearly, remembered.

'The piece of the machine ...' said Lena, an edge of anger, of panic in her voice. 'The lucky shard I told you to get from the derelict. Where is it?' But she gave Kris no chance to speak before she cried out, 'Leo, he's not broken anything!'

Startled by this sudden change in Lena's attitude, Kris watched her curiously as she seemed to teeter on the verge of hysteria, twisting round to kneel up in the wind-swept tent. He said, 'I'm sorry. I didn't know I had to get it so soon ... I just couldn't break anything ... I told you it was tough.'

'He didn't get his charm, Leo!' Tears flowed. She stared at Faulcon, seeking an answer in his impassivity.

Infuriatingly, all he said was, 'Calm down.'

Lena reacted with open anger. The tears dried, her face went white, her voice coarsened. 'You fool! Don't tell me to calm down! The kid's as good as killed us. He didn't break off a charm, and he's done for us! I *told* you. I told you so bloody *clearly* to get an amulet. What do you think they are? Games? Little indulgences?' She raved openly, and Kris nearly fell backwards as she made to hit him. Her face had turned livid, her eyes bright, her lips wet as she shouted. Faulcon felt helpless because he felt so afraid, but he reached out and tugged the girl back from Kris, forcing her to sit. Her fists clenched up as she tried to control the terrible emotion she felt. 'Damn it, Leo ... why didn't he do it when I said ...?'

Kris Dojaan, confused, lost: 'I'm sorry, Lena; Leo ... I'm so terribly sorry ... I just didn't realize ... what, I mean ... well, what's so important about them, about a bit of metal?'

'Luck,' said Faulcon stiffly. 'You brought us luck, Kris, by suggesting we came as far as the Sea. But the world will take it back, and us with it, unless we pin it down, pin that luck down by getting it into our life frame.'

Kris shook his head, the hint of a smile on his face. 'But that's nonsense—'

Lena wrenched herself from Faulcon's restraining grip, and struck at the boy with the open palm of her hand. The blow resounded loudly, and Kris's startled cry was almost a scream of confusion. But the physical violence seemed to calm Lena. She grabbed for her sand blaster and narrowed the focus until it was effectively a weapon. She thrust the gadget at Kris and said, very stiffly, 'You get out there and blow something, anything, some piece of metal *off* that hulk. *Do it!*'

'I'm going. I'm going.'

'Maybe it's not too late. What d'you think, Leo?' She turned, and was suddenly lost again, becoming tearful. Faulcon hugged her and watched as Kris strapped on his face mask.

'I think it'll be all right,' he said. 'It's not too late. If you can get a good shard, Kris, not too big, it'll bring that luck with us wherever we go. I think it'll be all right.'

With difficulty through the improperly aligned face piece, Kris said, 'And who's going to explain the damage to Steel City? I'm not.'

'Just do it!' shouted Lena, drawing away from Faulcon and using the back of her hand to slap the boy on the arm, a more friendly blow. Kris crawled through the lock and out into the night. Lena looked almost embarrassed when he'd gone, smiled at Faulcon and feigned the slapping of her own face. Faulcon laughed. 'When did *this* happen?'

'What, the change?'

'All this hysteria, this insecurity. This isn't the real you.'

Lena agreed. 'I suppose it must have been that storm just before we left to come out here. Remember the change? I didn't see a *fiersig*; it wasn't that physical, not much of a light show, but there must have been one hidden behind the dust. I woke up from it feeling very on edge. I've managed to keep it under control quite well, until now. I'll change back, of course.'

'I certainly hope so.' But Faulcon knew she was right. Mood upsets were never permanent in their extreme forms, although each electric storm that brought the *fiersig*, the power-fields of change, twisted and distorted the stable mind just that little bit more, scarring the mind irreversibly in a way too insignificant to note at the time, but with mounting effect over the months and years. They were fools to stay here, Faulcon knew, but then what had he lost, how had he changed from the man he had been a year ago? He didn't get excited by ruins; he was no longer thrilled by the dead past. Not much of a change, he thought. Nothing to concern him as much as the more physical upset that might occur if he got caught by a time squall.

But he thought back to the storm that had hit the area of the valley, and the human installation, just before they had embarked on their seven-day prowl through the Ilmoroq mountains. Mood changes were not normally connected with dust storms, even if there was electrical activity about. There was always electrical activity in the atmosphere of Kamelios, but infrequently did it blossom into the spectacular *fiersig*, the drifting sky fire that worked its mysterious force into the minds of men and turned Steel City into a focus of human fear and desperate resistence. The storm had obviously concealed a small *fiersig* and the City had not realized its effect until the following morning, when patterns of behaviour were manifestly altered.

'I got away this time,' said Faulcon. 'I didn't really notice any change at all. Felt good when I went to bed, felt good when I got up.' He grinned boyishly, and Lena touched a finger to the tip of her nose. *Get lost.*

'I don't know that you're good for me,' she said. 'Sometimes I love you, sometimes I don't. Mostly I don't. At the moment I particularly don't.'

Faulcon grinned, but before he could speak there was the sound of a discharge, and a peculiar grating sound as of metal being riven. Faulcon called out, but the tent, and the wind, must have stolen his voice; Kris did not answer. 'I bet he brings in a piece about six feet long, just to spite us.'

'He doesn't believe yet,' said Lena. 'But he'll learn. I just hope he doesn't learn the hard way.'

They waited for Kris then, in moody, contemplative silence. Faulcon felt very tired and wanted to sleep, but he wanted the ritual with the charms even more, and he grew impatient waiting for the youngest member of the team to return. After half an hour he abruptly felt uneasy, and picked up his face mask, activating the radio. He called to Kris Dojaan, but there was a static-filled silence, and he guessed that some sort of electrical disturbance was happening out in the cold night world.

'I'm going outside,' he said, and strapped the mask on properly. Lena nodded agreement, but made no move to follow.

As he emerged from the tent the wind tugged powerfully at him, and as he stood erect so he felt himself flung heavily against the sheer wall of the derelict. He clung on for a second and watched, by Kytara light, as sand and shards were whipped up into scurrying vortices, and sent into the darkness by this 'night breeze'. He had never known such a strong wind blowing in such localized fashion, and though he knew the tent was safe with its deep 'roots', he felt a moment's concern for the boy who might well have been caught off-balance and knocked against the metal machine so hard as to render him unconscious.

When the wind dropped a fraction, Faulcon leaned into it and made his way carefully about the wreck, until he saw the gleaming ocean, its sluggish movements highlit by two of the moons, Kytara, of course, with its crescent of pinkness where enigmatic Merlin slyly watched the world below, and

Threelight with its three shining dust deserts, higher and brighter than usual. Tharoo, he noticed through the swirling sand, was low against the horizon, half full, seeming to hover as if waiting its moment to sweep across the sky.

He called for Kris, and continued to call as he worked his way precariously about the entire perimeter of the hulk. He realized, with some concern, that Kris was nowhere to be seen.

Beginning the circuit for the second time, he soon discovered the place where Kris Dojaan's shot had struck the hull. The metal was twisted inwards, the side of the machine opened in a long and narrow split. The shot seemed to have half-caught an entrance-way, because Faulcon could see the twisted remnants of some intra-wall mechanism; beyond the hole was a passageway, narrow and of pentagonal cross-section. He could see only a few inches into the interior, Kytara being bright but not sufficiently bright.

A wash of purple light made him stand, startled, and become aware that the wind had dropped. He looked up into the heavens and saw the tenuous flickering purple of some stratospheric activity. It was pretty, though not startling, and moved away to the south, discharging two magnificent strikes of forked lightning down onto the ocean.

Lena's voice in his ears whispered, 'Is he there? Has he got a shard?'

'I think he's gone inside the machine,' said Faulcon stiffly. 'He's opened some sort of passageway. I've tried calling him but he doesn't answer. Maybe he's screened somehow.'

In the stillness, but still wary of a sudden squall, Faulcon backed away from the hulk and peered up at its tiny windows, hoping to see some movement. He saw nothing and felt a moment's thrill at the thought of where inside that vast ruin his colleague might have been, and what sights he might have been seeing. *I haven't lost it all; not yet, not yet.*

There was a sound down by the ocean and he glanced that way; it had sounded like an animal splashing in the water's edge and his body chilled as he imagined something creeping up the shore towards him. As he saw movement in the darkness he felt a second shock, and backed away a little. The creature came between him and the bright reflection of Kytara on the ocean's surface, and he saw that it was a man; after a moment he recognized Kris, walking steadily towards him.

'I thought you were inside the machine,' said Faulcon evenly.

'I got a six-skip,' said Kris, laughing stiffly. And he held up his hand. 'I also got my lucky charm.' Light reflected weakly off a small fragment of opaque crystal, star-shaped and precise.

Faulcon said, 'Then you didn't go inside ...?'

Kris hesitated just briefly before he said, 'No. No, I didn't go inside.' And he walked past Faulcon to the tent.

CHAPTER TWO

It was the end of spring, and time for the city to move. Spring on Kamelios, whether in the northern or southern hemisphere, was a season, no more, no less, dry and windy than any other time of year. But for the last three Kamelion months – longer than a Standard Earth month, but the year on Kamelios was divided up into the same twelve units – there had been a noticeable darkening of the native flora, and changes in the behaviour of many of the beasts that inhabited the lands about the valley. And for three months, too, the crop-fields of the various human settlements, from Valley Edge and Chalk Stack, to Touchdown and Hawkman's Holding nearly two hundred miles away, had begun to show a rapid growth, and would soon be ready for harvesting.

For Steel City, the end of spring meant a change in position, a move of fifteen miles along the edge of the valley known as Kriakta Rift. It was mere ritual, and as such was never missed.

From a high ridge of ground, west of Steel City, where a tangled forest of the white and purple tree-form known as sun-weed made travel difficult and habitation all but impossible, Leo Faulcon watched the city rise on its engines, and hover almost silently above the blackened crater that had been its home for the last quarter year. Behind him, Lena Tanoway guided her byke through the snag-toothed trunks of the forest, and brushed blue and grey fragments of leaves and pollen from her black travelling suit as she stopped by Faulcon and watched the manoeuvres several miles distant. Kris Dojaan could be heard, distantly, cursing and shouting as he failed to ease his way through the forest. They should have come by the marked track-way, Faulcon knew, but they had been in a hurry to get home, and this short cut, close to the scientific station at Chalk Stack, had seemed like a good idea at the time. They had forgotten the date, and the ritual shift of base location; they would not be able to enter the city until dusk, and they could easily have taken the longer, more leisurely route along the edge of the valley.

To Faulcon's surprise, when Kris finally emerged from the stand of sun-weed, dishevelled and covered with the fine, powdery exudate from the plants, instead of complaining he gasped in wonder. Climbing down from his byke, still brushing at his arms with abstracted gestures of his hands, he walked to a chalky outcrop of rock, stood upon it and gazed across the land laid out before him.

Faulcon recognized instantly what Kris was feeling, and realized that he had been right to suggest the short cut. Was he getting so jaded that he could overlook the simple pleasures of tourism? He smiled as he walked to join the youngster, and as he looked at the distant city, and the land surrounding it, he felt, for a moment, the sense of awe he could remember having experienced a year before when Lena had taken him up into Hunderag Country, to the foothills of the Jaraquath Mountains. There, close to the many territories of the manchanged, the view to the south, across the rift, had been even more startling than from Chalk Stack.

'You think it's so barren, round the city; when you're inside, looking out, it seems so desolate and dry. But it isn't, it's beautiful, it's rich, really rich. And that valley!'

Faulcon smiled, half watching Kris Dojaan's dust-and mask-covered features as the boy enthused, aware of the expression in his eyes, even though the goggles effectively hid his features from view.

They were not high enough to get a clear view into the valley, and they could not get a real view of the spread of the land; but they had sufficient vantage to see how wide the valley was, nearly a mile across, with its wind-scoured bluffs and ridges covered with all manner of gleaming, indistinguishable junk. It looked vegetated in parts, and Faulcon, through binoculars, observed that a wide spread of now-dying forest covered several miles of the valley's bottom, ripped there from a future time, no doubt, when the valley had been eroded away, and a stand of these high, tree-like plants had grown upon a marshier soil. Two spires rose from that green and brown foliage, and a movement upon one of them told Faulcon that a team was crawling about those ruins, logging everything. It did not make him want to be there, back in the valley; but it made him remember how thrilled he had been the first time his Section Commander, Gulio Ensavlion, had allowed him to join a Section 8 team shortly after a time wind had blown through the gorge.

The valley was two hundred miles long, in places so wide and low that it seemed like no more than open land between rolling hills; at the far end, the eastern limit, it was deep, narrow, dangerous; here, close to the western extreme, the 'beach' was wide and shallow, marking the place where the east to west flow of the time winds blew themselves out. From their vantage point they could see some twenty miles of the valley's snaking form, as far, in fact, as Riftwatch Station Eekhaut, the ruined observer post that sat on the sharpest of Kriakta Rift's bends, at Rigellan Corner. ·

Along each side of the winding valley ran a ten-mile strip of essentially uninhabited land, varying from a tangle of jungle life along most of the southern perimeter, to the more barren reaches of Gaunt's County, the western lands where Steel City spent most of its restless life, and across whose forested borders Faulcon and the others had just passed. Only installations from the military section of the Galactic Cooperative, or Federation as it was more familiarly known, were allowed access to this so-called Valley Zone, although there was a small and vital tourist trade, and for the purposes of more practical trade and communication there were trackways passing from the various counties beyond the Valley Zone up to the huge, brick-built Exchanges that were scattered along the border. Those counties were the neocolonial settlements. Gaunt's County, Five Valleys, Seligman's Drift and Tokranda County were the nearest to Steel City, and the only inhabited regions that Faulcon had visited.

Here lived the first and second generation colonists, human settlers not prepared to undergo the same drastic engineering as the manchanged (which would adapt them, ultimately, to Kamelios in all its poisonous, pollen-saturated glory), but rather hoped to evolve a natural tolerance. The nearest of the manchanged lived in the high lands, in Hunderag Country, the foot-hills of the Jaraquath Mountains, and were rarely seen in the counties. These low lands were mainly devoted to agriculture, and quite intensively farmed; the fields made an octagonal checkboard of colour, and the darker shapes of the towns and villages were scattered almost regularly between the small-holdings.

The area of habitation ended at Chalk Stack, close by, with a sprawling scientific installation, built below, up and across several weather-worn pinnacles of a white and flaky limestone-type rock. The place was well known to Faulcon from a few months ago when, his relationship with Lena broken for the while, he had known a girl called Immuk Lee. She lived at Chalk Stack, now, with the station controller, one Ben Leuwentok, who had often induced sleep in Faulcon with his interminable, and no longer fascinating, seminars on man, moons, madness and the native life-forms of Kamelios.

Six counties, Faulcon explained to Kris Dojaan, and six major towns; at their edge, moving between them, using them for food and supplying them with consumer goods of a more idle kind, was Steel City, an immense, domed monster, overshadowing the townships, shifting restlessly as it crossed the border between Gaunt's County and Five Valleys, and onwards, along the rift, until it turned and came back again.

It began its fifteen-mile drift now, away from Faulcon and the others, towards a place in cleared land where already a site had been marked out for it. Through his glasses Faulcon could see the winking lights, the scurrying shapes of rift-suited men, and the bulkier, spidery gleam of digging machines. At this time of day the sun was high, more orange than red, and the land was bright and green; the rift valley appeared as a reddish and grey streaked channel, bordered by greywood forest and the more colourful jungle, a treacherous land that reached hundreds of miles into the hazy distance to the south.

'Time to go,' said Faulcon, and they returned to their bykes, and the patiently waiting leader. Kris acknowledged her with a slight movement of his hand. 'Sightseeing completed?' she asked, and Kris nodded: 'It's a great view.'

'Wait until I get you hunting,' said Faulcon, 'up in Hunderag ...' He stopped speaking as Lena punched her byke into noisy life.

They trailed the city for several hours, passing around the gigantic crater where it had recently nestled. The city floated ahead of them, the whining of its motors growing in volume as they closed the distance. Soon they had to turn their heads to see the full span of the floating hemisphere, with its bulbous traverse units – five of the six – clinging to its lower half; where was the sixth traverse unit, Faulcon wondered idly, and as if to answer his question his eyes caught the flash of light on the tiny mobile installation, miles away, and crawling home, still a week away after some expedition into the far lands of the east.

From satellites, from air cars, on bykes and from segments of Steel City itself, from all these things was VanderZande's World studied and explored; an enormous team of men and women, dedicated to following the time winds, and picking up the traces of those who had gone before – and those who would yet arrive on the world, at a time when Steel City had long since corroded.

By mid-afternoon the city had reached its new location, and settled noisily and chokingly to the ground, promising an earlier entry than Faulcon had at first believed; the cloud of dust and smoke remained about the installation for several minutes, and by the time it had cleared the Riftwatch Tower had emerged, sliding upwards from the central core, its disc-shaped observation platform already turning.

Faulcon watched the city as it settled and was still again. He lounged back on his byke, scarcely aware of the muscular control he exercised over the intricate and complex mechanisms of the speeding machine. Moving at more than a mile a minute was not a particularly hazardous occupation, but on this terrain, with its hidden clefts, and sudden gusts of wind, it was far too fast for common sense. This was why Lena and Kris were now trailing him, concerned over his obvious relaxation. Faulcon was fascinated by Steel City, though. He thought it was incredibly ugly, and with the gaping gash in its side where the crawling traverse unit belonged, it was both ugly and lopsided. He could never understand why so many thousands of people opted to live within its glassy shell (calling it Steel City was just a way of describing its antiglare appearance) and had not set up townships within the Valley Zone.

Convenience, he supposed; and the sense of transience it brought to one's stay on VanderZande's World; that was why he himself had secured quarters in the city. Nobody with any sense ever came to this place intending to stay. Which was not to say that people who came to Kamelios ever left it.

The city, then, despite its hideous presentation, attracted Faulcon in an indefinable way. It also promised good food, proper rest, proper bodily hygiene, and a fat bonus, in old-fashioned credit chits, which he had every intention of spending with as much irresponsibility as possible. With Kris Dojaan on the team, he had managed to convince himself, they were the luckiest team on the world. When credit ran short they could always follow the youngster's nose.

The three-day journey home had been a reasonable approximation of hell. Food had virtually run out, and the expected catch of edible life-forms in the Ilmoroq passes had not materialized; meat compress and nutrient paste can become a most nauseating prospect when it is all there is to look forward to. He preferred to eat sand; he bitterly regretted the loss of the real carrot. Lena had seemed less bothered by the discomfort, but then she was a real old hand – or so Faulcon thought of her. Surprisingly, too, Kris had seemed unconcerned by the agonies of the return trip, and for one whose stay on Kamelios was still measurable in days, that showed remarkable self control. What puzzled Faulcon was that, for virtually the whole of the trip, Kris had done little else but complain – at not being able to visit the valley straight away, at the primitiveness of the masks and bykes – or gasp in awe, as when they had come through the Ilmoroqs, for example, and later, when they had hit the Paluberion beach. But from the moment they had started coming home he had seemed a different man. Certainly he had inquired almost endlessly about the human habitation and setup on the world, and Faulcon had swiftly grown tired of exercising his own rather shabby understanding of how the world functioned commercially, and how it was governed. But there was nonetheless something curiously different about the boy, a sense of detachment.

In whispered tones Faulcon had confided his concern to Lena, who had agreed with him. There were two possibilities. That Kris had lied when he had denied entering the derelict, and that what he had seen inside it had upset him, or altered him in some way. Secondly, that a tentative, rather weak mood change had swept them during that last night by the ocean; whilst Lena, and Faulcon himself, had not sensed any subtle change in their psychological presentation, Kris Dojaan, raw and fresh, and un-tampered with by the world as yet, had been badly affected.

There was, in fact, a third possibility: that all this was pure imagination; that Kris's early awe and the sense of his being overwhelmed by place and discovery, had worn off; that he was a controlled and inquisitive young man, with a great deal more sense than credulity, in contrast to the way he had earlier appeared.

As they circuited the perimeter of the installation, waiting for an access bay to lower from the core, Kris's soft voice again crackled through Faulcon's mask radio, expressing disbelief that anyone could be so obsessed with luck that they would move a whole city.

Faulcon had explained the reasoning behind the location shift a few hours earlier, and even then had found himself laughing in agreement with the boy. It *did* sound ludicrous, no matter how you expressed it, that every three months, by VanderZande's time, the city should lift up its skirts and scurry to a different place on the cliff approaches. It did not in the least reduce the chances of being caught by a time squall. It *did* give observational access to a different section of the valley, and Faulcon supposed that there was something to be gained from watching the time ruins regularly from a different spot. But anyone – and he was thinking most emphatically of Mad Commander Ensavlion – anyone who wished to watch the valley with a curiosity bordering on the obsessional had only to climb into a rift suit and go down to the valley's edge. If you'd paid your money to come here you could do what you liked – within reason, rules and your own scant spare time.

Steel City, Faulcon explained as they rested, close enough to the building to hear the low, grumbling sounds of its various systems, had a second escape-ploy, should a destructive wind rear up and out of the valley and swoop towards it. The traverse units, the six mobile domes that were effectively mini-cities on their own, could move considerably faster than the crawl with which they circuited the continent. They could, if required, lift vertically at only just less than bone-breaking velocity. If the klaxons went – signifying a time wind's approach – the populace could drain into the six units in literally thirty seconds, through any one of hundreds of drop-chutes from the main city body. The longest drop was from the observation tower that was raised so high in the air. Thirty seconds down, and the traverse units would explode upwards and away to safety, though the main city would be lost.

'A time wind,' Kris repeated, the tone of awe back in his voice for the moment. He had seen a derelict, an ancient machine ripped from its own era and cast, lifeless, upon the shores of a red-lit ocean. But he had not seen the wind that had brought it, and he was impatient to witness such a phenomenon. Faulcon explained that in the year he had been on VanderZande's World he had observed a time wind on only a half-dozen occasions, although he had once come close to being caught in an eddy, the sudden appearance of a tiny, transient focus of distortion. But the main winds blew in the deep valleys, and in the nearby valley most of all. If he was patient, he would see his wind; but there was no predicting them.

CHAPTER THREE

Two hours after their return to base, Faulcon was comfortably attired, cleaned inside and out, and replete after an uncomfortably generous meal of charcoal-baked tongue and boiled vegetables. He sprawled in his small room for a while and considered the state of his existence. For a man of thirty-two, with – time winds permitting – more than sixty active years ahead of him, he had not done so badly. He owned this room, although it had cost him two K-years' service pay to acquire it. The first year had passed: one to go; and of course every bonus he earned was his to keep, and he rarely went short of anything. Being, in this sense, freelance, with no regular income, was a spur to his activities in the field – it made him work all the harder. It galled him sometimes to meet explorers, traders, dieticians, administrators, any and all of the hundreds of functionaries on VanderZande's World who had signed on for the same brief spell of service and who were already, after one or two years, regularly amassing small fortunes and would leave Kamelios rich. He himself would have nothing to sell save his room, and the value of that asset might have changed radically. His consolation was that on a world as insecure as Kamelios this nest of security, this huddling place that was unobserved, impenetrable, his and his alone, was at the moment of immense value to him, and not just in a financial sense.

He would marry Lena whether she liked it or not. One day, one year, they'd sort themselves out, and in the meantime they were two people with their own rooms in the belly of Steel City, who shared a lot of fun, a considerable amount of love, and who were both as blank about the future as each other. Except for the desire to live together eventually they looked forward to nothing beyond the excitement, and risk, of VanderZande's World. Lena had lost her awe of the place, and Faulcon was well aware that he himself was changing, becoming jaded. Lena had bought her room outright, with money left to her by her parents, both of whom had died in a fire on New Triton, a world they had come to from Earth when Lena had still been in her infancy. So perhaps it was the fact that he was *working* for his special possession, his forty feet square of apartment, that kept his regard for Kamelios somewhere in between the extremes of feeling represented by Lena and Kris Dojaan. Unquestionably he experienced the same lack of concern, the same indifference to the scattering of alien artifacts that had been dredged up by the time winds that Lena and all the long-termers on the planet had come to feel; but equally he had found himself sharing in Kris's excitement, his eager concern with the wonders of other times. Faulcon was the bridge between attitudes in the team, fluctuating between those extremes according to whose company he found himself sharing. Like Kamelios itself, like all who lived in Steel City, Faulcon was a unit of change, an unfixed star, someone whose emotions could twist about in an instant for reasons other than the effect of the world upon him.

Despite the pleasurable anticipation of a small wallet containing his bonus – perhaps two or three thousand chits, the Kamelion unit of credit, on good, old-fashioned plastic notes – Faulcon decided he could not face Commander Gulio Ensavlion just yet. By rights, and by tradition, he should have gone straight to the section head to report on the expedition, and to answer questions. In practice there was always an hour or so delay before such debriefings, but Faulcon would have preferred to keep Ensavlion and his bizarre obsessions at bay for a whole night-day cycle. He called through to Lena but received no reply; checking with administration, he found that she had been summoned peremptorily to Ensavlion's office, and had been with the Commander for nearly an hour. As team leader it was not surprising that she had been called alone in the first instance, but it *did* mean that there was more to the mission than would at first seem obvious. It was not routine, Faulcon imagined, but he could not think what could have been so different about it that the leader should be summoned on her own. Surely not the discovery of just another derelict? Unless the damage that Kris had caused to the interior had got her into trouble, but that was most unlikely.

Suspecting that he might himself be summoned imminently, and still unwilling to face Ensavlion, Faulcon called the dormitory where Kris was billeted. The youngster also was unobtainable, but one of his room mates suggested that he might have gone up the Riftwatch Tower, to get the view from those wind-shaken heights before dusk settled.

So Faulcon left his room and made his way along the level until he came to the main plaza. Here there were colourful, spacious lounges, comfortable and quiet save for a distant susurration – the air conditioning – and the occasional drift of attractive, alien music. Voices were muted, though attention could be drawn across a distance by the careful use of speakers built into the ivory and jade columns; purely decorative structures, with no supporting function at all, the columns rose from the plush flooring into the hazy distance of the roof space, and served to give a sense of territory to the area. The lounges were crowded, and in one corner, muted behind a translucent screen, a celebratory party was occurring, with dancing and not a little drunkenness. Moving rapidly about, and giving to the plaza a certain sense of panic, were teams of repair men, and engineers, and a few medical personnel, hastening from damage point to damage point in order to seal and secure the city before the next Kamelion night.

Faulcon navigated this confusion, and resigned himself to the unpleasant sensation of the lift-chute in the plaza's centre, that whisked him from stable ground to a point five hundred feet above the lounge area on what appeared to be no more than a whim of warm air. But abruptly he was on a solid surface again, and stepping into the swaying platform that was the observation zone of valley and surrounding lands. A circular area that could support five hundred persons, it was now relatively empty, despite the city's change of location. Its motion had stopped and Faulcon walked around its inner path, away from the jutting windows; he was uncomfortable in the sun's glare, despite the fact that no harmful rays, nor distracting light, could reach him; but he had spent several days beneath the blinding disc – very unred in its passage across the heavens, and showing its age only at dawn and dusk – and he preferred to remain out of sight of that warming sphere unless it was absolutely necessary.

He spotted Kris Dojaan, and hastened towards him.

Kris was now robed casually in a short red tunic and thigh-hugging half-jeans. His feet were bare, and his hair was tied back in several elaborate ringlets, a fashion that Faulcon himself adopted. He was leaning against the restraining bars that kept observers from the thick, faintly tinted windows. His eyes were narrowed as he peered, without the aid of any of the several telescopes, at the distant valley.

As Faulcon came up beside him, the youngster turned and nodded acknowledgement, almost as if he had been aware of Faulcon for several minutes. Faulcon noticed the alien shard, now slung on a thin, leather necklet. Again he felt disturbed at the sight of the amulet, its regularity, its manifest deliberateness. Kris touched the tiny star and smiled, never taking his gaze from Faulcon's face. For a fleeting moment Faulcon had the sensation of being in the presence of a mischievous child. Kris had said that the object had been lying just inside the passageway exposed by his thoughtless discharge. He had seen it, grabbed it, become filled with a senseless panic, and had run down to the ocean, dropping to his knees and shaking for several minutes. Only Faulcon's arrival, searching for him, had calmed him down. But having taken the relic, nothing would make him give it back.

Now he fingered the object almost reverently. 'It's warm,' he said. 'Here. Feel. It has some sort of inner warming mechanism.'

As he held the amulet towards Faulcon, Faulcon found himself almost reluctant to touch it. But touch it he did, and he felt a thrill of fear, a shiver of apprehension, as his fingers communicated the information to his brain that the amulet was ice cold to the touch; ice cold.

After hesitating a moment, he closed his mind to the insistent voice that told him to say nothing, and informed Kris of the sensory contradiction.

'Cold?' Kris, who had seemed vaguely amused, now was puzzled for a second, stroking the star and staring at Faulcon as if it was taking some time for him to decipher the brief words. Then he looked away, out across the evening-lit surface of Kamelios. 'I suppose that's not surprising. You're already cold towards this place. You're as cold as Lena, like all of this city. Something like this, like this piece of history, well …' he struggled for words to express what was subsequently revealed as a garbled thought. 'I'm sure that things like this star respond to emotional warmth. To a sort of feeling of wonder, a feeling of respect and love for this world as it once was. Maybe Lena is right and I'll lose it, but if this jewel is warm, I guess that means for the moment the world is on my side. Does that make sense, Leo?'

Faulcon laughed, a gesture not without humour, but with an edge of considerable regret. He bit his lip before answering, framing words carefully. 'It makes as much sense as anything on this planet. But you're wrong to say I've lost my respect for the place. It gets covered up at times, but with you around ...'

Kris grinned, and in his face and manner there was a disquieting hint of patronage as he prompted, 'With me around ...?'

'It brings it all back,' Faulcon concluded. 'The sense of the ancient. The sense of the alien. The sense of excitement.'

'Touch the pendant,' said Kris encouragingly. Faulcon shook his head – a gesture of resignation – as he reached out and laid two fingers on the ice-cold crystal. Perhaps there *was* just a hint of warmth there.

Instantly afterwards Faulcon learned the reason for the relative desertion of this highly popular viewing platform: one of the traverse units was about to detach itself from the mother city, and the Riftwatch Tower would be withdrawn. The announcement had already been made and those who remained obstinately on the high level were now chased to the lift-chutes by several irritable security men. Faulcon hustled along with the small crowd, and when they were back at level four he dragged Kris by the arm and led him towards the museum.

Here, presented in something akin to organized chaos, was a cross-section of everything of interest that the time winds had dredged up on Vander-Zande's World, from the smallest 'toy', a wheeled object that had perhaps been the model of some land transport carrier, to the largest coffin-shaped enigma, four hundred feet long, still sealed along all edges, and according to every sensory probe used against it, filled with nothing but an assortment of small, differently shaped boxes, all lying free. Function, like the function of nearly everything in the museum: unknown.

Kris Dojaan's amazement at many of the things he saw, in particular some of the human-looking artifacts, his almost boyish energy, had a dramatic effect on Faulcon, charging something within him until he not only recalled the near-hysteria that had accompanied *his* first tour of this junk yard, but actually relived it. He led Kris through the galleries, round the cases, up to and away from the reconstructions of the planetary surface, as far as they had been elucidated by the enormous teams of geologists and topographists; and eventually, almost breathless, they arrived in the biology section.

In silence, reverent, awed, they peered at the main exhibit, the preserved carcasses of two carapaced, winged creatures that had lived upon this world perhaps fifty million years before, or which might yet be born to occupy it at some age long after Steel City had vanished into desert dust. Dredged through time these two unintelligent (it was believed) creatures had died quickly in the awful air of Kamelios. The rift team had lost two men to a following squall as their duty members had dragged the twisted corpses out of the deep valley.

Still staring at the largest of the two creature's enormous, dulled eyes, Kris said, 'And they don't know where they came from?'

Faulcon shook his head. He was trying to imagine these beings in full flight above the rich, forested lands of primeval Kamelios. They looked heavy, the carapace being thick, and armoured, all wings and the long-necked head protruding from beneath it. It would have been difficult to make exaggerated flying motions – the drawings in the next display demonstrated that – but gliding was the most likely main motion of the beasts.

'The trouble is, you can't date things that are swept through time as new. The only way you can get an idea where they came from, or rather *when* they came from, is by looking at what gets dredged through with them. Bits of rock, perhaps whole rock scarpments, dust, things like that. The geological history of this planet has been reasonably worked out, and you can sometimes match a time-torn rock with a dated and recognizable rock formation close by. Again, the trouble is that the rift valley itself is such a mess, such a mixture of different ages, that any sort of dating work is just guesswork.'

There were other creatures labelled as 'extinct'; they were mostly small, insignificant-looking things, conforming basically to a 'spring-limb' structure, with several scrabbling and holding limbs, often much modified, for example into the carapace of the winged creatures. And there were displays of the existing life of Kamelios, animals that had been named in the early days of the colony: skarl, snake-hare, easiwhit, olgoi, and the gigantic gulgaroth, shown only in holographs, and frightening even so. There was too much information on life-style and symbiotic relationships – the strange olgoi-gulgaroth sexual relationship especially – for Kris, restlessly fascinated, to stay long at any one display.

Ultimately he was disappointed in the display of the ancient, extinct (or successional, as yet unevolved) life of the world. What was missing, of course, was any life-form manifestly intelligent …Where the hell? … Nothing? 'No thinking creatures at all?'

They walked back to the tower, now that the traverse unit had departed. 'There obviously *were* intelligent creatures here … over a span of thousands of years almost certainly.'

'Obviously,' Kris repeated irritably. 'What I meant was, where are they? Surely somewhere, *something* got caught by a time wind.'

They had reached the chute and made the stomach-churning ascent to the top of the tower. 'You'd certainly think so, but no one has ever found such a creature.'

'Or seen? No sightings?'

Faulcon smiled and glanced at the youth. 'That's a matter of debate. There have always been sightings, claims that are never backed up with hard evidence. Everybody would like to see an intelligent alien, and it's just too easy for the mind to fill in the missing image. Everything's been seen over the last few years, from God to giant squids; and some things that aren't quite as amusing as that.' Faulcon ceased to talk, unwilling to volunteer what he knew without further prompting. He always hated to talk about the pyramid, and the sighting of a year ago. Why his mouth should go dry, why Ensavlion's unwillingness to drop the subject should upset him so much, he often found difficult to answer.

Kris, ever inquisitive, said, 'Have *you* ever seen anything?'

Faulcon smiled and shook his head. 'I've seen it all, Kris. And in a year, so will you. I see things in my dreams that ought to drive me insane. And there are some who say that every waking hour on Kamelios is a dream.'

'So you've never seen a real, live, indisputable alien?'

Faulcon couldn't help laughing at Kris Dojaan's eagerness. 'Only one man on Kamelios persistently claims that privilege; usually the certainty of the sighting fades with time, but this one man ...'

'Tell me about it.'

'I think not. I'll let the man himself tell you. It's more fun coming from him.'

Kris sensed Faulcon's meaning instantly and looked suitably impressed. 'Commander Ensavlion, you mean. That makes it tough, though. I mean, what I've heard about him isn't exactly flattering. Some call him mad, others deluded.'

'A bit of both,' agreed Faulcon as they walked to the edge of the platform, facing the darkening Kriakta Rift. 'And it's the sighting that turned him. But as I say, he'll fill you in on the details, I'm sure. He's always glad of a new boy to talk to.'

The plump man who had been using the telescope nearest to Faulcon suddenly swung the instrument round on its housing and walked away from the viewing platform. Faulcon moved swiftly into possession, and slipped a coding disc into the slot, pressing down on a small red button on the body of the binocular magnifiers. 'As long as you like,' he explained to Kris, 'but if you take your finger off the button you have to pay again. Yes, I know ... it's like something out of an old film.' Kris was looking vaguely horrified at such a primitive viewing system. 'Everything on Kamelios is old-fashioned and clumsy. You'll find that out soon enough.'

Before allowing Kris access, however, Faulcon himself took a slow and steady look at the distant valley, sweeping the field of view from the small, squat Riftwatch Station at the head of the gorge, right along to the distant gleam of some spiral structure which, rising a few yards above the edge of the cliffs, marked Rigellan Corner, where the valley curved round to the south.

As he peered across the mile or so to the rift, so Kris followed his gaze, squinting against the distance and the growing darkness. He said, 'Why wouldn't they let me trip out to the rift? It was the first place I wanted to see ...'

By way of an answer Faulcon swung the viewscope and focused on a jagged rise of purple rock and scree which seemed almost incompatible with the surrounding dun-coloured landscape. 'Take a look,' he said, and when Kris had looked, and was still staring through the binoculars in some confusion, Faulcon said, 'That was once a Riftwatch Station ... You can still see part of it. Between one windy gust and the next it had gone; that small crag, the result of some future movement of the planetary crust cracking the valley wide open, and then being eroded down ... That lump of rock is all that remained. To go to valley's edge is to invite a wind to snatch you away.'

Kris pointed out the hundreds of dark shapes moving darkly along the top of the valley, some of them quite obviously dropping over the cliffs and into the hidden deeps beyond.

'But they're all in suits,' said Faulcon. 'Rift suits – we call them r-suits. Have you had any practice in an r-suit yet?' He knew the answer of course.

'I tried one on,' said Kris. 'Why?'

'Because a rift suit is a life-saver. And it takes a lot of practice to learn how to respond to what the suit does. Until you've practised you won't be allowed within shouting distance of that wind channel down there. No one goes there naked. Not unless they're stupid. You're not stupid, are you Kris?'

Kris Dojaan's only reply was a contemptuous – irritated – snigger; but he kept his eyes to the viewscope, and Faulcon noticed him frown. 'No one goes there naked, eh? Well, what about him?' There was a moment's silence. Faulcon sensed the sudden shock that struck Kris rigid. The boy said only, 'It can't be ... it can't be ...'

'What the hell are you looking at?'

As Kris Dojaan drew away from the viewscope, Faulcon saw tears in his eyes, a frown of disbelief on his face. 'It can't be ... not so old ...' as if imploring.

Faulcon had tried to stop the machine cutting out as Kris's pressure eased on the red button; he failed. He slipped his credit disc into the slot again and peered into the distance. After a second he noticed what Kris had seen, and he couldn't restrain a laugh. 'That's nothing to be afraid of,' he said. 'That's our phantom.'

'I don't understand.' Kris's voice was quiet, worried.

'Our time phantom,' explained Faulcon. 'Or at least, so it's said. He's wearing the remnants of a Steel City uniform, and he first appeared out there, by the valley ... oh, I don't know. Before my time. Ten years ago? You can't get near him. Either he teleports, or there are hidden burrows that only he has discovered – or he vanishes into time … Nobody bothers him, and he doesn't bother us.'

Even as he said the words, so Faulcon recognized the death of wonder in his statement. He felt a prickle of cold sweat as he glanced through the great windows at the wind-swept landscape, and the distant figure – indistinguishable from the waving vegetation in which he crouched – that was the phantom. Nobody bothers him, and he doesn't bother us. The words seemed to mock him. A man who could travel through time itself! But he doesn't bother us. Faulcon's gentle laugh was impossible to read. We don't understand him, and on VanderZande's World that's the same as losing interest! The coldness clawed at his stomach. He looked to Kris Dojaan, and might have said something about the sudden terror he felt, the sudden focus upon the process of dehumanization, but Kris was speaking, responding to Faulcon's words of the second or so ago.

'He doesn't bother you? That's nice. Well let me tell you, Leo, he bothers me. And it's a damned shame that he didn't bother someone in Steel City, because he might have been saved a lot of agony.'

Puzzled, but aware that Kris was fantasizing about, or identifying with, the ancient relic of humanity that was crouched out by the deep valley, Faulcon focused again on the phantom, and reappraised the man. It was some weeks since he had last seen the apparition, and to be fair to Kris Dojaan, he *had* at first been excited at the thought of the man who had apparently conquered time.

The time phantom was an ancient, shrivelled figure; it was difficult to make out detail in the fading light, but he seemed to be staring straight at Faulcon as the viewscope peered down upon him, staring from shrunken eyes hidden in massive wrinkles of flesh and twisted facial muscle. His nose was squat, giving every appearance of having been crushed; it seemed to twitch as if he smelled Faulcon's scrutiny, but this was almost certainly imagination. His hair was lank, long, grey as ash – though there were those who said the phantom had hair of a different, darker hue – and from this distance seemed filthy; it blew, in the breeze, straggling and unkempt. By way of breathing apparatus he seemed to wear a corrupted respirator that covered the lower part of his face, held in place only by the pressure of his lips.

Suddenly he had risen to his feet. Stooped with age he began to lope along the edge of the valley. Now Faulcon could see that he was tall and withered, his arms skeletally thin when glimpsed through the ragged fabric of his clothes. When he crouched again he seemed to fold up into himself.

His garments were the fading remnants of a body suit, the clothing worn beneath the bulky rift suit. He could see no identification tag, nor any insignia.

The man was an enigma, and, excited by Kris Dojaan's freshness and the youngster's interest in all he saw about him, Faulcon re-experienced the thrill of mystery about the phantom. He was a man who no longer talked, who no longer allowed any contact from his fellow human beings, but a man who had undoubtedly once been of the city. He had been snatched by time and flung somewhere, somewhen, some place and time where he had screamed and not-quite-died ... a prison where the walls were centuries, where time itself was his gaoler.

And despite all that, he was a man who had come back!

Whether he had been lost from Faulcon's time, or from a time several or many generations hence, it was impossible to know. The man said nothing, and always ran from company as it approached. He was to be seen only on occasion, and had the knack of vanishing into thin air. The belief that he *was* one of the timelost was based more or less on this fact of his sudden appearance and disappearance, but it was true that he might well have been able to teleport; on a handful of colonized worlds such latent talents were more sharply pronounced than on Earth.

Faulcon cared to believe that the time phantom was just that ... a time traveller. He had been in Kriakta Rift a few weeks before when the man had last been seen by a crowd. All work had stopped, all eyes turned on the enigmatic, aged figure, as it had scurried along the base of the cliffs, darting between one piece of alien ruin and the next. There had been a slight breeze blowing, an ordinary wind, bearing with it no sign that it was concomitantly blowing through time. But abruptly the phantom had vanished, and the conviction was that a time squall had taken him. But a week later he had been sighted at the southern end of the valley ... more than three weeks' walk away!

Faulcon had found himself in considerable awe of the man, a man who could somehow ride the time winds, ride the whole of time itself.

Kris agitated for access to the viewscope, and Faulcon stood back, keeping his finger on the operating button. Kris, as he stared across the distance, was silent for a long time, although his breathing grew more pronounced and Faulcon saw that he had begun to sweat. All the while he fiddled with the star-shaped amulet, already developing Steel City superstition.

Quite suddenly Faulcon's body turned cold; he felt chilled to the bone and began to shiver. He wrapped his arms around his body and frowned, shocked by the suddenness of the sensation, then increasingly apprehensive. He took a step back from Kris, his gaze shifting between the stooped youngster and the haze of distance and dusk that bordered Kriakta Rift. He knew what was happening, not by virtue of any experience, but by having heard so often from older inhabitants of Steel City that this sudden awareness was one of the most frightening tricks that VanderZande's World could play.

Faulcon wanted to shout, but he kept determinedly quiet; he felt sick; his head was spinning, and cold panic began to drain the blood from his face. If Kris should have looked up at that moment he could not have failed to see the mask of shock that twisted his colleague's face. He would have asked pertinent questions, and Faulcon knew that he would not have been able to hide the truth from the boy.

Kris continued to watch the phantom, unaware of the deepening sickness in the man behind him. He himself was still agitated, upset by what he could see, recognizing, or identifying something about the distant figure, and Faulcon wondered whether Kris was gradually coming to realize just *why* he was experiencing that feeling of familiarity.

Faulcon began to walk quietly away from his team mate. He felt the rigidity in his face, the expression of bitterness (Kris was so young, it was so unfair!) and the deeper shades of unease. There was no question in Faulcon's mind, however, that those in Steel City who preached the strangeness of the world were right; there had always been those who held the view that within a few weeks of arriving on the world, certain senses expanded, certain sensitivities became more acute. It was said that you could tell the moment when a man's destiny linked with time, the very instant at which fate decided a man was to be lost into Othertime, even though the event may have subsequently taken a year or fifty years to come about.

Kris Dojaan was a marked man, marked out by the world to be swept into the greedy maw of years. Faulcon heard hastening steps behind him, realized that the boy was hurrying to catch up with him. But he wanted distance. He felt very sick, and there was a sharp pain in the pit of his stomach: tension. To be on the same team as a man whose death you have discerned is a terrifying ordeal, for once the team is formed it is formed until the end. Where Faulcon went, outside the City, Kris would also go, and Lena too, and one day a breeze would come, and perhaps as it took Kris Dojaan away into time it would spare a gusting afterthought for the others of the team as well. There was comfort in the simple action of raising the leathery piece of skin, his amulet, to his lips, wishing away the evil gaze of Old Lady Wind.

He stopped, then, and turned to face his colleague, not surprised to see tears in Kris's eyes. Not knowing what else to do he patted the youngster's arm, then began to walk with him towards the lift. 'You know, then. You've realized ...'

In retrospect Faulcon realized how cruel those words might have been, because surely Kris Dojaan had not had time to hear about the acuteness with which humankind on Kamelios came to be aware of time, and all its tricks. His words had been as cold, as thoughtless, as fleeting as a sudden bitter breeze.

He nodded his agreement, miserable, yet somehow resigned, now, to his new knowledge. They dropped to the lower levels, and began the lengthy walk to where the Commander of Section 8 would be waiting for them. Kris said, 'I should be at least grateful that I've seen him, even though he's ...' He broke off, shaking his head, perhaps shaking away tears. He slammed the amulet on his chest. 'I was so sure I'd find him, and then I felt so elated – it never occurred to me that what I'd find would be ... oh hell!' He laughed bitterly, then, and went on, 'I came here in the desperate hope that I would find out what had happened to him. The letters we received were not very specific, but I think we all guessed what had happened. Someone had to come and find him again. I dreamed of him, one night, I could hear him talking to me, telling me to follow him to Kamelios. You can't just sign on for a stay here, but I found a way of getting accepted quickly, and I came out.' He turned anxious eyes on Faulcon, who was by this time disturbed by the fact that he had misunderstood Kris's distress. He was also apprehensive, for he was aware of the youngster's fate when Kris Dojaan himself, it now seemed, was not. Kris said, 'Leo, I must get out to the valley. He's alive out there and I suppose that's all that matters. I'm sure that's him, and I'm sure he'll recognize me. I must get out to the valley ...' Faulcon saw him shiver, saw doubt touch his features. 'And yet, I'm reluctant to. Deep down I don't want to face him, not like that. But I must ...'

'Who are we talking about?' asked Faulcon carefully. His own agitation was growing. 'Your father?'

'My brother,' Kris said, as if surprised that Faulcon could have thought differently. 'My elder brother, Mark. He vanished nearly a year ago.'

'Mark Dojaan,' Faulcon said, and he felt clear-headed and ice cold as the name sprang out at him from among the lists of the timelost. In his months on Kamelios over forty men had vanished into time; incautious behaviour, perhaps, or the unpredictable time squalls that were the bane of the Rift-watch Stations, and the men who staffed them, catching them unawares. Faulcon knew all those forty names, could have written them out when drunk. You never remembered the names of those who had disappeared before your arrival on Kamelios; but you never forgot the names of those who disappeared while you were there.

So Kris was now convinced that the time phantom, the wizened enigma out by the valley, was his lost brother Mark; and Faulcon thought he knew for sure that the phantom was Kris Dojaan himself, thus accounting for the boy's sense of familiarity with the dimly seen figure. Both beliefs, both ideas, were unreasoned, unreasonable, unshakeable. Faulcon felt torn as to whether or not he should tell the youngster of his feelings, and whether he should tell him tactfully, or bluntly. One thing, he realized, was essential, and that was to take Kris out to the canyon as soon as he could, to let him get as close as possible to the man he believed to be his brother.

Another part of the strange lore of Steel City was that a man who is about to die at the whim of the time winds can always sense it, out there where the cliff walls dropped steeply to the alien lands below. He can stand there and hear the wind that will take him. When Kris Dojaan heard it he would know, of that Faulcon was sure. Kris was a man destined to be lost, and perhaps to be found again, found as an aged and withered creature whose movements and existence baffled and frustrated Steel City's security.

Faulcon wanted to be with his colleague, and yet he was afraid to be near him. This was the terrible paradox of Steel City, and the time wind teams; the terrible irony of friendship on this strange world.

CHAPTER FOUR

Between and above the six domes of the traverse units, the central city core was a great bulbous construction, divided into twenty-four levels, each with an area of a quarter of a square mile. Each level was equipped with its own scattering of lounges, 'open space' illusion, tight-packed living quarters, and less cramped administrative centres. Winding corridors linked extremes of each level, interlinked levels themselves, and connected the whole city mass with the traverse units, and with the utility sections in the wide stem of the central core. From most levels it was possible to look inwards and outwards across the vast, central plaza.

Steel City was crowded, often claustrophobically so; only 5 per cent of its population ever ventured out to the alien world with any real regularity. What had drawn them here, what kept them here, what motivated the fact of their contentment with VanderZande's World was something Faulcon had only vaguely ever understood. And even though he sensed it might be important to understand the reason for this massive commitment of human energy to such an apparently worthless existence, he had long since lost that natural inquisitiveness that might have led him into deep, psychological waters.

This was not to say that everyone on Kamelios, or in the city, or out among the neocolonial towns, was kept here for no apparent reason. The communities were genuine long-term settlements, granted by Federation Charter, supplied by Federation ships, listed with the Galactic Health Organization, and granted full rights under Galactic Law. The same was not true of Steel City, which was officially a 'military installation', still part of the same Federation, but responsible to a different Earth-based Committee of Interstellar Affairs. And even in Steel City itself, among that aimless population of clerks and cooks, cleaners and doctors, musicians, writers and entertainers of every sort, maintenance engineers, troops and the rich élite who had spent a fortune to buy the boredom of the mobile city on VanderZande's World, even here there were those who knew exactly why they stayed, whose whole lives depended on, and functioned because of, the quirks and mysteries of the planet beyond.

Commander Gulio Ensavlion was, among these few, the most manic, the most obsessed, the most fascinating.

As leader of Section 8, the exploration and monitoring section of which Faulcon was a member, Ensavlion lived, brooded and planned in a vast semi-circular office on level nine. One side of the room was a single, tinted window, overlooking the land between Steel City and Kriakta Rift. The curved wall seemed taken up not with gentle pictures, or soft, relaxing colours, but with maps, designs and charts: contour maps, detailed and precise, of practically every square mile of the main continents of the planet; satellite photographs of the world; meteorological charts of the wind flow, cyclone distribution, rain belts, earth-quake zones. Colourful, confusing, convincing, the man was surrounded by VanderZande's World in so much detail that it was doubtful if he could ever finish the exploration of his walls, let alone the real world outside.

One map display above all dominated the room: a one to ten thousand aerial map of the rift valley, all two hundred winding, enigmatic miles of it, taking up yards-long rows across the middle of the wall. The map seemed blurred at first, until Faulcon realized that each display was in fact several views of the valley taken at different times, showing the effects of each of the really powerful time winds that had blown through it over the last few years. The regular geometric patterns that laced the valley were the ruins, the structures of other times and other beings. Of some of these Ensavlion had pictures and plans: the towering temple-like building that had popped into view almost two whole years before, only to be snatched away a month later; the cubes, and spires, the domes and twisting, unaesthetic structures, hollow and more often than not empty, sometimes filled with such meaningless garbage that might be found in any building – containers, vessels, objects of decorative nature, supporting structures and a plethora of incomprehensible, ostensibly functionless trivia. Ensavlion's office was filled with such things, many in cases, some on open display. He even had models of a few of the more elaborate ruins in the valley.

As Faulcon led the way into the room, at last, summoned by the Commander, Kris Dojaan's eyes lit up. There was something even more exciting about seeing such junk in Ensavlion's office than in scrutinizing a carefully labelled display in the museum. It was as if the fact of its presence in the room of a Section Commander lent an aura of importance and mystery to the objects.

The door closed silently behind the two explorers. Faulcon relaxed, probably the effect of some ease-inducing chemical in the air, and smiled at Lena, across in Ensavlion's small interview area, away from the enormous desk where he worked. She was stretched out in an easy chair, legs sprawled, hands behind her head. She looked bored, tired, and extremely irritable. She raised a hand and waved at Faulcon, but her face never changed its expression of total fatigue. No doubt Ensavlion had been questioning her with great enthusiasm. The hazards of leadership.

Kris Dojaan, Faulcon noticed, had eyes only for Commander Ensavlion; he did not even acknowledge Lena. And to Faulcon's mild surprise Ensavlion himself seemed to find the young Dojaan an object of irresistible interest. The two exchanged a long, intense, mournfully solemn gaze. Abruptly Ensavlion smiled. Kris, who had seemed in awe of the older man, gave a quick little bow from the neck and his face hardened. Faulcon thought he saw a hint of anger there.

Gulio Ensavlion was an impressive-looking man, not particularly tall, but strong in build; his legs, in particular, were noticeable for their musculature, and though Kris could not yet realize the fact, Ensavlion's physique showed all the signs of one who spends hours, even days, in a rift suit. Older than his visitors, Ensavlion was nonetheless of indeterminate age. Faulcon thought he might have been in his sixties, on the declining side of his prime, but with a good forty or fifty years of active life before him. His face was drawn, deeply lined; his black hair was greying; swept back, and tightly bound in a small, greased plait, it seemed to shine darkly, strongly. He wore his green under suit, an outfit designed as a wear-anywhere, but which was particularly designed to be worn underneath an armoured rift suit. Kris was no doubt puzzled – whereas Faulcon was slightly impressed – to observe no insignia of rank, of achievement, sewn upon it.

'Welcome, gentlemen,' Ensavlion said, extending his hand to each of them. His grey eyes regarded each in turn, a nervous, hesitating gaze, and though he smiled he was apparently uneasy with them. 'Follow me, will you? We'll eat the cream before talking about the cake.'

Faulcon echoed Kris's empty laughter with a nervous smile of his own. He fervently wished that Ensavlion could relax more. But then Ensavlion had isolated himself so much from the human community that perhaps there was no hope of him ever regaining human attitudes.

Lena rose to her feet as they gathered at the main desk, came across and courteously shook hands with Faulcon and Kris, something they never usually bothered with. Ensavlion picked up two red plastic folders, slapping one into Faulcon's outstretched hand, and the other into Kris's. He laughed abruptly, staring at Faulcon who was greedily weighing the fat wallet and its traditional, plastic chits. 'Heavy, huh?'

'Generous,' Faulcon agreed, wondering what value was coded into each strip. It would have been improper to check the value of the bonus here and now; fifties or hundreds, certainly, and therefore five or ten thousand g.u.'s. Faulcon could scarcely bring himself to accept the possibility of the higher figure, but when he glanced at Lena she flickered her eyes heavenwards, and made a facial expression implying she was overwhelmed.

Ensavlion had slapped Kris on the shoulder, a hesitant but friendly gesture, and waved him to a seat. 'Sit down, Leo. Lena … Mister Dojaan.' He waved to a third chair. Sitting behind the desk, and leaning forward with his hands clasped on the work top, he looked at the two men and nodded. 'Very good work, gentlemen.' And to Kris Dojaan. 'May I assume the liberty of calling you Kris?'

'By all means,' Kris answered, while Faulcon winced: *may I assume the liberty!*

Ensavlion relaxed for the first time since they had walked into the room. He looked through slightly narrowed eyes at Kris. 'I've heard a lot about you. It's good to have you on the section. Good. Need vigorous young men, people with an interest, a compulsion …'

A compulsion to what he never said, but spent a moment nodding thoughtfully and appraising the youngster. 'I remember your brother. A good man and a tragic loss.'

It was possible to tell, from the way he chewed at his lip and sat up, that Kris was about to interject something on the subject of the phantom. Faulcon caught his eye and gave the merest shake of his head. Kris frowned, but relaxed again. Ensavlion said, 'I know you've come looking for him. I know that's very much on your mind. Well, maybe you'll find him. I can say this, Kris … I hope you do. I hope you find him, and I hope … I hope things work out fine.'

Faulcon noticed a certain shared grimness between Kris and the Commander. He glanced at Lena who was staring across the room at one of the maps; aware that Faulcon had glanced towards her she raised an eyebrow in query, but Faulcon shook his head and turned away. Ensavlion was saying, 'Always the need for young recruits, coming here from other worlds, distant worlds. We have an important job here, a vital job … a job that needs to be done, and I guess it's true that … I think that young men and women bring freshness, young ideas. And that's important if we're ever to … if we are to complete our mission here, and find out just what they are, these … these creatures, these beings. We need all the ideas we can get, all the good ideas and insights because, you know, they *are* there, they're out there, out there in time, and we need them, and we know that they watch us sometimes and know we're here, and maybe as I've often said, maybe that's because they need us.' He laughed suddenly, briefly. Falling solemn again, he stared across the room at his wall charts and diagrams. 'They need us, gentlemen ... and Lena. I beg your pardon. They need us, and that's something other section Commanders ... well, they forget the mutual need aspect. We can help, we can exchange ... ideas, you understand; cultures, insights. We *have* to find them again, and I think that ... I think that if we can just get out there and be ... and be positive, then maybe we'll benefit, maybe we'll advance our relationship with the Galaxy.'

He stopped talking, pushed three fingers across his brow and looked at the moisture he had rubbed off onto them. He was embarrassed, and suddenly in a state of extreme tension. Kris looked horribly uncomfortable, and Faulcon sympathized with the lad, wishing that somehow he could convey to him that Ensavlion always broke out into a sweat when he talked about *them*, and that there was nothing to worry about.

Ensavlion laughed suddenly. 'Hot,' he said. Faulcon agreed. The room was indeed stifling, but now that Ensavlion had finished speaking, had got this routine speech out of the way, an air of relaxation descended.

Ensavlion knew full well, of course, that he was regarded in a variety of ways by other Sections, even by his own: with amusement, or with contempt, with frustration or apprehension, and very occasionally with interest. There *were* those who believed he had seen what he claimed to have seen, the timetravelling creatures from the ancient days of this world. But the believers were few and far between.

It was a paradox that Faulcon occasionally found nagging at him. With a valley full of relics, and a land surface that was forever presenting new junk, new time debris to the inquisitive minds of men, it was difficult to comprehend how people could deny so aggressively the passing through of those who had once lived here, and who had constructed some of those objects. It was as if all the artifacts of another age were no more than toys to a child, a child who would find it hard to comprehend the stages, and hands and minds that were once occupied in constructing the playthings.

Behind Ensavlion, where the wall was blank over a fairly large area, a light flickered into existence, and a moment later, on the blankness, appeared a map of that part of the continent that included the vast inland Paluberion Sea, and the Ilmoroq mountains, with their dense forests and deep gorges. Ensavlion turned, reaching for a light pointer, and flashed the tiny arrow onto the screen, waving it in a wide circle. 'Recognize the view?'

Faulcon found himself nodding thoughtfully, but disturbed by something. He realized abruptly that the vast stretch of fairly featureless land reaching back from the foothills of the Ilmoroqs had been omitted, so that the end of the rift valley, the western beach, seemed far closer to the ocean than it was. A huge, multi-branched arrow was drawn across the ocean, its path curving both up and down. 'This is a prediction of the time flow that caused your machine to appear. Based on surface disturbances, and a more intense look at the sea bed now that you've drawn attention to the likelihood of a wind in this area, it looks as if we have a dual-channel flow. The machine could have come from either of them.'

Lena asked, 'Are there other ruins, traces on the sea bed?'

'None,' said Ensavlion. 'No traces at all, in fact, except for some strange topographical features. But no remains.'

'Just our derelict,' said Faulcon, suddenly realizing the full importance of the find. Normally such a discovery, leading to the prediction of a nearby time-flow, would be the first discovery of hundreds, or thousands, as full survey and excavation teams moved into the area. With the ocean, of course, they would be submarine teams, from one or more of the units that crawled along the ocean's edge, working in conjunction with deep-water orbital surveying satellites.

Ensavlion had turned about, and looked at Faulcon, something of a smile, something of concern on his face. 'Not *even* your derelict,' he said.

All three reacted with surprise, Faulcon leaning forward, and Lena shaking her head in bewilderment. 'I don't understand,' she said.

Ensavlion touched the small button built into his desk and the map view of the continent vanished, to be replaced by a satellite photograph of the shoreline. The tracks of their bykes, practically obscured by drifting sand, were none the less clear. Where the machine had been stuck in the rise of the sandy shore now there was nothing. Faulcon clutched his wallet of money tightly, wondering whether its continued association with him was now in jeopardy. He had actually stared at the machine-shaped impression in the sand for some moments before he became aware of what it was, and he relaxed.

'It went away, then,' he said. 'Good God. It must have crawled away again after we left, back into the sea.'

Another photograph appeared on the screen. This one clearly showed the hulk, and the marks of the three explorers who had walked so excitedly about it. Faulcon felt safe, now. The extra bonus was no doubt a personal gift from Ensavlion for their having found something that actually *functioned*.

'It had gone between one orbit of the viewSat and the next, a period of thirty minutes. Something went wrong with the geo-synch as it moved into place, the morning you left; it made another loop, and when it got back the thing had gone. No tracks left, but the wind might have obscured them on the ocean side of the ridge. Did any of you get inside the machine?' How confident and clipped Ensavlion could become when not indulging his encounter with the aliens.

Faulcon shook his head, then dropped his gaze as he waited for Kris to respond. Kris, however, denied having been inside the derelict. Faulcon glanced uneasily at Lena who shrugged almost imperceptibly. Then Kris said, 'But I'm afraid I damaged the side of the thing, trying to ... trying to clear sand. I set my blaster too high and gouged out a piece of the hull.'

'Did you enter it?'

Kris said no. He touched his amulet almost lovingly. 'I removed this from just within the confines of the machine. I reached my hand inside to do so.'

Ensavlion sat back, staring at the youth. 'It's possible, then, that your damage triggered some mechanism that eventually set the machine into motion. Is that what you think?'

'Delayed action ... up to ten hours later, following a freak shot?' Kris shook his head. 'That doesn't sound very likely to me.'

Ensavlion was staring at the amulet. For the first time he was realizing that the regularity of the shape meant it was an artifact, and not a shard. And of course, it was all that remained of the derelict. He drew a deep breath, selecting his words carefully, then leaned forward, hands clasped before him. 'Kris, you're new on this world, and we have codes of behaviour, and ways of doing things that may seem a little strange at first. I expect Leo has been filling you in ... telling you all about it. That's why you're on his team. You've broken a code of behaviour out of ignorance ... I should be angry with you, Leo, for letting him.' Kris paled, Faulcon noticed, but kept calm. 'You've taken an artifact as your charm, and not a shard. Artifacts are commonly taken as charms when there are several of them. Single artifacts are not.' Kris fiddled with the necklace, shaking his head almost imperceptibly: *you're not taking it away from me.* Ensavlion went on, 'However ... once a man takes his charm, it's taken. It belongs to you. To deny that would be to deny your right to life. There is nothing that can ... nothing that will be done to, do you understand, pressure you into allowing an examination of that piece of history.' He was beginning to sweat again, his coherence going as he succumbed to discomfort.

Kris had immediately caught his drift, however, and was obviously eager to cooperate now that he knew he would not have to lose the jewel. Had Kris so quickly become ensnared in the world's superstition? He said, 'But if I *allow* a study ... that's all right, is it? And I get the charm back?'

Commander Ensavlion nodded his agreement. 'Would you be prepared to do that?'

'Yes, of course.' Kris made to remove the amulet; he seemed vaguely amused by the whole discussion. Ensavlion quickly stopped him from lifting the necklace over his head. 'No, no. Don't take it off. Never take off your charm, Kris. Always wear it, keep it close, keep it soaking up your life spirit, guarding you. We'll conduct an examination *in situ*. I can only thank you for your help.'

How strange, thought Faulcon: over the last few minutes, except for the occasional moment of discomfort, Gulio Ensavlion had relaxed more than Faulcon had ever seen him relax in all his time on Kamelios. He obviously liked the boy, was recognizing, or reacting, to something about Kris Dojaan; this was good for Kris, and it was good for this tiny team. It was also good for the Section, because it had long been the considered opinion of the thousand persons who comprised Section 8 that Ensavlion needed someone to bring him gradually, delicately, but firmly back to the harsh realities of life on this confusing, changing world. Maybe Kris Dojaan could do it. Maybe the boy was a walking focus of luck.

Ensavlion slapped his hands together, then laid them flat on the table, staring at his knuckles. As Faulcon watched him in the silence he suddenly realized that the Commander wore no visible amulet. It had never occurred to him before, but now that he thought of it, he had never ever seen a shard or a necklet on the man. Before he could take the point further in his mind, Ensavlion said, 'The question is, to return to the problem at hand ... was it the jarring effect of the shot that sent the machine moving again; or was there someone ... or something ... on board. We'll never know, I suppose. The machine hasn't been spotted in the ocean ... it's a big ocean, mind you, and the bed is craggy and scored with deep, overhanging rifts. It could be hiding down there. More likely, it got caught up again in a flow of time. The ocean seems to be an active place, despite its quiet surface motion and unspectacular tides. Gentlemen ... Lena ...' He settled back in his chair, his gaze going beyond Kris to the wall maps. 'I think we may have encountered the travellers again.'

Oh dear God, thought Faulcon. Not the lecture. Please not the lecture.

Faulcon's fervent prayer was heard and granted. Ensavlion rose from his seat and gestured to Kris to follow him across the room. 'Come and see this, Kris. The others are probably fed up with hearing me talk about it, so they can start thinking of the report they'll have to make.'

He led Kris away across the room, to stand before the diagrammatic map of the present valley. Faulcon heard him describing the rift, pointing out the ruins of past, and some that were thought to be future, showing him the paths of the time winds, and the gullies and crevasses where squalls of time flowed and scurried almost constantly. He described his own visits to the interesting buildings, and to the less interesting structures; he stabbed at places where strange, living animals had been seen – always elusive – and where dead ones had been concerned him most, the place where the pyramid had come and gone in the twinkling of an eye, and yet in that twinkling ...

Although others had seen the structure, only Gulio Ensavlion had glimpsed, through the wide, unsymmetrical window, the movement within the machine of intelligent beings, the creatures who had once owned the world, who had left their ruins in abundance, and who journeyed through all of time to see what had come after them ... and perhaps to monitor it with some unknowable purpose in mind. They had paused in the valley for just

44

a second, stepping through the shimmering walls of their vehicle, perhaps aware, as they journeyed on, of the human eyes that watched them from the cliff tops … not staying to exchange greetings.

Ensavlion's audience of one was watching and listening, fascinated, mouth open, Faulcon imagined, eyes wide. Lena came over and sat next to Faulcon, whispering, 'Six thousand g.u.'s!'

'Six thousand!' Faulcon shook his head, almost in disbelief as his wildest dream came true. 'And for a machine that walked away! The old man must be crazy. Crazier, I mean.'

Lena laughed quietly, then nodded down the room where, to nobody's surprise, Ensavlion was telling Kris in great detail the story of that sighting he'd made, just less than a year back. 'Many good men lost out there, Kris. Good men, brave men. Seeking the aliens, seeking to make contact with them, and some of them went out once too often and never came back. But we've got to find them again, we've got to flag them down, so to speak. Man has learned to live on this planet, Kris; he's learned what to expect and how to react; there are no surprises except … except what's in the valley. There's danger there, certainly, and yet there's a goal there that makes no danger too great, no loss too heavy to bear. The valley, Kris. Have you been out there yet?'

'Not yet. Apparently I have to train first.' There was a hint of irritation in Kris Dojaan's voice as it drifted through the stillness to the silently listening Faulcon. And then an abrupt change of subject that caused an awkward exchange of glances between Faulcon and Lena. 'Commander … about Mark.'

'Mark?'

'My brother. Mark Dojaan. You know, the man who was such a tragic loss. Mark, for God's sake!' The sudden anger disturbed Lena Tanoway who turned to watch Ensavlion's reaction. Like Faulcon, all she saw was a stiff embarrassment on the Commander's face.

'What about Mark? A good man.'

'So you already said. But your letter told us nothing. Just that he was lost, dead … but how, why? Who was with him, Commander? Did he go bravely? If you thought he was dead, couldn't you have said that he had died without pain? You can't know the agony that letter caused …'

'Mister Dojaan.'

'No! I'll finish!' Ensavlion's face was red, now, and his skin gleamed with sweat. To Faulcon's surprise he stood his ground, watching the youth, watching the anger, taking it. 'You told us nothing, nothing but his death.' Kris suddenly relaxed, glanced at Faulcon. 'He's not dead, you know.'

'Isn't he?'

'I *know* he's not. But that's not the point. It's taken me months to get here, months even to start to find out why he failed to "survive", when you could have been so straight with us from the beginning. Mark was a strong man, a clever man; he was a natural survivor. So what happened, Commander? What went wrong for him?'

As if suddenly aware of the two listeners, Ensavlion glanced down the room at Faulcon. Faulcon and Lena rose from their seats and made 'about to leave' gestures. It was appropriate; they would have to submit draft reports within twenty hours, and there was a lot of writing involved.

Ensavlion gently propelled Kris back across the room. 'Kris, I can understand how upset you are. I really can. For the brevity of my letter, I apologize; and for failing to patch the information into the GHO network, yes, I apologize for that too. To be truthful, one gets forgetful … so many good men are lost here …'

'Right! You forgot about him. He was nothing to you but a name and a rank, that's the truth of the matter, isn't it? A routine loss. You don't even remember him now – you just checked his records.'

Angrily, no longer prepared to tolerate Kris Dojaan's emotion, Ensavlion silenced the man curtly and authoritatively. Kris fell sullenly silent, and when Ensavlion said quietly, 'That will do, Mister Dojaan. That will do,' he began to look slightly abashed. Ensavlion relaxed again, smiled nervously as he moved with the group towards the door. 'The sooner you get out to the valley the better, I can see that. Get in a few hours' training in a suit, and get out there. Look for your brother, if you really think he's still alive, and look for the travellers. Watch hard, watch constantly, watch carefully …' he glanced towards the darkness beyond the window, '… because they come and go, fleeting, like a breeze.'

The door slid back, squeakily. Cooler air from the neon-lit corridor was refreshing to Faulcon. Ensavlion shook his hand. 'Look after the boy. Talk to him, explain to him. He's bringing luck to Section 8 – if a little impatiently.' Faulcon forced a laugh at the strained jokiness. 'And maybe we'll catch a glimpse of the travellers when he's around. I've waited a long time, long months, and I've waited patiently; and now all of a sudden,' he shook hands with Lena and Kris, 'I feel they're just around the corner. Goodbye, gentlemen. Lena.'

CHAPTER FIVE

'Are you always so tactful?' Lena led the way into a credit registration booth, barely wide enough for the three of them to squeeze in together.

'I don't want to talk about it.' Kris Dojaan watched as Lena operated the automatic teller. 'This is a really stupid routine,' he observed as she slid the thin chits into a slot labelled with the same denomination and watched her credit tally mounting on a screen before her. She punched instructions – 20 per cent to be transferred to her personal account on New Triton, 10 per cent to her tax account, automatic settling of her dream-dome bill.

'We like it,' she said.

'We certainly do.' Faulcon kissed his wallet, pocketed one of the smaller chits – 'for a souvenir' – and shuffled round to gain access to the register. 'That's the trouble with progress; it forgets that people *like* the way they do things.' He started to register his bonus. 'If I were you, young Kris, I'd salt some of those g.u.'s away for a windy day.'

'Why? I'm not going to need it.'

Sullen, depressed. Faulcon looked at him, and at Lena, who shrugged.

'It's going to be a real fun evening, I can see that.' He punched buttons. 'Ensavlion's a fool.'

'Yes, well there are those who say he is, and those who say he isn't. Whatever you've got against him, somewhere there's a man who would disagree with you – violently. So I'd keep my irritation to myself, if I were you. Your go.'

A while later they stood outside the registration console and watched the bustle of life within Steel City. Kris was fascinated by peering upwards through the vast central well of the core, to where the different levels could be seen; for several minutes he was content to watch the movements of men and machines, passing around the huge open space above the plaza. Lena suggested they ate dinner together after night-fall, to celebrate their new luck. She had had no time to herself as yet; she scratched her torso and murmured something about a dream trip, a quick freshening up of the dye of her hair, a long bath – did Faulcon want to join her? Was he sure? Okay, she wouldn't press – and they could meet in the Star Lounge at chime nine, nine-thirty. Faulcon and Kris were agreeable, although both had stuffed themselves with junk food at the first opportunity earlier that afternoon. Faulcon explained that the Star Lounge was deliberately set aside as being too expensive for more than the very occasional visit, dealing as it did mostly in exotic imports and expensive trivia. It was Steel City's most attractive prospect, at least as far as food was concerned, and it was the quickest and easiest way of recouping a bonus into City funds.

Lena slipped away, into the crowds; Faulcon thoughtfully watched her tall, lean shape, her body moving with the stiffness of fatigue, her long hair gleaming, blue-tinged gold, in the bright, artificial light. He felt a momentary pang of some emotion as he realized that because he had refused to go with her, now, she would probably spend time with someone else. He couldn't help feeling that their relationship was getting a little too casual.

He turned back to Kris, his unease with the lad effectively damped by the protective walls of Steel City. His first panic gone, it was nevertheless with some misgivings that he anticipated the external training schedule that he would have to undertake with the new recruit. 'Do you want to be alone until we eat?' Faulcon enquired, not certain, because of Kris's quietness, whether he was intruding on the youngster's solitude. Kris shook his head, and declared quite brightly that he wanted to get drunk. Drunk straight away? Or first laid, and *then* drunk? Kris thought for a moment, wiry body hunched as he looked about him at the restless population, perhaps seeking inside his mind and body for some stirring of interest at the prospect of going up to the dream-dome. He decided just drunk would do fine, so Faulcon led the way up to a sky bar, with an outlook towards the gloom-shrouded valley. Kris sprawled out in the quiet and relaxing lounge, watching the lights of the world come on, while Faulcon acquired two bottles of a green, translucent liquid that he told Kris was *baraas*, a rare distillation and among the most expensive drinks in the Galaxy. They tucked in with enthusiasm, although after a while decided that *baraas* would taste better flavoured with lime.

During the evening Kris met a handful of Faulcon's acquaintances and section colleagues and exchanged increasingly slurred pleasantries with them. He perked up quite noticeably when Faulcon introduced him to a dark-haired girl called Immuk Lee, who sat for a while and shared a glass with them. She was an old flame of Faulcon's, and Kris was quite evidently attracted by her. Down from the biology station at Chalk Stack, she was staying overnight. She'd brought in several specimens of gulgaroth body fluids for a more detailed analysis in the laboratories of the City. Kris Dojaan, for thirty minutes, discovered an amazing interest in the blood of native carnivores. When she left she invited them both to visit Chalk Stack. Kris watched her go, then slumped in his chair, mournful and distant. When he recovered from what he revealed had been an incapacitating surge of desire he began to ask questions, many of them conversational (and about Immuk), a few of them to answer things that had puzzled him since his arrival on Kamelios.

Why, for example, did Lena speak so peculiarly, so liltingly? Faulcon had long since ceased to think of Lena's speech as being unusual, but of course she *did* have a strong accent, and that accent was colonial New Triton, her planet of origin. New Triton was a world where InterLing was spoken with reluctance, the main language being that primitive version of inter-Lingua, French: she had come to the Galactic language with facility, therefore, but had never bothered to try and work away the clipped, lilting accent of her natural tongue. Some people, Faulcon hinted strongly, found that trait attractive. He was slightly disturbed when Kris declared emphatically that he did not.

But why, he asked, did she wear her hair so long, like a man's, with those ridiculous transplanted side-burns curving nearly to her cheeks? The way he described them, in an exaggerated, almost comic fashion, made both men laugh. But Faulcon pointed out the high incidence of transplanted cheek and chin hair on the female population, some worn bushy, some shaved very close, and he made it clear that Kris's awareness of Lena's modishness was only because he was more aware of that one woman among all the hundreds who inhabited Steel City.

Faulcon spent a while instructing Kris in the arts and versatilities of Steel City tastes, and how attitudes and clothes, make-up styles and hair arrangement, changed not from year to year, but almost from a fourteen-day to a fourteen-day. Sometimes a group aestheticism would emerge from the chaos of styles and modes, and then it would linger longer, and permanently establish a group of men and women who would forever wear that style, for although fashions changed frequently, there were always minority groups who settled for one 'look'. At the moment, Faulcon explained, pointing out examples in the bar to illustrate his words, the mode was for women to wear their hair long, like Earth women, and to seek skin grafts with bright orange or red hair on them, to give their side-burns an interesting contrast to the green or purple staining of their natural locks. He pointed out the high incidence of male pigtails, with natural colours being more obvious than the occasional streaking of silver, an outdated fashion that had lasted several months, about a year ago. Body hair, of course, was dyed in personal choice colours, and often grafted or shaped into elaborate patterns. Faulcon opened his shirt slightly, and showed Kris the abstraction of his own chest hair. Kris laughed, frowned, and swallowed his *baraas* quickly, refilling his glass almost as if the stimulant would make him immune to Steel City's bizarre behaviour. He had led a very sheltered life on Oster's Fall.

He was glad to hear from Faulcon that, whereas on many civilized colony worlds voice and pigmentation transplants were common, on VanderZande's World such extremes of body art were frowned upon.

Gradually Kris brought the idle conversation round to the subject of the great valley, and its ruins, and in particular its human ruin, the phantom. He repeated his feeling of urgency that he should get out to the lip of the canyon and look for that fleeting figure against the wreckage-strewn landscape. He glanced at Faulcon. Could he go out the next day?

Faulcon shook his head, concerned for the youngster, and concerned for the flaunting of Steel City rules. 'I'm afraid not. It takes several days training in a suit … You can't just put an r-suit on and away you go. And the rules of the City are quite explicit about it; we had a lot of difficulty clearing the Ilmoroq mission so soon after you joined us, but we never underestimate the danger of the valley.'

Kris looked first crestfallen, then angry. 'But Commander Ensavlion said I should get out there as soon as possible.'

'Which is a three-day at least. Two if you really work hard.'

'Ensavlion implied quite strongly that he thought I should go out to the valley *today*! *Tonight!*'

One glance at the impetuous Kris told Faulcon that this was a lie. Besides which, he'd heard no such implication, although he *had* heard Ensavlion encouraging the boy to train quickly so that he could become a fully fledged member of the team.

'Steel City has the final say, not Ensavlion.' And by way of changing the subject and bringing the pressure down, Faulcon told Kris something of the team he'd joined.

When Faulcon had arrived on VanderZande's World, Lena had already been here a year. He had come with more than a hundred other rookies, a very bad error of application on his part, since it meant he had been assigned to a large, inexperienced team, led by one old hand, well-satiated with the wonders of Kamelios. It had taken a month to get his first circuit of the valley, and two months more before the team was allowed its first run down to the cluttered lower slopes of the rift. Thereafter, for a few weeks, he had worked as part of Ensavlion's ten-man team, the Commander at that time being head of Section 3. At his own request, and against Lena's better judgement, he was finally taken on in Section 8, assigned to the team that had Lena as middle-runner and a man called Rick Kabazard as leader. By coincidence, Ensavlion transferred command at the same time.

Most of their trips down into the gash in the crust were for the purpose of investigating 'hollow boats', the City nickname for any building or structure with an r-suit-sized opening in it, and a very dark maw. Most of his work, he told Kris, had been spent walking or crawling in dark and cramped corridors from one boring end to the other, or perhaps to a dead end at which point, frustrated, the team turned round and came out again. Where entrance-ways were tight it was traditionally the middle-runner who climbed out of the r-suit and squirmed in naked.

There was precious little by way of bonus for that sort of work, and Faulcon, and indeed Lena herself, began to get very restless. In fact, what was happening to them was perfectly common, and their feeling of being a bad-luck team was shared by virtually every other team in Section 8. Then, just twenty days or so ago, a time squall had thrown up several oblong structures, piled in random, chaotic fashion, and thought at first to be crystal formations of geological interest only. With a geologist from Section 14 the three of them had 'run the rift', dropping down into the canyon some way from the object of exploration, and moving towards the destination in a wide line, wary for the sort of swirl of wind and time that had thrown the artifacts out of past or future. The obsidian crystals were some four hundred feet long, and forty wide, and were piled in threes, so that they towered well above the team. It was immediately apparent that the smooth surfaces were pitted in an artificial way, and that underneath, where the juxtaposed faces were not always aligned, there were knobs, buttons and panels.

Kabazard and the geologist discovered a low entrance-way, where the squall had unevenly fetched the object from its natural time; part of the back of the structure was sheared off, exposing thick, crystalline walls, and for men in r-suits an uncomfortably narrow tunnel-way in. The two men had entered, despite Lena's protestations that because this was not a geological feature it should be she who went inside with the leader, and not the man from Section 14. Her protests ignored, she and Faulcon had continued exploring those parts of the outside of the feature that the view-probes in orbit and on the canyon-lip could not see.

The squall came back, a rising eddy of air and dust, and the dizzying blurring of features, and flashing of colours about an area of total black, that tells of the opening of the time gate. Faulcon could not forget Kabazard's screaming as the first eddy had sheared part of the structure away, and part of the leader's body. Faulcon was already hundreds of yards away, his suit obeying his unconscious instinct to run, and since he was now under total control of the cerebrally-linked servo-mechanism, he was able to turn and watch as the obsidian enigma was again swallowed by time, but in two bites, as if it were too large to be ingested in one go. And for that terrible instant, as the eddy veered away and then back, he saw Kabazard's bloody figure, cramped up inside the warren of tunnels that penetrated the structure, his right side sheared clean through, and the suit jerking spasmodically as it tried to function and failed. A second later he had flickered out of sight. By that time their r-suits had taken Lena and Faulcon well out of range of that danger spot.

'We didn't know it,' he said to the silent, attentive Kris, 'but Ensavlion had just accepted your application form, and logged you down for Section 8; you were already on your way, of course.'

'I don't understand ... I don't understand the connection.'

Faulcon grinned. 'Your luck, man! Your luck. It had reached across space and wrapped its arms around me. By rights it should have been Lena in that object, with the geologist waiting outside. By rights both Rick Kabazard and Lena should have died. And on this world we have special rules, as Ensavlion tried to tell you. If two of a three-man team get swallowed up by time, well ...'

He had stopped, but Kris had comprehended. 'He has to go too; he has to sacrifice himself.'

Faulcon nodded. 'It's a tradition that has grown up over several generations; it's a rule of the game, a code, an unbreakable code.'

'But it's unhuman! It's stupid!'

'It's an inhuman world, Kris. It's a hard world and makes hard rules.'

'I didn't say *in*human, I said *un*human. It doesn't sit right on man to agree to such self-sacrifice. It's wrong for man.'

'This whole world is wrong, Kris. It's a world of constant change and it changes man along with it. If you spend long enough here your body and mind will be twisted and torn until sometimes you'll be walking when you're sitting and awake when you're asleep. Unless you fight it, like we've all fought it. Resist it, resist the change, resist until sometimes you'll want to scream. We've adapted to Kamelios, all of us, all the survivors. We've worked out our relationship with VanderZande's World, and we've mastered it. And the changes are all superficial, Kris – they don't get in deep down. Like Ensavlion said, we've learned how to live here, what to expect, how to react. Now we can get on with the business of exploring the alienness.'

Warmed and slightly dizzy from the *baraas*, Faulcon felt a peculiar sense of pride in being on the world. Kris Dojaan watched him carefully, perhaps looking for some facial gesture that would belie the words. He said, 'So man has no fear of Kamelios, or of time, or of the ruins.'

'There is a gut fear of the time winds – they're dangerous. You don't treat danger in a casual, careless fashion. I'm afraid of the time winds, I'm afraid of being swept away – and I behave carefully, respectfully. That's how I behave with loaded weapons, with gulgaroth, with everything that has a dangerous potential; especially with the winds. Nobody wants to go into time.'

Kris's eyes lowered and he swirled the drink in his glass. 'Nobody?' he said. 'Surely there must be a few adventurers, men sufficiently disillusioned with our world to kiss it goodbye and go to other ages.'

Faulcon said, 'You might think so. I think I remember thinking so myself. I think. To be honest it's hard to remember, but it certainly seems a ludicrous idea to me now. And a terrifying one. You'd literally have to be out of your mind to risk being swept away … The evidence of what animals we pick up in the valley, and where other winds blow, is enough to tell us that the atmosphere of Kamelios has altered vastly over the ages. You'd have to be mad.'

'Or obsessed?' Kris was looking hard at his team mate, his youthful features tense, almost agonized, Faulcon thought. Was he referring to Ensavlion?

'Commander Ensavlion wouldn't risk it,' he said. 'The man is obsessed with his aliens, but he wants to see them here and now; he wants to invite them to Steel City for drinks and supper. He wants the glory, and you don't get glory if you're stuck a billion years in the past, or embedded in primeval sedimentary rock, with just your face plate gleaming through as erosion works its way down to you. There is such a corpse, Kris. It's at the farthest end of the valley, and it's been there a long time. I tell you, one look at that "fossil" is enough to put anyone off stepping deliberately into the path of a squall; it lets you know that the time winds are death winds … when they take you, you *die*. Forget the romance. I can't forget Kabazard.' Faulcon hesitated, conscious that his voice had risen, and his speech had begun to slur. 'Besides,' he said, 'back to Ensavlion for a moment. He believes in the travellers, the alien time-travellers. Why risk death in the unknown when the travellers could teach us all we want to know? It's neat. That's why Ensavlion is not alone in his belief.'

Silence, then. A brooding silence, despite the babble of conversation, and clatter of glasses in the extensive bar. Faulcon was thinking of Mark Dojaan. Was it Kris's brother who was emerging from the valley wall under the eroding influence of rain and ordinary wind? Most unlikely. And it was not Mark who was scurrying darkly about the canyon, Faulcon was sure of that as well. When Kris found the fact out for himself, what would his next step be? Faulcon was almost certain that it would be a step into the path of a wind, a deliberate suicide in the hope that it would not be suicide, but rather a mission of rescue.

Which of course it would not be. It *could* not be.

'How do you know', said Kris quietly, 'that hundreds of men and women, trained people, people fully aware of the dangers, and the certainty of being forever lost, how do you know that there aren't hundreds such going out to the valley every night and slipping away into Othertime?'

It was a disturbing thought, and Faulcon felt the hair on his neck prickle as he tried to picture such teams slipping out in the darkness, descending the canyon walls, and stringing out, grabbing squalls and winds with joy, popping out of sight, some perhaps being sheared completely in half, or losing limbs, or bits of protective clothing. He had been out at night, and had never seen any such movement. There was no talk in Steel City about such events. But the rift valley was hundreds of miles long, and there were stations along its rim every twenty miles or so, stations big enough to accommodate a large population if that population was just passing through. And some of them had landing sites for the cargo shuttles from orbiting supply ships.

He said, 'I give up. What's the answer?'

Kris laughed. 'You don't know, is the answer. You can't know. Nobody in this steel-hulled hell-hole knows anything about what's *really* going on on VanderZande's World. You get up, go out, get a bonus, get drunk, get laid, go to bed ... sleep. And in the night the world could stop, do a somersault and spit a hundred explorers into the world's Cambrian, and in the morning Leo Faulcon would still be thinking of *money* for *artifacts*, and how to survive another day, and what's he going to have for breakfast.'

Faulcon poured himself another drink and wondered what was coming – hysteria, contempt, anger? It was difficult to gauge a man whom he had only known without a mask for a matter of hours.

He said, 'I'm sorry if you're angry, but that's the way it is. I don't believe in your moonlight missions, because I don't believe that Steel City has a secret side to it. We hear about everything that goes on—'

'And don't give it another thought, right?'

'That's as may be,' Faulcon agreed mildly, settling back and staring hard at the boy. Kris's face was white, his lips pinched, and Faulcon guessed that it was a recurrence of the grief he had felt at losing his brother, a grief now tempered with desperation ... and yes, maybe a little contempt for Faulcon's mercenary, easy-going attitude. 'That's as may be,' he repeated, 'But the point is, we've heard nothing. There are three-man teams, there are eight-man teams, there are solo riders, there are sections set up for liaison, for geology and chemistry, and there's a section kept ready for that much desired first contact. There are no time-travelling sections. I could account for every room, every level, every section, every Commander, every man, woman and child in Steel City and its environs. I could stop *anyone* and get a response from them as to what they're doing on the world, and it would fit with the routine scheme of things. Kamelios is not the last great frontier, Kris. There are no pioneers here, no covered wagons heading through the misty wall of years, back into the untamed lands of yesterday ...' he briefly shared Kris's smile at the purple shade of his prose, '...the planet is an anomaly. The people here are monitoring that anomaly. A few are trying to understand it. Earth awaits their findings with interest, but hardly with baited breath.'

Kris Dojaan shook his head, as if in sympathy with Faulcon's short-sightedness. 'I can only assume that something about this place, or the society of men in Steel City, blinkers people like you. I hope it doesn't happen to me. I shan't be around long enough to find out if it will.'

Faulcon waited quietly, watching his colleague. 'What does that mean?'

'I mean, when I find Mark I'm going home. That's Mark out there ... old, frail ... maybe no longer the brother I knew in mind, or experience. But it's Mark, and I've come to take him home. To find him and take him back, because that's what my family wants, and it's what I want, and it was what Mark said to us before he left. He said to find him if anything went wrong, and when it went wrong he called to me and repeated his plea.' Seeing the quizzical expression on Faulcon's face, he shrugged. 'We have this thing, this contact ... a talk-space in our heads. As kids we played chess across half a planet's distance ... we lived apart for a while, when our parents were split up. I'd always know the move he wanted to make, and he'd know mine. We're not twins, we just have talk-space. I heard him, Leo. I don't expect you to believe me, but believe that I *think* I hear him ... he communicated with me, he called to me. And I've come a long way, and practically signed my life away, to get him back.'

Quietly, Faulcon said, 'Is a brother so important then?'

Kris's eyes were tearful. 'Yes, he bloody well is.'

Faulcon thought: what do I do? What do I say? The man is right to be wary of my motives, to be contemptuous of me. But what do I say to him to convince him he's being foolhardy? Kris Dojaan had reached across and was draining the *baraas* into Faulcon's glass. He smiled thinly, almost ashamedly. 'I'm sorry, Leo. I shouldn't take it out on you. It's not your fault. I'm sobering up too fast. Let's have another bottle – this stuff's good.'

Before he could turn to attract the attention of a waiter, however, Faulcon said, 'That's not your brother out there, Kris. That's not Mark.'

'You've implied that before.' Kris was not hostile, just quiet, thoughtful. 'If it's not Mark, then who is it?'

Faulcon stumbled on the words, not really wanting to antagonize the boy, to spoil the evening's celebrations; he was aware that Kris would probably react scornfully to the idea of Faulcon's truth, but he was afraid that the boy would be contemptuous, almost aggressive at what he might see as Faulcon's delusion. Before he could verbalize that truth he felt he should tell Kris, Kris said, 'It's Mark. I just know it is. Mark had that survival streak in him, you know what I mean? He was a winner, a natural winner. It made me mad, sometimes … jealousy, envy, call it what you like. But others fed on his strength. You talk about luck, and me spreading luck; with Mark around, as kids, even in national service, everything went right; he was so confident, Leo. He made life a challenge, and he made it rich. And if anyone came back from Othertime, it was Mark. That was the sort of man he was. He was a winner, Leo, an absolute, survival-orientated, winning-streak of a man.' He smiled. 'That's why I know instinctively that it's Mark … he came back, Leo. He was lost, and he came home again. And he communicated to me … mind power, his mind power reaching across all those light years.'

'Is he talking to you now?' asked Faulcon, but the dead tone of his voice was a sufficient indication of his cynicism to make Kris's face darken. The point went home. Faulcon moved quickly, sensing that it should be now or never, prepared for as many reactions from Kris Dojaan as he could foresee. 'Kris, that's not your brother out there, it's you. You. Kris Dojaan, the young man of twenty who, in a few weeks' time, or a few years' time, will be snatched away by the winds, and will somehow make it back. The time phantom is you, yourself.'

If Kris was momentarily stunned, laughter soon swept through him 'Me? *Me*? Oh come on, Leo, come on. That's nonsense and you surely know it. Don't you think I could have sensed myself out there …?'

'You sense your brother,' Faulcon said stiffly. 'But what you sense is something personal, and you are rationalizing it as your brother.'

'I don't believe it. Anyway, what makes you so sure it's me? What makes you so sure it's anyone? I've got an empathy with Mark, and whilst I wouldn't call that any sort of *psychic* power, it's strong enough to … you know, it's an *affinity*. That's what I mean, an affinity, a spiritual affinity between us …'

'Talk-space.'

'That's right, that's what we called it at home. And it communicates in some way other than by senses. But what are you using to be so damned sure it's me, and not Mark, or you yourself?'

Faulcon almost shouted with frustration. He placed his glass down on the table, glanced around guiltily as he realized that Kris's outburst had caused an embarrassed silence in this part of the bar. Gradually heads turned away, conversation resumed, and Faulcon faced Kris's aggressively triumphant features. The boy was drunk, that was clear enough. He was also getting very angry, very concerned. Faulcon didn't want to talk seriously in conditions such as this, but he felt he had no choice.

'Look, Kris. On the one hand you're claiming powers of empathy, on the other you're denying them. If you can believe an affinity between two brothers, living light years apart, why can't you believe in a heightening of extra-sensory powers on a world like this one, whose second name is Kamelios, think about that ... Chameleon, the inconstant one, a world of changes, a world where nothing remains the same when it gets here. And that goes for people too. I came here thick and dull, sensually that is. Within a year my senses are sharp. I can hear better, I can see better, I can smell better even though I wear a mask outside, and I can *sense* better. Everybody here can do it. No, that's not true. Not everybody, perhaps not even half. But so *many* people experience it that it is a definite phenomenon. We develop special senses. Come on, Kris, it happens all over the colonized galaxy. Worlds have auras, and those auras impose different psychological constraints or enlargements upon an alien population.'

'I know about that,' said Kris, testily. 'Homing, the shroud, all of that stuff.'

Faulcon had not thought of Homing for a long time, and now, just briefly, he experienced it again in all its clenching, nostalgic, desperate sharpness – fields, cities, the smell of earth, the aura of Earth: the earth shroud within which man had evolved, the aura of the world that had become so deeply interpenetrated with the cells and substance of the animal body. It had marked humankind as belonging to a single world, and when they left that world the tie of the shroud was only broken with difficulty – it tugged at heart and mind, and could break spirit; it could destroy, and yet it could be destroyed itself. Homing. Homesickness. The voice of the earth, weakening, but always there.

'All that stuff,' Faulcon echoed quietly. 'That's right. And how do I know it's you out there? I felt a strong sense of familiarity myself. I felt it suddenly, and agonizingly. A little voice in my head told me that you were doomed. I'm sorry to be so blunt, but it's one of the phenomena of this world that when someone gets "marked down" for taking by the winds, when fate decides you're going to be lost in time, it communicates to some of those around you. It really does, Kris. I can't explain it, all I can say is that if you're here long enough you may well come to feel it yourself.'

Kris stared at Faulcon, expressionless, but obviously intent. 'What are you saying, Leo ... that suddenly, a few hours ago, you felt, you *sensed*, that one of these fine days I'm going to slip into Othertime?'

'And the coincidence of your own familiarity with that phantom ... it seems to add up, Kris.'

'What I want to know is, why didn't you sense the impending doom of Kabazard? Your old leader.'

'Rick Kabazard. Yes, a good point, and one I did wonder about ... briefly. A man like Kabazard, doomed, doesn't sort of "radiate" his fate; perhaps I gave that impression. There is a moment when your life takes a turn, links up with Kamelios. It's at that moment that you can "feel" his fate, sense it. It had happened, with Kabazard, before I met him, before I spent time with him. He knew it, he must have known he was doomed, but he said nothing about it.'

'All right, Leo. I'll accept that. I don't want to talk about it now, but Leo ...' he smiled and leaned forward; the amulet swung free and struck against the glass he held with a short, ringing sound. Kris raised the star to his lips just briefly. 'Leo, it should be *obvious* to you that I'm going to slip into Othertime. For God's sake, that's the whole reason I came here. I've got to find Mark. I came quite prepared to chase him through Othertime, to seek him out. I still am, and I know that I may have to pursue his withered body through the years, to give him the confidence to return. I shall do it. So of course you sensed my impending "doom". But what makes you so sure that the *phantom* is me? I don't understand that.'

Faulcon shrugged, *baraas* dimming his vision and his faculties.

How to explain that sudden surge of understanding, that moment's intuition? And how often that intuition had been proven wrong. 'You identified with the phantom, I identified you as fated to be lost to time. I think two and two make four. I agree, we could both be very wrong. You *want* to find Mark, and I don't comprehend the way VanderZande's World affects my mind. Or anybody's mind, come to that.'

'Here's to madness!' Kris, having replenished their glasses from a new bottle of *baraas*, raised his drink towards Faulcon, who responded, smiling. 'To madness.'

The long Kamelion dusk ended, the light outside Steel City deepening from red to grey as the ancient sun was swallowed by the mist-shrouded mountains of the west. The nearby land was an eerie nightscape of scattered lights and winking green signal-points, marking danger zones and trackways through the jagged rocks. Steel City was a brilliant jewel, glowing with internal light, yet still reflecting the redness of Altuxor; a fire-lit ruby, the installation entered its evening phase. From the bar where Faulcon sat he could see the warm glow of life in the cabins and restaurants below them, and in shops and workplaces in two of the traverse units. But as yet, though he tried, he could not see the stars.

At the musical disturbance of nine chimes they rose from the bar and made their way to where Lena Tanoway had just arrived in the Star Lounge. She was dressed more casually, now, in wide trousers and a green, many-layered shirt, the folds of cloth tumbling across her breasts most erotically, as far as Faulcon was concerned. She had trimmed her hair, and tightly curled it about the rim of her skull. The sideburns that Kris found so idiotic were hardly in evidence. She smelled faintly of musk, faintly of soap, and Faulcon felt his mouth go dry. Raw jealousy, the belief that Lena had been up to the flesh farm since he had not gone with her, made him angry with himself; the drink made him emotional; his maleness made him resentful.

Inside he twisted up as he said, with affected relaxedness, 'It's good to see you. And you look gorgeous.'

Lena smiled at the compliment, and as they took their places in the lounge she cast a cynical glance at Faulcon and said, 'One bottle or two? Each?'

Faulcon made a gesture with his hand: more than one, less than two.

'You reek. Both of you. I'm surprised you're still standing.'

'We've been arguing,' Kris observed politely. 'And now we're friends again. Isn't that right, Leo?'

'Kris won't believe that we sense certain things,' explained Faulcon, and Lena stared at him hard. 'Won't he?' she said, and it was apparent to Faulcon that she was less bothered by the cause of the argument than by something in Faulcon's demeanour, his behaviour; he sobered quite abruptly, met her gaze coolly. *Please don't say anything, not yet, not yet.* She said, 'That's enough of that, anyway. I want to eat, to talk about our next few days – we have to train Mister Dojaan here to ride an r-suit, but on the other hand it *is* our vacation, and only three days to offload a vast number of g.u.'s. That's going to take some organization, gentlemen.' She looked at Faulcon again, but the hardness was gone; Faulcon felt himself go tense, and then warm with love. She was smiling very faintly, but her eyes communicated more than she ever allowed her words to say. 'After dinner, Kris, you will excuse us I'm sure.'

'I suppose so,' Kris said glumly. 'But haven't you got a sister?'

They toasted a good week's work. The two meat-eaters ate snails in their shells, imported from the farms on nearby *Cyrala* 7 and cooked in garlic and tasselroot sauce. Faulcon indulged himself, then, with a white meat called *beliwak*, from a non-terrestrial animal with an analogous amino-acid structure to Earth animals (the *beliwak* had probably been seeded in the early days, and no record kept), which had a strong taste, and made Kris blanch as Faulcon offered him a morsel. He said it smelled rotten. Faulcon explained that it was allowed to deteriorate in a special liquid containing herbs and bleaching for nearly two months. Kris blanched even further. He himself, being a principled vegetarian, ate a spiced dal made from lentils grown in the colonial communities hereabouts. He was particularly taken with coddle-neep in red wine sauce, a native root plant and a recipe acquired from the manchanged colonies, high in the foothills of the Jaraquath mountains. Its flavour was not unlike strong game-bird (although only Faulcon recognized this fact). Kris thought it was excellent, and seemed doubly delighted to be eating an 'alien' plant, since on Oster's Fall everything was earth-seeded.

The meal for three came to eight hundred g.u.'s, ten times what they would normally have expected to pay.

Kris excused himself eventually, and Lena and Faulcon walked hand in hand down to the occupation levels, and to Faulcon's quarters. Lena was warm, communicative. Perhaps the tension of leading the team for a seven-day had drained away, leaving her relaxed, aware of those parts of her body and mind that were not concerned with VanderZande's World, and work, and aliens; parts concerned with love, and Leo Faulcon.

In the soft light of Faulcon's room her body lost much of the hardness imposed upon it by training and life on Kamelios; they stood in each other's arms, close, warm, eyes shut, lips playing gently on each other's skin as they fed on the peace and tranquillity of this first embrace since the mission.

Lena kissed Faulcon on the mouth, then said, 'You followed me to this world ...'

'I wasn't going to lose you. I was determined about that.'

'I know. You followed me here, I suppose it's only right that I should follow you away from here, to your own world.'

Faulcon smiled. 'I don't mind where we go. The problem is, how can we break with Kamelios?'

They drew apart and hand-in-hand stood by the window, looking out across the brilliantly-lit slopes and surface walks of the city. The nightscape beyond was visible only as a series of red and green lights; their own shapes moved, ghostly, tenuous, in the glass. Above the land Merlin showed its face from behind bright Kytara, the two planetoids skipping ahead of tiny, pale-faced Aardwind – the moons were insubstantial half-discs, seen as in a pond.

'Do you realize', Faulcon said quietly, 'that we have just acknowledged how trapped we are by this planet?' It was something they had never discussed, something, a knowledge, that all on VanderZande's World denied. Faulcon realized, now, that the denial of this particular reality had been a barrier between them, indeed, was a barrier between all men on Kamelios.

Perhaps trapped was the wrong word, with its connotation of imprison-ment and desire to escape. Lena said, 'We've become masters of Kamelios, we've learned to live on the world, to use the world, and we've changed. We've both changed, Leo. Our ambitions are the ambitions of just about everybody who ends up in Steel City, and not on the farms: discovery, investigation, the finding of *something* ...'

It was a feeling with which Faulcon was well familiar – the sense of having a goal, of seeking something, even though he could not voice, or articulate, exactly what it *was* he was seeking. And the thought of leaving Kamelios was terrifying – the thought of distance between himself and the valley and time and ruins. What contrary creatures we are, he thought – on the one hand cold, contemptuous, uninterested in time's derelicts, but trapped by the need to discover something within those remains.

'Perhaps we should just go – right now,' he said. 'People *have* left Steel City. We should just drive out to the landing strip and wait for a shuttle. What do you think?'

Lena said, 'That would be the only way. Just up and go. Don't think about it, don't think of the valley. Just leave; Leo, I truly want to leave here, to go somewhere dull and simple, Earth perhaps, or any farming world. Why don't we do it?'

Faulcon found himself in the grip of a sudden panic, a claustrophobic sensation, the room closing in, the air straining his lungs, the beast of blood through his head loud and physically violent. 'We should do it tomorrow,' he said, and there was no real heart to his words. 'Why don't we see how we feel in the morning?'

If Lena felt like laughing she restrained it well. Hugging Faulcon, she agreed quietly. 'We change our minds so often, Leo – we really will have to move fast when we move.'

'We've adapted to the world, as you say. We're in control here, but the price has been heavy, very heavy.'

Sometime during the early part of the night a *fiersig* drifted from the hills, and across the valley, causing a change to pass through Steel City. Faulcon felt it without realizing what it was for a while; the shivering sensation, the sudden change of mood, the sudden feeling of irritation, excitement, a quickening of heart and mind, a livening of the spirit.

Immediately he began to breathe deeply, heavily, his eyes shut, his mind fixed on the idea of permanence. With each second that passed he felt the vaulting, tumbling mix of emotions, a confused and frightening jumble of anger and fear, of humour and indifference. He bit the flesh inside his mouth as he resisted the probing fingers of the *fiersig*, fought to keep the mood of love and determination he had shared with Lena just hours before.

He began to groan, then cry with the effort of resistance, but he was winning – he sensed he was winning, he *knew* he was beating it. His cries woke Lena. 'It's all right,' he said, and then was quiet, deciding against further words, for words were dangerous while the *fiersig* passed.

Lena sat up, not looking at him, disturbed by the change herself. Faulcon stepped down from the couch and dressed. His mind was fresh and alert, as it always was during a mood disturbance; he left the room without a glance back, aware of the sounds of Lena's efforts to block the change, and walked up to the Skyport at the top of the Riftwatch Tower.

The strange lights in the alien sky were brilliant, and crowds of people were drifting up to the lounges to observe them: streaks of red and green breaking across the night and fading, then the spirals and circles of yellow, sparkling gold, zigzagging between the stars, racing across the nightscape from one horizon to another, it seemed, in the twinkling of an eye ... more reds, breaking and dividing, curving about and dissipating in startlingly bright explosions; then winking, flashing purples, drifting between the gold and red-streaked chaos in serene fashion. The whole fiery display of atmospheric energy passed above the city and away into the night in a little over half an hour.

Faulcon heard laughter, then, and some shouting: the usual heated debates as to whether the *fiersig* might be intelligent life-forms; the usual empty arguments. The restaurants and bars were closing down as temperaments altered and relationships shifted in the delicate balance of intellect and instinct that had brought people together a few hours before. People needed time to adjust, time to think. Clothes were shed, bodies and souls bared to the unseen, unknown fingers of Kamelios, defying them to try and wreak change upon the individual. Figures walked naked, unsure, through the corridors and across the softly undulating floors of the relaxation lounges.

Faulcon saw Lena there, moody, depressed. He walked across to her, and tried to speak to her, but she shrugged him away and walked back to her own quarters, all her earlier energy dissipated in an instant.

PART TWO

The Phantom of the Valley

CHAPTER SIX

An immense black shape, manlike yet not a man, passed out through Steel City's southern gateway and moved swiftly across the brightly lit land surrounding the silent installation. Within seconds it was entering darkness, its form visible only by the occasional reflection of light on its smooth metal bulk. Soon it was gone.

An r-suit could move fast under direct human control, but at night the terrain between the City and the deep canyon was hazardous, and the man moved slowly, following, after a while, the lines of green and red lights that marked out smoothed trackways to the lip of the gorge. In the windless night the servo-mechanisms of the suit made distinct whirring sounds, but as he drew near to the valley a fresh and gusty breeze blew up, and only the fleeting glimpse of a tall shape, or a momentary rattle of rocks, told of the passing of the stranger.

At length the alien canyon yawned before him, and even the suddenly activated light from the helmet of the suit showed only blackness. Bright stars, and the glow of the moon Three-light, permitted glimpses of the structures below ... Here a gleaming, greenish plate, there a twisting spiral of blue and silver, fragments of sparkling red catching the eye from among large, amorphous areas of nightblack.

The man turned and began to run his suit along the trackway that bordered the canyon's edge. Soon the city was a long way behind, an area of bright yellow light that reached up into the sky, and gave the horizon behind him an eerie glow. In the distance, on both sides of the valley, were the smaller, less inviting lights of the Watch Stations. A sedately moving light in the sky, passing across the Kamelion constellation of the Axe, was the great orbiting refuge known as Night Eye Station, but it was well to the west, and its banks of cameras would not be directed here, not so far away from its present route across the world.

The rift suit moved on, seemingly of its own volition. The man inside relaxed physically, but remained watchful for movement on the canyon's rim, and for movement and light in the darkness below him. The suit had run this route many times before. It reached into the man's mind, snatched its instructions from the imprinted repetition of activity it found there. It powered the legs and the helmet, it kept the arms comfortable, and it sniffed and probed the ground ahead, all in the twinkling of a star, each movement a coordinated movement, happening between mind and machine, taking the man on his circuitous pilgrimage about the gorge.

Soon it stopped, bracing itself almost at the very edge of the drop. Although viewing from within was easy through the wide, outwardly curved face plate, the helmet turned. Through the darkness the man could almost see the shapes and shards that crowded the deep cut in the world, the cubes and spheres, the girders and jagged edges of once-proud, once-living structures. But to his eyes, and to his immediate awareness, there was only blackness.

And yet not so long ago …

His eyes, and the helmet of the r-suit, found the place where the creatures had come, where the golden glow of their machine had lit the dusk with a different fire to the red light of Altuxor. The emanation had seemed to fill the valley, to radiate to heaven itself. The glow had been warm. His r-suit had consciously adjusted its temperature to maintain the comfort of the startled, overwhelmed occupant within. Then the shapes had gone, the golden machine had vanished into time. The moving creatures, glimpsed so quickly, so imperfectly as they stepped through the sloping side, had taken their minds and their awarenesses elsewhere in the cosmic vastness of the single world; to times beyond.

Darkness. He watched that darkness, and hours came and went, and soon he moved on, further from Steel City, disappointment drying him, and choking him, nagging him as it always nagged him, distracting him as it had distracted him a hundred times before. They had not returned; but surely one night they would. They *had* to return, they *had* to.

And so as he ran, as the darkness passed him by, as the r-suit plundered the miles, its monotonous movement regular and steady, so his mind went out: upwards to the stars, downwards to the earth, sideways and inwards to the rift, to the unconscious minds that he *knew* must be listening from the eternal void of time.

I'm here, I'm here … please show yourselves … please come back … please communicate …

But Kamelios answered him as it always answered him, with wind, with stillness broken by a gusting breeze, with the cold light of stars, with the chasm and the dead things that lay therein.

He passed widely by the ruined Riftwatch Station Eekhaut, and returned to the edge of the world of man. Suddenly he began to run faster, looking away from the valley, away across the hills to the north where – had he the necessary magnification on his face plate – he might have seen the tiny lights and fires of one of the human townships.

And gradually the suit stopped, and turned back to the gorge, though the man inside the machine was anxious to pass on. And yet he had sensed it would stop, just as he sensed that there was some meaning to the sudden hastening of the suit's progress whenever he passed the ruined Riftwatch Station.

It stood there and watched the darkness of the deep void, and the man watched that same darkness, and felt the suit's arm raise and point to a place in the emptiness where he knew he had been before.

Aloud he said, 'Move on,' but the suit stayed still, its arm pointing, its helmet turned sideways, looking down, so that he could stare through the clearest part of the visor at the place where the wind ... where the screams ...

He could hear the screaming now, a banshee wailing, the sound of awareness of death, the sound of a drowning man.

'Move *on*!'

Standing silent and still, the r-suit disobeyed the verbal order, but in truth it disobeyed nothing, for it drew its power and its commands not from the voice but from the mind, and in his mind the man did not want to move; he wanted to stand here and remember, and relive, and become aware again of that thing which he had forced from his mind, that inaction that he had expunged from his existence, and had thus taken from that area of responsibility and morality that dictated to his conscience.

The time winds broke distantly, booming and thundering, darkening the sky. They swept close, bringing time and change, bringing destruction and creation, driving away the ordered ruins in a fleeting moment of visual chaos, only to vanish westwards up the gorge leaving a new order, a new stillness. The arm of the suit pointed in the darkness, the stiff metallic finger an arrow of guilt drawn tense in the bow, ready to discharge itself into the man's heart. Through the dark quiet he could hear the wind, he could see the struggling shape of the man, caught in the tight angle of two alien structures. Through the suit receiver the voice was hysterical, fear-filled, terrified: help me, for God's sake don't just stand there, help me!

They might come, they might come behind the wind

Help me!

I saw them before, golden creatures in a golden machine, they came behind a wind for

For God's sake!

a second, they were there, a second, golden, creatures, second

Don't just!

after the wind, watching me, watching them, intelligent time-travelling beings

Stand there!

I must watch, I must watch, I can't go down ... the wind too strong too fast ... I can't go down ... get free, wriggle free ... creatures coming, golden machine

HELP ME! HELP ME!

I can't. I won't! I might miss them!

The arm of the suit dropped. In the stillness the man's voice was a strange keening, that broke into the sound of sobbing, that suddenly cried out through the dark night, that gave vent to its frustration and fear and guilt. 'He had to come! He had to remind me!'

The suit moved away, running fast and furious, the man's legs drawn up to his chest so that he rode within his machine in a crouched position, the mechanical legs pounding the cliff top at speeds faster than a human limb could tolerate. He tried to race his shame, to outrun his fear, to leave behind the need to tell the boy, to say something, to tell him how his brother had died, and how he had seen the death, and how he had stood there and done nothing. But all these things were carried by the suit as well, and the faster he ran, the faster they spun in his mind, and blurred his vision, and dulled his senses.

But soon his blood cooled and the tears on his face no longer tickled their message of weakness. The suit slowed, and stopped, and turned about, facing the distant glow of the city, staring there now because the man wished to stare there. And when it moved it was because he wished to go home.

CHAPTER SEVEN

Kris Dojaan's impatience to go out to Kriakta Rift, and seek out the time phantom, made him a willing trainee, a hard worker, and an exhausting student; it also boiled over, on several occasions, into an anger of frustration, against which Lena was forced to pull her rank. Much of the next two days was spent in silence, the sullenness almost physical. And Kris was tired, too, Faulcon couldn't help but notice that, the weariness and pallor in the youngster's cheeks. Yet he worked hard, and could give his team mates no cause for dissatisfaction.

Lena and Faulcon took it in turns, three hours a session, to teach the boy the function, structure, use and dangers of the rift suits, the protective armoured mobile-environments that were often all that stood between a man and the endlessness of Othertime.

The suits were not just bulky, they were immense. Even a largely built man seemed no more than a stick insect within the voluminous confines of the machine, his arms padded and cushioned in the severally-jointed upper limbs, his body supported naturally and comfortably within the body space, surrounded by tubes, the ridged coverings of crystalline power transmuters, the brightly marked 'organs', each the dispenser of some survival ingredient.

Inside the suit it was soon easy to forget that you were riding a structure half again as high as your own body, with five times your body's volume; your legs dangled free and comfortable into the cavernous thigh of the suit – the 'idea' of walking was enhanced by the slight pedal pressure available if a normal walking action was undertaken. The silent, swift response of the suit, walking as you wished it to, belied the power available to it if escape action was needed: at two hundred miles an hour it gripped you somewhat more firmly, pulled your legs up to your chest, free of the limbs which now moved like pistons, almost blurringly fast, taking the body away from danger as an athlete sprinting for the finish line.

On the first day, after completing their mission reports, they introduced Kris to his personal r-suit, sealed him in, and let him experience the frightening disorientation, and uncoordination, of a machine that was overwhelmed by his conflicting conscious orders. They were in the special environment, in one of the low levels of traverse unit *Pearl*. Kris's preliminary running-falling-turning-tripping activity was hilariously funny to watch, although Kris himself was less amused. Nevertheless, that first training session helped to lighten the moodiness that was still residual from the passage of the *fiersig*, the night before. Kris had been violently affected by it, he said, and had thought he was going out of his mind. Perhaps that accounted for his tiredness, Faulcon thought, and reassured him.

Within a day, after that shaky start, Kris was making good progress, at ease with the suit, and with the irritating skull contacts that always pressed harder than expected, and which could become a source of intense itching, or aching, or other psychological manifestation of newness and new awareness.

On the second day, again ignoring Kris's protests and claims that he was ready and able to go out at least *near* to the rift, they took him on a south run, through the hills and stumpy forests of Tokranda County, and along the wide, stone roadways that linked the townships. Immediately on passing out of the protective walls of Steel City Faulcon felt his unease at being close to Kris Dojaan surface again, the awful fear of time's grasp that can infect men close to one whose fate has been ordained. But as they put distance between the rift and themselves, the concern fell away, itself outdistanced, perhaps.

Kris had little time, as they ran, to observe the sprawling areas of wood and brick houses, smoke rising from primitive chimney stacks, animals and men practically indistinguishable against the muddy backgrounds of their communities; even their clothes, skin and farmhouses seemed stitched into the visual fabric of Kamelios. The towns were often this primitive, although they drew much in the way of luxury and services from the Federation installations around them, in particular Steel City itself.

The people who lived here maintained close links with their home-worlds, and the governing and economic bodies that had, in part, financed their colonization. The simple use of primitive building materials was as much due to the smallness of those financial contributions as to the widely felt principle that it was important to build using the world and its resources, and not depend from the outset upon the imported materials that could make an air-tight, heat-tight living unit. It was true, also, that most external finance was channelled into medical supplies, for while the hundreds of tiny communities in each county could support themselves from their hunting and farmlands, they were unable to produce that natural resistance to disease organisms and pollen that the manchanged (whom they loathed) could achieve. These low-land communities had opted for the middle ground, a toughing-it-out type of colonization, more integrated with Kamelios than the 'instals' of Steel City and its associated supply and watch stations, but not prepared to undertake the violent, and grotesque, bio-adaptive processes of the manchanged, whose territories were well away to the south.

The lowland farmers wore breathing and eating masks against the organic ravages of the world, but within their houses they took advantage of technology to maintain a tolerably low organic level, and by generations, and agony, would come to terms with the environment.

The mountain road through Tokranda County meandered through the settlements, then turned to run, no more than a track, along the edges of the dusty, white-wood forests. Faulcon led the others along this track, in a suit-programme designed to test each and every reflex in their new team mate's body.

Kris ran and walked and became adept at living within his suit; he became expert at controlling it. He learned to relax as the suit's internal mechanisms gently manipulated his body … Turning, for example, made him feel as if four hands were pushing him into the direction of the turn. Starting to run gave a sensation of being lifted bodily. To slow gave pressure on chest and back, and made him feel as if gentle hands gripped his skull. The final prac-tice on the run-back that second day was allowing his body to be squeezed into the crouched position preparatory for a rapid run. His suit was not yet programmed for that, but he went through the motions of snap-shutting his eyes, opening his mouth and letting his legs be painfully pushed up out of the thick, highly-motored legs of the machine. Each time this happened he found his knees jarring agonizingly on the front of the thigh region of the armour. Buttock to knee he was two feet in length, and the suit, built to accommodate the longness of this body section of his, was dangerously close to inefficiency with its mid-quarters so bulky.

The mechanism demonstrably worked, however, and when the suit decided to move Kris out of danger, it would work again; it would skin his knees, maybe even break them (this was not unknown); that discomfort, Kris was assured, was far better than the alternative.

As they moved at forty miles an hour, back through the farmlands in the hills, towards Steel City, Kris complained bitterly that he would have to spend a third day training, this time at the bone-wrenching speeds of 150–200 mph. But, since there was no escape from a time wind in an upwards direction, this was the suit's primary function, and it was the hardest function to live with.

He was still bitching when they crossed the dirt trackway that skirted one of the townships and came suit to face with a straggling band of manchanged.

'Who the hell are they?' rasped Kris, the surprise and revulsion clearly evident in his voice. Faulcon was still moving along the track, towards the hesitant group. Now he stopped, turned, and snapped at the youngster, 'Keep your mouth shut, Kris. These are manchanged.'

The manchanged were a group of twelve individuals, six males, four females, and two drawn-faced rather ragged children. Faulcon thought he recognized the leader at once and lifted a hand as a gesture of greeting.

The whole group stopped, visibly tensing. Enormous, bulging eyes stared at Faulcon, mouths opened and closed, taking tiny gasps of breath. Skin, white and unpleasant looking, flushed slightly, a bluish grey colour, not the red flush that Faulcon was used to. They looked, otherwise, perfectly human, and of course that was exactly what they were. Humankind, changed to accept the organic poisons of the world, to be able to see without their eyes melting away, to breathe without corroding the linings of their respiratory tracts.

The sight of three towering, threatening armoured-suits was discomforting them greatly. Manchanged were rare visitors to the lower lands, especially to the communities and installations along Kriakta Rift. They brought sun-dew, of course, bright yellow crystals that formed in the deep earth, and were useful – though not essential – to the power supplies of Steel City. It was diplomatic trade, and the only reason for a manchanged group to be this far north.

Faulcon saw the several sacks of the precious substance, carried by the men. It would have been a long walk from their plateau. They would be glad to get rid of the crystals.

Switching on his exvox, Faulcon said, 'I'm sorry if we startled you. Please don't be afraid. We're only training.'

The older man who led the group stepped forward and raised both hands. 'We're not afraid. Just startled, as you said. We're taking sun-dew to the City.'

'So I see.' The nagging familiarity of the man's face made Faulcon strain to remember where he had met this particular manchanged before. 'Are you the man Audwyn? I seem to recognize you.'

The manchanged smiled; his face could not show surprise. 'Yes, I am. I am Audwyn.' He came right up to Faulcon's suit and stared into the helmet. 'The gulgaroth hunter – is it you in there?' He seemed pleased.

71

'Leo Faulcon. Yes. Hello again.'

As best they could, manchanged and armoured-suit shook hands. Much of Faulcon's unease slipped away in those few moments. He stood and stared at the strange man before him, half wanting to get away from the unpredictable creatures, half remembering the occasion, those months back, when his presence in the foothills of the Jaraquath mountains had marked a meeting of destinies, his and Audwyn's; his snap-shot had caught the rogue gulgaroth in mid-leap, saving the unsuspecting manchanged from the particularly hideous death that the beasts imparted to their human prey. Gulgaroth did not usually feed on man, but somewhere in the half-awareness of their brain-masses they felt resentment for the alien intruders on their domain.

Behind Faulcon, Lena murmured, 'Let's go, Leo. We have a lot to do. Come on.'

Perhaps Audwyn sensed the restlessness, the discomfort of the group of rifters. A hint of a smile touched his lips, making Faulcon feel at one and the same time both guilty and irritated. There was little love lost between the two types of human – didn't rifters refer to the manchanged as 'manks', a particularly unpleasant epithet – and little trust. The manchanged were withdrawn, hostile to outsiders, and hid away in their plateau-based communities, learning their own rules about VanderZande's World.

'Would you carry our crystals to the City?' asked Audwyn. 'It would save us a day's walk, and your suits …'

'Can carry tons. Yes, of course, we'd be happy to. But don't you want paying … trade?'

Audwyn said, 'This is final settlement for several boxes of metal shapes. Thank you.' And he turned from Faulcon, gesturing to the rest of his band. The group turned and began to walk back towards the far mountains.

There were five sacks of sun-dew and Faulcon carried the single, largest. They continued on their way towards Steel City, just visible in the distance, beyond the band of tall, twisted chalk formations that was Whitefinger Row. The nearest of the colonies to Steel City lay the other side of the desiccated area, on ground that rose slightly towards the edge of the canyon. As they ran, Lena queried the occasion on which Faulcon had previously met the manchanged. 'I didn't know you went off alone so much,' she said, as Faulcon described the unexpected turn of events during his routine stalking of a male gulgaroth that had left its forest haunts and climbed into the foothills.

'I like to be alone at times—'

'Don't I know it.'

'I went hunting more in the early months. I found it relaxing.'

Lena made a sound like a laugh, but without humour. 'You didn't seem very relaxed when I came with you.'

They arrived back at the City in mid-afternoon, all three of them sweaty with effort, although the suits had kept them otherwise comfortable. They powered into the shedding lounge and switched off suit power. Instantly the three towering structures froze into silent stiffness. The backs opened and with difficulty Faulcon hauled himself out into the cool room, shivering as the fresh air around him made the clinging sweat of his woollen undergarment cold and clammy.

When Kris was with him Faulcon stared up at the r-suit helmets and said, 'Are you beginning to get the idea that if Steel City regards these monstrosities as necessary for survival, then the rift valley is not quite the day-trip, picnic-view area that you seem to think it is?'

Kris grimaced as he stared at the suits. 'They're so damned ugly.'

'You should have seen the man who designed them,' said Lena coldly. She was still moody, and slightly depressed, but the worst effects of the abrupt changes brought about that evening, two nights before, had mellowed as her real personality inched through again. Faulcon himself felt tired, short-tempered. He had not slept well, mainly because he had been eating rich foods, and drinking too much *injuzan*, an alcoholic drink with a high caffeine content. Similar indulgence was possibly the reason for Kris Dojaan's weary features, and his constant, nagging complaints about the continuing denial of his access to the valley area.

Later that day, during the slide show in which the final structural and functional suit mechanisms were explained to the bored and drowsy recruit, Commander Ensavlion stepped into the room and stood silently watching the small company. When Lena noticed the man she switched off the projector, and Faulcon and Kris rose to their feet, uneasy with the intrusion.

Ensavlion had been a frequent observer during Kris's training. On the second day his loping form, r-suit clad, had dogged their tracks for several miles before vanishing, presumably to change course and head back to the valley, to stand and watch, awhile, for a sign of the travellers. The Commander had said nothing and in no way interfered, but it was apparent that he was taking an immense interest in the new recruit, and equally apparent that something about him was disturbing Kris.

'He makes me shiver,' Kris had confessed the evening before, whilst they were still out on a short run. 'He just watches me, and never smiles, just frowns. Then he waves and walks away.'

'He's taken an interest in you,' said Faulcon. 'He's not the only one. The story of the luck you've brought our team is quite widespread now. You're a minor celebrity.'

'I don't think it's anything to do with the machine we found,' said Kris quietly. They had been resting, still in their suits, and were preparing to make their way back to the City. 'I think it's my brother. I think he knows something more about Mark's loss into time and he doesn't know how or when to tell me. It has to be that, doesn't it, Leo? He was Mark's Section Commander, and it was Ensavlion who wrote to my family, telling us of Mark's heroic death during an assignment. Now he seems to fight shy of even mentioning my brother's name; but it's obvious he hasn't forgotten him. I know you only knew Mark in passing, but can you remember anything that happened back then, anything between Mark and Ensavlion?'

'It's easy to forget things on VanderZande's World,' said Lena quietly; she was uncomfortable with the discussion.

Faulcon laughed bitterly as he agreed. 'And when you forget caution, you forget everything. But you may be right about Ensavlion. It may well disturb him that you've come. One man dies, and his brother comes almost to take his place ... I'd imagine the old man is feeling the responsibility he may have to bear if you fall foul of the winds.'

It was Kris's turn to laugh. The pale features that regarded Faulcon from behind the gleaming face plate seemed almost stretched into a smile. 'Do you realize you said "if" and not "when"?'

'So I did. I must be taking you for granted.'

Now, in the Visual Education room, Ensavlion waved Lena back to work: 'Please carry on with the programme. Leo, would you step outside a moment, please?'

As the room darkened again, and Kris settled glumly back in his seat, eyes fixed on yet another cutaway of an r-suit, Faulcon followed Commander Ensavlion into the passageway, and the two men walked slowly towards the main through-way.

'How's the training programme going? Well, I hope.'

'He's very adept, very keen,' agreed Faulcon. 'He's half an inch too long for total comfort in an r-suit.'

Ensavlion seemed slightly amused. 'Cumbersome bloody things. And so damned impractical.'

'So Kris Dojaan has been pointing out to me for two days. He's overwhelmed by how primitive much of Steel City is ... masks, bykes instead of air-platforms, force-fields only on the entrance-ways. You'd think he came from Earth, the way he misses technology. But the r-suits, they annoy him most of all.'

Ensavlion shook his head. 'He has a dream about how advanced it's possible to be; he'd never even experienced spaceflight before he came here, and he's disappointed not to be able to float around as if by levitation. And he has no idea of cash flow in the Galaxy. He thinks force-fields grow on trees. As for the suits, there'll be a new design up from Base Seventeen soon; hopefully it'll be less restrictive – and smaller in size.' He was silent for a moment, and Faulcon wondered whether he should stop his slow amble, indicating his wish to return to the VE room. But Ensavlion said, 'What stage is he at?'

'Kris? He takes a fast run with Lena, tomorrow.'

'And the canyon the day after?'

'Or later in the day. He's itching to get out there; he can't understand the delay and our refusal to let him just go and see it, to peer over the edge.'

Ensavlion slapped his hands together behind his back, turned to Faulcon as he stopped walking, and Faulcon saw the mixture of pleasure and concern in the Commander's face. 'That's good,' he said. 'The boy has a good potential. But you won't let him go to the canyon until he's fully ready; you won't flout the rules, will you, Leo?'

'Of course not, Commander.' He didn't add that it had been Ensavlion's encouragement that had given Kris high hopes of a rapid access.

Ensavlion looked back towards the room. 'I wouldn't want anything going wrong. I don't think he fully comprehends the danger, and the nature of death on this world, not yet, not fully. You'll help him understand that. You didn't mind taking over the training yourselves, did you?'

'Good heavens, no,' said Faulcon, but Ensavlion was carrying on along his own train of thought: 'I trust you, you see, Leo. I trust you to look after him. I don't want us to lose the man.'

Ensavlion's stare was hard, and yet Faulcon detected the concern behind the grey eyes, a more personal concern than just a Commander worried for the well-being of an impetuous recruit.

Faulcon knew his own face was pale, and he could taste bitterness himself; the blood seemed to have stilled in his body as he stood with the Section chief and contemplated the nature of Kris Dojaan's tragedy. Finally Faulcon said, 'With respect, Commander ...'

Ensavlion silenced him with an abrupt shake of the head, and a hint of a smile. 'I know what you're going to say, Leo. I must talk about his brother Mark. I must take the boy aside and talk about Mark Dojaan, and let him know that we *do* care, that we *do* live with our responsibilities; and our tragedies; and that a man like Mark Dojaan isn't wasted for nothing. Have you said anything to him yet? About Mark?'

'Very little. He seems to be expecting more from you.'

Faulcon saw the alarm in Ensavlion's mind, a brief glimpse of the passionate unease that he wore with such outward calm. 'I'll be frank with you, Leo. I don't know how to do it; I am afraid that the words will not come, and I dare not show weakness to the youngster. You and I, Leo, we know each other; not well, but we have worked together, and we have seen through each other's masks. But Kris Dojaan has come here with an image of his brother, with a belief in his brother's strength of spirit, and we must keep that belief alive, for his sake; and he must not see Kamelios and Steel City as they really are until he has come to comprehend the nature and facts of his brother's death. But how do we explain to him without shaking his belief in the orderly and directioned existence of his race on this world?'

Much of the agony that Ensavlion was attempting to communicate was lost on Faulcon, who had concerns of his own, and he let a long moment pass when the Commander had finished speaking while he tried to divine what was the best course of action now. He finally decided to tell Ensavlion of Kris's belief in the return of his brother Mark as the so-called phantom. Ensavlion was surprised by that, and then concerned again. 'It's not possible. Keep an eye on him; the phantom is still about, so I heard ...'

'The phantom is *always* about. Somewhere, someone sees him ...'

'Right. And if Kris hears he might take it into his head to slip out this evening. I will have to hold you responsible for that if it occurs ...'

Dully, Faulcon said, 'Yes, sir. I understand.' And slightly angry at that condescending flourish of authority, he turned and walked back to the room, and his colleagues.

CHAPTER EIGHT

At the end of the session they made their way to a small restaurant and ate a light meal, relaxing for an hour afterwards before picking up one of Kris's barrack mates, a jovial, blond-haired, Earth-born youngster called Nils Istoort, and playing some sport, two rounds of handball, a twenty-one of badminton. Quietly, when he had an opportunity, Faulcon mentioned to Nils that it might be a good idea if he kept a close eye on Kris Dojaan for the next few hours. The two of them had planned to go up to the Sky Lounges and drink some of Kris's bonus, anyway, and Faulcon and Lena thus found they had a few hours to themselves. They went immediately to Faulcon's quarters. For a while they sprawled out on the cushioned floor and talked.

'What did Ensavlion want?'

'He told me to keep an eye on Kris. He doesn't want him rift-running before he's ready.'

Lena shrugged, uninterested, tired. 'From what you say he's on his way in any event. Do you trust that other kid to look after him?'

'I think so. Besides, I'm meeting them both later—'

'Oh I *see*! This is just an interlude in your drinking!'

Ignoring her, Faulcon went on, 'Meeting them! For talk! And I don't propose to let Kris out of my sight until he crashes out. I don't think he'll disobey me, though. He has a sense of responsibility, and he knows he'll be a free agent as from tomorrow.'

'A sense of responsibility,' repeated Lena, and laughed as she mocked

Faulcon, 'Just like you?' Then, more seriously, she said, 'What's Kris doing to you, Leo?'

'How do you mean? Doing to me? He's not doing anything to me.'

'Yes he is.' She moved off her cushion and wriggled up next to Faulcon, unclipping his shirt and stroking his chest. 'He's having quite an effect on you.'

'What sort of effect? I hadn't noticed anything.'

'For a start, I've only ever once known you to spend so much time with a person other than me—'

'Don't talk about that, Lena. Please.'

'I wasn't going to. Kris is a very different person. I know you're sympathetic, and I know you're trying to relax the boy, and make him feel at home – but Leo, after a mission we *always* spend time together!'

'And we didn't this time. I know – Lena, I'm sorry about that—'

'I don't need your sorrow, Leo. I'm a big girl. I just need you to recognize that Kris has far more of a hold on you than you seem to think.'

'As you say, I'm trying to welcome him, that's all. To make him feel easy. To be a friend to him.' Faulcon took Lena's roving hand and lifted it to his lips; she watched him warmly and he asked, 'Moodiness all passed?'

'Thank God. Don't change the subject. What's going on in your head, Leo? What has our young man from Earth done to you?'

Faulcon didn't answer for a moment. He stared across the room, trying to find some order in the confusion of thoughts and emotions that was conjured to mind whenever he tried to assess his relationship with Kamelios. 'It's excitement, I think. That sense of excitement, of wonder. The sort of feeling we had at school when people talked about other Galaxies, and all the worlds in our Galaxy that had only been recorded, never explored. It's imagination, the feeling of mystery that you get when people tell you stories about distant islands, hidden asteroids, secret locations, secret lands where things are strange, and where we're infiltrators, or strangers. There's something so magic about the unknown, and I remember that it was the sense of the unknown, and the desperate need to penetrate that unknown just a little, that brought me out here. And then it went, and everything became so routine, and the canyon was just a canyon, and the aliens were just aliens, and so what?'

'And then Kris Dojaan. The child, his eyes filled with awe, with wonder, and Leo Faulcon finds his humanity again. I understand. You're very lucky.'

Lena was quiet. Her hand rested on Faulcon, but she no longer communicated her desire for him. She lay staring away from him, and he put his arm around her shoulders, gently stroked the soft skin of her cheek. 'You think you're too dulled, is that it?'

'I was dulled a long time ago. I can't feel that wonder. But I sense the loss, do you know that? I do sense the loss … of something, of a part of me. This is a killer of a world. We have to get away, Leo, before it kills us completely.'

Faulcon squeezed her tight, and she looked up; her eyes glistened with tears. Faulcon kissed her on the nose. 'I love you, Lena. I really love you.'

'Say it again.'

'No.' He grinned. 'That's your ration for tonight.'

'Cheapskate.'

She lay back on his chest. It was pleasantly still and silent in the room, and after a while Faulcon's eyes closed.

Later he checked on the young Kris Dojaan and found him sleeping soundly in his bunk, his barrack mate finishing a bottle of *baraas* and quietly reading. Faulcon took a midnight stroll about the Sky Lounge, but it was a quiet and dark night, and there was little happening. After a while he found a deep armchair, leaned back and slept.

In the morning, shortly after the huge red-haloed disc of Altuxor had crept above the eastern horizon, he made his way back to the barracks, intending to fetch Kris – who no doubt would complain at the earliness of the hour – for breakfast, a good feed before the final, most intense part of the training.

Kris was not there. His barrack mate, Nils, was still asleep, sprawled half out of bed, snoring loudly; the place reeked of drink. Faulcon stood for a while wondering where Kris might have gone, what he could possibly find to do at such an early hour. Watching the dawn was one possibility, or already at breakfast. A thought nagged at him. It wasn't possible, was it, that he could have decided to take an early morning walk … out through Steel City's public ramp …?

He suddenly realized that he was being paged, the voice a soft and insistent repetition of his name, almost lost against the growing activity and bustle in the barrack corridors. He glanced around and saw a wall phone. When he picked up the receiver and identified himself there was the briefest of pauses before Lena was on the line, telling him curtly, almost angrily, to move himself down to the suiting and shedding lounge.

He ran down the levels, and burst breathlessly into the room, pushing among the lines of r-suits, seeking Lena. The ramp was out, leading down to the planet's surface, and only the faint whining of the preservation field across the opening prevented Faulcon from diving for a mask. A bulky shape stood there, a rift suit, its legs braced apart, the details of its insignia lost against the bright light of the outside world. But behind the tinted face plate it was obviously Lena. When the suit moved, deeper into the lounge, he saw her face inside the helmet. She looked tired, almost exhausted. And she obviously had bad news.

Her voice rasped on the exvox. 'Suit up. Our child team member, despite his *fine* sense of responsibility, has gone out to the valley.'

'Surprise, surprise,' said Faulcon dully.

'And he's gone out in a touring suit! We'll get docked our bonus and more if he gets himself caught by a squall, or even breaks a limb. Suit up. Don't just stand there gaping.'

All love was gone in the face of professional anger. As Faulcon hauled himself into his suit, wincing at the stinging of the control probes easing into his skin, he thought for the thousandth time that he must have been mad to have accepted a position in the same team as Lena. Mad. It was difficult enough to love the woman with mood changes upturning relationships every five minutes. When she was forced every day into a position of leadership, into a command position, it put an often unbearable strain on them.

Which was not, he silently acknowledged to himself as he sealed himself in, totally true. He was tired, she was tired, their moods were bad. Most of the time they worked well together. It was times like this that he could do without.

And Kris was going to get a rift glove slapped across his face, Faulcon was sure of that.

When Faulcon was ready Lena turned and raised an arm to the monitoring technicians. The preservation screen collapsed, lights winked on; in his headphones Faulcon heard Lena's instruction to move out of the city. He followed her up the ramp, and down onto the planet, and when they hit hard ground they began to run.

Lena led the way at a compromise speed of ten miles an hour, not uncomfortable, but involving some actual physical effort to control the suits. They dropped down into a flat-bottomed gully, which was crowded with transport vehicles of various kinds, taking supplies and specimens between the city and the Riftwatch Stations. After a few minutes they were pounding along the valley road, parallel to the rift, but some way below the rocky approach slopes.

They passed by several Watch Stations, including the ruins of Eekhaut, and Faulcon began to wonder what Lena had in mind. Before he could voice his question, however, she abruptly changed course for the north, up the approach track, and close by to Riftwatch Station Shibano.

At once Faulcon found his heart beating fast, his mind and body light, a sensation of floating. He had seen this valley so many times ... but he suddenly knew that he was going to see it differently, or more accurately, that he was going to see it again as he had first seen it, through the eyes of wonder, with the imagination of the young.

They were at Rigellan Curve, where the canyon turned to the north, widening and deepening and boasting its most fabulous array of ruins anywhere along its length, a fairground, of Othertime, extending miles into the distance. Within seconds they had reached the edge of the rift. In silence they looked at the breathtaking view.

Here was such a farrago of alienness that Faulcon found himself growing dizzy every time he shifted his gaze. He always found it hard to convey the baffling impression of lights and shapes, the jagged and the smooth, the towering, twisting, stooping structures of another race and a thousand other times, all interlocked and tangled in ways for which they had never been designed. His attention lingered on several, translucent towers, their enormous heights shaped and beaten by wind and rain, sparkling and glittering in the bright, red-tinged light of high Altuxor. He was fascinated by an immense, sprawling spider's-web, complex in design, its broken strands jutting and quivering as if they sought that part of the web that had been lost to them. He could see wide, half-familiar roadways, one raised above the ground on steel pillars: this road began and ended abruptly, and it had been shifted by wind and change so that it had skewered the web at its mid point. The other end rested awkwardly upon a cubical black structure, in and out of which moved several city-robots, no doubt documenting and removing the contents now that a human team had been inside. The whole valley below them was a junk-yard of alien buildings and huge half-severed, half-alive machines, snub-nosed and wide-winged, or on tracks or wheels, upturned to display their gaping rocket jets, or plunged nose first into the substrate of the valley so that just their ends rose into the still, cold air. Shimmering walkways trembled in physical breezes, spiral structures that ended hundreds of yards in the air.

Most of the remains were clustered at the very bottom of the canyon, on a wide, scoured plain, where once, perhaps, a river had flowed. Now it was substantially forested, the colourful, confused afforestation that results from the overlapping of native species from different ages; predominant were the thrashing red and green masses of broad-flails, not native to present-day Kamelios, and expanses of the white and hornified plants known as skagbark. On the wide ledges that separated the several scarpments of each cliff side, it was scagbark that dominated, roots twisting out into the void in their search for water in the thin soil of the slopes. Above the ledges the pattern of stratification rippled, twisted throughout the valley in a geological jigsaw. The deep rift meandered into the distance, into haze and obscurity. And Faulcon and Lena Tanoway were minute black shapes against that vastness.

Faulcon suddenly realized that Lena was talking to him; her voice had been gently insinuating itself into the sensory confusion in his mind, and now he looked at her and saw her pointing across the canyon. Faulcon turned up the magnification of his helmet and the bulky shape of Commander Ensavlion appeared clearly before him, recognizable from the insignia on his armoured suit. He stood close to the rim, above a sloping escarpment, below which were the covered tents containing the dead life that had come out of

Othertime, unintelligent forms, of course, mostly animals, with a smattering of organisms that were unclassifiable in terrestrial terms. Ensavlion stood stiffly, his head bowed as he scanned the valley bottom. He seemed unaware of the team that regarded him from more than a mile away.

Faulcon knew that Ensavlion came to the valley every day, sometimes for just a few minutes, sometimes for hours. He came and he stood and he watched, and one day perhaps he would again see that small, glowing pyramid; it would flash into the canyon, appearing from nowhere, and the tall, hovering shapes would materialize through its walls, moving about the valley for a minute or so before returning to their machine and vanishing into time. Although the travellers may have been constant visitors to this place and time, only once had they materialized before a group of men, one of whom had not been running when they came, a man whose memory of that event was so distorted, by time and the need to review the occurrence, that the pyramid had increased, in his account, to something twenty times as large as it had been, and the creatures had become almost godlike, manifestations of the super-race he so obsessively sought in the Universe.

As Faulcon watched Commander Ensavlion, strangely disturbed yet fascinated by the man and by the turmoil of feeling that seemed to be plaguing him since Kris Dojaan's arrival, so the distant figure turned and vanished below the approach slopes of the canyon. Faulcon switched off his helmet's magnifying plate and returned to the task of seeking his team mate.

It was nearly four hours before they spotted him, seated on an outjutting of rock, some hundred yards down the sloping inner edge of the valley. He appeared to be contemplating the infinite, his head turned, his gaze obviously somewhere out above the distant reaches of the rift. His knees drawn up, his arms tightly folded around them, he might have been any sightseer on any gorge on any world. The irresponsibility of his behaviour incensed Lena, and she almost shrieked at Kris, but the boy remained motionless, and perhaps his tiny face-mask radio was not operating.

Faulcon remained on level ground while Lena, her rift suit sliding in what seemed to be – but was not – a most precarious fashion, came up behind the youngster. Kris turned at the last minute, but did not seem alarmed. When the r-suit picked him up as easily as if he were a cat, he remained motionless and unbothered, and waved at Faulcon as he came up the slope in the arms of his team leader.

Lena deposited him far less gently than she had picked him up. Faulcon eased down the volume of his radio as the woman's voice shrieked angrily through his head-set. Kris said, 'Ease off. I'm safe, aren't I?'

Before Lena could react with a possibly damaging blow – and Faulcon felt such an event was looming – he stepped in and said, 'Let's get him to the nearest station. Maybe Ensavlion need never find out.'

'Good idea,' said Lena, and they picked Kris up between them and ran the mile or so to Riftwatch Station Shibano.

In the warm, spacious interior of the station Faulcon stepped out of his suit, and helped Lena from hers. The two on-duty station crew, ageing, rather unsociable men, remained at the Valley Monitoring Console, listening, always listening, for the sudden atmospheric crack, the electromagnetic symphony that heralded the abrupt appearance of a time wind. The winds did not begin at one end of the valley and blow through the gorge to the other. They could form anywhere, and though they usually blew east to west, they had been known to blow in the opposite direction as well. The valley was watched constantly and with great concentration.

'That was a stupid thing to do,' said Faulcon. They sipped hot soup and sat in a small circle close to the wide window overlooking the valley; the thick glass was tinted in some way, and the dome's interior seemed slightly blue. On Kamelios, where the ageing sun cast a red shadow across everything, the effect was slightly disturbing.

'It was a bloody irresponsible thing to do,' snapped Lena glaring at Kris. 'On my team you obey the rules. You've not only put your own life in danger, you inconvenienced and endangered *me*, and I resent that.'

Kris, quite pale, seemed unrepentant. He drank his soup, holding the cup in both hands, and stared out through the overlook. Finally he said, 'I guess I'm sorry.'

'That's a shame,' said Lena stiffly. 'If you'd known you were sorry I'd have liked you a lot better.'

'I *am* sorry,' Kris amended, looking at her. 'It was dumb of me. I'd ask you only to crawl inside my head for a moment, to have a sniff around and see what's there.' Imploring eyes turning on Faulcon, reasonableness oozing from his youthful features. 'You've got to know what it's like … what it *was* like … to have come so far to find Mark, to see him, and to be denied access to him because of … because of a *danger*, a dangerous thing, that in my days here I haven't seen, or heard, or even got wind of, if you'll pardon the feeble joke.'

Lena dismissed the levity with a contemptuous glance. Kris tried to ignore her and looked at Faulcon. 'I saw the phantom, Leo. I really did.'

'A lot of people have seen the phantom.' Faulcon could recognize that something in Kris's expression testified to more than a distant sighting. He wondered how close the man had got, but he didn't want to push Kris for information, not in the present hostile atmosphere.

Distantly the two observers laughed at some shared joke; their console had been making crackling sounds, the sound of communication with something or someone out on the planet. Faulcon watched them for a second, then let his gaze drop back to Kris Dojaan, who was chewing at his lower lip, distracted and thoughtful.

'I know a lot of people have made sightings from a distance,' he said, 'but I've been right up close.'

Now Lena looked interested too. 'How close?'

'As close as this,' said Kris. He was being infuriatingly unforthcoming. 'The first night I didn't get very close – I saw the figure and it ran away.'

Faulcon was horrified. 'The *first* night? You mean you've been out every night since we came back?'

Kris grinned. 'Do I get my wrist slapped?'

'Imbecile,' said Lena quietly, and Kris shrugged.

'I'm not the only man from the city who goes out at night. The first night I saw someone in a rift suit, running like a mad thing along the edge of the canyon, and yelling, I think. I could hear sounds coming from the helmet. I was a long way away, and he didn't see me. I was hiding. But he *was* in a rift suit and if he was looking for the phantom he was destined to be unlucky. A rift suit moves too fast and the phantom doesn't take a chance. Me, out there practically naked, well, I was trusted.'

Lena said, 'I doubt he was looking for the phantom. A golden pyramid more like.'

'Commander Ensavlion, you mean? Yes, that makes sense.'

Faulcon watched him solemnly, quietly, and finally said, 'What about the phantom? What did you learn?'

'Too much,' said Kris quickly, not meeting either gaze. When he had said no more for several seconds, Faulcon prompted, 'Was I right, then? Have you come to understand a little more about this world?'

'Do you mean is it me out there, running around in rags?' Kris neither smiled, nor frowned, but his voice became sad for a moment. 'It isn't Mark, at any rate. I was so sure it was Mark, and it wasn't, and so I've still got to go after him. But that's all right. That's why I came here, to Kamelios. It's in my contract.'

Faulcon and Lena exchanged an uneasy glance. In his contract? His work contract? There was surely no such clause that required a man to sacrifice his life into Othertime. But Kris was not elaborating.

Putting that last cryptic statement aside for the moment, Faulcon persisted: 'If it's not Mark out there, who is it? You must know if you've spoken to him!'

'I'm not sure that I do know,' said the boy. 'And I'm not saying what I think. Don't press me, Leo. Please. I really don't want to talk about it.'

Exasperated with him, Lena stood, smoothed down her tight-fitting undersuit and shook her head. 'I'm going back to the city. There'll be a cargo transport passing here in two or three hours, so I'm told; you'll ride back on that. Is that clear?' Kris nodded. Lena looked at Faulcon. 'Are you coming?'

'Later,' said Faulcon, and Lena was puzzled for a moment, watching him curiously. When he made no effort to explain further she turned abruptly and went to the alcove where her suit was standing. Before Faulcon could rise and help her she had swung into the machine and was walking to the airlock.

'I really don't want to talk about it,' said Kris as she went, looking at Faulcon with an expression of slight embarrassment. He had obviously assumed Faulcon had stayed because he thought Kris was uneasy with Lena. He hadn't. Faulcon smiled at his team mate, and observed how tired Kris looked.

'I'm dog tired. It's true. The training – the sleepless nights – is taking its toll.'

'Then sleep,' said Faulcon, and Kris walked to a couch and curled up gratefully. Faulcon watched him for a while, then rose and fetched the face-mask from his suit. The two observers watched him sourly as he strapped the face piece on, and one of them said, 'Against regulations to go out there without an r-suit.'

'Report me, then,' said Faulcon bitterly. 'But first, let me out, will you?'

Reluctantly the station crew obliged.

Running. It was like running through time. It was an exquisite freedom, and experience so terrifying that it was almost intellectual; the relinquishing of responsibility, the dispensing-with of the protective suit, the running through this backwater of time's great river was a religious thing, and Faulcon wanted to sing its praises, to scream the sweat that covered his body, to sing the tension of the wires that moved him.

He went down the canyon slopes, and the sun was lost to him; the cloak of deepening red became a darkening night, a land of shade, where structures and decay were highlit, then brightlit, then redlit, then instantly in darkness; and as he moved through alienness so he found an incomprehensible beauty in the moving of one ruin against another, the red crystal spire that was suddenly a towering dark shape, moving across his field of vision and showing him the wonder of mindless cubes and pyramids of green and red-lit colours of the rainbow.

Deeper; darker; a shard of life in the barren sediment of time, running through the ages of the world, crawling down the eons, the rocks and fossils of the strata scattering and crumbling and making their own way from some para-permian to a sterile cambrian, and deeper still, to the scar-ridden flat lands in the deepest part of the half-lit gorge.

Before he reached the bottom, more than an hour since he had started his descent, Faulcon's resolve gave out, the thrill of fear overwhelming him, and he sat down heavily in the stillness. The smile behind his mask was of triumph – to have got so far, to have overcome fear to this extent! All his unease at being so close to Kris Dojaan had gone. The fear he faced was that terror of anticipation of being lost in time that had haunted him since his first days on Kamelios. Naked to the winds he could gauge the extent of his courage; in his months here he had never before dared to approach the valley without a suit, and gradually that suit had become a mask to his apprehension, a crutch that had almost grafted itself to his body. For the first time in a very long time he was starting to find out how it really was between him and VanderZande's World. He felt the gusting, tugging fingers of some natural breeze that heralded the coming dusk. With a view down the valley, into the western distances, he sat as Kris had sat, and contemplated the farther wall of the canyon, and the minds that had designed this carnival of ruination; and he examined, too, the nature of his fear, and the sense of ecstasy, and excitement, that had suddenly greeted his contemplation of the alien land before him, a land he had observed so many times before, and always with a bored indifference, a mercenary-seeking of anything that might pay well.

Yes, much of the coldness was the fault of the rift suit, the stable environment, the human-made machine enclosing the fleshy thing that was the intelligence, and bearing it about its business secure in the knowledge that the suit was increasing its survival chances, to such an extent that the odds were highly favourable. And when the sense of danger goes, perhaps the sense of awe follows. A full appreciation of mystery demands the linking of the soul, and the r-suits cut off the soul as hard and definitely as they cut off the wind, the air, the waves of energy, the very breath of time itself.

He was free now, and his soul and his heart soared out across the void of the canyon, settling on this structure, then that, winging its way from city shard to city shard, never knowing whether there was a billion years of difference in the simple visual hop from a spire to a stone arch and back to the ground again.

Where are you then? Come on, show yourself. I haven't got all day.

A long time passed and Faulcon remained still, searching the canyon and the buildings for any sign of movement. The day grew redder, darker. He knew that soon he would have to move back up the slope or risk spending the night in the valley, exposed to any time squall that might whip up over the next few hours, and exposed to the terrible night chill of Kamelios. His undersuit would keep him warm or cool within moderately intense fluctuations. But night would creep through the fabric with steady, ghoulish cold.

A movement, distantly, made his heart stop. He peered hard to the west, towards Steel City, seeing some few miles up the canyon before the curvature of the valley cut off his view. He gradually realized that the movement was caused by twelve rift-suited figures racing across the canyon bottom, and disappearing into some invisible structure on the far side. Faulcon could not imagine what they were doing here. He had always thought that all missions returned to a station or the city when dusk came down.

He had managed to worry over the distant figures for no more than a few seconds when he heard stones tumbling, and the unmistakable sound of something moving across the ledges above him. He remembered, with chilling hindsight, that this part of the valley was a favourite hunting ground for the male gulgaroth, and that unprotected humans were by no means outside the range of such creatures' tastes if they had not fed for several days. He stood quickly, turned, and stared hard against the sky, seeking the sleek, gleaming shape of the creature. As he did so he suddenly felt his skin crawl, imagined for a moment that he was being watched from the deeper valley. The presence was so strong that he cried out, but when he turned there was nothing to see and the sensation faded. He looked back up the slope. For a moment he saw nothing but the rising cliff, and the waving motion of sparse vegetation clinging to the easier slopes. Then something, too small for a gulgaroth, darted off to the left. He thought it was another animal at first, but when it slipped slightly, and stopped, he realized he was staring at a man, an old man, wearing the ragged uniform of Steel City and a small survival mask. Faulcon knew without hesitation that it was the man he sought. He shouted for the figure to wait, but his own face mask inhibited the sound. He waved. The man turned to watch him briefly, then ran along the slope of the canyon, behind a jagged outcrop of sparkling rock.

Faulcon went in pursuit, up the incline, and calling as loud as he could. The phantom scurried away from him, but Faulcon came close, closer than he would ever have thought possible. Whoever this man was, he was reluctant to invoke the mechanism of his vanishing trick. He wanted Faulcon to come close, and yet was afraid to confront him, to face him.

'Please wait! You spoke to my friend, speak to me. For God's sake wait ...'

Why am I so afraid? My eagerness is fear, isn't it? Of course it is.

Quite suddenly the phantom was before him, cowering, crouching, hands lifted to face, fingers spread and hiding those features of the aged face that the mask did not conceal. Faulcon wondered if he looked frightening, inhuman in the narrow mask he himself wore; perhaps to remove it, to show his full face, would emphasize to the phantom that his concern was genuine. He removed the faceted goggles, gagging on the atmosphere of Kamelios for a second before he could get the respirator back into his mouth. Now he could breathe but not talk properly. 'I'm a friend!' Patronizing words, and difficult to achieve: remove respirator and speak without breathing; respirator back; blink away streaming tears; rack with the choking sensation induced by whatever organic compounds made the Kamelion atmosphere directly unbreathable. The cowering figure of the man was silent, all the whimpering, strangely animal noises gone.

'Who are you?' said Faulcon, learning how to speak and breathe without choking. 'Please tell me.' Breathing. 'I'm not just inquisitive, I really care.'

The shape turned away from him, the fabric of the tattered suit stretching tight across its back. The phantom held up a wrinkled, trembling hand, held it out towards Faulcon, stretched his arm for the most direct and fervent gesture possible: please stay away.

Faulcon approached, only to hear the phantom cry out, a strangely old, high-pitched voice, the voice of a very, very old man, almost child-like, almost desperate. The hand shook, then was snatched into the body, and the figure seemed to shrink even further. Faulcon drew his hand across his eyes, trying to clear his vision, horribly aware that less than a minute of exposure to the Kamelion atmosphere could start to corrode the cornea.

He realized he was about to lose the time phantom, and even as he shouted, 'No, wait, please ... I must know who you are ...' so the figure blurred through his tears, seemed to dart out of sight, and was gone as abruptly as that, as cleanly, as completely as any fleeting breeze, Faulcon found himself staring at bare rock through his goggles, still in an attitude of appeal, still working to fix the mask on properly. He straightened and looked around. Bitterly disappointed, and yet elated somewhere inside that he had achieved so much more than for years had been believed possible, he began the slow climb back up the cliff.

A long while later, in the last hour of Kamelion's rich red dusk, he re-entered the dome of Riftwatch Station Shibano, and dabbed a special ointment to his weeping eyes. Through his blurred vision he noticed that Kris Dojaan was not in the main lounge. He asked the crew of the station if the cargo-transport had taken him back to Steel City and was told that the transport had been delayed.

A pang of disquiet silenced Faulcon for a second and he regarded the observers with blank features. 'Where is he, then?'

'One of the Section Commanders turned up. Just came, just this last few minutes.'

'Ensavlion?' asked Faulcon, and the man grinned.

'The very same. He's been out looking for aliens, and he's popped in for a drink.'

The observers found that very funny. Faulcon remained impassive. What was Ensavlion doing here? Coincidence? He would certainly have known that three of his team had checked in, the observers would not have broken regulations and *not* reported the arrivals. Or had the Commander followed them yet again? And what was he saying to Kris that he felt he had to hide away from the main lounge, and the possibility of being overheard?

'They're back there,' Faulcon was told, and followed the man's glance to the relaxation and TV room, now lit up. The door was slightly open and Faulcon walked quietly across the floor to stand just outside, carefully peering in.

Kris was seated, his back to the door. Commander Ensavlion was leaning against the ebony box that housed the TV player, looking away from the boy, and away from the watching stranger outside the room.

CHAPTER NINE

'I should have spoken to you before, I know that. I'm sorry about it. I was glad when Leo Faulcon suggested you go straight out on a mission. I thought it would help settle you psychologically to Kamelios, to come to understand the place to a certain extent. Then I thought it would be easy to talk to you about Mark, about the mission, about me ... about why Mark died when I could have prevented it. But it wasn't easy. I should have spoken to you when you came. I must confess that I am afraid to speak to you even now. I wonder what you must think of me ...'

Kris sat stiffly and watched his Commander. For some minutes the conversation had been strained, and trivial. Ensavlion seemed incapable of looking at Kris Dojaan, but cast furtive, fleeting glances at him; and furtive, fleeting smiles, as if always divining for sympathy, always trying to elicit a warm and friendly response from the young man who sat so solemn, so passive, so embarrassed. And Kris *was* embarrassed. And he was also angry. He was confused, and this world and its people confused him worst of all. If Ensavlion would come out with his statement it would be so much easier for all concerned. If he would say: I let him die, I was irresponsible, I am to blame, I shot him, I pushed him ... if he would just say whatever it *was* that was eating at his soul, the atmosphere in the room could become sweeter, and Kris would relax; and maybe then they could talk sensibly about a brave man, about a 'dead' man, more accurately about the man who had gone into time ... and had not come back. Mark had *not* come back; he was not the phantom, it had been a stupid dream, a clutching at straws of the first magnitude. Mark, nonetheless, was the survival type, and if anyone could survive the hostile future – or past – Kris was certain it was he. Mark's survival instinct was far greater than that of either Leo Faulcon, or Lena Tanoway ... far greater. He thought of Faulcon for a moment, a fleeting moment, a distracted instant in the silence following Ensavlion's stilted, awkward confession. Poor Faulcon. Poor man. He felt close to Leo, close enough to regard him as a friend. He felt a sympathy for him that he could not have felt for Lena. Sweat prickled on his face and he tried to put the terrible thought aside, let his attention swing back to Commander Ensavlion.

'I sent him out, you see. I sent him out when I knew it was unsafe. There hadn't been a full scale wind for weeks, but there was a spate of squalls, sweeping the valley; totally unpredictable. Quick, clean, the flash of an eye. They often herald a major wind, and there were structures appearing in the valley that were lasting only a few hours before vanishing again. I wanted so desperately to see everything, to get a glimpse of everything that was time-flung. I sent a lot of men out, and most of them did an hour in the rift, then fled. Mark was a strong-willed man, and he behaved by the book. I told him to go out, and he went out, and when the wind came he was stuck … he got caught.' Ensavlion glanced at Kris, his face white, his eyes dim behind tired lids. 'There was nothing anyone could do. I'm convinced of that. There was nothing. Please believe me. If your brother could have been saved, then, as I'm sure you know, he would have been. I'm sure you know that …' He was staring at Kris queerly, a steady gaze, now, a searching stare. He wanted comment from the boy. He wanted his psyche patted better, a kind word, a forgiving gesture.

Kris, comprehending that it was unfair of him, nonetheless did not feel that he wanted to put Ensavlion at his ease. He could scarcely credit that this trembling, weak, fearful man before him was his Section Commander, and the leader of the mission that had brought Mark seven hundred light years to participate in; and which had brought Kris himself along the same interstellar route to join in place of his brother.

He said, 'I'm sure everything was done that could have been done. I don't understand your feeling of failure.'

Ensavlion paced awkwardly in front of the seated youth. 'He knew I was wrong to order him out. But he went out, him and others … I forget exactly who, now. Afterwards we tried to forget about it, to put it from our minds. I had no cares for his safety, but he never found the words, or the disobedience, to correct my instruction.'

'That's a mistake of war, Commander. Every Commander is responsible for the life and death of his men, but it isn't as if you stuck a knife in him. You were wrong, and my brother was caught off-guard; if I was convinced he was dead it might make me more bitter towards you. But he's not dead. I know he's not.'

Ensavlion laughed in a way that suggested relief (at the change of subject, perhaps) and just a little appreciation of Kris's dogmatic adherence to what must surely have been a lost cause.

'You mean the wizened phantom of the valley … well, I appreciate your enthusiasm, and your imagination, but you really should start to think—'

Kris cut in. 'Not the phantom. Not the phantom … I know that now, and I realize I was wrong, and I'm angry at myself for being wrong. Not the phantom …' he touched the amulet about his neck, drawing reassurance from its cold, smooth feel; Ensavlion followed the minute motion with his eyes. 'Not the phantom, but something the phantom said … I know my brother is alive. But whether I can find him is another question.'

Kris was amused by the expression of shock that touched the otherwise dull and expressionless features of his Section Commander. Ensavlion pushed himself away from the TV unit, his hands behind his back. Dramatically he turned round, peered down at Kris. 'Are you telling me you've spoken to this person?'

'Not exactly spoken. Exchanged shouts, snatches of words, sentences. A rather unforthcoming piece of time flotsam, the phantom. Enough exchanged, though, for me to shed a tear or two, one for grief, one for joy. What I sensed about the phantom was not the actual identity of my brother, but the transmission of that identity. When I was on Oster's Fall, my home world, when we got news of Mark's death, I had already been dreaming of him, and when the news came I dreamed harder. I heard him speaking, I'm convinced of it. It was something similar when I first came here. There were moments when I felt Mark calling to me, desperately loudly. He was alive, but trapped. The phantom was relaying that telepathy—'

'Telepathy?'

'Or whatever. I appreciate my senses, Commander. I don't try and constrain them with reason. If I smell something I smell it, I don't start questioning whether I smell it in my nose or my olfactory lobe, or even whether I've smelled it at all, but rather am smelling something because of a visual association working subconsciously. If something stinks, it stinks. If something speaks in my mind, it speaks in my mind.' He frowned, then laughed as he noticed Ensavlion's cynical expression. 'What I'm trying to say is that I'm a slave of my sensory input, and I don't worry about it. It keeps me going, as it has kept many a so-called crank going, through the centuries when people laughed at teleportation – remember that? – and now certain planetary environments enhance that power, right? And through times when people thought that there had never been animal God creatures on Earth, and now there's been communication with the creatures on Earth, which live out of phase with humanity, the same beings who inspired all those legends and myths, right?' Ensavlion was nodding in agreement, conceding the point. Kris said, 'And of course, through times when people scorned time travel.'

Ensavlion's eyebrows rose slightly. 'We still don't have that, you know. There is nothing to say that the phenomena we are observing in the valley, on VanderZande's World, are not in fact something else, some perception trick, or spatial orientation trick.'

'Do you believe that? Do you believe in cosmic tricks?'

'No, I don't,' said Ensavlion, wiping a hand across his face, and smoothing back his hair; he was hot again. 'I don't because I've seen them, the causes, the travellers. I've seen their machine. But despite what my colleagues say, I am not blind to their argument, and indeed to those who argue against a point blank acceptance that the time winds are time *travelling* winds.'

Kris felt smug in his special knowledge. 'It *is* time travel, and you are right and they are wrong. I'm convinced of it, and I've spoken to someone who has hopped through time with the same ease as you or I might hop into a car. That's why the Catchwind Mission is so important. That's why I'm puzzled as to why it hasn't happened yet.'

'Ah,' Ensavlion turned away again, considering the statement with something akin to embarrassment. 'Yes, you are quite right to query that. Your brother was part of the original team, and he was here for some months, and we did not go; and it is months since he disappeared and still we haven't gone.'

When it seemed that Ensavlion would be content with stating the obvious, Kris prompted, 'But I keep seeing men out in the rift. When I was out last night I saw movement. Not the solitary figure that keeps running along the valley's rim. That's you, I guess.'

'Me?' Ensavlion smiled. 'I do spend rather a lot of time out there, I must confess. But go on, you've seen men. Men in rift suits?'

'Of course.'

'Men and *women* in rift suits, to be precise. That's the team. Every few days when there is a sort of wind eddy, or dark cloud, or electrical disturbance that sometimes, but not always, is associated with a time wind ... out they go. But they would abort the mission without instructions from me.'

'And that's happened several times.'

Ensavlion looked horrified, then angry. He took a step towards Kris and his face flushed with suppressed rage. Then he smiled grimly, slapping his hands behind his back and looking away. 'By God, Mister Dojaan, you've been nosing around to an impressive degree. Out on the rift where you oughtn't to be, not yet, and asking questions that by rights should be unanswerable.'

'Are you angry?'

Ensavlion considered that, calming during the few seconds of silence. 'I don't think I am, now.'

Kris decided that he should tread prudently and pick his words with care. 'I thought I might have touched on a sore point. I haven't been nosing, and that's the truth. I was talking to one of the Section during my suit-training, and I suppose he divined that I was the new Catchwind recruit. Maybe something I said, or did, or implied, gave it away.'

'Your name, probably.'

'He told me straight that we're not supposed to talk about the mission, but also that he was part of it. That they'd been waiting for over a year, and they'd always been available when the wind blew, but that you've never given the word. And you never explain why. And they're getting very fed up waiting, which is why there is such a need for replacements.'

Ensavlion watched the boy and hardly a sound was heard, hardly a breath was drawn. Kris felt the terrible imminence of the question, and his heart began to stammer as he wondered what he should say when it came.

'They say, I suppose, that I'm afraid. Commander Ensavlion is scared to death of the mission, and because of his streak of yellow is denying the Universe the possible benefits of the first organized and considered venture into Othertime. Am I right, Kris?'

Kris said nothing, did nothing, but sat in embarrassed silence. 'They think you're scared,' he confirmed after a while. 'As if they're not scared themselves.'

Ensavlion obviously appreciated the softness of that, the generosity. If it was not totally honest on Kris's part, and if Ensavlion realized this, nothing was said, only, 'Everyone's scared of course, that's only natural. But those men and women were prepared to risk death; they signed on for the Catchwind mission, and they were prepared to go through with, it, exhausted with fear, damp with fear, sick with fear, they'd nonetheless have done it.'

'Why *are* you so afraid?' asked Kris, aware, now, that all ice was broken, and that Ensavlion and he had grown closer than was good for two men of such different ranks and such different age; but close they had grown, and there was no denying or escaping it.

The Commander shook his head. 'I've never fully understood, Kris. One day I watched a time wind … a magnificent sight. I can't begin to describe it. The most fabulous, the most incomprehensible sight in the whole Universe, an art form so distinct, so natural that it fills me with joy, such joy that I want to sing with that wind, always sing, always become a part of it. And for years I fought, and argued with the Federation, with the financiers, with the governing body of this Sector to allow a "suicide mission" into time. I got volunteers and I said it was madness not to send an expedition into Othertime. They always came up with the same argument: no one has returned, and therefore no one will. No information has been received from Othertime, and therefore no information will.'

Kris was momentarily confused. 'That makes no sense.'

'I agree. They argued that any successful expedition would indicate a control of the random time-flow in the valley … Do you see what I mean? That time would flow from specific point to specific point, and everyone going *into* time would follow the same path. If such control existed then men, lost or expeditionary, would have turned up, and been turning up for years …'

'One did.'

Ensavlion laughed. 'I don't think the phantom would have been very good support for our cause. In any event, the council eventually agreed to the formation of a small task force, to be maintained in strict secrecy, everyone working a normal job, and waiting for *their* say-so, for *their* word to go. Then, when I saw the pyramid – and I was not alone although I am the only one left alive who saw the travellers – official opinion was swayed sufficiently. I was put in charge of the mission, with full authority to call the task force out into the valley. Secrecy was maintained. After a few weeks the interest in seeking the golden pyramid declined, and I became … I don't know, a laughing stock perhaps? That wouldn't be so far from the truth.' He smiled thinly. 'Then two things happened, two terrible things. In fact, perhaps a third thing happened, a change on Kamelios, one of those electrical storms that addle the minds for a few days and impose different personalities upon us. I don't know. Perhaps world and fate conspired to take the steel from my nerves, but whatever happened, the confidence was suddenly ripped away from me. Though I was afraid for myself, I was as afraid for the people I was planning to take into time with me. Suddenly I couldn't do it.'

'What happened? Or is it too …'

'Is it too what? Too difficult to talk about? Not any more. It was at first, which is why I didn't. Oh yes, your brother's death was one of the things. You should know that.'

'But not the main thing …'

'I don't know. Who can quantify these things? And what good would that do, anyway? Mark's death happened two days after I'd led an expedition up the valley to a place called Ridge Seventeen. You can't see it from here; it's forty miles or so to the east, well away from Steel City. There are Watch Stations there, but that's all they are, Watch Stations. They monitor the winds, and give us warning of time squalls, electrical upsets. They're not equipped to send men down to the valley, at least, not on more than preliminary surveys. Something interesting turns up, out goes Section 4 with the scientific groups, then my section, 8, with its three-man, careful-study groups, then the big Sections with the scientists again. All very complex, and often not adhered to. Well, just before your brother got swept away I'd gone down with one of the eight-man teams, a rapid survey group attached to geology, to see some particularly fine structures, and formations, thrown up by a time-eddy – that's a persistent flow of time through a small area; it has no physical manifestation, beyond the sound, a sort of high-pitched screaming. Time flows fast and furious and all you can really see is sensory impression, and feel the occasional vibration through the ground – you know about that, about the fact that the valley seems physically separate from the land around, although it is apparently connected. We went down into the valley a few hours after it had fallen quiet. Experience teaches us that these rapid-flow time fluxes burn themselves out. I was with the geology group and I saw what looked like a fossil in a stratum of sedimentary rock, and, as you've probably been told, fossils are rare. I went up closer and thought I was looking at a crinkled, pitted shell-form. It swam into focus suddenly, the same colour as the rock around it, a sort of smoky grey; it was a rift suit helmet. When you looked hard you could make out the vague shape of a suit lying horizontal as you'd expect. It was very crushed, but clearest of all was the shape of the five-fingered glove, curled up. You can look at that shape and argue for hours as to whether it *is* a rift suit. All the features are much obliterated, and the face plate lay turned into the cliff from the valley. We were looking at the back of the helmet. It's still there. No wind has touched it since. No one's ever gone and dug it out.'

'Why?'

'Why? Why won't a man go out without his amulet? Why does the loss of a team member result in an elaborate ritual of exorcism for the others? Why does every rifter scrub the dust off his suit before he leaves the vicinity of the valley? Because to do otherwise would be bad medicine. Because on Kamelios we don't invite Old Lady Wind to supper. Because we respect the dead, and we respect Othertime even more.'

'I understand that,' said Kris, and added, 'You don't wear an amulet, I've noticed.'

Ensavlion smiled, just briefly. 'I don't need to, Kris.' He touched his skull, above his eyes; by looking hard Kris could see the thin line of a surgical operation. 'I wear my shard inside.'

There was a moment of silence. Kris thought of rifters turning up from other times not as phantoms, but as vague outlines in deep sedimentary strata; crushed and twisted by planetary forces, they outlived, in their new stone form, the flimsy, fleshy shards of life that busied themselves over the monumental trivia and enigma of the alien ages that filled this deep cut in the world.

He thought of Mark.

'And a few days later, to add to the deep concern this fossil human filled you with, you pushed Mark to work the valley and heard that he had perished.'

Ensavlion looked grim and cold as he silently agreed. 'That's about it. When I heard that Mark had been swept away I was upset at first, then angry, then just very, very depressed. I couldn't spend a night without thinking of him. It took me three weeks to write the letter to your parents – I couldn't bring myself to use the direct link – and what a terrible, and trite, letter that was. I'd written such letters before. Of course I had, many times before. Section 8 is a spear-head, a dare-devil group; they go everywhere and they die everywhere. I've written letters to a thousand worlds, and a thousand homes, and a thousand men and women whom I have never seen, and who, for all I know, never got those personal notes, but found out the details by u-fax. But all of those dead went out on missions that were approved, and sanctioned, and they knew the risks, and they took the risks voluntarily; it hurt when they were lost, but there was a greater stake, and it was easy to be cold.'

'But Mark knew it was wrong to go out, and he made you know without objecting at all. You forced him, and he obeyed. He was a fool.'

'He trusted me. Don't you understand that, Kris? He trusted me, he obeyed me, because, even though he sensed the risk, the danger, he decided that I was a man to be trusted; he could not find it in himself to doubt that if I was insisting on him going, then I knew something, or I had a different, more rational, more experienced instinct. Your brother went into the valley because I had as good as said that nothing would happen to him; my credentials were experience, my rank. And there was no experience. He died. I wonder if he died thinking of me, wondering if I had done it on purpose, if in some way I had felt contempt for him that I could waste him so. And I didn't. He was like you, Kris, like you in many ways. And as I feel a bond with you, so I felt a bond with him. Rank meant nothing. We shared an enthusiasm, an awe of this place. A sense of the alien, a gut-wrenching sense of wonder that people usually lose on this world, like Lena and Leo, your colleagues. They're dead, like steel, polished, sharp, but cold, cold. Not you. You are not sharp yet, and not too polished, but the vibrant energy in you is almost tangible. You came looking for Mark, and you found a world that thrilled you. I could sense it in the sweat smell of you the first time we met. Pungent, aromatic, the most wonderful stink in the world, the stink of excitement. It was the same with Mark. But I pushed that poor bastard, I pushed him because I was half afraid to do my own work. I sent him to the valley whenever I should have gone myself, if anyone was to go at all. Because the valley is our enemy; it is our death; it is to be respected, and there are rare moments when it is totally safe. There are too many moments when it is comprehensively dangerous. I abused his trust, and his awe. I killed him.'

Kris watched Commander Ensavlion, feeling a terrible cold chill deep inside. He could not think of his brother as a man who would mindlessly obey; his brother was a survivor, all the Dojaans were survivors. And Mark would have had the instinct to know when not to go to the valley. He wouldn't have trusted Ensavlion so, not such a weak man. He would have seen that weakness and questioned that order. And yet, he believed in obedience. He hated rank, but always respected sensible, genuine, considered rules; and orders were rules; orders drew on the rules of a place, or a game, or a situation. He might have been torn, then, torn between his contempt for Ensavlion – for surely he could not have respected this sweating, trembling man – and his respect for authority, for rules. Could Mark have made a mistake? Could Kamelios have so affected him that his judgement had been dulled? It was a possibility too reasonable to deny. Kris felt anger, now. It was irrational, certainly, but as Ensavlion wiped a pad across his face, soaking up the great sheen of wetness that had formed from hairline to chin as he had spoken, so Kris heard a voice saying, 'Kick the bastard, kick him now, when he needs you to kick him! Get it out of your system.' But he remained quiet, and still. He obeyed the rules. He sat stiffly silent, sensible that on Vander-Zande's World, with its never-easy double name (the confusion of identity stretching to the very world itself!), he must always keep his emotions, and his reactions, in tight check. You beat this world by always comprehending the nature of the forces that worked through you. He knew that, now, and all he needed was the experience of those forces. He would make a start by allowing Ensavlion no let-up in his embarrassment, because he would not melt again, he would not show tenderness again. Survival was what it was all about, as Faulcon had said to him twice during the training. Kamelios hates our guts, and wants to mentally castrate us. Fight it. Shout at the devil and you win. The meek shall inherit the time winds, the unwary shall inherit a body sheared in half by a gusting squall.

Ensavlion had sensed the hardening of Kris Dojaan's spirit; he seemed uncomfortable again, on edge. He leaned back against the TV unit and the look on his face was one of considerable uncertainty. But he had committed himself, now, and the story was finished. He had laid his soul bare to the youngster – or at least, had appeared to – he had expounded the factors of his fear, and perhaps, by so doing, had expunged them. Kris said nothing, sitting quiet and straight-faced, his gaze as near unblinking as was humanly possible, and fixed upon Ensavlion an arrogant gaze, a contemptuous consideration of the elder man. When long moments of this strain had passed, Ensavlion looked away, looked down.

'Well, Kris, now you know. I don't blame you for being a little surly, but perhaps when you have been on Kamelios a short while longer you will be a little more sympathetic to the pressures of responsibility.' The stiffness in Ensavlion's voice, Kris realized, was a reaction to his own hostility. He must have been sitting there looking melodramatically grim, and he tried to relax. Ensavlion was right. This world was an important factor in any assessment of men and the value of the experience they might have acquired. It was unnecessarily harsh, and naive, to judge Ensavlion as if this were Oster's Fall.

'I apologize, Commander. I suppose … I suppose it's hearing about Mark, and seeing how the world itself has had a hand in his fate. It makes me go very dry, very tight.'

'I know. I can imagine.'

'And perhaps it's also a reaction to the silence on Mark since I came here. I really thought that the moment I stepped from the shuttle someone would come up to me, take me by the arm and say, I knew your brother, great guy, tragic death, lots of friends, come and have dinner, talk about him, see what we can do about him. You know, a sort of "friendships formed in the teeth of tragedy"; people *caring*.'

'People don't care, on Kamelios. At least, not after they've been here a while.'

Kris shook his head, 'That's not always true. You care; you plainly care. About the world, and about your men, and about the possibility of tragedy.'

Ensavlion conceded that. 'Yes, you're right. I was generalizing of course, but even so, even I, even Leo Faulcon have been dulled by the world. People get *control* of VanderZande's World – we can become its master, but at a cost, a terrible cost.'

'You said Leo was sharp, just now.'

'Sharp in a different way. Sharp instinctively. Sharp in that he has got a nose for the planet, and a reaction time to it. I imagine, though, that he had forgotten much about Mark before you came, and then probably felt as awkward as I, talking about it.'

Now Kris was confused. For a second he tried to remember what Faulcon had said, those earlier days, out in the mountains, and more recently during their long, lazy chats. 'I don't think Leo Faulcon knew Mark at all. He'd heard of him, of course, but he didn't seem to know much about him.'

'That's strange,' said Ensavlion thoughtfully. 'What's Leo playing at? I agreed with him that for the first few days he would say nothing about Mark, giving you time to settle into the world, and get to know Leo himself. But I thought I'd made it quite clear, the other day, that I wanted him to talk to you about their friendship, to break the ice a bit. Perhaps he misunderstood me.'

Kris had risen to his feet, frowning, taking a step towards Commander Ensavlion, and then stopping, crossing his arms as he let the full impact of Ensavlion's words sink in. 'I don't understand this at all. Leo and Mark were *friends?*'

'The best of friends,' said Ensavlion quietly. 'I wonder why he said nothing?'

'He not only said nothing, he specifically and adamantly denied knowing Mark. Why would he lie so intensely?'

Ensavlion shrugged. 'As I said ...'

'No! I don't believe that. For the first few days, yes, perhaps he would have thought it best to let me get acclimatized. But we've spent so much time together ... we've talked, we've got drunk, we've trained ... he's had ample opportunity to say something to me when the moment would have been right. Are you *sure* he was friends with Mark?'

Ensavlion was uneasy, yet firm. He gave a barely perceptible nod. 'Of course. You'd better ask him about it. The whole reason I assigned you to his team ... kept him and Lena waiting for a recruit for several weeks ... was because I knew you were coming ... the whole reason was so that he could help you understand what happened, and get a sympathetic picture of Kamelios, so you could comprehend what Mark had signed to do, and what you have signed to do in his place.'

Had Ensavlion used the young replacement as an excuse for holding up the mission into Othertime, Kris wondered, as he followed his Commander through into the main lounge of the station. Only the observers were there. Had there been a whole string of excuses, and delays, each and every one sounding terribly reasonable, in fact just a mask to hide Ensavlion's own fear? But why had Faulcon said nothing to him? There had to be a reason, and because it was possible that Ensavlion was right, that Faulcon had wanted his young colleague to discover certain truths and certain facts about his brother on his own initiative before talking to him in more personal terms, Kris reluctantly decided that he should approach Leo Faulcon with care, and consideration, and not with fists flying.

CHAPTER TEN

At first they thought it was some gigantic sea beast, seen through the night lens of an immobile camera and barely visible as its decaying, scaled bulk settled deeper into the sand, deeper into obscurity. But when the projected image was sharpened and brightened it could be seen for the machine it was, lying slightly askew on the uprise of the shore. The ocean was a glimmering spread of movement in the far distance. A figure walked across the red, blurred image on the screen. It passed across the field of view from right to left, and vanished; then it came back, further from the camera on the byke and stood, its head turning and lifting as it stared all about the hulk.

'That him? That must be Dojaan, right?'

The disembodied voice startled Leo Faulcon. He felt Lena's sudden start as she sat beside him, eyes fixed on the well-remembered scene of their discovery. Faulcon said aloud, 'That's right. He'd forgotten to get an amulet shard and Lena – Leader Tanoway – sent him out. We were angry and upset and he went out fast.'

As he spoke Faulcon glanced around, and by the projected light from the film room he could catch glimpses of the rows and rows of white, impassive faces behind him. It was impossible to tell who had spoken.

They were deep in the heart of Steel City, somewhere below the great plaza, at least half a mile beyond the restricted-travel barrier on level four. This was an administrative centre that Faulcon had only guessed at before, a silent, solemn area, well guarded and uncomfortably clean. The people he had seen working here had all worn prominent identity tags. He had not seen many amulets.

The same voice behind him said, 'He is unaware of the camera? You're sure?'

'Almost certainly,' said Lena testily. 'He was unfamiliar with normal routine at that time.'

'Besides which,' added Faulcon, 'it's very easy to forget normal routine procedures – I forgot I'd been filmed until we got back.'

On the screen the shadowy shape of the youngster, moving in an exaggeratedly jerky way, blurred even more as he obviously went down the beach and around the machine. For several seconds there was stillness before their eyes, the strange, gentle motion of the sea being difficult to focus on, causing confusion – was it a photograph or not? Suddenly there seemed to be a flurry of motion before the camera eye. The wind had begun to get strong again, and sand swirled in brief-lived vortices about the derelict. The camera eye trembled slightly. Faulcon couldn't remember if the bykes had fallen during the night, but he felt sure they hadn't.

'Has he gone inside?' came a woman's voice. 'What the hell are we looking at?'

Faulcon exchanged a mocking glance with Lena. They decided comment was unnecessary.

Difficult to see against the dark, rising wall of the machine, Kris eventually reappeared, holding onto the metal hull, and inching his way back into camera shot. His body seemed thinner, more ghostly through the redness and the haze of sand. For a long while he stood, irritatingly at the edge of camera view, and stared at the hulk. Then he seemed to fumble with something in his hand, staring down at it but casting quite apparent glances towards the nearby tent. He raised his hand and the screen flared briefly as he discharged a bolt of energy into the wreck. The hull splintered and fragmented; a brief cloud of smoke was rapidly swept away by the wind. Kris edged forward and dropped to a crouch, peering in through the gap he had made.

'Watch now. Watch carefully. The film gets a bit dark here and we want to be absolutely sure we are agreed on what happens.' The voice, alien to Faulcon, was worrying in its implication of how often the attached mentality had observed this strip of film.

On the screen he could see Kris Dojaan leaning into the hulk, but his body and the machine were difficult to distinguish through the raging storm of sand and wind. Faulcon glimpsed the boy's figure by brief, dull reflections from his faceted goggles as he looked towards the tent, and by occasional, more clearly resolved, movements as he leaned back and looked up the wall of the wreck.

Suddenly he was gone. 'There,' said the same voice. 'He went inside. Did you see that? He went inside.'

Faulcon felt cold. He had instinctively known that Kris had been lying about not having entered the hulk, but here, before his eyes, was the hard, blurred evidence. And yet, when Lena whispered, 'What's all the fuss about? So he went inside. So what?' he had to admit that his feeling of anxiety was irrational.

For several minutes the room was heavy with the concentrated silence of its occupants (save for the coughing, shuffling and nervous whispering of those only peripherally interested in the events); the screen remained a view of an ocean, a windswept shore, and an alien machine that seemed to change its appearance the longer the gaze was fixed upon it. Faulcon grew hot. Lena, beside him, touched his hand, but any meaning, or shared sympathy, was lost on him. Eventually there was a rapid, startling motion on the screen, something huge passing in front of the camera, out of camera-shot, and then back into view. Faulcon himself, coming to find out what had happened to his young team mate. He battled against the wind, round the hulk, and back into vision again, then peering into the hole in the machine's side.

'Has anybody seen any activity to or from that gap until now?' The voice was the woman's voice, and Faulcon cast a quick glance backwards and saw the person sitting on her own.

There was a murmur that signified 'no'. Faulcon watched himself back away from the hole and look around, at the tent, at the ocean, up into the night sky, then back at the machine. And quite suddenly there was Kris, rising from the shore, a dark shadow, insignificant, moving and standing and achieving a significance of high priority. The figure ambled towards Faulcon who suddenly saw it, manifestly jumped with fright – which caused a ripple of mirth among those who perhaps had not seen the film before – and then walked a few paces to meet the boy.

There were a few seconds of motionless, silent communication, and then Kris held out something towards Faulcon.

Brilliant blue light washed across the screen, ceasing abruptly and leaving an intense after-image on Faulcon's eyes, although the Faulcon on the screen – several days ago – had been unaware of any emission from the star-shaped shard that Kris had shown him.

The film was stopped there. The lights in the room came on and Faulcon and Lena swung round in their bucket chairs. Now they sat in the initial arrangement, as part of a square, facing a desk behind which sat two men and a woman, making notes and murmuring quietly to each other. The room was filled with doctors, psychologists, geologists, section Commanders (Ensavlion was not among them), and the dark-suited figures of two Galactic Commanders, the overseers of all planetary colonies. These two men said nothing, and would probably continue in the same vein. They were here as observers, and the only function they served was to take information back to the Federation. But they worked closely with the tripartite structure that controlled VanderZande's World, representatives of which were the three stony-faced individuals who sat before Faulcon. The woman was from the offices of the *Magistar Colona*; she was youngish in looks, with fine features and carefully plaited hair, and she spent a while reading through her notes before she said, 'Did Dojaan give you the impression that he was lying?'

'About going into the machine?' Faulcon thought back, trying to remember exactly what it had been that had made him uneasy with Kris Dojaan's behaviour out by the ocean. 'Yes, I think he did. He hesitated. He seemed guilty. And it seemed unreasonable that he should *not* have gone into the machine.'

'But you didn't go inside yourself,' said the sallow-faced man who sat on the right of the woman from the *Magistar Colona*. He was from the Office of the Provincial Secretary, and as he watched the proceedings his face hardly moved; Faulcon was hard-pressed to observe him blink.

'I felt afraid,' he said. 'And I was looking for Dojaan outside.'

'Guilty? Or confused. Dojaan.' This contribution was from the other man, older, grey-haired and very overweight; Faulcon had seen him before, Marat Inhorts, adviser to the *Magistar Militar*. 'Could he have been confused? Addled? Unsure of what *had* occurred to him?'

'Yes ... yes, I suppose he could have been.'

A nameless psychologist said, 'That would fit with the speech and behaviour pattern that Faulcon reported. He may have deliberately entered the machine, and subsequently been confused, perhaps even mind-blanked.'

Faulcon said, 'He was certainly not possessive towards the amulet, the artifact that seems to be linked with his entry. He was quite prepared to give it to Commander Ensavlion so it could be analysed.'

'But Ensavlion stopped him taking it off,' said Lena. 'I think it was analysed *in situ.*'

The council all nodded as one, and the woman held up a sheet of paper, staring at the words written upon it. Behind her, as she touched a small desk button, appeared a transray photograph of the star, showing a jumble of small tubes, circular structures and geometric – crystalline? – formations. Under higher power, it could be seen that the internal face of the star was literally covered with small scratches, linking and crossing, a micro-circuit perhaps, of crude and clumsy design.

Inhorts said, 'As you can see, the artifact has a detailed, mostly incomprehensible, internal structure. It is apparently very inferior to our own technology, a crude mechanism for producing energy at all wavelengths, and under a sort of external pressure and heat control; these microcircuits are quite alien to us, but very crude; the crystals fulfil a sort of channelling and reverberation function and are unnecessarily enormous. It's a child's toy. A stupid thing, functionless.'

The woman said, 'Shortly after the encounter between team and wreck, the machine vanished. There is a generalized belief that it crawled back into the ocean, and then disappeared into time, perhaps in an undersea current, or squall, or perhaps by its own volition. The lack of track marks, and the failure to observe any small disturbance whatsoever in the ocean during the hours following, also suggests the possibility that the machine may have vanished from the site of its shore-line presence. There is, again, little sign of any disturbance of the shore. We have to consider the possibility that this was a deliberate contact, for purposes we can't understand.' She held up a photograph, which Faulcon thought might have shown Kris's amulet, 'Surely not for this, this toy. Although ...' she shrugged, placed the picture down, and looked abruptly at Faulcon, her face hardening. 'One question that intrigues us, and this is the real reason for your presence here, the question of coincidence: the fact that you, Faulcon, are now the only person we know who has – apparently – been exposed to the monitoring life-form twice.'

As the words had come so Faulcon's head had started to ache, and the room had seemed to close in about him. Beside him, Lena's presence grew out of all proportion. He could hear every breath, every heartbeat, every frown, every silent query, every flush of anger and confusion. When he looked at her out of the corner of his eye she was staring straight ahead at the council, but her cheeks were bright red, and her chest rose and fell rapidly, a sign of the emotion she was feeling.

Trying to ignore Lena, Faulcon said, his voice not steady, but hopefully under reasonable control, 'I don't really understand the meaning of that ... What are you implying?'

The woman laughed humourlessly, as if she had only contempt for Faulcon's defensiveness. 'We're not really implying anything, rifter. We have here a satellite plot of your route, the three of you, during that last mission. We have your instructions as well. For several days you explored the mountains and part of the desert, approaching the northern shore of the ocean; abruptly you changed direction, south-west through the forest lands, a very large change in direction and one that takes you arrow-straight to the alien derelict, even though at the time you could not possibly have seen it; and even though, as best we can see from the scattered, rather uninteresting satellite shots, the hulk was not in evidence for several days before you came ... it wasn't there. It seems to have come out of the sea to greet you. Whose idea was it to change direction?'

The room was almost totally silent. All eyes were on Faulcon, all faces solemn, all solemnness belying the deep mistrust and inquisitiveness that beat in thirty breasts around the room.

'I don't know,' said Faulcon quietly. 'We just did it on impulse, I think.'

Before there could be any response to that, Lena said quickly, sharply, 'In fact it was Kris Dojaan's idea. He wanted to see the ocean, and we knew that the view from the north was across salt flats. We changed direction while we were in the mountains and just followed the sun. When we made the discovery we attributed it to our luck, brought on by lucky Kris Dojaan.'

The council talked quietly together for a few seconds, and during that momentary pause Faulcon tried to attract Lena's attention. Irritatingly, and worryingly, she remained staring steadfastedly ahead; but she was aware of Faulcon's worry, he could tell that. She was freezing him out, and he knew exactly why.

'Rifter Faulcon?' He dragged his attention back to the council, to the woman who had been insistently calling to him for several moments.

'Sorry. I was miles away.'

'Something has to be explained to you, we have decided, to both of you, in view of your relationship, and Leader Tanoway's existing security clearance. This world, this time, this whole installation, is watched. Who or what is watching us we can only guess. Why they are watching us is something else we cannot at this time answer. It seems, however, that they do make contact; they make contact in a variety of ways, or at least, we assume they do. The amulet may well be an example of one form of contact, a subconscious calling to a site and a sort of "handling" process … in this case Kris Dojaan, although almost certainly both of you were scanned in some detail while you were there. The visual sightings are another contact; or so we assume. And there are other suggested ways that we needn't go into here and now. We know, of course, that you have officially denied seeing the travellers –' she was addressing Faulcon direct. 'Or indeed their machine. At the time your section Commander saw both, and when others of the team, now dead or insane, also made visual contact, you claim to have been unconscious. The fact that you are neither obsessed, nor dead, nor indeed committed, suggests that you are telling the truth; your story holds up. We know, of course, that you are lying, your scan-debrief following the incident told us all we needed to know, that you saw as much as Ensavlion—'

Again Lena caught her breath sharply; no doubt she was wondering what would come next, what other falseness and deceit would be revealed. Faulcon could only sit in hot, terrified silence. He had not even *known* they had scanned him at his debriefing. He felt angry, hostile at the invasion of his privacy.

'—Ensavlion's obsession, his public bragging, is an embarrassment, but is also useful. There is an impression that only he has seen this structure, and the travellers, this visitation, but in fact it is a well-documented, and often-sighted phenomenon. Whether or not the travellers are fact or fantasy we can't judge yet …'

'Why don't you scan him, like you scanned me.' Bitterly, the blood hot in his cheeks.

Inhorts shook his head, 'You gave permission on your arrival form that if you made a contact we would scan you. Ensavlion did not. We don't abuse our technology and our position of responsibility, rifter. Although I can see you don't believe it.'

The man was right! He *had* agreed to *viscan* debriefing if he should be unconscious, or incapable following a mission.

'Besides,' said the woman, 'we are not so concerned as to what you saw as to whether or not what you saw is real.'

Lena said, dully, almost mechanically, 'Did you *viscan* Kris? Did you peer into his skull to see what *he* saw?'

Inhorts nodded thoughtfully, staring at her. 'He gave permission. Nothing but intense, high-resolution images of his brother, and the ocean … the Paluberion Sea. It was impossible to tell if he even went into the derelict. The images were not helpful …'

'What the man means is …' the woman in the middle, almost sardonic. 'Kris Dojaan appeared to be deliberately blocking his mind to us.'

What *are* you up to, Mister Dojaan?

'We're telling you all this, rifter Faulcon, Leader Tanoway, because you are now part of a greater project.' As Inhorts talked, he slowed his speech, enunciating the words with almost comic clarity, as if anxious that their full import should sink into the minds of the commoners before him. 'You will continue your work with Section 8. Although your commanding officer is security cleared, henceforth your orders will come from us; Commander Ensavlion will not be aware of the fact.'

Aware of its pointlessness, Faulcon half-heartedly protested: 'I'm not full military; I'm freelance; slightly.'

'Not any longer. Law forbids us to watch you, to monitor you in private – unless you give permission? No, I didn't think so – in public, however, you will be overseen constantly. You know the routine: if you have any objections they must be received on tape, by Central Judiciary, within five days, supported by a representative of Section 8. Incidentally, you are forbidden to mention any of this to any representative of Section 8—' a sense of humour, thought Faulcon, and actually smiled himself. 'What you have heard here today, what you now know about Kamelios, and the valley, all of it is classified. If you talk about it, if it is suspected that you have talked about it, you are liable to transport and confinement in solitary. I hope that's clear. As you leave, pick up grey security identification discs. Carry them, concealed, at all times.'

Faulcon nodded dumbly, watching the impassive faces of the council. The woman said, 'This is the first time you have been before the council. It is also the last. But we shall never be very far away.'

Faulcon rose and followed Lena to the door. 'That's very comforting,' he said, as he stepped out into the cool passageway beyond.

CHAPTER ELEVEN

Bright sunlight filled the central plaza of Steel City as Faulcon and Lena walked quickly and silently through the milling crowds, towards the sloping corridors that led to the living levels. There was a fair taking place, probably a trader fair from one of the older colonized worlds, bringing strange goods and strange acts. Faulcon could see two highly colourful men balancing on a tightrope and fighting each other with mock swords. The plaza was a vast arena, and there were hundreds of people gathered by the open spaces; it was difficult to make out more than just a flash of colour and movement.

As they walked up the sloping hill, winding round the outskirts of the plaza and glancing down to the soft green floor below, Faulcon became very aware of the tiny dark spots that were the traffic-monitor eyes; he had no doubt in his mind that those same eyes were now linked to his personal profile, and the relevant views being passed to a bored official in some sprawling, white, personnel-watching room, somewhere in the deeper layers of the city. Lena was also super-sensitive to the idea of being constantly regarded. When Faulcon tried to speak to her she shut him up with a curt and angry comment. She strode ahead of him, tense and upset. Faulcon, not even knowing if she would let him into her room, followed resignedly, assuring her that she was overreacting, expecting nothing else but the silence he received by way of answer.

She opened the wide door of her suite and turned to prevent him entering. Faulcon took a step forward. 'Lena, let's talk about this—'

She cut him short with a vicious, and painful, slap across the face.

'You *stupid* bastard.'

'I knew you were going to do that.' He forced a smile as he tenderly touched his cheek.

'Well, aren't you the clever boy. But lying and deceit isn't clever. Lying is stupid. *You* are stupid. You've lied to Kris Dojaan, and you've lied to me. I thought we were close, Leo ...'

'It's such a trivial thing, such a small lie—'

Her voice was choked with rage. 'Small! Don't you even understand now? It's not the lie, but the fact of the lie. Suddenly I don't think I like you very much.'

'Let me talk to you, Lena.'

She slammed the door in his face.

There seemed no alternative but to get out of Steel City for a while. He knew Lena well enough to recognize a full day's sulk, and there would be no reasoning with her until the next day at least. He was wrong, he knew; her anger was fully justified. What made him furious was the frustration of being unable to account for himself to her, to put her in the picture. As he made his way carefully down the levels, until he entered the walkways around and above the plaza, he reflected ruefully that now, more than at any other time, was the right moment to say the things to Lena that had haunted him for so long. And she had slammed the door in his face. He would have to wait, and it made him apprehensive when he entertained the possibility of the rightness passing, of the moment becoming wrong again; of the haunting continuing.

For a while at least two things were for sure – he had no Lena to turn to, and he had to avoid Kris Dojaan. If it would have been appropriate to speak to Lena at this time, the same could not be said for Kris. The lad was full of questions, full of restrained anger, full of resentment. And Faulcon could not blame him for that either. But what he had to say to Kris could not be said now, not until he had exorcized a particular ghost. Not until the past was cleared in his mind.

The most sensible thing at the moment seemed to be to take his leave of Steel City, a byke ride perhaps, a night-trip out to the hills and back. An escape. First, though, he ate in a tiny, out-of-the-way bistro, then dialled his apartment recorder for messages. Kris had called twice. And there was a message from Immuk Lee. Was she still in the City then?

Immuk. Faulcon thought of her warmly, and of the help she had been to him before. They had been very close, shortly after Mark Dojaan had been taken, at a time when Faulcon had needed a good friend; they had been lovers in an unsatisfactory way, ultimately deciding not to continue the affair, but remaining close, almost amused at the failure of the sexual dalliance. Lena had been distant from Faulcon at that time. He had not even tried to turn to her. He had known intuitively that it would be a redundant effort.

Immuk Lee, yes; it would be good to talk to her. The only thing that worried Faulcon was that Kris had shown great interest in her. Were they together now? He decided to take a chance. She was down in Biolab 5, and he began to make his way there.

Immuk was on her way out of the science complex as their paths crossed.

'Leo!' she said brightly, and stretched to kiss him. Her oriental eyes sparkled as she looked at him, but she withdrew a little, apparently concerned. 'What have you been doing to Lena?'

'You've seen her?' Immuk nodded.

'There's a confrontation looming,' Faulcon went on. 'At the moment she's upset.'

'At the moment she's probably still in the Sky Lounge getting drunk. I saw her an hour ago; I spoke to her and she eloquently told me where to go.'

'She's in a bad mood.'

'I'd never have guessed. What are you doing now? You need a talking post?' She smiled.

'I could do with one. But more than that I just need to get out of the City for a while. I need to get my mind off its current preoccupations. How long are you staying here?'

'I'm leaving right now, although I'll be working here permanently from the end of the seven-day. I'm going up to Overlook. Ben's up there, Ben Leuwentok—'

'Yes, I know. The olgoi watcher.'

'He's doing some good work, Leo. And not just on olgoi. I've got some charts for him, information on the moons. Why don't you come along up?'

Faulcon required less than a second to agree. 'Thanks. That's a very good idea.'

Within the hour they had checked their bykes out of the hangar and were speeding west, away from the city, following a route close to Faulcon's return route of a few days before. But Immuk suddenly turned inland from the valley, and up the steep, chalky hills that led through Chalk Stack, to the wind-eroded bluff known as Overlook. The station there was a cluster of dull, cubical houses, grouped around the taller dome-shaped laboratory and observatory building. It looked very run down, and very quiet, but as they drove into the compound, and turned to get a good look at the forest spread out below them, Faulcon heard the sounds of revelry from one of the huts, and gradually became aware that the place was humming with activity.

Ben Leuwentok was a man in his middle age, weather-worn and grizzled; very tanned. The area of his face that bore his mask, when outside, was a striking white streak across his nose, above his eyes and reaching into his cheeks. Faulcon couldn't help chuckling as he saw the strange colouration. He had forgotten that Altuxor emitted a good deal of UV light, and that at the equator a tan was almost as easy to achieve as on Earth, where legend held that pale skin bronzed in hours. But what Faulcon noticed most about Leuwentok was his intensity. His brown eyes gleamed as if with their own light; his face, lean and hard, was never still – he laughed, regarded intently, thought, then broke into rapid chatter, explaining his work to Faulcon, taking immense pride in what he was doing. His hands were as restless as his body, secure only when thrust deeply into the pockets of the green lab-coat he wore.

'The main work we do here is on the native life of Kamelios. My particular interest is the olgoi-gulgaroth symbiosis.'

'Symbiosis?' Faulcon was following Leuwentok through a narrow corridor and into a foul smelling, but spacious, animal room. There was a sudden fluttering, darting action on all sides as creatures, large and small, reacted to the intrusion. 'I thought the gulgaroth *ate* the olgoi, except when they send them up the hills to feed the females with their seed. Where does the symbiosis come in?'

Leuwentok had busied himself cleaning trails of evil-smelling excreta from the walls of the lower environments; the exudate had dripped from higher, open-fronted (but barred) cages where the sullen, beady-eyed forms of four olgoi squatted, watching the humans. 'Somebody'll get sent back to Steel City for letting them get into this state,' he said irritably. And to Faulcon. 'Symbiosis – well of course – have you ever tried to capture an olgoi in the lowlands? They're protected, they're fed, they're kept warm, they're transported to where their females are. There's a lot of life on Kamelios that would enjoy an olgoi for dinner. But when half a ton of razor-clawed and dagger-toothed arachno-form comes as dessert, you think twice. The olgoi are only vulnerable during the six-moon run.'

'That only happens for a few weeks of the year, doesn't it? I know there's a limited hunting season.'

Leuwentok looked appalled. 'Are you a hunter? You hunt olgoi – shoot them?'

Faulcon shrugged, glancing uneasily at Immuk Lee. 'Why not? They're good sport, and good eating. You can't get olgoi in Steel City, the communities won't touch them because they're taboo, and the manchanged don't kill enough even for their own use.'

'That's disgusting.' Leuwentok was quite sincerely appalled. It had genuinely never occurred to Faulcon that a preservation instinct prevailed on Kamelios with regard to the fleet-footed little animals that scampered, for a few summer weeks of the year, up into the territories of the female gulgaroth. He decided against mentioning how his main reason for hunting was to get gulgaroth trophies – claws, teeth, shearing plates, and the coloured gulzite crystals that their bodies manufactured for decoration. Leuwentok went on, 'I suppose I shouldn't expect any different from a rifter. But it's bad enough that the manchanged set traps in the high country – Hunderag Country is one of the four main route-ways of the species, and manchanged colonies intercept as much as 20 per cent of the betweenings!'

'The betweenings? What's that, slang for migrating olgoi?'

'Very perceptive,' said Leuwentok grumpily. Immuk smiled at Faulcon from across the animal room. The largest olgoi made a keening sound and came to the front of its cage, chewing the bars with the four, triangular cutting plates in its round, deceptively weak-looking mouth. Faulcon thought its four tiny eyes were all swivelled to watch him. 'Aren't they beautiful creatures?' Leuwentok continued, suddenly relaxed.

'Yes,' said Faulcon. 'Do they bite?'

'Do they bite!' Leuwentok glanced, half amused, at Immuk. He held up his left hand; the little finger was missing, and still obviously healing, and there were deep, red-rimmed scars in the palm and on the meat at the base of the thumb. 'Just occasionally,' he added.

And yet, despite these appalling wounds, the man abruptly opened the cage and shot his hand inside. The olgoi all hugged the back of the environment, but the bold one, the one that had come forward, was firmly grasped by its neck. Leuwentok closed the cage and held the shrieking, defecating animal up to Faulcon's face. The smell was unbelievable, a richly chemical odour that turned his stomach – sweet, sickly, overwhelming. Leuwentok laughed. 'You've probably never noticed, but that's the way the world smells; up here, in the forests, at least.' The olgoi, in its ungainly attitude, dangling from the biologist's hand, reminded Faulcon of a green and blue plucked chicken, save that its feet were viciously clawed; the animal made high pitched sounds of objection.

'That smell,' said Leuwentok, 'is not its own. It's gulgaroth. I caught this one as it began its run. Every year there's a small percentage of olgoi that begin to move up into the mountains when only five moons are dancing. Merlin is the main influence, of course, but only when all six are thirty degrees or more above the horizon do the really big changes happen to the fauna here. I think it depends on the gulgaroth more than the olgoi. The olgoi are just carriers, as you know, and they're programmed by the symbiont. When a male gulgaroth discharges its seed into the olgoi, the olgoi takes off, no matter how many moons are up.'

He held the creature close to Faulcon again, and pulled apart the muscular orifice that ran the length of its underside – Faulcon found himself looking at a slick, purplish grey cavity, covered with yellow-tipped nodules, and coated with a translucent and highly unpleasant jelly. 'You know how many gulgunculi are in there, how many thrashing sperms? About four. Ridiculous isn't it? Germ plasm in the throat, and four sperm; and they can't even be bothered to inseminate the female themselves. How the hell do they expect that to work biologically?'

'But it does.'

'Of course it does.' At long last Leuwentok released the olgoi, which ran, panic-stricken and senselessly, around the cage. 'Any eco-system that is literally programmed by the movements of six moons is bound to be weird, and bound to work in a weird way. This reproductive process, using a go-between, works – quite what would happen if a male and female gulgaroth ever got together is something I'd dearly like to know.'

Immuk had slipped out of the room, Faulcon noticed, and now Leuwen-tok led the way back to the cluttered workbenches. Coffee was stewing in a conical flask. Coffee! Faulcon bent to sniff the imported drink, and found the aroma to be everything he had imagined of such an expensive luxury – weird, but wonderful of necessity. He declined a beaker-full, however (he didn't really understand why), and watched as Leuwentok sipped a half-glass him-self. Immuk came into the room, holding several rolled charts which she placed on the small desk at the end of the room. 'I hope these are what you wanted. They have to be returned within a two-day.'

Quite suddenly Faulcon felt out of place, an intruder. He had got away from Steel City, and for a while had forgotten about Lena and Kris Dojaan. But now Leuwentok had work to do. Faulcon excused himself and walked alone across the station grounds, and up the chalk bluff. He decided against risking a quick smell of the real, raw atmosphere. He sat there for a long time, watching the sun creep down towards the horizon, watching the wide land redden and darken and take on a very different appearance, somehow more alien than the familiar world of the day. At dusk he began to sense movement below him, in the forest, and in the deep shadows of several of the towering crags of white rock. He was on the point of returning to the station, for safe-ty's sake, when he saw Immuk a few hundred yards away, darting between the seemingly petrified trunks of ancient skagbark, among the strands of powdery sunweed. He rose, stretched, and scrambled down the easier slopes until he was on the spongy land that approached the thin forest. He couldn't see her among the trees, but Altuxor's red disc made a part of the forest un-seeable, setting everything into silhouette. He shouted through his mask, calling her name, and her answering cry was almost frightened. 'Leo? Is that you? For God's sake go back to the clear land!'

'Where are you?' A breeze had confused his senses. He wasn't sure he knew where her voice had come from; in these conditions the mask's small ear-plugs, designed not to affect sound reception, could not have helped. He stood among the skagbark, conscious of the darkness, aware of the surrepti-tious movements of small animals. It suddenly occurred to him that he was being very foolish indeed, and that he was unarmed. He had never, in all his sorties through these forests, seen a gulgaroth – but he had never been through at dusk.

He turned back to the bluff, intending to walk up to its top and wait for Immuk to come to him. He continued walking towards the cliff, noticing the dark area at its base, and thinking for a second that it was a shallow cave. The sound, as of several twigs snapping, brought him abruptly to a halt. Blood drained from his face. His heartbeat quickened. It was a familiar sound, that snapping sound – claws clicking out of their pads. The next instant an olgoi shot away from the patch of dark, shrieking horribly. Faulcon was so startled that he felt he had been punched; he froze. He was partly aware that he should be reaching for his holster, partly aware that he wasn't wearing it, mostly aware of the huge shape that was rising onto eight, spider-like legs, and turning its head towards him.

Several eyes sparkled in the forest of black, spiky hair that covered its head; sensory tendrils on the bloated, shiny body quivered frantically, sniffing him out; a gaping hole opened in the face and cutting edges passed silently across each other.

The gulgaroth made a throaty, rattling sound, and took several rapid steps closer to Faulcon, then stopped and began to weave from side to side, its head turning from Faulcon to the sky. It should have attacked instantly, Faulcon knew. The male gulgaroth never hesitated. It should be chewing its way through him by now, not eating, just killing. It was twice as tall as him as it stood on four legs, its other limbs reaching towards him, stroking the air between them.

Behind Faulcon the forest rustled as two human forms darted out of concealment. The gulgaroth made a deep sound, a click-spitting noise. It took a step back! Faulcon heard the sound of a hand-weapon being made operational, and Leuwentok's voice, 'No. Don't shoot it!' The man sounded disturbed as he called loudly through his mask.

'Are you mad?' Immuk; angry.

'Don't shoot it!' Leuwentok insisted, and a moment later he tugged on Faulcon's arm. 'Move slowly, round to the right, and up the bluff.'

'Why doesn't it attack?'

'Look behind you. Easily, not jumpily.'

As they edged away, the gulgaroth hesitantly turning with them, Faulcon looked over the forest; in the dusk sky five moons formed a diamond pattern – tiny Aardwind at the top, the heavily pitted twins Kytara and Tharoo at the sides, and green-glowing Threelight below; nearly fully emerged from occlusion by Kytara, the striated red disc of Merlin was an unfamiliar, and brilliant, addition to the pattern.

'It's beginning,' said Leuwentok cryptically. They had put distance between themselves and the gulgaroth, and Faulcon noticed with some relief that the giant animal was slowly turning back to face in the direction of the moons.

'Saved by magic,' he said.

'Merlin's magic,' Immuk murmured, expanding Faulcon's point unnecessarily. They climbed the bluff – the gulgaroth had vanished by the time they were peering over the cliff for it – and watched the double moon slowly break away from the pattern, Merlin's disc paling quite noticeably, and shrinking a little as Kytara came to cover it again. A few minutes later an eerie howling rose from the forestlands that dipped down towards the barren area of chalk stacks and scrubby, brush-like vegetation. Darkness was approaching quite rapidly, now, and the moons were assuming more dominance in the sky, only pale Aardwind dropping away to the horizon and losing distinction. Magrath was just visible to the north.

Leuwentok said, peering downwards, 'I think that's our gulga – quite a long way off. Let's go back to the hide. But go quietly, and keep your eyes open. These masks don't let us smell a gulgaroth like the other creatures can.'

The 'hide' was a small, pre-fabricated hut, double-walled and strong enough to withstand an attack by the giant animals it was designed to observe. Grey stippling was its only attempt at camouflage. Inside was a single, spacious room, with wall bunks, desk area, eating area, and a closeted convenience that Faulcon used with much relief. When he stepped back into the main room, Immuk and Ben Leuwentok were sitting close together, poring over some figures. They were holding hands. Faulcon was aware, again, that he was still intruding. He wished he could be back at Steel City, and he wished above all that he could talk to Lena, right now; get her back on his side.

'You take the top bunk,' said Immuk suddenly, and in that moment all thoughts of leaving the hide were taken from Faulcon's mind, although he said, 'I'd thought of riding back to the city ...'

'With Merlin showing so much of his face? I shouldn't.' It was Leuwentok who spoke. 'It's coming time for the moons to part, and that's hunting time for all you trigger-happy rifters – it's also problem time for the gulgaroth. They'll guard their little go-betweens quite savagely once they've broken Merlin's spell. Like that fellow out there, right? High on Merlin, but only for a few minutes. You're safer here. We don't mind.'

So Faulcon found a chair and sat with them at the table. He was hungry, distracted by the gnawing emptiness inside him. As if reading his mind – or perhaps hearing the rumbling of his stomach – Leuwentok grinned and said, 'Vegetable stew. It's heating up; won't be long. Meantime, come and look at this.'

As Faulcon moved around the table, to look at the several graphs, Leuwentok looked at him quizzically. 'You're hiding out, Immuk tells me. Is that right?'

'Lying low for a while. Personal difficulties.'

'I thought you might have been checking up on us. Steel City occasionally sends people out to see if we're coming up with anything really *interesting*. Intelligent life, in other words. But you're just curious, right?'

Faulcon shrugged. 'Fascinated. Curious. Intrigued. It seems much more alive out here than the science section in the city.'

'It is,' said Leuwentok, in a tone of voice that suggested he had little more than contempt for the city scientists. 'We're a part of Section 2, the peripheral part. Oh, the city's data is useful: migrations, sightings, specimens. But the real work is done here, in the field.'

The sheets of statistics were all concerned with the movements of the six moons, related to single and multiple behaviour patterns of the olgoi, gulga-roth and assorted other creatures. 'The moons are really important – that's something I never really understood; I *knew* it, but it had never sunk in, if you see what I mean.'

'Merlin is most important of all. Quite why I don't know.' Leuwentok searched through the sheets until he found a plot of olgoi mating activity, related to the various emergence phases of Merlin from behind the disc of Kytara. He made his points one by one in rapid succession, stabbing the paper with his finger, giving Faulcon no chance to think hard about any single fact: that a hormone called *attractin* increased dramatically in the olgoi body fluids when Merlin was first seen as a crescent in the early spring months; that male olgoi responded to the first half-face of Merlin by produc-ing quantities of germ cell fluid; that females held fertilized embryos in stasis until Merlin was more than half obscured again, in late summer, but that the final trigger for development was the first time that all the moons were in alignment, vertically, following the Merlin factor. And the gulgaroth, too, showed physiological and behavioural changes all closely related to the occlusion, waning and waxing of the red moon, in particular their seed-mating as Merlin was almost fully seen, the ritual insemination of the olgoi occurring – and there were many results for this conclusion – the moment Merlin's full disc had emerged, and at a time when the olgoi's own reproduct-ive cycle had finished. Some, like the pair they had seen this evening, behaved differently, early, futilely, responding to a wrong sky-sign, perhaps.

'The moons form a highly intricate and complex programme. The pattern of movement is identical year to year – I can show you correlations between the colour change of whip-weed and bladderlash fronds and the distance above the horizon of Threelight. I can show you a thousand correlations – life on VanderZande's World jumps to the pull of the moons' strings, and does so to a degree that is quite staggering. But Merlin most of all – that's the main force. Perhaps for no other reason than that it's hidden for so much of its year. Certainly there are no measurable, or should I say yet-measured, rays from it, no forces reaching down to grapple with physiology. Visual cues are supplied simply by its appearance and disappearance, and Merlin's combined gravitational tug with Kytara probably acts as a non-visual cue.' Leuwentok sat back and looked up at Faulcon, who shook his head, partly in bewilder-ment as he scanned and rescanned the columns of data, partly from a sense of guilt – after all, Leuwentok had explained all this during those early seminars – and partly from a sense of surprise. The question he had been burning to ask at last found voice.

'There's nothing here about man. Do we escape?'

Leuwentok chuckled. 'I could see that question coming a mile off.' He moved papers aside until he found what he was looking for. 'This is a correlation between the so-called *fiersig* and the position of the moons. Inasmuch as *fiersig* affect man, the moons affect man. You can see that we get spates of the activity when there are four moons high. *Fiersig* tend to pass south-north as you know, they come from the direction of the mountains, and drift away across the valley. As they move they follow a line towards either Aardwind or Tharoo, changing direction as their target moon sinks or rises obliquely. And don't ask me what any of this means, because I have no idea, and I don't think anybody ever will – if we were going to demonstrate that the *fiersig* were life-forms I think we'd have done it by now. The whole thing is cosmic linkage, moon to world, moon to life. Earth experiences a similar linkage, but in a much simpler way since it only has the one moon, and most life on Earth is programmed by daylight. But that moon does have *some* effect – dogs howl at it, physiology can be shown to fluctuate with it, sea-tides are much the result of it. On Kamelios we have all of that six-fold.'

'That's why there are no dogs here,' said Immuk knowledgeably. 'They howl themselves to death.'

Faulcon frowned as he looked at her. 'Really?'

She looked embarrassed. 'It was a joke, Leo.'

Leuwentok went on, 'Incidentally, there is no correlation between moon and the time winds – not as far as anyone has determined. Nor between moon and the time squalls, or eddy currents or swirlwinds – whatever governs the flow of time through the valley is responding to something other than the obvious climatic and environmental triggers.'

'And the sightings of the pyramid?' Faulcon felt a moment's unease – he had stayed quiet about the pyramid for so long, tried to put it from his mind so totally, that he felt himself fighting against a powerful internal resistance to even mentioning the subject.

Leuwentok stared at him thoughtfully, and with just a hint of apprehension. Guessing what was the matter, and taking a chance that what he was doing was not against regulations, Faulcon drew out the small security disc. At once Leuwentok rose to his feet, walked up to Faulcon and took the piece of plastic. 'Good God – he's got a grey clearance. How did you get this? You *are* a rifter …?'

'I made a sighting. I've been sworn to silence on anything I see, hear or do, on pain of isolation.'

'Well, don't take too much notice of that,' said Leuwentok, and showed Faulcon his own clearance. Immuk waved hers. 'A grey clearance doesn't mean much; it does mean I can talk to you about the aliens. Even so, nothing you hear on the subject of sightings should go out of this room. Olgoi, gulgaroth, moons – that's fine, that's education. But someone in Steel City doesn't want the sighting, or our ideas on them, talked about. They're trying to keep it all to rumour level; no hard facts. What they don't want is a generalized *belief* in an alien presence. Not yet, at least.'

'Do you *know*, then, that Commander Ensavlion's sighting – an alien machine, with travellers aboard – is a genuine sighting of genuine creatures?' Faulcon was hot, the flush in his face burning him.

'Have you experienced them?' asked Leuwentok quietly. 'I mean the aliens, not these so-called humanoid creatures, these time-travellers. I mean the *real* aliens. Have you sat in that valley and sensed them?'

What do I say, Faulcon wondered, and his head whirled in confusion. Did he admit things or not? Did he make the decision now that the experience of the alien in the valley the previous evening – something he had felt several times before, but only when naked to the world, at times such as his hunting trips – that that experience was real? Or was it just imagination? He said, 'I've felt something – something close. As if I was being watched. Yes.'

'Have you seen the phantom?'

'Certainly, more than once.'

'How about the timelost, the shadowy figures crawling up the side of the valley?'

For a moment Faulcon was puzzled; he had not even heard of such sightings, and said as much. Leuwentok agreed. 'They're a rarer sighting, and they tend to be very disturbing. It only goes to show that more is going on in the world than even an old-timer like you knows about.' Faulcon had heard that before, somewhere. Leuwentok pressed on, 'What about the whirligigs?'

Faulcon had heard talk of the whirling forms that swept through the valley occasionally, but he had always thought them to be tricks of the light, or a form of the *fiersig*. He had never seen one. Leuwentok nodded thoughtfully, asked quietly, 'What about God?'

'God? The white-robed man? That's just nonsense – that's a joke, a Steel City joke.' The tall, rather arrogant-looking ghost that walked through the ruins, his feet hidden in a swirl of dust. Faulcon had shared the joke – on Kamelios you get to see everything if you wait long enough, even God!

'They're no joke, Leo. They're genuine, and terrifying, sightings. The old man himself, his arms outstretched to welcome you into his kingdom. And a surprising number of people go – and get lost.' Faulcon said nothing, watched and waited. He was now beginning to feel a little dizzy. He had *seen* the phantom, but he had never thought anything at all of the wild reports of spiders, gods, whirling shapes, spirals and shimmering alien forms that made a man feel nauseous to see, so indefinable and confusing was their appearance. It was Kamelios folklore, the sort of nonsense that accumulates on any world.

But in the next few moments Leuwentok put him straight on that particularly blinkered attitude. 'You'd be surprised what, people report that they've seen – in the valley, on the edge of the valley, in the hills and faraway. A lot of it is classified. A lot of people have left Kamelios in a disturbed state of mind; most just keep quiet. The people who live in the township, miles from the valley, well, perhaps they keep quiet too – but regularly there are medical teams which go out and, so to speak, "cure the manias" of a few townsfolk who have seen things, or who feel compelled to undertake irrational, or dangerous tasks – long walks seeking an enlightenment, or a rendezvous with something, or someone from their past lives. The townspeople are all affected in one way or another by a conviction that others of their family are on the world, and waiting for them, lost, alone, frightened, perhaps crashed in one badland or another. It's very strange.'

'I'd never noticed. They always seem calm, uninterested, learning to live with the world in their own way, rather unconcerned about us and our valley-edge city.'

Immuk spoke for the first time in several minutes. She had been poring over the charts, making marks by certain figures. 'Most of the community folk are fed huge doses of some form of repressant, something to stop them being as restless as we are – something to stop them wandering off in search of their dreams. It's all official; they asked for the treatment.'

Leuwentok laughed as he watched Faulcon's solemn face. 'And that's it, Leo. Dreams. You feel an alien presence because that's what interests you. We are all at the mercy of some form of desire fulfilment. We see lost kinfolk, lost friends, lost images from our past – we see treasure, aliens, religious manifestations, and mostly we see enigma, we see things that excite us because of their mystery. It holds us here more strongly than gravity. We are not conscious of it because consciously most of us become dulled, uninterested, as if incapable of excitement. And yet, deep down, we can't give the world up – we can't run out on our need to see those images, to visualize our dreams, or our fears.'

It did not ring true for Faulcon. 'This is just your idea?'

'Just my idea. Except that – you asked about the effect of the moons on man – well, the number of reports of sightings of different images fluctuates quite remarkably – it correlates with Merlin's appearance. As Merlin shows from behind Kytara, M-Z-alpha neural activity increases; so does leucocyte mobility in the tissues, but I don't suppose that's important. At the same time, man sees the ghosts of the Kriakta Rift.'

'Some of those ghosts have been holographed – the phantom, at least.'

The point was not lost on Leuwentok. He hesitated a moment. 'That's true, of course. The phantom may be a different phenomenon ...'

'A time-travelling phenomenon, perhaps?'

'Maybe. It is the only image that *has* been holographed. The so-called pyramid, which on hypnotic description turns out to be a much less pyramidal structure than you might think, has been photographed several times – only nothing showed up. That shape is a very powerful human symbol, more powerful than people often realize. And gold is a powerful symbol too – it isn't surprising that they show up in combination as an enigmatic sighting by people searching for just that.'

'And yet it is not a pyramid at all – is that what you said? Why would people imagine one shape, and be aware of something different?'

'Dreams,' said Leuwentok. 'Deep desire, deep-seated images – no alien has been seen, despite that one man's claim. And yet something is dreaming along with man. I believe that. The pyramid is the dream image of something non-human, the alien presence that we all seem so aware of on a non-intuitive level. We share its image – we change it to our own; but we're not only chasing our own dreams on Kamelios, sometimes we're chasing something else's.'

CHAPTER TWELVE

Faulcon travelled back to Steel City in the morning, having slept fitfully and uncomfortably. Leuwentok had worked late, and was still asleep at dawn when Faulcon made himself a small breakfast and left the hide to pick up his byke. Immuk, sleepily, wished him good luck.

Lena was in her apartment, still in night attire despite the lateness of the morning. She had spent a night every bit as restless as Faulcon's; the anger, and after-effects of excessive drinking, showed clearly on her: rimmed eyes, dishevelled hair, listlessness. She opened the door to Faulcon, stood silently for a moment looking at him (he said nothing himself), then stepped aside to let him in.

'I went up to Overlook,' he said as she closed the door, but she ignored him, walked across the room to her small window and stood there, sullenly looking out across the sloping surface of traverse unit Opal, watching the activity of hull engineers laying external cables. If she had behaved differently Faulcon would have known he had lost her; but this stiff disappointment was an invitation to speak for himself, to convince her that she was wrong to be so angry.

The trouble was, Faulcon reflected quite grimly, she was absolutely right.

He went to her dining ledge and sat down, hands clasped before him. He could watch her, and also gaze ashamedly at his hands, depending on how he felt. 'Okay Lena, I can understand your bitterness. Honesty is what we promised, even if the *fiersig* turn us head over heels. It's never easy to keep a grip on everything that happens inside, especially here, on Kamelios; but somehow we always managed ...'

'*I* managed,' said Lena stiffly, not moving from the window. 'You led me to believe you were Leo Faulcon. But you're not, you're a different man. You have the same name, but you're not the man I've known for five years, on and off Kamelios.'

For a second Faulcon was sufficiently confused to think she was implying something far more significant than she was: that he was in some way a substitute, had killed the real Faulcon and slipped in in his place, a spy, an infiltrator. His grasp of the metaphoric way she spoke reasserted itself and he wondered how to begin to tell her that he loved her, that he loved her very much indeed; that he had not always loved her, but that was not his fault, that was Kamelios playing games with him; that if he couldn't explain to her what had happened to him here he would be heartbroken to lose her, because increasingly she was the focus of his life, and he had looked forward to the day they quit VanderZande's World for several months, now, and had even made preliminary application for a place on the non-established colony of Tyrone's World, not so very far from New Triton.

No words formed to explain all this. How could something so familiar, so easy, so true, be so difficult? He knew the answer. Mark Dojaan. Bloody-minded, star-forsaken Mark Dojaan. She didn't even know him, had probably only seen him in passing when he had worked with Faulcon. And yet he was interfering in her life just as he had interfered with Faulcon's; and just as he had interfered in everybody's life, wherever he went, and no doubt, knowing Mark, whenever he went.

Unexpectedly, Lena walked back across the room and sat down across the dining ledge from Faulcon. He had been miles away, running through the rift valley, sharing – and this is what still shamed him, despite the other shame – sharing Mark Dojaan's destructive enthusiasm, caught in the whirling vortex of his mercenary vigour as he prowled and kicked-over and upturned and sneaked-inside the structures and ruins.

Lena said, 'So many lies, Leo. So much deception. Do you blame me for going off the handle? I keep asking myself, what next? What else? You know me, Leo. I can't cope with things like that. I have to have my life straight, orderly, above board. I need honesty like I need food. I not only depend on it, I thrive on it. I suppose I've been aware of the lack of honesty in you for months; I didn't know what it was was, but I've not been thriving. I've been wilting. You've commented on it yourself, that I've seemed moody, depressed, too easily upturned by the mood ripples.'

'There are no more lies to confess to,' said Faulcon quietly. He reached out and took Lena's hands across the ledge. She didn't pull away, but she didn't respond either. 'There are elaborations, insights, facts that come out of the lies. But there are no more deceptions, nothing waiting to spring out at you.'

'Thank God for that. Leo, I'm not at all sure that I want you to tell me any more about it; and yet I know that I'll not be able to relax until you do. You'll have to explain at least why you felt it necessary to deceive me. And then I suppose you should tell Kris about his brother. He's been here twice, looking for you, asking questions. I said nothing of course, but the time has come to admit you were friends with Mark.'

'That's going to be hard. He has an image of Mark, and I've got to crack that image. Kris idolizes his brother. I'm not so sure I don't have the power to crack him wide open himself. I'm just not sure.'

'You shouldn't have lied to him about knowing Mark. That was stupid. I knew you wanted to keep it from him out on the mission, but I assumed the reason the two of you wanted to be alone that first evening back – remember? – was so you could talk to him about Mark. It never occurred to me that you hadn't. If we hadn't spent so much time rift-suited up I'd surely have dropped you in it inadvertently. Then Ensavlion did it.'

Faulcon managed a half-hearted laugh. 'I thought my head was going to explode. I really did. I left that station on tiptoe. I thought that if Kris caught me there he'd do violence before I could get a word in.'

'You are the most god-awful coward.' But she liked that, because she was a large percentage coward herself. That's why she and Faulcon were still alive, when men like Leader Kabazard were dead. Cowardice, caution, the same side of a coin, and Leo Faulcon and Lena Tanoway were also on the same side; Faulcon knew that, unless he said something tactless, or got self-righteously angry, or unless a *fiersig* hit the city during the next few minutes, he had got Lena back.

Drawing her hands away from his she pressed a small panel on the wall by the uncomfortable dining ledge. The wall blinked open and displayed the well-stocked drinks cupboard. She knew Faulcon's taste in drink and drew out two small containers of *baraas*, nicely chilled. 'Here's to the worst liar in the world … about to come clean.' She filled and raised a glass.

Faulcon responded, and said bitterly, 'Here's to Mark Dojaan. May he rot in the swamps of VanderZande's Cretacious.'

As Lena sipped at her *baraas* she watched Faulcon carefully, thoughtfully. 'I had no idea you had such hate in you, Leo. I had no idea that you and Mark were such enemies.'

'We weren't enemies,' said Faulcon, 'My hate came after he was swept away. Reflected hate, reactionary hate.'

She nodded as if she had somehow divined the darkness in Faulcon's mind, which of course she could not have done. 'Tell me about the travellers, anyway. That's what's made me angry. Mark Dojaan is your problem with Kris.'

'It's all connected,' Faulcon said, and drained his glass. The *baraas* went through him like fire, made his muscles tense for a moment, then over-relax. He stepped back those several months as easily as he might step across a threshold; vivid, detailed memory projected before his mind's eye after months of being hidden away, repressed. He went white with cold. Lena said nothing, and in his own time he told her of that first mission.

'I'd been out to the valley before, during training. But I'd not been given clearance to go down, so I spent a lot of time staring at the view, and watching the ordinary winds and the men grubbing about among the ruins. I expected that at any given moment a time wind would be blowing, but I never saw one. People described them to me, and most of all they described what happened to people who got caught at the edge of them. I began to feel as if I *had* experienced a wind. But I also started to jump every time it gusted strong on my naked skin ...'

'I remember. You were really on edge for the first few weeks.'

'That's right. On edge, because I spent so much on *the* edge, looking down into the valley. The anticipation, the suspense, was agonizing. People talk about time winds as if they blow fresh every day, with autumn breezes every evening. I sat or stood or ran and I watched and I watched, and inside I was getting more and more twisted. I asked you why I was going through this and you said, "adjustment". We all go through it, you said, and I was too glad to hear those words to think that you might have been making empty platitudes. No, don't interrupt. Just listen. I need you to understand something. I need you to understand what happened the first time I went down into the valley. For God's sake, Lena, it's as if it happened yesterday again; I feel just like I felt then, all the tension, all the fear, all the guilt and confusion. So let me explain it, and try and understand it.'

'I'm sorry, Leo. Go on. I'll keep quiet.'

'I hardly knew Ensavlion. To me he was a man in a rift suit who gave orders. I was training with a Section 3 team, stripping removables for examination, but at first I wasn't allowed more than two-thirds of the way down the valley walls. Ensavlion was with the section, as Commander – you remember that – and he was *never* out of that valley. He was always there, and he even went down with other sections. He was obsessed with the idea that one day there'd be a sighting of the intelligence that made these ruins; they'd find a body, or a message. He was convinced that somewhere in all that junk they'd find a living Kamelion, still eating breakfast. Nobody thought in terms of controlled time-travelling; or at least, if they thought of it they kept quiet. It seemed a huge jump from natural time distortion to free and safe travel through time. You've experienced this yourself, you know how it is. Madness, maybe, but that's the way minds work on Kamelios. A particular day occurred! I was to go down to the valley floor for the first time. There were about ten men from the section with me, following Ensavlion, while many more spread out up the valley. There had been two squalls, apparently, and several new structures had appeared during the night. Even as we reached the bottom of the canyon there were warning sirens going. We all stopped and listened, and in the far distance you could actually see the sky darkening, and those immense purple flashes of light over the far horizon. There was some debate as to whether or not we should get the hell out of there, but the older team members thought that was stupid. We had rift suits, and we could clear the area easily ... why all the fuss? You got several minutes warning of the wind channelling down the valley. Ensavlion agreed and we started to move fast. I ran in the middle and I was scared as hell. That darkness seemed to be getting closer, but it must have been miles and miles away. What was of interest, what Ensavlion wanted to look at before it was swept away again, was a whole house. I mean, that's what it was. You've seen the pictures, I expect, a real brick house, with a roof, and obvious doors and windows. Nothing like any house you've ever lived in, mind you, but a house, a real dwelling place, ancient, all closed up and all intact. You could almost hear Ensavlion thinking, there might be a couple of aliens in there, still in bed, still in *coitus tempora interruptus*. We approached it like a pack of wolves, staggering and powering between walls of rock, and round the ruins, and through damn near sheer gullies, some still with water in them. The whole place was a geological nightmare. You couldn't even glance to one side without seeing something that didn't fit with something else, some stratification, or sedimentation, or boulder, or glacial deposit that just didn't belong where it was. How the crust survives these upsets I just don't know. But this was nightmare valley, and even the rift suits were having a job keeping balance.

'And there was this little brick building, really weird, standing askew, it must be said, and obviously beginning to crack where the stress had broken its main structure. The team gathered round the place in something like ecstasy. And in they went, with me photographing outside, and Ensavlion calling stupid instructions like, "If they're there, be courteous. Back away and make no sudden moves." I mean, it was really pathetic. It was still calm in the valley. Ensavlion reckoned we had almost ten minutes. But the rift suits let you know every breeze and draught and that was something I wasn't used to. Every time it gusted, my stupid heart stopped with the whining noise the wind on the sensors evokes. I was a nervous bloody wreck. I don't think I've ever been so scared in my life.

'And then a hell of a wind sprang up. Not a time wind, there was no klaxon blare, no darkness; just a healthy wind, the sort that you expect to precede a time wind by several minutes. Nobody reacted. They went on working, and over the radio I could hear them laughing, and talking as if there was no danger … and I suppose at that precise moment there wasn't. But at the time I had no idea … I saw that dark pall in the distance, I heard the racket in my headphones, the sensors, and I went crazy. I went so crazy that I must have screamed my panic, and so confused the rift suit that it whipped my legs up into rapid-motion position, but started to run around in circles. There I was, berserk in a berserk r-suit, and the rest of that team just howling with laughter. They stood there, watching me, and you'd have thought they'd never seen anything so funny in their lives. And they probably hadn't. Ensavlion stepped in; he came over and shot a tranquillizer from my suit into my arm. I felt the sting. I was still yelling. As the suit calmed and I calmed he said, "It's all right, son. In a few weeks you'll get your own back on some poor rookie who'll do just the same. Let's get you up to to the cliff top." I felt, you might say, something akin to a fool. In fact I felt quite suicidal. Maybe the drug had something to do with it – it was certainly giving me blurred vision – but the sight of those r-suits swaying about as their occupants laughed at me was crippling. I was crying when Ensavlion got me to the top of the canyon, and it was a reaction to that awful fear, the feeling that a wind was going to snatch me at any second! And then guess what happened …'

'A time squall, of course,' said Lena. Throughout Faulcon's narrative she had sat stiff, silent, solemn, slightly irritated by the way he filled in on detail with which she was well familiar – that much was often apparent to Faulcon – but perhaps piecing together in her own mind the events of those many months back. 'A time squall?'

'A swirlwind,' said Faulcon, 'The first and last I ever saw. Maybe I had some survival sense working, I don't know. But that wind came out of time in a flash. Those poor beggars down in the valley had about eight seconds warning, long enough for those closer to the ledge system to bounce up out of the valley. Three men got out. I forget how many died. I saw two go up on jet power, straight up into the air. It didn't work, of course, they vanished into the squall … no, not like a squall; it was like a real wind, a real time wind, but generating out of nowhere and spreading out in both directions. To us, it seemed like a time wind that had come without warning. The brick building vanished. I dragged myself away from the edge, and all I could hear were screams, and the whining of the wind, and the exploding sound, the booming of atmosphere. It was so dark, like being trapped beneath a blackening sky. Ensavlion stood on the cliffs, looking down, watching the men die.

"Then the whole air was filled with a sort of golden glowing. It was like a bonfire at night, the radiant light filling the darkness, but not pushing it away. Ensavlion was saying things, incoherent things. I could hear him, but I couldn't understand him. He kept standing there, staring down into the canyon. I crawled towards him, unable to get the rift suit to stand properly. I was still shaking, still crying I suppose, my eyes blurred with tears and dizziness. And I looked down into the valley and yes, I saw it: a tiny, tiny pyramid, giving off an immense amount of yellow light. There were shadows and movements in it, nothing I could discern, but then you often get that in the ruins that are time-swept … you know, decorative, or the way the light passes through the different densities of crystal in some structures. I looked at that pyramid and I was watching it as it vanished, really abruptly, vanishing from that great swirl of confusion and time change happening around it. You couldn't help thinking that it was the pyramid that was causing the wind, dragging things through time with it as it was afterwards talked about. But at the time I didn't think of it as a time machine, or any sort of machine. It was just a magnificent, and beautiful, and awe-inspiring piece of time-junk.

'I backed off from the cliff edge again and managed to get the rift suit up to its feet. Ensavlion came running over to me and I realized the golden glow had gone. He started to shout at me, "You saw them, you must have seen them!" I shook my head. I said I'd seen nothing. Everything about that vision was becoming just that … a sort of vision, a dream-like memory. I found myself not believing I'd seen anything. The sky brightened, a faint pink again. The sound of the wind had died away and my head was throbbing and felt slightly unreal. I watched Ensavlion standing, staring back at the rift. He kept saying, "Somebody must have seen them. Somebody, one of the others." At this time I didn't know that more than half the team had been lost. He came up to me and started to question me about whether I'd seen anything. I agreed that I'd seen a golden *light*, but for some reason I didn't admit to seeing the pyramid. I suppose I thought I hadn't really seen anything, and didn't want to get involved with what I detected as being an obsessive interest in this man, even then. But Ensavlion had seen more. He'd seen godlike figures, moving in and out of the pyramid through the very walls. I didn't see any such thing, all I saw was shadows. But he insisted that those figures had appeared there, and he kept on about it, and sometimes, when I think back, I can resolve humanoid shapes from those shadows, and I wonder if he was right; but the more he insisted at the time, the more I hid what I'd seen. I kept thinking, I knew it was going to happen. I could have warned them, I could have shouted; or perhaps I did, and they died because they took no notice of me. I survived and they died. Every day that passed I got more ashamed. People kept coming up to me and asking me why I'd survived, a rookie – always the first to go – when their mates had been taken. Was I in the canyon, or skiving? I lied and lied. Others asked if I'd tried to help. I lied and lied. Others had heard about my panic, and they thought that was really funny. Ensavlion kept on about those stupid figures. The other three who'd survived had only seen the pyramid – so they said. And within a week they'd all got lost, one of them going up to the canyon's edge and falling in. He hadn't gone to find the pyramid, he'd just lost his mind. So it was Ensavlion. And me. And even Ensavlion came to believe I'd seen nothing. But I'd been close, you see … close. And so I got taken under his wing. Just like you saw him with Kris, so he was with me. Protective, friendly, fatherly. Concerned. And just like he was with me, so he had been with Mark Dojaan, and continued to be so after the event.'

Lena looked a little surprised. 'I've gone adrift – wasn't Mark one of those killed by the swirlwind?'

'He wasn't with us that day. I met him a few days later, through Ensavlion. You were on the islands, remember? Poking around down there with some section or other, digging up fossils and not contacting me.'

Lena smiled thinly, rose from the ledge and walked to the soft vastness of her couch. She flopped down and put her feet up, staring at the ceiling. Faulcon watched her, wondering with irritating insistence what life would be like without a Lena featuring in it. He said, 'The frustrating thing is, it probably wouldn't have made a damn bit of difference if you'd known that I was scared silly, and saw that pyramid. Not a bit of difference.'

'You're undoubtedly right. I thought the revelation would hurt, but why should it? There is nothing nasty in it, nothing too shameful, nothing to make me think less of you, nothing to make me think that for those events alone you'd have kept quiet about it, told me nothing, upset me because of the *fact* of the deception, which of course is at the root of my anger. In other words, Leo, that's not the whole story. In other words – and I realize you haven't actually said "that's all" – I expect to hear something else from you, something that makes it seem sensible that a man would deny even to himself the memory of such an event as glimpsing an alien time machine.' She raised her head and peered at him, then after a moment shuffled onto her elbows. 'I imagine Mark Dojaan is about to rear his handsome head.'

'Mark Dojaan!' Faulcon exploded with bitterness as she spoke the name. Perhaps the *baraas* had reduced his emotional responsibility, but suddenly he was desperately angry, and the glass in his hand seemed functional only to be cast against the far wall of the room. The sound of the shattering vessel was wonderful, shocking. Fragments glittered and scattered about the room and Faulcon felt some of the tension drain from him. 'I'm so sick of hearing that bloody name,' he said, his voice soft, icy. He stared at Lena who shrugged non-committally.

'It means very little to me. I hardly knew him.'

'And yet … though you didn't know him he's still there, behind you, overshadowing you. He's in your life whether you like it or not. He's like this bloody planet, always there, always watching, always with a finger firmly up the rear-end of your life. Mark Dojaan! How I wish to God he'd died before I knew him.'

Faulcon's sudden anger fed Lena's. She swung her legs off the couch and stood, walking to her sleeping closet and stripping off her night clothes. 'No more lies, eh Leo? No more deceptions to be revealed.' Faulcon watched her coldly, partly wanting her as he stared at her nude body, partly afraid of her.

'There's nothing more,' he said, but he knew she could hear the silent prayer he offered with that awful statement. She turned, dropping a flowing kaftan across her shoulders and billowing it out. There was no love in her face, no understanding. For a second she was silent, then she said, 'What is it you're so afraid of, Leo? That he might be listening from Othertime? Is that it? Are you afraid he'll come back and dominate you again, make you feel like an idiot, laugh at you? That's what he did, isn't it? He got you under his thumb like a good little dog-like friend. Here Leo, there Leo, do this for me Leo, that's not funny Leo, enter your ten-minute embarrassment phase. You followed Mark Dojaan about as if you were on a chain. Did you think I hadn't seen? Do you think I'm blind?'

'It wasn't like that. For a while we were close friends—'

Lena's laugh was bitterly cynical. She walked towards Leo, standing in the bright light of the Kamelion day, and the expression on her face was malice. 'You fool. You star-struck fool. Friendship? Do you know, do you *really* know what friendship is? Friendship isn't coming back time and time again and forgiving. Friendship isn't seeing who can vomit *baraas* furthest over the edge of the rift. Friendship is sharing the private part of you; *sharing*, Leo. Not giving, not taking, but exchanging. Friendship isn't one way, one giving, one taking. And that's exactly what you and Mark Dojaan were. I know that, Leo. I could feel it in you, and I heard it. I kept clear of you during that "friendship" because I was afraid that if I tried to interfere he could damage what you and I had far more than I wanted. Perhaps something inside of me *was* afraid of Mark, though I didn't know him, perhaps I was warning myself against him all the time. Maybe you're right, Leo, maybe he was more powerful than most people ever realize. He had his doggy friend, giving his all – did you give your all, Leo? And you were too friendship-struck to realize that he was using you, and baiting you, and making you do things that your better self must have been screaming objections to. And this is why you hate him now, you hate him because you loved him, and you loved him because you were afraid of him, and in awe of him, and you rationalized everything about your relationship by calling it "close friendship", and there's something about that bastard that lingers on, you're right, Leo, it's here, it's all around, the power of his mind, because you're standing here, your face white, your body shaking, your heart thumping, and you're defending someone and something that just moments ago you were screaming hate for. He's got you head over heels, Leo; you haven't shaken him off even now.' She reached out and touched his face gently, then reached round to stroke the back of his neck. She came into his arms and felt the despair in him, and the rapidly surfacing tears.

'I loved him,' he whispered.

'I know you did.'

Faulcon involuntarily squeezed her tighter, and though she couldn't see it his eyes were tight shut, and his teeth crushed together as he drowned out, and fought against, the sudden furious desire he felt to scream and hit out and cry like a baby.

Lena said, 'I've been waiting for you to find the way of getting this off your chest. This is why I was so angry Leo, I'm sorry. I knew you had this terrible thing weighing on you, and even though you should know it's not so terrible for me ... I'm from New Triton, remember? Everybody believes in love without constraint there. But I knew you didn't, and I knew this was hurting you, and I could see you had blanked it out. But I'm human too, Leo, and I couldn't help wondering what else, what other deceptions were being gradually erased, buried in your super-active unconscious.'

Faulcon relaxed his grip. He drew away from her and kissed her lightly on the lips. She smiled and kissed him back, long, hard, trying to express in that simple action the depth of her love and regard for him, no matter what, despite all.

Faulcon walked up to the window and leaned his forehead against it, staring out across the city, looking at the activity, but not seeing it.

'He was a criminal; he was a mercenary, merciless, power-struck kleptomaniac son-of-a-bitch. He looted the valley and he got me to loot it too. We used to go in there in our suits and hide anything small, and commercially saleable, in the spaces in the legs and body. It made the suits difficult to operate, but we walked carefully out of the valley every time and over a few weeks we got quite a little export trade, working through another friend of Mark's, a shuttle pilot operating a food drop, the sort of thing that gets a dismissive glance from the port guard. God, he had that so well worked out. It seemed such a good idea ... give the Galaxy a bit of VanderZande's World ... Why the hell should it all be stuck in one city, with only a fraction on display in the museum. By what right did the Federation prohibit the removal of artifacts off-world?

'And then one day we were working a standard rip-off, ostensibly part of our routine examination of ruins, and as usual we'd slipped ahead of the team a bit, and I went up the slope keeping an eye on the leader, while Mark darted in and out of the ruins, looking for removables. And a bloody wind came. Well, we had the usual notice, several minutes. I was damned glad to be up the side, and I called the warning down to Mark in case his suit was being screened from the sirens. He popped out of the ruins he was in, looked into the distance, checked my estimate of time before it struck – we reckoned five minutes – and went back in. He'd found a pile of small objects that looked like they had machinery inside them. He was loading his suit. He took two minutes. The sirens were going and I could see the rest of the team making an orderly ascent of the canyon. Mark was easing himself out of the jumble of metal and crystal structures when suddenly he called out that he was stuck. "What d'you mean, stuck?" I shouted. "Get the hell out of there!" "I can't," he shouted back. Some of the junk had dropped through his suit and was jamming a mechanism somewhere. He was caught there, in his suit, unable to move. I just stood there feeling sick, feeling terrified, and thinking to myself, the travellers … they might come back, Ensavlion's godlike creatures. In a split second I became obsessed with seeing the pyramid again, following in the wake of the wind. Mark's screaming faded away, just like the sirens, and the clatter of wind-sound on my suit's sensors. That bloody wind struck, and the moment it struck I turned away. I didn't even watch him go; I can't even remember what abuse he was shouting as he was cut off in mid-word.'

'So you killed him, and you killed your guilt, and then you had to live with what you'd done, and you killed that too.'

'I guess so. It hardly took any time at all to erase Mark Dojaan from my mind, to put what I'd done aside, to regard it as a dream. Then Kris came, and it all came back, really intensely and frighteningly. I felt so torn with him, so close on the one hand, and so afraid, so distant on the other. And I sensed his tie with the wind, when it happened, a few days ago, and that hasn't helped.'

Lena put her arm around him. 'I think it might perhaps be as well not to tell Kris any of this. You're right when you say he has an image of his brother, a good image, the image of a man of courage and honour. Kris shouldn't be punished for Mark Dojaan. What do you think?'

Before Faulcon could answer, however, there was a loud, almost angry knock at the door. Faulcon turned, puzzled, and Lena shrugged and walked to the door switch. 'Who is it?' she called.

'Kris. Let me in, will you?'

Exchanging an uneasy glance with Faulcon, Lena nevertheless opened the door to her apartment.

It all happened almost too quickly for Faulcon to comprehend. Kris swept into the room, his face white, his whole body rigid with tension. 'You bloody lying bastard!' he screamed, and ran at Faulcon. He punched Faulcon hard on the mouth, then slapped him about the head until he sank to his knees. 'You're a liar! A bloody liar!' And he kicked viciously up at Faulcon's chest, sending his team mate toppling back towards the window. Lena was suddenly behind the youngster, and one jerk of her arm had Kris sprawled on the floor. He jumped to his feet and smiled with a sort of triumph. There was blood on his lip. Faulcon had stood up as well, clutching his chest and breathing with difficulty.

'Get out of here,' said Lena to the boy.

'Mark was a good man,' said Kris, speaking slowly, deliberately. 'I don't know why that bastard said all those things, but they're lies, and he's a liar, and he's hiding something, and if he says one more word about my brother I shall kill him. And you'd better believe that, Mister Leo liar Faulcon.'

Lena took a step towards him and slapped him hard and stunningly on the face. 'I told you to get out of here.' Kris turned about and ran from the apartment. Lena swore softly and went to a drawer, searching around among the junk until she found a small metal box, a detector. In a second she had found the small needle, fixed above the door, with which Kris had heard their every word.

'How the hell did he get hold of that?' said Faulcon. 'Unless Ensavlion gave it to him.'

'Damn,' was Lena's only comment as she snapped the needle. 'He must have hidden it there when he came looking for you.' She looked anxiously at Faulcon. 'Do you really think Ensavlion would have okayed him eavesdropping?'

Faulcon eased himself down into a chair, clutching his stomach and dabbing at the blood on his lips. Lena suddenly mobilized into action, shedding her kaftan and taking out her grey overalls. 'Never mind your aches. You deserved every punch. Much more to worry about is that we've just done a stupid thing, letting Kris go like that. He can put you in the disembowelling chamber if he decides to tell what you just told. You may have learned to live with the fact, and kept it quiet, but you are guilty of a crime against the Federation – and I doubt if you told council about it? No, I thought not – right, you're guilty of criminal abuse of the responsibility assigned to you when you were allowed to the world. We've got to talk to Kris, and we've got to secure his silence. And don't forget, the council will have eyes on us, now. So behave calmly. Clean up and let's get after him.'

CHAPTER THIRTEEN

After searching in lounges, corridors and exit stations for nearly an hour, Faulcon did what he should have done at the outset; he checked with the suiting lounge and learned that Kris Dojaan had suited up and gone out to the valley. Furious with himself, and taking that anger out on the technician in the lounge – 'Didn't you ask for his identity? Didn't you check that identity and find out that he hasn't been fully *trained* yet? Are you stupid or just lazy?' – he climbed into his own suit, waited impaitently for Lena to prepare, and then ran out into the red-tinged afternoon.

The canyon was a mile away and they arrived in less than two minutes, having broken the law on speeding, but not by much. After watching the activity in the area for a minute or so, scanning each rift-suited figure for the clue that would identify Kris, they decided to move along the valley rim to the east, to where the phantom had last been seen. Faulcon was sure that Kris had come back to find the time phantom again, perhaps for reassurance, perhaps to find out how to travel into time himself.

Lena was not so sure; she was worried about Kris's safety, even though she felt more irritable at this repeat of their earlier pursuit of the boy. As team leader that safety was her responsibility, and she was proving inept at the job. She accepted the fault, but was determined there would be no consequences for her. Kris was going back to Steel City if she had to sling him, rift suit and all, across her shoulder.

They passed two stations, contacting the observers only to learn that they'd seen nothing. They asked about winds, or signs of squalls, or atmospherics: nothing yet; and so they passed on, Lena less worried now, but Faulcon deeply apprehensive of being close to Kris Dojaan inside the volume of the valley itself.

The canyon widened, the valley walls sloping more gently. Wind and rain had scoured strange formations from the rock sections of the valley wall, columnar pinnacles of yellow rock that widened towards the ground and were lost in the heaving strata of some lake-bed sediment, perhaps, that swept about the pinnacles and seemed to be consuming them. Jewels glittered here, small structures, some crushed beneath the rock, some embedded in it.

And something moved.

Lena saw it first, the fleeting movement of a human figure, far down in the canyon, and lost behind the twisting walls of a leaning tower. As she saw the movement, Faulcon spotted the rift suit, standing on a narrow ledge where the canyon walls were less steep than usual; the suit's arms were extended, and the back hatch was open. Kris had used it to descend almost to the bottom of the valley, and had abandoned it before entering the canyon's deeps.

'He's a damned fool,' said Faulcon loudly, and he recognized the anxiety in himself, the worry for Kris, despite the throbbing ache in his jaw and ribcage.

'There! See, Leo? Right down there.'

Faulcon followed the direction of Lena's raised arm and after a second glimpsed Kris; now he was crouching watching something that neither

Faulcon nor Lena could see from on high. A moment later Kris looked around, looked up, the sun flashing on his mask. He must have seen the two stiff, bulky figures above him, because he suddenly rose to his feet and made efforts to conceal himself.

'Let's go,' said Lena, and she jumped from the ledge, using vertical power to descend the first steep hundred feet, to land on the natural trackway below. Faulcon's suit obeyed his similar unvoiced instruction. He landed lightly, ran a short way, and then followed Lena over a much greater drop; the ground fell up towards him, the tangle of alien buildings sweeping in an arc towards his slowly turning body; he felt himself guided between quivering girders and jagged projections that tried to snatch at him, and after a moment the suit deposited him jarringly on level ground, and returned main control to him.

There had hardly been time for him to re-orientate himself, and to accept and ignore the irritating pain in his knees, before his head was filled with the siren screeching of danger.

He froze, staring into the distance, to the growing darkness. The sound went through him like a knife, cutting his body into neat pieces, penetrating to his every cell. Whining, throbbing, rising and falling, the voice of panic, preceding the voice of the wind.

'Leo … move it!' Lena's voice was sharp, angry, He realized she was standing near to him, the rift suit braced ready for action, her face a white blur behind the face plate. 'What's the matter with you?'

Faulcon powered forward, far too fast, forcing himself to slow. The whining siren made his heart race, made the sweat break from him as he moved through the ruins. He couldn't wrench his eyes from the gloom in the far distance. I'm afraid, he thought. I'm terrified, but I'm still here. I'm not running.

He saw movement to his right and Kris was there, fleeing between the crowded walls and girders, and rugged shards of rock. Faulcon couldn't follow him exactly, and nor could Lena, and they moved where the suits would allow them, getting deeper into the morass of channelled space between the time-flung ruins.

'Kris!' Lena's voice was shrill as it came through Faulcon's headphones. 'Stop running, Kris. Give it up. We've got to take you back, and you know you've got to come back.'

Kris's sour laughter was unmistakable. Faulcon stopped, looked around him, between walls, panels, girders, rocks … He saw Kris just briefly, the insectoidal mask flashing light as he turned to look at Faulcon.

'Can't you hear the sirens?' shouted Faulcon.

'Tricks is it, Leo? Trying to trick me out? Why don't you just leave me be. Go back to your fantasies.'

He slipped away and Faulcon had to retrace his steps until he could move through the junk yard again. With a sudden awful comprehension he realized that Kris did not have the siren-tuner, the special receiver that carried the siren wavelength so that it would not interfere with the ordinary voice communication.

'Lena!' he yelled. 'He can't hear the wind. He'll never get out of here, we'll chase him until it hits.'

'Then we chase him until it hits!' she shouted back.

Raw panic surged through Faulcon. He started to shake and the suit behaved badly, not yet ready to take over the survival function, confused by Faulcon's lack of control. He looked into the distance, saw the darkness rising higher into the pink sky; he could see the moving shapes in that darkness, currents of air rising and falling, sweeping about as if the very clouds lived and writhed as they crossed the centuries.

'We've got to get *out* of here,' he screamed, and the suit began to run, struck a wall, bounced back.

'Calm! Leo, calm,' came Lena's voice. 'If you throw a fit you're dead for sure.'

Kris's baiting laughter; his voice: 'Calm, Leo, keep calm. Don't be scared, poor little Leo. Just get out of the valley and go and stand and watch and see people die, just like you saw my brother get swept away ...'

'Shut up, Kris.' Lena, anxious, the edge of panic in her own voice.

Relentlessly: 'Poor Leo, so shit-scared his rift suit is all fouling up. But don't worry about me, Leo. I'm all right. You can watch me without helping me any time because I don't want your fucking help. Go and stand and tremble and remember how it was when Mark called out for help, and you were too scared to lift a hand, too shit-scared to find out if you were really a man, so you just stood there while my brother called for help when his suit failed him, and got swept away. A brave man, Leo, and a man with all the instincts for survival. Just think about that, think about how it is to trust someone, to make the mistake, the noble mistake, of putting your faith in someone who isn't worth a damn. Just think of it, and think of all that fear-crap deep down in your belly, and think about all those times you go running at night, and stop and scream your fear when you look down and remember how fucking shitless you were that day. Oh yes, Leo, I know it was you that I saw running that night, running and screaming and vomiting your fear. It wasn't Ensavlion, like you tried to make me think. It was you! How many nights, Leo? How many hours screaming, how many buckets of tears?'

Faulcon moved towards the movement he could see. Kris's voice was a grating whine; it had jarred and stung, and then it had angered and hurt, and then it had become just the voice of a man in deadly danger, a man who was clinging to a dream, who needed help just like his brother had needed help, and maybe more so … There was nothing wrong with Kris Dojaan, except that he didn't know what was about to happen to him.

Faulcon moved after him, now, and the pathways between the crowded ruins widened; abruptly he was out into the open, running down a slope, and into an area of area of high, misplaced rocks and crumbling brick and stone walls. He glimpsed Lena some way away, but moving in the same direction. The siren wailed, and he forced himself not to look into the distance; already his suit was beginning to sing its wind-song, the rattling whining of surface sensors reacting to the physical wind that was building up outside.

'Why don't you just leave me to myself!' cried Kris, and Faulcon imagined that he was addressing Lena; there was anxiety there, not hostility.

'Can't you see that darkness?' came Lena's voice. 'Wise up, Kris. Your life is in danger.'

'I want to go. Just leave me … I'm going after Mark …'

'The hell you are.'

Faulcon listened to the interchange and felt terribly cold. Now he could hear the booming of the wind, the deep thunder of atmosphere being wrenched and twisted against the fabric of stable time. His head spun, his mind became nothing but dizziness and determination; he seemed to run in a dream, his legs hardly moving. Even if he'd wanted to he felt he could not move fast enough, now, to escape that wind.

He saw Kris run out of sight behind a sphere of translucent green material; he could see the boy *through* the structure, standing there, breathing hard as he tried to think where he should run to now.

Faulcon moved after him, and quite abruptly he came face to face with the time phantom, the ragged, wretched figure, now standing beside him, staring at him. He stopped and stared into that wizened face, saw beyond the mask of age and into the very soul of this timelost. In the instant of indisputable recognition he felt a sobering shock.

His stomach heaved; sour bile rose into his mouth, flooded down his chin. His stomach clenched, stopped the vomiting, hurting as the muscles contracted and tugged and shrank, pulling his body down against the resistance of the rift suit. He was a man shocked to immobility, and the suit took over.

The time winds boomed again through his headphones, louder now, seeming to approach far faster than was usual; the siren was a persistent and frantic reminder that somewhere in the valley, men and women were scattering like frantic herds, that Steel City was swinging its observer stations round to watch, that photographs were being taken, that cars and trucks and shuttles were shifting into positions to get as much from the winds as they could, that teams were being called up, suited-up, instructed ready for the swift mission following in the wake of the time winds; and above their heads, in the deeps of space, satellite crews were swinging out of hammocks, crawling down to their cameras and view-stations and monitoring consoles.

And somewhere nearby, perhaps, Operation Catchwind was moving into place, waiting for the word from Ensavlion, the word to go.

All this was happening, and Faulcon stood and stared at the time phantom, remembering Leuwentok's words, but unable to make any sense of what he remembered, conscious only of that face; he felt his body moved finally by the gentle suit, moved away, moved almost out of eye-shot, just sufficient vision remaining so that he could see how the phantom appeared to fade away, to become insubstantial, ghostly.

He took control of the suit, conscious that the machine, itself aware of his shock and growing hysteria, had not relinquished full control to him. He moved out of the clustered rocks back into the open spaces, and Kris darted from hiding, and stopped, staring at him. There was something about the boy, something about his bearing, his posture ... he was exhausted, his chest rising and falling heavily, his skin, the naked skin of his hands and cheeks, glistening with sweat; his mask was dirty, his vision impaired by dust. Lena appeared close by and began to run towards him. He heard her and started to move again; whatever he had been thinking as he had stood, staring at Faulcon, Faulcon would never know. Kris Dojaan took two steps away from Lena when he noticed something beyond Faulcon and stopped again, this time turning fully round, then backing away, his body cringing, his face creasing with a sudden, shocking fear; he ripped the mask from his face so that he could see better, and his voice was almost hysterical as he screeched his panic, choking as the words came, 'Oh *God*! What's that ... Oh my *God*!'

'Get him, Leo!' shouted Lena, and moved in on Kris. 'Come on, Leo, come on, for God's sake. My suit won't let me hang around much longer. *Leo!*'

Faulcon had turned. He could not hear her. He was listening to the screaming gale, the frightful booming and wailing, the thunder of the physical wind that came with the silent wind of time.

And he was watching; above the valley hung a great black cloud, rolling and breaking and flowing towards him, a hideous rolling caricature of the most fearsome night imaginable. Below it the valley was changing faster, more confusingly than the eye could follow – the land and the structures upon the land rippled and distorted, twisted and vanished as they were swept into some unimaginable future, Faulcon watched as white towers winked out of existence, to be replaced by moving spiral shapes that radiated redly as they turned. He watched as an immense spider's web of girders was torn from vision, flickering a moment as a time squall knocked it into Othertime and back, and then it was gone and a hideous shape stood there, the carved, gargoyle-decorated gateway of a primitive era. Then that too had been swept away and its place taken by bulging domes, then decayed concrete block-houses, then a vast tree-like plant, its branches laden with green and juicy fruit.

Everywhere in the valley the shapes were changing, the valley walls themselves shifting in colour and texture and dust rising from the incredible conflict of time and matter that was occurring.

And this terrifying storm of change was gaining on Faulcon, overreaching him, perhaps the most powerful wind that had ever been witnessed on Kamelios …

Faulcon's rift suit took command; perhaps it had comprehended the danger, both from the wind and from Faulcon's frozen fear stance. It turned him round and began to run him away … faster and faster, until his legs were jerked into the rapid run position and he was carried forward at an almost bone-breaking speed. In a matter of instants he had passed Lena and the petrified Kris Dojaan. If Faulcon heard her voice, 'Leo, stop and help … help me carry him … he could do nothing about it.

But after a moment as the terrain fled past, as the suit whined and groaned its effort, Faulcon snapped out of his shock and twisted about. He saw Lena running after him, the limp form of Kris Dojaan cradled in her arms, the towering dark, the flickering wavefront of change, close behind her. She was still screaming at him, still calling to him. But his suit would not stop; his suit had only one thing in its mechanical mind: the survival of its occupant. It was running him to safety, to the safety of the sheer wall up whose length it could leap in four or five jet-powered bounds. He was a passenger in that man-shaped survival machine, running forwards, looking backwards, watching appalled as Lena's suit, not prepared to live with the encumbrance of its passenger any longer, let Kris drop to the ground. Faulcon's ears blanked Lena's horrified scream from his mind; one glimpse, one imagined view of the disgust and helplessness she must have felt, was enough. Kris sprawled on the ground, then scrabbled to his feet. He looked about him, anywhere, everywhere but at that sheer wall of dark that was reaching above him. He began to run, and as if it might somehow protect him from the wind he had so quickly come to fear, he flung himself into the lee of a cubical grey building in whose translucent walls automatic shapes moved as they had moved a million years distant.

An instant later the wave front of distortion swept across him; the cube vanished, to be replaced by a towering crag of rock, Kris flashing into Other-time and a spinning, gleaming, indefinable shape appearing in his place, the dust of the ground a different hue, and where he had cowered, sensing death so close, just the swirling of dust, and age, and time …

Lena's yelling changed to the genuine screaming of her fear. Faulcon joined her, the flood of panic dissipating in a few welcome shrieks of terror. The wind boomed, the suits moaned as the wind tickled their sensors, Lena gained on Faulcon, and the edge of the canyon, the safety point, seemed to get no closer to either of them. Faulcon could see dark shapes scattering up the canyon walls in the very distance, suits mostly, but a few two-man craft rising vertically, and earning their price for their drivers. He could see the sparkle of light on steel, and knew that the monitoring cameras were in place all along the ridge. And as he looked into the distance, so it appeared before him in the winking of an eye, the pyramid, the time machine of the enigmatic creatures that Ensavlion believed policed this world out of sight of those who watched. Faulcon's suit veered to the right and he was powered past the faintly vibrating golden structure in a few instants. But as he passed so he turned to watch as a figure seemed to rise from the ground before the machine, a wrinkled caricature of a human shape, rising to its feet from a crouched position, a figure he recognized, having seen it only minutes before.

Faulcon could only assume that as the phantom rose to its feet it met the eyes of the woman who raced towards it, and in that terrible instant of recognition the shock, the surge of confusion and of comprehension that passed through Lena must have stopped the motion of the suit. Faulcon was half a mile beyond her as he strained to see backwards and saw her sprawling on the rocky ground, the time winds swirling around her and taking her in the gusting of a sudden breath.

Abruptly Faulcon's suit was veering to the right even more, running diagonally across the approaching wave-front of the wind. He reached the canyon wall and rose up, his body twisted and jarred by each rocket-powered ascent and every clumsy impact on ledge, or outcrop, or less hostile slope. Screaming for speed, helpless, fearing that he would not make the canyon's rim, he was stumbling across the lip of the valley before he knew it, tumbling end over end, being braced and grasped by helping hands. The time winds swept past in the canyon, darkness overtaking him, thunder, lightning, and the screeching of wind turning the safelands into a nightmare of their own.

It was gone then, and there was quiet, and the darkness lifted as it sped away to the east. Faulcon lay in his suit, on his back, for a long, long time, staring up at the afternoon sky, waiting for the shaking to begin and the tears and the shock. Somewhere he was sure he could hear the phantom laughing, her voice so horribly familiar to the man who imagined it.

PART THREE

Manchanged

CHAPTER FOURTEEN

He realized that he had never known true loneliness. He experienced, now, an aloneness, a discontinuity, that physically hurt him until he cried, or vomited, or dulled his senses with alcohol and drugs. There had been many times in his life when he had categorized the particular feelings of frustration and solitariness that he had been experiencing as 'loneliness'; now he accepted that he had merely been in transit from one moment of aliveness to the next, and that what he had been feeling was impatience. Loneliness had never truly entered his life before, and now he found that he could not confront it, only succumb to it; the loneliness washed through him like the change winds, poked icy, mocking fingers into every nook of his body, shouted to him through the echoing void inside his skull. He was alone, totally alone. There were people around him, but they were not with him; there were two Universes of sensation that overlapped, theirs and his, but there was no communication. He was a Galaxy away, literally a Universe apart. When they smiled at him, those ghostly participants in Kamelios life, the smile was not for him, for he was no longer the body that people saw. He was carried by it, but he was not a part of it. He was alone even from himself.

For five days he haunted the corridors and plazas of Steel City, drifted through bars and lounges, and finally curled up in his silent quarters. After a while he became aware of the feelings of hostility being directed towards him. Abruptly he realized that the early expression of sympathy, in regard to his personal losses, had somehow transformed to an expression of anger that he was still not lost alongside of them. The rituals of Steel City came back to him with startling clarity, filling him with the coldness and bitterness of fear. He recognized that his presence was not only resented, but his death was rapidly required. Fear and loneliness combined to empty his mind of everything but panic, and on the sixth morning, at the break of dawn, he left the city; afraid for his life, he was pursued every step of the way by the silent guardians of Steel City ritual, the angry few who remained unseen as they followed him, but whose presence he could discern quite clearly. They hesitated round corridors, hid among machinery, and hovered among the limp suits in the suiting and shedding lounge. He signed out his byke, rather than his r-suit, and rode out into the gusting dawn wind. The moment he was out of easy eye-shot of the city, he turned away from the rift.

He rode up into the wide lands to the south, through the limestone and chalk drifts, then travelling beyond the sprawling forests to Hunderag Country. In the foothills of the Jaraquath mountains he came to a high plateau where a large and thriving settlement of manchanged had long been established. The journey took five days and he did not eat in all that time. His only drink had been mouthfuls of warm water from a flask. Hunger had been an insistent pain every ten hours for the first two days; now he was aware only that he ought to eat to sustain his strength. The only hurt was the hurt of his loss.

So he approached the settlement, his byke making low noises as he crawled between fences and areas of cultivation, wondering where he should stop, and for how long. In the distance he could see the clustered buildings, white upon white, rarely more than two storeys high. The houses were huddled together about a wide compound as if they were insecure, unsure of themselves, and had not yet found the courage to spread outwards a little, to find their own space. He could see people working in the fields of green and purple crops, and as he rode past they glanced up, but quickly turned back to their work.

He was always discomfited by the appearance of these fourth and fifth generation inhabitants of the high plateaux, their bulging eyes shining unnaturally, their arms ridged where the purifiers beneath their skin showed through the lean flesh of their arms. They had not yet achieved full independence from technology; Kamelios was still a strange land to them, but slowly they evolved in the modern way, and soon men would walk about this hostile place and be able to say that they truly belonged here.

Faulcon stopped his slow ride some hundred yards from the township. He had not yet seen the only manchanged he knew. He dismounted and walked through the buildings into the compound, aware that he was watched from windows, conscious that he was causing something of a stir. Few rift-folk ever came this high up into the mountains, and Faulcon knew that he was not welcome. And yet he was abruptly surprised as a slim, dark-haired young woman walked from a barn-like building, through the doorless exit and into the compound, waving to him as she came, and smiling. Behind her appeared a tall, muscular looking man, his hair turning white, his skin weather-beaten and leathery. Behind his mask, Faulcon smiled as best he could.

In this way, grateful for the persistence of the human faculty for friendship, despite the adjustments to the alien, Leo Faulcon made the proper acquaintance of Audwyn, and his young wife Allissia.

'I wasn't sure if it was even the right plateau,' he said, nervous and uneasy. 'I need food, that's all. Just something to eat, and a little rest, and then I can be on my way.'

'You'll stay until you go,' said Audwyn with a smile, leading Faulcon into a small, claustrophobic house, two-roomed, with a table, bed and cooking area, and precious little else; the toilet was outside.

'Well, that's very kind of you,' said Faulcon. 'If you're sure …'

'Try doing otherwise,' said Audwyn with a chuckle, and waved Faulcon to a stool at the table. 'It seems to me you rifters believe everything you hear about the "manks" … That's what we're called, isn't it?'

'I assure you that it is,' said Faulcon, leaning on the table and watching as Allissia began to cut thick slices of grey meat from an unappetizing-looking joint. Audwyn himself drew drinks from a wooden barrel, three clay mugs of a green liquid that smelled sweet and tasted sweeter. With the steaks taking care of themselves, Allissia sat down. Faulcon was less relaxed with her than with her husband, and he knew this was because she was a lovely-looking girl below and above the enormous, sheathed eyes. But as he regarded her he noticed the flexing of her nose and the glisten of hard, yellow substance, the poisons and dusts of Kamelios that were gathering within the cavity. During the next few hours he grew quite accustomed to the way she and her husband would turn to the left and delicately eject the hardened, colourful mucus onto the floor.

Before they ate, Faulcon fetched his gear from the byke, and pushed the machine into shelter. He approached the task of eating with some apprehension, since the mask was not an efficient filter when it was being used in this way. He ate very little, and felt queasy even as he was finishing; but his digestive system was able to cope with the native meat, and two mugs of the sweet, alcoholic drink helped enormously. He was amused, as he ate, to notice the flickering of light in the room that told of the surreptitious staring-in of the locals. Whenever he looked up they had vanished, but he felt their watching eyes and minds.

After the meal Allissia watched him sympathetically, assuring him that if his stomach rejected the food she could find vegetables that might be less poisonous. Faulcon thanked her, but declined, and after a horrifyingly sweaty and cold few minutes the nausea passed away and he relaxed, replete, and grateful for the dizzying effect of the drink.

'Why aren't you working?' he asked Audwyn, and was told, 'We are. We were settling calcas, a fleshy root crop we grow up here. Settling means we were burying it in worm-soil. In a few weeks the worms will have processed the roots into a more digestible and solid cake which we then use both as a winter staple for ourselves and our animals – we even have a few adapted terrestrial animals, pigs, horses – and also for making the brew that you appear to be enjoying.' Faulcon smiled as he leaned back in the only straight-backed chair in the house; he raised the mug appreciatively to his lips and felt a shock of revulsion as he saw the bloated shape of a small worm floating close to the bottom. Flavouring, Audwyn said, apparently innocent of the appalling effect such detritus could have on off-worlders. Faulcon carefully picked the offending corpse out of his mug.

'Now that you've come we're still working, being hospitable. Only when the fields need furrying – that's clearing them of parasites – do we have to be out all day. How about you? What brings a rifter so far from his metal womb?'

Faulcon wondered quickly what he should say, how much he should say. When the silence had begun to embarrass him he murmured, 'A friend of mine died. I had to get away from Steel City, get out of myself for a while.'

As he spoke he was not unconscious of the almost amused glance that was exchanged between his hosts. Whatever it was they shared they didn't share it with him, and he wrote it off as part of the strange behaviour of these mountain farmers. Only later did he discover what had tickled them; he was introduced to a younger man, a cousin of Allissia's, when he was on his way out to the fields to participate. 'This is Leo Faulcon,' said Audwyn as Faulcon and the youth shook hands. 'Mister Faulcon is only partly here, some of him is still down by the valley. There's enough of him to work, though, so show him how to furry-up pulp-scab, and perhaps root-up as well.'

Faulcon enjoyed the work he undertook for the next two days. It was hard, and the pulp-scab parasites that crawled through the crops were small and elusive. There weren't many of them, but they were highly destructive to the maturing crops. Faulcon came to understand how delicate and dangerous was the balance up here between success and starvation.

The work enabled him to shed his tears inside, and in silence. He fought against crying out loud, but too often for his liking he gave in to emotion, feeling ashamed and embarrassed as he realized his weeping had been heard by others around him. He noticed, however, that they took no notice, and made no sympathetic gestures. Occasionally he would stand, leaning on the wooden-handled furrying tool, and stare across the plateau to where the lands to the north were green and grey, rolling and rising from hill to mountain, the valley forming a recognizable network back towards the crop-lands around the canyon where time was master. As he stared at those distant, natural sights, he saw Lena; over and over again he saw her, walking towards him, or sitting quietly and moodily, trying to shake off the effects of a *fiersig*. He missed her with all the pain in his body, and all the reaction of the nerves in his torso, and all the coldness that his spirit could muster. He worked hard and furious, letting anger rule him, enjoying that anger, and shouting at the parasites that wriggled in his grasp as he squashed them between thumb and forefinger, letting their sticky juices spread their stink across his flesh.

Each night, as he shuffled around in the blanket roll that Allissia had provided for him, he spoke through the open door between the two rooms to his hosts, themselves quite comfortable and unbothered as they lay or loved in their own bed. 'I'd better not impose another night. I'd better leave.'

Audwyn said, on each occasion, 'You're welcome to stay until you leave,

Leo. One thing's for sure, there's not a chance in a million that you'll still be here after you've left.'

On the third day he cut his hand very badly, and walked up to the village to find Allissia. As he made his way between the houses he was again uncomfortable, the stranger in this tight and unfriendly little community. He had met only a handful of people and they had been friendly and communicative, but he sensed their distance, their unwillingness to commit themselves to him; they were friendly because that was the way to be. But they watched him, and wondered about him, and many of them resented his intrusion here. He knew he would have to leave soon, because he knew he was upsetting the delicate balance of life in the community.

He found Allissia in the small forge, working on a complex-looking tool whose spirally curved blade had sheared in two. The forge was hot, the brazier of organic rock glowing bluely as she operated a small bellows with her foot; she was hammering the metal blade with remarkable proficiency, and Faulcon stood and watched her work until the thin line of the join had vanished and she seemed reasonably satisfied with the job. 'It'll do for now,' she said, smiling at Faulcon. She noticed the blood on his hand and said, 'You've been using your fingers and not the furrier.'

'That's right,' he said. 'You have some vicious stones in your soil up here.'

'They're sun-dew crystals, and they're quite rare in the fields. Show me where you were working, later, and we'll dig the thing up and send it back to the City with you.'

He followed Allissia into the small house and found Audwyn hard at work riveting a large, skagbark barrel. He was unsympathetic towards Faulcon's wound, but Allissia smiled at him as she cleaned the gash and bound it with a dark, rather pungent linen. 'Have a drink before you go back out,' said Audwyn, banging the last rivet into place and reaching for the mugs.

Faulcon said, 'You'll have to give me another job. I'll have to rest this hand for a while.' He sat down at the table.

Audwyn smiled as he splashed the sweet drink, which they called *calcare*, into the earthenware mugs. 'Defeated by a shard of crystal, Leo? It amazes me that with an attitude to life like that, you could have reached the age you have. I'm surprised you didn't succumb to the first discomfort that ever got the better of you.'

Faulcon was grateful for the warming glow of the drink; the plateau was cold and exposed. As he savoured the drink, alert for worms, he said, 'I couldn't operate the furrier if I wanted; my hand won't grip at the moment.'

Audwyn laughed and shook his head. 'You rifters ...'

'I'm an off-worlder.'

'That's even worse! Don't you know that you can do anything if you really want to? Don't you know, didn't anyone ever tell you, that a man is bigger and more magnificent than a piece of dirt? I guess they didn't, eh Leo? Pain, discomfort, irritating circumstances, they're all bigger than you, aren't they?'

Unwilling to provoke an argument, despite the throbbing pain in his hand, Faulcon said, 'I can certainly try and hold the furrier …'

'I don't want you *trying* to do anything, Leo. If I try and talk to you I don't talk to you. If you try and hold the tool you don't hold it. If you *hold* the tool you hold it. I don't mind you doing that. I don't mind you doing what you're doing, but it seems pretty pointless to try and do something that you're not doing if all that's going to happen is that you're going to go on not doing it.'

'Give me another drink,' said Faulcon dully, and watched, frowning, as his mug was filled. His hand hurt like hell, and he was feeling silently angry at what seemed to him to be an unforgivable carelessness on Audwyn's part. 'Are you saying that you'd go out and work again with a four-inch gash across the palm of your hand that is stopping your hand clenching, and causing you considerable agony, and stopping you being efficient?'

'Well, why not? If I trip over I don't lie there saying, "I've been overwhelmed by Mother Earth who has thrown me down, so I'll just lie here for the rest of my life and acknowledge that I'm insignificant against the huge presence of circumstance." I don't do that, Leo.'

'I hardly do that myself, but—'

'You've been doing that all your life, Leo! The hell you haven't. You've been totally content when you were happy and totally discontent when you were miserable; you've evaluated the moments of your life into good and bad, and you, and the billions like you, have never comprehended that there are no good and bad moments, only moments when you're alive, moments when you're experiencing life, being *with* life, no matter whether you're in pain, or pleasure, or depression, or solitariness. It's extremely easy, as you will no doubt be the first to acknowledge, to be happy when you're happy; but it's so damned hard to be depressed when you're depressed – you've always got to fight it, right? You've always got to treat depression as something to be got rid of, to be resisted, when in fact it is a commonly known truism that nobody is ever not depressed when they're depressed. Nobody ever has a pain in the hand when they don't have a pain in the hand. The point is, are you bigger than that pain; are you prepared to shrug your shoulders and say, so I've got this throbbing, hurtful, agonizing pain in my hand, so what? You see, Leo, that's the way we lead our lives up here, and we find it works rather well. We do things, we don't let things do us; we get hungry, but we don't let hunger get us. I can tell you with absolute certainty, Leo, that there's not a man, woman or child on this plateau who isn't hungry when he's hungry. The difference between us and you, Leo, is that here on the plateau hunger is a part of our experience, part of the life we lead, part of living; to you it's an ache that has to be satisfied in order to make it go away. Hunger gets you every time you get hungry ... it distracts you, it nags you. Up here, when we get hungry we get hungry, and later on when we eat we eat, and when we sleep we sleep. Do you follow me, Leo?'

Faulcon drained his mug, adjusted his mask afterwards. He felt bitter, quite angry. He didn't like this nonsense talk from the frog-eyed man who sat so smug in front of him; he didn't like Allissia's self-congratulatory smile, the way she watched him from a point of total subjugation to her husband's words. He said, 'How can you pretend to know so much about we ordinary mortals?'

By way of answer Audwyn rolled up his sleeves, then pulled apart his robe at the chest. Faulcon stared at the hideous scars, the swollen, lumpy inclusions in the man's body, far greater than he normally associated with the process of manchange. 'I was not born a manchanged, Leo. I lived among men, in the lower towns, in your city, for several years. I'm no older than Allissia—' Faulcon was taken by surprise. He looked twice her age. 'The process has an ageing effect upon a matured body, which is something I know, something I accepted. I *chose* to come here, a first among the fourths and fifths. The gatherers brought me when I was alone and wandering in the mountains. I don't regret a day in my life. I don't regret the waste of time when I oversleep, I don't regret the missed opportunity, the lost love, the failed work. My memories of man are of a constant process of dissatisfaction, of regret, of resistance to anything that does not seem as if it's going the expected way, of not *living*, Leo, of not ever being 100 per cent a part of *life*. I remember men as being a breed forever resisting its very humanness – its weakness, its flaws, its failures, its imperfections. Such resistance is the quickest way to self-destruction. It's the easiest way to become trapped by the very weakness you try to avoid.'

As Audwyn arranged his clothing again, Faulcon said, more angrily than he intended, 'If you're so damned alive up here, why are you so bloody unfriendly?' Restless, he rose from the table.

Audwyn exchanged a curious glance with Allissia. She said, 'Who's unfriendly, Leo? Haven't we made you feel at home?'

'You have, and I'm more than grateful for that. But these mountain communities are so insular, so hostile to strangers. Why the hell do you think so few people come out here? It isn't because you're all leading natural, content lives, it's because you're inbred and suspicious of strangers. Maybe you can't see it from where you sit, but it has certainly been very apparent to me.'

Audwyn rose from his stool and followed Faulcon to the door. 'I must say, Leo, that from where I sit I see only that you came into our community and we made you welcome ... I know we put you to work, but we do that to everybody who comes out here; if you want to stop work, then that's fine by us. Please feel free to do just what you want. But Allissia and I have opened our house to you, I've introduced you to several others. I don't see where this hostility lurks that you seem so conscious of.'

They were out into the crisp day. Faulcon's skin-tight suit was uncomfortable in the strong wind, but he noticed that Audwyn was shivering slightly inside his patterned jacket and grey pantaloons. He was watching Faulcon curiously, staring at his eyes behind the glasses that covered the upper part of his face. Faulcon waved a hand around at the houses huddled about their small open space. 'Why didn't they come out and welcome me, then, when I drove up? Why did they hide away as if they were afraid? I walked in here and I felt every eye on me, I saw people peering at me from behind the windows. I came here and I scared everyone to hell; a man from the lowlands, an outsider. And in the days I've been here I've not changed, I'm still the outsider, and I'm still distrusted to the point of fear.'

Audwyn laughed, 'Except by myself and Allissia. Everyone in the town is terrified of you, except two of us. Wouldn't that make us outsiders too?'

'You're part of the town. And I don't suppose I mean terrified ... uneasy, suspicious.'

'We're a part of the town, Leo, yes indeed; but we're a part of life. Tell me, are you uncomfortable when you're on your own, walking out through the houses to the fields? Are you uncomfortable now?'

Faulcon tried to flex his gashed hand and failed, looking around him as he did so. 'I feel I'm an object of curiosity and suspicion, yes. I'm not exactly uncomfortable because I'm with you. But it would help if there was some life and communication going on here, if people weren't shuttered up in their houses.'

Audwyn said quietly, 'Leo, there's no one, not one soul in any of the buildings. A handful of us have remained here, to pick away at the lower fields; most people are up in the high fields, and in the game forests. This is Moondance Season, a time of hunting. When you came here a few days ago there was just myself and Allissia and those few out in the fields. You were welcomed by the only two people around to welcome you.'

'Are you telling me I was imagining being watched?' Faulcon looked around him, disturbed by the implication of what Audwyn was saying. The houses looked as they had looked three days ago, deserted, lifeless, empty ... and yet he had sensed the eyes watching him, the furtive movement of people, insecure now that their territory had been invaded by a lowlander. 'I don't understand, I'm sure there were people when I came, when I walked past the houses.'

Allissia laughed, and laid a gentle hand on his arm; Faulcon thought he recognized the humour in her wide, staring eyes, but now he was not sure. She said, 'How lovely to be able to see people when they're not there. How sad to be able to see only frightened people.'

'What other sort of people should frightened people see?' said Audwyn. 'Poor Leo, so afraid that he frightens himself. So uneasy with the world that there can be no world in his eyes that is not uneasy with him.'

'You make me sound like a victim ...' Faulcon tried levity, but somehow there was nothing in what Audwyn said to make light of. 'I guess we're all like that, down by Kriakta Rift.'

Audwyn nodded his agreement, watching Faulcon earnestly. 'That's the first step in getting rid of your status as victim. Keep working on it, Leo, and soon you'll see that you don't have to be victimized by anything, least of all your own shadows, and you do have shadows, don't you, Leo? So many shadows. Allissia and I have seen so many shadows crawling around in you that sometimes we thought the lights had gone out. There are more dead bodies in your past than there are in the time valley ... all those friends, eh Leo? All those people you let down, deserted, denied, deceived. We can see them, and we can hear them, because they're all you, they're all your own illusions, just as we are your illusion, and the people that were watching you were your illusion. You make your own ghosts, Leo. Nothing you can do or say is going to change one molecule of anything in the damned Universe, so is there really any point in brooding about it, or worrying about it, being beaten to death by it?'

'I suppose not, except that I'm a rifter, remember? I eke out my existence down by the valley where the time winds blow. My whole life is about survival. The moment I give into inevitability, which is what you do—'

'Which is what you *think* we do. I've never said that, Leo.'

'Okay, you've never said it. But what you're telling me is that there's no point in worrying about anything because everything is inevitable and nothing can be changed, so don't even try.'

'That's what you *think* I said, Leo. That's how you've interpreted it, but that's all right. Everything's all right as long as it's the honest and real you we don't mind what you feel, or do, or say as long as you are completely *you* in the feeling and doing and saying of it. You see, we like *people*, Leo, not "roles", not "labels" – not survivors or victims, or manipulators or aggressors. We like people and the reason this township is so alive is because there are no masks, there are no denials, no hidings ... if we're afraid, that's fine. Did you ever know anybody who wasn't afraid when he was afraid? But you've spent all your life *trying* not to be afraid when you're afraid, denying yourself the opportunity to experience your real and mortal fear, and by so experiencing it, and allowing it its full expression and place in your life, by doing that, to be its cause, not its effect, to rule *it* and not vice versa. Your whole life is fear, even your shadows are afraid, even your words are afraid. Survival. That's it to you, isn't it? Kamelios is a world of change and sudden death, and so the off-worlders who come here have to immediately take it on, survive its changes, survive its hostility.'

'If we don't survive we die.'

'Exactly. Have you ever known anyone who wasn't dead when he was dead? No, of course you haven't. So what's to survive? Do you think that you can do anything, anything at all that will delay your death by even a millionth of a second? Is there something you can do that when the moment comes that you drop dead you can stand there a few seconds longer and say, "Well here I am, dead as a doornail, but you'll notice I'm still alive." Of course not. A survival machine, Leo, is surviving until it doesn't survive, at which moment it dies. There's no such thing as a survival machine, there are only machines with short and long life spans before they die … death machines. You approach Kamelios as if by doing what you do you can stop or delay something that is going to happen when it happens whether you like it or not. You survive, you take it on, you scream and struggle, you hide and deceive, and you have talked yourself into the idea that by doing this you can delay death, but when death comes, you're dead, and nothing you've done has changed it one iota.'

'Except delayed the moment at which it comes.'

'How in the hills do you know? How in the world do you know anything about what hasn't happened yet? And besides, don't you see that by delaying death, if that's what you believe you're doing, you're eking out your existence from the point of view of fear of death, rather than from experience of life? You exist because you're being buffeted about by just about every circumstance that the Universe can throw against you. We *live* up here because we create our own circumstances, we accept responsibility for everything. You fight against the inevitable … if you're going to walk into the time winds, do you think you can do or say one thing that will change that? Of course you can't. So why fight it, why be dragged fighting and screaming through the inevitable, only to emerge on the other side bloody and breathless, saying, "My God, I made it through." Don't you think you'd have made it through anyway? *And* how much more enjoyable the passage would have been if you'd relaxed and experienced what was happening to you.'

For the last few seconds Faulcon had not been listening; he felt shocked and surprised at the reference to walking into the winds, and now he could not help himself saying, loudly and vehemently, 'How the *hell* did you know that? I never said a damned word.'

Audwyn smiled and shook his head. 'Don't fight it, Leo. How did we know? People like you don't come up to the high plateaux very often, you've remarked on that yourself. When they come here, to one or other of the communities, they are coming here to think, and what they've come to think about *always* involves the winds, and their relationship to the winds, and the necessity of their destruction by the winds. Leo, you're one of many, and we've seen you all.'

'Enough,' said Faulcon, disturbed and dizzy with the calm statements in favour of inevitability. He had wanted to be alone with the agony of his decision, to come up into these hills and think, and instead he found himself transparent to the people he had come among, and he wasn't sure if he liked that at all. Allissia smiled reassuringly at him as she turned away to her work again. Faulcon flexed his hand and walked silently through the deserted town, out into the fields, to where he had left his furrier. As he passed by people they acknowledged him, but they were tired and sweaty, working hard and furious, and had no time to talk.

He worked into the red dusk, almost until the last edge of Altuxor was below the far horizon. His hand was hurting him but he had ignored it, and the hurt was no longer a threat to his work. He had learned how easy it was to operate the tool with his left hand. He had dug out the crystal shard that had cut him, and stood for a while turning its exotic shape over in his hands, and seeing how the deep-grained colour changed with movement, an attractive thing as well as a useful thing. He touched the small, leather amulet around his neck, held it before him and stared at it, wondering whether or not he should remove the one and replace it with the crystal. There was a fear inside him that to take away his luck, even for a second, would bring death that much closer, that much quicker. And yet he was half convinced by Audwyn's quiet, simple argument that if he was to die he was to die, and why fight it, why resist it? But the amulet was strength; around his neck it interacted with him and was strength. To remove it now would be to act against his genuine wish, and so he left it around his neck, pocketed the crystal and resolved to wait until he felt the time was right to change his charm.

He heard his name called, and when he looked through the twilight he could see the slim figure of Allissia, stretching up and waving to him. He shouldered his furrier and with a last glance to the north, to the place where Steel City was an occasional transient gleam during the brightest part of the day, he walked back along the winding ridges between the crops and to the trackway that led to the town. Allissia waited for him, and as he drew near he realized that there were many more people around, both in the compound and still walking in from the hills that rose beyond the community; the hunters were returning, and he could see that several of them carried beasts of varying sizes slung across their shoulders; he numbered three olgoi among this prey, and looked around quickly in case Ben Leuwentok should be watching. His attention, as he did so, was snared by the full face of Merlin, red and bright, its twin a paler gold beside it. The moons were rising.

'Is the hunting season over so soon?' he asked Allissia, as she took his arm and walked with him towards the village. She was smiling.

'No, no, not yet. This is Moondance Eve, the time of celebration for what the earth and the air have donated to us. The hunters return, the gatherers come in, and those in the fields abandon their tents for the one night. They bring animals, samples of the crops. If the Grey House has a lonely man in residence he comes out, his first contact with us.'

'A lonely man? Grey House? What's that?'

Allissia frowned slightly. 'The Grey House is where we are born, Leo. Surely you know that. Birth for a manchanged is a little different from birth for you. It's a hospital. A lonely man is like Audwyn ... one of your own who has wandered away from the city. The gatherers watch for them throughout the Moondance Season, and bring them back to be manchanged if that's what they desire. No, this isn't the end of the hunting season, it's the beginning. At the end of Moondance Eve everyone goes back to work. Audwyn and I will go up to the high fields this time and another couple will take over the job of settling, and holding the town.'

'Waiting for people like me, who come here direct, eh?' She squeezed his arm. He was a little disturbed by the affectionateness of her, wondering whether this was the way with these people. Where he himself came from there were restraints on public demonstrativeness, especially between a man and his host's wife (or husband). But Allissia clung on to him firmly, walking beside him, her body in close and quite intimate contact. As they approached a great brazier that was burning in the compound, Faulcon saw Audwyn working huge chunks of meat onto a spit and laying them across the fire. He acknowledged Faulcon with a cheery wave, a cry of 'How's the hand?' and a laugh when Faulcon replied that he'd hardly noticed it all afternoon.

They went into the house and Allissia took Faulcon's wounded limb and removed the dressing. The gash was congealed and ugly. It hurt as he became aware of it, but Allissia now had a thick blue ointment, highly unpleasant on the nose, she said, and Faulcon grinned behind his mask. She washed his hand again, and smeared the balm along the cut. It hurt for a moment, and then tickled. Allissia laughed as Faulcon winced with the strange feeling. 'It's a root pulp that I prepared this afternoon; it will help the skin and muscle to knit together, and it will also make your hand more flexible. We'd run out earlier. You see, we do have medications ... We don't walk around in pain or with disease when we can do something about it.'

Faulcon said nothing. He was very aware of the girl, now, and although by his eyes she was hideously ugly (because of *her* eyes) he found that the ocular features of her face could not detract from the warmth he felt for her, and the strong feeling he had that he would like to kiss her lips. His respirator allowed him to notice that her breath was very sweet on his face as she laughed, and she had some simple body perfume that was subtle and intriguing. Beneath the colourful tunic he could imagine her body, small, girlish, not full, yet manifestly womanly.

Perhaps Allissia was aware of the beginnings of his arousal. She seemed embarrassed for a moment, glanced towards the door then down to the floor as she knelt beside the chair where he sat.

'I'm fifth generation,' she said, and her wide, staring eyes fixed upon him, and he knew this was a question: are you aware what that means?

'Fifth of the manchanged, you mean. I understand that, yes.'

She shook her head. 'It means I was not born like I am, changed for the world ... physically changed. You know we are not *really* changed, not the people that we are. We change our clothes, and we change our bodies to live here more comfortably, but the people inside are not changed. I came from the womb of my mother and I was altered in the Grey House, where all the machines are locked away. A lot of me was born genetically changed ... a lot of the altered me was passed from my mother to me through the genes. But not everything, not yet. They think it will be the tenth generation who will be born pure. I shall be long dead.'

'I don't understand how these things work, but I always thought they programmed the mind to accept the form, the new form ...' He had imagined she was distressed because she was abnormal in appearance, compared to the appearance of Faulcon, the natural human form. He had even thought: 'So much for acceptance.'

Allissia said, 'They don't. Part of the adaptation is to evolve psychologically. Here on the plateau, in all the communities in the high lands, we have come to accept what is, and we live and we are alive, and when we have doubts and fears we accept that we are doubting and fearful, and experience it. Nothing about us is so contrived that we cannot cry, or feel an agony at the ugliness we must appear to people like you. And I feel it very badly, Leo. I had to tell you this, I am so afraid of what I look like to you.'

'You look ... lovely,' he said. 'Your eyes are not lovely, but *you* are lovely.' It was true, he thought. It's what I've been feeling.

'You are like gods to us,' she said, and reached to touch his face. Faulcon waited for the gentle touch on his skin, and realized the moment he sensed her fingers on his mask that what she was seeing was a man in glasses and breathing tube. He frowned, wanting to remove the mask for a moment, but there was an expression of such passion in Allissia's face that he made no move; she moved her fingers over his cheeks and the glasses, across his hair, and the leathery binding of the mouth-piece; she curved her fingers about the ridged pipe that extended two inches from the mask, where the filters were housed; she seemed to caress something that was to her more erotic than lips.

'I dream of faces like this, real faces, the faces of men,' she said.

'I'm a man wearing a mask,' he said. 'The real me is underneath.'

'In our stories the great men are masked, the masks are golden or red or black or white, and some of them are strange, and some look like faces over faces; but this is how we remember the time of the first men, unrevealed, and yet unchanged by the masks that conceal them, just as we are real and unchanged. You are beautiful, Leo, and I am going to miss you so much.'

'That sounds perilously close to regret, Allissia. I thought regret was frowned upon.'

She shook her head, 'Not regret, Leo. Just honesty. Just true feeling.'

I look like an insect, he thought, and this is how she knows me, and this is how she will remember me and miss me. I must show her my face, all of my face … not once while I've been here have I taken off my mask …

He reached up to remove the eye-covers that kept the stinging atmosphere of Kamelios from his sensitive corneas; Allissia made a sound of panic and raised her hand to stop him taking the action.

Faulcon took her hand gently and smiled, wondering if she could see that smile, wondering if she had ever realized he had smiled. 'There is a greater distance between your people and mine than even you admit …'

'Perhaps.'

'You would never come to Steel City, never mix with rifters.' It was neither question nor statement. There was something of regret in his tone.

'No, I don't suppose we would. This is our living place. When we trade we go on the long walk down, and if any of us felt like staying, then he would stay. Usually we just want to make the long walk up.'

Faulcon leaned forward, close to the strange eyes that regarded him with such warmth. 'But can't you see how frustrating it is – how difficult – when you stay up here, and we stay down there, and come to regard each other with fear and contempt?'

'Speak for yourselves, Leo.'

'But you have things to offer – life to offer, warmth, experience. Don't you ever regret that no one can share the experience of your life, the love of life?'

'We don't regret it, Leo. What more do we need than you to take our life beyond the plateau? You share our lives for a while, and experience our love and our minds and our traditions, and you go from us and take that with you. You will never lose it. What more could we need? What more could we ask for? A few people carrying our lives in their hearts.'

Outside there was a great cheer, and laughter, and the two of them turned towards the door, the intimacy suddenly broken, the night of celebration stretched before them, suddenly demanding their attention. They both laughed, nervously, perhaps with a certain relief. Arm in arm they went out into the compound; the fire burned high, blue and yellow, with the occasional licking of a deep red flame into the night. Sparks flew up to the stars, and the skagbark crackled and charred, noisy and alive. Faulcon wished he could smell the wood, and the sizzling joints of meat, but his mask allowed him only a hint of a smoky odour, and a continuing memory of Allissia's perfume.

And so they celebrated Moondance Eve, the night of the hunters' return. The meat they ate was exquisite, like nothing Faulcon had tasted before; it was not the grey meat he had eaten for several days, nor was it the meat of imported terrestrial food animals; it was, he was told, the flesh of some creature they called a pathak, a large, fleet, man-eating predator that had been evolved for Kamelios from the stock of old-earth cats; it was an experiment in domestication that had gone wrong. Faulcon ate so much of the non-poisonous meat that he was sick anyway, leaning against the wooden walls of the house as he held his mask clear and voided his stomach contents with an amazing force; Allissia laughed at him and wagged a finger at him for his unnecessary indulgence. The drink was good, too, mostly *calcare*, but supplemented by three large china flagons of *baraas*. He threw up some more, and his mind grew euphoric with happiness, alcohol and a clearer understanding of what he was and what he had to do; he would experience everything, from the revolting sensation of nausea, to the final, heart-pounding moment when he stepped into the path of the time winds. Not a moment would pass when he would not be alive and aware of the simplest, most transient sensation. He would go to his death more alive than he had ever been in his thirty-two years. And when he died he would be dead, and there would be no resistance, there would only be fear, and that fear he would experience and know that he died Leo Faulcon, and not a man denying the innermost agony of that final moment when he found out what really lay beyond Old Lady Wind. Perhaps not death at all, but a new freedom; and Lena.

The fire was burning low, and all the meat had gone; the drink was as bountiful as ever, probably because half the community was slumped quietly, or chattily, about the brazier, or in shadows, by the houses. It was well after the midnight hour, and Faulcon was on his back, close to the dying warmth of the skagbark bonfire, half listening to Allissia talking to her husband, half watching the incredible spread of stars, the wide, white band of the galactic centre, the twenty dazzling blue stars that were the Twioxna Lights, a cluster with an abundance of inhabitable worlds. He was just deciding that he would close his eyes and sleep, right there beneath the sky – even though he would wake up dew-covered and frozen – when distantly there was the low rumble of thunder, and the terrifying crackle of an atmospheric disturbance. Above him the stars seemed to ripple for a moment, as if seen through a pool of water.

'A *fiersig*,' he said aloud, and sat up, then stood up, staring into the night, watching carefully until at last he saw the purple glow, moving towards them across the hills. It was a wide band of flickering light, with golden and red whorls chasing each other in frantic displays about the night sky. Below the activity, the land was eerily lit with an iridescent green, that changed to yellow and blue each time the thunder rolled and the leaping shards of lightning struck down to the earth.

Around him the manchanged had fallen quiet, and slowly, one by one, were standing, watching towards the south and west. But as Faulcon looked around him he realized there was none of the apprehension, or fear, or defensiveness that he would have expected as these strange manifestations of Kamelion interference approached. People watched as if impatient, as if the approaching phenomenon, and all it implied, was something that was interfering with their celebration, and which they would be pleased to get over with as soon as possible. Allissia was still murmuring quietly to Audwyn. Audwyn noticed Faulcon watching them, and a moment later Allissia turned as well, and the two of them rose to their feet to approach him.

'Are you afraid?' Allissia asked, and Faulcon said, 'Not at all. But it will end the pleasantness of the evening. These changes hit so hard that it's easier just to go off alone. I'm disappointed, that's all. I was enjoying the tranquillity.'

'Don't resist it,' said Audwyn. 'Just let it happen, let it pass. It's irritating that one of these things has to come tonight of all nights, but so what? It's here, let it pass through. The best part of the celebration is yet to come … at dawn, you'll love it.'

Faulcon thought to himself that at dawn there wouldn't be a person in the compound talking to anyone else, because there was no way of resisting the ferocious, mind-tearing effects of these electrical storms. But he said nothing, turned back to the thunder, and the flickering lights in the heavens.

Faulcon's skin began to tingle; he felt a wave of change pass through him, the alertness, the freshness, the turmoil in his head seen through a crystal glass; he held onto his amulet, focusing upon it, concentrating on it. At once he felt bright and cheerful, then a wave of sadness, then a sudden terrible panic, emotion piling upon emotion, over and over again panic insisting its way into his heart so that it raced and his palms began to sweat coldly. Around him there was silence for a long while and he was aware of the community watching restlessly as the lights swept steadily towards and above them, the centre passing out across the fields, but the full sweep of the flickering area of the disturbance taking in the clustered houses and huddled peoples of the plateau.

Quite suddenly they began to wail, the sound starting softly, a few heads hanging forward, only a few voices participating in the rising wave of despair; the wailing grew louder as more of the manchanged joined in, and soon Faulcon was in the centre of a howling mob, resisting his own emotional upheaval and fascinated by the racket that surrounded him. He saw Allissia, her head thrown back, her eyes closed and bulging against the thick lids, her mouth open, her voice lost in the greater sound of screaming. But Audwyn, standing near her, was angry, shouting, his voice insisting its way through the noise so that Faulcon could make out his words, the incoherent babbling of his fury; others still were laughing, or weeping, but over all there was the whining sound of a hundred manchanged experiencing some common feeling, and as Faulcon thought of this so he began to understand what might have been happening.

The change passed over and left Faulcon alert, slightly apprehensive, a small alteration to his previous mood of relaxed acceptance. He was nervous as Allissia, smiling broadly, came up to him and suggested a drink. Around him people were shuffling back to the fire or the places where they had been sitting, and the sound of laughter and chatter was loud and unexpected. Even those who had been crying were wiping the wetness from eyes and cheeks, and talking as if they were doing no more than brushing a stray hair back into place.

No lingering after-effects, he thought. They went through it and emerged unchanged.

When he said this to Allissia she frowned and shrugged, 'Why do you always question things, Leo?'

'Because I'm puzzled, and interested. You seemed in deep despair, but now nothing has happened to you. I feel all tight and on edge. I know people in Steel City who would have been knocked out by that change; for days. I know, I know ... people in Steel City are not the best examples in the world.'

'You said it,' said Allissia, and added, 'I feel a little tense, now, but that doesn't matter. It'll pass away in a few minutes; most of it passed through me as the *fiersig* passed overhead. These changes aren't permanent, but the more you resist them the longer they stay.'

'But in Steel City it was proved that if you didn't fight the things you got addled for weeks – upset for weeks ... There must be a reason ...'

'Reasons!' Allissia snapped the word, a touch of that residual tension emerging in a moment of frustration. 'You can work out reasons for anything, Leo – it's the human facility. Reasonableness can kill you quicker then anything. Reason is a liar.'

Faulcon said no more, nor asked another question. Allissia drifted away from him to talk with friends, and take part in a quiet, almost sleepy dance in the dying glow of the fire. Faulcon crept into the house and curled up in a corner, sleeping quite heavily; at dawn he was woken by the sound of laughter, and, peering out of the window, watched the manchanged dancing almost frantically, carrying colourful paper, or cloth, streamers. He did not feel in the mood to join in, and returned to sleep, his last wakeful thought being of the time winds, and of Lena, and of the way he would go to follow her soon, and of the excitement that he was suddenly feeling, the determination to fulfil the terms of his agreement without fear, without restraint, without tears.

He slept late into the morning and rose to find the house and the village deserted. The hunters had moved back into the hills again; the fire still smoked greenly, a wide patch of charred ground and ash showing where it had spread beyond the metal brazier. There was no sign of Audwyn or Allissia, and Faulcon felt quite pleased about that. He wrote a brief note on a piece of torn paper he found in the house, and then walked to where his byke stood in the shelter of a small, empty barn.

The noise of its motor must have resounded about the silent village, but no one appeared to watch him go. He rode slowly through the fields, winding along the tracks towards the wide, dirt road that led to the steep, descending path to the lower lands. Several manchanged were working here, and those that saw him stood and waved. He waved back, increasing his speed all the time. The last of the villagers that he saw was a woman, bent to her work, her back to him, her body slim and small beneath the wind-whipped garment she wore. She remained unmoved by the sound of the byke, and Faulcon remembered that Allissia was supposed to be working in the high fields. He waved anyway.

PART FOUR

Walking on the Shores of Time

CHAPTER FIFTEEN

At the first break of dawn Faulcon rose from his damp and chilly sleeping place and walked to the edge of the canyon. Here he stood for a few minutes, staring down into the gloom of the valley, discerning the shapes and structures, watching as the slow rise of Altuxor brought shades of pink, then yellow, to the alien confusion below and beyond him. The wind was fresh on his naked cheeks, and the dampness of his night's sweat was obtrusive and cold beneath his outfit. He watched the heavens as the stars expired, noticing that the last to vanish behind the red-streaked day were the winking lights of the geo-stationary satellites, watching the rift valley, probably watching him.

He felt no fear. He ached for Lena.

In his hands he held his old amulet, the small fragment of leather, smoothed and worn by his constant touching. He had carried this object of art around his neck for far too long; it had come to embody Mark, he realized now, and to throw it from him would be to detach one of Mark's fingers from their frantic grip upon his arm. Around his neck, now, he wore the crystal shard, carefully contained within an unobtrusive, platinum holder and slung upon a strip of the dark linen that had once bound the gash in his hand. He was not a man to spurn the slightest sentiment, not Leo Faulcon. Allissia was in his mind, and she was slightly in his heart. In the days since he had left the man-changed, she and Audwyn had grown in his life. They were warmth to the planet's cold; they were certainty to VanderZande's uncertainty; they were resolve to the inner fear he acknowledged, experienced, and realized could not control him.

And yet he could not cast away this strip of leathery skin, this piece of him, this part of his past. He dearly wished to consign it to the oblivion of the canyon, to watch its fall into the vast unknown, to await the next time-sweep of wind from beyond.

'Throw it you fool; break the spell once and for all.'

Faulcon had been unaware of Ensavlion's approach. He turned, now, and saw the man in similar garb to his own, an off-white service outfit, reasonably warm, designed for less risky environments than the canyon edge. Ensavlion's rift suit stood awkwardly a few hundred yards back along the track; Faulcon could see it, standing twisted as if staring at him.

'Commander,' Faulcon acknowledged. 'What brings you here?' Yet another chance for the Catchwind mission missed, quite obviously, but Faulcon said nothing.

'You, of course,' said Ensavlion, his face working behind the thin mask, his eyes clearly narrowed behind the goggles he wore. 'I tried to find you in the City, but you must have spent only a moment there. I wondered where the hell you'd got to these last few days.'

This declaration of Ensavlion's concern for one of his junior rifters disturbed Faulcon; what he had to do, what he faced, was something solitary, something that no man could be a part of. But he said, hoping to pacify his commanding officer, 'I took absence without leave.'

'That I know. I signed papers giving you official leave. You're off the hook, but where did you go?'

Cynically Faulcon glanced at the older man. 'You mean you genuinely don't know? I thought you had eyes everywhere, Commander. You certainly had them in Lena's room.'

Ensavlion appeared unabashed; the area of cheek that showed beside his mask did not flush; on the contrary, Faulcon thought the man was positively amused. Ensavlion said, 'I heard nothing myself. I make no apology. Consider us to be square, me for allowing Kris Dojaan to eavesdrop your conversations with Lena, you for taking unofficial leave. Where did you go?'

'Up to the lower plateaux, in Hunderag Country. I stayed at a manchanged colony. They made me realize the foolishness of bending to fear ... of bending to anything. They made me aware that I, Leo Faulcon, am ten times bigger than fate. Fate may call the tune, but I dance the way I want to dance.'

Ensavlion clapped his hands together three times, slowly. 'Bravo, Leo. Three cheers for the man who has stood up to destiny. And still you'll jump into the path of a time wind, and still you'll be swept to an unimaginable future. What you mean is, the persuasive, and hallucinogenic ways of the manchanged have rid you of apprehension; no, not even that. It's made you accept that things are the way they are, that nothing will change, and you might as well go timeswimming with a smile on your face. I think that about sums it up.'

Irritated at the tone in Ensavlion's voice Faulcon said, as coldly as possible, 'I think you're right, yes, that sums it up. Why the sarcasm, Commander? The approach a little too simplistic for you?'

Ensavlion prodded the leather amulet in Faulcon's grip, his glassy eyes meeting Faulcon's and doing their best to communicate reasonableness from mask to mask. 'Simple or complex, who the hell cares? All I wonder about is a man who professes such acceptance of the inevitable, such control over circumstance, who stands fondling the one thing that promises to trip him butt over elbow the moment he takes a step. Throw the damned thing away. Don't you think it's been a weight about your neck for long enough? Throw it away, you fool, now, quick ... quick!'

And Faulcon, his heart racing, drew back his arm and pitched the amulet out into space, watching the leather thong twisting behind as it plummeted out of sight and clattered off a ledge, somewhere below.

Faulcon returned to Steel City on his byke, following the towering form of Ensavlion's r-suit. He reported to his section to terminate officially his unofficial official leave, and waited a few minutes in the lounge, aware that the silence in the place was the silence of embarrassment. He remembered the mistake he had made in the plateau township, the belief he had that he was regarded with hostility, a stranger, a threat to them. So he walked to one of the older Section men, who sprawled in an easy chair reading a news sheet. He acknowledged the man who looked up at him without a flicker of a smile and said, before Faulcon could initiate a conversation, 'Get lost, Faulcon. And I mean lost.'

'In my own good time,' said Faulcon stiffly, feeling the flush rise to his cheeks. Around the room others, men and women both, had looked towards him, their faces pale and angry. The man he had addressed said, 'We lost young Cal Reza to a wind because of you. The sooner you go the better. There's not a rifter in this room can walk safe while you're alive. If I had my way, you gutless wonder, I'd kick you over the canyon myself.'

A man whom Faulcon only vaguely recognized said, 'You made an agreement, Faulcon … your integrity is on the line; you're betraying your very humanness!'

'Do it, for God's sake, Leo,' said a woman behind him. Faulcon felt instantly cold as he turned to face Immuk. She came into the lounge area and sat down heavily in an easy chair, spreading her legs and gazing up at him coldly.

'Do you think I don't intend to?' he asked.

She said, 'I don't give a damn what you intend to do, just do it. The sight of your face makes me want to throw up. I'll like you a whole lot better when you're dead.' She grimaced in disgust. 'You're such an appalling coward. You'll end up with your neck being broken and your body being thrown over the edge, and I shan't shed a tear for you, not one single tear.'

'It frightens me to hear you talk like that. It makes me realize how much this world has got into our blood, has changed us.'

Someone sniggered and Faulcon felt his face flush. Immuk said, 'That's fine, Leo – you didn't think that way before, a few months ago when you helped escort Opuna Indullis down to the valley. But when it's you who has to show the colour of his courage, oh it's a different matter then. It suddenly seems so reasonable to remember that we have peculiar rules, peculiar rituals, and to invoke them as a sign of our madness. You make me bloody sick!'

Before Faulcon could retort, two section wardens appeared from the other end of the lounge. Faulcon turned away at the sight of their yellow uniforms, unwilling to make a scene, or be the cause of one. As he walked towards the door he was aware of the two men running quickly after him. He had hardly decided to turn before he was pushed hard in the back, and flung heavily against the wall, a hand on the back of his head making sure that his nose was blooded painfully before he was kicked twice in the groin and unceremoniously bowled out of the lounge, into the public way.

'See you in hell, Leo,' was the last voice he heard, Immuk's voice, followed by her cruel laugh and the thud of the door sliding back into place.

He brushed himself off and limped to a san-closet to attend to the blood that was gushing from his nose. When the flow was staunched, and he had sealed the small gash in the membrane that had split, he went to his room, changed his clothes, and then made his way to Ensavlion's office.

Gulio Ensavlion was expecting him.

'Can you blame them?' he asked, after Faulcon had briefly described the attack. 'A rifter called Cal Reza was swept away by a time wind because of you, and these things escalate, as you well know.'

'Cal Reza was caught because he was careless,' said Faulcon bitterly, touching his nose tenderly. 'He *must* have been careless. I'm beginning to despise all this "lucky" crap.'

Ensavlion laughed. 'That's why the scene this morning with the amulet. Oh sure, Leo, you've seen the error of Steel City ways, sure you have.'

'Damn it all, why this hostility from everyone? I've made clear my intention to fulfil the agreement of my contract. I'm going to do it, but why should I be pressured?'

Ensavlion was cold and pragmatic. 'Because you're a coward. Oh, you may realize that you're not, but your section doesn't. Your team mates were swept away, and the correct thing to have done would have been to impart luck in a long and generous good-bye, and within a two-day to go down to the valley and wait. If you'd done that you'd have had every man and woman of the section down there with you, waiting with you, making sure that your last days and weeks in the valley were spent with the best of friends. But no, you had to run, up into the hills. And two days ago Cal Reza died in a squall, and that was because of you, and so is it any wonder that your section would like to string your guts across the canyon from one edge to the other?'

Faulcon brooded silently for a moment or two, staring at the huge maps of the world, letting his gaze flicker uninterestedly from picture to map to screen and at length down to his spread hands, resting lightly on his thighs. 'It's so bloody stupid,' he said, trying to forget the two occasions when he had participated in, and insisted upon, this exact same rule of life, the compulsory death of one man and one woman after circumstances not dissimilar to those that had now made his own 'suicide' imperative. He knew, and he repeatedly told himself, that there was no hesitation or doubt in his own mind that he would perform the act of willing self-destruction; but this need

to be hurried, this denial of a man's right to pick his moment and place ...
this began to anger him. It especially angered him that he should be held
responsible for a young rifter's death, or loss, by carelessness.

He repeated this to Ensavlion, who shook his head and then banged his
desk with a flat hand and almost shouted at the resentful form of his junior.
'Cal Reza went out into the valley thinking of you, thinking of bad luck, the
bad luck that you had become. In other words he went out there with death
on his mind, with his survival attitudes blurred; you know how it is, you've
been around long enough. Reza was vulnerable, and a man is always ten
times as vulnerable as he thinks he is.'

Grimly, angrily, Faulcon accepted the reprimand, accepted the point. He
felt an unaccustomed stubbornness jostling to remain the prime motivator
of his behaviour, but gradually, breathing deeply and trying to rid himself of
the sense of hurt and disloyalty he had received from his one-time friends, he
came to experience a pleasant calm, a lingering moment of resignation. His
willingness to face the time winds was reinforced, and the prospect seemed
almost unworrying again ... and exciting: the chance to find Lena and Kris,
the chance for life beyond what appeared to be the dark wind of death.

Ensavlion seemed to observe the relaxation, for he too relaxed, toying
with a small alien artifact that he used as a paperweight. 'Is there any reason,
any reason at all, why you can't go out to the valley now, and sit there and
wait for a time wind?'

There was, but Faulcon found his mind choking on the idea of telling
Ensavlion.

'I'm waiting,' Ensavlion persisted, an edge of irritation showing in his
voice. Faulcon refused to meet his gaze. There was perspiration on the Commander's face again, the sign of his growing tension. 'Any reason, Leo, any
reason at all? If there is I want to hear it.'

Abruptly, tearing his gaze away from the corner of the room, Faulcon
decided to be straight with his Commanding Officer. 'One reason,' he said. 'I
want to see Lena before I go. I think she'll be expecting me.'

Ensavlion frowned, staring at Faulcon. The paperweight turned faster in
his fingers, the harsh room-lights reflecting sporadically from the uneven
surface. 'Lena? I don't understand what you mean.'

'The phantom,' said Faulcon stiffly. 'It's Lena. She survived the sweep of
Othertime, so can I. I'm going to minimize the risks by talking to her first.'

'The phantom is different things to different men. You know that.' But
Ensavlion was deeply curious, almost shaking with excitement.

'Do I? Kris saw the phantom that night he went out alone. I thought he'd
seen me, from the elusive way he behaved afterwards, but it was Lena. It must
have been Lena.'

'You don't know that. The way I read it, Kris saw a phantom that reassured him about his brother Mark's survival. He saw someone who made it clear to him that beyond the time winds was life, survival … and Mark.'

Fleetingly, Faulcon remembered that flickering, devastating wave-front, the tiny, sprawled form of Kris Dojaan vanishing in an instant. He wondered where Kris had gone, and whether, moments later, he had struggled to his feet in an alien land: and he wondered what he had seen there.

To Ensavlion he said, 'Then maybe there are many phantoms. Maybe you're right. But I saw Lena. I saw her as close to me as you are to me now. And the young Lena saw her old self, and fell into the wind because of it. Don't even think of that, about its implications. There's something more than coincidence working here, Commander. It's just too easy to see the phantom, and recently it's been too easy to come *closer* to a phantom who turns out to be someone known to you.'

'The travellers, you mean; playing games with us.'

'Or something.' Faulcon couldn't control the hint of a smile that he felt touch his lips; Ensavlion was in deadly earnest, his eyes bright, his body tense with expectation. 'I keep asking myself what the hell was Kris up to? What was it about our encounter by the ocean that made him so secretive – or did he really not know he'd gone into the machine? He claimed to have had contact with Mark *after* Mark had been lost, but he never talked about any communication with Mark after he arrived here looking for the man. Games may be right, Commander – but Kris's games? Mark's games? Or something else's, something using the wind, hiding behind its destructive front. Maybe there's a whole world of time travelling beyond the wall of present.'

'Of course there is; I *know* there is.'

'Yes, but we also know the time winds can kill; perhaps they kill 90 per cent of the time. Perhaps someone, or something, only wants a *few* people to pass through them.' He leaned back, watching Ensavlion, but seeing only the valley. 'That's why I want to encounter the phantom before I go – I don't know what it is, what it means, but it means *something*. I'm sure of that. I want a head start on everyone else who gets sucked into the void. That makes sense, doesn't it?'

'Very good sense indeed,' said Ensavlion. He stood up behind his desk and walked round to lean against the front edge of the table, close to Faulcon, folding his arms across his chest. 'And I suppose you'll want to be alone when you try and see her?'

Faulcon concurred. 'She'll not wait around while anyone else approaches. Why?'

Ensavlion said, 'Because whether you like it or not, you're part of the Catchwind Mission now. When you go into the valley, I'm going with you. Talk to the phantom – to Lena – all you want; but when the wind comes to take you, you're going to have company.'

Faulcon rose from his chair and faced Ensavlion. He felt confused. He had been afraid of the prospect of his solitary trip for so long that for a moment or two he could not adjust to the idea of his 'ritual death' becoming a part of a larger mission. Then pleasure, and security, and the warmth of excitement washed through him, making him smile, making him relax. Trying not to let too much relief show through, he said, 'I can't think of any better news I've had in months. Commander, we're going to take time apart at the seams.'

Ensavlion grinned. 'And we're going to be the second to do that. But we're not going to come back like the phantom, aged and withered. We're going to breach time, explore time, and we're going to walk up to Steel City afterwards and tell them a story that will blow their cosy world apart.'

CHAPTER SIXTEEN

And yet, the strength of his resolve to commit himself, body and soul, to the time winds was still a strength tempered by doubt, by the nagging voice of fear. The unexpected and welcome excitement of his visit to Ensavlion, the thrill of realizing that he would be a part of an expeditionary force into Othertime, soon passed away. It did not upset him that he could react so positively to the idea of a burden shared, for this is indeed what had occurred to him: that what happened to him in Othertime would happen to someone else as well; that the pleasure or agony of the exploration would be received in company, and not in solitary. Solitariness was the wall around his life that he feared to contemplate, the hell within his soul. The manchanged had significantly affected his attitude to aloneness, had reduced his isolation by making him accept it, rather than resist it. But the shadowy spectre of the Timelost chilled him, for he identified with the terrifying loneliness of men lost a billion years from their own kind. With Ensavlion, no matter what happened, no matter where he was flung, he would have the companionship of another soul. This made the prospect bearable; it did not alleviate the apprehension.

In a most impressive and determined fashion, Commander Ensavlion immediately set about arranging for the first, and most definite, plunge into the mysterious winds from Othertime. He told Faulcon to leave all the preparations to him, and to get out to the rift and seek out Lena. When he came back his r-suit would be fully provisioned, serviced and ready to go. Faulcon agreed to this and made his way from Steel City by byke, taking only enough supplies of food and water for two days. He made straight for the Riftwatch

Station close to which, just days ago, he had seen the phantom for the first time at close quarters.

The valley was changed now; where it curved through sixty degrees, its wind-scoured bluffs and crags rising to obscure vision from the long, straight tract that reached towards the north-eastern horizon, here there was now an immense gate of dull metal and dark patterning; although it did not span the rift completely, it rose hundreds of feet above the dying vegetation that here, and in its own time, covered the valley floor. It was built into the rocks of the south wall, but sheered and broken a good way from the north; like the rising immensity of a dam, this gate watched him through the eyes of its doors, and the sparkling profusion of its tiny, circular windows.

Faulcon watched this bridge with interest. During the first day of his vigil on the rim of the canyon he saw movement in the body of the wall, the swift passage of some shape behind one of the open doorways. He rose from where he had been sitting and ran along the cliff top to where the span of the gate stretched away from him, and here he could see how wide was that wall, the width of a major roadway, and peppered with shafts and vents and small cylindrical structures. Braving the physical wind that blew strong and dangerous in the middle of the valley, Faulcon walked out across the gate, peering down into the gloomy interior of the structure, calling and shouting for Lena, and listening in vain for the hollow echo of his voice as it was sucked down into the alien place and lost. He returned to the edge of the valley and passed the night, frozen and uncomfortable, beneath the stars. Rift Station Shibano was close at hand, but he was apprehensive of asking for shelter; he was afraid of them refusing him.

He passed the second day in like fashion, walking slowly along the valley, riding to different access points, noticing, where he could, the new routes down that had formed since the last wind. For the most part he crouched within the span of the canyon, a few hundred yards from the cliff top, but close enough to the outer world to reach safety if a wind blew up. He had given up calling for Lena. He willed her to appear, but the canyon moved only with the dark shapes of rift suits, and the cumbersome and bored exploration by robots.

With two hours to go before the red twilight settled into black night he returned to his byke and, almost overwhelmed by his bitter disappointment, he rode back to Steel City. He ascended the access ramp into the towering, star-lit shape, and for a moment thought he must have approached the wrong entrance, for the door-seal failed to respond to his identity. He backed off a few yards and saw that he was in the right place. The sheer, curving wall of the traverse unit was a grey, monotonous surface above him, he a small, dark shape on the wide ramp, calling to be allowed inside.

The door remained closed.

He contacted the Watch on his mask speaker. He heard sour laughter, an obscenity, a curt instruction to get away to hell, and he knew that his disobedience of the unwritten rules of Steel City had reached to all corners of the installation. He was an outcast, now, and at the mercy of the world. He could not reach Ensavlion, although he tried, and his request to be put in touch with the man was greeted by a mechanical noise with a crude connotation. He was dirt in the eyes of the men of the Watch. Dirt was given no favours.

Resigned to his fate, and to a second night beneath Kamelios's brilliant spread of stars, he rode away from the City. Minutes later, as he debated where he should sleep for maximum comfort, he remembered the ruined Riftwatch Station, Eekhaut, and made his way there.

Station Eekhaut had been built too close to the edge of the valley. It had been constructed in the early days when the men who explored Vander-Zande's World still argued about how the geological structure of the world could be changed and bastardized by the phenomenon of time flux. They watched stratification and igneous insertion dancing hysterically before their eyes, and somehow it made no sense when considered against the might and axiom of Universal laws of conservation. It happened, though, and if Riftwatch Station Eekhaut had been built with an egocentric denial of the wind's true power, it had rapidly been taught the lesson of its lifetime; a gusting squall had ripped it in half, taking men and women with it, leaving the half-shell with the edge of metal as clean and smooth as if it had been machined; later, the valley edge had reappeared, three hundred yards of it, but the remains of the Station had not been a part of the refashioning.

Faulcon parked his byke in the shelter of the jutting dome; he walked through the gaping mouth, into what remained of the operations room, and found the doorway into the small sleeping quarters. He used the light from his byke, and with the door closed behind him, could fill the room with atmosphere from the still functioning air-supplies. He would not take the chance of failure while he was sleeping, but while awake, and sprawled on the floor, he took off his mask and enjoyed the smell of nearly natural air, just a certain staleness, the traces of animal life that had prowled here, reminding him that this was not home. It was all a part of taking risks, this breathing naturally, all part of putting survival in its place. He found his mind occupied with thoughts of survival, of the maintenance of the bodily status quo. He realized that his whole resistance to the rule of the rifters was a part of his enormous survival mechanism, his instinctive denial of the intellectual readiness to commit a self-sacrifice. And as he thought about this, as he allowed his mind to play with the words and images of the past days and weeks – even years – so he calmed in body and mind, found his own space and drifted. He was hidden here, tucked away from human eye, a man alone, and yet without having lost that recent gesture of friendship and support from Gulio Ensavlion. Faulcon was glad of this solitude, glad of the chance to let his mental defences down, and to look inside himself to see how he really was ...

Afraid; truly afraid. Great. He was glad to meet his fear, to shake its hand, to let it wash through him. He liked the way his stomach churned, and the beat of his heart increased its pace. He acknowledged the residuum of his terror, and his unwillingness to die; he enjoyed acknowledging the coward-ice in him.

Then there was his integrity, and his determination to live honourably. He had made the agreement when he had first come to VanderZande's World. He had thought it nonsensical at the time, agreeing that if his team mates died he would die too. But who ever considers the possibility of being forced by principle into suicide? He had been unable to envisage the necessity of his voluntary death, and the agreement had been easy to make, along with all the others. (And, of course, they had never talked in terms of 'death', but of 'going into the wind'.) Now that fulfilling the terms of that agreement was a harsh reality staring him in the face, he resolved to honour it; he hated and resented those who had questioned his honour. He accepted both the questioning, and his resentment. He accepted that his fear had certainly made him pull the punch; there was right and wrong on both sides. Acknowledging this was a relief, and the pain of the last two days went slowly away.

But what would not go away were the words that he remembered from a time talking to Kris Dojaan; the youngster had brought to VanderZande's World a healthy excitement, a welcome expression of awe, and a nicely restrained cynicism for some of the wilder aspects of local life. Faulcon recol-lected only too clearly Kris's amazement when he had been told of the rule of suicide: 'But it's unhuman; it's stupid!'

'It's an inhuman world, Kris. It's a hard world and it makes hard rules.'

'I didn't say *in*human. I said *un*human. It doesn't sit right on man. It's wrong for man.'

And Faulcon felt a moment's wry amusement as he remembered how that conversation had continued, how he had said to Kris that the whole world was wrong; it was a world of constant change and it changed man along with it. If you spent long here your body and mind became twisted and torn until sometimes you'd be walking when you were sitting and awake when you were asleep. Unless you fought it, that is, like they'd all fought it, resisting it, resisting until sometimes you would want to scream.

How had that conversation ended? Maddeningly, Faulcon realized that intoxication had made the exchange less of a conversation, more of a passing splutter of words. Why had that brief exchange insinuated itself into his awareness now? Was he trying to tell himself something? Faulcon grinned at that and sat up on the floor, stretching forward to test the stiffness of his back. He had been lying down for some minutes, and the floor was cold and hard. He was amused because all mental conversation was meaningful. It was too easy to dismiss that scattered memory, or imagery, or wordery that drifted through the waking mind as being mere day-dream indulgence. The fact was that internal conversations were often pointers towards important resolutions. And Faulcon knew that something about the valley, and the nature of Othertime, was disturbing him; it was not his fear; his fear was symptomatic of the uncertainty he felt, the feeling that he was committing himself improperly to the unknown, when in fact he should attack Othertime with considerably more foresight.

There had been another time when the word humanness had been brought up in angry dialogue; it had been those two days ago when he had gone to the lounge and had been attacked by his section colleagues. 'You made an agreement, Faulcon … your integrity is on the line; you're betraying your very humanness.'

Integrity maketh the man, he thought. I know that; I know the extent to which I can experience shame, and guilt, when I break an agreement, when I let my selfishness grow larger than my integrity, my basic humanness. *Opposite view*: for God's sake, what's more important, life or integrity? Certainly history is replete with suicide-warriors, and altruism of the highest order, the noble sacrifice for the greater cause, so what? What greater cause is served by my death now? This rule is based on fear; a man who dies to save his platoon advances a cause, the cause of more lives saved for the cost of one. The rule of suicide on VanderZande's World is a part of the luck/bad-luck obsession, the appeasement of something we have anthropomorphized: Old Lady Wind. Kris was right, it *is* stupid, a stupid rule, a senseless rule, but a rule that has now taken a grip upon us. Men *can* die if the rule is broken, because they are obsessed with the unfairness of a man like me who apparently flaunts the code of behaviour. It's called distraction, and distraction kills when the world is as unpredictably hostile as this one. But Kris was *right*. How simple to see the madness of suicide under these conditions; how hard to have seen it before. All that's keeping me determined to attack Old Lady Wind is my integrity; this is what's on trial here, my decency, my honour, my willingness to self-destruct for no other reason than that I have agreed that I would do so.

It was cold in the station, and he climbed to his feet, stretching his limbs to try and shiver some heat into his cooling flesh. He strapped his mask on and stepped out into the windy night. Movement was the best defence against cold, even though the night temperature was dropping rapidly towards a few degrees above freezing. As he walked towards the valley he noticed that all the moons were high; Merlin was full, and with Kytara, its twin, formed a strange, fascinating structure in the night sky, a double lens watching the world.

He kept well clear of the edge of the cliffs, for despite the glow of the moons, and the Galactic Centre, he found it difficult to judge the precipitous lip of the valley. As he walked he relived moments up on the plateau, in Hunderag Country: the warmth of the fire, and of his hosts, especially Allissia. He remembered something she had said to him: you can work out reasons for anything, it's the human facility. Reasonableness can kill you quicker than anything. Reason is a liar.

Is that what he was doing now? Reasoning why it was good to be a coward, to break his word? Using reason to ease his conscience?

He remembered something else that the manchanged had said to him, that the quickest way to self-destruction was by resisting the basic nature of humanness. They had said that resistance in any form was an active statement for a point of view, and that if the opposite point of view showed up, then such a man would be trapped by it. Inevitability and acceptance allowed for freedom, for an escape from being manipulated whether by powerful men or circumstances.

He had become convinced that to simply accept what had to be was the best way to experience it, to live it, and to live through it; all his 'reasoning' was a form of resistance, and was a certain pointer to the inevitable failure of Leo Faulcon to survive the time winds.

The sudden thought of the winds from time made him stop, listen keenly to the high howling of air currents above the canyon, and the distant moan of wind as it blew and gusted between the eroded pinnacles of rock, and through the deep, winding gullies that riddled the lower valley walls.

He could not escape the fact that everything he thought and did was connected with his death, with his willing sacrifice of life to wind. That thought grew larger, twisted all about, seemed to come back at him again and again. Was it right that a man should be obsessed with his death when his death was all that tomorrow could promise? Of course it was. More reason, he said, more bloody reasonableness. A man alive should be concerned with life, not death. He could think of death after the event, when it didn't matter anyway. But that, he acknowledged, was not the human way. It might have been the way of the manchanged, but they were educated in the art of calm acceptance. To them both future and past were functions of the present; all were records, memories; past memories were true memories, whereas future memories were flexible, changeable, all draining gradually towards the tight neck of time where the bubble of the present moment existed, declaring some records true, and most records fantasy, showing the way things were, no matter how things had been hoped for. And once something had occurred it was unchangeable, and therefore unremarkable. This was the manchanged, and Faulcon knew it was the true state of human-kind; but millions of years of intellect and concern had masked the deeper intuitive faculties, allowed man no space to breathe, save when he was discontent.

Death. Integrity. Discovery. Three factors in the complex equation that was Leo Faulcon, three factors that were not in balance, that did not add up, three factors that he thought about, and worried at, and as he attacked them so it seemed to him that he was watched; and that the watchers were testing him; and that he was a game to them, and this made him angry, very angry.

He turned around, staring into the darkness, looking up to the stars, then down to the vague patterns of light on metal that told of starlight on ruins. The wide chasm of dark before him was no invitation to him, was a sinister hidey hole for those to whom Leo Faulcon was a one man show, the raw meat of his existence on the table, prodded and dissected by inquisitive, alien minds.

He started to shake. Never in all his months on Kamelios had he felt the presence of the alien so strong, so close. He ran through the darkness and stumbled on a rock, jarring his toe painfully and sitting up, clutching his foot while he stared, wide-eyed, terrified, into the gloom. It was all about him, engulfing him, spreading dark limbs around his shivering body, drawing him into its maw. He rose to his feet, crying out as pain shot through his toe, and began to run back towards the starlit shape of the Station. The alien presence followed him, riding the air about him, moving effortlessly as he weaved and dodged, as if it rode upon his back and watched across his shoulders.

Abruptly he stopped. His heart was thundering and the blood in his temples was surging so hard, so fast, that his whole skull felt as if it would burst. His vision was bright, swirling, the stars moving through the sky in impossible patterns, the ground about him rippling and twisting, a carpet of living tissue. *This is madness. I'm generating all of this. There is nothing here at all.*

He dropped to a crouch and looked out towards the windswept canyon. He could see a ridged bluff of rock rising above the rim, and something shone steadily from a point half-way down the towering shape. The light, he knew, was just moonlight on a sheet of polished metal, a piece of wreckage cast onto the wall of the valley and waiting for the tide to whisk it away again. The claustrophobic presence of something alien had dissipated slightly; it seemed to him that he was watched from afar, again; that eyes were on him from within the canyon, peering over the sheer wall, shuffling restlessly as if waiting for his next move. He could hear its breathing, the noisy rhythmic flow of wind from east to west and back again, surging through the gullies and channels of the valley, whistling through the lung spaces between the crags and bluffs of time-scarred granite.

They are there, he thought. *This is not in my mind, not in my battered human psyche. They are really here, and they are watching me …*

Out of eye-shot, somewhere in the depths of the canyon, a light glowed golden for a few seconds; he saw the brightness in the air above the valley, as if a match had been struck and flared up, before slowly dying again and leaving the place in gloomy darkness.

A night creature called its message through the black, a throaty gargling sound followed by a high-pitched clicking. From across the valley came an answering call, and Faulcon let his gaze follow the sound of wings beating hard as something launched itself towards its mate. He listened to the night sounds for about an hour, wondering if he had imagined the sudden flash of light, wondering if it would return, wondering what it had brought to the valley, what it had left below the rim.

The movement caught him by surprise. He had been staring straight ahead, half expecting something to appear before him. A human shape started through the moonlight to his left, dropped to a crouch so that he finally saw it only by the sheen of light on its mask. .

'Lena?' he called gently, but was answered by the darting motion of the figure away from him, towards the valley's edge. He ran after her, picking his way carefully, straining to see a path, a safe place to step. He was belly flat and peering down the slope of the canyon before he knew it, and the phantom was some way below him, still moving away. Resigned to the danger he wormed over the edge and let his body slip and slide down until, some hundred yards or so away from the safety of the land above he came to a level ridge, and here he rested so that he might catch his breath.

I mustn't lose her!

Movement below him again and his heart fluttered; was she leading him down to the very bottom of the canyon? *I'll not be tricked. I'm going to stay right here.*

Tricked by whom, and to what ends, he wondered idly, as minutes passed and his body began to shake with cold. He *was* afraid of being tricked, and the thought of being tricked brought images of Kris Dojaan to mind. Never unwilling to entertain his idle thoughts in serious discussion, he asked himself, quite consciously, was Kris Dojaan tricked? Is that what I think?

He had no answers for himself, but was curious at the way he had first thought of himself as being on show, then had distinctly felt the presence of some alien awareness – perhaps nothing more than the closeness of Lena to him, before she gave herself away – and now started to think in terms of tricks, and games ...

Movement; a rock dislodged and clattering for a few yards until its further downward progress was across a scrubby carpet of vegetation.

Again he called, 'Lena? Are you there?' And this time he was answered by the frail voice of the phantom, 'Hello, Leo. Aren't you cold?'

'Not now. I'm burning up. Where are you?'

'On the ledge. In front of you.' He looked hard. There she was, crouched and hunched, watching him. He made no move to get closer; instinctively he wanted to hold her, to hug her, but the image of her whiskery, wrinkled face was hard and grim in his mind. The Lena he wanted back was *his* Lena; that she would ultimately end in the valley, chasing her young lover, was not as important to him as finding her and sharing time with her, time when she was young, time before whatever tragedy would bring her back to the valley as the wizened object of man's curiosity.

'Are they here?' he asked. Lena said nothing. Faulcon imagined she had not understood his question. 'The aliens, the creatures that ride up and down time, watching us. Are they here? Our gaolers, our monitors, our guardians? I saw their machine, the golden colour of it, anyway. Are they here, Lena? Watching us now?'

There was a wind-disturbed silence for a moment, and Faulcon, his gaze somewhere out across the dark void, frowned, and turned back to the vaguely defined form of the phantom. Before he could speak again, or repeat what he had said, Lena's voice whispered, 'But you *know* they're here. Didn't you feel them just a while back? Why ask me about what you already know? They're always here, they always have been. The question is, why?'

'The question is why,' he repeated. 'That's a good question, Lena. But I don't have an answer, so perhaps, would you mind ... could you answer that one yourself?'

'Can I ever answer anything you can't answer?'

Faulcon laughed, feeling a sudden intrusive chill through his clothing. 'Not if you're a function of me, no. I had wondered about that. I'd wondered about the phantom, a figure that's always one of those enigmatic features of the landscape; so familiar in one respect that the wrongness tended to get overlooked. Everyone knows that the phantom changes; no one ever really bothered to try and link a healthy, rational, human nuts-and-bolts explanation to it.'

'Does it need an explanation, Leo?'

'No, not really, not after a while.' Faulcon huddled down on the ledge, arms round his legs, chin resting on knees, eyes sad, yet resigned to what he felt, intuitively, was not a real encounter at all. 'Kris was convinced you were his brother; I thought you were Kris; later you became Lena, and Lena saw herself in you at the same time as I saw Lena in you. We see what we want to see, or what our minds want to see. Isn't that right? There might be hundreds of phantoms in fact, but it's strange how no two ever show up at the same time. You're a sort of mind's eye symbol, a deep-rooted image. Something archaic, archetypal ... the dead returned, the lost returned.'

'Don't you find that interesting?'

'I don't understand how the mind works, Lena.' He looked at her, and he felt moved to tears, and moved to shout. He felt angry. He had wanted denial;

he had wanted reassurance; he had wanted evidence of her tangibility, of her realness; he had wanted to know that time was controllable; that somewhere she still lived, young, alive, passionate, waiting for him to reach her. 'You're not real.'

'What is real? How do you assess realness?'

'Measurability,' he said without pause, 'I can see you, but that's not measuring. You're not physical; only physicalness can be measured.'

'Aren't dreams real?'

'The fact of the dream, yes, the electrical activity; the events of the dream – the Lena factor – no, that's not real.'

'How do you measure physicalness, Leo?'

'With instruments. Physicalness cannot be denied; physicalness is reality.'

Her voice was a mocking whisper in his head, a tiresome distraction from his growing mood of depression and anxiety. 'How do you measure the instruments, Leo? How can you measure real if you need to assume reality to measure it? Reality is what you see, Leo. There is only one realness, and that is what your mind tells you is real; there is a consensus, a general acceptance, that realness shared on a large scale is more real than realness observed alone. Don't question my realness, Leo, when nothing is real or unreal except inside your head. Don't you know that everything that happens to you is generated by you, everything you hear someone say is said by you, everything you see someone do is imagined by you –' *Audwyn's calm, insistent tone of voice! He recognized the shape of the words, even though they came in the frail voice of the phantom.* '– What does it matter if there *was* a state of existence in which an unconnected life-form actually altered the air, and made sound waves that communicated a word to you. If it doesn't happen in your head it doesn't happen. So whether or not I'm real, everything about me is you, and if there's one person in the Universe you should listen to, it's the ego-tripper inside your own skull.'

Faulcon couldn't help smiling as he realized, abruptly, that he was recalling the words of his training supervisor, years back, when his whole attitude to perception and belief had been run through a mill of simple paradox, naïve logic and gradual argument, leaving him sometimes breathless, sometimes sceptical, sometimes angry, slowly more aware of how little he had actually *thought* about the nature of his own existence. The insights gained had rapidly fled; the human mind was too rigidly evolved to be changed by education, by the words of the great thinkers of ages and cultures going back to the beginning of Man; only over generations, only by social conditioning over hundreds of years, could the mind be made to expand, or contract, and to see round the corners of logic and reality, and thus travel outwards from its existentialist base.

'Are you alive?' he said finally, quietly, and the phantom answered, 'I live.'

Faulcon looked at her. 'Can I ever get to Lena, to the Lena I knew?'

'Of course not. The past can never be recaptured. The Lena you knew was gone from you the instant she was gone.'

'I meant', Faulcon insisted patiently, 'the Lena who is young, not the Lena who is old. Can I ever get to her, get her back?'

The phantom made a sound that in the darkness Faulcon could not identify ... laughter? Sadness? He wasn't sure. She said, 'I was lost; I was alone; I grew old; the years; the aloneness; I grew old, then older; soon I will die; I was lost; I was lost. What is it you want, Leo? Do you want to wind me back, to reverse me like a car? Do you want to push me against the flow of time and watch the wrinkles fall away, and my breasts become firm again, and my legs lean and hard, and everything you liked about me reappear? Or do you imagine that there are millions of Lenas, all at different ages, from birth to death, and somehow you can walk into a room and pluck down the one you like, dust her off, put some clothes on her and take up where you left off? What is it you want, Leo? What is it you want to *do*?'

'I want Lena. I want the young and lovely girl who a few days ago was snatched from me, and who therefore is just a few days older than she was and can surely come back to me as young and lovely as she was.'

'But I'm not young and lovely, Leo. I'm old, withered. Time has passed Lena by. Not your time, but her time. What makes you think that her time and your time are the same time? Where's the book of rules?'

'Oh God,' Faulcon let his head fall forward, let a tear form in his eyes. 'You're a figment of my mind. So why am I even talking to you?'

The phantom laughed. 'I reflect your confusion. I reflect your desperation to understand something, the winds ... the time winds, the nature of time on VanderZande's World itself. You approach the study of time from a point of view that says: I don't have a clue about anything. That's not a good way to study anything, Leo. You have already decided that you are generating me, and that assumption has no room for the possibility of Lena actually existing and contributing to that generative imagery. You're so trapped in your neural pathways that whether or not you like it you are resisting the world that is trying to show you something. Have you thought of that?'

Faulcon looked up, wiped his hand across his eyes and started with surprise when his gloves hit his protective eyewear. 'Okay, answer me this. What are the time winds?'

The phantom laughed again. 'That's the wrong question, Leo. That's not the question at all.'

'It's the question I came to Kamelios to help to answer. How can it be the wrong question?'

'It's the wrong question. Try again.'

He said, 'How do the time winds get generated?'

The sound of the phantom's humour, so reminiscent of her younger laughter, made Faulcon's stomach knot. 'That's still the wrong question; what, how, why, what the hell does any of that matter, Leo?'

'I was about to ask *why* the time winds blow. I was about to get some motive into my questions. I thought you might find that more acceptable.'

'Wrong question, Leo. Always the wrong question.'

Exasperated, Faulcon shouted at her, 'What question, then? For God's sake don't play games with me. What question should I be asking? Tell me!'

The phantom, he thought, had moved away a little, slipped out of what meagre view he had. At once he called, 'Don't go. Please don't go.'

'I'm not going. How can I go when I was never here?'

'I don't know what to do, Lena. I have to go to the winds. I have to, but I want to know ... I want to know what to expect, how to handle them. I want to know how to survive them, how to find you.'

'Poor Leo, can't ever let go. Can't ever let go. Didn't Allissia teach you anything?'

Faulcon was stunned. How could the phantom, Lena, how could she have known what he had done up on the plateau ... he rose to his feet, staring at the crouched shape along the ledge. He felt cold, almost desperate. So she *was* a projection from his mind; she was not real at all. He had clung to the faint hope that she might have been ...

The phantom said, 'I can hear the clockwork, Leo. All that reasoning, all that explanation. She said that, so she must be this. She did that which means this is true, therefore that, therefore this, therefore that, therefore this. Give it up, Leo. Get rid of it. I'm old, old, old. I've had time to be everywhere, every-when. I know all, Leo. And I know nothing. Every reason you come up with I can come up with a counter-reason. Reason is a liar. Natural knowing is all there is; natural knowing is the only truth.'

Faulcon shivered and dropped to a crouch again to try to conserve his body warmth. He teetered a moment on the ledge, and felt a passing panic as he thought he was slipping; his eyes flickered out into the darkness, down to where the fiercest part of the time winds blew, and he thought of the next wind that would come, and of how he would be there, with Ensavlion, petrified, yet determined, and he would flicker in and out of objective vision, and then be gone. And people would wonder where he had gone to, to what age, what vast future, what bleak past.

'Nothing helps,' he said quietly, almost self-pityingly. 'The next wind that sweeps through the valley is my Charon, taking my soul; it will sweep me to hell and I shall have to go. I don't want to go, but I have no choice. I *have* to go into time, and I desperately want to know what to expect. My God, Lena, I feel like I'm being tested, torn every which-way. Surely there's no reason for you not to tell me whether I can survive or not, whether it's death I face, or a new life?'

'If it's a test, Leo, surely it would be cheating to tell you that?'

'But a test for what? What the hell do the time winds mean to man, Lena—?'

'*That's* the question, Leo.' She laughed delightedly, and moved away. 'Or at least, it's part of it.' Faulcon rose and walked towards her, but already she was darting through the darkness, down the slope, towards the sheer drop that he knew was below Station Eekhaut. Through the blackness her imagined voice came once more. 'Never mind me, and what I am or represent. Think about Mark Dojaan, *think* about him for once in your life. Don't keep blocking him out. Think about a man who was so *different* to two people who were so close to him. Think about the sense of that, and then do what you need to do, and do it *alive*.'

He called her name through the bluster of the night; over and over he called for her, but she was gone. Slowly, and sadly, he made his way back up the valley wall and into the cool shelter of the ruined Station.

At first break of dawn he rode back to the city, determined to gain access and to stand no nonsense from the entry Watch.

CHAPTER SEVENTEEN

Three hours later, Faulcon was uncomfortably seated in a small studio room, at the edge of the vast area of the records-unit; on a wide, curved screen before him there was a coloured picture of a sprawling farmhouse, built on the side of a hill. It overlooked a rich, cultivated valley, its crop well lit by the double yellow sun that was sinking towards the horizon of the world, Oster's Fall. Faulcon stared at the scene, trying to imagine the young Mark Dojaan running from house to barn, and then down the winding trackway that led to a low, rickety-looking fence demarking the area of cultivation. In his head a machine voice whispered facts about the farm. It was of little interest to Faulcon and he reached out to change the image on the screen; the words ceased, then began again as a new picture appeared.

Faulcon's knuckles stung as he straightened his fingers. He had not bothered to dress the grazes and cuts in his skin. The jagged wound across his palm had opened up again as well, and he had tied a white cloth about the gash. On the screen a picture of the Dojaans' parents had appeared, young people in brightly coloured clothes; they were standing at a gate, against a backdrop of strangely stunted trees; two boys swung on the gate, one taller, fairer than the other; both smiled broadly towards the camera.

Behind Faulcon the door of the studio room opened and closed; ignoring the machine-prattle about Mark Dojaan's early childhood, Faulcon glanced round, acknowledged Gulio Ensavlion as the man peered over Faulcon's shoulder, then sat down on the second chair, before the visual display console.

'I thought you were going to kill them,' he said, and Faulcon grinned. 'I enjoyed every punch, and I'll not hesitate to do the same again.'

'I never knew you had such violence in you, Leo.'

'I surprised myself,' Faulcon conceded. He rubbed his bruised hands. 'I had to get back into Steel City and I couldn't depend on you pulling strings to get the unofficial blockage stopped.'

'I got you access to private files, didn't I? If you'd just asked, this morning ...'

Faulcon glanced curtly at the older man. 'If I'd asked, I'd have waited for days. I know you too well, Commander. You have a great talent for indecision.' Ensavlion looked slightly stung by the unexpected vitriol in Faulcon's voice, but Faulcon went on, 'With me around, Commander, there will be no chance to screw things up. I'm close to something, God knows what. I've spoken to Lena ... I think; I've tapped my subconscious memories ... I believe; in no time at all you and I will be changing the course of Kamelion history, I imagine.' He smiled at Commander Ensavlion. 'In other words, I'm quite determined in my confusion.'

Ensavlion looked at the screen. 'Mark Dojaan's records,' he stated; 'anything yet?' Faulcon shook his head, touched the change button and thereafter summoned images and spoken records quite fast.

He saw Mark Dojaan's history in fleeting glimpses. The machine voice was confusing, but after he had looked at the endless supply of photographs he could visually inspect the written records on the man. He would, if needs be, sit here for a week learning about Mark Dojaan, because somewhere in this file there had to be something to make clear what his mind-generated image of Lena had meant.

Ensavlion had been in the studio for no more than ten minutes when he came to what he was seeking.

The picture was of Mark Dojaan, a youthful-looking version, probably a teenager, sitting at a workbench, fiddling with something. The machine voice whispered, 'Hobbies display; subject a keen musician and crystal artist; techniques learned from great great grandfather and inherited through paternal lines.'

Faulcon leaned forward and stabbed a red button: further information.

A second picture appeared, a close-up of the first, Mark working with a small electric point, fashioning a human figure from a green shard of crystal, perhaps emerald. The picture changed, Mark and his brother Kris, still very young, working on a model of an Interstellar Liner, the Pan Galactic insignia clear on the hull; a third picture, a display of Mark Dojaan's artwork.

Quite literally, Ensavlion gasped; he leaned forward and stabbed a finger at the screen. 'That's that bloody amulet!'

Faulcon put the display unit onto 'hold', and stared at the star-shaped amulet that sat among the intricate and exotic carvings on the screen. 'Well I'm damned,' he said, and then, 'Or am I damned?' and laughed.

Ensavlion was shaking his head. 'So Kris was playing games with us all the time. He never found the amulet inside the machine, he brought it with him. Why would he do that, Leo?'

'I don't think he did,' said Faulcon. 'He came to VanderZande's World to find his brother. His brother found him: Mark left that amulet in the hulk for Kris to find. That's why Kris was so confident his brother was alive. It was a fine game; he didn't let on, of course; why should he? This was his private and personal trip, and that's why he could so happily face the prospect of a trip into time. Whatever Mark was, or is, up to, he couldn't show himself direct, but he wanted to contact Kris, and he used the jewellery he brought with him to the world ... What was Mark's amulet, can you remember? Did he have one?'

Ensavlion thought for a moment. 'It's a long time ago. I can't remember if I even saw one on the man.'

Faulcon called up a picture of Mark Dojaan on Kamelios; he felt a passing chill as he found himself staring into that serenely confident face, the shock of fair hair falling across the forehead and nearly to his eyes, the smile just hinted at, the figure, photographed against a view from the city of the rift, so arrogant, so self-aware. Between the parted neck flaps of the shirt, a crystal fragment gleamed, and when Faulcon ordered a close-up he could see the hint of a star shape. The photograph had been taken on Mark's arrival, probably within the week, as soon as he had finished his basic training. Faulcon called up a second picture, and on this one it was readily apparent that Mark was wearing no amulet at all; and then, later still, a few months into his time on VanderZande's World he was wearing a spiral of metal, a real amulet, a real piece of luck. And here too he seemed to be showing the face that Faulcon remembered so well, the slyness, the self-centredness, the appearance of a man who is taking what he can. Mark Dojaan had really gone through the changes on Kamelios, and Faulcon felt a tinge of sadness about that. Why sadness? He experienced the desire to cry, wondered about it. He thought it was because Kris had been a straight and genuine man, and Mark had perhaps once been the same; but Kamelios had beaten him down far more than most were beaten; it had wrenched Mark around and around and made him into something hard, something calculated, something whose greed was greater than any other consideration.

His empty words to Kris came back, words about how superficial the changes on Kamelios were, how no one was changed deep down. What a terrible self-deception that must have been. And Faulcon found himself wondering how deeply *he* had been changed, without him realizing the process, without him being aware of it. Should he draw his own file from the bank? Should he risk the watching of his earlier self, the sight of Leo Faulcon, the youthful Earthman who had followed his closest friend from New Triton to Kamelios, and thrown himself head-first into the restless tide of change, and had denied himself the luxury of intelligent appraisal as to what was going on within his skull, within his very soul?

He thought that he would not look at his own records. He concentrated on the screen again, on the image of Mark Dojaan, and when enough time had passed for him to treat the image as just that, and not as a haunting voice shouting abuse at him, so he checked to see whether the amulet had been among Mark's private possessions, after he had vanished; it had not. He had been carrying it with him on that fateful day. Faulcon summoned up the display of Mark's jewellery again, and settled back in his chair.

It was clear enough to him what must have happened. Kris and Mark had a closeness not measurable by traditional means; they were linked in spirit, a not unusual phenomenon, unusual only in that this linkage had worked through space and time, calling the younger boy to this place of Mark's 'death'. Kris had come, unsure, uneasy; but on his first expedition, watched from Othertime by his brother, he had been taken to a place where Mark could contact him, using a time-swept machine, and the amulet that he would have known from his days on Oster's Fall. Faulcon remembered how quiet Kris had been, how secretive, how vaguely amused. He had tricked Faulcon and Ensavlion and even the Council into thinking this was a real discovery, and no one ever questioned the fact, because on Kamelios the world was full of junk.

He had played a game with Faulcon; he had made Faulcon touch the jewel and demonstrated its warmth. He was so confident of finding his brother, of sharing the experience of travel in time, that his childish humour had overtaken him. No wonder the interior structure of the thing had seemed so primitive, a silly colour-producing mechanism, and Steel City had not seen beyond the charade of alienness.

And only at the moment of decision, the final moment that he had been waiting for, the riding of the time winds, only then had he allowed a moment of doubt to surface, seeing that depthless black, and the swirl of change, he had been frightened ... and Faulcon could not blame him for that.

'Mark is out there, in Othertime. My God, knowing that makes me feel quite dizzy. And not just Mark, surely not just Mark ... all the timelost, all of the "dead" ... all the "dead" of VanderZande's World.'

Ensavlion had leaned forward onto the console, and sat awkwardly, staring vacantly past the screen, lost in his own thoughts. Faulcon watched emotion and concern walk across the man's features, the slightest of frowns, a movement of lips, the restless flicker of his eyes. At length Ensavlion said,

'You make an assumption: you assume that it was Mark who put the amulet there. It is possible that Kris had the amulet himself, and was pretending to have discovered it. That *is* a possibility. It is possible further that it was not Mark who placed the jewel where his brother would find it, but the creatures who watch us. That is another possibility, is it not?'

Faulcon considered Ensavlion's careful words for a moment or two. On the screen the images of the jewels and carvings seemed to blur and flicker. 'I don't think Kris brought the jewel with him. Something put it there ...'

'But an alien, perhaps.'

Faulcon recalled the presence of something, some force of watchfulness during the long night previous. 'Yes. Perhaps. But even so, whether alien or human, it seemed a deliberate act, designed to make contact. Don't you see, Commander ...? It's a sign that time *is* occupied; it is evidence that time *is* under control on this world. If there are aliens, there can be men. Why not? Why should we doubt that men can survive in Othertime?'

Surely something, or someone, was communicating through time. On a world where time was periodically wrenched apart, where all hell let loose from past and future, it made good sense that creatures who understood the mechanism of the destructive forces of their Universe should patrol the ages, and make sure that intelligent life was not recklessly destroyed by its own, initial misunderstanding of the situation.

Lena, or whatever the manifestation had been, had hinted so strongly to him, hinted that he should think of Mark Dojaan, and she had been directing him to the evidence he needed that time was safe, that what was missing was the eloquence of communication between man and the guardians of VanderZande's World. He had seen the star jewel on Mark in the early days, and had forgotten it consciously; he had directed *himself* to the clue that time was safe! And time *was* safe. He knew that now, and the great weight of fear lifted from him.

CHAPTER EIGHTEEN

Think about a man who was so different to two people so close to him!

As Faulcon followed Ensavlion's rift-suited figure along the top of the valley towards the Riftwatch Station where the others waited, so he thought about that man, and about the difference. It was comforting to him; Mark was no longer the threatening, haunting presence in his past; rather, he had become the focus of his courage, his determination. The face of Mark Dojaan that he saw now was the youthful, pleasant face of a younger man, Mark as he had been two years ago; the resemblance between him and his brother Kris was close. And Kris was grinning at him too, and Faulcon knew that beyond time there would be no anger, no hostility. Fear and frustration had caused the row, the hurt, the tragedy. With Kris and Mark reunited all bad feeling would be transformed into support and closeness again. And Lena would be there ...

What would happen to her that would bring her back to the valley, a wizened creature of indeterminate age ...?

The jarring thought chilled Faulcon as he paced along the cliff top. Even now, even in his contentment, he was uncertain about the phantom, about its nature. *Had* he spoken to Lena, to the real Lena, or had she been the phantom image of his confusion, a projection put up before his consciousness to help him resolve the conflicting facts and images in his own skull? The phantom *did* exist ... there were physical records of that fact; but was Lena that phantom, or merely a convenient image for his ravaged psyche to grasp, and present to him? She had stepped into the valley when Kris had been lost, real, ancient, frightened. He had seen that.

His mouth felt dry. Ensavlion's rocking form some yards ahead progressed towards Station Epsilon with monotonous regularity, the dust rising from his feet, the reddening sun making his suit darken into a silhouette; dusk was two hours away. The valley was still.

He couldn't get the image of the aged Lena from his mind. He would find her, of course, and he would find her when she was young; there was no doubt in his mind about that. But would *something* happen, something that would allow her to live for years, when he had gone, and Kris had gone, and Mark had gone? How long, he wondered, would they have together?

I was alone; I grew old; I was lost ...

The sad words sickened him; he slowed to a walk, then stopped. Ensavlion sensed the cessation of movement and turned. 'Come on, don't hold things up. If there's a wind tonight, we'll be swimming in time before dawn. Come on, Leo.'

Faulcon urged his suit forward into a gentle trot.

I was lost; I was alone.

That suggested that she had *not* found Faulcon. But then, he reminded himself firmly, the image in the rift that previous night was not necessarily the real Lena, the real phantom. It was Faulcon's own feeling of aloneness, of isolation, his feeling of fear that had put the sad words into the sad projection of his own mind last night. The real phantom was the last of them to survive their lives in Othertime, a life that might well – he clung to this hope! – bring them *all* back to Steel City at some short time in the future. That Lena would end her years in the valley, watching her younger self, in no way denied the certainty of their youthful rediscovery of their lives and passion and love.

He caught up with Ensavlion as they approached the bright Station, light spilling from its overlook window; Faulcon saw dark shapes inside, and as they approached the airlock so the door slid open, and the entry light winked on.

The Catchwind Team comprised eight men and four women, all of them with at least a year's experience on Kamelios, and all of them hardened and cynical about the valley and its remains. The one thing that linked them, and which tended to separate them from all other highly experienced rifters, was that the idea of *time* still fascinated them. They were determined to explore the furthest reaches of the world, both past and present. They had waited patiently for their Commanding Officer to give them the go-ahead, but after so long a wait, and so many delays, it was apparent to Faulcon, as indeed to many others, that they would soon take their fates into their own hands.

They had not heard of Faulcon's 'cowardice', keeping themselves fairly isolated from Steel City as they went about their normal routines of exploration and mapping while awaiting the word. They welcomed Faulcon pleasantly enough, most of them having seen him about, and two of them actually having spoken to him some months before. He was not a stranger; but he noticed how much of a stranger Ensavlion was to them. They were courteous to him, but distant. He stood apart from the sprawled or seated team, watching them, watching Faulcon, and then studying maps and notes. He spoke very little and seemed inordinately unrelaxed with any of the team save Faulcon himself.

For most of his waking hours, during the next three days, Ensavlion hovered above the monitoring screens and signal posts, watching the flickering lines and circular scans for a sign of a squall.

On a shimmering green screen, in a darkened room, bright yellow lines flickered briefly and faded; from a speaker there came staccato sounds, crackling sounds. They came in waves, sometimes quite dense, sometimes slowing down and then disappearing altogether. In the long moments of silence that followed, only Ensavlion's breathing could be heard; the screen remained blank, the speakers quiet. Then a flash, a yellow line, darting across the field of vision; then the sound of static, and silence again.

'What the hell *is* that?'

The man at the control turned slightly towards Faulcon and shrugged. 'Wish to God I knew. I don't think anyone knows. It's one of the scanning features of the valley, but it doesn't have anything to do with a wind. Or a squall.'

Faulcon said, 'Something must be causing it … something …'

'We've never found out what,' said the man at the controls, reaching forward to gently stroke a strip of heat-sensitive green fabric. On the screen the scale magnified slightly. The man seemed satisfied and leaned back. Yellow lines flickered; noise crackled from speakers. Ensavlion leaned closer and shook his head, watching the enigma; not understanding.

Five days passed in this way, the valley quiet, the storm-winds pitching hard against the Station, blowing dust and debris against the walls; but never a squall from time; never a moment that could panic the Catchwind Mission into suiting up and racing down into the rift.

On the sixth day, shortly before VanderZande's blood-red dawn, a wind began to generate two hundred miles away in the west; within seconds it was blowing fast and furious through the valley, and Station Epsilon was alive with activity.

As the team moved out of the building and into the brightening day Faulcon sensed the disbelief in the group, the expectancy that Ensavlion would order the whole team back into the Station; he heard the words of several of them, the whispered agreement that this time there would be no going back. But Ensavlion was ahead of the team, a solitary figure fast-jumping down the valley towards the beginning of the sparkling ruins.

Faulcon opened all his communication channels and listened to the booming of the winds, and the whining of sirens, giving warning of the foul wind that approached. He found the sound excited him; his heart raced and he tasted salt on his lips. He began to run faster, jump further, and his abrupt motion spurred the rest of the team into a faster run. Soon they were gaunt figures, kicking up dust and slipping down the slopes as if they were a group of children, running to the water's edge.

Ensavlion fell behind, spoke to Faulcon through the radio. He was not breathless through effort, but was gasping with excitement, and the paternal hand that slapped Faulcon's rift suit hit with such force that Faulcon was glad of the armoured protection.

As they jumped on rocket power down hundred-foot gullies, and sheer faces, so the distant sky changed from red to a sombre black again, a frightening darkness in the bright day. The team stopped for a moment to watch and listen as the time winds thundered towards them.

Within minutes they were spreading out across the flatter ground at this chosen spot, where the walls of the valley were only a mile and a half apart, and the chaos of alien debris was confined to the edges of the deep valley; where they stood the land was flat and empty, ridged and raised in places, but still one of the most barren parts of the time valley.

Ensavlion's voice was firm and clipped as he called out orders: 'Spread out, keep in twos, when the wind hits don't move. Keep your signal beacons on and sounding wherever we get to and we'll hope to regroup at the other end of time.'

As the dark wind swept closer, reaching high into the heavens now, causing the day to darken substantially, so Faulcon and Ensavlion stood together, twenty yards from each pair beside them.

A deep calm took hold of Faulcon; he could hardly feel the beat of his heart; he felt almost joyful as he watched the wind's approach. Ensavlion was silent too, the man about to achieve his dream, to plunge into the unknown and to come face to face with those whom he had waited for, the creatures he had sought during his long years on VanderZande's World. They would be waiting for him, and Lena would be waiting for Faulcon himself. In this act of death there would be a discovery and a return that would bring new life to their existence, new passion to the emptiness that both he and Ensavlion had become.

Somewhere along the line of rifters a man shouted, another man cried out in panic, concern tempered with excitement. Distantly, towards the east, the landscape flickered and changed: Faulcon saw a spire appear, growing out of the slope of the valley, and in the flicker of an eye vanish again; a dark shape remained there, something sombre and malevolent from the more ancient past of Kamelios.

'Here she comes!' The universal statement of the obvious, and now at last the blood in Faulcon's body began to surge, the chemicals of his blood sharpening, adrenalin making him go cold, tense, wide-eyed, wary.

Ensavlion repeated the statement, over and over again, and each time the words rattled through Faulcon's transceiver so that he could sense the rising pitch, the taint of fear, the beat of fear, the rising storm of fear in Ensavlion's body and mind. Here she comes ... she comes ... she comes ...

And elsewhere in the line of motionless black shapes a man cried out, 'God protect us ... God watch us ...' and a woman's voice, calmer than her predecessor, shouting, 'Into the wind forever, with luck ... luck to us all.'

Faulcon found his hand at the crystal shard that was tacked to the outside of his rift suit. He touched the jagged edge, and looked slightly to the left, and saw Ensavlion looking at him and smiling. Sweat tickled Faulcon's face, irritating him intensely, but the distraction was momentary. The wall of blackness, the vortex of time disruption, filled his eyes, his head, his Universe.

It swept towards them. The valley changed, he could see the change, see every detail, every shape and structure that came and went as the wave-front rolled through the valley, channelled towards the twelve who waited. He said, 'Stay close,' and he was surprised at the energy of his words, surprised almost at the words themselves. And Ensavlion's reply sank in, and was welcomed, although it said little: 'I'd hold your hand, but it isn't done.'

Faulcon heard himself laughing, a sound cut short as he licked salt and wetness from his upper lip. 'Dear God, let her be there ...'

'She'll be there, Leo. They'll all be there.'

Thunder. The sensors on his rift suit reacted to the wind, screaming their siren warning above and through the sound of thunder, that bass booming that preceded the actual wind itself. The blackness was practically absolute in front of them, the light from behind lost in that depthless dark. Faulcon watched that blackness, trying to penetrate to the life beyond; he wondered, fleetingly, whether he looked into the future or into the past, or just into the void of space, or into the void of no-place and no-time. He sought a golden flare; he sought a tall and angular girl, walking towards him, her arms stretched out to hug him as he was bowled through the years into her love again.

There would have been seconds left, and as if his body and mind were reacting to the idea of death, he began to see, vividly and passionately, scenes and moments from his life; he could smell the smell of his home world; he could taste the food that his mother had cooked using the spices of Earth, ancient recipes, hot and sweet; he could feel the erotic silence of Lena's room, feel the smoothness of her body, taste her sweet breath; his tongue tickled as her own tongue darted into his mouth; perfume aroused him; laughter tormented him.

'Lena ...'

Seconds ...

He had a sudden, explicit vision of the time phantom, the wizened, stooped shape scurrying away from him as she had scurried from him a few nights before; it hurt for a moment, but his imagination was his worst enemy now, and that night when he had interacted with Kamelios to 'see' Lena as the phantom, that had been imagination's triumph, his deeper, darker mind breaking through to him, pointing the way clear to this mission, showing how all along he had known that the time winds were not death winds, as long as one was taken complete; there was always that chance for death, like Kabazard must have died, but he could survive the actual *fact* of journeying through time.

Her words were the comforter. Think of a man who was so different to two people so close to him.

And he thought briefly of Kris Dojaan, and of Mark, and he knew that they too would be waiting for him, themselves reunited.

Seconds ...

Think of a man ...

I was lost; I was alone ...

(the bitter memory of his own sadness, translated into imagery)

His suit shook as a powerful physical wind began to buffet him, trying to rock him; but the rift suit could stand against winds far more powerful than anything Kamelios could throw against them.

One of the team began to whine, expressing fear in his own personal way, but not moving, standing his ground. The voice grew until it was as loud as the shriek of sensor, overwhelming the booming and thundering of the raw wind itself. Others laughed or joked, or spoke aloud in words, lost against the howl of the time wind, that Faulcon nevertheless intuited as being prayers. So many Gods, these days, so many deities being summoned for strength, for courage.

He said only, 'Watch for me, Lena … watch over me, Allissia …'

How strange that he should invoke Allissia's name. He chilled—

Moments!

Allissia seemed to run towards him; he could see every detail of her, the round face, the smile, the hideous eyes, her thin gown pressed against her body by wind, her arms waving as she ran. She was saying something, and the words flooded back, jumbled, then clear.

Reason is a liar, she had said. *You can make reasons for anything … for anything …*

And Lena – the imagination's Lena – and the words he had said to himself: *the clockwork … all the clockwork …* figuring things out, rationalizing … you can get reasons for anything …

Reasons for living; reasons for dying; reasons to confront a danger confident of survival … of survival!

He felt suddenly sick; he experienced an upsurge of emotion, a sudden reliving of the fear of the alien he had experienced that evening when he had confronted his mind's image of Lena; he felt again that sense of being watched, and tried, and tested …

Reason is a liar …

Games! Games! Testing, trying, torturing …

Games!

There were less than seconds … there were only instants. And they had tricked him, after all his care, after all his bid for survival, they had tricked him into death, and he was about to die …

They were here: He could feel them, all around him … touching, probing, searching, questioning …

'A trick!' he screamed, his voice lost against the roar of the wind. 'Ensavlion, they've tricked me, they've been playing with me all along, testing, testing me … Get out of here … *run!*'

He turned his suit and began to run; the motionlessness of the action was jarring, for his suit didn't move. Panicking, still crying out in desperation, he tried to shift the suit manually, but the bulky armour remained braced against the wind, facing it. The thought fled through Faulcon's mind: the damn suit is working against me … it *wants* to destroy me!

His panic, however, had reached through the few feet of distance between him and Ensavlion, and the Commander was turned and beginning to run. His howl of terror was one more note in the rising wail of sound. Faulcon turned his head and watched him moving away down the valley, but he was not running fast, and the arms of the suit were raised awkwardly; in seconds the suit had turned and was running its occupant about the valley in tight circles, like a hen without a head … like Leo Faulcon on his first trip down, all that time ago.

A sudden swirl of dust came between Faulcon and the dancing figure of Ensavlion; he looked back towards the wind, and the darkness reached past him, enveloping him. The thunder reached a deafening pitch, the whining of the rift-suit sensors seeming intolerably loud for just an instant.

The wind had struck.

He saw the valley as it had never been in the time of Steel City – green walled and sun-swept, with opalescent spires rising from the undulating sprawl of a living city; creatures and machines moved almost lazily about the whiteness, and as Faulcon watched—

Blackness, and a sudden silence, and

A rain-swept view, a dark gate, snarling faces carved in stone, and the procession of fire that marked a ceremony, or a war, or some unknown purpose –

And then the blackness was absolute, and the sound of life was gone; Faulcon was immersed in a silence so profound, so clean, so pure, that he felt at once shocked, and at peace; his body gave in to that silence and he found himself incapable of resistance, as if all of life and all of movement was a constant pull and push against sound, against music, and wind, and speech, and vibration, and with that universal noise gone, there was nothing for life to work against, and he began to evaporate, to drift, to disseminate. There was not even a ringing in his head, not even those neuronic echoes of the earth-sounds that, instants before, had assaulted him.

He tried to cry Lena's name, but his voice was a soundless movement of lips and even that movement existed only within his mind; he tried to clench his teeth but there was no sensation; he tried to move his arms, but they were stretched out to infinity, great lazy sails, drifting through the void.

For an instant he fell, seeing no difference in the darkness, sensing only the way the blood shifted in his body, loving that moment's awareness of nerve ending, and pressure centre, loving the sensation; he twisted and turned, battered and buffeted by a feelingless, soundless wind; he spun, a leaf in the sky, a life on the wind; he drained upwards and down, his legs stretched to the ends of time, his head drawn out, and twined and twisted like a rope, then unravelled and whiplashed out so that his body undulated and snapped taut: no pain, no fear, no sensation other than that of the standing wave of sound, and light, the violin string struck and alive with energy, then snapped *taut*, and dead again, and drifting:

Colour now, but no colour he could relate to. Perhaps red, yet a bluish red, and swirling and changing, and something like red, yet not red, more – he thought, as thought faded, his last thought, the idle thought of a dying man – more the colour of laughter, streaked through with shades of tears, and the sparkling brightness of love, and here the tints and shades of childhood.

Through it all – last moments, last pulses of nerve and mind – through it all, the golden glow, the points, the faces, the lines, the twisting panels, the multi-dimensions of the pyramid, spanning space and time, and reaching into his eyes and ears and fingers and feet: the pyramid, the darting golden enigma, and Lena, yes, she was there, reaching to him, death-dream Lena, dying-thought Lena, long-dead Lena, so lost, so alone, so aching for the memories of her youthful lover, now falling after her, through the golden blackness, the silent roar of time, of endless time, of non-existent time, and downwards.

No touch, no temperature, no fear, no pain, no sound, no sight; and soon, as nothingness sucked all emotion from him, soon there was no thought, no sleep, no awareness, no existence. And it ended with peace.

CHAPTER NINETEEN

After the storm had passed, the valley lay almost uncannily quiet, its stillness seemed unnatural. Dark rain clouds had been gathering in the north, and they swept across the land, now, covering the world in a mournful grey and orange cloak; the rain came, fine and gentle at first, then heavier interspersed with thunder and electrical discharge. It rained for an hour, and because of tradition there was none who would venture out into the wet until it had passed completely.

The susurration of rain on steel faded and was gone; the sky brightened and the blazing disc of Altuxor peered through the dispersing clouds; above the valley, elusive red shapes, vortices and spirals, danced for a few minutes, insubstantial light-forms rejoicing in the passing of the rain.

Men moved out of Steel City, and from all the Riftwatch Stations, weaving and walking their way towards the valley. They came in rift suits, and in tractors, on air platforms and small copters; they came in ones and twos and sometimes in whole teams. They didn't hurry, but they were intrigued to know what time had left on the shores of their world.

The men from Station Epsilon were the first to arrive at the lip of the canyon; it was they who were closest to the Catchwind Team, and they went down to search for the fragments of those who might not have made it, who might have been uncleanly swept by the time winds. They were surprised by what they saw through the magnifying plates on their suits. They were very surprised indeed.

A single rift suit stood in the deepest part of the valley, turned to face the direction of the wind, its legs braced apart, its form quite motionless. Of the others there was no sign. They had all been taken.

The identity of this lone survivor of the mission intrigued the rescue team that descended the rift for no more than a few minutes. Half-way down they could make out the markings on the suit.

Behind the face plate, staring out as if in wonderment, Leo Faulcon was at first thought to be dead. His staring eyes, the lips of his mouth parted as if crying, the cheeks tugged in as if withered, the crusting of salt down the sides of his nose and eyebrows, all showed the man had died of shock, and in terror. And yet, as the rescue team circled the frozen suit, so the expression on Faulcon's face changed, and the hint of a smile touched those twisted lips.

And then the eyes closed and the suit whirred for a second, powered two paces forward, its head bowed, its form finally sinking to its knees.

Faulcon was immediately hauled out of the back of the suit, and his shivering, ice-cold body wrapped carefully and taken up to the Station; from there he was transported to an infirmary in Steel City.

Hardly breathing, his heartbeat so slow that at times the pacemaker console was forced to squeeze a response out of the sluggish tissue, Faulcon lay in the coma for three days; his dreaming was monitored on an encephavid, something that would normally have required an authorization from Faulcon himself, but under the circumstances ...

To begin with, the flickering images on the screen were quite lucid, showing a beach, a restless ocean, the movement of some bulky creature just below the surface. The image frequently broke up, corresponding to a dampening of the amplitude of various neural frequencies. When the activity returned, becoming more normal, the image returned. Faulcon responded to his own name with an image of his face; he responded to sudden noise in the room with an image of fear, the inside of a tiny chamber, windowless, doorless, dark shadows in the corners that moved about like ghosts.

It was after one of these fear-images that the basal image changed abruptly. The beach dissolved; Faulcon's alpha readout began to fluctuate erratically, and his whole body began to tremble. When body and mind were calm again, the screen showed a picture of swirling clouds, brightly lit and colourfully confused; all the blues and reds of a *fiersig*, but stationary, now, and settled on a hillside.

Whilst the inside of the room remained quiet, colourful, intensely focused, outside, in the wider spaces of Steel City, there was mayhem. Word had leaked out that the coward Faulcon had *still* not made his sacrifice to the winds. That he might have been into the wind and come out again was not a possibility that anyone thought to entertain. His own section was the centre of the trouble. They tried to storm the hospital area, and were kept at bay by guards, whose numbers were tripled. Scenes of such anger had rarely been seen in Steel City. Faulcon's existence, his presence, was outrageous. It destroyed the smooth working of Section 8; it upset men and women on all levels. He was a core of bad luck in the city. There was public demand for his death, for his burning, for his ashes to be scattered in the valley.

Inside the room the men who watched and waited for Faulcon's return to consciousness were unmoved and unbothered by the noise and anger outside.

Within two days a second group had arisen, a quieter group who made their feelings felt in a peaceful way; to them, Faulcon was pure in spirit; he was God-given luck. They believed he had gone to the winds and returned; he was the turning point in the history of Man on VanderZande's World. The contradiction of emotions outside the hospital managed to cancel out the greater part of feeling; by the third day there was peace. Faulcon lay quietly, breathing once every minute, and behind his closed eyes his pupils were wide, as if he watched a scene of great pleasure.

And yet, on the screen of the encephavid, there was nothing new, nothing but the image of a motionless *fiersig*, its colourful tenuosity hovering against a cleft in the hillside.

Had he gone into time, or had the wind avoided him? It seemed impossible that a man could be swept away by a time wind, only to be redeposited on precisely the same piece of ground that had been his waiting place; and yet Ensavlion, whose frantic form had been dancing only feet from Leo Faulcon, had gone, and the winds were not so precise that they could distinguish in the matter of a few paces.

At last one of the nurses picked up the crystal amulet, turned it about in her fingers and raised a question: had the amulet protected him? Had they found a way to survive the winds that had been available all the time, but had never been used as anything but a crude source of power? It was definitely a crystal of sun-dew.

Towards dusk on the third day someone came to a conclusion: 'The crystal, in a way we don't as yet understand, has shielded the man from the effects of time. We can test that easily enough, but for the moment it seems a reasonable explanation. It would seem that Leo Faulcon never went into time. The winds ignored him.'

Faulcon opened his eyes and smiled.

'Not true,' he said, his voice soft, slightly hoarse; he struggled into a sitting position, propped on his elbows. He breathed deeply, almost gasping, almost hurt by the sudden in-draught of sterile air. 'I went into the wind, and I came back. They brought me back.' He gasped for breath, beginning to laugh, and fell back onto his pillow. He stared at the ceiling. 'They brought me back. My God, they really did ... and now I can find her. I can find them all.'

His eyes closed.

He slept again, fitfully, sporadically; while he was awake he said nothing, did nothing, just lay quietly, staring at the ceiling. When he slept he dreamed chaotic dreams, and only on occasion did the encephavid show a glimpse of hillside, and *fiersig*, or beach and rock, the images that had dominated his read-out for so many days.

One morning, when the nurse came in to inspect him, and to bathe his sleeping form, she found Leo Faulcon standing naked by his bed, his eyes not fully alert, his hands shaking. As she gently pressured him back to the bed he gripped her wrist. His eyes focused; the grip relaxed. 'Get me my clothes.'

'I can't do that, rifter. Not without the proper authority.'

Faulcon conceded the point. He smiled, let go of the nurse completely, and began to run around the room. 'I'm starving,' he said abruptly, standing, hands on hips. He slapped his stomach and thighs. 'I've lost more weight than is good for a man.'

The nurse laughed, staring at his red-blotched body. 'You've certainly got bony in the last few days. I'll get you some breakfast.'

As she walked past him to the door he took her arm, leaned close to her. She blinked and recoiled a little as his breath was stale and sour. Faulcon knew this, but couldn't help his lack of freshness. He said, 'Get me a suit; or a robe; or anything. And a doctor. I'm ready to leave.'

He ate breakfast, sitting naked on his bed; he used the tray for mock modesty when the medical team swooped upon him, testing eyes, mind, heart and musculature. 'May I leave now?'

By late afternoon he had been allowed his clothes, and, whilst being watched on the Steel City internal communication system, he was walking free through the plazas, corridors and lounges. No one took much notice of him; he was fortunate in not crossing paths with anyone who knew him well, and who might have drawn attention to him.

He refused, point blank, to talk about what had happened, not to the medical team, nor the psychologists ... and not to the representatives of the council who pestered and plagued him. 'All in good time,' he said over and over again.

At the end of the day he went to the byke hangers and tried to sign out his rift-byke and a mask. He was refused. Angry, then canny, he found a corner, dropped a cushioning of under-suits into it, and sat down. He spent the rest of the evening and all of the night there, staring blankly ahead of him. Early in the morning two technicians approached him and informed him that exit clearance had arrived, and that he was free to depart from Steel City. He smiled at once, climbed to his feet, stretched and busied himself with preparations for a long journey. The technicians watched him, but made no move to interfere with him.

'I *will* be back,' he said as he wheeled his byke to the exit ramp; he said it to the technicians, but he intended the monitors to hear him. For a while, at least, he felt he wanted to be alone, unfollowed, unwatched. All except for Ben Leuwentok, that is. For it was to Chalk Stack that he was headed, now, to find Ben, to talk to him, and to bring him up to Hunderag Country.

CHAPTER TWENTY

He skirted the valley, hardly glancing at it; the land steepened and the track-way wound away from the rift and up towards the chalk pinnacles which rose among the dense forestlands. Skagbark and the threshing foliage of comb-fern had soon surrounded him, and he rode carefully, and alert, towards the semi-camouflaged hide where he was sure Leuwentok would be working.

Near by, quite suddenly, there was the sound of an animal panicking. A high-pitched cry was followed by a small, dark shape rushing headlong from the comb-fern, running across the track, then stopping. Faulcon braked hard and turned off the byke's motor. The silence was quite startling, although he became aware of the thrashing sounds in the distance, and the rustling of wind in the fragile branches of the skagbark.

An olgoi stood before him, its four eyes wide, its beaky jaws apart, gaping, drooling. Its whole body, supported on its muscular hind limbs, shook with fear as it stared at the human and his machine. In its tiny hands it was grasp-ing the limp, probably dead, form of a slug-like forest animal. The olgoi's belly was not properly closed; glistening pink showed itself to Faulcon in a vertical gash from throat to crotch; fluid had dribbled down the olgoi's thighs.

The creature was beginning its mountain run. Almost unconsciously Faulcon glanced up and saw Merlin fully emerged from behind its permanent partner; in the bright day the moons were faint outlines, colourful. As Faulcon's gaze was distracted from the creature, so the olgoi snapped at its prey, biting and chewing a huge chunk of the shapeless mass in its mouth. Faulcon was con-cerned to pinpoint the gulgaroth that had at last released this little symbiont, but the big animal was probably a long way away, now, moving towards the valley, or to whereever it had chosen as its place of rest or death.

The olgoi swallowed, squawked, and vanished into the undergrowth, evi-dent by its noisy passage for a few seconds before it had disappeared towards the far hills. 'See you very soon,' called Faulcon, and laughed.

'Well, if it isn't the olgoi hunter! Hello, Faulcon.'

The voice caught Faulcon by surprise; he twisted round, looking back across his shoulder. Ben Leuwentok stood there, smiling from behind his thin mask; he carried a shoulder bag and camera, and was dressed in white and green safari clothes. He walked up to Faulcon and they shook hands.

'I was coming looking for you, Ben.'

'I heard you'd been ignored by a time wind. You're a lucky man.'

For a moment they exchanged a long, searching gaze. He knows, Faulcon thought. He had probably known all along. 'I wasn't ignored,' he said quietly. 'They took me and they brought me back. In the wink of an eye, so I'm told. In the wink of an eye.'

Leuwentok shrugged off his shoulder bag and put it on the ground. He closed up the camera, taking time about it, concentrating on the actions, although his mind was clearly elsewhere. 'I was following the olgoi,' he said. 'Merlin's bright, now. The migration is beginning in a big way.' He looked up at Faulcon. 'How long did they keep you? Hours? Days?'

'I don't know. It seemed like no time at all, and yet I recall an age of floating in their minds. I was disembodied, and yet I could feel everything. I touched their hearts, their souls, their memories. I came closer, I think, than anyone has ever come. We exchanged thoughts, and I suspect it was for the first time, although they must have come close with Kris Dojaan.'

Leuwentok looked up sharply. 'That's a familiar name ... Mark's brother?'

'That's right.'

'I remember Mark. A vicious man, totally unprincipled.'

'That's true,' said Faulcon, 'but it's not important. Mark was taken by the winds, but there was something that existed between his brother Kris and himself, an empathy that kept them in touch ...'

Leuwentok was familiar with such rare, but undeniable, linkages. 'Personality fifteen,' he said, 'ego links, instantaneous awareness of each other.'

'That sort of thing. Kris knew his brother was here, and alive, and his dedication to the task of finding Mark was almost tangible. The creatures of this world responded to him almost at once – they tricked him with an amulet that was one of his brother's artistic creations; they convinced him to come into the wind because they made it seem as if his brother was waiting for him. And when they made contact with Kris, they made contact with me, and with Lena Tanoway. We should have been honoured – we were a special study to them.'

Again Leuwentok fiddled with his camera before glancing at Faulcon. 'Why are they doing it? And why did they let you go? And why have you picked me to tell this to? Why? Am I next?' His face was white behind his mask, his eyes wide, his demeanour that of a man suddenly afraid.

Faulcon laughed. 'Get on the byke. There's something I want to show you.'

Leuwentok obeyed, squeezing onto the saddle behind Faulcon's thin form. 'Why you, Ben? Why not? You were very close to understanding the immense life-form that dominates Kamelios ...' He punched the byke into action, shouting above the roar of the engine. 'In fact, I suspect you knew all along. You certainly knew more than you let on last time I saw you.'

'I have ideas, that's all.'

'That's as may be.' Faulcon guided the byke in a tight circle, cutting between shadowy trunks of skagbark. Leuwentok clung on too tightly for comfort. 'There's another reason, though. I want you to come up to Hunderag Country with me. I want you to see what I see, and then you'll know everything. I might have to wait there a while, and it will be up to you to report to the *Magistar Colona* and the others.'

As the byke lurched along the track, back towards the valley, Leuwentok shouted, 'I don't mind that. I don't mind at all.'

They came close to the gentle slopes of the valley; here, where the valley was nearly at its end, the span of the gorge was wider, but the drop was shallow. A few dusty, rather disappointing derelicts were scattered about the slopes and flatlands below: buildings, mostly, and unimpressive. The winds usually blew themselves out some way before this 'beach', as the whole area was known.

As they stood, looking out across the rift, Faulcon said, 'There.'

'I've seen it before. Ruins.' He looked at Faulcon.

'Not ruins,' said Faulcon quickly, and tapped a finger against his temple. 'Thoughts. Images. Dreams. Pictures from the mind of a creature that is several creatures in one, and which flows through this valley from one end to the other, almost a reflection of its own breath of life. It doesn't respond to the moons, or the daylight; it responds only to its own whim, rolling between the cliffs, seeking out the tiny life-forms that it has been watching for years – seconds by its own standards – and which it is still watching now.'

Leuwentok was silent behind his mask for a while. He shook his head slowly, then, and Faulcon imagined that he was putting together pieces that had never quite fitted before. 'I'd wondered about that. I thought the wind itself might be some by-product of the passage of the creatures: I always thought there were several creatures, I always thought of *them*. And I thought they moved through time, dragging these artifacts with them, and creating dream images. But I suppose they don't move in time at all.'

'They aren't as tightly constrained by time, by the present moment as we are. But there is no span of billions of years. A moment to them is perhaps a few of our months, and they are free within that span of time. All of this, this whole valley, is a sort of crease in their ego; the ruins are the memories of other creatures that visited this world, and perhaps even lived here. There are even a few human ruins if you watch closely, a few human memories, twisted and changed just enough to make us blind to their real nature. Intelligent life has visited Kamelios for thousands of years, being taken in the same way as we have been taken. The creatures down there looked for memories, for life; they watched structures being built, and later they recreated them, made them into solid forms and beached them on the shores of their own collective mind.'

'Tolpari,' said Leuwentok. 'Thought into substance. It never occurred to me. I was convinced that most of the strange manifestations were from an alien mind. But I linked the ruins with time, and accepted them as real.'

'We all did. Very solid images, very real. They seemed something apart from the pyramid, and God, and the phantom.'

'Tolpari *are* real. They're a phenomenon that some say we experienced on Earth more than we realized: space craft, figures, animals, all created by concentrated thought and given substance, and even life – *how* is something I couldn't tell you. They always decayed, though. The artifacts in Steel City haven't.'

'Same principle, different intensity,' said Faulcon, and thought of the very solid phantom, the one that showed up on photographs: turned on and off by the group mind that created it.

Leuwentok put his hands to his head and stood, for a minute or so, staring into the distance. Then he said, 'But why are they doing all this, Faulcon? Why the tricks? Why these images? Are they trying to communicate in some way, throwing up echoes of our own minds?'

Faulcon relived that moment of close consciousness, floating so still, and feeling the contact of awareness, *becoming* for a while a part of the wind, seeing in an instant the longings and the memories of the natural inhabitants of VanderZande's World; he felt dizziness, a slight nausea; he felt his body teeter on the edge of the cliff, and stepped back, at the same time shaking his head to clear the sudden sensory assault that threatened to upset his equilibrium.

He said, 'In one sense, yes. They *are* trying to communicate. Only their definition of communication isn't the same as ours. To them communication is part of reproduction, and it comes out simply as: "Carry my life, my existence, my awareness, carry all of this, some mental part of me to *another* me on another world." And part of that communication involved finding out the answer to a simple question: what will make a man die? What one thing would make us all sacrifice our lives to the wind when we happened across this creature's mate, a thousand light years away, a thousand years in the future. Was jealousy the key? Or passion? Intrigue? Curiosity? How they got us with curiosity! They gave us buildings, apparitions, life-forms – never an intelligent one, and how tantalizing *that* was – pyramids, they gave us anything and everything to whet our appetites for the unknown. They addled our brains to see what remained constant, what drive existed so deep rooted that they could find the 'lemming-factor', the all-jump-together button. They seemed to tune into the most psychically aware of us. Those without that particular openness of mind are probably dead. These creatures just didn't understand us, because they were responding almost instinctively, getting us ready to aid their reproduction. We're olgoi, Ben; messengers … To the wind-creatures we are star-travelling olgoi, to be primed with the seed of their lives and dispatched to other worlds, other winds, there to give up that seed – and our lives – in a splendid moment of "mating"; mating not for the reproduction of the physical form of the creatures, but for communication … the spirit of life communicated to another of their kind, a replenishment, a linkage of existence. All of these last few years they have been working out what to prompt us to do, how to programme us to behave in a common way whenever we encounter their kind on other worlds. They sent phantoms, and they entered our heads with a different sort of phantom. They had us running about like headless chickens, pecking at enigma, seeking lost times.'

Faulcon was breathless; he dropped to a crouch and dug out a small piece of stone from the earth, tossing it idly over the cliff and watching it roll away down the slopes. Leuwentok had wrapped his arms about his body, stood silent, intense. Faulcon thought he might have been afraid to speak, in case it should stop him fully understanding what Faulcon was saying, communicating what he had learned during his wild ride.

'Whatever Mark's brother, Kris, saw in the valley – he saw a phantom – and whoever it was, it made him more determined to go into the time winds because it reinforced his belief in the possibility of survival beyond them. The same happened to me. My own fear had to be overcome by *reason*, and at the last minute, as I was about to be caught by the trick, as I finally convinced myself that I *could* travel in time, I saw through it! The creature responded to that particular panic because it was like an enormous blast of mental energy – it was a communication as we understand it, and which they finally came to understand themselves. Quite suddenly they could see that we were not biological machines, that we no longer had some common, animalistic drive that was there for them to programme. An immense, intangible creature, trying to communicate with us: carry my life, my existence, carry the spirit of my life to others of my kind on other worlds. Only we couldn't do it; we're too diverse, too different from one another. The deep drives are just ghosts, now; phantoms. We've become a superficial race, aware of transient, passing things, fixed to a moment of time, busy evaluating our individual worlds. The deep world, the link between man and earth, has been destroyed by inutility. There was nothing for the creatures to grasp, to key into; nothing but scattered dreams, desires, images, different things to different men. They failed and failed. They trapped a few rifters, and killed many through misunderstanding. They found no key to the trapping of us all, and therefore no way to programme us to commit suicide, or at least "union" on another world. Those failures that survived, those who were lost, they moved in their own way to a sleeping place, a long way from us, preserved because it didn't know what else to do with them."

'You know that for a fact?' Leuwentok's voice was unsteady.

'I know it.'

'You've seen them? Where have you seen them?'

'In dreams, Ben. As yet only in dreams. But I want you to come up into Hunderag Country with me.'

'I'll do that, Faulcon. You know me. I've worked for years to try and come to some sort of ecological understanding of Kamelios. I thought I'd got it. I understand the moons, the fauna, I thought I understood that mankind was responding to alien dreams, that our unfulfilled dreams and those of some creature, some entity, were interlinked, causing the chaos of Steel City and all its departments and failing scientific studies. I thought we were shallow creatures trapped by the deep drives, the ancient parts of our existences, the left-overs. Now you tell me that there are no deep parts. We are superficial creatures trapped by that superficiality: I want to know, I want to have, I want to touch, to experience ... always I *want*. And I want to *know*. Is knowing such a superficial thing? Is knowledge so empty?'

Faulcon turned away from the valley, stretching his cramped limbs and leading the way back to the byke. As he walked he said, 'I can't answer that, Ben. The manchanged made me realize something when I was with them last. They said that natural knowing is the only knowing.' He glanced at Leuwentok, who walked hunched and frowning beside him. 'What you are born with, what you die with, that which is the very life you are. Natural knowing. All else, all we learn, all we strive for, all of that is garbage. Our species has lived for so long trying to find some reason to learn that we've now lost that ability to know without effort, to know naturally. Our friends in the valley, the creatures that are the wind, have never experienced anything like us, such empty things, such transient life-forms.'

Leuwentok made a sound, perhaps a bitter laugh. 'There's truth in that, and there's nonsense. Without science, without striving, we wouldn't be here, across the Galaxy from Earth, on an alien world; without disease.'

'Or we would have been here a long time ago; without disease. We are an impatient, edgy species, Ben. We can't wait for things to happen; we have to *make* them happen. We've put our lives into *trying*; *trying* has become a religion to us, something honourable, and we've overlooked the fact that trying is *failing*. Ultimately our success, our understanding of our microcosm, comes generations late, and when it comes it is a truly superficial thing.'

The byke had fallen over; together they heaved it upright, and brushed dirt from its panels. Leuwentok said, 'I don't really believe that. How can I? I'm a "modern" man. The Age of Roses is long since past for me.' He shrugged his equipment pack onto his shoulders again, then hesitated and grinned, the mask wrinkling slightly. 'A few minutes ago when you asked me to come with you, I was afraid. I felt horribly afraid.' Faulcon said nothing, just watched the biologist. 'So you see, Faulcon, I *do* believe what you said. Quite apparently I do, quite obviously. But I'll only admit it to you. I'm certainly not going to admit it to myself. How can I? I'm a modern man.'

Faulcon tapped his temple twice, then laughed. 'Get on the byke. First stop Overlook; then the Jaraquaths and the sort of food you've had nightmares about.'

CHAPTER TWENTY-ONE

Allissia was working in the lower fields, digging furrows in the stony earth ready to take a new season's calcas. She saw them as they rode above the distant edge of the plateau, and for a moment manchanged and rifters regarded each other across the distance of half a mile or more. It was late in the day and the wind was strong, blowing hair and dust and sweet pollen from the high forests. Shading her eyes, Allissia finally decided that one of the pair was Leo Faulcon. She jumped up and down three or four times, then stopped, then jumped some more. She waved. Then she stared hard into the distance, puzzled as to why the figures on their weird-shaped machines had stopped so still.

Across the intervening land came the sudden, repeated roar of the bykes; one of the men waved and Allissia cried out delightedly, dropped tool and earth sack and turned to run and fetch her husband.

Audwyn was in the high field. Allissia ran through the village, stopping just for a moment in her own house to make sure that she had all the food she would need for the guests, and then she took off like an olgoi, bounding and tripping, through the skagbark woods, and out into the busy field where harvesting was in progress.

Audwyn was close by. He stopped his work as Allissia shouted to him. Several of the manchanged gathered about her, their bodies reeking with the smell of sweat and dirt, their faces creased and content, but tired, very tired after this exertion. Audwyn wiped the earth from his blade, and kissed the cold steel. He laid the tool at the edge of the field, pointing inwards, the promise that the time he was absent from the harvest would be made up twofold the next day. But there was none who resented his departure.

Audwyn loped ahead of the sprinting form of Allissia, and they reached the house in a panting race. Faulcon and Ben Leuwentok were waiting for them at the edge of the village, and the manchanged caught their breath and went to meet them.

'I've come to ask your help,' said Faulcon, his voice tired as it sounded through his dusty, choked mask. Allissia took his arm, led him back to the house with Audwyn walking beside Leuwentok and hearing of the journey up to the plateau. Leuwentok seemed quite relaxed with the manchanged.

'Don't even talk,' Allissia insisted, 'until you've both eaten and we've drunk a toast to our pleasure at seeing you.'

They seated themselves around the wide, wood table. The sight of food made Faulcon's mouth water, simple vegetables and boiled meat though it was. Leuwentok seemed slightly apprehensive of the meal, but relaxed more as Allissia allowed him a pre-taste, which he found, to his surprise, to be very tasty. Naturally enough they joined Audwyn in raising a mug of *calcare*, draining the sweet liquid and pressing hands to sternum as the burning went on and on, all the way from throat to fingertips. 'Excellent brew,' said Leuwentok, and removed his mask for a moment to smell the drink. They ate, then, and the meal that had taken scarce minutes to prepare, took scarce seconds to vanish from their plates.

When they had eaten their fill, and Audwyn and Allissia had taken a small meal for themselves, Faulcon suggested a stroll up to the high field to watch the harvest. Leuwentok had come over slightly queasy and decided to lie down for a few minutes. Faulcon and the others walked easily through the woods, listening to the scurrying movements, of dusk creatures venturing into the deep, reddening shadows. From afar, from the mountain lands beyond this plateau, came the solitary, mournful howl of a female gulgaroth; the sound made Faulcon shiver. This was the time when the females came down from their mountain haunts, seeking the olgoi. It was not unknown for them to wander as far as the farms of the manchanged.

Audwyn had noticed Faulcon's sudden hesitation, the way his head had lifted to regard the distant cry, the narrowness of his eyes behind the wide, clear-glass goggles. 'Is that where you are to go, then? To the mountains?'

They were at the edge of the wood, now, and in the breezy dusk the fields glowed orange and moved in colourful rhythm before the gentle winds. All but a few of the manchanged were finished with the day's work, and stood in groups in the stubbly clearings, resting on their long-handled farm tools, or seated, arms around knees, staring into the setting sun and talking in quiet voices. They seemed unperturbed by the sporadic, but insistent, crying of the gulgaroth.

'The mountains,' Faulcon agreed as he focused hard, intent upon the white peaks and the dark slopes that now seemed almost a part of the sky. 'Not to the tops, certainly. Not to the snow. But to a deep Galley that looks towards twin peaks. What is sleeping there is what I seek.' He looked round at Aud-wyn, who was noticeably uneasy. The man's wide, staring eyes were rimmed with pink, and though he smiled, though he affected composure, Faulcon realized that the thought of a trek through the territories of the gulgaroth was deeply disturbing to him; or perhaps it was as simple as Audwyn having divined Faulcon's purpose in coming to the village first, and despite the man-changed philosophy that they were all far greater than the circumstances that affected their lives, he was nervous at the prospect of going into the valleys. Faulcon watched him carefully, wondering what spark of memory, what hint of the past, might have been nagging at Audwyn, making him respond with a very human fear.

There was no time for subtle suggestion. 'I need a guide, Audwyn.'

The manchanged smiled. 'Of course. But you shall have two guides. Allis-sia must come.' He reached for his wife and put his arm around her waist. Allissia melted against the tall man, and her eyes too showed the passing concern, the moment of fear before the fact of acceptance.

'What a confusing man you are,' she said, and Faulcon frowned his ques-tion. She shrugged almost imperceptibly. 'The last time you were here you were seeking the courage to walk into the depths of the rift valley. Now you seek guides to the high lands.'

'There is a connection,' said Faulcon. 'I went to the valley. I went without hesitation. I went with others, and together we faced the time winds, and together we travelled into their realm.'

Audwyn and Allissia exchanged a startled glance. Audwyn shook his head, the transparent gesture of confusion, as he said, 'You rode into time, on the wind? You went and you came back? How can that be?'

'I wasn't wanted,' said Faulcon simply. 'I suppose I was needed here. I was to have been a messenger, but I decided to keep my message to myself for a while. I wanted to see for myself where time's tide has been leaving its debris.'

Audwyn looked back at the mountains. 'The high land. Very well, we shall go and prepare to take you. The journey will be long and dangerous. It's the gulgaroths' time of seeking, and they are more vicious at this time of year.' Faulcon, perhaps Audwyn too, remembered that occasion nearly a year ago when their respective paths had crossed that of a seeking gulgaroth, and Audwyn had escaped death by mere seconds.

Allissia had stepped ahead of Audwyn in understanding what Faulcon was searching for. She said, 'The place where time has left its debris ... to seek what sleeps there. The timelost. Is that what you mean?'

'There are no timelost,' said Faulcon. 'There are just those who are lost. And Lena is among them.'

'I don't understand,' said Allissia. 'You were far-flung into time like the others of the timelost, and you are back … Were they all brought back to this world and this time?'

'Allissia, there is no time but the present; there never was a wind that blew from past to future, only a wind that blew memory and desire, and those things on a scale beyond our understanding, almost. Concrete memories, and heartfelt passion, and a desperate attempt at communication with those that were seen as couriers. The *lost* were taken into the fabric of creatures that fill the valleys and the deep seas. I don't know what was done to them, but they have been changed, more changed than you, much more. They were placed by the guardians of VanderZande's World in a valley, in the high land; they have been cared for, out of the way, asleep. The guardians have recognized the nature of their couriers at last, and I think they have realized that we are useless to them as such. It has taken a long time for them to come to this understanding, but now I think there will be a stop to the taking of men into the winds.'

By their faces neither Audwyn nor Allissia could understand the flow of words from Faulcon. He smiled suddenly and began to walk back to the village, the manchanged following him closely.

Audwyn said, 'I know the valley that looks towards twin peaks.'

'I know you do.' Faulcon glanced back; Audwyn was troubled, remembering something but not enough. When Faulcon said, 'We must keep our eyes keen for lonely men,' Audwyn almost jumped, his face whitening in a quite startling fashion.

Allissia did not know. She said, merely, 'If your Lena is going to be so changed … why do you wish to find her again? Why not leave her in peace?'

Because I can't! Because I cannot control anything in my life, least of all my selfish concession to curiosity, even less my human need to complete the pattern, to see Lena again, to prove to myself that they really are what they say they are, these wind-creatures of Kamelios. Because without Lena I am a shadow; because with her, in whatever form she is, I can make a pretence of completeness; a part of my mind can rest again, the human part, the insecure part, the loving part.

'Because I am incomplete without her,' he said aloud. The woodland area was noticeably darker than when they had walked up this way; night winds shifted the spidery branches against the red sky above.

'Are you not complete within yourself?' murmured Allissia, and when Faulcon looked over his shoulder, staring pointedly at her hand, clasped in the larger fingers of her husband, she grinned. 'But I'm still an individual. Without Audwyn, if I were totally alone, I would live on, I would survive. I am complete within myself.'

Faulcon shook his head, swinging down a steep bank by hanging onto the leaning trunk of a skagbark. He reached up to catch Allissia's hands as she jumped down; Audwyn descended on his rump. 'It would seem that way, I suppose,' said Faulcon. 'Even as I followed Lena to VanderZande's World, even as I became obsessed with finding her again, even as I drew the friendship of ... someone else, another man, drew it into me like life itself, still I thought that I was an individual, indulging the social rituals. But I don't think that now. When I hunted olgoi alone I felt not solitary but cut off, severed from some part of me that exists not in me but in you, in everyone. I'm a part of more than me, and Lena contains most of that which is outside of me. I'm incomplete without her. And I must find her.'

After duskfall Faulcon stood at the edge of the village, listening to the sounds of night, watching the distant lights close to the rift valley, and the darkened heights of the mountains to the south. In the village there was a celebration somewhere; he could hear the sound of a weird string instrument, accompanying the awful clash of untrained voices. A blacksmith was mending tools, the sound of hammer on heated metal muffled behind the closed doors of his forge, but still punctuating the music. Faulcon could smell the odour of the coals; lifting his mask for a stinging moment he smelled the sickly odour of skagbark, and the pungent aroma of cooked food.

It was very cold and he was glad of the extra clothing he had brought on this trip. When Audwyn finally stepped from the house and walked through the village towards him, the manchanged's breath frosted. Faulcon watched him approach. Nothing had been said since their arrival back from the woodlands, and the high fields, but he had known that Audwyn would want to talk to him, quietly, privately.

'Your friend is very ill, I'm afraid.'

'Ben? He'll get over it. Too much synthetic food is his problem.'

Audwyn made no response except to say that Leuwentok would be unfit to travel the following day.

Faulcon said, 'It isn't important. I think I'd prefer for just the two of us to go.'

'Agreed,' said Audwyn, and he tugged his coat tighter about his neck as a freezing wind suddenly sprung from the east. For a while nothing was said, Faulcon remaining quiet as the manchanged found the right moment to confirm the idea that must have been worrying at him. Above them, above the village, the moons were bright, Merlin the brightest of all, tugging at Faulcon's attention, catching his eye every time he looked around.

At last Audwyn reached out and took Faulcon's arm, leading him slowly into the lee of one of the houses, where the night was not quite so fierce. 'What was my name?'

'Darak Iskaruul. I only had a few moments to scan the records; I saw your face and recognized you at once, but I had little time to read about you. As far as I can tell, all else that you remember of your time in Steel City is the same.'

Audwyn hunched a little; he was angry, Faulcon could see that, and he was allowing that anger its full expression. 'The same, except for the manner of my leaving. I didn't mind not knowing my name, but I don't understand why a false memory was given to me.'

'But no one would have known where you came from. You were a wanderer, and someone suggested you had wandered up from the city, and that is what you remember. There was no deception, I'm sure of it.'

Again silence, and then, 'When was I lost? I came here five years ago.'

'Then you must have slept for nearly a full year. Did you arrive here in the spring, can you remember? When Merlin was full?'

Audwyn nodded and Faulcon smiled slightly. 'The moon has a strong effect on animal life … and on man. When Merlin is full, and the olgoi are chasing up into the hills to fulfil their role as carriers of life, at that same time a few of the sleepers wake up and wander through the high lands as lonely men, choking their lives away. A few survive. Your colonies a long time ago must have found them and helped them, not knowing where they had come from, no doubt assuming they had come up from the rift valley. Perhaps the manchanged thought they were doing the right thing, saving the lonely men's lives, changing them, adapting them, allowing them to forget. Now it is done quite routinely. You remember quite a lot of your early life, but not the events that led you into a time wind. But you *are* beginning to remember something now; or am I wrong?'

Audwyn straightened and shook his head, his gaze beyond Faulcon, out across the night lands below the plateau. 'No, you're not wrong. I remember the valley where I slept. I remember it clearly … a bright light, like a *fiersig*, yes, a *fiersig*, hanging on the side of the valley. I passed through it and into the brilliant daylight, and saw the lights when I looked back. I remember choking and weeping and feeling as if I was going to die … And then a manchanged, a gatherer, covering my eyes and bathing them, and asking me where I'd come from, and would I like to become a part of their community, a part of this; and I can recall how welcome I found that suggestion, and how good it was to sleep in the Grey House, and to come closer to this world.' It was too cold to stand talking any longer and they began to walk back to the house, to the warm fire, to a long night's rest. Audwyn said, 'I had had no idea. Until you mentioned the valley looking towards two peaks I had remembered nothing. Allissia never knew. I think you're right, Leo; no one here knows where the lonely men really come from.' He laughed gently. 'It's ironic; some of the timelost have been among men for years, and none of us ever realized it.'

In the house they found Leuwentok, wrapped in his bed roll and propped against the wall, white and uncomfortable, trying to conjure up a spell for sleep. Allissia was already preparing the packs for the long journey. She made no objection when Audwyn told her she would not be coming.

FINDING

It was not the valley that he remembered from his dream, but the clouds were low and the twin mountains hidden from view. It did not have the brightness, the freshness of the land he had experienced in his time of contact. It was drab and wet, the dark stones sombre and unpleasing, the plant life tangled and uncomfortable.

Yet Audwyn was quite confident that he knew where they were. Calmly, resisting Faulcon's assertions that they ought to travel further round to the east, he led the way down the difficult hillside, between boulders that towered high over their scrambling figures, and eventually out into an open space where Faulcon could see more of the spread of the valley. Without a word Audwyn waited for Faulcon to see the *fiersig*, and grinned as he heard the rifter's gasp of surprised delight.

Colours and shapes, almost static, hugging the earth below an overhang of rock: high on the far wall of the valley, a long climb away. There was a cave there, although its entrance could not be seen through the swirl of its guardian.

It was time for Faulcon to go on alone. Perhaps the creature in the great valley could have brought him here direct, but he had not wished that – he had needed Ben, and Audwyn, and Allissia, he had needed to draw something from them, to convey something to them; he had needed their company before he began the long wait for Lena. Now it was time for solitariness, time to lie down beside Lena's sleeping form and wait for her to stir, and wake.

Audwyn began to pitch the tent. He would wait for a few days and then go home again. Faulcon felt sure he would not be going home alone.

Audwyn was a tiny shape in the lower distance when Faulcon turned for the last time and waved to him. If the manchanged responded, Faulcon was unable to see. The *fiersig* was brightness around him and above him, and as he stepped into its insubstantial form he was immersed in colour and tranquillity; he felt a gentle embrace and knew they were with him. Deeper, through a place of darkness, he could see floating human figures.
He stepped towards them.

EARTHWIND

for Kath and Bob Holdstock

As one with the knowledge and magic of the source
Attuned to the majesty of music
They marched as one with the earth

Jon Anderson,
The Ancient: Giants Under the Sun

PROLOGUE

Some of them died in the cave, died of cold or of hunger, unable to find the spiritual strength to carry on through the winter. Others died out on the snow-covered plateau as they hauled fragments of the ruined ship into the barren cavern in the middle of this ice wilderness; instinctively they knew that they were high on the side of a mountain. When the snow clouds occasionally dispersed they could see into the distance, and though ice crystals stuck their eyelids together, and made blue-skinned statues of them, they could see the green of the lowlands.

A woman led the way, a woman who had once been important to the group, and who was now just a name. They followed her blindly, those who had decided to leave the remains of the crashed ship. Others stayed behind, secure in the vacant mountain cave, slowly starving.

Those that went had already forgotten what the ship meant to them – they had forgotten what they were and who they were, where they had come from and where they had been going; the blinding, driving snow chased these memories from them, but nothing mattered now, nothing but the green lands below them.

And the pattern in their minds, the bizarre and frightening alien image that began to haunt them ...

RITUAL

one

She dreamed of the Stone Age again, and on waking felt a sense of disappointment as the images fled rapidly from her mind, leaving just coldness and strange alien smells. How vivid the recollection of the great tumulus had been, how piercing the imagined sounds of ancient chisel on rock, echoing through the still summer air. Then there had been familiar faces, crowded in a small chamber, and the babble of excited voices, sounding hollow and unreal in the dank confines of the tomb. A flickering light had illuminated the surfaces of the rock that lined the passageway ... there had been a sense of pain, and of pleasure ... words, meaningless as she thought about them on waking, had left her with a sense of great age, of great enigma, of bizarre activity in the dawn of civilized man ...

The dream decayed but for some minutes Elspeth Mueller lay waiting for the after-images to dissolve fully, allowing her sideways view of the forest to assume importance. The sense of pleasure evaporated, but not the pain. The pain persisted.

After a while, in order to examine her ankle, she sat up as straight as she could in her low-roofed cawl, a hastily erected tent of blue-bark and dead vegetation. The cut was deep and blood had run everywhere. It had dried on her calves and soaked into the white leather of her moks, which had taken her hours to make and of which she was very proud. She pulled the shoe from her wounded foot, hating the leather's greasy waterproofing because she remembered where the grease had come from. Tentatively she touched the gash and managed to open the wound again.

A spike of blue-bark, part of the curved frame of the cawl, had driven into her ankle as she slept. Perhaps it had sprung out of position, and at some time during the long night she had impaled herself, not waking, but sensing the pain even in her dream.

The feeling of pain that had accompanied her unconscious revisitation of that Stone Age tumulus came back to her. How bizarre the way two elements of her life, separated by many years, could combine in such a totally inaccurate but such a very coherent way during one short dream, one brief transcendence of normal time. An agony of her childhood, and an event from her recent past (the exploration of the tomb) drawn together in the half-light of her sleeping mind.

With pain she was well acquainted. The ritual agony of her girlhood, the final almost unbearable attack upon her, initiating her, bringing her to womanhood, defining her as a particular type of woman – a *magda*, breast-less, childless – those moments, those terrible, beautiful moments, haunted her sleeping hours more and more …

As if my mind senses the fading of memory – touching her breast – *as if it knows how soon I'll forget* …

There had been no pain when she had been in that ancient valley on Earth. The pain of laughter, of jokes, directed at her almost alien strangeness – that pain, yes: and friendships, maturing naturally into love, but frustrated, defeated, by her ritual lack.

The passage of years, her twenty years in normal society, had poisoned the beauty of her initiation. She thought of her home planet, now, as a brutal place, with barbarian habits, a horrifying world that was as primitive, beyond its glass and steel shutters, as Aeran with its stone and slings.

And yet – again she touched the two glittering jewels that were sewn tight, deep, in the skin of her chest – *and yet the earth is in me, in all my kind, earth and stone, intimate with the red life of my body* …

Perhaps that was why Darren – such a young boy to be such an experienced hunter – perhaps that was why he felt so strong an attraction to her.

'Stone lady' he called her, and it was a name given out of respect, and out of affection. And more recently it had started to become *my* stone lady.

She smiled at the thought, staring out through the wide entrance of her cawl to where huge, damp fronds of blue-bark hung limply in the dense forest, absorbing the dawn mist and waving gently in the unfelt breeze that filtered down through the canopy. To love an alien, to mate with a *nue*, with a beyonder, with a naked-skinned black-skinned stranger from beyond the air and sky …

What was it doing for his reputation in the crog? What thoughts filled the air behind those earthen walls? For the most part they had accepted it, his elders, the seer, the singers of earth and wind and stone; they had not condemned him.

Noise: the noise of wind, high above the forest, not really penetrating this deeply through the tangled growths, the purples and greens and reds, and the flickering tendrils of light-gatherers, reaching into the air above the canopy, thousands of them, like the darting tongues of snakes.

Noise: the chatter of skitch, migrating away from the winding river for an hour or so in search of certain juicy 'worms' that emerged into the hot undergrowth during the night, before coolness and dawn drove them back into the mossy soil.

Noise: the explosive gasps of a gup, jumping backwards from branch to branch as it escaped some unseen terror, a plate-toothed vine, perhaps, or a snapdragon (yes, a snapdragon – she could hear the staccato snap of those slimy monsters, a squad of them, she imagined, swarming through a blue-bark, consuming all that had made the 'tree' their home).

After a while, into this symphony of alien forest sound, came a new noise. Voices, the babbling laughter of a girl, the grunting anger of a boy. They weren't as close as they sounded; the blue-bark fronds, with their peculiar resonating ability, could retransmit forest sound for miles. The group could be miles away, just leaving the crog, excited at the prospect of a full day's hunt down-river on the scree plain bordering the marsh.

Elspeth stretched out her legs so that her feet extended beyond the protection of the cawl. Blood from the ugly gash ran freely on to the moss that covered the soil of the clearing in a thick, spongy bed. And, like a sponge, the frondmoss absorbed and digested the strange alien fluid, leaving no trace but the odour of raw meat.

Am I raw meat? To an animal any other animal is just that – living, raw flesh. Blood is the taste of meat. I am the taste of blood. Natural flesh, living, pulsating, stinking like decayed meat. I am decay. How strange.

Staring at the wound, experiencing the pain, the sight of her bodily loss.

Strange. So long since the last time …

Her ship – faithful servant, a sailing star among the stars, so far above her – the ship had protected her for twenty years, preventing pain, preventing wounds, preventing disease. She had almost forgotten what it was like to function normally. For the first time in her adult life she knew what it was like to be fully human.

Where are those kids?

She could hear their voices, drifting, echoing through the saturated jungle. They were running through the mist, following instinctively the unbeaten track to the small clearing where Elspeth and Darren had built the cawl. They sounded more than usually excited, perhaps because today was the day they would show the beyonder, their strange, hairless female friend (and the 'marked woman' of the older youth, Darren) how to snare blackwing.

She had waited so many hours for this moment, so many desperate hours …

That sudden thought of how long she had spent on Aeran made her heart miss a beat and she glanced at the tiny watch she still wore on her left wrist. The green figures flickered on and off, checking the seconds as they drained away. Nearly one hundred hours. She had been on the surface nearly one hundred hours.

Long before she had arrived in orbit around Aeran she had known that her time on the planet would have to be restricted or … well, it was still a fanciful thought, even if the evidence was overwhelming. (Remember Austin, screaming his fear, his gradual destruction, an insane man filled with a desperation to cling to the last vestiges of what he had once been …?)

She had set that arbitrary limit of a hundred hours as the time of her total stay if she was to remain unaffected by whatever had destroyed Austin. She had been in orbit over two standard months, spending a few hours on the outskirts of the crog, or with the marked couples on their hunting trips; but now, aware of the privilege she was being granted, she had been a full Aeran day in this tiny clearing, sheltered by her hastily made crawl, naked but for a pair of moks and a leather belt from which hung a roughly chipped bone knife. It was part of the preparation for her first hunt, her first taste of alien ritual. And it had used up her time, almost to the full.

Ten seconds, nine, and she watched with growing horror as the last moments of safety drained away.

Five seconds and the voices of Darren and the others grew loud. Two seconds and she shook her head, reached out to the watch and began to remove it from her wrist.

A hundred hours came and passed and she tore the watch from her arm, flung it deep into the bush in front of her, sat trembling and waiting for her friends.

She didn't feel any different, certainly, save for her now total resignation to death. Not death in the physical sense; she was well aware that death was always present, that from the moment she had slipped from the womb she had begun a slow, then increasingly rapid, slide down the road to decay, and would soon crawl back into the womb of the Earth Mother. Not that sort of death, but the death of everything she had been, everything she was, everything she might have hoped to be. How long remained to her she didn't know. She had never discovered how long Austin had been on Aeran before he had realized what was happening. That arbitrary figure had been based on nothing at all. Even a hundred hours might have been too many. But what the passing of that self-imposed limit meant was that she had resigned herself to obliteration, and had done so cheerfully, and without remorse.

She would have to watch her own past very carefully, and monitor the way it faded.

Easing herself out of the crude shelter, Elspeth drew up to her full height and stretched her limbs. The cold, the damp, the cramped position did not bother her, she had found that out very quickly. The nightlife of the forest had been a nuisance and her calves were covered with white blisters where yellowspins had fed on her during her light sleep. The blisters were not the result of the bites but her body's immune reaction to the whip-like parasites that the yellowspin had injected into her. None of them had succeeded in penetrating very far. The ache in her muscles soon vanished and there was just the natural and persisting pain of the gash on her leg.

Elspeth Mueller, standing at her full height, was over six feet tall, a head at least taller than Darren, who was a tall male. Her extra height in no way affected their relationship, although it had prompted much discussion of her ethnic origins, long weeks before, when she had told the young hunter just exactly what she was and where she came from. It had not been a good thing to do, she had realized afterwards, since it constituted cultural interference, but the crog's special interest in her had soon faded.

Her brown skin was naturally sexually unattractive to the males on Aeran, who found her colour amusing; but Darren had penetrated beyond the superficiality of the strange *nue* (hairless humans of either sex) and Elspeth had no doubt that Darren was experiencing something not far short of desire for her. He had, after all, asked her if he might be her marked man, as obvious a declaration of desire as any she had experienced in her short life. She had not yet agreed, but saw his point that it would help her enter the inner dune of the crog, where she was at the moment forbidden to go.

Quite suddenly Darren came bounding out of the undergrowth, grinning and breathing heavily, holding on to a crystal knife that hung round his neck by a thin leather cord. Two other males followed him and behind them came two younger-looking girls. The two youths she recognized as Engus and Laurian. They were both heavily built youngsters and rather bloodthirsty; she had seen their proficiency with stone, sling and spear, but they were not as highly regarded as Darren. Laurian, in fact, had failed his initiation ritual and was hardly thought of at all, but in time he would try again. In the meantime Darren and Engus both demonstrated a pleasant fact of Aeran life – friends were made to last. They had not rejected Laurian as Elspeth might have supposed they would had she not been here witnessing life in the forest at first hand.

Darren was the most slender of the three, and also the tallest. He had to look up to Elspeth, something he didn't like, but towered over most of the rest of the colony. He was good-looking beneath his long yellow hair that hung limply, and dirtily, all round his neck. His body hair seemed tighter than that of the others; deep yellow (in some places almost orange) it looked not so much like fur as a tight-fitting yellow garment. Only his face, above the jaw, was pink and bare. And, at appropriate times, his sex organ.

The two girls were identically furred, save that the younger was still obviously pubescent and large areas of her breast and shoulders were still naked. This girl Elspeth didn't recognize, although she knew the older girl, Brigedd, the marked woman of Laurian. She was unhappy with that status since Laurian had failed to complete the rigorous initiation programme (more a test of physical stamina than anything), whereas she had managed easily. As a consequence, even though her acquaintance with the couple was brief, Elspeth had a picture of a constantly fighting and very unhappy match. Darren talked casually about 'stealing' Brigedd before too long – he always said it within Laurian's range of hearing and the non-warrior grew furious, but was not allowed to do anything by way of issuing challenge.

The group gathered about Elspeth. 'This is Moir,' said Darren, putting his arm round the youngest girl's shoulder. 'My sister.'

Moir looked up at the tall negress and moved her lower jaw in the side-to-side motion that signified wary greeting. *She's very pretty*, thought Elspeth. *Without the fur these people are really beautiful.*

'Elspeth is a friend,' snapped Brigedd, and the younger girl smiled self-consciously. 'Hello.'

'Hello Moir. Your first hunt?'

'She's not hunting,' said Engus darkly. (Why was he always so bad tempered?) 'She's watching. Which means I'm watching.'

Elspeth realized, quite suddenly, that this was Engus's marked woman. Darren's sister! Was Darren unhappy about the fact? She couldn't decide.

Elspeth noticed Darren and Engus looking her up and down. She felt herself flush and fought not to drop her hands to conceal herself. 'You're making me uncomfortable.'

Darren smiled, fixed her with his blue-eyed gaze. 'Why?'

'Never mind. When do we start?'

'As soon as we can,' said Darren.

'She hasn't scratched any symbols,' said Brigedd. Elspeth's heart raced. The girl was smiling at her, knowing of her fascination for the symbols used by the people of the crog. For the first time since they had arrived Elspeth noticed Brigedd's arms – badly gashed and only just beginning to heal. She'd been in a very bad fight. Seeing Elspeth's scrutiny she touched her left arm almost tentatively. 'Duel,' she said. 'I won.'

Obviously, thought Elspeth, bearing in mind the finality of Aeran duels. The duelling system, here, was complex and was one area of the culture she would not fully understand until she was accepted inside the dune walls.

'That's right,' said Elspeth loudly, returning to the question of her carving the symbols of the hunt. 'I haven't done my duty yet. Who's going to show me?'

'I'll show you of course,' said Darren. He too knew how excited she got when she saw, or watched the production of, the complex symbols that the colonists (was that term appropriate any more?) used at every junction in their lives. He probably also knew that she was less interested in the black-wing hunt than in making the symbols for herself and having him explain them. Today, with luck, she would make a small breakthrough in understanding what had happened on this world, Aeran. And today, with any luck at all, she would take a large and important step towards understanding something that had been a mystery, a tourist-attracting enigma, for more than seven thousand years.

She bound up the gash on her ankle and then they ran through the fast-rising early morning mist until they came to the river. Here they found movement less difficult and wound their way, with the meandering water course, through the dense jungle of the forest, until at last they had left it behind. The land rose into a series of rolling hills, boulder-scattered and deeply incised with the valleys of rivers which ran from the distant mountains, through the forest and into the marshes.

Here, on the hills, a deep and soft layer of frondmoss made running very comfortable. They left the river and climbed over the top of the valley slope so they could look down at the thread of silver and out to the brown and glistening swamps. Lakes and mudflats, the inhospitable land between the crog and the vast salt ocean was a place where no Aerani had ever ventured, an area of carnivores and maneating mud-pits. There, at the edge of the swamplands, the eyes and hands of dishonoured Aerani were committed to decay, denying the spirit its rightful consummation by fire. And there, too, the ground seemed thrown up into ridged humps, like peculiarly fashioned graves – but the graves, occasionally, moved and revealed themselves as the beasts they were.

'This way,' called Darren, leading the group away from the direction of the river and further across the frondmoss plain. The air was crisp and cold and a strong wind, blowing up across the hills, carried with it the rich scents of the crowded forest. Elspeth, breathing deeply to compensate for the low oxygen content of the atmosphere, found the smells exciting and sensuous. She became dizzy with the effort of breathing and stopped, for a moment, to stare across the green and purple mat of foliage, the flickering snake tongues, the darting animal shapes …

Behind the forest rose the mountains …

Partly obscured by clouds, white with snow, jagged and sheer: the mountains. They cast their shadow across the land, the shadow of snow, evoking memories of her past, and a fear that had been for so long buried beneath her trappings of adulthood.

Fear surfaced – blizzard/blood … the coldness, the deathly chill, the needles of ice …

The terrifying memory receded, but her panic remained; she ran after Darren and the others, a silent scream echoing (silently) through her mind. While the mountains watched …

Eventually they came to a great causeway, dipping into the earth, running for nearly a mile and flanked by sheer cliffs.

Hanging from the cliffs, dangling almost effortlessly, were thousands of dark leathery shapes. Blackwings.

Laurian and Brigedd vanished, running silently over one cliff-top to get to the other end of the valley. Engus and Moir crept off along the other edge of the causeway so that the girl could watch the procedure of the hunt with Engus explaining. The youth was annoyed at having to waste this hunt in such explanations; Engus was always bad tempered, and his disapproval of Elspeth and her involvement with the colony (she was a *nue* after all, he often shouted) always made his presence unwelcome.

'If we can't catch one of that lot,' said Darren, pointing to the sleeping blackwings, 'then we ought to be ashamed of ourselves.'

They lay on their stomachs and stared at the silent valley. Blackwings hunted in the early afternoon; two or three hours of frenzied feeding, and then back to the 'roost' for the rest of the day and all of the following night, hanging motionless but not quite fully unconscious as many an unsuccessful hunter had discovered to his cost.

'You'll need your own snare,' said Darren, and slid out of sight behind a jagged rock. Elspeth crawled round after him and squatted on her haunches, staring at the desolation of the frondmoss plain. It was a stark land, rolling brown turf, scattered with boulders and the clumps of tangleweed that the Aerani hunters used as snares. It was not an angry land, it was an inhospitable land, and its bleakness chilled Elspeth more than the cool wind on her naked skin.

The wind had dropped to a whisper, and at the far end of the causeway a thin veil of mist remained, clinging to the valley and making shadows of the activity there. Elspeth could hear Moir babbling her questions, and Engus's occasional angry grunt that silenced the girl for a few seconds. Suddenly, however, a new sound came from Moir's direction; the sound of her voice singing.

Elspeth was taken by surprise and she listened intently to the song as it spilled across the valley, not loud, not shrill, not alarming, just a gently fluctuating note, quite entrancing and quite beautiful. Elspeth had heard singing from the walls of the crog – several songs, by several different Aerani – but this music, coming from the girl above the cliff, was unfamiliar.

'She'll scare the blackwings, won't she?' she said to Darren.

The boy shook his head, abruptly, decisively. He was watching his sister through narrowed eyes, a hint of a smile on his lips.

'It's an earth song,' he said quietly. 'She's adding to it in her own way.'

'What does it do?'

'Wins the earth,' he said matter-of-factly. 'The blackwing like it, they think all is well. All we have to do is capture the wind for a while.'

'Singing?'

'No!' said Darren, shocked. 'Not singing! Can you sing the wind song? Would you dare?'

Elspeth shrugged. 'We'll carve it, then. As a symbol.'

'Not even I can do that,' said the youth. 'Not yet, anyway. No, we'll make simple offerings to the wind ...' he trailed off, staring upwards. 'Listen to her voice.'

Drifting, soothing, the note perfectly held, perfectly pitched. Darren watched her, distantly. He seemed full of pride, full of love.

They walked to the nearest clump of tangleweed. Seven whip-like arms trailed limply on the ground and under Darren's instruction Elspeth lay across the clump; but although one strand moved slightly the weed remained, on the whole, uninterested. They walked to a second plant and here had better luck. As Elspeth stretched her body, stomach down, across the heart of the weed, so two of the whips shivered and wrapped around her limbs, drawing tight.

'Take your pick,' said Darren. Elspeth reached for the longer tendril and gently detached it from the moss, shaking the clinging matrix from its three thin roots. 'The roots can be broken off.'

'Is that necessary?'

'Not necessary, but they'll burrow into you if you don't.'

'Oh.' She gently snapped the roots and the plant coiled and uncoiled for a moment, then wrapped around her arm.

'It likes you,' said Darren, grinning. He swept back his hair and looked around. 'My turn.'

He reached out to the same clump of tangleweed and they all wrapped round him. He gently disentangled himself and uprooted the longest strand. The plant flexed and twisted as he practised with it, and the motions grew faster and faster, the expression of intensity on his face increasing. Eventually the tangleweed was moving too fast for Elspeth to observe. 'Are you watching, stone lady? Are you watching? This is the sort of proficiency you need to make a snare.' He seemed proud. 'Try it.'

The tangleweed raced in Elspeth's grip. Darren nodded, satisfied. 'With luck you'll catch a blackwing and be inside the crog before night. Once the weed has a hold it's up to you to keep your grip. That's when it gets dangerous. But once the blackwing is snared it only takes a few seconds for its heart to stop. You'll see.'

Moir's song faded away and mournful wind sounds drifted out of the causeway.

'When do I carve the symbols? Now?'

Darren laughed. 'All right. Come on, let's use that piece of bare rock.'

Crouched by a boulder, that grew out of the moss at the very mouth of the causeway, Darren removed his leather necklace and eased the crystal knife out of its binding. He passed this precious weapon (the gift of his initiation into warriorhood) to Elspeth, who cradled it in her hand.

With its tip she gently scratched the diamond-shaped pattern that aroused the forces within the rock. Three diamonds in a chain and Darren seemed satisfied. He stared at the boulder as if seeing more than its surface, and then directed her to add a fourth figure to the other three.

She scratched the rock, the lines coming out wavy and uneven, but her hand shook so much with excitement that she could hardly even think what she was doing …

This is how man carved the stones of Ireland seven thousand years ago … did it mean then what it means now?

Satisfied with the offering to the earth Darren took back his knife and licked the dust from its point. The knife was his greatest pride and he carefully slung it back around his neck.

'What do they mean?' Elspeth asked, smiling as she touched her shallow scratches.

'You have put yourself into the wind; the shape allows for the passage of your hunter's soul into the earth and the wind by way of the boulder. In water it would be different, through the forest different again. The rock itself is the most direct way of offering. Now the earth may return your favour by helping you snare a blackwing.'

Simple, really. Elspeth pondered the shapes. One more symbol for her answer book. The number that she understood was growing, and the repertoire of rock carvings was not vast. But this was the first that she herself had carved! Simple it may have been, but it was a great step forward for her.

She bent forward and kissed the symbol she had carved and Darren grinned. Then they ran back to the blackwing sleeping-grounds and lay flat on the spongy moss, staring down into the rift.

'Before we came we asked our seer for a prediction,' said Darren quietly. Interested, Elspeth glanced at him.

'What did he come up with?'

'Good fortune. New beast,' said the youth.

She remained quiet for a moment, then turned back to regard their potential prey. 'That's the trouble with your oracle, it doesn't leave room to figure out what it means. Now where I come from there's an oracle—'

Darren waved her silent. 'There's your blackwing!'

One of the leathery creatures had dropped from its sleeping position and flown a few yards out into the bottom of the causeway. It curled up on a rock and wrapped its membranous wings about its body, buried its globular head in the skin wrinkles on its torso.

'Aim your snare for the legs.'

'Right.'

Elspeth, clutching her tangleweed tightly, walked quietly into the valley, ducking behind exposed rocks wherever she could, and bent almost double as she approached the creature. She realized she was sweating and the gentle breeze on her naked skin made her shiver with cold. There was something excitingly primitive about this sort of hunting, using parts of the environment to catch parts of the environment, matching strength with strength, speed with speed. One blast from her Kiljarold automatic would dispatch the blackwing to a better place in a split second. But there was no excitement in that.

Five yards from the creature she stopped, caught her breath and tried to calm her body. She was deep in the valley, the wind blowing quite strong now, and as she walked she could feel the dried blood on her calves cracking and irritating her skin. The gash was still painful, but she didn't care. All around her the motionless black shapes of the blackwing population hung silent. High overhead, where the sheer cliff was a jagged grey gash against the brightening sky, two faces peered down at her. At the other end of the valley both Laurian and Brigedd were darting swiftly from rock to rock, approaching two susceptible blackwings as they snoozed on small boulders.

Stepping forwards gently Elspeth closed the distance between herself and her prey. The tangleweed in her hand seemed to tense with her, as if waiting for its instruction. She could see the beast's throat moving as it breathed, hear the dull triple thump of its 'heart'; pinflies, the animal's natural parasite, moved across its body in apparently aimless activity. At any moment the blackwing might wake up, see her, and vanish in that bizarre mind-jumping flight that made the animals on this world so difficult to catch.

It had to be now.

Slowly she raised her arm, holding the tangleweed towards the animal. A moment later the blackwing's eye opened, its head turned to look at her, and she squeezed the whip.

The plant uncoiled almost effortlessly and wrapped around the blackwing's leg; the creature screeched and flapped into the air, but the tangleweed kept its grip. Elspeth felt her body swung into the air, and for a second she panicked …

Let go.

She hit the rock full face, grazing nose, forehead, jewelled breast. Sprawled across the boulder she watched the blackwing flicker away, leaving her in bursts of here/not-here; it covered the length of the valley in a few seconds, darting in different directions, almost defying her efforts to follow it with her dizzy gaze.

Miraculously the valley remained still, only a few blackwings actually flying off in panic pursuit.

Shaken, hurting where her skin was grazed and raw, Elspeth ran back to Darren and knelt beside him.

He was laughing. 'You let go.'

'I know I let go! I nearly bashed my skull in.'

He reached out and touched her grazed nose. 'You'll have to be more determined than that if you want to catch a blackwing.'

'Are you sure we drew the right symbols?'

'You and your symbols.' Amusement. 'Yes, we drew the right ones. The only thing that went wrong is that you lost your nerve.'

'Well, I won't lose it again.'

'We'll have to wait for a likely prey – look, down the valley! Quick!'

She stood up and stared down the gorge. Distantly, only just in eyeshot, one of the two hunters at that end was snaring a blackwing successfully. The great beast had its wings at full stretch and was beating the air, flying in short jumps with the tiny human form gripping it securely at a distance of some ten feet. For a moment beast and man (woman?) vanished, and reappeared some way distant, but still the hunter held on, and the blackwing collapsed to the ground. A second later it was motionless and the hunter (it was Laurian) was waving at them.

'It mind-jumped while he was still attached.'

'A strong beast,' said Darren thoughtfully. 'It's a strange sensation, especially if the beast changes direction mid jump.'

'And all the animals on this world can do that?'

Darren nodded. 'All except us. But then, we have the Earthwind.'

'The Earthwind? What's that?'

Before Darren could answer, however, Engus and Moir raced by, Moir laughing as a well-aimed kick from her marked man found her furry rump.

Darren called to them to be quiet and they both dropped to the ground, looking apologetic, although Engus's remorse was only momentary as he met Elspeth's gaze.

'Nice try,' called Moir. 'We've seen enough. We're going to hang for a while.'

They were gone, then, racing across the frondmoss until distance and the vapour barrier hid them from view.

'Hang awhile? What does that mean?'

Darren glanced at her. 'We'll do it later. You'll see. I'm not letting you go this time.'

Sex, thought Elspeth. *It's their term for sex. I've been here all this time and I still haven't learned their most basic colloquialisms.*

A sudden deafening beat of wing against air dragged their attention back to the valley of the blackwings. A huge male blackwing, with a span of nearly twenty feet, was settling on to the boulder beneath which they crouched. Darren fell backwards in surprise as the great single eye turned to look at the two humans, but Elspeth jumped to her feet and flexed her tangleweed so that it flickered outwards …

The air before her face was disturbed violently as the leather-winged creature slashed at her, but perhaps because of her unfamiliar dark skin, perhaps because of her unconscious movement backwards, the razor-sharp claws missed her. The blackwing, before it knew what was happening, had a tangle-weed around its left leg.

It screeched, stretched and struggled into the air ...

'Hold it this time,' yelled Darren, scurrying away as the great beast swung down to the earth, unable to pull itself into the air as easily as it had expected.

'Help me,' screamed Elspeth as she felt her body dragged forwards and upwards.

'Do it yourself!' shouted Darren, delighted.

'I can't! Oh God!'

'Keep holding!'

All she could see was the immense black shape stretched out before her. The tangleweed was biting into her wrist where it had wrapped itself around her arm before snaring the blackwing's leg; she ignored the pain, tried to ignore her fear that the primitive beast would turn on her at any moment. The blackwing was too busy panicking, however. The thunder she heard was the beat of wings. The wind she felt was her body being half dragged across the stony ground as the beast tried to fly.

Sudden nausea!

She shook her head. Her stomach had turned over and the dizzying sensation of impending sickness had flashed through her skull. What had happened?

It happened again! And again!

The cliffs seemed to jump as if they were being displaced by split seconds. A boulder flashed by and was gone, not smoothly, just vanishing. She screamed. The blackwing too began to screech, in its horrifying high-pitched voice; loudly, angrily, beating the air, but fallen, now, to the ground.

Elspeth kept a tight hold on the tangleweed, but maintained her distance from the threshing animal. Slowly she climbed to her feet. Her whole body was trembling, her stomach hurting with the wrenching sensations of sickness that had accompanied the flight. She knew what had happened but was almost too confused to think about it. The here/not-here dance of the blackwing had carried her with it, instantaneous transportation across several yards at a time. She had teleported. She had jumped through space hanging on to the beast's mind by the vegetable whip that had served her so well.

The blackwing died.

Its threshing ceased, its eye began to bleed, sepia blood running down its shiny black skin. Elspeth released her grip on the tangleweed and the plant curled about her arm like a passionate snake, gripping her tightly and bury-ing its tip in the warm wetness of her underarm. She wiped her hands on her thighs, stared at the smeared blood from the broken skin on her right wrist. Darren raced up and dropped beside the dead blackwing. He looked up into the sky, stared at the cliffs where large numbers of the animals still hung calmly and disinterestedly.

'You were lucky,' he said. 'That final screech usually makes them attack. That's the one thing you have to fear, the blackwing calling for help.'

'It panicked a few of them.'

'But they didn't attack.' Darren stared at her, reached out to touch the tangleweed and let his fingers run over her ebony skin. 'Perhaps this, perhaps your own darkness ... I've never known them not attack before.'

They stared at their prey. Its wings had begun to shrivel as body fluid drained out of them and into the slowly distending body cavity, and after a moment Darren crawled over and took a hold of the skeletal structure of the blackwing's upper limbs. He snapped the bones with a great deal of effort and ripped the wings from the body. Using the sharp end of the bone he punctured the body cavity and glistening green fluid spurted across the ground, bubbling as it drained into the moss.

'Help me,' he said.

Elspeth gripped one of the beast's legs, and with Darren hauling at the other they dragged their hunt back to the entrance of the causeway. Breathless they squatted for a while and laughed. Their laughter became more excited, more childish. Elspeth said she thought that she must have looked really funny being dragged by the blackwing. They laughed. Darren said that she had. They laughed some more. Elspeth said she'd never been so frightened in all her life; they shrieked with laughter.

Some of the blackwings left their sleeping places and beat a noisy track out towards the distant weed-clogged lakes of the nearer marshlands; haze and mist consumed them as the two hunters watched, silently contemplating the morning's events. Elspeth ran her fingers along the faint symbols she had drawn, tracing the shaky lines of the lozenge patterns. 'Thank you,' she whispered, feeling strange as she said it, watching the rock as if some reply might miraculously appear on its grey surface.

'We'll come back tomorrow and chip them in deeply,' said Darren.

'A successful hunt,' said Elspeth proudly. 'My own permanent symbols.'

'It's a great moment,' agreed Darren. 'If you go on like this you'll soon be carving the Earthwind.'

'What *is* that, Darren? You mentioned it before. What is the Earthwind?'

He looked at her in surprise, then glanced at the spidery symbols scraped on the stone. 'The Earthwind is ... well, the *Earthwind!*' He smiled, looked at her and shook his head. 'It's the symbol that gave us life, and gives us the earthsong to guide us.'

'The oracle!' said Elspeth loudly, making some slight sense of what he was trying to say. 'You call the oracle "Earthsong". Is that right?'

Darren seemed uncomfortable. He traced round Elspeth's symbols with his forefinger and frowned. He said nothing.

'But Earthwind,' insisted Elspeth. 'Darren, what *is* that? I mean … well … show me. Please, show me.'

'I can't show you …' Darren trailed off looking awkward. 'The Earthwind, it's …' He struggled for words. On his face, above the fur, a thin sheen of sweat appeared.

Suddenly he jumped to his feet and ran back to the dead blackwing. 'Come on, let's get him to the forest, out of sight of the rest.'

Elspeth sighed, but decided to live with her intrigue. There was plenty of time yet. She looked down the valley and realized there was no sign of Laurian and Brigedd. 'Where are they?'

'Doing what we should be doing,' said Darren. Elspeth felt her stomach knot; Darren seemed matter of fact.

'Hanging?'

'Hanging. But not with this beast lying around for any hunter to pick up and claim as his own.'

They dragged the carcass back to the river and from there back to the forest and the tiny clearing where they had all met earlier. Darren was out of breath, his yellow-orange fur saturated and matted with sweat. Elspeth just felt cold. Her wrist was hurting and she wished she had just a pair of shorts or even a decent pair of tall boots. The leather moks she was wearing rubbed her heels and slipped about with the sweat from her feet. Nakedness had its shortcomings.

Resting, squatting on the ground, Darren unwound his tangleweed and flexed it a couple of times. He looked at the vegetation wall all around and finally spotted something. He pointed. 'Look there. See?'

Peering through the tall plants, the great divided trunks of the blue-barks with their precisely straight branches sticking out like vanes, she saw what looked like a large net. It was difficult to discern exactly what she was looking at … a sort of cocoon hanging from one of the lower branches – orange laced through with black …

With a start she realized what it was and it made her heart race. Engus and Moir were hanging from the tree, locked together by their tangleweeds, legs trailing limply, faces together in a long, almost motionless kiss; each had one hand on the branch and they were tied to the girder by one end of each tangleweed. They swung slowly round, completely still, completely unbothered by anything.

Darren became very excited. Elspeth became very anxious. She was several inches taller than the youth, and a lot heavier, and she didn't know whether or not she liked the idea of having sex whilst dangling from two whips. But then what was she here for if not to become a part of these people until she could fully understand the symbols of their culture?

She rose to her feet and took a deep breath. Darren grabbed her hand and almost dragged her to the nearest blue-bark.

'Do what I do,' he said calmly, and reached up so that his snare could wrap itself around the lowest branch. Elspeth did the same and the two tangle-weeds curled down and reached around their bodies. With a jolt, and a gasp of surprise, Elspeth felt herself lifted from the ground, her body, the jewels in her breast, her belly, still tense with anticipation, locking against Darren's furry torso.

For a moment she felt the breath squeezed from her body, but as the tan-gleweeds dragged them upwards and her right hand locked on to the stability of the branch, the plants curling further down and creeping around buttocks and thighs to support her, so she began to experience an unexpected sensual-ity. Darren's lips pressed against hers and she closed her eyes, felt his warm tongue in her mouth touching her own. He penetrated her with some diffi-culty and she unconsciously hauled herself higher so their height difference became lessened. The tangleweed contracted and she felt herself securely held.

He moved very slowly, almost too slowly for her taste, but as they started to spin, first to the left, then back, blown by wind and the slight movements of their bodies, so her body began to whisper its pleasure, her heartbeat became a solid, impassioned thumping and her kissing motions became wild and uncompromising. She wanted to do so much and there was nothing the tan-gleweeds would let her do but gently twist and turn, moving ever so slightly, focussing all her awareness on the touch and interlocking of their bodies.

When they returned to the clearing Engus and Moir already had the black-wing cut into easily transportable chunks. They were sitting on the ground and Moir was watching as Engus eased the blackwing's teeth from its gaping mouth. As Elspeth walked over to them and knelt, without saying a word, Moir giggled.

'What's funny?' asked Elspeth. Her right arm ached and the skin was raised in angry weals where the tangleweed had failed to take all the pressure from her body.

'Nothing,' said Moir, glancing at her but looking embarrassed.

'She's laughing at us,' said Darren, inspecting the divided carcass. 'Good. You've done a good job.'

'Did we look funny?' asked Elspeth self-consciously. Engus smiled and ignored her. Moir stuck out her lower lip and stared at her brother.

'Well?' said Darren in mock severity. 'Did we?'

'Just a bit,' said Moir.

'You shouldn't have been looking,' murmured Elspeth. She was about to say that anyway they'd both looked funny too, but she didn't.

Taking as much of the blackwing as they could carry Engus and Moir left the clearing to return to the crog. Darren helped Elspeth widen her shelter slightly and she squatted inside it for a while, watching the youth tying the remainder of the blackwing to a long piece of bark. Her intention was to return to the crog for a few hours and take immediate advantage of the fact that, having snared her first blackwing, she would now be allowed to sit on the inner perimeter of the earthworks, with the other initiates who were slowly working their way back into the heart of the settlement. She would then fly her shuttle back to the orbiting ship and record her experiences and few discoveries; then – a long bath, spend an hour in the medical unit, and sleep for a day. She was bitten, bruised and shaken, and that was too much for a girl to bear all in thirty or so hours. A tactful retreat was called for.

As she watched Darren working, so she thought of what she had learned. In all of her previous visits here she had remained outside the giant earthen walls with the two or three juveniles who were beginning their programme of self-proving. Here she had talked with both youths and adults, getting their trust and their interest; she had even been allowed to walk around the outer compound, which was nothing more than the ditch between the double walls of the crog (the dune-trench, they called it). In all that time she had struggled and worked to pick up hints as to the cultural meanings of everything she could see about her. There were omissions and additions, certainly, but the colony on Aeran had done nothing less than completely recapitulate a particular Stone Age culture; at least, the tomb-building and rock-decorating aspects of that culture. And those decorations, those symbols, were tantalizing. She had seen them in Ireland, preserved on the timeless face of stone, and she had wondered then what they had meant. But imagination is reason's worst enemy and she had left in an agony of incomprehension. Now they were alive again, living symbols of a living culture. She *had* to understand what they meant and what had happened here ... But all the time she was faced with a single problem: linking names and meanings to shapes and designs. She had interpreted only seven symbols in more than forty hours, and if Austin had been right then time was already running out for her.

And there was one symbol that she had never seen and, until today, never even heard mentioned. The Earthwind.

When Darren had mentioned the Earthwind he had seemed uneasy, uneasy at her lack of understanding as if it was something he couldn't believe was true – a person not fully comprehending the symbol. He had said it was the symbol that had given them life. An earth symbol, obviously, or a womb symbol. But equally obviously it was something of basic and paramount importance to the Aerani. Her next task *had* to be to pick that symbol out.

Making her mental plans she hadn't noticed that Darren was standing out-side the cawl, looking upwards and away to the south.

'Finished?' she asked him. (Was he angry because she hadn't helped?)

'Quiet. Listen.'

Elspeth crawled outside and stood up. Immediately she heard it, the sound that was bothering him. A whining, moaning sound, very distant … but coming closer.

She looked up through the thin canopy of this part of the forest, into the grey skies where the spiral clouds whirled across the jungle, away from the lakes and up into the snow-covered mountains. The sound carried beneath them, riding the winds, opening out across the forest.

Louder.

The rhythmic beat of pulse-engines pushing a ship forwards at sub-sonic speed; the moan of a stabilizer field, the shriek of metal cooling against the wind … familiar sounds to Elspeth; terrifying sounds to Darren.

The youth was white beneath his fur, and he looked at her in panic, but when she didn't panic he stood his ground.

'Do you know what that is?' he asked, the words almost choking him.

'Yes. Yes, I do …'

'A beast? A new beast …' He was remembering the oracle's prediction. New beast. Something from the swamps, he was almost certainly thinking. But it wasn't from the Aerani swamps that the flying beast had come.

The ship never entered their field of vision, riding away to the west. It was flying towards the crog and the clearing around it, and the changing rhythm of the engines made it obvious that it was slowing to land.

As it passed from earshot Elspeth found herself trembling almost as much as Darren, who walked across to the blackwing and crouched, his head bowed in silent contemplation.

'It's nothing to be afraid of,' she called to him as she walked behind him. *What a terrible thing to say. Before I even know what they're doing here.*

A fleeting memory of her childhood: the sprawling metropolis of New Anzar on Pliedase IV, the perpetual rumbling of rocket ships passing above the tribal city. On that day of her great pain, the ritual mastectomy that she had borne before the cameras without a whimper, without a tear, the great ships had been pouring through the skies, bringing the invader to the deserted lands in the northern hemisphere. Against the roar of the ships she had seen her body mutilated in a beautiful barbaric way. The glittering jewels sewn into the raw meat wounds. The hymns, the scream of rockets, the stench of ozone, the shuffling, crying, moaning amorphisms of the thou-sands of tribes crammed into the giant city, dancing and laughing, and celebrating the initiation rituals of their various ethnic groups.

She remembered her friends, so many friends, so many tears …

But as she tried to remember their names, their faces, so she found those memories were gone; there was just the agonizing motion of the knife, the deafening thunder of rockets, the wet lips of the surgeon, slashing, slashing …

Her friends had gone. The moments before that ritual were gone. As she strained to remember, to recall her life before the initiation, she turned away from Darren and began to scream. Her scream echoed through the clearing and carried away through the forest on the resonating fronds of the blue-barks. Darren watched her with shocked surprise, then ran to her and shouted her name.

She continued to scream. In her head there was a blankness, a darkness, an emptiness that she had only just noticed.

Ships …

Sobbing …

Shuffling, agony, pain …

But nothing before it! The past was slipping away already. She had known it would, and she had expected it, but the fact of its passing was a shock that could only be borne by screaming.

When she stopped sobbing Darren was still holding her. It was dark. Something had crept out of the forest and stolen the remains of the blackwing.

two

The vehicle wound across the landscape of Aeran, slowly weaving through and around the forest, crashing through dense undergrowth, skirting jagged rock formations and plunging nose first into bitterly blue rivers; rode downstream with the currents, rising and sinking, all the time watching and listening.

It emerged on to the bank of one river where shaped stone posts suggested a long-disused landing station, primitive and crude, yet still intact against the winding spiral of time, the gusting winds, drenching rains. Perhaps a hundred years since this small station had been used to moor a boat, or a raft. The vehicle shimmered yellow, creaking its disused moving parts as antennae turned, and cameras extended, swivelling in a slow circle, taking in the view of the world.

Then moved on its way, groaning, burning vegetable life as it laboured up steep slopes; cracked the air, the oxygen, leaving the tang of ozone, electric discharge snapping at the unturned, richly mineralized earth.

Miles distant its eyes were the eyes of Karl Gorstein, ship-Meister of the *Gilbert Ryle*, seated in his plush, warm quarters, the lights turned low, a hint of rose in the air, ventilation rustling, ruffling the red and blue drapes which moved almost imperceptibly giving their static life force a dynamic energy; animals and landscapes rippled and changed on the walls.

'Turn left,' murmured Gorstein into the quietness, and the eyes turned left, showed him mountains half hidden by blue tree-forms; a black shape winged across the foliage, dropped swiftly out of sight. The sun glanced sharply from scattered crystal outgrowths on the distant slopes. White caps, the white of snow: gleamed.

'Turn right,' he said softly. From the screen came the dizzying sensation of rapid movement as the vehicle pivoted; green and purple, the unobservable low-growth swept past his vision; flash of glass; crystallized earth essence, perhaps quartz, perhaps mica, perhaps diamond, or the shards of a broken emerald, smashed by geomantic forces, scattered above the living earth. The vehicle would tell them when it returned.

Turned right. Showed shipMeister Gorstein the flowing waters of the river, widening back along the route the vehicle had already followed. More black flying shapes were settling distantly, out of sight behind the forest. There was movement nearby, almost imperceptible. As he watched, so that movement resolved into a running shape, orange, furry, small and lean. It darted out of sight and did not reappear.

'Turn right.'

The light catching the smooth hull of the ship, a mile and a half distant. Beyond the ship the earthen wall around the colony rose starkly from the high-ground clearing in the heart of the jungle. Smoke drifted above the wall, spiralling on the wind vortices, dispersing into the vast sky. Blackness, thinning, a vein of fire quickly returning to earth.

Behind Gorstein the door opened and closed softly. Knowing this was the rationalist he ignored the sound for a few moments.

On the screen a woman darted from the nearby undergrowth, stared at the vehicle for a second, before running away out of sight. Gorstein leaned forward and instructed the vehicle to follow her. The image on the screen shifted along the river and then lurched as the robot mobilized its pursuit.

After a minute, as the screen showed a dense wall of vegetation approaching, into which the woman had run, Gorstein realized that for the moment he would have to make do with that single glimpse.

A dark-skinned woman, very tall, very lean, very beautiful. Her hair had been cropped short, and there had been jewels sparkling on her chest. She had been naked but for a pair of crude shoes. She did not, he felt sure, belong on Aeran.

'You sent for me?'

The rationalist's voice was calm, old. Without turning to face him Gorstein nodded slowly. 'Yes.'

He rose and crossed to the draped window. Pulling back the patterned curtain he found himself staring out across a flat, almost barren field, dull brown vegetation, lowly and struggling. But at the end of the field the impressive earthworks of the colony rose almost sheer for twenty feet, before curving over to form a rampart above which the spiralling smoke strand was still battling through the wind. There was no one watching. Through the gap in the earthworks all that could be seen were the brown, gentle slopes of a second ring of earth, a wall within a wall, a double barrier against the invading eyes of the ship.

As he stared at those walls so his apprehension returned. It was impossible to explain this nervousness, this sense of wrongness, and yet as he stared at the colony on Aeran he knew that things were not right; he was acutely uncomfortable.

Turning, he faced the rationalist. The smiling man who stood there showed unmistakable signs of his distant oriental ancestry, but the features were overlaid, now, with the mixed expressions of many generations of racial intermixing. The tracery of red blood vessels that covered his whole body (a pressure accident some years before) further obscured the fact that he, of all the rationalists that Gorstein had ever encountered, was closest to the race which had brought awareness of the cosmic *tao* so absolutely into the human psyche.

Peter Ashka: white-haired, a thin white beard around the angle of his jaw; deep-set brilliant blue eyes, housed in heavy lids, in a face as richly lined as it was veined. He stood, slightly bowed, staring at the floor before Gorstein's feet; his hands shook as he clutched his black cloth bag to his chest. Bare feet showed beneath his blue and green ship-robe; the robe was gathered about his waist and displayed the man's total thinness. It was the thinness of age, not race, and yet for all his feeble appearance Peter Ashka was a strong and vital man. And a great comfort to Gorstein who leaned upon that strength more often than he leaned upon the strength of sex.

Gorstein motioned the rationalist deeper into the room and indicated that he should sit on one side of the communion mat that had been laid and prepared in one corner of these quarters.

Ashka walked forward, still silent and bowed with respect, and took a position on the south side of the mat so that Gorstein could sit facing that pole, the strong pole of any revolving planet. When they were both seated and had smiled at each other (and the difference in status had been formally dispersed) Ashka relaxed and placed his cloth bag on the mat before him. He looked up at Gorstein and motioned that he should strip. Gorstein undid the belt of his robe and let it slip from his shoulders, leaving the warm material gathered about him, but allowing the rationalist's expert eyes to survey the muscles and angles of his body. 'You look strained,' said Ashka calmly. 'Tense. Yes, tense. You look apprehensive. Yes. I'll certainly be able to help you.'

'Thank you,' said Gorstein with the faintest of smiles touching his lips. *I wonder. I wonder if your little magic book can help me, or if it is just your relaxing presence …?*

He stared at the items on the mat, several small, patterned plastic jars, smooth to the touch, indefinable to the eye as the subtle lines of decorative colour twisted in and out of the fabric of the containers, almost imprisoning the awareness of the casual observer.

'I have caffeine, liquified and flavoured with chocolate, I imagine. There is mescal,' he tapped the smallest of the jars; touching a third, 'this is neurobyn, probably not advisable at the moment. And this one is …' he broke off and picked up the last jar, frowning as he studied it. After a moment he shook it and smiled when it rattled. 'Button cookies. Very good. Do have some. There is also sweet starch, and this protein slab is genuine meat.' He waved his hand across the food. 'Please feel free to take what you want.'

Ashka regarded the delicacies enviously, then glanced up at the ship-Meister. 'Will you eat first as well?'

Gorstein declined. He wasn't feeling hungry, and didn't want to risk a stimulant. Ashka seemed disappointed and looked briefly at the protein slab before raising his hands. 'Thank you, but I will also decline.'

Gorstein removed the food from the mat and Ashka placed the cloth bag in the centre of the ring of *ching* hexagrams that had been hand-sewn into the fabric. Purely decorative, it was nevertheless impossible to deny the stillness, the calmness that they extended to the seated observer who regarded them. The pattern, just a collection of threads, was so evocative that it was as if some intangible essence flooded from the mat to the mind, a drug that worked its magic in the moment of looking.

Opening the bag Ashka unpacked the contents, laying them out before him, neatly, precisely, letting his fingers linger for a moment or two on each item:

– Tarot cards, thumbed, worn, ancient. The pack was a twenty-first-century *Marseilles* pack, and though the edges showed signs of their passage through time, the colours of each face were bright and alive; with age, with use, meaning had become instilled into the cards. Ashka treasured them, even though he rarely used them.

– A memory terminal, a small screen, surrounded by ebony wood, notched and carved over the years in Ashka's personal way. This was placed to one side, its earth lead touching the metal strip that ran round the base of the walls. At the top of the screen a tiny red light glowed on signifying contact with the ship's association-memory bank.

– A small red cloth which Ashka opened and the contents of which he spilled on to the mat to his right. Bones, small, white, very fragile. They had been with him for many years, inherited from the shaman who had been his first teacher, who had inherited them in turn, and so on, back through the centuries, before there were rationalists, before the rational Universe was even understood. Bones. The disarticulated framework of a small extinct bird. Gorstein had only once asked why the bones were so important to Ashka, and whether they were an oracle in their own right. Ashka, then a few years younger, had merely smiled, then explained in all seriousness: 'They are the bones of an extinct water bird of Earth; the *moorhen*, which swam on the waters of Earth, flew in the air currents and winds of Earth, and used the earth itself for its nest, burrowing into the river bank for several feet. Such a bird was one with all the environments of the old world, and in its bones are memories of those environments. When I throw the bones they adopt a pattern on falling, the vertebrae thus, the leg bones here, the wing bones so … or perhaps a different configuration. From their arrangement it is possible to read many things. I rarely use them, and never in my capacity as rationalist.' Gorstein had stared at the fragments of that long dead bird and slowly shaken his head, breathing softly as the implications of the rationalist's ability sank into his mind. When he had glanced at Ashka there had been just the hint of a smile on the rationalist's lips. Just a hint, vanishing quickly. Gorstein had felt slightly piqued and had not asked again. (Had that simple joke been the beginning? The start of the corrosion …?)

– Last item on the mat, the most important. The bound copy of the *ching*, still wrapped in its traditional black silk covering. Ashka placed this carefully before him, unwrapped the covering, exposed the ancient book, its leaves yellowed with time, treated to preserve them. It was written in an ancient language that few but rationalists spoke, the language that formed the basis for the more complex interLing that was the Universal tongue.

Ashka finished his delicate array, working slowly and with suddenly steady hands. Gorstein had long since ceased to smile at the man's fad for the traditional approach to the *changes*, and to all the oracles he used, for that matter. The rationalist was too successful for there to have been no point in the tradition. Gorstein knew that it didn't matter *how* the oracles were consulted, or where, or under what circumstances, but the comfort of the rationalist was all-important. So much of the consultation comprised the professional interpretation of the luminary – so much from his mind into the life of the questioner – so much influence on the basis of the throw of a coin – so much interference …

He allowed the doubt to filter away and returned to the moment, stared at the composed figure of his friend (how many years had they been friends? It seemed like a lifetime, but it was a mere forty seasons, ten years out of fifty!)

As always, as he watched the meticulous old man, Gorstein felt unhappy at the thought that Ashka's life was coming to an end. *Why did you do it, Peter? Why? No man's destiny belongs to himself alone. You should not have asked …*

How he had done it he had never explained to Gorstein, save to say that it had nearly destroyed his relationship with the *ching* – but however it was done, Ashka had asked for an absolute prediction, he had asked for his moment of death. And he had been told. The *Book of Change* did not predict, it guided, but in all the thousands of years that it had been added to and expanded it did not surprise Gorstein to discover the power of prediction entering its pages. Ashka remained thoughtfully (perhaps tactfully) silent on the point. All he knew was that he would die peacefully, and that his remaining time, now, was as little as seven months.

It posed a bureaucratic headache for Gorstein, who would soon have to begin the long and tedious process of selecting a replacement, and all of Ashka's trainees on the ship were still too young to take on the responsibility of rationalist.

'Well now.' Ashka seemed satisfied with his arrangement and looked up at the shipMeister. 'Tell me why you've sent for me. Identify your problem.'

'Since landing here ...' how difficult to put feelings into words without their sounding trite, almost childish. 'Since landing here I've felt uneasy. Very uneasy. Perhaps apprehensive would be more accurate.'

Ashka nodded thoughtfully. 'Concerning what?'

'Concerning ... the mission, I suppose.'

'You're not sure?'

'It's difficult to tell ...' As he spoke so he grew more uncomfortable. What would it look like to the junior ranks, the shipMeister squirming with embarrassment? But then, the rationalist was a rank apart from the rest of the ship. It was senselessness on Gorstein's part that he felt uncomfortable exposing his fears to this man above all. 'Yes,' he said more convincingly. 'Yes, the mission. I'm apprehensive about the mission.'

'And which aspect of the mission do you think is worrying you most?'

Gorstein was silent for a moment, eyes closed, thinking hard. His face grew darker as he frowned. He was aware of his hands clasping and unclasping in his lap. Self-consciously, feeling that his nervous motions would draw attention to his nudity, he drew his robe across his lap. As his eyes flickered open for a moment he noticed Ashka smiling as he stared at him. Gorstein smiled back.

'Christ, Peter. I'm tense. What can I do?'

Ashka shook his head. 'Your penchant for archaisms is very disconcerting. What can you do? Become less tense. Simple procedure—'

'Breathe deeply. I know.'

'For just a few moments.'

After a minute or so Gorstein felt his body relax, his heart slow down and his painful sense of embarrassment faded away, leaving him feeling slightly foolish. 'Which aspect of the mission? Yes. That's a good question. I have no answer. Perhaps this is where I need clarification.'

The rationalist smiled. Then: 'When did this unease develop? Before or after landing?'

'After. Immediately after.'

'Before or after you first saw the colony?'

From where he was sitting Gorstein could not see the earthworks, but the mention of the colony made his stomach tense – he could visualize that calm structure, the smoke spiral curling through the wind.

'After.'

'Then what can I do for you? You are worried that the mission will run into difficulties. It's a common apprehension – from examinations to missions, the thought of failure is very frightening, sometimes irrationally so.'

'No!' Gorstein felt momentary disappointment make him momentarily angry. 'No … it's more than that. I've performed too many of these missions for our new masters to let one more bother me. It goes deeper. I'm sure it goes deeper.'

Ashka smiled and reached for the small memory terminal. 'I think I understand – you want to satisfy yourself that your unease derives from within you and not from some outside force.'

Very tidily put, thought Gorstein. It was obvious to him, now that the rationalist had enunciated it so simply and precisely. Was he subconsciously avoiding the idea of outside forces? Was it an intolerable idea to the quieter Gorstein that lay below the conscious mind of the loud and authoritative one? Perhaps he should go into that with the rationalist at some later date.

'I should like you to consult the *changes* for me.'

Ashka seemed surprised, then shook his head, slowly. 'Why? It would be meaningless. To ask a question about something you know very little about would result in only the broadest answer possible – a trend, a prediction since you like the word so much, that could mean many things. The *ching* will be useful after you've got to know Aeran on a real gut level. You know this, shipMeister. Surely …'

'Nevertheless …' Gorstein began firmly.

'I refuse!' snapped Ashka, suddenly angry. He immediately regretted his outburst and smiled apologetically. 'Relax, Karl. Relax and I can do you some good!'

Gorstein relaxed, moodily, and watched the rationalist at work. The memory bank was too simple, too simple by far. Ashka never related to anything but the *changes*, at least, never related in that out-flowing, all-enveloping way that managed to put Gorstein so much at his ease. A book or a friend? Which was important? He stared at the *ching* and then at Ashka. He closed his eyes. *I just don't know. I just … don't know!*

There was movement in the corridor outside the shipMeister's quarters, a hesitation, then the movement went away. No doubt a landing party request;

it wasn't often that they reached a world quite as amenable to survival as Aeran, and the crew had been cooped up in the *Gilbert Ryle* for a good long time now. But there would be no 'earth leave' just yet. Not with a giant earthworks staring the ship in its camera eyes, and not a sign of civilization to be seen around what should have been a conventional, if fairly backward, colony.

Ashka was at work, drawing Gorstein's recorded personality from the ship's memory log, crossing it with observations to date on the planet Aeran Aurigae IV, and placing his questions. After a moment he frowned and glanced at Gorstein. He placed the memory terminal in the middle of the communion mat and asked his question loudly, the words appearing in glowing blue at the very top of the screen.

'Does shipMeister Gorstein's unease derive from his own personality?'

A second to process, then the answer, brief, unequivocal: No.

'Does shipMeister Gorstein's unease derive from forces outside the ship?'

Unequivocal: Yes.

Gorstein started forward, about to speak, but Ashka silenced him with a wave of his hand.

'What are these forces?'

Red light answer: Not yet known.

'To what degree of certainty do you state that the forces derive from outside the ship?'

Ninety-three parts certainty.

'Is there value in consulting the *ching*? Correction ...' the screen was covered with waving lines, indicating misunderstanding 'is there value in consulting the *I Ching*?'

A longer moment to process. Then, flashing on to the screen in a split second: There is value in consulting the *I Ching*, since the area of unease within shipMeister Gorstein's psyche may emerge and be relatable to observed elements on Aeran. Caution is urged in interpretation.

Gorstein smiled. Ashka seemed content enough; he was not humbled by having been proved wrong in his earlier recommendation. How could he have known?

Something outside the ship ... intriguing. Something outside the metal walls ... something to do with the planet, or with the colony, or both. It did not occur to Gorstein to be frightened.

Ashka unwrapped the book and placed it before him. He opened its pages and removed three silver discs from between the leaves. These he passed across to Gorstein who studied them for a moment. They were very old coins, a woman's head drawn on one side, and a strange and confusing pattern of plants drawn on the reverse. They were all dated 1961. The inscriptions were in two archaic languages, one of them an early form of interLing. Gorstein had asked a long time ago what precisely the coins had been. 'Sixpences,' Ashka had replied cryptically and with an almost tangible pride in his voice. 'Very rare European coins from the age of Pisces. Twentieth century after the Christ.'

That old!

Gorstein studied the coins now, and warmed them to his external body temperature. A sickening feeling of apprehension was rising inside him. His heart was beginning to race and Ashka's calmness seemed a thousand miles away. Then, gradually, a deep-felt reassurance overwhelmed him; the pressure of the coins against the skin of his clenched palm; the bitter, metallic smell of them as he held his fist to his nose; the sound as he ran the coins across each other, exploring their carved surfaces with his finger tips. It always worked like this, the coins becoming a focus of his tension, draining it away from him, absorbing his emotions in some purely metaphorical way. He opened his hand and stared at the moist coins, the mythical woman's head, the plants, the strange runes, their meaning lost in the dark centuries of time ... such power, such awesome power from these fragments of an almost forgotten past.

As Ashka had explained it to him, years ago when the two men had first become close friends, growing to know each other as intimately as was necessary for the rationalist to be useful to the younger man, there had been a time when coins had not been used to consult the *changes*. Thin sticks had been thrown, over and over, and a complicated routine of counting them out in fours had gradually built up the *ching* hexagram that was the answer to the question. It was Ashka's greatest desire to locate such a set of original sticks, but time and confusion would have destroyed the fragile things. Wood, unlike metal, could cast a shadow down a mere few hundred years. Metal could see further into time. The sticks (he had called them stalks) had been a biased mechanism, Ashka had explained, since they gave the yang element a slightly better chance of being thrown. The ancients had imagined this bias to be the driving force of the *ching*, but their understanding had been limited by their concept of the Universe, an incomplete concept (and often an irrational one); they had taken no account of the cosmic tides, and little or no account of the nature of time itself; and most especially they had consulted the *changes* in a detached fashion, not using the deeper levels of their minds at all. How much they had missed! (Ashka said).

'When you're ready,' said the oriental, smiling, breaking in on Gorstein's reflections. 'I've worked out your question.'

'Very well. I'm ready.'

'This is an *insular*, not a direct question to the *ching*. Do you understand?'

'Why not a direct question?'

'There is no direct question you can ask. But if the *ching* can help, then with me here it *will help*. Understand?'

'What's the *insular?*'

"'Why do I feel so apprehensive?'"

Gorstein repeated the question to himself, and closed his eyes. He sat motionless and silent for nearly ten minutes, thinking the *insular* over and over, examining its every insinuation, every innuendo, every hidden facet – future and past he could recognize, internal and external queries he could recognize … it was a very simple, very obvious question; the answer would be an indication of any area of conflict that could be working on him through his natural human facility for premonition, for sensing alternatives. With Ashka guiding the flow of probability, harnessing his own mental energy to the projection and widening of Gorstein's non-present awareness, the question might evoke the relevant passage of *ching* text to give him an idea of what was wrong.

He opened his eyes. The small room seemed dark and unsteady, the walls rippling, the floor and ceiling flowing outwards from the centre; but Ashka was still calm and smiling before him. Slowly the shipMeister's body achieved its greatest balance (yang and yin, he thought to himself – all those hormone levels changing, parasympathetic clicking into action, sympathetic responding to my unconscious commands to switch off; body systems relaxing, muscles toning, body fluids ceasing to race … Balance – it all comes down to balance. Internal, external; ride the winds, the waters, the flow of time. Everything is related to everything else, overlapping, intertwining, matter and time as products of the structure of the great tao, each man a fragmentary side effect of that same structure …)

'Now,' he said to Ashka and the rationalist rose and came behind him, reached down to his wrists and neck, took Gorstein's pulses, and assessed the tension of the ligaments. 'No. Bad distribution …'

'But I feel quite relaxed,' protested Gorstein.

'It comes down to far more than that, Karl. Your body is depressed.' He fumbled in his cloth bag and withdrew a tightly rolled strip of cloth. Unwinding the green material the light of the cabin reflected brilliantly off a thousand tiny needles.

'Depressed? Too much yin I suppose.' Cynical.

'If you want to be traditional, yes. If you would like the electrochemical figure for your skin …?'

'No, no. I never understand all that sodium flow nonsense. Too much yin will do fine.' He watched as Ashka selected a tiny needle, almost invisible save for the glitter of its diamond-dust plating. Gorstein leaned forward and felt the tiny prick as the needle entered his skin. Could the slight depression of his spirit be the sole reason for his unease, for his troublesome neurosis? How embarrassing if, as the body energy surged and redistributed, he found himself feeling quite happy about the mission. How embarrassing if he had called on the rationalist for something that he should have known to have done himself!

There was a flowing sensation from the area where the needle had pierced his adipose tissue; Ashka was twirling the tiny instrument, his eyes closed, his fingers spread across Gorstein's skin, moving subtly, feeling and sensing. After a while the tension ebbed from Gorstein's stomach and limbs; he had felt so relaxed in contrast to a few hours ago that he had not noticed this residual tension until it left him. The room grew calm; he smiled.

Ashka took his pulses again. 'I didn't know you were having liver trouble. You really shouldn't drink so much.'

'A slight fibrosis, well under control. I stopped infusing alcohol a long time ago, as you well know.'

Ashka sighed and shook his head. He was still dissatisfied but probably realized that acupuncture would do little more to affect Gorstein's natural body rhythms. He removed the needle and wrapped it in gauze before returning it to his pack.

'You're as ready as I can make you,' he said. 'Go on, proceed.'

Speaking his question aloud, Gorstein watched the words appear on the small screen; when he spoke the word '*ching*' the screen flickered with light and six vertical spots appeared, ready to change into the lines that he threw. With a last glance at Ashka, and a momentary reflection upon the question, now large and prominent in his mind, he threw the coins on to the communion mat.

Their silvered faces flashed in the cabin's soft light as they fell, and the mat absorbed their motion. The bottom spot on the screen changed to a broken line.

Scatter.

The coins rolled and fell, glinted as they came to rest.

Scatter.

Ashka watched fascinated as the coins formed their apparently enigmatic message; Gorstein felt his face become wet with perspiration. It ran from his brow and became cold on his hairless chest.

Cast the coins; (roll, scatter, rest). Heads and tails, tails and heads, values of eight and eight, then six and seven, and as the coins sped across the mat, his hands jerking as they released the metal discs, the fifth line was filled with a seven, and both men stared at the display, and knew what the *ching* was telling them.

'Throw for the last time,' said Ashka softly. 'Put thoughts of the outcome right out of your mind. Repeat the *insular*... repeat the question ...'

Gorstein repeated the words to himself, let them echo in his mind for a moment, now less dedicated to that one query and becoming preoccupied with the terrible choice that his last throw would make. For there were but the two alternatives: a broken line for success, an unbroken line for failure ... stagnation ... hexagram forty-five. It was terrible to realize the choice in advance, but it was impossible not to recognize those two hexagrams, the one so favoured, the one so feared. (By Gorstein.)

He threw the coins.

Stagnation!

'Oh my God,' he said aloud. He felt as pale as he imagined he looked, as dead inside as his drawn face would have looked outside. His apprehension raced away, his unease vanished, to be replaced by such a sensation of disaster that he almost fell backwards into the folds of his robe and screamed.

It's just a book, said a voice inside him, but confusion made an enemy of any calm questioning of the book's value.

He remained sitting, absolutely solemn, while Ashka stared at him looking vaguely exasperated. 'Such an irrational man, Karl. God does not exist. He was merely how your forefathers saw the tao. And anyway, why the depression? Can it still be said that after fifty years of life, and thirty with rationalists at your call, you still have not grasped that the *ching* warns, outlines trends, does not predict dogmatically? Can that still be, Karl?'

'What does the text say? What does it say in the book, Peter?'

Ashka said, 'Karl, you are a fool. You are affected by the oracle in the wrong way, and neither I, nor the oracle, can change you ...'

'Read me what it says!' said Gorstein, sharply, and even as he spoke he was thinking ... *Why? What does it matter? It's just a damn book, a crutch – why can't I shake it off, like rain, like a clinging woman?*

Ashka picked up the book; he didn't open it but held it before him, cradled in his two hands. 'There is no understanding. The great are going, the small are coming.'

'And what do you think that means, Peter?' *Do I care?*

Ashka placed the book down before him and stared at its withering covers. 'Unless you find your natural, stable position in the vortex, unless you can adapt to your situation and consciously examine it for whatever trend has caused this prediction, then I think the oracle is predicting a failed mission, and somehow you are aware of it. It is also, I must say, the sort of advice I would expect if you were heading for a worsening relationship with the crew of this ship. The ambiguity stems from your premature use of the *ching*. In any event, you are heading into deep water. Karl ... you *must* remember that the outcome is now in your hands. Success or failure depend on you. The future is not fixed, so take no chances, Karl. Assume that everything is going wrong, and find out why, and *stop it.*'

'Something outside the ship ...'

'No, Karl. Something outside your mind!'

'We can be more specific. We can ask the *ching* which alternative it was getting at. We can ask what exactly it sees as going wrong.'

Ashka shook his head angrily. 'No, Karl. No. We cannot. And if we could it would be too dangerous.'

'You've said that before,' snapped Gorstein. 'You've said that so often before. How do I know that it *would* destroy you and the *changes* to ask it something specific?'

'Why would I lie to you, Karl?'

'Because in some way, in that enigmatic rationalist's brain of yours, you may have decided that specific predictions are too easy. You may be thinking that it increases character, builds strength, to be faced with alternatives and to have to make decisions. But I need to know *facts*, rationalist. Hard facts. What is going to go wrong, how, why, when? Tell me those facts!'

'What would you do if you knew them?'

'What do you mean?'

'How would you act?'

Gorstein stared at the calm man in front of him. Ashka was smiling, just enough to register amusement, not enough to be insulting. *Facts*, thought Gorstein. *Facts or nothing at all. Of what use is anything in between? This book is crippling us ...*

'We've had this argument before, haven't we Peter?'

'So many times, Karl.' Now Ashka grinned broadly. 'Why can't you ever seem to understand the nature of the *ching*? Why you alone? Everyone else seems to have their own relationship with the oracle, but not Karl Gorstein.'

'Is it my fault that the *changes* ... the *ching*, sorry. I must be respectful. Is it my fault that we never grew close?'

Ashka shrugged. 'Impossible to say. I know other men – and women – who have never been able to merge fully with the oracle. With them, as with you, I am not merely a mechanism of focus, but an actual channel, a controller. I have to work very hard with you, Karl. I have to become you, rather than just sitting and supervising from a distance. You're a great trouble to me.'

My crutch? My helping hand? Keeping me on the straight and narrow?

'I know, Peter. And I appreciate you the more for it. Without you, well ...'

'You'd be flotsam, Karl. Mere flotsam, at the mercy of waves, of the currents, unable to control or direct your existence from one moment to the next. It would be so much easier for me if you would at least try and *understand* the *ching*. It really is very simple. But your persisting belief that it knows absolutes, and can dispense them, is ... well, an aggravation to both myself and the oracle.'

'It *can* dispense absolutes. I know it can, and you know it can.'

He was feeling argumentative now. He felt only coldness when he looked at the *ching*.

There are no absolutes, Karl. Nothing is immutable. It can merely be more specific, and you can choose to ride the waves. I could change the fact of my death, but I have no wish to. I shall ride calmly towards it because that is my wish. Not absolutes, Karl; specifics. And those only at terrible cost. Terrible cost. The *ching* is a sensitive and particular oracle, it is in us all and we form our relationship with it by reading the philosophy it has expressed through men across thousands of years. The words on the paper don't matter, it is the significance in your mind that is important. And to grasp that significance, and to couple it with your future-awareness, you must understand and love the oracle. And you don't, Karl. You neither understand, nor love it. But it understands you, and yes, I believe it loves you, and with me as mediator it is guiding you. But we would both appreciate so much if you could ...'

'Understand it.'

'Yes, Karl. Understand it.'

'I'll try.'

They looked at the hexagram again. 'What does the moving line say? The six?'

Ashka hesitated, then said. 'He hides his shame.'

Gorstein felt the blood drain from his face, but he kept calm.

Shame! What am I letting this man do to me? Shame! This is intolerable.

'The complete bad news,' he-said aloud, trying to sound fatalistic. 'Personal disaster, would you say? Stemming from a failure during the course of the mission?'

'If it is, then don't let it be. Besides, I have very strong doubts as to the accuracy of this consultation. It is essential, Karl, that you achieve an internal balance before asking the *ching* anything more on the subject.'

'Yes,' said Gorstein solemnly. He rose to his feet and went, naked, to the window, stared out at the silent earthworks of the Aerani settlement. 'Thank you, rationalist. Thank you for your time and energy.'

'The consultation isn't finished,' said Ashka, sounding surprised that Gorstein had abandoned the oracle before he had heard the full outcome.

'I said thank you. That will be all.'

Ashka stared at Gorstein's naked body, darkly silhouetted against the bright light of day. Gorstein was a powerfully built man, running to overweight on his thighs and hips, but still muscular and supple. But as he stood by the window he seemed to grow older, stooping, becoming loose, his contours losing their firmness. Ashka looked down at the screen and said, softly, 'change'. The hexagram flickered and altered to accommodate the change of the moving line.

Hexagram thirty-three, Withdrawal, an indication of favourable communication and success in the event of persistence.

Ashka understood one possible implication only too well, but he remained silent and gathered up his equipment. When he picked up the *ching* he paused and held it in his unsteady hands, feeling the coarseness of its fabric, sensing and enjoying the smell of its ancient pages. The tangible sense of awareness he gained from the book was very strong. Just a key, he knew – just a key, a gateway into the real oracle, and yet it was always strongest when the book was in his hands. There was a perpetual sense of anger, but an imprinted sense – as the sculpted lines of a man's face might reflect anger at all times, even though anger might be far from his heart. The anger of the *ching* was because of the other oracles. Its silk covering screened it from the Tarot and the extrapolative function of the ship, but it knew they were there – it was unhappy about it, but the grumble was always very faint.

As he held the *ching* now, watching Gorstein but unaware of anything but the sensation of the tao as it focussed through the book, he felt a stronger anger, an almost tangible emotion that had to be jealousy …

Was there an oracle outside? If so it was a powerful one to affect the *ching* so much. He wrapped the book and gathered the rest of his equipment. Without saying a word he backed from the room and left Gorstein to ponder his next few movements.

three

Warmer, now, dressed in a short, loose kilt and jacket, Elspeth crouched in the small cawl she had made two days before and waited for Moir.

Where *was* the girl? She had promised to return the moment she heard when the visiting aliens were on their way to the encampment. That had been hours ago, literally hours. Surely no ship of Earth would spend so much time just sitting, watching?

But of course, they weren't just sitting, watching. They had sent robot eyes prowling across the terrain, and one of them had spotted her early this morning as she had run back to her shuttle to return to her orbiting base. What, she wondered, had the human monitor made of her? A black woman on a world of furry humanoids … chaos added to confusion, no doubt; the puzzlement at finding no ordinary colony compounded by her ebony form streaking along the river shore to where the small vessel was securely hidden inside the bush.

Come on Moir! And why had Moir insisted that she wait here, in the heart of the forest, and not in the dune-trench?

The trouble was there was no way she, alone, could get into the heart of the crog to see what these people, the new beasts, wanted. As an outsider she would not necessarily have been precluded from the Fire Hall – there were many nomadic groups on Aeran (mainly *nues*) who turned up occasionally to the crog that had turned their ancestors out; they were accorded great civility by the encampment – provided they were peaceable – but that didn't help Elspeth any. She wanted to become part of the crog society. In view of this the Ungenn, the elders, the advisors to all the families within the earthworks, had recommended that she approach the Fire Hall in that series of circular routes that was the initiation programme for the young would-be warriors: round the outer wall of the crog (this she had quickly done) and then into the dune-trench, the deep ditch between the earthen walls; once here she could make no further progress into the camp until she had successfully snared a blackwing. This was now done and she could pass through either of the two gates in the inner wall and enter the outer perimeter of the fireglow, the open space around the outside fire pit.

But there were still the circles of the inner corridors to pass, the labyrinthine circuits of blue-bark and stone-lined passages that wound around the great Fire Hall and the perpetual fire that burned inside it. Here, the beyonders, the aliens, would be entertained. There, then, was where she had to be. And she wasn't allowed ...

What Moir was going to help her do was a stupid thing, and yet she was desperate to learn the reason for the ship touching down on this unimportant colony world. If she was discovered she would lose everything she had gained, spoil everything she had achieved.

But she felt – perhaps irrationally – that it was a risk worth taking.

Moir appeared from the bush, running and sweating. She dropped to her knees in front of Elspeth and smiled, catching her breath.

'What's the rush?' asked Elspeth.

'They're coming *now*. We'll have to hurry or people might start coming out through the tunnel before we can get in.'

'A tunnel? I see ... I wondered how you were going to smuggle me in.'

'And take your clothes off too ... they're too bright and obvious.'

Elspeth laughed. 'And my skin isn't?'

'Well ...' Moir seemed confused. She looked at the kilt and the jacket and a very thoughtful frown passed over her youthful features. 'Is everyone really a *nue* where you come from?'

'Mostly. We don't have time for idle chat, do we?'

Moir looked horrified. 'No, we don't. Come on, I'll lead you.'

As they ran through the forest Elspeth was again impressed by the speed at which the Aerani youngsters could move. Moir's pink and orange body almost vanished from sight several times as the girl jumped branches and pitfalls, plunged into clusters of dangerous looking plants through which Elspeth herself plunged with her eyes tight shut, and her stomach tense in anticipation of being suddenly surrounded by fleshy jaws. But the forest jungle was safe enough for a creature of Elspeth's size. It was only her legs that were letting her down. They just wouldn't move fast enough.

She came into the wide clearing almost without knowing what had happened and bumped into Moir who was catching her breath. They both fell sprawling, and Moir laughed.

'Did I run too fast?'

Elspeth shook her head. She could hardly speak with the pain of her straining lungs. 'Whatever gave you that idea ...' hitting her chest to ease the agony. 'I was only ambling along.'

Moir giggled again, climbed to her feet and scratched her belly unselfconsciously. After the slight hostility of yesterday the girl had warmed to Elspeth with lightning speed, making an especial effort, this morning, to find her and talk. Perhaps Darren had made her ashamed of her coolness; or perhaps the joke about the 'hanging' had in some way made Moir accept Elspeth without further thought of discomfort. At any rate, what Moir was doing could only be construed as the favour of a friend, for Moir stood to lose more than just her achievements if Elspeth were spotted in the Fire Hall and it was discovered that Moir had led her there.

In the clearing was a mound, perfectly regular, perhaps fifteen feet high and thirty feet across. It was ruddy brown coloured as a particular variety of moss had grown over it in the centuries since it had been built, and when Elspeth looked closer she could see that some of the earth had slipped; originally this mound would have been several feet taller and narrower.

The clearing was natural, she realized, like the area of higher ground on which the crog had been erected. The forest crowded on all sides, but the depth of earth was insufficient to support the dense jungle and it merely watched the man-made monument in its heart. As she looked carefully around the open ground, Elspeth could see the now-shallow trenches from which the mound's covering earth had been excavated.

'How long has it been here?' she asked Moir who stood staring at the tumulus.

'Don't know. Ages, I expect.'

'Is it a burial mound?'

'It has a passage in it, and a tunnel into the crog. Burial?' She looked puzzled. 'Why would anybody be buried in a big hump like that?'

'But a long time ago, perhaps. Before people were taken to the marshes and the blue-bark cemetery.'

Moir shook her head. She obviously had no idea what the mound might have been used for. She led the way round its contour and crouched to enter through a small hole. It was a tight squeeze, and very uncomfortable. The passage was only two feet high and less than two across, and was made of small fragments of stone piled on top of each other, capped by several slabs of a more crystalline rock. After just a few feet the faint light that penetrated the passage could do no more than give a slight reassurance when Elspeth, stretched on her belly, looked awkwardly over her shoulder.

After a few yards the tiny tunnel opened out and Elspeth found she could stand up straight. She reached up and could just touch the ceiling of what she sensed was a circular chamber, some ten feet high. A hand in the darkness felt her breast, withdrew: Moir gasped with embarrassment, or perhaps with shock at feeling the hard diamond of Elspeth's jewels.

'Are you looking for my hand?' whispered Elspeth. *Why am I whispering?*

'Yes,' said Moir. 'Why are you whispering? It's quite safe here.'

Elspeth shrugged, a futile gesture. 'This seems like a holy place. Where are you?'

Their hands touched and gripped, Moir's a small warm palm encompassed by Elspeth's cold one, fingers shaking with ... fear? Expectation?

'This is one of the ancient exits from the crog,' said the girl. 'It's still used in certain rituals. There's a pit in the floor ...'

Elspeth dropped to her knees, still holding on to the girl. Sure enough, they stood on the edge of a sheer drop. Elspeth found herself breathing a sigh of relief that she hadn't blundered any further when the tunnel had so abruptly ended and she had suddenly felt less restricted.

'There are steps somewhere down the side, down into the caverns. We'll have to feel our way along until we get to the upwards passage. Are you afraid of the dark?'

'Not at all,' said Elspeth reassuringly. 'Only of what might be hidden in it.'

'Me too,' said the girl. 'But if we keep together they may not do anything to us.'

'What? What mightn't do anything to us?'

Moir's grip increased convulsively and she seemed to be making 'keep quiet' sounds. *It's like being blind*, thought Elspeth as she explored the floor of the chamber with her free hand. *What have I let myself in for?*

Her fingers touched some soft substratum in one corner of the chamber. Soft and gritty ... She picked up a small handful and hid it in her pocket. If she had picked up the ashes of human cremations she knew she was going to feel a little queasy afterwards ...

Letting go of Moir's hand for a moment she felt her way along a short length of the rock wall and explored the cold surfaces for any symbols and carvings. There were a few simple sun shapes and the flowing, weaving lines that looked so much like maps of a river, but had a more subtle interpretation that Elspeth hardly dared think of ... and most thrilling of all was the unmistakable shape of a tight double spiral, two spirals each with a common centre, weaving outwards in parallel. Before she could fully explore the design in the pitch darkness Moir tugged at her sleeve.

'Come on.'

Reluctantly Elspeth turned away from the rock wall and crouched by the pit. *This* was something that the old tombs of Ireland had never had, she reflected, unless the slab floors of those prehistoric tumuli were in reality trap doors?

The sense of cold and confinement, and the musty earth smell, were so similar to those enigmatic barrows on far distant Earth. So much was familiar, so much was even identical – it made her shiver just to think about that fact. To wonder about what had happened here, on Aeran, to give rise to that familiarity made her head ache.

'Come *on!*'

'Are you sure this isn't a burial place?'

Moir shivered. 'Who would want to be buried here? It's so … cold.'

'But burned remains … you burn the eyes and hands of the honoured dead, don't you?'

'But those ashes are kept below the earth floor of the person's cawl. They wouldn't do any good here, in this place.'

A long time ago, then, thought Elspeth. Before the tradition of eyes and hands: burned if you died in honour, left in the marsh to rot if you didn't. The corpses were slung in the blue-bark cemetery to be consumed by the spirits of the earth. Elspeth had seen that cemetery on her first visit to the surface, and the sight had repulsed her. All forest hunting was forbidden for two days after a death so the spirits could consume the torso, in their disguise as blackwings, and make safely away again. Thus the *body anima* was taken away to safety, leaving the spirits of eye and hand to guard the family.

Moir had found the steps and they lowered themselves into the pit, carefully, painfully (the rock surfaces were sharp), fifteen feet or so until they stood in an underground passageway. Holding hands again they felt their way along, touching the ice-cold rock walls, stumbling, exclaiming, coming closer to where the cavern passed underneath the earthworks wall around the crog. At times Elspeth's fingers touched the pecked carvings of symbols she recognized and had already interpreted. Occasionally there were unfamiliar shapes carved in the stone and she spent a moment scrutinizing them with her fingertips, until Moir tugged her along again.

Water rushed, distantly, and once, as they passed through a wide chamber, a passageway opened up to their right at the end of which light glimmered.

Elspeth whispered, 'What's that?'

Moir almost screamed for her to keep quiet, slapping her tiny hand over Elspeth's mouth, murmuring intensely and pulling the beyonder away from the passage and the enigmatic glow.

'The Seer,' she breathed.

And they came to the tunnel leading up, Moir climbing first and peering through the tiny egress before crawling through and turning to motion Elspeth on. She hauled her body through the tight entrance and found herself surrounded by carved blue-bark and stone, a dark corridor, deserted, with gaps on the inner wall that looked through into a second corridor. Distantly there were voices.

She was in the Fire Hall. There was no turning back.

Crouched low, watching always for observers, they cut between the corridors and arrived in the passage that ran around the very centre of the Fire Hall, a large space with the perpetual fire burning high and fierce to one side; cooking pits and vats lined the walls and a meeting circle had been dug out of the floor in the middle of the room. Three aged women, fur deliberately blackened with charcoal, crouched near the fire, watching the flame and occasionally throwing fragments of chipped stone into the heat.

The walls of the inner hall were the broken stone slabs of what might once have been a ring of henges, the lintels removed and replaced by the sloping mat ceiling. A few faces peered from between the stones, but the corridor was mostly in darkness since it was not used for movement, merely for ritual, and in this shadow Elspeth felt fairly safely concealed.

The beyonders were there, seated stiffly and uncomfortably opposite the three Ungenn and several other family representatives, the eldest of each of the three generations of the main families. Darren was in the circle, looking cold and hostile, seated next to his father who was playing idly with his gleaming yellow bone sword. There were over twenty Aerani, some young, some as old as the oldest Ungenn himself, Darren's grandfather.

Opposite them: four men and two women. The tall, thick-set man, dressed in the richest robes, flowing cloak and skirts, studded belts running across his chest, this man was surely the leader of the group. He was striking to look at, deep set eyes, long dark hair drawn back into a wide and elaborate pigtail. The men and women who sat around him were less splendid, though attired similarly and all with the same intensity of expression – an intense blankness. Were they hiding fear?

There was one other, an old man who walked around the edge of the Fire Hall and scrutinized the weapons and carvings with an almost professional interest. He was walking towards where Elspeth and Moir were crouched. Would he see them?

The fire crackled loudly, its brilliant illumination setting off the carvings and symbols on the stone walls in stark and fascinating relief. As her eyes took in everything, absorbed every detail of the Fire Hall, she came to look behind the Ungenn, at the largest stone of the inner wall.

Her stomach turned over, that gut reaction that follows total surprise. A magnificent symbol, and one she had not seen on this world before, but one with which she was well acquainted: a vast three-spiral pattern, not a continuous line but three spirals close together in triangular formation, and each spiral itself a double spiral, a double centre radiating out in parallel, defying the eye to follow the tight curves, the repeated twists of the arms as they reached from eternal smallness to outer vastness. A symbol she had seen on Earth, a rare symbol, an enigmatic symbol. The spiral was common, the double spiral well known, and spirals in association with each other had been found all over the continental lands of Western Europe; but this display of three was rare ... it was rare on Earth, and she had not seen it on Aeran before now ...

She turned to Moir, pointed to the spiral shape and questioned.

Moir glanced back, puzzled, perhaps, that Elspeth should be asking the obvious.

'The Earthwind.'

Said simply, said without thought, without concern. The Earthwind, the symbol which had given them life, but more than a symbol, something that went deeper into the past of Aeran, into the roots of these natives. Darren had become uncomfortable when she had questioned him about the Earthwind. Moir seemed unconcerned, but Moir was younger, perhaps less aware than the other youngsters she associated with.

Elspeth felt like quitting this foolhardiness right now and just slipping quietly back to her ship to think ...

Moir gasped.

She looked up. The old man from the ship was standing above her, on the other side of the ring of stone, staring. His eyes were narrowed in an expression of puzzlement, but he said nothing. A moment later a second figure joined him, but didn't follow his gaze.

Elspeth recognized the local Seer, an old man called Iondai.

Between the two men there seemed to be an unspoken, possibly unconscious, recognition. They looked at each other and smiled, turned to where voices were being raised in the discussion a few yards deeper into the hall. The blazing fire, whose warmth Elspeth could feel even this far away from its crackling embers, set curious shadows dancing on the rock pillars and across the dry earth floor. The features of the ageing earthman above her seemed to change subtly as he turned his face this way, that way, as if the flesh were not fixed but lived on its own, expressing a subtler mood than the man himself realized. It was the fire, the light, the flickering flame, bringing out the hidden surfaces of those who grouped in earnest in the confining arc of its warmth.

'A world reached through the Absolute Darkness.'

Iondai had spoken the words softly, without inflection or indication of to whom he was addressing them. The stranger glanced at him. 'I beg your pardon?' The Aerani language, so close to interLing, nevertheless spoken with a certain awkwardness.

'Your strange world – I was listening to the man in the middle of your party.'

'Yes.' The stranger stared at the discussion. 'A huge cloud of dust. It obscures many of the stars.'

'The Absolute Darkness,' repeated Iondai thoughtfully. 'It had never occurred to me that there might be stars beyond it.'

'Oh yes,' said the stranger. 'Many millions. In a few centuries the brighter of them will begin to shine through the cloud.'

Iondai laughed softly. 'I don't understand. But it's fascinating. The Absolute Darkness was the birthplace of the Earthwind,' he glanced towards the three-spiralled symbol. 'I have often wondered what that birthplace was.'

The stranger stared at the rock and Elspeth again found her eyes drawn to the giant carving. Her skin tingled.

The two men turned back to where the discussion continued, and slowly they walked away from Elspeth. She breathed an audible sigh of relief, glanced at Moir who was shaking visibly, despite the darkness behind this concealing pillar. Edging forward so that her face would have been in view, counting on her dark skin to give her that extra degree of protection from any sharpeyed warrior, she listened to what the men from the ship were saying ...

Moir was tugging at her arm ...

Abruptly Elspeth turned to face her, angry at having had her concentration disturbed. It was difficult hearing everything that was spoken from this distance. 'What is it?'

She was taken by surprise to see Moir's eyes filled with tears, her face a mask of terror; the girl's hand slapped across Elspeth's mouth as she looked anxiously into the Fire Hall.

'We've got to get out of here,' she whispered urgently. 'Oh please, Elspeth, come with me ...'

Elspeth shook off the girl's frantic grip, glanced back at the circle of men and women. A few faces were turned towards her. 'Why? Have they seen us?'

Moir, silently hysterical, pulled at Elspeth's jacket, gripped her arm and tried to tug her bodily. Tears ran down her face, but she uttered no sound.

'What *is* it Moir?'

'Come *on* – you don't know what you're doing!'

'What am I doing?' demanded Elspeth. She felt her fury speaking; it was enough to make her murder every human in sight, what she had been listening to, and this girl's irritating behaviour was going to bring her rage to its full force.

'You've been shouting, Elspeth. They've heard you. If they come over and see who we are we'll be killed. *Please come.*' Terrible anxiety, her voice now loud, attracting attention.

'Shouting? I haven't been shouting ...' she kept her voice at a whisper, but couldn't deny that the discussion had stopped, puzzled faces watching their place of concealment. No one moved.

'You *have*. Elspeth! They'll kill us.'

Suddenly she realized that two of the old women fire-tenders were walking across the Fire Hall towards her. Darren had risen to his feet and seemed to be waiting for permission to come and investigate the disturbance himself.

Elspeth's heart jumped, and raced; she felt a sudden, almost incapacitating, sickness. It was a sickness at what she had been listening to, and at what she had been doing, making a noise, unconsciously shouting out her anger at what she had heard ... drawing attention to herself when she should have been sitting quietly and fearfully, unobserved and unobservable.

Moir jumped to her feet and ran. Elspeth, panicking, raced after her, through the dark corridors and to the escape tunnel. They squeezed through the narrow entrance and reached, in a few seconds, the caverns below the encampment. Were they being followed? There was no sound of an immediate pursuit. Moir's urgent grip on her hand pulled her away from danger. They ran back the way they had come, hands on walls, breathing loud, searching for the way back to the clearing.

They reached the pit and climbed into the mound; less difficult going up than coming down. And then the final crawl through the stone-lined passage from the corbelled chamber to the small clearing.

Cold air, the tang of the mossy vegetation; no sounds of anyone following them.

Moir burst into tears and Elspeth, crouched on the dry ground, filthy with dirt and grazes from their terrified flight, put her arm around the girl and tried to comfort her.

'You promised you'd be quiet,' sobbed Moir.

'Yes. I'm sorry, I'm really sorry. I just got so ... so angry!'

Moir wiped a hand across her eyes, the fur on her wrist matting with tears. She stopped crying, tried to dry the wet hair with her fingers, rubbing it vigorously. After a moment she looked up at Elspeth and smiled, then shook her head.

Elspeth said, 'I really gave us a fright, didn't I?'

Moir nodded vigorously. They both laughed, but Elspeth felt less like laughing than crying.

Those bastards!

What did they think they were *doing*? They would spoil everything, ruin all her work, ruin the Aerani people … but how was she going to convince them they were wrong? They *had* to be made aware of the destructiveness of what they had proposed.

But she recognized the signs, the symptoms, of that most motivating of emotions … fear. Pure fear, ingrained into those men and women, down to the last cell of their brains, the last fibre of their muscles. The fear of retribution. Elspeth had seen it coming as a young girl in the centre of the Federation, living on a world where the old regime was already in the minority and the security forces had virtually ceased to worry about the insurgent behaviour, the revolutionary groups … it was taken for granted that the old ways were going, the old order being kicked out, the centre of power being shifted from the beaten down old world of Earth to the new bastions of civilization around Electra.

Elspeth had seen it coming, observed it happening (the rockets over the tribal city … and within a year the tribal city just a vast ruin, its centuries of tradition and ritual trampled beneath the foot of the new intolerants) and deep down she had not been afraid, nor had borne any regrets. She had not expected *this* turn of events, however.

'Everyone got so angry,' said Moir. 'I don't like to see that. We have too many duels, too many people get killed. I don't like arguments.' She shivered. There were no families, Elspeth knew, that did not have a record of death in the immediate past, vicious slaughter for the sake of honour. On the inside of the inner dune were hundreds of depressions in the earth … each depression concealed a head, severed for honour, honoured by burial, watching the life of the encampment from its privileged position in death. There were few Aerani who did not hope to die, one day, in a conflict of honour, rather than of old age when they would end as ashes below the cawl of their children.

'Do you really blame them?'

'Even the Ungenn got angry,' said Moir, looking up at Elspeth. 'They should never get angry, but they did!'

'Do you blame them?' repeated Elspeth. It was strange how this small girl's depression, her anxiety, had calmed Elspeth down.

'I didn't understand what was said,' murmured Moir. 'I didn't understand the words. They didn't mean anything …'

'I think very few of the adults in the circle understood some of those words,' assured Elspeth. 'But they understood well enough that they were being asked to house a spy.'

The language had been spoken perfectly, of course – there was no hardship involved in embedding the slight variation of the Aeran tongue over the standard interLing which the visitors almost certainly spoke. But to explain what they had tried to explain in a language that had lost so many words –

like the word 'moon', meaningless to a world without such a satellite, and no doubt swiftly forgotten ... such a task was forbidding, and the discussion had sounded awkward, uncomfortable, terribly patronizing. The shipMeister ... Gorstein, Elspeth believed was his name ... had done well to keep so calm and collected and to present his mission as clearly as he had presented it.

But such a mission!

'These ... things ...' Moir began, her face creased with the difficulty of remembering.

'The monitors?'

'Yes. What do they look like?'

How does one describe a human mind? 'They don't look like anything, Moir. They're just – thinking units—' *Units.* How difficult not to use words in specialized ways. 'Look, Moir ... you have a physical body, yes? And you have a thinking bit inside the body. Understand?'

'I think in my head, not my body.'

'Yes of course. Anyway, that thinking part, without the head itself, without the flesh and bone, that is what the *monitors* are.'

'And those people want to put extra thinking parts into our heads. How funny ...'

'It's not funny at all!'

'I didn't mean that,' said Moir, looking apologetic. 'I meant, it must be strange to have two thinking parts in one head. That would be like me and Engus all being inside me ... well, he often is ...' she giggled, but forced a straight face again when Elspeth looked severe.

'It wouldn't *be* like that.' Was she being teased? 'The extra mind – the thinking bit – would be quiet, unnoticed. But it would be experiencing everything you experience, and since it's also thinking in another body somewhere miles and miles away, upwards ...' Moir was losing her, as she had obviously lost Gorstein as he had tried to explain. How could one put across the concept of trans-spatial-cortical-resonance to a people who still had failed to grasp the concept of levers? How could one explain clearly the sort of fear that could make a government want to keep an eye on even the most insignificant of colonies, making sure that no uprising ever occurred against them ...?

'Besides,' she went on, changing the subject. 'That is not the point. No one has any right to tamper with a culture like yours.'

'They were saying that we were all part of the same people ... that there are millions of us, not just this one crog and the mountain nomads.' Moir seemed upset. 'But they, you too ... you look so different. It doesn't make sense. We can't all be the same race.'

'Well ...' it was getting cold, and Elspeth still hadn't come to a decision on what to do. 'It would take too long to explain, but I'm afraid it's true. Hundreds of years ago your ancestors came to the crog from a very much bigger encampment. And they looked … well, mostly pink, light-coloured skin, like your shoulders. Your own body hair is something we call *drifting* – the stars in the sky, the movement of the earth you sit on, the differences in the air and the food you eat, all that makes a different …' environment? What could she substitute? '… a different *surroundings*. Every one of us, me too, is in harmony with everything around us. When you change those surroundings bizarre things happen to our bodies. Like fur, or thick skin, or … hundreds of things. We call it *non-critical eco-cosmological genetic channelling*. How about that?'

Moir's eyes popped open. 'What was that?'

'Never mind. The sad fact is that you people here are very different to what the beyonders expected to find, and you're different in ways that none of us understand. You don't remember your origins. Aeran is a very strange planet, and those men in the ship are likely to upset you in a very big way.' Moir's face was blank. Planet, ship … the words probably meant nothing, although the Aerani used them in different ways. 'I've got to convince them to go away and leave you all alone. The damage is done in one sense – a myth has been established, an uncertainty … and …' she trailed off, cradled her head in her hands. 'Listen to me. I'm doing it too. I'm telling you things you ought never to know.'

Moir's touch was gentle, affectionate, brushing the hair from her neck and delicately stroking the soft skin. Elspeth shivered with pleasure. 'That's nice. But you're the wrong sex.'

'I don't like to see you depressed.'

'I don't like to be depressed, Moir.' She turned to look at the young girl. 'You were hostile to me yesterday. You resented me.'

'I was frightened of you.'

'But not any more?'

Moir shook her head. Smiled. She ran her hand down Elspeth's neck and traced around the opening of her jacket. Where the skin was taut and sensitive around the two small diamonds, Moir's fingers were tantalizingly tentative, touching and leaving, feeling the folds and the junction between softness and crystal hardness. Leaning towards her, her body thrilling to the youthful touch, Elspeth pressed her lips against the girl's. Moir didn't pull away but closed her eyes, probed Elspeth's mouth with her tongue, let her hand rest more firmly on Elspeth's body.

Pulling away, Elspeth smiled self-consciously. The two girls stared at each other, then drew apart completely, turning to look at the wall of vegetation which uttered strange sounds before the growing wind.

'I don't understand anything,' said Moir quietly. 'Not a thing. It's all silly. But it's also horrible. I'm very glad that the Ungenn and all the families were so angry about it all.'

'Aren't you the contrary one! You just said that they shouldn't have got upset.'

'Did I?' She rested her head on her knees. A parasite, a small shining black creature, crawled up her leg and she reached down quickly and picked it off her fur. Slowly dismantling the tiny creature she said, 'Well, I changed my mind. I'm glad they did, now. It seemed to frighten the beyonders.'

'It certainly did,' agreed Elspeth, watching the fragments of parasite as they fell between Moir's legs. 'It's a fright that doesn't really make sense, but they *were* frightened. They were frightened when the Ungenn were so adamant in their refusal to accept the mission, but they weren't frightened when the tangleweeds disarmed the two guards. Did you notice that?'

'They didn't know what had happened,' laughed Moir. 'It was so fast.'

'But it made the shipMeister very resentful. I thought Darren and his father – your father – were going to assault him at one point when he was provoking them.'

'My father makes me very angry,' said Moir testily. 'He and Darren don't obey the oracle, or at least, they obey it when it suits them. But the oracle knows, and they ought to take more notice.'

They both fell silent and after a moment Elspeth reached into her pocket and scooped out some of the material from the tumulus. Staring at it, and feeling a little uncomfortable, she finally let it trickle through her fingers on to the ground. Ash – unmistakably ash, and powdered bone.

A moment later both girls heard the sound of someone crawling through the tunnel in the mound. They turned to stare at the earth bank, waited just a second, cast a terrified glance at each other and were up and running.

They entered the forest at full speed and stopped, stared back at the clearing, and then began a very serious and painful retreat.

'We'll have to split up,' Elspeth yelled, wondering why she even bothered to say it when Moir was already yards ahead of her.

Elspeth changed course and ran towards the river. When she paused for a moment to listen she could no longer hear Moir, but could pick out the sound of pursuit quite clearly. Probably one, maybe two, but following her – fast.

She closed her mind to the thorns and sharp edges of certain leaves that she usually jumped or skirted with great care. She barged through the forest, noisily and breathlessly, fearing the worst if she was caught; she was determined to escape. Along the river, concealed from sight, was her shuttle. It would be touch and go whether she made it or not.

The man or woman who pursued her gained on her steadily. When she stopped for breath, wondering why she couldn't get her second wind, she could hear the person coming very fast; it was almost certainly a juvenile, and that was *worse*, she knew. The juveniles had little tolerance for the flagrant breaking of the ritual law.

She reached the thinner bush along the bank of the river and increased her pace towards the disused landing station and the deep gully where she had hidden her craft. Her kilt was a hindrance but there was no time to remove it. Her legs had gone numb, the muscles of her thighs taut and agonized, but she worked them remorselessly, knowing she would pay dearly even with the ship's robot masseur working on her afterwards.

With a start she realized that the gleam of light she could see distantly was the exposed wing of her shuttle; hadn't she concealed it properly the last time she had landed? She felt sure she had. Stopping for a moment, glancing over her shoulder, she took two deep and luxurious breaths, and then felt her hopes sink.

There was a shape moving by her shuttle, darting from concealment to concealment, but not before she had spotted the flowing robes of one of the beyonders. Hands on her hips, conscious of the thudding steps of her pursuer now racing towards her along the river bank, she resigned herself to a fight. She gauged the man's approach – she could just hear his controlled breathing, and knew there were seconds before he was on her. Her hand went to the belt of her kilt and unlocked the tiny stiletto she kept concealed there.

She turned, ready to draw the weapon and flick it at her attacker.

'Darren!'

Without stopping Darren bowled into her, and before her hands could come up to protect her face his fist had thudded against her jaw and sent her flying. Dizzily, feeling the sharp pain in her face subside into a dull and intense ache, she climbed to her hands and knees and tried to focus on the ground. She touched her jaw and jerked her hand away as pain shot through her skull. Slowly the world became oriented and immediately her legs turned to jelly. Looking up she saw Darren standing over her, obviously furious.

'Get up,' he snapped. She reached out a hand for help. '*Get up!*'

Easing herself to her feet she worked her jaw a moment, meeting his gaze as steadily as she could.

'You're stupid, Elspeth. *Stupid!*'

'And you hit me too hard, you bastard.'

'I should have killed you!'

'You nearly did,' said Elspeth feeling the anger rising through her astonishment at being treated so roughly. Her jaw began to swell, blood in the tissues leaking slowly from ruptured vessels. The pain grew worse; tears filled her eyes. 'A human head isn't made for blows like that.'

And to her utter amazement she found herself spinning round and plunging into the icy water of the river; just her upper body, hitting the cold currents so that the bitter shock drowned the pain of the second blow, delivered to the other side of her face by a fist she never even saw coming.

'*Stop it!*' she screamed as she felt Darren's hands haul her from the water and pull her roughly to her feet. Her hand grappled at her belt, seeking the deadly blade, but the movement was too obviously defensive and he gripped her wrists and tore them from the buckle.

Elspeth sank to her knees and groaned, cradling her jaw in her hands and closing her eyes.

'Why did you do it?' shouted Darren. He sounded as disappointed as he was angry.

'I wanted to know their mission,' she murmured; the effort of talking involved pain, and the pain was growing worse. She couldn't look at the youth.

'I would have told you what you wanted to know,' he said angrily. 'I would have told you everything. You didn't have to act so stupidly. You *knew* you were doing wrong.'

'You wouldn't have understood what they meant,' she said quietly. 'I had to be there.'

'I could have told you the words. I could remember them and you would understand what they meant. No, Elspeth, it was stupid to come into the Fire Hall. Stupid.'

'Well, I'm sorry, but it's too late now ...'

'Yes! Too late.'

She feared the worst. 'They'll kill me if I go back to the crog, I suppose.'

Darren sneered at her as he said, 'No, you can go back safely enough. No one knows it was you. And I shan't tell them ...'

She looked up at him, feeling both relief and an enormous tension. Darren's face was drawn and lined, a face far older than it should have been. Fury, upset, panic ... mixed in his features, jumbled, so that what emerged was almost indefinable, and yet all these emotions could be seen. For Darren, for a reason that Elspeth could not understand, there had been a turning point, and he could not go back; she felt a thrill of fear when it occurred to her that she might now have been cut out of his life.

He wouldn't kill her, she knew that since he had said as much already. But he might no longer help her, and that would be a great loss.

'Darren ...'

His hand slapped against his mouth loudly, and away. His eyes remained cold. It was a gesture that was unambiguous by anybody's terms.

'If you do nothing else,' he said quietly, 'get your beyonder friends off this land. Get rid of them!'

'Darren, I can't just ...'

He turned on his heel and ran away, a tensely muscled figure vanishing into the protective darkness of the forest. Elspeth watched him go, watching, with her fingers touching her aching face, until there was no sound left of the youth's departure. Then she started to cry. It seemed like the easiest thing to do.

A hand, out of nowhere, touched her shoulder and she screamed with shock.

four

Blinking tears from her eyes Elspeth stared up at the old man.

'I'm sorry if I startled you,' he said.

The effort of trying to move her jaw to reply was too much; pain lanced through her cheek muscles and she gave up, sufficing to shake her head. The old man seemed unsure as to what he should do. He fixed her with the same gaze she had seen in the Fire Hall when he had stared at her through the rock pillars. Puzzlement, concern … intrigue.

'I saw what he did to you.' Glancing after Darren. 'Very brutal. Very brutal indeed, but then …' he hesitated for a moment. She stared at him blankly. There was something about him, something she recognized, and yet something indefinable … 'Well,' he went on awkwardly, 'I thought it sounded like a lover's quarrel more than anything, so I didn't use my automatic.' He patted the small red pouch that hung from his belt. Her attention drawn to his belt, Elspeth realized how thin the man was, how frail. His red and green robe billowed in the breeze and she could see the skeletal quality of his legs through the semi-translucent material. His face was etched and wrinkled, age upon age, brilliant eyes that had seen many decades.

Almost immediately she realized what he was. Her mind, befuddled by the beating and still painfully aware of her bruises, finally pieced together the visual and character clues and came up with the obvious answer.

'Rationalist …' she murmured, wincing. The old man dropped to his knees and touched a finger to her lips. His face became earnest, intense, almost boyish beyond the time-weathered contours.

'Don't speak until we disperse the blood. Here …' He swung a small cloth pack round from where it had been hanging behind him, opened it and fumbled for a moment. He seemed upset when he couldn't find what he wanted. 'I'm sorry, I don't seem to have—'

She reached out and touched his hand; smiled. 'Don't worry,' she said. 'My ship … there …'

'I'll help you.'

He stood and reached down for her, but as she tried to climb to her shaking legs her weight was too much for the small man and he buckled at the knees. He laughed when he heard her chuckle, and shook his head. 'I never was very strong.'

'I bet you got picked on as a child,' said Elspeth slowly as she climbed to her feet and stood, for a moment, getting used to the sensation. She looked down at the old man. He was smiling.

'I was too clever. I talked my way out of trouble.'

'That's what …' she winced. 'That's what … you're supposed to be good at. My face is *killing* me …'

'I'm not so sure these days, which is why I carry my automatic. Here, lean on me if you want.'

She looked at him and he gave her a wry glance. 'Perhaps not,' he said.

'I don't think I'll trust the engineering,' she commented. 'But I thank you for the thought.'

Her shuttle was almost as she had left it this morning, halfhidden by dead vegetation and the camouflage net she had dragged across it; but it had been forcibly entered, that much was immediately obvious. Shuttles were not designed to be burglar-proof; rather, they were designed to grant easy access to any explorer careless enough to lose his entry disc. There was nothing of value in the shuttle, of course; but such robbery had not been the vandal's intention.

The old man looked embarrassed as he stared at the open hatchway. 'We watched you landing this morning. I came straight here after the meeting broke up and this is how it was.'

'Beyonders!' she muttered. 'What odds that your shipMeister has removed the flight lead?'

'He has. He wants to know who or what you are. I'm sure he'll behave sensibly, though, and give it back to you.'

I'm stuck here, was her first thought. A chill fled through her body, was gone before she had fully realized her involuntary fear reaction. But did it really matter? It was too late anyway to prevent the slow dissolution of her remembered past. The rot had set in already, and if what had happened to Austin was representative, then whether she left or not, the rot would continue.

'So the meeting broke up …'

'In some disorder,' said the old man with a smile. 'We were thrown out. A very puzzling colony …'

'Yes.' She found herself nodding in agreement. 'There's a medikit just inside the first locker,' she said, changing the subject abruptly, 'Get it for me, will you?'

She sat down by the river and waited for the rationalist to join her. From her vantage point, low down on the sparsely floriated bank, she could see only jungle; distantly she could hear animal cries, but couldn't identify them. The air was pungent with the smell of plants, slightly fetid odours that were soon ignored, in the same way that the low oxygen content of the atmosphere could be easily overlooked after the initial discomfiture of a newly arrived body.

'My name is Peter Ashka,' said the old man as he sat down beside Elspeth and handed her two white pads.

'Elspeth Mueller,' she murmured, and pressed the pads to each cheek, blinking as the myriad tiny needles penetrated her skin and began to inject and absorb. Ashka reached over and shook her little finger with his own. She smiled.

'Am I so obviously a ship's rationalist?' he asked. His body almost closed in upon itself as he hunched up next to her and he seemed to vanish into the folds of his totally unsuitable robe. He must be freezing, Elspeth thought as she looked sideways at him. She nodded.

'Not so much the "ship's" as the "rationalist". It took a moment, though. To recognize you, I mean. I've been out of touch for a long while.'

'Out of touch ... what, with civilization?'

Elspeth laughed, and immediately regretted the action. 'Yes. Civilization.' She hoped her cynicism didn't sound too corny, but the value of the term seemed remarkably restricted since she had met the Aerani culture, a lithic culture yet very highly civilized by the only standard that seemed to matter to her – the extent to which they communicated, cooperated with and utilized nature without precipitating some drastic ecological change.

She found herself running the definition through in her mind, five-syllable words and glossy print. She often thought in definitions, a left-over from her intense book-learning youth.

'That might account,' said Ashka thoughtfully, 'for the fact that I cannot determine precisely who or what *you* are. That's a question, by the way, phrased very cleverly.'

'So as not to seem like you're prying into my life. Ah, the diplomacy of the rationalist.'

'We work on levels most people don't even realize they have.'

Old rationalist joke. Elspeth laughed since it was easier than embarrassing the old man. She felt a warm trickle on her wrist and removed the pad from her right cheek. Dark blood had run from the absorbent pad on to her skin and she semi-vocalized a curse. 'I always pick the leaky ones. Always.'

'Your face looks a lot better. Is it still sore?'

She realized that the pain had gone. Funny, she reflected, how the departure of pain can be unnoticed whereas its arrival was so central to anyone's awareness.

'Feels a lot better, old man. A lot better.'

'You can call me Ashka, if you like ...'

Elspeth felt terrible. She hadn't realized what she was saying, had fallen back into the casual mode, the attitudes she had lived with, grown up among ... disrespectfulness was almost a way of life and she had discovered it to be a refreshing evolution when, after some years' absence from her home world, she had lost the habit. 'I apologize Ashka. I truly do.'

Touched his hand, but there was no hurt in his face, no loss of composure or cheerfulness. He was a rationalist after all, he would know better than to let other people's weaknesses in any way relate to that private level of his mind that was his and his alone. 'I bet you know where I come from now,' she added with a grin.

'New Anzar, yes. I think I half knew it just from your appearance.'

'Tall, you mean. Well, that's not *so* unusual.'

'I was referring to your tribal cuttings. Are they diamonds?'

She drew back her loose-hanging jacket so the weak sunlight caught the slightly dusty facets of her breasts. Ashka stared at them for a long time; Elspeth felt slightly uneasy at the prolonged scrutiny, but finally he looked away and shook his head. He murmured something that she thought might have been 'barbaric'.

'It wasn't the worst that was done in the tribal city. Some of the initiation rites for the equatorial city clans could result in death. Others were very beautiful. At the time I was very proud – I remember being very proud ... and in intense pain ...'

Blankness ... she deliberately put the past from her mind, not wanting to find that more of her childhood had been eaten away.

'You know why we're here,' Ashka said at length. It was a statement, not a question. Elspeth affirmed silently. When she said nothing he went on, 'How long did you say you've been out of touch?'

'Years. Not all spent on Aeran, of course. But – out of touch.'

'So you know nothing of the Great Struggle?'

She looked at him. 'Of course I do. I saw it beginning. It frightened me. It frightened me partly because I knew what would happen to Anzar if the Electra gained power, and partly because ... well, I had a feeling that there would be a more Universal repression with the Electra than with the old Federation. I was right, wasn't I? These monitors ...' she shook her head. 'That's real fear isn't it? Fear of all the tiny and insignificant colonies they can't see, protecting themselves against the trillion to one chance that a super power will emerge from a tenth generation colonial world.'

'That is undoubtedly the case,' said Ashka solemnly. 'The old fleet, the old crews, have all been drafted into this task and there are terrible consequences for failure. The Electra know our feelings about this sort of invasion, and know we would reject it if possible, so they have made it virtually impossible for us to disobey; there is only one man on the ship who does not live in constant fear of failure of these missions.'

'Yourself.'

'Myself. I have no family anywhere in the known Universe. My death, peacefully, is a marked day on the calender in my room.'

'But I am just the rationalist on the ship, and have nothing to do with orders.' He stared at Elspeth. 'You feel you must stop him.'

'Your shipMeister? Yes. I feel it very desperately.'

'I don't think you could succeed in such an attempt.'

Elspeth laughed. 'Perhaps I could read the *ching* about it. Perhaps I should try and make friends again …'

She removed the pad from her left cheek and discarded it on to the earth with the other. Within a few minutes the organic structure of the pad would start to break down for easy assimilation into the biosphere. Attracted by the unusual protein, seeping through the soil and into the water, a cluster of thin, yellow river beasts (skitch) darted about the surface, tiny legs paddling frantically against the current, sinuous motion reminding Elspeth of the snakes she had seen in various zoos.

Ashka said, 'What did you mean, make friends again?'

'With the *ching*. We fell out.'

'Did you try to come to an understanding? The *ching* can be very temperamental, you know. It persistently makes trouble with me for using the Tarot.'

Elspeth was amazed, and found herself laughing with surprise. 'I never thought of that. Jealousy. Are you telling the truth?'

'Absolutely. An oracle likes to think of itself as the sole personal property of the user. If you use other oracles there can be intense bad feeling and it takes a lot of rationalizing to get a tolerable understanding.'

'I never thought of that,' repeated Elspeth. 'I only ever used the *ching*, of course. So the problem never arose.'

'So how did you fall out?'

She shrugged. 'Only since I came here, to Aeran. For the last five years I've lived with the Edge Society, mainly studying prehistoric Earth. Most of the Edge people are so fanatical about their particular study, their *edge*, that I kept very much to myself. I didn't need to scrounge or fight for survival, like most of them … But I had fun.'

'And your *edge* was prehistoric society?'

'Early civilized Earth, I should say. Excavation, reconstruction stuff. You know … Then one day I heard about the Aeran culture. Someone had some pictures of the colony, and the symbols they use in their rituals, and I had to come and see for myself. Within a few days, spent largely in orbit, not down here at all, I found the *ching* was telling me nonsense. I'd ask it a question and it would reply something that triggered nothing at all in my head. Complete nonsense.'

'Did you ask it what was wrong?'

'That's complicated, so I may have done something wrong, but yes, I did, and still I got nothing. I felt very alone for a few days.'

'I'm quite sure,' said Ashka sympathetically. 'But I don't think the *ching* is angry with you in any way. It bothers me what you said about its nonsense replies. If the *ching* becomes hostile it always lets you know. It never confuses.'

'Maybe … maybe it just stopped working for me. We were never that close.'

'That is too obvious for words. That it stopped working, I mean. But I'm puzzled as to why. The *ching* is linked to the user and can usually adapt to the change in cosmic environment along with the user. Even the Aerani should be able to use the *ching* ... I have never ever heard of such a complete cessation of usefulness.' He was frowning, staring at the water, at the animals that fed on the invisible stream of blood plasma that was seeping into the river. Occasionally one of the beasts would flicker-swim away and vanish from its close proximity, coming to rest across the other side. Ashka watched the activity thoughtfully, chewing at the inside of his mouth, shaking his head as if he could hardly bring himself to believe what Elspeth had told him.

'If I ever lost my relationship with the *ching* I could not be advised better than to put a Kiljarold to my head and end my life in a moment.'

'It would be a fearful thing to happen to a rationalist, and to those who depend on him. I myself never depended that much ...'

'You're exceptional, then.'

They sat in silence for a while. Elspeth realized, belatedly, how well she had acted in being honest about her lost personal relationship with the oracle. If Ashka believed for even a moment that the presence of the ship on Aeran was jeopardizing its crew's relationship with the prime oracle then surely there would be no question of their immediate withdrawal? But how difficult it would be to convince even a rationalist that an Earth-type world with no obvious magnetic or gravitic quirks could be the cause of a solitary female's loss of *ching*-reliability. And yet ... it was a chance. If she herself went to see the shipMeister and pleaded with him to evacuate from Aeran, to explain what she had discovered to the new government, then perhaps all would be well.

As if reading her thoughts Ashka said, 'What *are* you doing on Aeran? What is it about their symbols?'

'I'll show you.'

They rose and Elspeth led the way along the river's edge. They clambered over exposed rock faces, and slid in mud, ducked under the low-reaching limbs of giant green-barks where the jungle crowded so close to the water that it actually tumbled over the edge of the land, in places, so that bizarre brown and yellow weeds waved from a watery root. Ashka began to breathe with difficulty; Aeran's atmosphere taking its toll of his unaccustomed muscles, and perhaps of his age too. They rested constantly. He asked if she couldn't just tell him what he wanted to know. She grinned and shook her head, and after a while they slipped and stumbled on, hugging the winding river, watching animals for anything that might be dangerous.

Ashka saw his first blackwing. It was floating on the river surface, wings outspread to maintain its position, head down and feeding off some presumably abundant aquatic delicacy. Elspeth threw a fragment of stone that she picked up from a patch of almost barren ground. The blackwing was startled by the sudden splash and rose shrieking into the air, moving out of sight rapidly with its split-second jumps through space as well as its frantic flying. Ashka marvelled, turned to Elspeth with his eyes wide, a half-smile on his lips. 'If I hadn't seen it I wouldn't have believed it.'

'Teleportation,' stated Elspeth. 'All the animals on this planet do it.'

'Yes ... yes, I noticed those fish things flickering, come to think of it. I thought it was the light playing tricks on me.'

Elspeth shook her head. 'No tricks. It's a beautiful escape mechanism. They can also change direction in mid-jump. There is no predator species that I've seen that has evolved a really good answer to it.'

'Teleportation,' repeated Ashka thoughtfully, staring into the far distance. 'I saw a man teleport once ... it wasn't like that blackwing, though.' Elspeth said nothing. She couldn't see the old man's drift. After a moment she reached down and picked up another fragment of stone, lobbed it out over the water.

'You've *seen* that? A man teleporting?'

Ashka looked mysterious. 'I've seen many things, and forgotten many things. All rationalists get to see the bizarre and the new at some time in their lives – it's part of our job, acting as witnesses to this and that and ... teleportations!' Smiling. 'It goes back into my past a long way, and that's an area where facts and events have an annoying habit of getting themselves lost.'

Feeling uncomfortable at the thought of it, Elspeth said, 'Anyway, shall we get on?'

In a few minutes they had arrived at a large, natural pool, through which the river flowed in an almost circular motion, creating surface patterns that were intricate and fascinating. The water seemed dark and Elspeth explained that here it was over fifty feet deep. Steep, naked boulders rose on both sides of the pool, and on the rocks, carved shallowly but permanently by anything but geological time, were hundreds of symbols. Some had been scratched, but others had been chipped into the stone by repeated blows of some pointed instrument.

'This is it?' asked Ashka, running his finger around one of the shallowly inscribed circles, then rising to his feet again and balancing carefully on the sloping rock. 'Circles, concentric circles, broken circles, circles with lines through them ...' he looked at Elspeth.

'Wherever the Aerani hunt, scatter the ashes of their dead children, or feel that a place is sacred, there they inscribe the rocks with symbols such as these ... and not just these. These are water symbols ... this one is "ashes in the water" ... this is to ask the water to return the anima of a man who drowned ... this is to ask for the giving up of a pool-dwelling beast for catching.' She rose to her feet, still looking down at the scattered carvings.

'Elsewhere there are air symbols, and tree symbols, and earth symbols. There is an enormous alphabet of carvings and I've been piecing together what they mean for the last hundred hours or so – that's more or less the time I've spent on the world.'

'I find it hard to relate to abstraction,' said Ashka, looking around him at the thick forest. 'That's something I've inherited from my forefathers, I suppose. I like to see the full picture and reduce it to its essence in my own mind's eye. These symbols ...' he stared down at the rock. 'There is something essential about them, certainly, but it doesn't trigger any great sense of meaning in my head. Give me landscapes every time.'

'The sleeping dragons ...' said Elspeth and Ashka smiled.

'Obscure though they are,' he said after a moment, touching one of the circles again, 'I am filled with a vague sense of familiarity.'

'Simple patterns, simple "essences", continually manifest themselves in different cultures ...'

'Ah yes,' said Ashka, rising again. 'And I think I understand your drift. Somewhere else you've seen not just similar symbols, but *identical* symbols. Is that it? Is that why you're here?'

'Very much so,' said Elspeth quickly, then paused. On the verge of explaining her excitement she realized how strange, how fanatical her study might sound to someone not only unfamiliar with, but possibly also uninterested in, the study of primitive peoples.

Picking her words carefully, therefore, she tried to put Ashka in the picture, trying to read his attitudes and reactions, ready to give up at the slightest hint of his becoming openly cynical. In fact, after a few minutes, she realized that far from regarding her as a fanatic, he was listening, fascinated and intense.

It had started when she had been living with the Edge Society, part of a small commune with whom she related well, although physically she kept herself fairly isolated, joining with others mainly to talk and exchange ideas. Short of ways to occupy their time and interest they had, *en masse*, gone to Earth and volunteered in the archaeological restoration programme in Western Europe. After the three-hour war of some centuries before, much that was of historical interest was still buried beneath dust, sand or rubble, and slowly those monuments of pre-history that had been so painstakingly recovered during the twenty and twentyfirst centuries were being restored.

They had worked in France, and then in Ireland, and it was here that she had first come across the ancient Stone Age crematorium in the water-shed of the now dried-up river Boyne. There were thousands of volunteers strung along the Boyne and most of them were unearthing the hill-top mounds of a people who had lived on these slopes three or four thousand years before Christ. There was a crumbled twenty-first-century tourist station, and contemporary earthworks of various descriptions including an excellent example of a *tar roadway* that now lay revealed for nearly four hundred yards of its length.

But surmounting all, towering above the road and the river, was the mound of Newgrange, a tumulus, the original white-topped *Brugh* that had been visible for fifty miles around. Now substantially restored, it still possessed its timeless ring of carved stones, a kerb of giant rocks built into the structure for some unknown purpose, presumably ritual, carved with symbols and patterns in those darkest of ages before even the legendary *pyramids* of Egypt had been built.

Fascinated by the carvings, which extended into the passage tomb itself, and could still be easily discerned behind the more recent overlay of graffiti, Elspeth had recorded as many of the designs as she could, spending days in the sun and rain, copying the symbols, and wondering about them, and wondering about that one symbol in particular, carved in the central tomb, watching over the remains of the dead ...

Then they had left, and interest had been buried beneath the necessities of living and finding a new *edge*.

'Until ...?'

'Until one day, when a small group of us were wind-diving on a hell-hole called *Sabbath*, a man named Austin was brought to us. Someone doing him a favour, I suppose. He was a friend of one of the group and he was losing his mind and his memory. He was semi-hysterical in his urgency to cling on to his reason for a few more days.

'Austin had landed on a world – don't ask me why – and found the colonists had undergone bizarre physical changes – which is understandable – but had also returned to a Stone Age, natural way of life. It was a world not particularly hostile to the adventurer, except that after just a few days he had started to forget things. He had landed, observed, enjoyed the sensation of the new planet, and had then realized that his mind was being eroded with each passing hour. That was when he got back into his shuttle and fled into friendly arms.'

'And Aeran was the world?'

'Yes. Aeran.'

After leaving the planet the process of decay had not stopped, and Elspeth had been with him as he died, killed by his own hand, a man unsure of what he was or where he had come from, a shell, a speaking body that failed to recognize friends, and knew only how to scream in anguish as he tried to reach for some memory, some event on the very edge of his mind, but just out of reach.

Before he died he saw Elspeth's symbol dictionary from Newgrange. He recognized the symbols, but since he could never have seen them on Earth, he must have seen them elsewhere. On Aeran? Perhaps, he had said, his eyes, blue, tear-filled, staring at her through shadows, through living death. Perhaps Aeran … perhaps …

'I was intrigued, as you can imagine I'm sure. I didn't really know whether to believe him or not – he was half insane, occasionally berserk, and not exactly coherent. But I came and I found … these,' she pointed to the rock. 'And others too – and a culture just like he'd described it.'

'And the symbols are the same? As the Boyne symbols?'

'Almost identical. There are a few symbols here that weren't there – as far as we know at least – and some that I found at Newgrange that haven't shown up here, but then how do you date a chipping in a piece of igneous rock? It's very difficult, especially when the rock has been dead for thousands of years. Lots of symbols might have been added quite a time after, perhaps as a mark of religious respect, or just plain vandalism.'

'Then how has it happened? How has a civilization, dead these last seven thousand years or so, managed to re-manifest its art at more than two hundred light years distant?'

'If you expect me to answer that one,' she gave him a wry smile, 'you must be a little space happy.'

'No ideas at all? No ideas as to what might have happened in the river valley all that time ago, or here in the last few hundred years?'

'I *have* been wondering along similar lines to those. To be honest, it's driving me half insane thinking about it. Have you ever known the like in all your wide experience?'

Ashka shook his head slowly. 'No, I can't say I have. Something very peculiar has occurred here, and something unique – I'm sure of that, if of nothing else.'

'Intuition,' said Elspeth with a grin. 'It's no substitute for hard fact.'

'Oh, not you too,' murmured the rationalist, obscurely.

Ashka sat very quietly for a long while, staring at the dark pool, at the spiralling waters. The wind was gentle, but cool; as the day advanced towards dusk the thick forest around this open rock and water space became noisy, mostly with the sounds of plants, but occasionally with the cries of animals, emerging from the undergrowth to prowl through the night.

After a while he said, 'There are two possibilities that come to mind. Do you object if I suggest possibilities?'

'Go ahead.'

'I assume, by the way, that the colonists could not have brought the symbols with them, say in a book, or photographs …?'

'It's a possibility, certainly, although the tombs had been lost for a couple of centuries when the original colonial settlement was established.'

'Then, firstly, it is possible that something happened to the human colonists here that also happened to the human population of Ireland. The symbols could be related to an Event.'

'Alien contact? Is that what you mean?'

'Possibly. There is some evidence for an advanced alien life form at large in the Galaxy. It *is* possible. The second possibility that comes to mind is that the symbols which have emerged here and in Ireland a long time ago, are something basically human, an underlying artistic expression that most human cultures obscure; but again, an Event has allowed that basic culture to emerge.'

Elspeth thought about the suggestions for a while. Something extrinsic or something intrinsic. Yes, that did seem to cover everything! They weren't very brilliant suggestions, really, but they certainly were provocative. An alien presence in Ireland three millennia before Christ, re-appearing on a colonial world? That was easy to imagine, easier than trying to understand how some intrinsic cultural phenomenon might be lying within every human individual waiting to emerge. And yet, whilst not understanding it, that latter was the more likely, wasn't it?

Aliens, or human psyche. Or ... something else? And what would they look for in the symbols that might give them a clue as to which was the real answer?

She shook her head, turned to look at Ashka whose eyes were closed, face pale and solemn.

'Most of the symbols are really very simple. Circles, squares, wavy lines ...'

'Hmm?' He broke from his thoughts and met her gaze. After a moment he said, 'Why would they be complex?'

'Oh, but some of them *are*.' She reached down and traced round an open circle. 'Earth symbols can be fantastically complex, often complex combinations of other designs, often based around the double-centred spiral ...'

Ashka asked, 'Do you think their use here is the same as their use in Ireland?'

'I wish I knew. I'm inclined to think so ... here, let me show you something else, just a few yards away.'

She stood up quickly and helped Ashka to his feet. Walking away from the pool they approached a monolithic rock, five feet high, quite fat. It rose out of the ground at an angle and looked as if it had been placed there by hand. Most eye-catching, however, were the lines that had been intricately carved across two of its four surfaces. Parallel lines, weaving and spiralling, running up and down the rock and then round, tapering off, and all ending abruptly at ground level. Like a giant fingerprint, Elspeth reflected for the hundredth time.

'What does that suggest?' she asked Ashka. 'What immediately springs to mind?'

Ashka was delighted with the carving. 'The flow of earth energy in the rock. That's all it can be. That is exactly how earth energy flows through a boulder. Amazing ...'

'The kerb stones of those Irish tombs were covered with this sort of patterning, and some of the stones had obvious foci upon them.'

'The single spirals suggest those areas, yes ... I should have realized ... and these single weaving lines are fault lines in the current. But ...' he looked at her. 'Several foci in one area? Several focal stones around the base of a tomb? They must have been moved there after carving, or after locking the pattern in the crystal structure.'

'Obviously. You're missing the point, though. How could a primitive people be aware of such a sophisticated wave form? Earth energy wasn't made discernible until thousands of years after the Ireland colonists passed away.'

They stared at the rock. Ashka said, 'It's a familiar question. Perhaps the answer is that a primitive people were naturally aware of earth energy, but gradually lost that perception with time; perhaps the question should be, why did civilized man lose his ancient perceptions?'

'To rediscover them through science, and then here, when he regressed again to a Stone Age culture. Yes. That too is a familiar question.'

'I'm a rationalist, not an innovator,' said Ashka pointedly. They walked back to the river. 'With such an awareness these people ought to have an oracle, a specific concept of time and prediction.'

'They do,' said Elspeth. 'You were with the seer in the Fire Hall.'

'Ah,' Ashka signified that his suspicions had been confirmed. 'I shall be very interested in seeing the oracle here. Is it at all familiar?'

'I've never seen it,' confessed Elspeth, 'although I've behaved in accordance with its predictions. I have a feeling it's very different to the *ching*.' Understatement of the year, she thought to herself. Should she tell him that the local oracle predicted absolutes? No ... it would spoil the surprise!

'A spiral,' he said as they scrambled through the forest along the river shore, 'would probably symbolize a concept of Soul – beginning with the infinitely small, growing to the infinitely large.'

Catching their breath for a moment, staring from the bush over the flowing water, Elspeth said, 'I'm not sure yet. What intrigues me is the variety of spiral forms. There are double spirals which must have a very different meaning, and there are groups of spirals in ocular-like patterns, you know, two eyes sort of thing. Well, what does that mean? And most of all ...' should she tell him?

'Most of all?' he prompted.

It grew dark very quickly.

'Most of all?'

'Three double spirals, interlinked, triangular.'

Peter Ashka stopped and Elspeth turned to look at him. In the Aerani twilight the entire world was alive with sound, most noticeable of all the sound of wind in the forest.

'I saw that symbol in the Fire Hall,' said the rationalist. 'A very arresting design.'

'They call it the Earthwind, and it means something very significant and far different from simple circles and spirals. But I don't know what. The natives seem … not afraid, exactly, but reluctant to talk about it.'

'A God symbol.'

'No. Something even bigger.'

'Is that intuition talking, or evidence?'

Elspeth smiled in the greyness. 'Intuition. But I've got to find out what the Earthwind is.'

'I was reminded of the triple spiral, signifying a special trinity, that appeared on many ancient taoist works of art – one spiral represented the *ching*, or change, which provided the aesthetic impulse, the motivating power of all inner artistic conception and inspiration. The second referred to the *shen*, the luminous inner spirit which comprised an individual's thoughts and sensations and his sense of personal identity. The third spiral indicated the *ch'i*, the moving vitality, the force by which all great innovators tuned themselves into the flowing of the tao. The *ch'i* is in us all, the original Soul, the Christian Soul, the link with God.

'Do you sense such … *meaning* in the Earthwind? The spiral is so obviously a sign of inner spirit related to outer greatness – can there be any doubt about that?'

'I am filled with similar ideas, dear Ashka. And I just don't know. I just don't know.'

'And this bizarre spiral pattern … was it present in Ireland?'

'Only once. In the main tomb, Newgrange, right at the back of the tomb itself; it had been carved on the right-hand wall of a small, central chamber, and the magic thing was that once, and only once, in every year the sun shone right down the length of the passage and into that alcove. Just once, and at the time of building that date was also the shortest day of the year …'

'A magical day?'

'The winter equinox. Yes. A day of great mystical significance.'

'I'm intrigued,' said Ashka genuinely. 'I'll run it through my memory, if you like.'

'I'd like.'

'I'll also try to get your flight lead back …'

Elspeth laughed sourly. 'It doesn't really matter any more. I don't suppose I have the time to go up to my ship. I have to convince your shipMeister to get off this world.'

'I'm very reluctant to stay here myself,' said the rationalist. 'If Austin really *was* affected by Aeran then the sooner we leave the better.'

They moved on through the forest.

For your own sake, Peter Ashka, I hope it isn't too late …

five

In the early hours of the morning, feeling very cold and very tired, Elspeth emerged from the forest and stood, for a while, staring up at the sheer, earthen wall of the crog. She could hear shouting and screaming from within the colony, and the bitter night air (it was two or three hours to dawn) was punctuated by the sharp crack of bone upon rock as the artists behind the dunes chipped patterns and symbols to allay whatever fears were growing in the Aerani community.

The squat ship stood a few hundred yards away, at the edge of the vast natural clearing, sprawled partly across the sparse vegetation, partly nestled in a shallow pit of its own making. Lights were on around its midriff, and figures moved to and fro about its landing cradle. The smell of frying meat was on the air and since the cold wind was blowing from the direction of the ship she guessed that something good was being prepared for breakfast. Her mouth watered uncontrollably. It wasn't so long since she had last eaten real protein, but it seemed like years. Blackwing, her staple diet for the last few days, tasted like nothing short of leather and had a texture to match. She had almost forgotten the aroma of 'civilized' foods.

Two human shapes stood on the outer dune, staring silently down the hill towards the alien. She couldn't recognize them, though she saw them to be men. One was old, the other seemed young, and both carried bone weapons in the form of curved swords that reflected an occasional flash of yellow ship's-light. Elspeth didn't move as these two men walked round the rampart, staring down at the clearing outside the crog. They didn't see her, and after a few minutes they stopped again, exchanged inaudible comment, and then vanished down into the dune trench.

Elspeth darted from concealment and ran around the base of the outer rampart until she came to the great gash that was the gateway. Her shadow was faint against the dark earth wall that rose beside her, thrown across the surface by the beacons from the ship. She was unbothered by any eyes that might have been watching from the beyonder's vessel. She was concerned only with avoiding her possible execution the moment she entered the compound. After all, she had to keep reminding herself, she was unaware of the extent to which her breach of law was known by the Aerani, despite what Darren had said.

There was no one watching the outer gate. This was an unnerving fact since it suggested the presence of the ship was already throwing ritual and custom into unfamiliar patterns.

As she came into the trench between inner and outer walls, so the sound of shouting and arguing grew louder.

Immersed in almost total darkness, although a flickering torch further round the inner dune threw some scant light into the trenchway, not to mention on to Elspeth's furtive form, she scrambled up the inner earthen slope and peered very cautiously down into the fire-glow.

The air was heavy with the stink of torches, which burned in a great circle around the fire pit and around the top of the inner dune. The fire pit itself was cold and empty and around it were grouped men and women, both old and young (many wrapped in the simple cloaks they made out of blackwing leather) and it was their voices that were raised so high. Outside this cluster, watching silently, the rest of the crog sat or stood in groups or on their own, ranks of impressive faces watching the conflict before them. Beyond the low blue-bark roof of the great Fire Hall a few fires glowed among the clustered cawls of the village. Somewhere among them the lone artist worked his stone with a noisy and echoing enthusiasm.

In the central group, below her, two men were facing each other in anger, and Elspeth thought she recognized Darren's angry features, but it was hard to say in the inadequate torch light. The other man, with his back to her, she couldn't identify.

Slipping down the dune and back into the trench she ran round to the inner gate and crept inside, unnoticed she hoped, even though she now had the right to be here. A hand touched her and she jumped with fright, but turning – ready to fight for her life – she saw a tearful Moir staring at her.

'They're going to fight,' she sobbed. 'Oh Elspeth, they're going to fight for honour and Darren is bound to win ...'

Fight for honour ... The words made Elspeth sick to her stomach.

After a moment she said, 'Darren's going to fight?' Looking over the crowd, but she couldn't see the youth. 'But if you think he's sure to win ... why so upset?'

'He's fighting Engus,' she said, and fresh tears filled her eyes. Now Elspeth placed the stocky character who had had his back to her. Engus, Moir's lover, her marked man. And Darren, her brother, with family ties being close and no way that the outcome of this duel could leave her unbroken ...

Poor Moir.

Elspeth hugged her for a moment, all thoughts of her own safety gone. The crowd pulled back after a while to leave the area of the fire-glow free. Only Darren and Engus remained, crouched at the edge of the fire pit, staring quietly at the dead ashes of the previous day's burning.

Elspeth sat down at the base of the inner dune, with Moir weeping silently against her chest. The Aerani, to a man, watched the centre of the fire-glow in silence but also with an unmistakable excitement. Elspeth found her gaze drawn towards the hundreds of pits on the earth surface, where the severed heads of the vanquished stared from their bony past at the fight about to begin. Somewhere along that rim of greatest honour, perhaps, a new pit was being dug at this moment. She could see no activity of that sort but felt that the outcome of this match was certain to be one death and that there would be no delay in making preparation for the ritual interment.

Who would stare through earth in just a few minutes' time? She could hardly bear to think of Darren's life being forfeit in such a duel, and yet she was haunted by a vision of his skull, grinning at her, worms in its orifices, earth replacing its brains ... the vision refused to go, as if some entity were fore-warning her, forearming her for the tragedy about to occur.

She closed her eyes for a moment, fighting back a sudden fear that crept into her bowels and refused to go away. Then she opened her eyes and made herself stare at the arena. Moir's hand interlinked with her own. The girl had ceased to cry. What vision was *she* seeing, wondered Elspeth? In her heart, no doubt, the child wished to see the success of Engus, her lover, even at the frightening cost of her brother's life. Was she, then, seeing a terrible vision of Engus's severed head? Was something preparing *her* for the worst?

Whatever that something was – and secretly she knew it was mere fantasy, her mind feeding on her anxiety – it really ought to know the outcome of the fight, for this strange world had absolute prophecy at its command ...

Where *was* the Seer, she wondered. Was he reading whatever runes he used at this very moment? Was he below the earth, in the mother's womb, secretly weeping over the death of one of her children, a death that she had seen in markings, or signs, or symbols?

Here's for Darren, she thought. *Come on kid.*

The ritual of death and honour began, and Elspeth hunched forward on her knees. The air had become remarkably still and quiet, just the singing of a high-stratum wind and the occasional crackle of one of the torches. The sound of chipping had stopped. The shadows of the two young men danced on the ground as they stood and faced each other, spiritual activity even though their bodies were motionless. They were naked, of course, and Engus looked hugely muscular to an extent that Elspeth had not noticed before. His long hair hung matted around his shoulders, swept back from his forehead which seemed to be painted with some dark stain. His face was a mask of hatred (and yet they had been such friends ...) his fists clenched as he stared at his opponent. Darren looked the weaker of the two, and yet he was the most impassive. His body was quite still, devoid, even, of the tension that was so obvious in Engus's stance. Elspeth wished he would glance across at her, but he kept his gaze firmly on the other man while their instruments of death were brought out:

– Long, curved bone swords, gleaming yellow, broader at the tip than at the 'hilt', although there was no hilt as such, just finger grooves notched into the thin end of the bone. The blades looked cruelly sharp. What animal they had come from Elspeth didn't know. Not a blackwing, of that she was certain; these bones were from something big.

– A tangleweed each, wrapped around the left arm, snugly tucked into the pits of their arms in these moments before the contest.

– A fragment of rock, sharp, pointed. Each man refused this splinter and instead unslung his crystal knife from around his neck. This he used to gash his right forearm and show the blood running freely from wrist on to sword blade, thence on to the dry moss. A moment later a spherical boulder, pick-dressed to enhance its almost natural ball shape, was rolled out by three older men and placed between them. Darren and Engus dropped to their knees on opposite sides of the boulder and began to smear a pattern on the rock, an intricate spiral pattern ...

After a moment Elspeth realized just how intricate that pattern was. Drawn in blood, but with not a stroke wrong, not a line or curve out of place ... three double spirals ...

A death symbol? Was the Earthwind, then, a death symbol, no more, no less than that?

They both rose to their feet, blood still running freely from their open forearms. Why didn't they begin, why didn't they get it over with?

It occurred to Elspeth suddenly that she had no idea of why they were actually fighting. She said as much to Moir, who looked up at her as if she hadn't understood the question.

'There must be a reason. Who or what is at stake?'

Moir looked back into the compound, spoke with a voice as dull as the skies, 'Darren is fighting for our family. Engus for his.'

'Yes, but why?'

'His family want the beyonders dead. They want to attack the sky building and kill all of them.'

Engus wanted *that*? Elspeth felt disappointed. It was such an irrational and primitive thing to want, the brute force destruction of an obstacle ... and of course, the Aerani would soon find out that the obstacle had some brute force tricks of its own. 'And Darren's family represent those who want to obey the beyonders?'

'Not obey them, but leave them alone.'

It was so pointless. These two youths were fighting for something over which they had no control anyway. But it was too late to change things, too late to convince them otherwise.

So … tight lipped, cold skinned and tense, she watched (with trembling Moir no longer crying) as Darren and Engus waited for dawn, to begin their private battle.

It was over almost before it had begun.

The sun rose over the forest and the sky brightened; the torches were extinguished and the two fighters rose to their feet. For a moment they circled each other around the boulder. Darren's tangleweed reached out towards his opponent, but Engus brushed the organism aside with his broad blade. His own tangleweed remained tightly coiled around his arm. Then there was the flash of light on polished yellow surfaces, and the air was filled with a loud crack as the two blades met above the rock and were mutually deflected. Darren ran, and Engus feinted, and again the bone swords smashed together as each man wielded his weapon, striking with huge force, aiming all the time for his opponent's head. Still Engus kept his tangleweed out of action, as if waiting for a moment to use it unconventionally. Darren seemed unbothered by the other man's reservation. He used his own tangleweed to try and grip Engus's sword arm, but Engus was too quick.

They circled the stone, eyeing each other, smacking their blades together and then making quick, darting thrusts while the noise of that contact was still sharp in the air.

There was not a sound from the audience, not a murmur, scarcely a breath. Darren's breathing was loud, however, and whenever they moved towards each other across the stone Engus grunted loudly with the exertion of the blow he levelled at the shorter man.

Then Darren's tangleweed found a grip round Engus's neck and tightened visibly, while Darren yelled for the first time and raised his sword. But Engus cut through the creature in a second and now his own tangleweed snapped out and found a secure and agonizing grip on Darren's body, pulling him round and towards the stone. Engus raised his sword ready to administer the death blow (– Elspeth screamed –) but when Darren hit the boulder – with a loud thud and a cry of pain – it was *his* sword that found its mark.

Perhaps he had been waiting for Engus to do precisely what he had done; perhaps it was just the superiority of Darren's duelling tactic, but in the second of Engus's triumph, so his head was rolling across the ground, staring at the watchers sightlessly, bloodlessly.

The decapitated body of Moir's lover collapsed across the blood-stained boulder, still gripping its bone sword and tangleweed with unbreakable strength.

Darren unwound himself and stood up, wiped the red smear from his gleaming blade.

Moir began to sob, convulsively yet so quietly that she drew no attention to her grief. Her arms wrapped around Elspeth and Elspeth found herself crying in sympathy with the girl, watching as the victor strutted around the fire-glow, waving Engus's staring head by its long, blood-soaked hair.

To give him his due when he saw Elspeth staring at him, tearfully, and recognized Moir in her arms, he rapidly concealed his trophy from view and turned away.

As the crowd dispersed, for the most part silently, Elspeth tried to analyse her own feelings about what she had seen and what she had seen done. How could she hate Darren? What he had done had been a part of his ritual heritage and quite natural and acceptable to everyone, Moir included. And yet, such viciousness, such primitive behaviour! She realized, not for the first time she had to admit, that she didn't like to think of someone who had made a sort of love to her being as barbaric as this. It was cultural snobbery, she supposed.

She should not feel badly towards Darren for executing one of his friends in this grotesque way, and yet, in the moments following his triumph, she began to feel sick. The final cruel blow occurred over and over before her eyes (one blow! what strength!) – each time the head, spinning through the air, staring that much more obscenely, the spray of blood (how brief it had been – not at all the flood she had imagined) reaching further towards her. Her recollection of Darren's face grew distorted too, his grin, his smile of triumph, growing into something more caricature than exaggeration.

She was sick, choking as she turned her head away from Moir, now quiet, quietly dying.

This is fear, she thought as the violence in her stomach finally subsided. This is real fear, this is the prime symptom of fear, a new experience. My second since coming here ... the pain of a wound, and the pain of fear. Am I growing or regressing as I linger here? Is this true humanity coming, or departing?

'Elspeth ...?'

A time on New Anzar, years before:

They had come to the end of the city. Now they walked, the entire family, along the transparent tunnel leading over the ice flow. Her mother was weeping, her brother holding the old lady upright in his arms, keeping the tears back himself with difficulty, glancing at Elspeth as they walked the road of the disgraced.

My father has disgraced himself. I should be ashamed of him, I should be abusing him, filling his ears with my contempt and hatred; but how can I? I love him. Alex should be beating him, taking out his own disgrace and shame on the man who has caused it. We shall be disgraced forever because of this man, and this walk to death should be our chance to assault him, to vent our feelings and our bruised pride.

But how can we? We all love him ...

Old man, twenty years past his prime, stooped, now, with shame, not age. He walked ahead of them, down the empty tunnel, occasionally looking upwards, or sideways at the driving ice shards, the spiralling snow. This far north, at the untenanted extreme of the Clan city, there was no warmth, neither emotional nor physical. No one lived here, not even a recluse. No man entered these tunnels save those who did not deserve to walk back.

My father ... my poor father ...

(She remembered the day with such bitterness, with tears in her mind if not her eyes. So soon after her initiation ... so soon after her great pride ...)

'I have disgraced my status,' he said to them. 'I cannot accept this challenge. I have no courage left.'

No courage left! A man who had fought in the northern clan wars, who had – more recently – demanded to die with the rest of those who had opposed the Electra, who had sworn publicly at his acquittal that he would never forget what had been done to the men and women who had spoken out against the invader. No courage?

To fight a duel of office at his age would have been suicide. The challenge, from a much younger man, had been made to amuse the council; there were more humane ways to settle replacement disputes. But since the challenge had been made, it had to be accepted, and he had not accepted. He had left office, and the shame had been too great.

He had denied suicide and now walked to suicide for the sake of his family name, and the continued status of his son and daughter.

Elspeth was still too young to understand fully, but she knew that she hated this city, and this world, she knew that she had to get away, to escape this ridiculous ritual barbarism. It annoyed her that Alex did not agree with her, that he called her a thoughtless child who didn't understand.

They walked.

At the end of the tunnel, without turning to face his family, without stopping to kiss or embrace, with just the slightest shudder of his body as he repressed a cry of anguish, her father had stepped into the airlock and closed the door.

Elspeth had run to the wall and hammered on the solid surface, screaming for her father to come back for just a moment. Alex had whipped her away, had screamed at her to shut her mouth, to observe the great courage of a great man, who was not dishonoured, who was without shame, no matter what the city had said.

Her mother collapsed: Alex laid her gently, comfortably, away from the chilled walls of the tunnel.

Stripped of his cloak, naked, bowed of head, her father stepped into the ice wind. Elspeth remembered watching his frail, dark-skinned figure, blown backwards against the airlock door; his shape was blurred through the thick transparent material of the tunnel, but she saw him walk back into the wind, leaning against it, standing motionless as the needles of ice flayed his skin, his flesh. Redness blew against the tunnel wall, whiteness obscured the spray of blood. After a few seconds the old man out on the vicious polar surface raised his hands to his face, then collapsed. Like a bundle of bloody rag his corpse was flung against the airlock door; then the fragment of human life was gone, blown away, into the snow mist, into the ice world beyond the city, buried, forgotten.

A thin early morning mist hung heavy, icy, across the earthworks. The air was foul. Bitterness in her mouth was an unpleasant reminder of where she was. As she swallowed, and blinked drying tears from her eyes, she realized that Moir was gone.

The area was quite deserted now, but Darren appeared from the Fire Hall, walking towards her. He seemed hesitant, unsure, staring at her as he walked across the turf, across the still-visible spill of blood. Elspeth looked away from him, found herself wondering about Moir, about what would happen to her, about what she might be required to do now that her marked man had been taken from her.

'Can you forgive me, stone lady?' He had dropped to his knees before her and now sought her gaze earnestly.

'What for? For killing Engus?' She shook her head. 'It's not my forgiveness you need, Darren.'

'For hitting you,' he said. 'It was the right thing to do, and yet ...'

'And yet you feel guilty,' Elspeth finished for him. All her instincts told her to play soft, to accept the youth's humility, but something obstinate within her, something that still disliked the thought of a primitive man combining sexually with her, made her act cool, almost sour.

'I've brought you a gift,' said Darren, smiling. The brutal warrior of minutes before had completely gone. There was a childish sparkle in his eyes as he held out his left hand towards Elspeth. She stared at the clenched fist (hours before that fist had sent her reeling backwards into the icy river).

'What is it?'

'Do you like gifts?'

'Yes I do,' said Elspeth agreeably. Darren opened his hand. A small crushed plant sat in the palm and as she stared at it so he smeared the plant with his thumb, held the hand closer to Elspeth who recoiled momentarily and looked at the youth with puzzlement.

'Smell,' prompted Darren.

She took his wrist in her hands and brought the open palm closer to her face, sniffed the fragrance of the plant. 'Beautiful,' she said as the perfume filled her head with its spell. Like no flower she had ever smelled, exciting as no perfume she knew had ever been. 'Is it aphrodisiac?'

'Is it what?'

'What does it do to me? Does it make me fall in love with you? What magic does it work?'

Darren laughed, realizing what she thought he was trying to do. 'Nothing,' he said loudly. 'It's just a nice smell. It smells like you when you come back from …' he lifted his eyes to the sky.

Elspeth smiled. 'Thank you, Darren.' They stared at each other for a moment. Elspeth realized she was still shaking, still upset by the killing and by the haunting memory of her father's suicide. Making a conscious effort to calm herself she grew more relaxed. 'Are we friends again, then?'

Darren hesitated, but it was obvious that this was his wish; he was confused about it, certainly, but he obviously regretted his actions of the day before. 'I'd like to be,' he said. 'For a beyonder …' he broke off. 'Well, you have a very strong effect on me. That's what you said to me a few days ago, wasn't it? A very strong effect. You're not like those others and I would hate to see you leave.'

'But the others … you want to drive them away.'

'I don't want to kill them. Engus wanted to kill them … he wanted to kill you too. We just don't want them in our land, by our river.'

Elspeth took his hands in hers. 'Me neither, Darren, and I shall be doing my best to encourage them away myself.'

'We won't accept what they say! We won't allow these *things* they want to put here.'

'I know.' She kissed the scented palm of his hand. 'It's good to be friends again,' she said warmly. 'I felt quite lonely without you.'

He nodded thoughtfully and for a moment the softness of his face became rough again, more manlike, more warrior-like. 'But you *must* do what I say in future. Is that clear?'

'Clear.'

She thought he still seemed troubled. There was a tenseness about him, an almost tangible unease.

'Darren …?'

He scratched his orange fur where it merged, above his neck, with the tight yellow fuzz of his adolescent beard. 'Moir is with the Ungenn at this moment, and will probably talk to the Seer as well. He'll be angry.'

'Because *you* didn't talk to him first?'

'Nor did Engus.'

Elspeth was confused. 'You mean you would have asked him who was going to win?'

And they would have found out too, with the oracle on this particular world.

Darren shook his head. 'That isn't allowed, but the Seer should have known, he should have known himself. It's the way with us.'

'So now he's angry. Why is Moir seeing him?'

'Probably for the same reason.'

Cold apprehension for the second time. Darren was performing some commendable bush-beating. What was it Elspeth didn't know? But then, what was it she *did* know about this society?

'Does Moir have to fight a duel of honour by return; is that it? Do you now have to kill your sister by law?'

He looked uncomfortable. 'I killed her lover in a duel of honour. Whenever that is done the marked woman – or man of course – can issue challenge to the marked person of the victor. That's ... that's you.'

Her astonishment at the thought of such return killing concealed, for a moment, a strange fact. It hit her suddenly. 'You mean you really do think of me as your *marked woman*? That's insulting!'

Looking as if he were acutely uncomfortable, Darren said, 'I know you're not really, but that isn't the point. The point is, only you and I *know* that. As far as my people are concerned you are my marked woman. And I'm your marked man. I thought you knew this ... how else did you think you'd been accepted so easily?'

It was a logical enough thought, and she should have realized the fact; what did his parents think of the match, she wondered, half amused.

And back again (her jumping thought processes) to the fact of the duel. 'Then ... Moir might at any moment issue me with a challenge.'

'At any moment.'

It was an abhorrent thought. To fight with swords, to whip with tangle-weeds, to cut, slash, to sever ... she couldn't do it, she knew she couldn't, and never in all the years that remained to her could she be trained or conditioned to be so cruel.

'I'll refuse,' she said simply, 'I'll not fight Moir.'

'You can't refuse to accept challenge!' Darren said, angrily.

'Can't I just?'

Darren stared at her and with each passing second he grew colder. Then: 'If you refuse,' he said quietly, 'I shall kill you. I would have to kill you by law – and I would not want it any other way ... *stone lady!*'

Elspeth controlled her rising disquiet. 'You presume too much, Darren,' she said, with equal menace in her voice. 'If I choose to end the pretence, to leave here and return to ... *up there*, then that's it, that's all there is to it. You have no further rights in my life than those upon which we mutually agree.'

He smiled, an expression almost identical to the smile of triumph he had worn minutes earlier. 'I will not face the disgrace of it, Elspeth. If you are challenged, you accept – or I'll kill you.'

He reached to the leather thong around his neck and felt for the knife that should have still hung there. Elspeth hadn't realized it was missing until now, and for some reason nor had Darren. He was obviously upset by its absence, and turned to look over the fire-glow. Elspeth took the opportunity to assess her situation. It was a long way to the exit from where she sat, and she could never scramble over both earthwork walls whilst fighting off a young warrior's fatal attention. There was no alternative but to brazen it out. Despairing, she said, 'Darren, I have no idea how to wield a sword. She'd kill me immediately.'

He looked back at her, fingers still on the leather thong. 'Not if you used your fire weapon.'

'You sound like you want Moir killed. She *is* your sister.'

He shook his head. 'She *was* my sister. The moment I killed Engus our blood separated. Unless she declines to issue challenge it will remain separated for ever. But none of our family would dare decline.'

The look between them was not hostile, nor warm; it was a look of mutual defiance, Elspeth's resentment at being labelled 'marked' emerging again to take a childish hold of her emotions, Darren quite obviously defying the older woman to embarrass him by not fighting his sister. They might have exchanged more words, were on the point of breaking the silence, when Laurian came running from the Fire Hall. He saw Darren, ran across, slowed and glanced at Elspeth. A less impressive youth than Darren in terms of stature and facial character, his fear was easy to read in the slackness of his lips and expression. Darren, still on his knees, looked up. 'Well?'

Laurian breathed heavily for a moment, glancing uneasily at each of them in turn. 'She ... she declines to challenge.'

For a moment Elspeth basked in an uncontrollable wave of relief (remember the relief when my father declined? Remember the sense of pride ... so swiftly drowned ...). Then Darren's angry shout startled her from her thoughts. Slowly, tensely, he rose to his feet, to stand staring at Laurian. 'She *refuses*?' he shouted again. His left hand fumbled at the leather thong and again his anger was momentarily interrupted as he failed to find the knife that should have been there.

Laurian said, 'I'm sorry, Darren. I really am.'

Darren turned to stare down at Elspeth. His face was that furious mask she had seen by the river, a few hours before, lines, tensions, adding years to him. He smiled, implying much in the sourness of the look he gave her.

'That's not all,' said Laurian. A small group of Aerani youths had slowly gathered around them and were watching Darren intently.

'Go on.'

'The Seer has consulted the oracle about the beyonders. The oracle has said we should accept what the beyonders want. The Ungenn are talking with him now ...'

Again, Darren's voice was a piercing scream of anger. 'Then it's worthless! Worthless! No oracle would ask us to do such a thing!'

'But it has,' said an unfamiliar voice. Darren turned and as he moved so Elspeth saw the Seer standing there, staring at her. Beside him stood Peter Ashka, smiling narrowly as he regarded her. Standing side by side Elspeth was amazed at how similar they looked – both old, both manifestly aged, both thin – the set of their eyes and expression of their faces giving tangibility to their special psychological abilities. Ashka, as usual, was lost in his billowing robe. The Seer, a frail man with white fur, was now wrapped in thick strips of blackwing leather, covering his legs and arms and a wide band of his torso.

Ashka said, still staring at Elspeth, 'The *ching* agrees. We asked it and it said the same thing – they should accept our mission.'

Somewhere around the wall of earth, out of sight, a woman began to wail, perhaps as she interred the head of her son, a son who might still have been alive if the seer had been consulted according to ritual.

RETREAT

six

Several hours earlier, shortly after he had left Elspeth by the river, Peter Ashka had returned to the ship, thoughtful and excited, worried yet intrigued. There were no service requests awaiting him, which he considered surprising, but it did at least mean he had some thinking time to himself. Entering his small room he turned off the light and walked to the large window. Outside it was dusk and the darkness was increased by the heavy cloud layer. Already, on the nearby earthworks, torches were being lit and for a while he watched the activity.

Elspeth Mueller, and what she had told him, was the cause of his concern. It may have been a mere quirk of fate, a chance in a million, that had caused her to part company with the *ching*, but something about what she had said still nagged at him; he had told her that he had never heard of such a thing happening before, but he realized, as he reflected on the full details of their conversation, that even at the time he had been aware that he was not telling the truth.

But where? When?

It was a snippet of information that refused to emerge and be identified. Some time in all his years of life he had read, or heard, of such a bizarre change in a human–*ching* relationship occurring, and had remarked it sufficiently for the fact to have lingered in his mind. But his memory, not frail like its possessor, but perhaps a little rusty, refused to behave decently.

How contrary a friend is memory, he thought to himself, that it waits until the helplessness of old age before it starts to play its teasing games.

His failing memory was his greatest anxiety; age, frailty, these things did not matter to him, and they did not matter even when he entered the company of youthful men and women, watched their vitality and energy, subtly deflected the insensitivity, the irresponsibility of youthful conversation that so often insulted him without meaning to do anything but put him at his ease. No, not the physical loss that he continued to suffer, not mental loss either, not speed of thought or general awareness, for in this area he was superior to everyone on the ship; he had to be, he was the rationalist. But memory, a part of the mind apart (despite appearances), an entity separate from the other possessing entities of the brain; here he felt a touch of jealousy, an uncontrollable ire when he found that he could not remember events or places from his middle years that younger men remembered clearly though they had been mere children at the time.

What memory he retained (and it was by no means small) he valued, almost treasured. Natural decay took its toll. There were too many times when he remembered a magic moment from his youth, a girl, perhaps, or a friend whom he had loved dearly, and the name would not come. The face was there, an attitude of body, the sound of a voice; there was the smell of snow, perhaps, or a hot, still summer, dry grass, sunlight filtering through alien foliage. A single scene, a few seconds of an experience that had lasted for hours but which had contracted to its essences. *Like a symbol, like the simple pattern that can mean so much, the bare design which contains a wealth of meaning, but can be stored so much more easily on our pattern-sensitive cortex.*

How irritating that his years of life were condensing into mere minutes. Each minute packed with meaning, of course, but adding up to such an insignificant span of time. It made him wonder what he had done with all the other hours and days. How often he had wished he'd had time to do this, or that, or visit a world here, or a city there, and how often time had defeated him; and yet … how much time he had wasted, searching for his inner peace, for his outer satisfactions, for his correct depth in the universal sea of time and change.

Memory. It was the key to his past and it unlocked only a fraction of the doors and windows; it restricted his backwards view and seemed to operate with a will of its own. He resented this, deeply and bitterly. His jealousy at the strength and resolution of youthful memory was merely a symptom of this resentment. A long time ago Peter Ashka, in the solitude of retreat, had come to terms with his social isolation, had realized that for him, because of what he was, both rationalist and unique human, he was destined to be the friend of all and none. All men enjoyed his company, no man would not call Ashka a friend; all rationalists were the friends of the race. But there was no one, not even Gorstein, who was truly the friend of the man. No one, save his memory and the *ching*, and these, comforting though they were, had their limitations.

To think of losing even such limited friends, to think of the relationships decaying because of something on Aeran, perhaps, struck a note of great fear in the vast spirit of the frail oriental. He had lost so much, he could not bear to lose more.

He had said that were he to lose his friendship with the *ching* he could be no better advised than to kill himself. His own words came back to him, loudly, frighteningly. He closed his eyes at the thought, but immediately the reassurance of the *ching* was there: seven months. His death was in seven months, and the *ching* had said it would be peaceful. Suicide was not peaceful. *Thank the tao*, he thought as he opened his eyes again, *thank the tao I took the chance and asked it.*

His spirits took an immediate surge upwards. Opening a small wall cupboard he withdrew one of his treasures, a flat photograph of a group of ten young men. The colour was blue with age, the edges, despite the material upon which the picture had been impressed, were cracked and torn; but the ten men were as alive as they always were, seated or standing, staring at Ashka down six decades. That blonde man on the end, his grin so wide it couldn't be anything but false, and yet ... not false. Lively eyes, stylish clothes, his bearing that of a man at superb ease. He wore a badge with a *ching* hexagram; this one was hexagram sixteen, Calm Confidence. The other nine wore different badges. There was Quiescence, a solemn man, his name forgotten, now, but his manner, his conversation still ... still largely remembered ...

(Ashka frowned.)

And there was his very good friend ... who? The name had also gone, but the badge Ashka remembered well, hexagram nineteen, Getting Ahead. The badges were jokes, of course, nicknames for the members of the conference of rationalists at which these particular ten youthful men were the new male rationalists of the year, newly graduated, ready to embark upon retreat for ... how many years? Had it really been ten? It seemed like ten weeks.

Turning the picture over, feeling the atmosphere of the convention in his blood, the noisy babble of voices, the smell of the pinewood tables, the way the green drapes in the rooms had rustled annoyingly during the nights ... turning the picture he read the words, New Recruits, Carnutes, 3577. It was his own handwriting. Carnutes? There was something ...

(He frowned again.)

He knew it was a joke, and yet he couldn't remember the joke. Carnutes. A name from history ... what name? Why did he know he ought to smile, and yet the name meant nothing?

Memory.

Tears filled his eyes as he looked again at the ten figures staring out at him in youthful splendor. Names all gone, save the grinning man and his Calm Confidence. *How I've changed. Do I still deserve to wear that nickname?* Thank the tao the rest of the conference was still in his mind ... the rustling drapes, the smell ...

His fingers tensed on the picture as he stared at the faces and willed himself to remember more.

The smell, the curtains, water ... water in a fountain? What else? What was said, what was done?

His face grew wet with perspiration: moisture trickled from the angle of his jaw, sweat and tears, emerging in silence as his mind strained to remember. He knew he should remember – the conference was always on his mind; he often relived whole parties, whole talks, whole conversations. It was impossible that the events of those days (weeks?) should have gone so completely ...

And yet they *were* gone.

He made a noise in his throat, half-formed words, half-vocalized cries. What was happening to him? How could he forget so completely? Surely not ... surely Elspeth Mueller hadn't been saying that *Aeran* ... Had he completely misunderstood her? Had she meant the planet really *did* destroy?

The conference, the greatest day of his life ... now there was nothing, just – pinewood, drapes, water – nothing else; the fact of the conference, yes, a half-remembered vision of men and women, a familiarity with the faces in the photograph, a friendship with the man standing next to him; and then nothing. Just blankness.

Terrified, shaking almost uncontrollably, Ashka opened the locker and flung the picture inside. He leaned against the window heavily, his brow finding pleasure in the cool glass surface, moisture misting the glass, running in rain-like trickles to the lower sill. He began to cry.

Later he noticed someone standing outside the ship, lit by the yellow glow spilling from the crew quarters next to his own cabin. He recognized the man as the Seer of the colony. The man was called Iondai, but that was as much as Ashka knew about him.

Iondai was searching the lighted windows in the sheer side of the ship. Whenever his gaze lingered for a moment on Ashka's window the man showed no recognition, but of course, he would have seen nothing. Was Iondai looking for him? Or just studying the alien?

Ashka switched on the light of his cabin. Now he found he couldn't see out, but for a second studied the dim reflection of his tear-stained face. He felt slightly embarrassed, allowing the irrational emotion to play out to its full before it faded away. Turning off the light again he saw Iondai staring at him, beckoning.

Gathering up his small pack, wondering what the Seer had on his mind and why he had come so obviously looking for his opposite number, Ashka hurried back on to the planet's surface. For a moment, as he stood at the bottom of the short ramp, he was puzzled; Iondai was nowhere to be seen. Ashka felt peculiarly vulnerable in the darkness, fully lit by the light spilling from the airlock behind him. Then he noticed a figure standing by the earthworks, round to the left, away from the gaping entrance. It was difficult to be sure but Ashka believed that the figure was Iondai, and acting on that belief he walked across the spongy scrubland, away from the ship.

By the time he reached the earthworks Iondai had vanished again; Ashka followed the wall around, feeling only a twinge of apprehension as the ship was lost from his sight. In total darkness he felt secure from the humanoid forces that were threatening him and his colleagues, but totally exposed to the natural life forms of the world which he couldn't convince himself did *not* have perfect night vision.

A sudden flare of light startled him; it was a torch being ignited in the distance. (How, he wondered, had that been done?) Held by a dim man-shape, the torch itself was waved beckoningly. Ashka pressed on, left the earthworks, found himself walking across open land and entering an area of bush and tree-forms. The torch bobbed ahead of him, weaving between the trees, vanishing and reappearing round upright boulders that Ashka, though he touched them and quickly explored them for markings as he passed, could not work out to be either natural or manerected.

He seemed to walk for ages, but only a few minutes passed before the light of the torch ahead of him cast shadows across a great mound, rearing out of the forest like the humped back of some sleeping beast. It was four or five times his own height and gently rounded in a fashion he was sure would be familiar to students of pre-history, but which he, in his ignorance, had never seen. Elspeth would understand the reason for its shape and size, this tumulus that no doubt reiterated the Stone Age culture with which she was so fascinated. To Ashka it was a man-made structure without fascination, but with a small entrance that would mean a certain amount of stooping. Iondai stood before this entrance and waited for Ashka, waving the torch as if the motion in some way helped the illumination of the difficult pathway.

Before Ashka could speak, on arriving at the mound, Iondai had ducked and entered the passageway. For a moment Ashka was aware of a richly decorated lintel at about waist height, and complex rock carvings reflecting what he was sure were earth currents in the stone, lining the first few feet of the passage. Then the light was a distant glow and he was crawling through the damp tunnel, stooped, uncomfortable, watching his breath frost in the icy air, feeling the cold, wet stone with tentatively explorative fingers; he felt a certain discomfort with the claustrophobic rock burrow, as if, when he touched the stone, some ghoul or ghost breathed down his neck. He drew his body into a huddle as he stepped further down the ramped passageway, descending, he was sure, into the bitter depths of the earth. The yellow flickering of the torch became his focus, his full awareness. It represented warmth and safety.

He was glad when he reached the great chamber at the end of the passage, which had extended, he was sure, for over two hundred yards. Iondai stood there, the torch in his hand, his face a mask, unsmiling, deeply shadowed.

'We're almost there,' he said as Ashka stood upright and looked around.

The next moment Iondai was vanishing down a side passage, the noise of his walking curiously loud and sharp in Ashka's ears.

He hurried after the strange Aerani, keeping closer to him, this time. After just a few seconds they went down a steep ramp and emerged into a cool but less icy chamber, well lit with wall torches and the floor covered with skins. The walls were decorated with earth current patterns and abstract shapes that Ashka couldn't begin to guess about. Other passages led off from this natural cave, but Iondai sat down on the skins and stared up at his guest.

Ashka too seated himself on the warmer floor and finished his close scrutiny of the cave. This, no doubt, was where the seer lived and carried out his predictions. One of the passages would lead to the inside of the earthworks, and Iondai had led the way down the exit to the forest: so where did the third tunnel lead too? Perhaps just another way out.

Iondai smiled as he saw Ashka's gaze lingering on the low tunnel. 'It leads to the Fire Hall,' he said.

'Ah,' said Ashka, smiling back, then shivering slightly as his body refused to adapt to the cool air. 'And that one? Where does that lead?'

'To the oracle,' said Iondai. 'To the Earthsong itself. Would you like to see it?'

'Very much,' said Ashka. Earthsong? It inspired a picture of no oracle that he had ever seen. Very interesting. 'Who built the mound?'

'There are several, scattered around the crog, in small clearings in the forest. Our ancestors built them as ritual entrances and exits to the Fire Hall. The earth below the forest is filled with caverns and tunnels and our old people often choose to go down into the earth to die. This chamber is the greatest chamber of all, and the Seer has dwelled here since before my grandfather's grandfather. Many generations.'

'Did they all use the Earthsong? The oracle?'

'My father was Seer, but he won the right by contest. I have never been contested, but have no children, so when I die there will be fierce competition for the honour.' He smiled narrowly. 'I don't propose to die just yet, however. Although I too have asked the Earthsong about my final breath.'

'I'm very anxious to take a look at your strange-sounding oracle.'

Iondai said, 'It has already predicted hostility.'

For a moment Ashka didn't understand what he meant. 'Hostility? You mean … what … between our two peoples?'

'Hostility among my own people because of your beyonder mission.'

Ashka fell quiet and thoughtful for a moment. He remembered his own *ching* reading for Gorstein, and the hidden implication of hostility; he remembered the strain of the first meeting between the two peoples, and a fight, a clash of anger seemed almost inevitable. 'We'll have to try and avoid it then,' he said.

'It is unavoidable,' said Iondai, almost sadly.

'Nothing is unavoidable,' insisted Ashka, 'If you know what you're walking into.'

Iondai seemed puzzled. 'The prediction can't be changed,' he said. 'There is nothing we can do.'

Ashka allowed his surprise to surface – if Iondai's oracle really worked (and Ashka was not prepared to believe that it did just on Elspeth's say-so) it was difficult to understand how the mutability of the predictions had not been noticed. If, by tradition, any prediction was adhered to it would, of course, explain the attitude that Iondai had demonstrated. But Ashka sensed that his opposite number was a deep and thoughtful man (a man with a rationalist's temperament, in fact) and it only took a slight dissension, an anger following a prediction, for the path of time to change, for the flow to alter in the way it so easily did. But then, so many human cultures which had developed prophecy had failed to realize what the ancient orientals had realized, namely that time and life were not predetermined, even though (if left to their own devices) they followed a fixed path, the path of least resistance.

Ashka was still wondering whether or not he had the right to educate subtly the Seer in the ways of the Universe, planting sufficient seeds, unnoticed, that within a short while correct understanding would bloom, when Iondai interrupted the lengthy silence.

'Which oracle do you use?'

The voice startled Ashka. For a moment he wondered if Iondai was joking – which oracle? Didn't the man know anything …? And then he remembered where he was.

It was as if he, Ashka, had slipped from reality for a moment – how strong the sensation – a living dream, a moment of detachment that seemed to have lasted for hours. The real world flooded back (how apt that metaphor!). In the torchlit cavern, the symbols and craggy rock protrusions moving in that bizarre semblance of life that an unstable light source can impart, Ashka drew his cloth bag round and on to his lap.

'We call it the *Book of Change*,' he said, drawing the silk-bound *ching* from among the assorted contents of his pack. 'A very ancient oracle that has evolved from several works of philosophy, each becoming embellished over the ages. Ideas, you understand – the ideas of many men that suddenly, hundreds of generations ago, crystallized into the key to the living oracle which it represents.'

'This very object,' said Iondai, reaching out to touch the silk.

Ashka unwrapped the *ching* and showed it for what it was. 'We call this a book. Ideas, advice, wisdom – all are recorded on these pages.'

Iondai was delighted. He watched as Ashka removed the three coins and began to turn page after page, pointing out words, symbols. Such simple excitement.

'And this is the oracle – you carry it with you! You must – forgive me if I sound awestruck, but you must be a very great seer!'

Ashka smiled. 'There are none who are great and none who are less than great.'

'But to *carry* the oracle!'

'This is not the actual oracle,' said Ashka. He hoped he wouldn't confuse the native. 'This is my connection to it – my way in. Through this book I consult the oracle itself.'

'And where *is* the oracle itself?'

'Everywhere,' said Ashka. 'The whole vast Universe is the oracle, the flow of time, the condensation of matter, the pockets of life, the tug of *gravity.*'

'I don't understand.'

'No one understands, Iondai. The *ching* – that is what we usually call the oracle – hides its true nature from us, whilst allowing us to come close enough to an understanding for us to be – frightened. Fear of the oracle's power means belief – belief is all that is needed for it to work for us.'

'The prediction, then, comes from within you – is that how it works?'

'In a sense.' It was, of course, obvious enough to Ashka, and to any child of Ashka's Universe, for that matter. But for the shaman of a Stone Age culture that simple statement represented a magnificent intuitive understanding. Magnificent.

'Vast is the tao,' quoted Ashka. 'Ultimate, universal, ever present, ever existent, embracing time and space, the beginning and the end, embracing man and the life that is lesser than man.' He broke off and stared at Iondai. 'The tao is an ancient word for – for the energy and matter that flow around us and through us, every one of us.'

'Winds,' said Iondai, 'Heat and cold, the forces that appear in our rock and stone, in the earth, the caught breath of time … yes, I think I understand.'

Earth current in rock …

'Can you really see …?' began Ashka, suddenly intrigued. 'The rock, the life—' he broke off. It seemed irrelevant, somehow, and he decided to question Iondai about it at a later date. Iondai obviously understood the concept of the tao, even if only in a primitive form.

Why the anxiety on the third level of his mind? wondered Ashka. It resided there, a nagging uncertainty, a mocking laughter – to what did it allude? Iondai? Was it Iondai who should have been explaining the nature of force and change to Ashka? Life in rocks, the flow of earth energy – seen by only the primitive mind, or by sophisticated equipment that itself reached into a dimension beyond the grasp of the normal human psyche. Behind his eyes, behind the bone and blood of his skull, locked in the bioelectric confusion of his brain, what secrets did Iondai conceal? He and his people all?

'Yes,' Ashka said aloud. 'Those forces are some of them. The night stars, they also exert their own force on everything around them, and between us and the stars is a void filled with the echoes of … of other voids, filled with tiny particles of matter that belong to several Universes, not just ours – all these things form an immense structure that fills our minds, our beings, flows in and out perpetually. Our life, we who are aware, is very intricately connected to this structure and we can ride the shifting currents of this vast flow. At times we are very much in tune with the energy around us, at times we are not. We can alter our physical balance quite simply by redirecting flow in the body, but the mind is more difficult and it is the mind that carries us through the slow processes of change. This, the *Book of Change*, tells us how we are heading and we can consider our path accordingly. It may be that we see the necessity to alter our relationship with the tao to avoid disaster or difficulty. By being aware of the future as it is indicated we can, of course, change it to one that is more productive.'

'So this – *book* – these symbols, they are a bridge between you and this tao.'

Ashka smiled, patting the book affectionately. 'Without it we are all just flotsam …' his favourite expression. 'The *ching*, this book, is just an object, but when being used it is filled with life. I believe, it *is* believed, that the book during use becomes something alive – a sentience somewhere between life and cold death.' He stared at the book, remembering his years in its company, the tragedy and joy they had shared, this book and he, the semi-living creature and the narrow human. Could there be any doubt that the oracle was alive, an extension of the questioner's awareness from the one side and an extension of that great Universal awareness from the other – the *ching*, at the temporary interface between material life and non-material life, a crystallized awareness that guided and encouraged, that warned and congratulated. A total friend.

'Our minds,' he said to the quietly contemplative Iondai, 'conceal much from our awareness. We are not aware of our intimacy with the cosmos – the tao – we can't feel it, we can't touch it, we can't smell it. For thousands of years civilized man believed himself to be flesh and mind, dead after bodily death, a container of reactions, an impenetrable bag, unconnected to anything else except by physical contact. It is still desperately hard to comprehend that we are all just dust motes on the shifting waves of a vast ocean; our mind reaches into that ocean without our knowledge, expressing itself in ways most of us never realize. In dreams we sometimes reach out a little into that frantic void, in language we find awareness surfacing and creeping into the way we form concepts in "words"… in symbols we express ideas—'

'My friend,' Iondai's voice was gentle. He was smiling as Ashka turned his distant gaze upon his darkly shadowed face. 'I regret – I no longer understand.'

Ashka laughed as Iondai grinned apologetically. 'I got carried away. I'm sorry.'

'Don't be. The oracle I use, the Earthsong, is far simpler.'

'I'd like to see it.'

'In a while. Your interest in my Earthsong is no greater than my interest in your *ching*.'

'Of course. Are you interested in consulting the *ching*? It *will* work for you.'

'I think we could both consult it in a moment. There is a question to which we need an answer. You will have to take that answer to your people and I to mine. So we shall have to ask both oracles.'

Should the mission go ahead? thought Ashka. The obvious question in view of the situation and the unexpected turn of events on Aeran. He smiled to indicate his understanding.

'But if I understand your meaning,' Iondai continued. 'Your *ching* will warn us of what *may* happen in the future. It doesn't tell us what *will* happen.'

'No oracle has that power,' pointed out Ashka. He watched Iondai's face for a sign – any sign – of puzzlement, but he saw none. 'The way the universe about us is constructed it is impossible to "see" the future. Life is not predetermined.'

'Then it could not tell you of death, or fire, or flooding, or birth ... it doesn't deal with things that will occur but only with a single person's relationship with things around him.'

Ashka couldn't disagree. 'In as much as people are usually involved with events the *ching* may be used to predict the possibility of disaster. As for death ...' He stopped speaking and let his gaze wander to the dark passage that led to the Earthsong oracle. 'Death,' he repeated. How strange that he had never before considered how close to breaking the rules his prediction of death had come; it was not an absolute, of course – if he chose to he had no doubt that he could delay his termination, his return to dust – s.a. therapy, perhaps, or comadelayed-death ... but why? Why not decline peacefully, relaxedly? There was no reason, and the prediction would come true, exactly as it had outlined the event. The specificity of both question and answer, however, had brought the *ching* and questioner perilously close to that awesome void where the tao was itself the echo of an energy-time system, rather than the matrix in which those bizarre echoes reverberated, allowing these occasional and very slight glimpses of a more factually defined outcome.

Every time Ashka thought of that question he trembled to think how near to destroying his own relationship with the *ching* he had come. It would be impossible to explain to Iondai.

'Death,' he repeated for the second time. 'There is no death in our Universe – cessation of body, certainly, but the mind continues forward. I have asked the *ching* how long to my body's death – it has told me seven ...' he rapidly converted seven months into Aerani time, 'twelve cycles of the torch. I shall not fight against it.'

It occurred to him, irrelevantly, that he had no idea what a cycle of the torch comprised, unless it was the ignition of the torches on the earth ramparts. How ignorant one could remain without being aware of it, without even seeming ignorant.

Iondai was shaking his head, staring at the *Book of Change*. 'How can an oracle work when it can't tell you precisely what will happen?'

As he asked the question so he reached out and picked the *ching* up from the floor. Ashka felt none of the anxiety at its being handled that he would have felt had, say, Gorstein or Elspeth touched the book. 'How do I consult it?'

'A sequence of random selections are first made. One throws these three discs and records the way they fall. This action is probably without influence from the questioner, but as I've said, during the consultation both questioner and oracle are intimately linked and the resulting prediction is due much to the innate …' clairvoyance? '…future-seeing ability that all humans possess. However,' he took the book back, fussily (unconsciously) smoothing over the places where Iondai's fingers had held the precious tome. 'However, most humans possess only a very slight ability in this way. This is where I come in. I assist in the interpretation, but also I can channel the disorganized thoughts of the questioner while he seeks among the several real and imaginary foresights for the correct alternative – the path along which he is moving at that moment. I am, of course, unaware of what occurs in his mind and I cannot see the outcome except through the oracle – but my influence is often important.'

'Briefly, then, how do I consult?'

It was impossible, Ashka knew, to explain the intricacies of the *ching*'s working in just a few minutes. He was not surprised when it took him a good half an hour – but he *was* surprised that at the end of that time Iondai already seemed to understand fully the oracle. (By now, Ashka realized, he should cease to expect anything other than first-class intuition from this elderly seer.)

'And your question?' asked Ashka.

'Concerns the wisdom of accepting the *monitors*,' said Iondai.

Ashka was taken aback – this was not the question he had expected. It was, nevertheless, an excellent question – it would seek prediction *and* guidance, no matter what the answer.

'Throw the coins, then,' he said, his awareness reaching out widely to encompass the old man. Iondai shook the coins for a long time, listening to the sound they made as they rattled together, the metallic sound of ancient nickel against ancient nickel, a sound never before heard by this culture where bone and rock ruled. He opened his hands. The coins scattered on the dry earth floor where he had pulled back the skins.

(Something was wrong. Ashka felt it very strongly as his own mind and the *ching*-Iondai awareness came close – something was very wrong. It was difficult to say what.)

Scatter: a six now, that Iondai scored as a broken line in the earth beside him.

(Not right – not linked – just random throws, with no influence, no value – Iondai was not linked correctly to the *ching* – the *ching* was there only because of Ashka's tenuous presence – it lay there, alive, sensitive, between them, doing nothing. Terribly wrong!)

Scatter – the third throw. Iondai was unaware that anything was wrong, but Ashka felt a sudden panic, his whole body going cold and tense ...

'Stop!' he shouted reaching out and scuffing the coins off the earth. 'Stop it! It isn't right!'

Iondai watched him, amazed. The sudden silence, the fixed stare between them, was almost embarrassing.

Ashka said, 'I'm sorry. There was something wrong – the *ching* wasn't working for you, not at all, not even the slightest. I don't understand why, but it didn't. I'm sorry.'

Iondai smiled uncertainly. 'Never mind. Why don't *you* ask your *ching* – you are the Seer, after all.'

'Yes.' Ashka stared at the coins, one of them half-buried in the fine dirt. 'I'm called a "rationalist" by the way, not a Seer.' He gathered up the coins, noticing that his hands were shaking. Or should I say irrationalist, he thought bitterly as he realized he was repressing his recognition of something else, a terrible observation that his unconscious mind seemed unwilling to allow him to consider fully.

He closed his eyes for a few moments, glad that Iondai maintained a respectful and understanding silence.

The *ching* was ill. What other word could he use? What he had become aware of, in those moments of consultation, was not the living awareness behind the symbols but something ... distant. It was as if the *ching* were receding, yet gripping the fabric of the Universe with as much strength as it could muster. It was being pulled, or pushed, out of time and space. It was suffering, suffering terribly ... He had felt it earlier, when Gorstein had consulted the *ching*, and he had put it down to jealousy, jealousy of the local oracle. But it wasn't jealousy, it was something far more final, far more destructive. Illness, sickness ... the beginning of death. Elspeth had told him what to expect – not in so many words, but she *had* told him, and because he couldn't feel it, because it didn't seem to be happening, he had put it from his mind. But she had been right.

'Oh no ...'

He opened his eyes, stared emptily at Iondai, who watched him impassively and asked, 'What's wrong?'

His impulse was to get up and run, to flee from Aeran as fast as the ship's drive would take him. But Gorstein would not listen to him. Panic was pointless.

'Everything,' he said. 'Perhaps nothing. Perhaps adjustment, acclimatization, nothing more. Perhaps much more.' He stared at the *ching*. His mouth was dry; his skin felt cold. 'My oracle is dying.'

'Dying? I thought there *was* no death.'

'Receding. It's as if … as if something is pushing it away.'

'The *ching* comes from within, doesn't it? Surely if something is wrong it is in your mind, not the symbols of your book.'

Ashka bowed his head. This primitive man had voiced that simple fact when Ashka himself had been unable to face the truth. He was right, of course. It wasn't the *ching* that was receding, it was he, Peter Ashka! But what did it matter? The effect was the same.

'Ask it quickly, while you still may,' said Iondai, and without thinking Ashka shook the coins and began to concentrate on the question.

Almost immediately he felt it, the *ching*, the great power of the oracle, alive, vigorous, only the slightest sense of insecurity present, and that almost unimportant. (*Perhaps it isn't too late yet.*) Ashka put his anxiety behind him, spent a moment correcting the psychosomatic balance of his body, and then let the question surface to his foremost awareness.

What would be the outcome of the Aerani accepting the monitors?

He cast the coins. Iondai drew the lines in the dirt while Ashka continued, and slowly the hexagram took form, assumed meaning.

Iondai stared at the finished symbol and smiled. 'A pretty thing. Meaningless at the moment.' He looked to Ashka for elucidation.

'Thirty-two,' said Ashka softly. 'Long duration. Successful progress and no error.'

'I think I can discern its meaning.'

'The oracle, if you choose to believe it, has just told you to accept our mission. There is progress to be achieved by so doing, and no error in the action.'

Iondai was silent, and in the dimly lit chamber he seemed to have become very pale behind his sparse white fur. Ashka read the full passage from the book. When he read the sentence 'movement in any direction will be fortunate' Iondai drew a sharp breath and said, 'I understand. It really doesn't matter whether we accept or not: there will be no error in either course. We might as well accept and remain on peaceful terms, as not accept and perhaps engage in hostility.'

'There is a proviso,' said Ashka, reading the passage for the moving line in position two. He laughed as he read it. 'All occasion for regret disappears.'

Iondai was almost incredulous. 'I can hardly believe it. Will there really be no consequences attached to accepting these monitors?'

'So it would seem. Perhaps your oracle can clarify the matter some more.'

'Perhaps,' said Iondai thoughtfully. He reached down and sketched the second hexagram that was created by the moving line.

'Sixty-two,' said Ashka, flipping the pages of the *ching*. He stopped and read. 'It reiterates what we learn from thirty-two. It says, however, that one must learn to distinguish between what is essential and what is inessential. What do you make of that?'

Iondai thought hard for a moment. Then he said. 'It is telling us to decide whether pride is important or not. Should we let our community pride prevent us from accepting the mission. Yes, I think that's what it means.'

Ashka smiled as he gathered up his coins. 'You'd make a damn good rationalist,' he said. 'Damn good.'

seven

They slept for a few hours, both men more fatigued than they had realized, then Iondai led the way along the low-roofed tunnel from the chamber where he lived to the oracle where he worked. They both had to crouch on occasion, and at no time could Ashka stand fully upright, which after a few minutes he found to be an intense strain. Iondai had not brought a torch (he refused to say why) and Ashka fumbled after the Seer in the total darkness, depending on Iondai's occasional warnings of obstacles to avoid sprawling headlong, or cracking open his skull.

With every step forward the air became colder, damper. Ashka coughed repeatedly as the heavy atmosphere tickled his lungs. His hands grew icy with contact on the sharp-surfaced rock walls. His pouch, dangling round his neck, beat irritatingly against his thighs as he walked unsteadily towards an oracle he could not imagine.

After a while, much deeper in the earth than he had hoped to come, Ashka picked up the unmistakable sound of wind. The air in the passage moved past his face with an unwelcome freshness, an icy draught evaporating the moisture on his skin and making him colder. He shivered, stood still for a moment and listened.

Iondai continued through the darkness, his breathing not as laboured as Ashka's. His shuffling steps, clearly audible, might have been the furtive movements of some inhabitant of this absolute darkness. And rising above the human sounds, the drone, the deep moaning, of a vicious wind, somewhere up ahead.

Encouraged by Iondai to press on (why was everyone on this world so keen on walking everywhere?) Ashka stumbled forward a few paces. He hit his head against the ceiling and cursed, dropped to his knees. There was water on the floor, trickles of icy liquid which he splashed across his now fiery forehead, cooling the blow. Looking up he saw light at the end of the tunnel, white light … daylight. The noise of the wind was a monotonous humming, distant but now quite loud.

He began to wonder, having forced the thought from his mind before, just what exactly the local oracle was. He began to have a glimmer of a suspicion. He began to get excited.

As the end of the tunnel came nearer, the ceiling sloping down again and forcing the two men into a very crouched position, the force of the wind ahead of them could not be doubted. It raged past the entrance to this passageway, singing through rocks and echoing through the great chamber that lay there. It was like the roar of machinery, a sound with which Ashka was well familiar from his days of retreat on more backward industrial worlds. The eddying effect reached violently into the passageway and Ashka felt his robe and short hair tugged and torn at by strong, aerial hands. His eyes dried over repeatedly and he found himself wincing and blinking against the thunder as he finally emerged into the gigantic chasm and looked up to where the cloud-covered dawn sky was the only roof in evidence. Gripping the walls of the passage, resisting his body's tendency to be flung before the incredible blast, he looked to where Iondai was pointing. At one end of the great roofless cave a second passageway opened out widely, like a yawning mouth, wider than it was tall, jagged round the edge where the wind and flung rock had chipped and eroded the smoothness of the old water-course away.

The noise was deafening, the low shriek of wind pouring from that tunnel drowning all sound but the noise of his thoughts. Iondai turned back and smiled, his face screwed against the cold. 'That it?' shouted Ashka, pointing. Iondai nodded violently.

'Not usually so strong,' he shouted. 'In a few minutes … die away … we'll wait.' He motioned back into the cramped passageway and Ashka turned and stooped and entered relative calm again. His ears still ringing with that gorgeous natural sound, his whole body shivering with the intense cold he felt, he crouched in the quieter tunnel and stared at the daylight.

After a while his curiosity about the source of the wind got the better of him and he began to crawl back towards the exit from this passage. Iondai reached out and touched his shoulder, shouted a word that sounded like 'Wait'. Ashka paused and looked at him, then turned back towards the daylight. At that moment the noise of the wind subsided and abruptly died away to become a mournful crooning, not at all thunderous – as if the earth had reached the end of a long and painful expiration, the tidal flow exhausted; a sound very like the last breath of a man passing peacefully into the tao, as Ashka himself would soon pass – breath and life, combining in a brief and instantly recognizable deathsong.

They emerged into the roofless cavern and Ashka was immediately possessed, possessed of that ecstasy of the soul spirit which accompanies the unexpected achievement of a dream, until then thought unrealizable.

He stood in the polarized wind current, felt it play around his body, passing through his robe and his skin and the muscle and bone of his body, circulating through those channels and pores of his body that no medical chart in the ship's sick-quarters would record.

He stared into the womb of the earth.

'The oracle! This is the oracle, the voice of the future – I can recognize it without your even telling me. I would know it anywhere!'

'Earthsong,' said Iondai. 'Carried on the wind that blows from the mountain cave where the Earthwind first came to us. Touch the water.' He stooped to the crystal clear stream that trickled beneath their feet. Ashka crouched and let his fingers touch the turbulent water sheet, the simple stream agitated to a frenzy of surface ripples by the powerful wind. Doing as Iondai did, Ashka touched the water to his lips, eyes and ears, staring always into the depthless maw of the oracle cavern.

Names filled his head, emerging from the past, the remembered and the half-remembered both – Lourdes, Wishing Wells, the Oracle at Delphi ... the caves and gaps in the earth from which the ancient prophecies of forgotten civilizations had emerged, the splits and rends in the gritty flesh of the earth mother, her cries of pain and anguish transmuted into a clear and frightening vision of the future – death, the winning and losing of wars, of women, of sons and daughters. Had they too, those dark oracles and magic places, issued the breath of the world? Had they spoken aloud, or through the minds of those who questioned? Had they really worked – or had they been a fanciful invention of a people sufficiently frightened of what was to come to desire to know their fate? And having learned it, had those people accepted it?

Ashka had never seen an earth oracle, had known of them from books but had always thought them a part of that splendid fantasy of *gods* and *hsien*, of *dragons* and of *middle earth* and all those other mystical beings whose violent tempers caused the rumblings and eruptions of fire and water from the hidden world below the skin of the land. As he stared at the mouth of Aeran, felt the breath of Aeran cold in his being, felt à stirring of consciousness in his mind that he had never felt before, felt the focussing of some unseen, awesome awareness, exploring his thoughts and his memories, and reaching to his soul's core, so he began to wonder if 'fantasy' had not been a cruel and unjustifiable label.

He had lived his life in union with the tao, looking upwards, outwards in the gigantic Universe; now he realized how much he had missed by not looking inwards, downwards, to the earth, to the gently protective femaleness of the rock and blood, earth and bone ...

So near – so aware of the world beneath them, yet so superficially aware. How swiftly the transient soil was forgotten in the striving to encompass the void!

'It is dangerous to stand here without a question,' said Iondai, and his voice was like a dream, emerging from some unreality, only achieving significance as the words ceased, echoed, and finally caught Ashka's attention.

'Dangerous?'

'The question,' said Iondai. 'You will have to ask the oracle too.'

The mood of possession momentarily broken Ashka looked up, looked around. He saw the chasm for what it was and for the first time his immediate environment registered on his mind as well as his sense organs.

A vast cave whose high roof had long ago fallen in and now lay fragmented, an organized montage of smooth surfaces and jagged fingers. The water from the passage flowed between the boulders, smoothing the lower edges, trickling through the tiny caves that the awkward juxtapositions of different fragments created, running over and under, linking the dead rock with the living breath and blood of the oracle. Some of the surfaces of the rock had been indelicately chipped with rough, unpolished symbols – lines that wavered and weaved, spirals that were as ugly in their amateur execution as the three double spirals of the Earthwind symbol in the Fire Hall were beautiful in their precision and confidence.

Intuition being his greatest gift Ashka did not even have to wonder about the roughness of the symbols – they would have been made early on in the new society that had arisen on Aeran. Anxious to exploit their new awareness to its full the artists of the first and perhaps second generations had tried to impart art to rock that no longer carried the vital flow of the tao. There was something sad about dead rock, stone that no longer bit the soil or carried the bizarre and reverberating echoes of the energy that spilled across its surfaces. It would probably have meant a terrified respect for this part of the world, where the rock was so different, where the magic sensations of oneness and flow ceased to be.

The sheer walls of the cave were still alive, but no doubt fear had meant their being left untouched, for no marks of man were discernible upon them.

High above, the circular pit looked down into the grey sky. Vegetation hung limply over the edge, probing up (down?) into the clouds, and down (up?) towards the roof on which Ashka stood, sensing and enjoying the strange invertedness of it all.

Behind him, facing the mouth of the oracle, was a narrow tunnel through which the wind continued, no doubt, although at full blast the upward current must have been sufficiently strong for it to carry a man out of the chasm and high into the air.

It seemed to Ashka that the wind, strong and cold, was building again. If it increased with the same suddenness as it decreased then this was a very unwise place to be. He couldn't imagine what geophysical process was occurring high up in the mountains to account for the phenomenon, but was quite prepared to accept that there was a rational cause for it. How easily he accepted the 'magic' of nature, the improbability of the atom and the chemical reactions in the landscapes they visited. It never occurred to him to doubt purple rain or fragments of rock scattering before him as if they sensed his coming – there were so many electromagnetic and chemical forces at work that nothing surprised him. He was concerned only with interactions and the vital flow – be they gravitic, electromagnetic or quirk – that formed the great tao, the cosmic forces of the Universe at large.

Wind blew, freezing, living. Ashka stared into the black mouth of the endless cave, let the sound of its booming voice excite his mind, drowning even his thoughts – like a sea cave on his home world, the way the gentle rushing of the ocean became something hollow and reverberating as it hit the walls of a rock cavern, eroding as it kissed the stone, booming as it squeezed into fissures and crevasses.

His thoughts lingered on death for a moment – he was aware of them, despite the sound in his skull. How sad that his life was so nearly gone, when there could be so much to learn …

I am a dying echo in the Universe …

Bodily, his reaction was to straighten in surprise. His face showed his puzzlement, his eyes never left the oracle. The sound of wind, funneling towards him, held him in concentration, held his mind as well as his body. He might have struggled to release himself from the spell, but he might have failed, so he kept calm and let the alien thought surface.

I am a dying echo in the Universe.

(Blackness – his mind seemed to slip, a strange feeling as if it were detaching itself, for a moment, from his cortex – shapes and faces whirled out of the dark abyss – symbols and sounds – something span among them, flashing before his mind's eye for just a second, long enough for him to recognize those three double spirals … gone, then, the haunting sense of something within his head—)

I am a child of time, but there is no time left.

The playground is behind me. The swings are still. The toys lie motionless. I run from the playground. I cannot turn and run back. Darkness ahead.

I am the last faint note of a flute. I am the last flicker of a candle. I am a dead man who refuses to attend to his burial. I am the tear of anger, drying on the angry face.

There are moments left.

Moments left …
Moments …

Wind. Cold; the sensation of shivering. Pain in his skull as his teeth chattered together. Iondai: 'Ashka …?'

A strong hand gripped his arm and tugged at him. He looked round. The native, cold and distressed, was trying to pull him towards the shelter of the small passage. Ashka, silently, let his body respond to the physical command. He left the coldness and crouched close to Iondai, staring at the lifeless rock through eyes that saw only darkness …

Moments left … darkness ahead …

'I had a premonition, a sense of almost immediate death. Strange thoughts, but not – not *my* thoughts.'

'You should have asked the question when I told you,' said Iondai quietly. 'That is the way the oracle works, speaking directly to you.' He stared silently at Ashka for a moment, his agile face, with its untidy covering of white hair, painting a perfect picture of uncertainty. Finally he said, 'I thought death held no fear for you. I thought your passing was already predicted.'

'It was.'

Moments left. Were seven months just so many moments to the driving power behind the Aerani oracle? *Moments.* He was disturbed, puzzled, uneasy. Something had looked into his mind and sensed, perhaps, his growing awareness of death, had interpreted it as an unvoiced question – *when will I die? And* had told him. And seven months was *not* long, no matter how much he convinced himself otherwise. Life was a collection of moments strung out along the thread of time. Here a happy event, there sadness, here adventure – and learning, always a moment or two of learning, of accumulation. He had lived for many moments, and now there were only moments left.

The Earthsong had merely echoed what the *ching* had told him. Its way of expression was different, more direct, that was all.

Ashka relaxed, then, and spent a moment tightening the loose belt of his flowing robe. The hem of the material was torn and wet and in contact with his skin was uncomfortable. Suddenly he remembered why they had come here.

'What did it say? About the mission?'

Iondai watched him for a moment, then said, 'It said there will be acceptance of the mission. It predicted the same as your *ching*. I have great faith, now, in your *book*. I had never realized that far-seeing power could reside elsewhere than in our own oracle. Between us we have understood something that we must make known to my people.'

'Yes,' Ashka said, without really thinking. 'They must, of course, listen to the oracles. The path they indicate is the best – to change direction would be a serious error.'

Iondai laughed for a reason that Ashka found he couldn't understand. 'My full question concerned not only the accepting of the mission, but also the outcome of actually telling them what the oracles have foreseen.'

'And?'

'Authority will stand between us. That is what the oracle has told me. Authority will stand between us.'

'Did it say a peaceful resolution?'

'No indication.'

'Then ask it.'

Iondai shook his head. 'I don't dare. To ask too much is disrespectful.'

'Nonsense!' cried Ashka. 'An oracle is your servant, not your master.'

'I can't accept that,' said Iondai uncomfortably. 'We are all the servants of the earth beneath our feet. It protects us, houses us, warms us, feeds us … and it allows us to know our destiny. We are humble beside it.'

Ashka had no argument. All earth-cultures would have felt the same, he was sure. It was rational, and he wasn't here to change their philosophy of life. And the *ching*, though not his master, was not really his servant either, It was his equal, and it was the most temperamental of the partnership of two. Ashka was respectful of that temperament, and Iondai was respectful of the powerful earth. In his primitiveness he saw it as a God, perhaps, a great being in whose bosom the Aerani snuggled. It was rational.

Authority would stand between them! What could that mean?

'I believe it refers to one of the three prime families. This particular family is hostile and angry by nature, and they are sceptical and cynical about the oracle. Not all of them, but the men. They perhaps,' he smiled narrowly, 'are a little like you, regarding the oracle as something to be subdued to a lower status. They may well cause trouble by rejecting the oracle's prediction. They were very hostile during the meeting in the Fire Hall.'

'Yes,' Ashka said and looked out at the mouth of the oracle. He thought he heard movement at the rim of the pit and glanced up, but saw only dangling threads of vegetation and the swirling clouds. 'Yes, I remember the men you are talking about.'

He was thinking of something else, however; of a consultation with ship-Meister Karl Gorstein, of a prediction made just a few hours before, a prediction that had frightened both the shipMeister *and* the rationalist, though Ashka had not allowed that emotion to show.

He hides his shame, the *ching* had said, and Gorstein had said, *personal disaster stemming from failure*. And Gorstein never fought the bad trends, never altered the flow of change and time to take him nearer the safety of the shore, away from the death-laden deeper waters. His inaction, or his thoughtless action to try to avoid any possible personal disaster, could well mean frustration of the mission.

Authority.

Yes, Gorstein was authority – he ran the ship and he ran the lives of those aboard the ship, and he ran Ashka like Ashka ran his correlative programmes. Ashka was the man's total servant, as were all the crew on the *Gilbert Ryle*, and yet, somehow that was as it should have been. There was no bitterness in the oriental's heart, no feeling of wrongness. All men were pawns, particles, shifting and bobbing on the surface of the tao, and external order came from internal order and Gorstein was a creator of order. In the way he ran the ship, in the way he commanded authority and exercised control over the bodies and souls of those around him, in all those ways he created order and stillness. Gorstein was not a symbol of authority, he was Authority personified, and to Ashka he was Greatness embodied, everything that Ashka needed to guide him on the earthly plane – Gorstein and the *ching*, the perfect duet of balancing forces.

Authority will stand between us.

ShipMeister Gorstein! It had to be!

A voice called Iondai's name and the two seers stepped into the wind current, stared up to where the solitary figure of a naked girl stood insolently against the skyline, staring back down.

'It's Moir, one of that family I mentioned. The pleasantest of them. She will be a great hunter in a few years; a great warrior.'

Ashka looked at the girl and wondered whether Iondai spoke from the experience of a prediction, or from an admiration of her firm physique, well muscled and strong looking, almost masculine, but masculine only from Ashka's cultural point of view.

'Leave us,' said Iondai and Ashka, disappointed, nevertheless obeyed, stooping to enter the passage and fumbling his way back to the chamber where Iondai lived.

A few minutes later Iondai arrived himself, distressed and agitated.

'There's been a duel of honour,' he said quickly. 'We must get to the fire-glow.'

Without asking any more, but puzzled by what the duel might have been about, Ashka followed the native through the third passage and up into the low-roofed shrine at the edge of the Fire Hall.

As they emerged into the dawn light the first thing that caught Ashka's attention was the great spill of blood on the ground nearby; and the atmosphere of excitement.

What had happened here? Who had died and why? He searched the fire-glow for anything that would give a clue as to his unvoiced queries.

Then he heard a familiar voice, a shout of anger that was unmistakably the same shout of anger he had heard yesterday, by the river, when that native boy had been attacking Elspeth Mueller.

He followed Iondai towards the group of youths. The voice said, 'The oracle would *not* predict such a thing!'

Had they found out already?

'But it has,' said Iondai softly and the crowd drew back.

Ashka started with surprise as he saw Elspeth sitting there, frightened and upset. 'So has the *ching*,' he said. 'I asked it.'

Her eyes remained blank.

Somewhere a woman began to wail. Ashka turned to see what was happening but he could see nothing.

When he turned back to Elspeth she was gone, and he saw her lithe form vanishing through the entrance to the outer earthwork wall.

He knew where she was going.

eight

The raft moved slowly against the current, moving up the river with inexorable patience, riding through the waters with that stillness that is associated with aimlessness. A glittering silver craft it nevertheless showed the unmistakable signs of decay, in the form of rust and other corrosion where plates of metal met or juxtaposed; its drive made a dull sound, a grating hum that fled into the unnaturally still forest, followed by the slight sussuration of the water disturbed in the raft's wake.

The alien craft might have been returning from a trip deep into the marshlands through which this river flowed; it might have been returning from a simple routine mission to where the forest finally thinned, defeated by untenable soil and the rock that bordered the foul-smelling boglands. It might have been on its way high into the hills, through the caves and tunnels which spewed out the streams forming this wide and often violent river. It might have been about to moor on the bank and return its burden of passengers to the ship that lay close by. Elspeth Mueller, watching, seated, from the river shore from a spot where the forest stood back from the water, had no way of knowing where or what these men had been or done. She felt unconcerned about it. She watched the man who stood at the front of the raft as it chugged towards her.

Whereas the other two beyonders sat and stared at the bordering forest, this man, whom she recognized as the shipMeister, stood rigidly at the very edge of the raft, his hands behind him, his legs apart, the gentle wind blowing his billowing robe tight against his body. His figure, outlined in colourful silhouette, was sturdy and muscular – his chest deep, his stomach running to rotundity. The tight knot of his genitals stuck out, almost obscenely, towards the waters that cleft before him. The sight, the symbolism of which did not escape Elspeth, amused her, because she guessed it had not escaped the ship-Meister either.

The raft suddenly angled towards the shore. The shipMeister moved back from the leading edge and seated himself on one of the low couches. The raft tilted a wing and left the water, running up the bank on a cushion of air, slowing from its sudden activity as it reached level ground. It rose two feet from the scrub and hovered. Elspeth, twenty paces away, watched it passively. The shipMeister stared at her without flinching, as did his two companions. After a moment Elspeth smiled and rose to her feet, walked across to the raft, felt its air cushion warm against her bare legs, the exhaust wind refusing to leave her loose kilt alone. The two junior crewmen found their gaze drawn to her revealed nakedness, but the shipMeister just stared at her – unnervingly.

Elspeth stared back, finding her gaze drawn deep into the fierce man's eyes; dark eyes, brown, the sort of eyes that encouraged relaxation, friendship – the eyes of a man to whom no one was too small or too unimportant; eyes to love, brown eyes, kind eyes … and yet on this man they were fierce, an immediate insight into his great strength and his great weakness, a solitary man, a man above the men he knew, self-important, self-centred, angry. And afraid.

The scrutiny lasted just a moment, a timeless moment that might have extended the space of a heartbeat, a gust of wind, the shrill navigational cry of a blackwing – an instant only – drawn out against some inner scale of time so that the pause, the flowing of spirit between Gorstein and Elspeth, seemed to last for hours.

Gorstein broke the silence. 'Abroad.'

Elspeth was startled by the man's abruptness. 'Is that an invitation?' She noticed the other two men smiling with amusement. At her? Or at the ship-Meister? Without waiting for a reply from Gorstein she climbed up on to the raft and sat down, holding on to a cargo-securing ring. The raft moved slowly off across the river-lining brush, rose above the forest so that the ship and the crog's stark earthworks could be seen distantly, then slowly sank down to land a few yards from the guarded ramp of the vessel.

Elspeth jumped to the ground as the raft fell silent and stared up at the squat and ugly *Gilbert Ryle*. A few hours ago she had been here, staring in the same way. She had been angry, still emotionally upset by the duel and its aftermath, the news from Peter Ashka that the oracles of both worlds were advising 'acceptance'.

Everyone listened to the oracles. She would be a single voice of unreason and yet she *knew* she was right. The oracles were wrong!

How frustrating it had been to find Gorstein was absent, up country riding out his own anger in some routine exploration. As she had sat by the river, waiting for his return, she had collected her thoughts, had broached the subject, of his quitting Aeran, in many different ways, none of which she could see as being sympathetically received when it came to the moment.

'Come to my quarters,' said Gorstein and she followed him into the extravagantly perfumed interior of the ship, walked along the high-ceilinged corridors, past open doors and the bustle of aimless activity. Faces stared at her, conversations slowed as she approached and speeded up as she passed. Her strangeness was obviously remarkable.

They ascended two levels of the ship and returned to the front of the vessel, where Gorstein's quarters occupied the entire length of the corridor. His office, his briefing room, his shower, his private study, his bedroom, his recreation room, his consulting room, his lounge …

Elspeth felt a faint amazement at this. She knew of no other ship where the Meister had commanded such an extraordinary quota of ship-space.

She followed Gorstein into the lounge and stood, just inside the door, feeling the freshness of the air circulator, remarking on the heady sensation of the natural atmosphere that she was suddenly breathing.

The room did not reflect the arrogant man she already felt she knew. For a moment she wondered if she had read him wrongly – this was the room of a gentle man, a soft room, the pictures and wall hangings being peaceful and aesthetically pleasing to her 'naturalist's' eye view. The furniture was all low and round, no hard angles or jutting curves. It was not the room she had expected.

As if to confirm that she had nevertheless made no mistake, Karl Gorstein said, 'I dislike this room intensely. It has no guts.'

'Why don't you put some guts into it?'

'I would,' said Gorstein walking towards her, taking a moment to study her in the flattering, if slightly false, light of the cabin. 'But my rationalist, you know. Peter Ashka. He's a very insistent man. "You can't be at peace in an unpeaceful room", he says. And he makes me hang these … these …' he glanced around at the wall hangings and grimaced theatrically. Smiling: 'Description eludes me.' He again met Elspeth's gaze. 'But I let him have his way with me on this point. It gives him a feeling of … what shall I say?… importance?'

'I've met Ashka,' said Elspeth quietly. She hated Gorstein's superciliousness in regard to the gentle man. 'I like him a lot. He's very perceptive.'

Gorstein considered that for a moment, staring at her quizzically. 'Been filling your attractive head with mystical starshit, I suppose.'

'Mutual, I think.'

His smile had something forced about it. 'Oh no, don't say you're a rationalist too.'

'Isn't there a little of the rationalist in us all?'

Gorstein was unimpressed and let his face show the fact. He turned away from her and walked to a wall closet at one end of the room. 'Very philosoph-ical,' he said sourly. 'I'm going to strip in order to change my clothes.' He looked back at her, pausing in his motion, something inquisitive in his eyes. 'I thought I'd tell you in case you wanted to ...'

Elspeth couldn't help herself. She laughed at him. Anger shadowed his face. She became solemn. There was a long moment of cold, the look between them letting each one know that hostilities were commenced. Gorstein, still staring at her, let his robe slip from his body. He was naked beneath it, and he seemed to be willing Elspeth to look him up and down, to make a com-ment, however derisory, to give herself away. Deliberately she looked towards the window. 'Impressive,' she said loudly. 'The earthworks, I mean. Don't you think so?'

There was almost tangible restraint in the way in which he closed the closet door. Gorstein, buckling on a pair of shorts, moved to the wide inspec-tion port. He looked out for a long while, his stocky shape almost silhouetted by the bright daylight flooding in. Finally he turned round and leaned against the sill. Elspeth didn't move from the door against which she herself leaned. 'Who are you?' he asked quietly.

'My name is Mueller. Elspeth, if you like.'

'That isn't what I meant.'

For a moment she was confused, then she realized what he was getting at. 'Oh I see,' she said coldly, loudly. 'You mean *who* am I? In what way am I to affect your destiny, is that it? Am I Angel of Death or Life?' She looked at him, suddenly angry. Her anger was due as much, perhaps, to her own blank incomprehension of why a man – any man – should behave so aggressively towards someone he had only just met, rather than the fact of that aggression. 'How very ... silly of you, shipMeister Gorstein. How very presumptuous.' She'd had enough presumption with Darren starting to think of her as *his* woman. How dare this man presume that in some way their destinies were linked!

She had hoped to anger him, either by her initial cynicism or her closing aggravation. If she didn't anger him then he might have laughed and relaxed, which would have been equally as useful in breaking the ice. But the ice remained. He took her seriously.

'I don't think it was a presumptuous thing to ask, Mueller. Not presumptu-ous at all.' He turned his back on her, staring at the distant crog. 'Destiny,' he said, seeming to take a moment to savour the word. 'I don't doubt that we will find ourselves affecting each other's destiny. I believe it is a foregone con-clusion. Ashka wouldn't like to hear me say that. Nothing is foregone, he would object. Nothing is as simple as intuition suggests. But some of us know better. Instincts cannot be denied and all my instincts tell me that you and I, Mueller, are heading for … for violence.'

She smirked, trying desperately not to laugh. The man was a fool! 'What, right now? Or may we talk first?'

Ignoring her he said, 'I saw you. Soon after we landed. I saw you for just a few moments as you ran along the river bank. You didn't see me, though you saw my "eyes".'

'That robot, yes. I saw the robot. So it was you at the other end. Well, well.'

'Something told me that you and I … whoever you were,' he again turned round. His persistent movement might have seemed natural to some observers, but Elspeth felt she could sense the restlessness, the turmoil in the man. The light from outside forced him round and round, alternately facing towards and away from the earthworks.

She said: 'That we would get it together and fight interminably. Ah, how romantic you are, shipMeister.'

'Not exactly,' said Gorstein, ignoring her tone. 'Not exactly so trivial. I'm a very sensitive man. I sense more than Ashka gives me credit for.'

'That still needn't be very much.'

'Don't mock me, Mueller. I *am* sensitive …'

Which is why, she thought with a shallow smile, you're going to such lengths to tell me.

'I sensed wrongness when we landed, two days ago. I sensed conflict, yes, conflict. I sensed it when I looked at the earthworks, and I sensed it in a different way when I found myself staring at a beautiful naked black girl, darting along the river shore.'

Silence. Elspeth couldn't find the words for a retort. Gorstein's stare was openly inquisitive, investigative. He looked at her body and he looked through her eyes for some insight, perhaps into her sexuality, perhaps into the nature of her personality (so far well disguised behind her obvious facade of cheap cynicism), some clue, some hint as to how that conflict would come about.

His interest in her sparked her own interest in him. He was not good looking, and yet he was commanding. There was an air of confidence about him, in the perpetual half-smile on his lips, the narrowing of his eyes which seemed not to regard her but to search her. He was losing condition fast, putting fat on to his arms and legs, but she suspected that this was probably the temporary fattiness of a man passing from youth to middle age and being taken by surprise by the slowing of his body systems. Gorstein was still quite young, still at a peak of his vitality. He would soon trim down again.

Standing only an inch shorter than Elspeth she didn't feel overbearing and he, when he came close, seemed unbothered by the woman's height. The manifest Gorstein was the master of all he surveyed and in total control of his own personality, projecting confidence and magnetism like heat or light. He was so obviously covering up for some deeper flaw that Elspeth felt like saying outright, 'confess'.

She wondered, half idly, whether or not Gorstein desired her. It was the sort of emotion that few men could hide, even if they wished to conceal it, but Gorstein was such a confusing and blinding projection of 'self' that she wasn't sure if she was being unfair to him, thinking that he was weighing her up sexually. She hoped he wasn't. In any case, if such *was* on his mind she would soon know; she prepared herself for a blunt attack, for Gorstein was surely incapable of subtlety.

'When shall we declare war?' she said, breaking the silence.

Gorstein laughed. 'Whenever you like.'

'I'd rather declare peace. There is much that I want to talk about.'

'I'm afraid not. Oh, we can talk, I don't mean we can't do that. But peace?' He shook his head. 'I don't trust you.'

'Oh?'

'Why should I? A strange girl on a bizarre planet. Running naked when she's not in company and not much less than naked when she is. I know you're from one of these barbarous backward Tribal Worlds ... Orgone? Phaedra?'

For a moment, just a moment, the name refused to come, the name of her world, of her home. For just a moment she felt a cold wave of shock pass through her, and might have reacted visibly had the name not come to her, to rescue her from despair. 'New Anzar,' she said.

'Oh yes,' he glanced at her breast. *If he touches me I'll hit him.* 'I thought I saw diamonds when I saw you first. You're a *magda*, yes?' She said nothing. 'New Anzar,' he went on. 'Well there you are, then. You're about as far away from the norm as it's possible to get. I feel such suspicion about you that I don't know why I'm even standing here talking to you.'

'The answer to that, shipMeister, is that you're also fascinated by me.' She smiled sweetly. 'Isn't that true?'

'I'd like to know what you're doing here.'

'Oh but that's easy,' she said in mock seriousness, 'I'm here to brush the leaves from your destined path, to lie down across the Chasms of Uncertainty along the way so that you can walk across my back in safety.'

Gorstein didn't smile, didn't react. After a moment of silence he said, 'I think you're here to kill me.'

She was surprised. 'To kill you? Why would I want to do that?'

'Simple. You want something; you want something that involves me. Or else you wouldn't be here. It stands to reason that I'm blocking something you want. It is therefore logical to assume that one possible way of getting what you want – whatever it is – is by killing me. How am I doing, Mueller? You're looking a little worried.'

'I'm looking a little sickened. Killing you hadn't entered my head. I came here to argue with you and to try to convince you of something.'

'You came to kill me. Or to plan how to do it.'

'How can you be so sure of that?' She felt quite perturbed by this strange paranoid insistence. 'I really *did* come here to talk to you, nothing else.'

'To put it on your wavelength, I consulted the great *ching*. I do understand it, despite what Ashka seems to think. Damn him. It told me what I already suspected, that death awaited me. I asked it to be more specific, but I don't know how to work that angle on the *ching*, but I already knew in my heart who it would be. So I asked about that person …'

'And it said me?'

'In it's tao-forsaken roundabout incomprehensible way, yes. You, Mueller, you yourself.'

There was something wrong. His intensity was without question, his certainty in what he had been told was undeniable, but since she knew, in her heart, that killing Gorstein had never entered her head (what good would it do? The mission wouldn't automatically abort just because the shipMeister died) she couldn't understand how the *ching* could have suggested such a thing. Unless …

I do understand it, despite what Ashka seems to think.

That was it, of course. Gorstein was a fool, a fool who couldn't be trusted to use the *ching* because he had no idea of how to relate to it properly. Ashka had to always be there. But now he had consulted the oracle on his own and had misread it, or misused it.

And he was still misusing it now – he was assuming that because, as he believed, the *ching* had said that Elspeth was hostility and a death threat, it had to be that way. He was obviously determined not to let the prediction come true – he didn't seem like a man who was facing the certainty of death – but Elspeth had a strong feeling that he believed his only way out was by killing her first.

And yet – he didn't seem like a man who was preparing for such a death either.

Talk it out.

'You really think I'm going to kill you?'

'I think you're going to try.'

'When? Now?'

'I don't know. I'll be ready for you whenever it is, though.'

This was like a bad dream, she thought. Or more aptly, like a bad holo-film …

'So you don't think I'll succeed?'

He shrugged. 'That remains to be seen. If you succeed it will be because you have deserved to succeed.'

A veiled threat. 'So you're not actually going to stab me in the back the moment an opportunity presents itself?'

'Certainly not.'

'Good,' she said. 'Then you'll forgive me if I take no notice of your phobia for a while. I came here for a very special reason. I'd like to get down to it.'

'That almost sounds like a proposition,' he said, very sure of himself.

'Well it isn't.' She had been right – no subtlety whatsoever. 'If you could try and get sex out of your mind for a few minutes I'd really like to discuss something with you.'

He was far too arrogant to let such a mild jibe bother him. 'Impossible,' he said, looking down at her half-exposed breast. He was grinning. 'In the presence of anyone even half as desirable as you, Mueller, serious conversation eludes me. Even conversation about killing. I'd much rather make love to you now and leave the war for a little later.'

Elspeth recoiled from the sudden and, she confessed, unexpected proposition. She had anticipated suggestiveness and innuendo, but such bluntness (such unpleasant bluntness) after so short a time together she found alarming and off-putting.

'Aren't you afraid I'd kill you at the height of your passion?'

'At the height of my passion? How romantic.' He grinned. 'No, I'm not afraid of that. I don't think you're ready to kill me yet. I think that, like me, you're more interested in knowing the nature of the beast. If you see what I mean.'

'Sorry to disappoint you, shipMeister, but,' she poked a finger into his stomach, 'fat men don't do anything for me.'

He was immediately angry. As he struck at Elspeth his face contracted into a furious mask which vanished as quickly as it had come. But between one moment and the next he had torn Elspeth's jacket from her shoulders, sending her staggering with the force of the blow.

Straightening up, holding her arms where the material of her jacket had finally torn, she found Gorstein triumphant, his anger having been catharized by violence. He looked at the diamonds that sparkled in their nets of drawn skin. Elspeth found herself hating this violent and unpleasant man; his behaviour was not just gross, it was unforgivable ... and unpredictable, and that, she admitted to herself, accounted for the fact that she felt slightly afraid of shipMeister Gorstein.

Fighting her natural instinct to cover herself against his gaze (that, she decided, would make him feel even loftier – how easy it was to sink to the level of such a strongly superficial man!) she said, bitterly, 'That was a stupid thing to do. You're like a child, shipMeister. I can hardly believe that you're in charge of this wreck.'

'Well I am, and don't let the *Ryle*'s appearance fool you. This is a fine ship.

A little old, but a fine craft.' He was still scrutinizing the diamonds. 'Those jewels, Mueller. They look very valuable. Am I right?'

She was disgusted. 'I can't remember.' It was an honest statement of fact, though she made it sound like uncooperativeness. 'You make me sick. Sick to my stomach.'

'Well isn't that a shame,' said Gorstein, and looked at her.

Her body went cold; her heart raced. The look in his eyes was as transparent as the crystal he had suddenly, in the space of a few seconds, come to covet. He wanted the jewels, he wanted to possess them. Perhaps, deeper in his mind than he normally went, he saw the possession of the *magda-stones* as possession of the *magda* herself. Perhaps he was just an ignorant and avaricious man.

She covered herself, now, her face showing the disgust and horror she felt. 'There is something horribly cruel in your interest,' she said. She didn't know whether to laugh at him or shout at him. Could anybody be this malignant? Was it just show, a deliberately contrived offensiveness calculated to throw her off course?

'I'm a very cruel man,' said Gorstein with pride in his voice.

'You're a very vain man.'

'I'm aware of my strengths, certainly.'

'Superficial strength, shipMeister. Why don't you look a little deeper?'

'I don't need to. There is nothing there to be ashamed or afraid of.'

'That's because there's nothing there at all.'

He laughed loudly, forced laughter. 'You're quite a bitch, Mueller. Quite a bitch. I feel myself losing control and you sense it and keep provoking. Put your jacket on, what's left of it, before I do you a mischief.'

Elspeth made no move to pick up her torn clothing. Gorstein pressed the button of a wall cabinet and sparkling glass appeared, filled with colourful liquids. He poured himself a drink, glanced at Elspeth as if to say, well? will you join me? She shook her head.

Closing the cabinet he walked back to the window and held the small glass up to the light, swirled the contents. Elspeth caught a hint of something acrid and unpleasant, a smell she associated with the primitive hospitals of certain worlds. The drink was probably a root extract, perhaps aphrodisiac, perhaps just a stimulant. He swallowed the drink in one gulp.

'Yes.' He placed the glass down on the sill of the window. 'Quite a bitch. Well, bitch, precisely what can I do for you?'

'Isn't it obvious? Get your ship off this planet. Take yourself and your monitors off the world. Leave it alone.'

'Did you think we were here to stay?' He stared at her. 'Of course we'll get off-world. Who'd want to stay here in their right minds? We'll be gone, Mueller, never fear. Just as soon as the mission is accomplished, we'll be gone.'

'Now! I want you gone now! I'm asking you, shipMeister, to raise the flag and go into orbit. Work things out from there.'

'I have a mission—'

'ShipMeister!' she cut in loudly. Was the man being deliberately obtuse? 'Look, the colony on Aeran isn't your usual, run-of-the-pack colony. Is it? You can't deny that!'

'I don't deny it. It's very bizarre and very provocative.'

'It has reverted to a neolithic way of life, right? Not even that, in many respects. And by so doing it has set itself up as being unique in map-space, right?'

'Absolutely. Unique, yes that's the word for Aeran, all right.'

'Well then!' she said, raising her voice.

'Well what?' he answered, equally loudly. 'Well why don't I leave it alone? Why don't I leave primitive Aeran to get on with its bone chipping? Why don't I leave the people to develop in their own way, without interference, without civilized man looking over their shoulders? Was that the question?'

'That was the question. It seems to me to be the reasonable thing to do, the humane thing.'

'Very easy to say isn't it? But you, my sweet Mueller, are speaking out of selfish motives, whereas I have to act out of responsibility!'

'Selfish! Responsibility! Responsibility to whom? To the Electra? Screw the Electra! The only responsibility you have is to the colonists behind that earthen wall!'

'No it is not!' he said angrily. 'I have to think of my crew. Do you know what the penalty for failing to accomplish a mission is?'

'But it wouldn't be failure!' she protested.

'Of course it would be failure. Do you know what the penalty is?'

'The Electra would understand!'

'They would understand nothing! *Do you know what the penalty is?*'

'I don't and I don't care. Those people are more important than any ... any *penalty*! They have the right to remain unbothered. And by careful observation we can learn more from their way of life than from a thousand years of digging into the past. You stand a good chance of destroying all that.'

'*We* can learn? Or *you* can learn?' His smile mocked her.

'What I learn others will learn.'

'Ah yes, but in the first instance it is Elspeth Mueller, is it not? You don't want these people left alone for their own sake, you just don't want to risk losing a degree of accolade for what you will find out from them about primitive man.'

'Not like that, you bastard. They're not just primitive, they are primitive in a very special way. Just take a look at their symbols, if you don't believe me!'

'Primitive is primitive, in my book.'

'Then try reading something other than comic books! These people are very unusual, and quite unique. You already admitted as much yourself. This ship, the mission, everything about you, is a threat to their lives, a threat to everything they are and could be, and it's a threat to the learning they could enable me to accumulate!'

He was triumphant.

'Selfish! I knew it. Your motives are totally selfish. Do you really think I can put the lives of a whole ship above the interpretation of a few scratches on rock? Oh I've seen the symbols you are so obviously fascinated with. Scratches, magic markings, meaningless except to the superstitious mobs who are ruled by the shamans.'

'You are ruled by the *ching*, and you don't call that superstition!'

Gorstein laughed. 'On the contrary, Mueller. Quite the contrary. The *ching*, those cards – all the other things that sweet old Peter uses, just superstitious nonsense. I've felt it for a long time and now I'm sure of it. Since arriving on Aeran a certain change has come over me, as if the planet had reached into my mind and said, come on Karl, one way or the other. Accept the *ching* or reject it, but stop walking the middle of the road. The *ching*, that damn book, is such an ingrained part of our lives! How difficult to throw it off, and how refreshing to have achieved that separation.

'It's all nonsense. I see it now. Blind faith, useful for blind followers. But me no longer blind, sweet girl. Me see great white light of truth. Try it some time. It's very invigorating.'

'Then all that about it telling you I would kill you ... just, what, a joke?'

'Not a joke. Well, a private joke, perhaps, but no, I'm deadly serious about that.'

'Well aren't *you* a contrary man. Do you or do you not believe what the *ching* told you?'

He hesitated before he answered her.

'I *felt* the conflict that lies ahead of us both. I felt it in some deep part of me, Mueller. What more does a man need to live his life carefully? I asked the *ching* just for the sake of it. It naturally gave me the answer I wanted. Isn't that what it always does? There is so much ambiguity in that damn little book, but with a good rationalist it all falls so *neatly* into place. But it doesn't mean a thing, does it? One always has a sense of one's own destiny, and whatever answer the oracle gives it will make the sort of sense you want it to make if you think about the answer long enough.'

'You obviously have no inkling of the value of the *ching*. But that's hardly important is it? I feel conflict too, shipMeister. I feel it like you feel it, but only because you obviously care nothing for the preservation of isolation where a culture's survival depends on that isolation.'

'I *do* care for it, Mueller, I care very much. I care enough to realize that you, with your empty words, are a greater threat to the Aerani than a thousand ships passing by the stars.'

'How? I've integrated with them. I'm almost *one* of them.'

'But you're *not* one of them. You know it and they know it. You're a game-player, Mueller. I've met your type before – you're all playing different games, and you're all hiding behind high ideals and fancy rationales, but you're all just insensitive game-players. *You're* playing the game of "understand the primitives; understand their symbols and their way of life". And what when you've finished the game? What then? Let people know? Why else would you be doing it? So people know and then they want to see for themselves. You are a threat, Mueller, a greater threat than I. You fume because of what the sight of this ship will do to them. I don't think we could do half the damage you've already done!'

Elspeth's heart was thundering with both excitement and fury, but this stopped her dead in her hostile tracks. She stared at the shipMeister, who was suddenly very calm. His words echoed through her skull for a moment, and gradually faded. The hiss of the air circulator attracted her attention.

The infuriating truth was that to a large extent he was right! She was no game-player, she knew that. She had no intention of publicizing her findings on Aeran – it was purely for the self-satisfaction of *knowing* that she was here. And even that desire for knowledge might have faded rapidly had it not been for one symbol: the Earthwind.

That one complex and beautiful carving nagged at her. It was a part of the repertoire of both cultures, the old and the new, and yet something set it apart – and if she were to define her mission on Aeran now it would be nothing more or less than to find out what that symbol meant to the Aerani, what it encompassed, what it reflected; its association with the oracle promised to make that discovery very interesting indeed. And that *was* a selfish mission, and perhaps – if she faced the truth – it was that selfishness that angered her most about the ship and its appalling mission. But she *did* feel for Aeran and she felt very strongly that it was wrong to bring technology (the monitors) to bear upon the people of the crog. And that, of course, made Gorstein right again! She *was* a damaging influence, however slight. She knew this already and it bothered her greatly and of course this was why she had gone to such pains to integrate herself into the paralithic culture on Aeran. But the fact remained that she had no right to preach the leaving alone of an isolated colony when she herself was busy sifting through their ritual and society for whatever she could learn.

Her moment of doubt passed. After all, she thought bitterly, I haven't in any way made the Aerani doubt or change their view of the Universe – I haven't tried to convert them to some obscure religion, or show them how to make guns or metal. I was just a stranger, a bizarre stranger, certainly, but strangers can always be accepted without causing change. This ship, and Gorstein's total insensitivity, could not in any way be considered similarly subtle.

'You may be right,' she said bitterly. 'But I've tried to keep a low profile and you have not. I *hid* my shuttle, you have not. I said nothing about any other world—' That wasn't true, she remembered guiltily. She had said much before she realized the mistake of so doing. 'Nothing of importance, anyway. Can you say the same? Can your own rationalist say the same? He spent time with the Seer of the colony. They exchanged oracles – how about *that* for non-interference!'

The arrogance drained from Gorstein's face and he stared blankly at her for a while, almost as if he didn't know whether to believe her or not. Turning to look at the crog he said, 'I didn't know that. When …? When did they exchange oracles?'

'A few hours ago. There was a duel fought over the issue of killing you or not. The moderates won the day, but there's a lot of very mixed feelings behind those walls.'

'We *have* rather … interrupted the flow of life. I have to agree with that.'

At last!

She said, 'But not irrevocably, shipMeister. Leave now and you'll pass into mythology. The Aerani will continue as they have for four hundred years.'

Gorstein was still silent and thoughtful. Elspeth guessed where his train of thought was leading.

'Have the colonists consulted their Seer about the monitors?'

'Yes,' she said. 'The Seer has said accept. But don't take any notice … please don't take—'

'Will the colonists take notice?'

'I don't know. I imagine so, yes, though there are several families that are aggressive towards the Seer and the oracle.'

Gorstein smiled. He leaned forward against the sill, muscles standing out across his shoulders and back, a sign of tension, Elspeth imagined. 'I suppose that means the Aerani are so blindly dedicated to their superstitions that even the orders of an incomprehensible silver ball from the stars will be obeyed.' He looked at Elspeth. 'They won't understand it, they'll be scared to death of it, it will alter their way of life forever, but they'll do what the oracle says. Yes?'

'Yes. You *mustn't* let that happen.'

'I wish there was some way I could stop it, Mueller.'

'Just don't implant the monitors. What could be easier to do than doing nothing?'

'Not that easy.' Gorstein shook his head. He seemed almost depressed. 'If they really believe now that it is right to accept the monitors, then what would happen to them if we refused? The oracle would have said something should be done and they can't do it. That might be even *more* destructive, don't you think?'

'No! The Seer could rationalize it away.'

That amused Gorstein very much, in a bitter sort of way. 'Of course. How remiss of me to have forgotten our wonderful shamans and their unfailing ability to explain and rationalize. You know, Mueller, there is something very sordid about that. I realize the fact now, having escaped from it. It used to be God, before God was replaced by the tao which is what God was all along, I suppose. Do you remember reading about God? You could make sacrifices to him and if your wish didn't come true all it meant was "God not pleased with offering". The whim of the all-powerful deity could rationalize *whatever* occurred in life. Now we have the *ching*. It says one thing looks bad and if that thing comes true – you didn't succeed in adjusting your position in the flow of the tao. If it doesn't come true, you *did* succeed in adjusting to avoid the trouble.' He laughed. 'Silly isn't it.'

'Pathetic, really,' said Elspeth coldly. 'That argument is the first thing that every infant meets in his educational programme. You're obviously a little late in your education.'

'Better late than never,' he said amiably. 'I wonder why so few people, share my point of view?'

'Because they know the tao exists, that the *ching* really works.'

'I never said it didn't. I said it was the tool of the superstitious, and super-stition is an attitude of mind not the functional ability or inability of the tool. Of course the *ching* works. It works if you want to believe it works. If you are not bothered whether it works or not, then you don't need it. The more I think about it the more I see the *ching* as a crutch for frightened men. I really must have a philosophical run-in with sweet old Ashka. I might even beat him for once.'

'I doubt it.'

Gorstein smirked. 'And why is that?'

'Because he sees what everyone sees, except you – that you're a frightened man yourself, that your brash, vulgar and almost hilariously egocentric sur-face hides a cowering shadow of a man.'

By degrees the amiability drained from the shipMeister's face as he fixed Elspeth with a gradually more irritated gaze. 'Is that so?' he said with restraint. 'And tell me, Mueller; of what is this cowering shadow of a man, that you have so expertly detected, of what is he afraid?'

'The penalty of failure perhaps?'

'Damn right!' Gorstein snapped, then laughed. 'You're damn right I'm afraid of the penalty of failure. Who wouldn't be? But I'm not trying to hide that fact. It's a fear we all face constantly. It makes me anxious, it makes me jumpy, it makes decisions easier, and conscience harder. Is that all I'm afraid of? Then I guess I'm lucky.'

'And I guess I was wrong, I guess you're not afraid of failure after all, not deep down.'

'Why thank you, Mueller. Now then—'

'You're afraid of something much more fundamental,' she went on. Gorstein groaned. 'You're mixed up, shipMeister. You don't really know whether to *believe* or not, you don't know if the future can be seen or not. You don't know whether to find out what fate has in store for you or to take your chances. That's it, isn't it? You don't want to believe in the *ching*, you want to believe in yourself, in your instinct and intuition; but basically you don't have any, and you're confused about the *ching*, so you've come adrift ... you're what Peter Ashka calls flotsam. The only security you have is aggression and the past. But the future ... you're so deeply afraid of what's ahead of you that you're withdrawing into a tiny capsule, bobbing along in the present moment, shutting the future out, trying to rationalize your own insecurity by rejecting the *ching* and the Aeran oracle as superstitious nonsense. You're a man without a goal, shipMeister, and somewhere inside you're curled up with fear.'

'Get out of here!'

'I'm going, don't worry. It's tough to take isn't it, shipMeister? The truth I mean ...'

'*Get out!*'

'... but you see, we who *believe*, we superstitious cranks who have our own association with the *ching* don't have to experience these sudden terrible truths. We know our weaknesses and our strengths and we don't have to hide them or brag about them; such things aren't necessary. We all lived in a sort of harmony that you have obviously never known – harmony with the tao and harmony with ourselves.'

'But you're *still* living a lie! Get out of here!'

'I'm going, I'm going.' Elspeth picked up her jacket and pulled it on, a badly torn rag that neither concealed nor hung in anything like the proper fashion. She stood her ground. 'I came to beg you to leave. You thought I'd come to kill you. Well I didn't, and you won't. I guess we've both failed. But if you have any compassion in you, shipMeister, you'll not carry through this mission. Leave the Aerani in peace.'

For a moment Gorstein said nothing. He licked his lips and turned away from Elspeth, walking back to the window. He picked up the empty glass and turned it in his fingers so that it sparkled brightly. During the seconds of silence he seemed, to Elspeth, like a man crushed by the hopelessness of it all, but that might just have been her own wishful thinking. Finally he said, 'Mueller, I have already issued orders to suspend operations on Aeran. It was the most unpopular decision I ever made, and I expect a lot of trouble from the crew. But I have issued that order. Don't look so surprised, it doesn't suit you. Everything you came here to beg I already had thought through. I'm not saying the monitors won't be implanted eventually, but in view of the nature of the colony, the mission is indefinitely delayed.'

She could hardly believe it. She didn't know whether to laugh or cry, to make amends or to run from the room.

'So all this argument … unnecessary. Pointless.'

'All quite pointless,' he agreed bitterly. 'All quite without cause.'

They stared at each other, solemn-faced, angry. 'Well,' said Elspeth. 'What's done is done. What's said is said. I'm glad you've issued that order. Very glad.'

She turned on her heel and left the ship, holding the fragments of her jacket together to protect her from the unwelcome gaze of the crew.

nine

She went straight down to the river, to where her useless ship was still hidden in the undergrowth, and jumped into the cold water, kilt, ragged jacket and all. She splashed for a few minutes, then sank slowly to the bottom of the river, in a vaguely seated position, arms outstretched so that she felt the water current moving past her. When she could hold her breath no longer she surfaced and gasped for air, struck out for the shore and crawled through the mud on to dry land. She imagined herself a castaway crawling out of the sea, hitting the land and crying aloud with joy and thanks. She cried aloud with joy and thanks, but this was not a part of the isolated and momentary game she played.

She felt a real relief. The battle was not won, but the enemy was half on her side already. What sort of a battle was that? She imagined that at any time she would hear the thunder of lift-off engines, and the whine of atmospheric drive, and good-bye Gorstein, monitors and all.

She laughed to think of her row with Gorstein, of her immediate dislike for him, of her obstinate refusal to pander to his egocentric whim, and of how close she had come to making him go through with the mission just to spite her. Funny how things turned out.

River beasts, probably skitch, nibbled at her toes, one of them quite painfully. She jerked her legs away and tumbled back into the water, swimming upstream again to where she had left the shuttle, washing the mud from her body. She climbed out along a vegetation bridge, stripped off her clothes and sat inside her ship until she was dry.

Later she buckled on an all-weather suit, tight down the legs, loose round the body, the sort of uniform that would keep her cool in the heat and warm in the cold. The leg tightness aggravated her and she slit the trousers up to her knees, without thinking of the damage it would do to the therm-stable mechanism stitched into the fabric.

Increasingly she was thinking about the crog and what was happening behind the earthen walls; who had been killed and who banished, she wondered. What decisions had been taken in regard to the beyonders – and what in relation to her?

She was about to run through the forest to see what she could see when she noticed blackwings rising into the grey skies, some miles distant. Like tiny birds their wheeling, flickering motion was eye-catching whilst maintaining an elusive quality that defied any precise determination of distance. But Elspeth had already been hunting and she knew that there was only one sleeping-ground in that direction, bordering the marshlands.

On impulse, suspecting that Darren and his (surviving) friends were the disturbing factors in that sudden angry sky motion, she changed her immediate plan and ran towards the mosslands that led down to the dry causeway.

Out of breath by the time she sighted the sheer cliffs and the scattered dark shapes of the blackwings, she dropped to a crouch and recovered her composure. She could see an Aerani, crouched in a huddle near to the rock on which she had scratched her first symbol. She thought that it might have been Moir, but it was hard to tell from this distance.

As her heart calmed and her breathing became more normal so Elspeth began to sense the mosslands as they really were. The sweet plant smell, the strange murmuring the wind made in the sparse vegetation, a distant clacking that might have been the beating of tangleweed against rock, or the snapping of a black-wing's leathery membrane as it rose into the wind to escape the human attentions being paid to it. Another sound, too, with which Elspeth felt aggravated; the crash, the incoherent grumble, of a robot vehicle moving away from the open land, back towards the river. (She saw light sparkling on its body, caught a glimpse of a track as it plowed its way through the scrub back towards the forest. Who had been watching, she wondered? Whose eyes were joined to the glassy probes of the mechanical parasite?)

And singing.

A sound that was the last sound she identified before she began to run towards the crouched figure in the distance, drowning all natural noise with the thunder of her own progress. Singing. High-pitched, girlish, the tremulous wailing of a rock song, but this particular song filled with inconsistency and uncertainty.

The voice *was* Moir's, she was sure. The song – even to Elspeth's untrained ears – was so imperfect that for a terrible few minutes Elspeth thought it might have been Moir singing her last song before death, and frightened by the thought, she ran.

But Moir was not dying, not in the real sense of the word. Elspeth stopped a few feet away and walked quietly round the small girl until she could see the youthful face, the wet skin, the faintly moving mouth. Moir had her eyes closed, her arms wrapped around her legs. She swayed to and fro, at times almost imperceptibly, at other times, when she sang louder, more climactically, the motion became exaggerated. The wind ruffled the tight fur on her legs, blew her hair in a stream behind her; vegetation and dirt lodged in the yellow strands; dirt smeared her skin; blood smeared the dirt on her face and on her arms. She had been badly beaten.

The song was terrible. It wailed through its sequences, some of which Elspeth recognized (she had often listened outside the crog to the dune singers within) some of which she thought she might have recognized, but were so badly performed that it was impossible to tell whether they were new expressions or old sentiments:

The rising half-tones that were sung when the rock spirits were told of sadness.

The three-tone trill, at the back of the throat, that expressed anger with destiny.

The repeated note, with its two-tone trill before and after the sequence, that imparted her family sadness to the rock she sat beside; the rock absorbed the tune, and imparted the emotion to the earth. The earth sang with Moir, the clouds and light danced rhythmically, but without meaning, across the heavens and across the empty ground, dark shadows scampering across the plain, covering her and at once leaving her.

Moir's lament ended abruptly as a deep booming roar shattered the stillness of the scrublands.

Both girls looked out across the plain, to where the land of tangleweed, rock and blackwing gave way to the deep, watery mire – a thousand miles of impassable swamp – lakes and liquid mud, seething and hissing in their gentle invitation to death.

Elspeth stood upright and stared into the hazy distance. The booming came again, the sudden, almost deafening expiration of air from one of the great leviathans that inhabited the deeper, completely inaccessible parts of the swamp. This beast, probably a female (or a beast in its temporary female cycle), had come inshore and was playing among the hornified maneaters that clustered near to the higher lands, never entering the firm earthlands, but terrorizing those who went down to the mire to hunt, or dispatch the eyes and hands of the dishonoured.

Elspeth could see the creature's triple body flexing and weaving a complex aerial pattern as it rose, almost lethargically, from the containing mud. Two or three hundred feet the shape rose, a grey, shadowy beast, indistinct in the haze and the slime that coated its body. Multijointed arms grasped and waved about each stalk; the light flashed off the transparent discs that covered its single giant eyes. More booming, and the playful beast subsided into the mud.

The blackwings nearby shrieked their annoyance (perhaps their panic) and flickerwinged upwards and away. Elspeth heard a masculine cry of irritation from far off in the valley.

'I don't think he's having much luck,' she laughed, recognizing the anger as Darren's. Moir jumped (almost literally) at the voice behind her. Although Elspeth had been watching her for some time, Moir had not realized she was anything but alone.

'It's only me,' said Elspeth awkwardly.

Moir's expression was unreadable. The girl seemed about to either burst into tears or attack the older woman. In the event she suddenly reached down and picked up a small leather pouch, turned on her heels and fled towards the distant marsh. Where she trod on clumps of tangleweed, lazy strands flexed upwards, reaching for the body warmth of what they believed to be a blackwing.

'Moir, wait!' called Elspeth, but the girl kept running. Elspeth cursed silently and gave chase. She might have lost the race had Moir not tripped and fallen headlong across a clump of tangleweed, from whose demonstratively affectionate tendrils she could not extricate herself. Elspeth thudded up and stood looking down at the sullen, tearful native, seated awkwardly and entwined by fifteen or so pale brown snakes, the seed of the unpredictable savannah flora. Laughing she helped the girl out of her predicament and Moir finally crawled away, leaving Elspeth to extricate her own limbs from the plant.

'Why did you run?'

Moir stared at her, one moment hostile, the next angry, then confused, then tearful. Elspeth put her arms around the girl and Moir accepted the embrace, pushing her face against the older woman's chest and shuddering once or twice with repressed sobs. She cried her confusion out of her system.

'Who beat you?' asked Elspeth, knowing the answer of course.

'Darren.'

'He's quite an expert at beating up women, your brother.' She glanced back towards the cliffs. There was no sign of the youth.

'Not my brother,' said Moir bitterly. 'I hate him as much as he hates me.'

'Oh Moir, that'll pass. You'll grow together again. Anyway, if you really hate him, what are you doing here?'

Moir looked at her as if she was mad. 'Where else should I be? Our blood has separated, but the Ungenn have banished me from the crog and only Darren can say a word in my favour.'

'So you'll just follow him everywhere, and hope he forgives you, is that it?'

'What else can I do? I can't survive out here.'

'And all this because you wouldn't fight me. Do you blame me for that decision, Moir? Is that why you ran?' The girl said nothing. 'Why did you decide to dishonour yourself, Moir? Were you afraid of my secret power? Or were you afraid that I would lose against you because I'd never hefted a sword?'

Moir withdrew from Elspeth's arms and stood staring against the wind, to where blackwings of all sizes were spiralling down on to the cliffs. The thunder of activity in the marsh had died away; a thicker mist was ascending from the vast glittering pools to the north, and rolling before the wind towards the group of humans. There would be very little vision left. Perhaps an hour, perhaps less.

Moir ruffled the fur on her stomach, parted the hair and turned to Elspeth. 'It still hurts, sometimes,' she said, and Elspeth looked at the wide, ugly scar that stretched across the girl's navel. It was an old wound, well healed, but had been deep when given and must have caused the girl horrible suffering.

Elspeth looked at Moir's solemn face for explanation. 'When I was less than half my age now, just a squatling, my mother fought a duel against the marked woman of a man killed by my father. I was strapped to my mother's back when she fought. She was a very great hunter, very skilled with weapons, and very skilled at duelling, but this time she lost. The other woman ran her through with her sword and the blade cut into me. My mother died, I lived. My mother's fighting spirit was transferred to me as our blood mingled at her death, and Iondai said I should be a very great warrior. The oracle confirmed his prediction. I was my family's great pride. I should have been a great warrior.'

'Then why didn't you fight?'

'Because I knew I would win! I'm *not* a warrior yet, but the moment I killed you I would automatically have been proved. No complex ritual, no great testing. To have killed you would have been fulfilment of the prediction. If I died ... Elspeth, I *couldn't* have died. The oracle is never wrong! And I didn't want to kill you, I really didn't.' Her eyes watered.

'Don't cry, Moir.' She crouched by the tiny girl so that she had to look up into her eyes. 'If the oracle said that you were destined to greatness, you still are. The oracle is never wrong, as you said.'

'Never,' said the girl quietly. 'But perhaps Iondai misunderstood the answer. Perhaps the way he asked it ... Darren has always said that the oracle is for the weak among us. He's always said that the strong shouldn't care what the future holds, but should fight and live without any fear at all.'

'It's a fairly common sentiment,' said Elspeth smiling. 'But Moir, the oracle should now be taken as a strength. It has forewarned you of your eventual return to the crog and of certain glory. You should be glad.'

'How can I be a warrior when I couldn't kill …' she looked at Elspeth with great fondness, 'for loving the person?'

Slightly embarrassed, Elspeth said, 'You'll just be a different sort of warrior, that's all. You'll have more compassion than your brother and the others. You'll probably find that the crog follows your example.'

Moir smiled, then looked back towards the valley. She grew solemn. 'But Darren still hates me, and I still hate him. I need him, but I hate him. He killed Engus.' Her fists clenched and she seemed about to burst into anger, but the anger subsided and her head lowered. She stared at the small black pouch that she held. 'He killed Engus,' she repeated quietly, and then fell silent.

'I know,' soothed Elspeth. 'I know what it's like …'

Moir glanced at her sharply. 'Do you have a brother?'

Elspeth started to respond. An answer seemed to come to her lips, but as her mind tried to link to the relevant facts and images from the past—

Darkness—

Blankness—

She felt the blood drain from her face. A brother? Did she have a brother? That man, boy – holding the slumped form of … a woman; mother? Sister? A youth, snow – blood on the snow – but a *brother*? Images fragmented, interwove. A city, streets, cars, people – a face seemed to bob among the crowds, a man's face which she knew she should recognize, knew she should love, and yet – it eluded her, escaped her, bobbed away, swallowed by the black faces of strangers. A brother?

'No,' she said, instinctively knowing that it was a lie, and yet unable to believe in the alternative. 'No, I don't have a brother.'

'Then you *can't* know what it's like,' said Moir. 'You can't understand.'

As Elspeth led the way back towards the rock she became obsessed with, a feeling of foreboding. The wind was growing stronger, colder, building, she was sure, into a fair-sized storm; the melancholy sound it made in the high atmosphere, the bleakness it instilled into the wide and barren frondmoss plain, were perhaps psychological foci for an emotion that was just a passing whim, but which remained, now, growing in intensity. She felt instinctively that trouble was looming ahead. For a while, earlier today, she had felt released from hostility; her argument with Gorstein had been a sort of catharsis. Released from the grip of tension, reassured by Gorstein's own sensitivity to the situation, she had felt for a wonderful few moments that trouble was at an end.

Assessing the situation more realistically, however, she realized that troubles might only just be beginning. Moir and Darren were in deep trouble with each other. The presence of the ship had divided them, and yet they were still linked together. Hatred was a potent link, and it was more than hatred that would hold them in each other's company – Darren was still responsible for Moir, despite her rejection from the crog. Acting with the instinct born of custom he would not shirk that responsibility; what effect the forced companionship would have upon them Elspeth could not guess. Perhaps warmth would grow again, perhaps friction would become unbearable. If the oracle had said that Moir was destined to become a great warrior, then since Darren knew the prediction, there would be the added element of fear eating away at the boy over the weeks and months as he watched Moir grow and become strong, and move inexorably towards the sort of self-reliance that would be required of her, surviving outside the protective walls of the crog.

And how would they both relate to Elspeth herself? A beyonder, one of the mysterious star people who had precipitated this antagonism in the first place. Suppose she was rejected, like Moir, banished to the lands outside the earthworks … suppose they refused to allow her to ask and probe and query and practise and learn … suppose she never discovered the nature of the more complex symbols, and that one symbol above all …

Suppose she died with the Earthwind still eluding her! Suppose she lived on, healthy, vigorous, without a past, with an uncertain future – faced actively and without fear – aware of the Earthwind, perhaps responsive to it, but not understanding the nature of the symbol, what it did, what it had done for her, where it had come from. Alien, or not alien … from within or outside …

She *had* to know.

She found herself running, her body tense, wet with sweat that trickled cold and uncomfortable down the inside of her savaged suit. Moir was padding along behind, unaware of the anxieties that had, as so often in the past, taken almost complete control of the tall beyonder woman.

Elspeth, returning to the windy causeway, had to smile at the way her selfish motivation could become so dominant and all-important. It was such an irrational frame of mind. Of what value, compared to survival, was the understanding of a single rock carving? Why was she so fanatical about its final resolution? It was as if something inside her, something that shouldn't have been there, that had crept in, perhaps, while she had slept in the forest that first night of her resignation to decay, a mysterious something in possession – urging her on: find out, don't give up until you know about it, solve it, elucidate it, find it … for tao's sake don't lose your grip … you must discover the meaning … for *my* sake, for *my* sake …

She smiled. An alien in her head? Some psycho-beast, or tiny parasite, hidden, painlessly, in a tiny recess of her mind?

There were no such things, of course. She knew that. Intelligent life was restricted to large, fleshy animals, the human variety, now very widespread, and those backward creatures on the other spiral arm of the galaxy, burrow-dwellers in the dawn of their civilized life. She couldn't remember their name. It was one more fact slipped out of her mind, into the highly absorbent earth, along with so much else. She hardly dared think back to the past now. The fear of what she wouldn't find was a fear far more intense than the remembering of some terrible deed.

As they reached the rock again, and looked down into the gorge, they saw Darren racing across the ground, darting from boulder to boulder, closing in on an unsuspecting blackwing. He had a tangleweed wrapped around each arm. The mist was already rolling in from the far end of the narrow passage between the up-lifted slopes of rock, and soon all would be obscured by whiteness. That would drive Darren to a frenzy, Elspeth had no doubt. Twice foiled by sound or motion, he would be desperate to make this third attempt at snaring a successful one.

Moir touched her arm and Elspeth turned; the girl was pointing back towards the distant forest. Following her gaze Elspeth saw a raft floating rapidly towards them, a single beyonder seated unhappily upon it. She recognized Ashka. Her heart stuttered and she felt a moment of apprehension. She knew why he was here.

Moir slipped quietly away, perhaps afraid to be so near to the sky craft, perhaps sensing that Elspeth would want to be alone. The raft dropped to the earth some way distant and Ashka, more sensibly attired now in a black tunic and wide, flared trousers, his precious oracles tied to a gaudy and wide belt, walked towards the woman. His face was calm, but his eyes – angry, very angry.

'If you're thinking of shouting at me, please don't. I've had enough shouting for one day.'

'So I understand,' he said coldly. There was no flicker of warmth in his face. 'I never raise my voice, Elspeth. Too hard on the vocal cords. Calm resolution is always superior to loud altercation.'

'You sound like the *ching*. You two are closer than I thought.'

Still no softening of the angry features. Moir watched him from a distance. The air became cloying with the first tendrils of mist; it would still be some time before visibility was affected, but the effusion from the swamp was already reaching its unpleasant fingertips beyond the causeway. Elspeth found herself breathing more heavily, disliking the clammy sensation of the humid air, the fetid odour that advanced with the fog.

'Gorstein would say very little to me, except that he has refused to allow the implantation of the monitors. You must have had a very pronounced effect upon him.'

'We had a very good verbal run-in, yes. But I don't think I influenced him that much. And it isn't hard to have an argument with your shipMeister. Thank you for warning me.'

'Didn't I warn you what he was like? I thought I gave sufficient clues …'

'Uh-huh,' she shook her head, pretending a certain irritation with the rationalist. 'You led me to believe he was a sweet and humorous man.'

'Gorstein?' Ashka laughed, then frowned, caught the sparkle in Elspeth's eyes. He shook his head. 'Very clever.'

'Don't be so angry, Peter. May I call you Peter? I really didn't say that much to him.'

'Enough,' said Ashka sharply. 'Enough to make him act foolishly, enough to make him decide upon something that will have dire effects on the colony.'

'I didn't, Peter. I really didn't. He'd already made up his mind.'

That puzzled the oriental. 'He'd already decided to hold back the monitors?'

'His reasons were almost the same as mine. He recognizes the strangeness of the Aerani, and he doesn't want to do anything that might get him into the Electra's bad books. I imagine he's making contact right now to see what he should do. They're bound to say "do nothing", so I don't see what all the fuss is about. He's merely using some of that initiative ships' captains are supposed to be loaded down with. Why are you so angry?'

'Because he hasn't consulted the only *important* source of advice.'

'The *ching*.'

'Of course. It is reckless of Karl Gorstein to act on his own initiative. Foolish. Suppose, for all its apparent commendability, he is acting wrongly? Suppose his initiative is wrong, his instincts misplaced?'

Wondering why she was defending the shipMeister Elspeth said, 'Can you really believe that it is? I mean, doesn't it seem the right thing to do, not to interfere with the Aerani?'

'No!' exclaimed Ashka. His face reddened. Elspeth was surprised by the explosive reply.

'I thought you never raised your voice,' she said.

'There are times …' menacing, then relaxing. 'Elspeth, don't you realize what he stands to do by his stupidity? Don't you realize what *you* are encouraging him to do by *your* stupidity? The Seer of the colony has recommended acceptance. The *ching* has said accept. Now Gorstein is preventing that acceptance, preventing those predictions, those guidances, from having any meaning. To a people as primitive as this the oracle must be seen to be true. The only acceptable course of action is to obey it.'

Elspeth shrugged and smiled at the disconcertingly agitated man. 'If the native oracle has made a prediction,' she said, 'then it *will* come true. They always do.'

Ashka shook his head in despair. 'It is the right alternative, but Gorstein is preventing that alternative from occurring.'

Elspeth laughed, now. 'Peter, there *are* no alternatives on Aeran. The oracle predicts what *will* happen. You surely know that by now. You've seen it at work, haven't you? It doesn't work like the *ching*, it *sees*, it sees whatever alternative will have been acted upon.'

'Impossible,' said Ashka. 'I hadn't forgotten what the oracle is supposed to do, it's just impossible, that's all. There *are* no absolute oracles; all oracles, throughout the whole of history, have dealt with probability, never with non-randomness. What I *do* agree, however, is that the oracle on Aeran is *believed* to be absolute, and like you I don't want to see that belief shattered. But that belief *will* be shattered if Gorstein doesn't implant the monitors.'

'No! That's intolerable, Peter. Intolerable. All these people want, all they need, is to be left alone ...'

She noticed that Moir was watching them, crouched tightly in the under-cut surface of a rock. The wind was very strong, now, and the encroaching wall of mist had already obscured the marshes.

Peter Ashka said, 'To be left alone believing that the oracle was wrong?'

'They'll forget that, or they'll rationalize it away.'

There was something very tired about the old man, as if the effort of arguing was draining his strength.

'Elspeth ... the *ching* has said that the implantation will be of no consequence. It has stated that precisely and without ambiguity. Put the monitors into the Aerani and nothing will change. Both sides will be happy, and nothing will change!'

'Did the *ching* really say that?'

'Yes!' he said loudly, immediately lowering his voice. 'You must believe me – the Aerani are on a path to disaster unless this mission is accomplished, bizarre to them though it is. They must go through with it.'

Elspeth was still dubious. 'Suppose having gone through with it their attitudes change; suppose they change paths, away from the easy path, on to an unexpected one. Then the *ching* prediction will change. After all, it has only indicated a likelihood, right? You seem to want me to accept your having both sides of it. The local oracle can't be an absolute because absolute prediction is inconsistent with the tao; but believe in the absoluteness of the *ching* in this instance because ...' she broke off and stared at him. He said nothing. 'Because what, Peter? Why are you so desperate for the mission to be accomplished? What does it matter to you? An oracle doesn't have to be seen to be true for it to be valid ... what is it Peter?'

She was perturbed by the shocking expression on Ashka's face, a haunted look, the face not of a man who was at inner and outer peace with the tao, but of a man who was so far from balance that he felt that at any moment he must surely plunge over some psychological precipice and dash himself to permanent death.

'You're right, of course,' he said after a while. 'It comes close to me, my fear, my desperation. This world is a terrifying world, Elspeth, and I am terrified of it, although why I am frightened I don't fully understand. I only know that I'm a weak man. I have never concealed this, nor have I ever been ashamed of it. My weakness was irrelevant because my strength in other ways was so great; it's like that in all of us, of course. But I approach death, death in short order, a matter of months. I am not afraid of that death, I am afraid of my human reaction to the nearing of it. I need strength in the next few months, outside strength, the strength of one man, because there is only one man strong enough to support me.'

'ShipMeister Gorstein ...'

'Yes. Gorstein. He has been my closest friend, my closest human friend, for the better part of my adult life. It's strange how the fact of friendship can be unrealized until a crisis, isn't it? I have only recently realized how much I need him to help me through my final months of life. Without him I believe I should die in a shambles. With him, however – peacefully. And a peaceful death is my greatest wish.'

Elspeth wanted to object in a tone similar to that which Gorstein had used earlier today, to rebuke Ashka for his selfishness, putting his own life before the lives of the colony. But she found she couldn't do it, and in any case she suspected that it was not the fact of the mission being accomplished that was important, merely the fact of the unity of feeling between himself and the shipMeister.

He said, 'I believe that Gorstein will become my enemy very quickly if the mission is delayed ... I believe it because of something the Earthsong oracle told me ... you cannot see from my side of this mortal body, but the prospect of Gorstein becoming my enemy is agonizing.'

'I sympathize with you, Peter. Believe me. But ...' She broke off, staring at the pale-faced man, his frail body trembling with cold, his whole bearing that of a child rather than of a deeply intuitive man.

What was happening to him, she wondered? How could he so consistently ignore the fact of difference on Aeran? Or was it she who was ignorant? Did she accept the difference so easily that she overlooked a more sensible alternative? She was thinking, of course, of the oracle, how the Earthsong, if it had predicted hostility between Gorstein and Ashka, had predicted what would actually occur, no matter how the relationship between the ship and the crog changed.

Poor man, she thought. He's heading straight for conflict and yet he clings to his belief that conflict can be avoided. How tragic he'll become. How sad ...

She felt a shiver of premonition. Looking, at Ashka she saw the man as he was, aware of death, frightened of the fact of death, frightened of losing those close friends that he had, frightened, in fact, of all the mortal, human things that he – in his function as rationalist – helped to control in others.

There was no one to help him.

She said, 'I'm sorry, but my feelings remain unaltered. If Gorstein hadn't already decided to delay the implanting I'd have continued to argue him towards that decision. And if he changes his mind I shall go ahead and argue again. There's too much at stake on this world to think any differently, Peter. Something strange *has* happened here, and it has happened to humans, and it may have happened to a human population a long time ago – and it might happen again. We really ought to find out what that something is, don't you think? How can we do that in the present climate?'

Before he could answer, or retort, Moir shouted, 'Darren's about to snare a blackwing. Come and see.'

With a last glance at Ashka, Elspeth ran over to the girl and crouched, watching the mist as it rolled nearer, already adding a fine veil of white across the hunter and his sleeping prey.

Ashka crouched silently beside Elspeth and she smiled at him. 'Watch this,' she said. 'It's quite spectacular.'

These are what the Aerani eat, is that right?'

'They eat the flesh – which is foul – they make clothes from the wing-leather, and weapons from the skeleton. All-purpose prey.'

'He's going to snare the beast with those whips? Surely he'll be carried up in the air. The animal is three times the size of the boy.'

'Just watch and see,' said Elspeth. 'You'll never have seen the like in your life.'

'There!' shrieked Moir delightedly. Elspeth stared back down the valley. Darren had successfully snared the blackwing with each of his tangleweeds. With two secure grips on the creature it was no wonder the blackwing failed to shake him off.

His cry of triumph was loud in the heavy, moist air. The blackwing reared, its wings beating hard and noisily, its own cry piercing the causeway, alerting the beasts on the cliffs. Darren rose with it and began to tug. Elspeth watched his sturdy shape stand its ground for a moment, and then lurch forward, dragged by the greater strength of the bird-form, and its enormous resolution to escape. The blackwing hit the air, and beast and boy rose, two, three feet from the ground, then touching the moss again, running, tripping, launched into the air; Darren kept his grip, his arms outstretched, the muscles ridged and straining beneath his fur, but holding on.

Then, the flickerwing tactic, the beast and its hunter vanishing for a split second to reappear further away, flickering in and out of vision, advancing across the causeway in that peculiar series of mind jumps that Ashka had already seen.

Even so, he gasped with delight – or perhaps with surprise, or perhaps … recognition? Something seemed to be exciting him.

As the blackwing vanished into the mist, still flickerwinging crazily, still shrieking deafeningly and causing much disturbance among the cliff-sleeping population, so Elspeth sat back and turned to Ashka, wanting to see what he had thought of the exhibition.

He was no longer beside her, however, and twisting round on her haunches she saw him running towards his raft.

'Hey Peter! Wait for me!'

She chased after him, caught him easily. He had stopped his fast withdrawal and was walking, almost hobbling, the last few yards.

'What's the hurry?'

'I remembered. Thank the tao I remembered!'

'Remembered what? Peter, will you slow down … what have you remembered?'

'I saw it before,' he gasped; he had reached the raft and clambered aboard. Buckling himself down he ignored Elspeth as she stood, astonished, intrigued, staring at him.

'You've seen what before?' she insisted. 'Blackwings?'

'That motion,' he called as he rose above the ground. Elspeth stood back, out of the suddenly icy exhaust air-draught. 'Not teleportation,' he shouted. 'I've got to go and think quietly or it will slip away again.'

'Let me come with you,' she called. 'If it isn't teleportation then what is it? Oh Peter, please, you aggravating man. Take me along.'

The raft drifted away, gaining speed.

'What is it?' she shouted.

'Time …' he called back, his voice faint against the wind and the noise of the raft's motor.

Time, she thought, puzzled. Time travel? Was that what he meant? That the blackwings could travel through time?

Where did that leave anything?

ten

After a while he felt a fleeting embarrassment when he thought of his dramatic departure. He must have looked very strange; he must have sounded almost bizarre, shrieking with excitement as he slipped away into the distance.

He had only wanted to be alone for a while, to slip away from the encumbrance of any other person standing close by and asking distracting questions. He had not meant to be dramatic, nor rude.

The mist had closed in about him, choking, cloying, an atmosphere full of the stench of marsh life. Simple nose-filters made breathing more comfortable and he sat on the raft, staring into the wall of whiteness that isolated him totally from his environment, allowing his mind to concentrate without worry on what he had seen and what he had remembered.

The first time he had seen a blackwing flying he had felt familiarity with the sight. It was not the movement of the black-wing itself, of course, but the strange flickering motion by which the beast covered ground to escape a source of danger. Elspeth had called it teleportation. Ashka had seen teleportation and it had not involved the fractional *absence* of the body from sight, it had been something instantaneous, a function of space, not time. This movement was like something else he remembered seeing, an experiment at which he had been a witness, an experiment not too distant in his past. The memory was locked in his skull, and lost to his conscious mind by the normal process of memory displacement; but it was still there to be rescued, to be aired and reconsidered. The planet had not yet claimed it forever.

It had been an experiment performed on Earth, some fifteen years before. He had witnessed it from a distance as one of his purely routine functions; rationalists were required to witness experiments and contracts at all times of their life. He had been present at thousands of each; his eyes had seen, his ears had heard, his fingers had signed the declaration, and then his mind had forgotten the events and he had moved on through his life quite normally.

This particular experiment had been witnessed by over twenty thousand rationalists because it was a fundamental experiment in an Institute devoted to research into the nature of time. He, and the others, had watched a man running across a vast arena: the man was wearing a heavy back pack, a chest plate of delicate machinery, a small head-covering, mostly steel, and thin crystal probes into his cortex. As the man ran so he vanished, to reappear again a split second later a little further on; thus, flickering, he had progressed across the arena, and then had turned and come back. Exhausted by the effort, the man had collapsed. Ashka had signed his declaration and left the observation booth. It had not been very spectacular, and it had not filled him with wonder or excitement. The same could not be said of many others among the witnesses. The air had been electric, with laughter, conversation, opinion and delight.

They had witnessed a man running through time, in tiny bursts of a fraction of a second, using mind and machine to draw close to some Universe where the inexorable forward flow of time was less inviolate than in his own. Ashka, at the time, had not stopped to consider the implications and later when he had been informed that the experimental subject had had to re-establish his relationship with the *I Ching* (*that* was where he had heard of Elspeth's problem before) even then he had failed to consider the implications.

In the wall of mist, alone and cold, but slowly understanding the world on which he was gradually losing his identity, Peter Ashka wished he had not been so impetuous and ignorant that day, fifteen years in his past. He wished he was not such an ordinary rationalist; he wished he possessed even a slight amount of innovative ability that he might have thought more deeply and more significantly about that experiment that had so bored him.

From his pack he withdrew the small, flat computer terminal that linked him to the vast memory and sensory accumulation-and-analysis centre of the ship. Uncoiling its attachment-lead he leaned over the side of the raft and pushed the terminal pin into the mossy earth, continuing to push it deeper into the soil until the screen glowed to life, signifying contact through the earth current.

Straightening up he stared at the screen for a moment, then spoke a request. 'Define the nature of time on the planet Earth.'

The glass flickered yellow for an almost indiscernible moment, then a dense block of words appeared:

Time on Earth, from empirical findings, is irreversible and sequential. It is further defined to be linear and constant in its flow, having the appearance of a wave-front moving from past to future. There is no absolute standard of time; the definition remains axiomatic and unprovable, labelling Earth time as an effective standard for practical purposes.

Satisfied that he fully understood the terminology, he wiped the screen. After a moment he asked, 'What is the nature of time on Aeran?'

A long pause preceded the reply. When it came the words thrilled Ashka, not so much because of what they said, but because of the implication that the mindless machines of the ship had known the uniqueness of Aeran all along, but had been unable to offer their information without the precise request from some human operator.

Time on Aeran and in the surrounding space may be meaningfully defined in terms of Earth time, once necessary relativistic adjustments have been made. In these terms, its behaviour is oscillatory. It fluctuates cyclically about the normal time flow, the amplitude of an oscillation being calculated at 0.02 seconds, and the frequency at 37.5 Hz.

That simple – that unique – that destructive!

Point zero two of a second stands between me and the awareness of my own death, he thought. Point zero two of a second explains it all, everything;

the vast, the minute – like the out-winding of a spiral, an insignificant point at the centre of a complex and vast pattern ... the infinitely small being indistinguishable from the infinitely large, for infinity has no dimensions, manifesting itself as space and time purely for the benefit of those who labour to define their surroundings.

I'm rambling ... my thoughts flicker forwards and backwards, like the beating of a wing, like ... like the catching of a breath –

The caught breath of time, Iondai had said – caught and held for an instant before it is completed normally.

Iondai knew, in his primitive, uninquisitive, down-to-earth way. He knew, as all the Aerani probably knew, but it had never occurred to them to define or question or analyse – they were not civilized enough to need such a sophisticated cage as an understanding of their insignificance to the vast universe.

The mist closed in tighter about him, isolating him completely from the raft, even from his own hands held before his face. It was wonderful confinement, wonderful stillness. The whiteness seemed to reach right into his skull, swirling and rolling down the hills and through the valleys, isolating thoughts here, memories there, pushing facts forward, blocking off irrelevant trains of reason.

A world where time was so fundamentally different to normal time that the *ching* wouldn't work, that the human mind found itself sinking, vanishing, receding from its natural home in the cells and circuits of the brain. An oscillating time front, a world, then, where at any one instant the past and the future were the same, held together in that past and preecho of the moment. When one acted one had already acted and would not act for a split second yet – a span of relative time too short to appreciate as the material body, the material brain, clicked into the rhythm of the motion without control; a span of time too short to be seen as anything but a bizarre flickerwinging phenomenon when an animal actively fought to ride the front of that wave, escaping by the unique combination of time and mind, apparently flickering because the observer and observed were moving in a different time pattern for those brief seconds of flight.

The ship had known. The *ching* too had known, but could not tell him without the correct question. Even Gorstein, strange man, strangely haunted man, even he had felt something wrong when they had landed; his insensitive mind, perhaps, was more receptive to the alteration of time than a more sensitive, and therefore more noisy, psyche. He had felt discomfort, a sense of something wrong. The *ching* had said, External, and Ashka had interpreted that as something from the colony, some foreboding of hostility. And there *had* been hostility, and he had believed his interpretation to be correct. But it had not been correct. Gorstein had sensed the wrongness with time; the *ching* had known it, had tried to explain it. Even the computer had tried to explain it, but how was the computer to know that what *it* detected as a strange phenomenon was what Gorstein also detected? Machines ... to depend on them was to depend on fools.

There was so much irony in the situation that Ashka gave way to the smile that had been begging for expression. Why, Iondai had even known that it was not the *ching* that was at fault, but Ashka's mind, and that made sense, of course. If Ashka's body could easily fit itself into the shifting flow of time on Aeran, his mind could not – the mind was something separate, the mind existed in its own Universe, and the smooth merging of body and mind was what the tao was all about, when seen from the human eye view. But no doubt even the mind could re-adjust – even the mind could sense its displacement and make adjustments, and as it adjusted, as it slipped gradually, inexorably, into the different space and time system, as it began to oscillate with the body that housed it, so it slipped away from the *ching*, so it ceased to relate, so the *ching* became meaningless, because it could not work. It had seemed ill when he had used it with Iondai – had that been jealousy, irritation with the vast oracle nearby? Or had it merely been a subjective assessment from a mind still close but sufficiently displaced, now, for the rough edge of non-functioning to begin to show?

And memory ... memory: nothing more (nothing less!) than a vibration in the nerve cell nucleus, a perpetual bioelectric wave motion determined by a particular crystalline protein structure beneath the nuclear membrane – a wave form that could be allowed to reach to the outer cell-membrane itself when that particular memory fragment was required and called for – a tenuous structure, man's past, his identity, his destiny, locked in a billion tiny reverberations – so easy to destroy. And Aeran was destroying them! Those intricate structures were a function of time as well as of space and no wonder they were decaying beneath the re-defined parameters of Aerani relativity. Gradual destruction, fragment by fragment, incident by incident ... as the mind made the transition, crossing over, so the accumulated experience of a lifetime was erased from the surface, from the templates, leaving them free and empty for the new acquisition of life and death.

Not all, of course. Language seemed to remain, the words and concepts, distorted by their passage from Universe to Universe, but still fundamentally the same. Words – speech – imprinted on one hemisphere where the brain thrust forward above the eyes; and on the other hemisphere?... symbols, yes ... if he remembered it well enough, it was geometric associations and symbols that were the responsibility of the other hemisphere. But all these things, unlike memory, had their cerebellar analogues – even speech! – and though the cerebral cortex was always active, there was little – in fact nothing, save memory – that was not divided between the higher brain with its complex cell structure and the lower brain with its more fundamental ways of recording and associating information.

So much was dark – so much was blank, blank like the wall of fog, indefinable, and yet with the subtle suggestion of shapes and faces, as if the memory that he believed he had lost was still there, in fact, but deep down, far out of reach, beyond the grasp of even the seventh level of his mind, the deep unconscious. So much that was a prisoner in the chemical codes of his brain – all those faces, all those times, cities, events, cast down to some hellish eternal darkness, leaving the tapes clear for new usage, in a new world, in a new time, giving him a new destiny ...

He felt inexplicably excited, his mind lagging behind his body following some spontaneous realization. Then he realized what it was.

Destiny.

Of course! That was why the *ching* could not work properly, why it failed to find a handhold on Aeran. Perhaps, then, it was not only the mind of the user that was at fault – perhaps when he had felt the *ching* to be troubled he had been right, making an error only in assigning that trouble to jealousy. The *ching*, the tarot, the several more obscure oracles he occasionally used, all were designed for a Universe where destiny was not predefined, but mutable, malleable – man and his future was an everchanging system, a moving wavefront which shifted position with each decision taken. There was no such thing as *prediction*, merely *probability*. No one could *see* the future, only a future possibility, because on Earth, in the vast Universe of normal time, there was no future until it arrived ... the *ching* could look into the void and see the trends. It did not see actuality. The likely trend could be obtained by bending to the tao, by ceasing to struggle for an ideal position; but nothing was certain until it was lodged securely in the past.

But on Aeran – on Aeran the future was ever-present. On a world, in a Universe, where time oscillated by even a billionth of a second, the future was already determined, because it always occurred before it happened. On Aeran destiny was absolutely defined, clear cut. Of course their oracle predicted absolutes! How it worked didn't matter – they used an earth oracle and the mind of the questioner felt the pulse of the future – it might have been Iondai himself, future-seeing quite literally, or it might have been something else, something vast compared to man – perhaps whatever lurked behind this Earthwind symbol ... the singer of the Earthsong itself? Ashka had no way of knowing. But the future on Aeran was predetermined. There was no escape from destiny, for on Aeran man was the servant of time, not merely a helpless passenger in its flow. The *ching* – poor oracle – could see as it had always seen, but it was meaningless when mutability was lost. What it had already said, before they had arrived on Aeran, would probably still hold good, but the longer they stayed here the less they could act effectively in accordance with the *ching's* prophecies which were dictating their lives and actions.

He had practically ignored Elspeth's earlier warning, but now he knew she had been absolutely right.

They had to get off the world. And fast.

He emerged from his reflective mental state, looked about him.

Hidden by the fog something was moving. For a second or two the muffled noise puzzled him – he stared into the whiteness (which was now beginning to thin a little) and tried to understand exactly what he was hearing. When he realized it was the loud approach of some animal his stomach turned over. The last thing he wanted to run into in this fog was a hungry maneater; oscillating through time or not, flesh was still flesh and Ashka was still a tasty morsel.

He reached for the key to the motor, but couldn't find it. It was not in his pouch either, and he unconsciously began to feel around on the damp metal floor of the raft.

The creature stopped.

It had been running in his general direction and now, still completely hidden from view, it had stopped and was listening, trying to sense him. Try as he might he could not cut his breathing to a gentle cycle of inhale–exhale. He gulped for air, to make up for his body's perpetual oxygen starvation. The creature began to advance – he could hear its footfall; he could imagine it searching the whiteness for some shape or shadow that would guide it to its prey.

Elspeth would never forgive him, he thought, if he wound up being eaten before he'd even told her a fraction of what he had come to realize.

Where *was* that key?

He found it, a small metal disc, cold and wet with the mist. He fumbled at the starting socket, breathing loudly, now, feeling a desperate panic as he thought of the potential cruelty of fate, wiping him out and his observations with it.

He might have remembered his *ching* prediction of a peaceful death, still valid on Aeran, but in the excitement of panic, isolated in the cold fog of this alien world, he lost all control of his reason. He fumbled at the starter and cursed loudly as the slick key slipped from his grasp again.

The creature came out of the mist. First a dim shape, weaving from side to side, then a grey form becoming clearer with each uncertain step forward.

Ashka watched, fascinated, as resolution gave the lie to his fear.

She emerged from the fog and also smiled with relief.

'I could hear you, but this mist is so deceiving.'

'Elspeth,' he breathed, calming instantly and closing his eyes to try and control his racing heart. 'I thought …'

She ignored the uncompleted sentence, advanced towards him and sat down on the raft. She fixed him with a determined look. 'Well?'

'Well what?'

'You've worked it out, haven't you.' It was a statement, not a question.

He laughed. 'Some of it. Just some of it.'

'This time,' said Elspeth, 'you don't get away so easily.'

eleven

Climbing out of the lowlands as the fog lifted, Elspeth watched the raft drift off across the scrub towards the distant forest. She had declined Ashka's offer of a lift back to the crog. Voices behind her attracted her attention and she saw Darren and Moir dragging the dead blackwing between them. She ran to assist, partly hopeful that communication had been re-established between brother and sister, but the talk was merely functional.

'Well done,' she said as she lent her strength to the task. Darren said nothing.

At dusk, in the crog, seated just inside the inner wall, away from the main group of Aerani, Elspeth watched a bloodless duel fought for the right to sing river-song. Moir was outside the crog and Elspeth had sneaked her out some small fragments of food an hour or so earlier. The girl was unhappy but not unduly uncomfortable. Darren had given her a blanket of blackwing leather and a small bone knife. The youth now sat sullenly to one side of the main group around the fire, his face mostly in darkness. The torches around the dune walls were being lit.

The duel won, the two contestants separated and the loser sat glumly in the outer glow of the fire. The winner crawled up the inner earthworks and squatted in position, singing the eerie river-song with its rushing sounds and vocal clicks. Tree singer was also in fine voice and the two sounds mingled and merged over the fire-glow, sending fragmentary images of her home world and of the quiet solitude of the countryside she had known on Earth dancing in Elspeth's mind's-eye. There was much she still remembered, and she was relieved to realize the fact – but her life on New Anzar had now almost completely slipped away, emerging only in fragments and only on occasions such as this when the earth singers entranced her with their song, or wind singer's mournful invocations brought back a sense of the wind that had scourged Anzar and made its unprotected surface so lethal. Wind singer was quiet tonight, she noticed. She was crouched some way round the rampart, staring down at the fire; occasionally she sang a few cadences, but she seemed bothered by the obvious tension of the group below. What was she responding to, wondered Elspeth? What did she sense on the wind?

Or was such belief in a mystical function for these strange songsters just foolishness?

Wind singer was the privileged one of all the earth singers. Iondai chose her and could dismiss her at his whim, but his whim, perhaps, was based on the way he himself read the wind. The other singers, river and tree, changed from torch cycle to torch cycle and everyone in the crog could hold the position for a while. Rock song was the prerogative of all who lived in the crog, at all times. A form of prayer, a winning of favour from the earth spirits, it no doubt had a cathartic function and little else.

The conversation round the fire was at times animated and violent. Elspeth found it difficult to hear very much and this was naturally irritating, but she dared not leave the edge of the fire-glow to get a clearer idea of what was being said – if the Ungenn still regarded her as a dune-runner in the middle of her testing, then they would kick her out without ceremony if she strayed from the spiral path.

Listening hard she gained an idea that the refusal of the beyonders to impart their 'bone spirits' to the selected few was causing major concern. Most were convinced of the value of such a possession in the crog, and they were convinced purely because Iondai had 'foreseen' it. There were dissenters – Darren, when he spoke, argued violently in favour of closing the entrances to the crog as they had when the *nue* raiders had come down from the snowlands. His father was sympathetic to his son's viewpoint, but the Ungenn of the family was not. Elspeth could detect the gradual increase of hostility towards Darren and his father. It did not bode well, she decided, and she didn't need an oracle to confirm her belief.

The sweet smell of cooked meat – blackwing meat – made her mouth water, despite her loathing of it. She had been given such a small portion earlier in the evening, and half of that she had given to Moir. She remembered her first taste of blackwing, the nausea she had fought, day after day, so that she could eat with Darren without grimacing. When she had had access to her ship, now a dead hulk in stable orbit four hundred miles starwards, she had been amazed at the length of time the medical couch had taken to flush the alien substances from her body. Eventually she had ceased to bother. There was nothing poisonous in the various foods that the Aerani ate, the blackwing, the rock-root fungus and that 'lucinogen' that grew in porous rocks … whitegum, she believed it was called. They could all be used by the human body without ill effect, and there was quite obviously nothing deficient in their nutritive value.

The night advanced, the fire burned high and the argument continued. Elspeth was half in the crog and half on some cloudy plane, remembering fragments of conversations, with Ashka, with Gorstein, even with Iondai.

Mostly she thought back to the afternoon, to the choking, stinking mist, and the intense oriental, sending shivers down her spine with the bizarre things he told her.

She hadn't understood much of what he'd said. The oscillation of the time wavefront she could 'see' by visual metaphor. But she had never before considered time as a wavefront and couldn't grasp how it might be nothing more than a manifestation of the balance between different cosmic forces. It all seemed so logically bound up with the tao, the way he had described it – the flux of energy, the distillation of matter, the currents of stress and strain that radiated from the stars and planets, and those unseen, unrealizable forces that had such lasting effects on the three-month-old foetus, marking each man and woman as a function of his Universal position. Astrologism, Ashka had called it, but the term was one of those vague rationalist's terms and she had not known it, and in the light of after-consideration, it didn't seem logical at all, just meaningless.

All these forces, he had said, interact in certain ways and where they overlap with matter, time is one of the products. Sometimes irregularities could creep into that balance and time changed – a man had once travelled through time by using machines and his own mind to induce an irregularity localized around the electric field of his own body. Here on Aeran, in the space around it, perhaps for light years, perhaps for just a few miles above the surface, there was such an irregularity. In one sense Aeran, though physically compatible with our own, was really a part of another Universe.

And what about Ireland, seven thousand years ago?

If (he had said) the common symbols of both cultures are a function of this irregularity, then yes, in Ireland there must have been a localized imbalance, lasting a few years, a few centuries, tied to that small part of the Earth by some particular presence, or perhaps – think of the running man – perhaps by the minds of the particular Stone Age people themselves. All this is just an idea, he said (though she intuited that he believed himself to be right), just an idea.

Time and symbols. Symbols and time. Were they related? How could they *not* be? How could a complex set of symbols re-appear after seven thousand years of obscurity unless it was related to the huge anomaly on Aeran? And if *these* symbols re-emerged, then didn't it suggest anomaly also in megalithic Ireland?

Her mental powers argued the case backwards and forwards, and she watched the procedure almost idly, almost without participation. Did logic decay with memory? Surely the answer was clear cut – time and the symbols of the Boyne valley and of Aeran were linked, were interrelated – without a change in local time there would not have been the symbols, either then in the dawn, or now in the dawn rebirth.

And why could she explain so many symbols (or felt she could) but not that *one*? Why did she feel she could explain *all* the simple patterns, the abstract representations of earth current in rock and water and wind, the lozenges, the circles, the triangles, the concentric circles, the spirals and the double spirals ... but not this one pattern, these three double spirals that etched themselves into the wall of her mind as some artistic hand had etched them into the tomb wall of Newgrange, a million lifetimes ago?

How magic that carving, how exciting that symbol, how deeply it had affected those who looked upon it, crouched in the dark chamber, closed in by slabs of rock and the heavy smell of earth. As their torches had shone upon it they had all fallen silent. Perhaps, in the time when Earth had been loved as home, perhaps a thousand generations had looked and marvelled at the Earthwind and asked themselves – what could it mean? Who carved it? What was he thinking as he picked away at the rock and left a piece of art that seems to reach into the mind and evokes a sense of prehistoric time like no other symbol or earthly structure of rock and sky?

Something Ashka had said that afternoon came back to her. They had been talking (just briefly) about the symbols again. Elspeth couldn't get them out of her mind, but Ashka was sufficiently unfamiliar with them to be unsure of his own ideas. But he *had* seen the Earthwind, and he had also felt that strange stirring of the mind – psycho-parasitic symbol? – an uneasy sense of familiarity and an unwelcome ecstasy as he had let his eyes follow round the complex spirals. Perhaps, he had said smiling, perhaps the great tumulus was erected not to bury men but to bury the Earthwind. A memorial, perhaps, or a prison ... a symbol they had used for years finally carved permanently, just *once*, and locked away.

At Newgrange, at the time of carving, the chamber containing the Earthwind symbol had been lit up by the dawn sun of the winter solstice, strands of light reaching over a hundred feet into the earth to touch the tomb of the spiral just that one day in every year.

So revered? Or so feared?

She liked the idea. The decaying tumulus in the jungle, where Moir had taken her to gain access to the Fire Hall, there too there had been a carving of double spirals – had it been the same? Had it been the Earthwind? The ashes of bodies might, as at Newgrange, have been a secondary burial, or even an offering. No light ever penetrated the Aeran tumulus, but then that winter sun was something peculiar to all the megalithic cultures of Earth, and not restricted to any one area.

And on Aeran, she had discovered, the Earthwind was associated with something else – with the oracle they used, with the gusting wind from the mountains, with the Earthsong that carried the vision of the future into the minds of those trained to consult it.

What one fact – she asked herself as she half-listened to the voices of the Aerani, and half-wandered through the rock labyrinth of a cemetery on Earth – what one fact links all that I know about the Aerani and the Earthwind? A symbol they seem reluctant to talk about – a symbol they paint on rock before a duel – a symbol carved over the fire pit, held at once in reverence and also in a certain fear ...

What did that suggest immediately? One thing. That the Aerani, like Elspeth, had no idea what the Earthwind was, even though it affected them deeply and they knew it meant, or had meant, something of extreme importance!

According to Ashka the cave of the Earthwind (she had never heard of this before) lay at the far end of that enigmatic wind current that was the oracle. There, then, she might find an understanding of the one symbol she felt would elude her for ever if she depended only on the Aerani and observation of their ritual.

Two sets of symbols, and not just one? It was more than a possibility, now. The symbols they used and understood, possibly just meaningless marks, without actual use except as some psychological manifestation of a greater awareness (but recapitulated!) ... and a second type of symbol, characterized by just one design, one expression, a fundamental expression, something so deeply ingrained in every single human that it could be at one moment completely taken for granted and the next – totally forgotten.

The fire reached crackling fingers of light high into the smoking air. The voices around the heat source grew unnaturally loud, but at the same time almost garbled. They seemed to be a noisy focus in an otherwise total stillness. River singer and tree singer crooned their magic song and the notes and images fell delicately and entrancingly across the fire-glow; somewhere a child mimicked a blackwing's courting song. A feeling of total detachment over-came Elspeth as she sat by the earthen wall, cold, yet unaware of chill, hugging her knees and watching the flames, and smelling the odour of burning flesh, listening to the gentle song and the murmuring voices of dissension ...

And gradually, starting as a faint idea growing with each beat of her heart, with each fluctuating note of the songs that mingled in her head, the river, the tree, the wind, the blackwing ...

She began to understand – she remembered something that Ashka had said that afternoon about man being evolved from pattern and essence, and for the first time she began to understand what had eluded her for what seemed to be a lifetime ... it began to make sense ...

An unearthly scream startled her from her meditation. For a moment, as she stared, unnerved, at the scene around her it was hard to tell that anything was wrong. Slowly she detected the change. All the Aerani were standing and Darren's father was collapsing to his knees, staring across the fire-glow at Elspeth herself, reaching out towards her as if begging support ...

Darkness stained his belly and chest, a criss-cross of black lines which parted, as he doubled, and were exposed as four ferocious wounds. Elspeth gagged, stifled the scream she would have much rather voiced.

The air began to stink, a sour smell, familiar yet unfamiliar, a smell that had revolted her only a day before. The smell of blood, of death.

Darren came running towards her and she began to struggle to her feet, but a thrown rock blade spun through the air so close to her head that she froze. Darren looked back, then at her (a split moment of decision) then raced to the exit through the inner dune. Elspeth noticed one of the older men prevent a heavily armed warrior from giving chase. She stared at the writhing body of Darren's father. Her whole body felt numb. As she watched, the man's living head was hacked away from his torso and flung unceremoniously on to the fire. The killer advanced on Elspeth, the stained bone-knife held menacingly towards her. She sat absolutely still, reasoning, with a suddenly clear mind, that she had no chance of escaping anyway.

A moment later the man was gone, walking swiftly back to the fire pit. A few of the older Aerani watched her from a distance, and then the Ungenn of Darren's family smiled at her. Wonderful calm, she thought. His son newly dead, his grandson driven out of the crog and there he sits apparently unconcerned. Can family ties, family love, matter so little in the face of dissension?

She was ignored, then, and left to her place of shadows, a hunched form peering in towards the warmth.

The decision had been taken, of course. There was no question in her mind that any other reason could account for the disintegration of Darren's family. Those who had clamoured for dismissal of the oracle had been dismissed in a very different way – those who had noisily opposed the 'bonespirits' had been acquainted with the total loyalty of the Ungenn and the majority of Aerani to the voice of time as it spoke through Iondai.

And there was Iondai himself, quietly smug, crouched in the inner warmth of the fire-glow, staring up at wind singer who now gave voice to a cheerless song, full of despair and cold. No one objected. Perhaps the noisy consuming of the vegetable fuel drowned, for them, the sad voice from the earth rampart.

How right she had been to dismiss her brief feelings of relief, after the talk with Gorstein. She might have been foolish, creeping away from the crog for a few days to allow the Aerani to get back to a normal way of life, and she might have returned and found the worst had happened. And she was now quite sure that avoidance of the worst depended on radical, drastic and immediate action. For with the Aerani ready and willing to accept the monitors, only Gorstein's uncertainty remained to protect them from the folly of their own ignorance. And how long would Gorstein's uncertainty hold out against Ashka's demands for immediate accomplishment of the mission and departure? The strangeness of the flow of time might sound unreal, but the ship knew and the machines would convince Gorstein where reason would fail. He would not argue with cold fact. He would find himself forced to decide immediately, not whether or not to leave, but whether or not to plant the monitors first.

And to return to those he so feared and to say to them, 'We didn't think it was right to tamper with them,' and to state 'oscillating time' as a reason?

They would probably laugh at him. Gorstein wouldn't risk it. He would act to give the Aerani what they now felt they wanted. It was the easiest solution for all concerned.

Madness was the master, now, and only Elspeth could act to prevent chaos. And chaos was how she envisaged the future for the Aerani if Gorstein had his way.

If it occurred to her that her strong sense of duty to protect the Aerani from themselves might have been misplaced patronization, she pushed the thought from her mind.

This was no time for self-criticism.

Unnoticed (or so she thought) she slipped out of the fire-glow and then out of the crog itself. She stood, for a moment, staring at the brightly lit ship nearly a quarter of a mile away, and when her eyes were accustomed to the sudden darkness away from the fire and the torches, she began to walk across the intervening land.

Darren was nowhere to be seen. She ignored Moir, who crouched against the earthworks, watching her. Moir called her name but Elspeth, even if she heard it, did not respond.

At the ramp into the brilliantly lit interior of the ship, she lied to the guard, saying that she was expected. The guard had seen her in the ship before, when she had been with Gorstein, and it apparently did not occur to him to ask for confirmation from the shipMeister. 'Go right in,' he said, smiling.

'I'm supposed to meet him at the monitors,' she said. 'I've got to describe them to the Aerani before they'll accept them passively.'

'About time too,' said the guard. 'Anyway, there's nothing to see. Nothing to describe. Not much, anyway.'

'You can't say that to them ...' she hitched a thumb back over her shoulder. The guard understood.

'You'll see a cargo-hold door labelled "sensitive". Go through there. Follow your eyes.'

She went up the ramp and with a glance at Gorstein's windows, all of which were radiating yellow light, she entered the ship.

She was through the cargo-hold door almost before she was aware of her racing heart and dizziness. Now, she knew, it was death if Gorstein found her. She would have to act quickly. If Gorstein came *out* of the ship her little game would be up; if the guard decided, on reflection, to check with the ship-Meister to make sure he was expecting Elspeth, her desperate ploy would be understood; she wouldn't stand a chance.

The corridor sloped downwards. Ship sounds filled her ears, deep thrummings, perhaps from the life support systems, or the Ames-drive which could never be turned off completely, even if an effort were made to do so.

As she walked through the white-walled passage she withdrew her tiny pin gun from her belt. It had not occurred to her to use the weapon for her own defence a few minutes ago … how strange the way the artefacts of civilization could slip away when inside the crog walls. She had not just decided against using the weapon, she had failed utterly to realize she possessed it.

She held it, now, pointed ahead of her. It had a single charge, which was very effective. If she had to use it for defence she would not have any attack strength left for the monitors.

And what *did* they look like?

At the end of the corridor, which was shorter than she imagined, she found the hold labelled 'sensitive'. Opening the door she stepped into a small, dimly lit room, warm, almost stuffy. Equipment littered the walls; faint lights covered the floor; a heady smell, ozone perhaps, sent unpleasant sensations through her body.

In the middle of the floor, rising to almost her own height, was a crystal cabinet, its body shot through with streaks of blue, complex, interlinked, grouped into twenty concentrations that were evenly spread through the housing. Could there be any doubt?

She raised the gun and pointed it centrally at the crystal. For a moment she hesitated, a stray thought entering her head – these are human minds … these are human awarenesses. Then she realized that they were not aware, although they did indeed house the echoes of human minds. But the humans who had donated these intangible pulses of energy were still alive and well, for the process did not involve any sacrifice. Like giving tissue, or love, nothing was really lost from the donor.

She aimed carefully (– a vaze would have been so much more effective, but it was too late now –) and opened the door behind her so she could dart out to avoid the blast.

She squeezed the trigger.

She hid in the forest for a while, trembling, choking on the fumes that had seemed to force their way into her lungs. How she had kept her mental and bodily cool long enough to leave the ship without arousing suspicion she didn't know. Now, stretched out on the cool earth of a tiny clearing, she gave release to all the tension that she had so admirably contained for the past twenty minutes.

The ship stayed quiet.

An hour later, recovered and feeling – at last – very pleased with herself (but recognizing that her life would not be worth living should Gorstein get his hands on her) she crept through the darkness into the crog. Moir called her again as she went past, a fleet shadow in the night, but again Elspeth ignored her.

If Gorstein's wrath peaked, and it was bound to, he might decide to take some aggressive action against the Aerani, and it was only fair that she should warn them. She realized the risk she ran, telling them about the death of the monitors, but the Aerani's marvellous talent for fatalism should help them accept what had happened, and they might even see that it was best. In any case, they probably already knew, for their oracle would know.

At the inner entrance to the crog she came face to face with Iondai. He barred her way, a frail, aggressive man, staring at her, and something in his eyes, something in his expression, told her what she had suspected.

He knew what had happened.

Nevertheless she said, 'The bone-spirits are dead.'

Iondai said nothing, merely stared at her. After a moment he stood aside and she realized what was about to happen.

twelve

For Peter Ashka life and the inevitability of death held no fear. With the element of uncertainty almost completely taken away from life by the *ching*, only the fact of death had stood between him and the peacefulness of existence he so desired. This was why, in his middle years, he had risked all and spent that long week in consultation with the *Book of Change*, asking questions and listing answers, probing and working his way towards an answer hidden far in the future, in that part of the improbable Universe where there still existed more dark than light. But the *ching* had reached and he had followed the *ching*, and at the end of the week he had possessed a series of equations from which he had discovered the exact date of his death.

If Ashka had had any major fault in his youth it was that he tended towards disorganization. Planning and scheduling were such chores that his life was often chaotic, and he sensed in this the strong possibility of death before full achievement. There was so much he required to know and to experience and only by knowing his limit of time could he organize himself to the correct ends.

That time was nearly gone, and though he regretted that the seven months were not seven years, he was not unhappy and was certainly not afraid, and this was how it had always been. A peaceful life and a peaceful death were assured to him, and peacefulness was his great wish. Gorstein was his Master and directed his life, the *ching* was his closest friend and directed his destiny. Life and destiny – what else was there? Only the past, and here and here alone Ashka found his heart occasionally filled with regret. But it was unimportant.

His life behind him was filled with memories of all the pleasures he had ever desired – new knowledge, new places, new questions. He had never married for that was one pleasure he had never desired. In many ways he was an abnormal man, but if his eccentricity of life, his dedication to the *ching*, set him slightly apart from other men, he was – nonetheless – an ordinary man, devoid of great creativity and lacking in innovative spark. He was good at his job, like so many others around him, but he was nothing exceptional.

He measured his own achievement not by his accumulated knowledge (this was his private pride) but by the achievements of Karl Gorstein. Gorstein – his master; and yet in one sense, his charge, for Ashka, over the past ten years, had guided Gorstein, helped him remain afloat, advised and consulted on his behalf, and watched the man rise to power, to ship-Meister, watched his strength flourish and consolidate, and felt all the time that Gorstein's strength was his own strength, that Gorstein's success was his success, that Ashka and Gorstein were closer than friends – they were almost one.

Which was why the prediction of Authority standing between him and success on Aeran had filled him with such anxiety. Deep in his heart (he had wondered) did he doubt Gorstein? Did he doubt the man's strength, his resolve? Did he feel, in some quieter corner of his mind, that Gorstein had failed, failed because he needed Ashka and therefore was less than a man?

To doubt Gorstein was to doubt himself – the whole thought was intolerable. Ashka and Gorstein, together. That was how it had always been. The rationalist and the shipMeister, the oriental and the 'westerner', the small man and the tall man, the weak of body and the strong, the strong of destiny and the weak, complementary halves of a single entity, yin and yang, the reacher into time and the clinger to the present. All sides of a whole that was greatness, that was advancement, progress and success …

To doubt Gorstein was to doubt himself. To doubt Gorstein was to admit to his weakness, his *own* weakness, his, Ashka's. Had he lived a peaceful life for all these years to question, less than seven months from death, the whole nature of his existence? No. He could not question it. Gorstein was … Gorstein was …

He *longed* to say *right*.

He bitterly, frantically, desperately wanted to say *right*, to know that Gorstein *was* right.

But if that was so ... then the *ching* was wrong! If Gorstein was right, if Gorstein was above doubt, then the *ching* was wrong, and that was impossible! The *ching* could not be wrong. The *ching* could not be doubted.

So Gorstein was wrong, wrong to reject the oracle, as he now had, wrong to dismiss it, wrong to dismiss Ashka, as he now apparently had ... Gorstein was wrong and Ashka's life was a lie, a bitter lie, an empty thing, an echo of greatness, of wholeness, a husk loosely disguised as complete.

Choice made a mockery of trust; decision made a liar of tears.

Gorstein or the *ching*, weakness or strength, truth or lie. Myself or myself!

And for just an instant Ashka rode the path of confusion, of uncertainty, of genuine questioning of the two values he valued most.

A moment, just a moment, just a second when his mind ceased to debate both sides of the argument and instead allowed itself to float, to bob on the waves of the tao, undirectioned, insecure ...

A heartbeat of treachery.

Moments left.

An instant of doubt.

Darkness ahead.

And then resolve: Gorstein was wrong! He was wrong and he had to be stopped. The *ching* could not be doubted – to reject it was folly, and folly was the prerogative of the ignorant. Gorstein *was* ignorant, of course. So ignorant that he had never understood the nature of time and change, had never related to the *Book of Change* and always needed a rationalist to be there. He was weakness of the worst sort; he was founded on the strength of another's principles.

He had to be stopped, his decision had to be reversed!

He might have said, 'Well, here I am. Reverse it.' But he didn't. He couldn't have known what was in Ashka's mind, but as Ashka reached his final decision so the door of his room slid silently open and Gorstein stood there. His face was white and drawn – tension, perhaps, or great anger.

'Karl ...' Ashka climbed unsteadily to his feet and looked earnestly at the shipMeister. 'Karl, why wouldn't you see me before?'

Gorstein stared at him for a moment, then looked down as he allowed the door to slide shut. He advanced into the room and looked through the window into the darkness outside (or at his own reflection?).

'I have no desire for an argument with you, Peter. Please forgive me if I seemed rude earlier.'

'I merely wondered,' said Ashka, 'why you did not allow me to see you?'

'Because I knew what you wanted,' replied Gorstein, a fine edge of irritation showing in his voice. He turned quickly to look at the rationalist, smiled, loosened the belt of his billowing red robe. 'There was – and is – nothing I could say to appease you, Peter. It is too late to go back and your very genuine concern for me would have been merely troublesome.'

'Troublesome!' Ashka could hardly believe the calm insult as it was delivered. 'Troublesome,' he repeated, and slowly sat down again. 'Ten years,' he murmured sadly.

'Hmm? Ten years?'

'That you and I ...'

'Ah,' Gorstein realized what Ashka meant. He sat down on the mat and nodded patronizingly. 'Yes. Ten years – many years, and I mean it when I say, Peter, that those ten years ... well, despite what you made me do, I *have* appreciated them, and I *have* appreciated you. I wish there were some way to thank you for that. A gift would be an insult, but there is one thing I can offer.'

'I need no offering. I need no thanks for those ten years.'

His eyes stung and he blinked as discreetly as possible. He felt reason slipping away fast, irrational emotion surfacing, unwanted nostalgia taking a firm grip on his mind.

Gorstein laughed apologetically. 'You misunderstand me. The thing I can offer is something very very dear to me – and I hope very dear to you too.'

'What?'

As if pleased with himself, Gorstein said, 'Continued friendship.'

Ashka said nothing. The shock he felt was almost unbearable. To have to offer it, to be aware of it, made it all the more a lie! Friendship? There was no friendship! Gorstein had never felt any such emotion for Ashka. How foolish he had been to have ever believed that such a relationship had existed!

'Thank you,' he said dully. Unable to help himself he wept for a moment, head hung forward on his chest, hands placed precisely on his crossed legs. The warm tears soaked between his fingers. Gorstein remained silent and when Ashka looked up, after a few minutes, the shadow of a smile vanished from the shipMeister's face.

He thinks I'm weeping for joy ...

Aloud: 'You said – *despite what I made you do* – what did you mean by that? The *ching*?'

'Of course. Like some ancient religion you fed me a diet of shamanism, directed and controlled me – oh yes, you did direct and control me, Peter – on the basis of prediction after prediction, never really allowing me to choose for myself – always the choices were given to me and all I ever had to do was decide the wisdom of each alternative – and often no alternative at all – do this or fail.'

'But – what was wrong with being told the alternatives?'

'Everything, Peter! Everything.'

'If you had considered everything on your own, Karl, you would have come up with those same choices! Where is the wrongness or the rightness of one approach compared to another?'

Gorstein said softly, leaning forward so that his intensity seemed to confine the rationalist, 'Whenever our race comes to depend on something it becomes weak. Dependence on machines or upon each other … it's weakness, and it's exploitable. The use of oracles is a weakness, Peter, it's a sign of our lost ability to think things through … every oracle in the empire predicted the downfall of the old Federation, and we all fell down. How much by loss of hope *because* of that prediction? I have decided purely and simply that the oracle is a crutch – I don't say that it doesn't work, merely that it is a crutch, and we are not lame, my friend … we are not lame if we only care to take a look!'

'But I don't see where the lameness comes in! There is no loss of free will. The *ching* doesn't decide *for* us!'

'Free will is more than just freedom and decision, Peter – it is much much more – it is the essence of our race—'

'No one doubts that!'

'But the *ching* smothers it!'

'NO!' cried Ashka.

'Yes, Peter, yes! With the *ching* used here, used there, man stagnates. Destiny is wonderful, the path is plotted, life is so easy, beware here and there, relax here and there, let life progress according to a *diary* – today I must control my anger or I shall fail, fall foul of the tao! It makes men weak, Peter. It makes them complacent and complacency is the enemy of the human spirit! I've seen it, why can't you see it?'

'I see no difference. *Ching* or no *ching*, I see no difference in the human psyche, or society, or shape or colour. Complacency is a symptom of personal weakness, not the *ching*. Would you deny yourself a torch in a darkened city? Would you deny yourself clothing on a mountain? Are you weak because you need such things?'

'Yes,' said Gorstein. 'Because I would die without them. But that's evolution, Peter. We can't help evolution. Technology helps us cope with evolutionary weaknesses. This is different, this damn book. It is acting to evolve us backwards! Clothes don't act to evolve man. They protect him. The *ching* is insidious, Peter. It's everywhere, reaching, controlling, weakening. I can see that now. We don't depend on the *ching*, we depend on what it represents – the easy way! You are infected with a disease, a disease called uncertainty. Elspeth Mueller accused *me* of harbouring that disease. A man with no knowledge of the future, she called me, and insinuated that I was afraid of that, and that I was weak because of it. But she was wrong.'

There was a moment's silence, broken by Ashka who said, softly, 'Perhaps we were both wrong. Perhaps whichever way you turn there is fear. Fear at knowing versus fear at not knowing.'

'Perhaps,' agreed Gorstein.

Ashka grew angry again, 'But you can't deny your own arrogance, Karl. Terrible arrogance.'

'How?'

'Your attitude, your whole manner, all is arrogance. I know that such is a requirement of a man in authority, but for ten years I have seen that arrogance as a mask, falling away when we were together, in private, friends. But now that mask is you, Karl. It has grown into you, or you into it. It hides that fear that Elspeth correctly saw in you – uncertainty.'

'No it does not,' sneered Gorstein, grinning. 'It hides nothing, Peter – there is nothing to hide ...' he fell solemn for a moment and frowned, an echo of some previous conversation, Ashka imagined, catching his attention.

'Arrogant,' repeated the rationalist. 'Deep down all men share that arrogance ... a lack of humility, an idea of greatness, a feeling of centrality, of causation; deep down men do not acknowledge the possibility of defeat, or the existence of a superior man. Mostly those primitive traits remain deep. In your case they have surfaced. Nothing can go wrong, can it, because some indefinable strength will see you through a time of trouble, get you out of difficulties ...'

'Yes,' said Gorstein. 'Some indefinable strength that is in us all, that can emerge to enable us to avoid mistakes—'

'Or to make them!' said Ashka sharply, angrily. 'There is no such thing as naked strength – always strength is tempered with weakness! This is why the *ching* is so immensely valuable. It takes all those considerations into account! You fool, Karl, you have rejected the *ching* for all the wrong reasons!'

His voice rang round the small room. The gaze they exchanged was intensely hostile but after a minute or so a mutual capitulation reduced the tension.

Gorstein laughed bitterly. 'If mankind was ever punished it was when his destiny was placed in the hands of unseen Gods.'

Ashka smiled; his nod was more reflex than conscious agreement.

'Karl ...' he said, feeling for a moment the old warmth creeping back into the relationship.

'Oh Peter, Peter ...' Gorstein seemed as confused as Ashka felt.

'Karl, my friend, my dear friend. Why do we fight? What has happened to us?'

'I don't know, Peter. Something ...'

Aeran, thought Ashka bitterly. This bloody world, it separated friend and friend and man from his past, and it would destroy them all unless they made a huge effort to leave, and soon.

'Peter, I came for a very special reason.'

The words hung in the air between them, cold words, delivered with all the deceptive warmth that Ashka had so recently come to expect from the ship-Meister. *A special reason. Not just to see you, or to talk to you, to explain or to beg understanding, but a special reason.* The man made a mockery of everything that Ashka cared for. A mockery! He was without compassion, without even a concept of compassion.

Gorstein might have broken the uneasy silence, but an all too familiar sound penetrated the thin glass of the viewing window and reached their ears.

'That was a scream,' said Gorstein, glancing towards the window.

'It sounded very like … Elspeth Mueller …'

They rose together, faded down the room's illumination and stared out into the alien night.

Ashka increased the magnification of the window and the body came abruptly into sharply defined focus. She lay sprawled on the soft ground, blood staining her short black hair, her arms out-stretched and fingers digging into the turf in agony. Face down it was difficult to tell whether she was alive or dead. A fragment of rock lay beside her skull, chipped and shaped, quite obviously a throwing knife that had glanced off her head rather than thudding in. Ashka thought he saw motion of her back – breathing.

'Send someone for her,' he said, and when Gorstein made no move: 'Karl?'

'Why do you want to help her? With Mueller dead an obstacle is removed from your path, no?'

'It had never occurred to me,' whispered Ashka, looking up into the smiling face of the shipMeister. 'Are you going to leave her there to die?'

'She's dead already.'

'She's breathing.'

'Then she would do well to stop breathing.' Still staring at the body Gorstein's tone and manner were filled with menace. He seemed to be considering what to do, torn between two courses and unable to decide. He glanced at Ashka and away, back at Elspeth's motionless form. 'What to do,' he said, and smiled.

'Shall I consult the *ching*?' Sarcastic, but only a mask for the confusion he was well aware he felt. 'Yes, Peter, I'd dearly love to drag her into the ship and cut her throat. But I'd better not. Not yet. Maybe not ever.' He glanced at Ashka.

What *does* he want, wondered the rationalist, and intuition began to fill his mind's eye with future situations that scared him considerably.

'So you'll leave her there to die,' he said loudly, letting the anger show in his voice. 'Well, I shan't.'

Gorstein's hand was a painful pressure on his arm, dragging him back to the window. 'You'll do nothing. Look.'

An Aerani youth, and the native girl he had seen at the hunt earlier today, were hauling Elspeth's heavy body away from where she had been struck down and into the darkness.

Gorstein smiled. 'She thinks she's safe.' Staring at Ashka, obviously thinking very hard. 'Whether or not she is depends rather on you, my old friend.' Said without a trace of warmth.

Ashka moved back into the room and contemplated sitting down again, but decided not to. He felt old, very old, and in the presence of Gorstein's youthful aggression he began to feel very sensitive and very battered.

Curse this world. If we hadn't come here none of this would have happened. I'd still be alive and vital, as I was a week ago. Now I feel more dead than alive. Is that what Iondai's oracle meant? Moments left because my spirit was dying and without the spirit what point in living is there?

'What do you want from me, Karl?' Tired.

'A reading,' said Gorstein carefully. 'A reading, a consultation with the *ching.*'

Is that all? Have I over-reacted? Has my self pity caused me to judge the man harshly? Feeling slightly uneasy he said, 'That is certainly my function. So what shall I ask it?'

'Two things,' said Gorstein. 'I want it to tell us what would happen if we resisted the colonists' wish to be placed under surveillance, or allowed them.'

Gorstein telegraphed his deceit almost before he had even started to talk. Ashka could hardly believe that a man's unsubtlety could manifest itself so starkly. His reluctance to rescue Elspeth, the monitors as a source of conflict, the *ching* as a tool, a powerful tool for the manipulation of men ... all these things merged into a single thought that Ashka allowed himself to voice, unbothered by discretion.

'She's destroyed the monitors!'

Gorstein's eyes widened for just a moment, and a smile of genuine admiration touched his lips. 'My God, Peter, sometimes your intuition borders on sheer genius!'

Ashka was horrified. 'She must have been insane.'

'She was dedicated to her misguided cause of protection. Don't call the game-player insane, Peter. I admire her courage and determination. A fool can be admired if she plays her game with uncompromised integrity.'

'But she has destroyed all of us!' cried Ashka. 'The Aerani, the ship ... everything!'

'Not *everything*,' said Gorstein calmly. 'I don't care about the colony any more. There is no need to. But I *do* care about us, you, me, the crew, the ship ... and this is where you come in.'

'Goon.'

'So far only I – and you – know of what has happened, a fortunate state of affairs due only to my having seen Mueller leaving the ship. But if the crew find out, then things will get very hot underneath my seat. Even worse, of course, if they discover the willingness of the colonists to surrender. And *that* they are bound to find out soon since the colonists will shortly arrive in force to demand the "bone-spirits" we promised them.'

'Do you think they tried to kill Elspeth Mueller because she objected once too often?'

Gorstein shrugged. 'It seems a reasonable assumption. Either that or she told them what she'd done to their precious spirits.'

'And where do I, and the *ching*, come in?'

'There are too many people on this ship for me just blithely to say, every-thing is changed – we're leaving Aeran and taking the monitors with us. I'll have to have proof that that course of action is the best course for all con-cerned. So I want you to ask those questions in the presence of several crew members.'

'Nothing could be simpler,' agreed Ashka. 'But firstly, since the monitors are dead the answer will be meaningless and will be seen to be meaningless, and second – how *do* you propose to explain the loss of the monitors?'

'That loss need not be discovered for some time. It is the avoidance of mutiny that concerns me now, not the consequences of failure.'

'Meaning …?'

'Meaning that this ship shall never leave Aeran. How can we leave and face the consequences?'

'Then what?'

'Peaceful settlement here,' said Gorstein, indicating the darkness outside. 'But for that I need the rest of the ship on my side and I need *you* to *get* them on my side. Once that has been established an accident can be arranged to destroy that cargo-hold and the main Ames drive. I am resigned to it. I think that you should resign yourself also.'

'And knowing, as we do, that the answers I will get to those questions will not be the answers you want?'

Gorstein laughed, humourlessly. He walked to the door and paused with his back to Ashka. 'I think you have missed a very important point, Peter. The answers will be that we *should* stop the mission, for everyone's sake. It is up to you to ensure that we *get* the correct answers. Now do you understand?'

When Ashka remained silent, Gorstein turned. Ashka looked from his face (which was white, angry) to the tiny pin-gun that the man held; as he watched so Gorstein raised his arm and sighted down the snub barrel, point-ing the weapon directly at Ashka's stomach.

'Do you understand?' he repeated.

'I understand what you say,' said the rationalist as calmly as he could. 'But I cannot, of course, do what you ask.'

The room seemed to swim before him, nothing holding still, nothing keeping its shape. His skin itched unbearably as sweat – the sweat of fear – ran across his body.

Gorstein laughed, shook his head. 'I beg to differ. The *ching*, however much of a crutch it might be, is still a powerful tool on this ship; the crew, if you convince them, will accept the *ching*'s observations.'

'I can't do it, Karl. If I ask the *ching* those questions, you will get the answers it gives and no other. There is nothing I can do.'

'The word, the thing you can do, is "fakery". Fakery,' he repeated, obviously very irritated by the rationalist's unwillingness to dispense with his ideals for a few minutes. 'It's an elegant word and a powerful concept. You can fake the answers. You *will* fake the answers ...'

Ashka shook his head slowly. 'I'm sorry. You ask too much. Don't compound your error by behaving foolishly, Karl. I beg you.' He was suddenly very calm, very sad for the shipMeister. He wished he could see into the other man's head, to root out the fears that were lying there, to chase them away; was Gorstein suffering the same sort of decay that he, Ashka, and several others in the crew were already suffering? Or was the shipMeister too insensitive, too chained to the moving moment of the present, to have noticed the erosion of his past? Ashka felt very sorry for the younger man, very bitter that circumstances were driving them apart. He knew he could help, if Gorstein would only give him a chance. Gorstein wouldn't kill him. Their friendship hadn't decayed that much, Ashka was sure. And besides, what did the shipMeister stand to gain by such an act? And again ... the *ching* had already told him that though his death was near it was not *this* near.

So he faced Gorstein quite calmly, now clear in his head, the distorted perception of panic having passed away as suddenly as it had come.

Gorstein said, 'I regret your decision, Peter. I regret it very much.' He was sad.

Ashka smiled. 'There is no need to. Come and sit down and let's talk it through. Please, Karl ...'

Gorstein shook his head. For a moment moisture sparkled in his eyes, but was gone, then, and the anger returned. 'There is no time to talk, Peter. You are too dangerous for me to permit you to live if you refuse to comply. You understand that ...?'

'There is no reason, Karl, for this senseless abuse of our respect for each other.'

'One last chance, Peter. One last chance. Please comply with my request.'

'I cannot. Karl – please sit and consider what ...'

The whole ground shook. There was a sound like thunder. Darkness, something was pressing into his back, trying to crush him, but he seemed to be standing his ground, and after a moment the pressure went away. The noise went away.

Stillness.

Had there been an explosion? Had the Aerani attacked? Where was Gorstein? Was he dead? Unconscious?

Ashka tried to see through the gloom. Slowly his senses ceased to reel, his vision cleared (the room was not in darkness) and he became aware of the cabin.

The pressure had been the wall against his back. The thunder had been the explosion of the pin gun.

He was sitting against the wall, his legs stretched out before him. There was a smell ... the smell of protein slab being burned ... like the roasting of a synthetic steak ... a rich, bloody smell, a mouth-watering smell ...

He tried to get up.

Nothing moved.

He lowered his head, and stared at his body.

Smoke rose from the hole in his belly. A glistening green and blue snake was slowly uncoiling from within that hole, piling on to his lap.

This is death, he thought. *The moment of darkness, the exhaustion of the spirit.*

He was calm. Blood flowed, heart beat. His mind closed off, shutting down, preparing him emotionally for the end of his existence.

A single thought pushed forward: seven months!

At once he was pulling out of the whirlpool of death, sharpening his focus, resurrecting the already dead parts of his awareness.

He was not due to die! His death was seven months away, and therefore he would *not* die now.

He felt pain and it made him scream, but he choked the sound back and concentrated again – this time, however, on the desperate task of repair. He let his mind close off from the environment (darkness, cool, the receding of familiar objects): he monitored his heartbeat. It was slow, but not slow enough. He willed it to a sluggish but strong beat. He went deeper into his mind, into the deep concentration mode he had been trained in, taking control of as many autonomic functions as his little strength would permit. He restricted the blood vessels around the gaping wound; the seepage of blood turned to a trickle, then ceased altogether. He activated the marrow within his bones; hormone flowed through his system, calming here, exciting there.

He drifted into his body and inspected the damage.

A torn body wall, a shattered kidney, lung damage, liver damage, torn, irreparable nerves to his left leg and side ... and much much more, but nothing that was as severe as the organ damage. He closed off the dead kidney, and tightened the muscles along the split in his abdomen, and that was all he could manage to do, but he felt it was enough. The process of death was halted, he was sure, long enough for someone to discover him and effect simple superficial protection until he could be carried to the surgery.

Now he relaxed, remaining in deep concentration, but no longer worried.

He had saved his own life, and only because of the *ching*. If he had not known that it was not his time to die if he cared to fight it, he might have allowed the life to drain from his body; or if he *had* fought he might not have had the ability, or determination, to muster his full reserves of mind to the task ...

He wished he could tell Gorstein the outcome of his earlier action, the way his attempted murder was supplying absolute evidence of the full importance of the *ching* ...

He wished he could see Gorstein's face when he found the frail oriental hanging on to life. Gorstein would reverse his opinion, wouldn't he? He would have to acknowledge that he had been wrong ...

That he had been wrong!

That he had not been right!

That ...

Ashka's heart speeded up, against his wishes.

Blackness began to consume him. Gorstein's imaginary laughter was triggering his auditory nerves. A powerful wind was murmuring in his mind. *Moments left!*

Not seven months' worth of moments, but *moments* ... a few minutes, a few hours ... an oracle that looked at absolutes had seen his absolute death within moments of its prediction.

And all because he had doubted.

He had doubted the *ching* for just a few seconds, just a passing flicker of thought. But he had *doubted*. In doubt there was change; in questioning there was the setting up of alternatives, alternatives that could be followed or fought against; he had known his death was due, and he had accepted it, but in that instant of doubt his relationship with the *ching* had altered, his own life had forked unexpectedly ... he had taken a course that the *ching* would have previously dismissed as being too improbable, an alternative life where his death had become imminent unless he had obeyed Gorstein.

If he could have summoned a cry he would have cried. As it was he remained silent and descended again into his body. He was depressed, but was aware, for perhaps the first time in his life, of how truly subtle was the oracle of change, and how disastrous had been his moment of conflicting interest, so few minutes ago. He relaxed his tense control of death, and let life flow out of his body along with the dark red blood that had been held back behind his mental dam.

RECKONING

thirteen

She was running up a steep slope, grabbing at the tight grass and hauling herself upwards towards the sharp ledge above her. What lay beyond the ledge was hidden from view, but she knew that if she could make it over the top of the hill she was safe. Behind her some alien, unseen creature loped in pursuit. She could hear it and she feared it. Its breath was icy. For a second she seemed to be frozen, desperately trying to haul her body up the last few feet of the bank, but she was paralysed, unable to move; the fearsome thing behind her was shouting her name, closing for the kill. There was a sound like thunder, a deep booming that made her look up. A column of icy, white snow was rising above the ledge, ready to pour down the hillside and engulf her. She screamed, but a second later the avalanche erupted outwards and downwards, encompassing her body, burying her, carrying her downwards encased in a bitterly cold tomb. The snow was in her mouth and her nose, choking her, strangling her, holding her arms and legs out-stretched as it seeped between her clothes and her body, compacting about her skin so that she slowly froze ...

A shape danced before her. Three double spirals arranged in a tight triangular formation. The pattern hovered in front of her eyes, spinning first to the right, then to the left. She reached for it, feeling immense warmth, great friendship, but the shape darted away, remaining just out of reach. She ran after it, calling to it, needing it, but the alien danced this way, that way, always eluding her, always slipping out of her fingers as she touched it. Darkness loomed from behind, the shadow of some terrible alien being, a fearsome creature, closing in to devour her; she ran from it, chasing the shadow of the spiral, reaching, begging, but the shape slipped away, and vanished into the distance, and the cold breath of the dreadful thing behind her touched her neck, riveted her to the spot ...

A boy was staring down into her face. Behind him an unseen monster groaned loudly and terrifyingly as it crept towards them, ready to devour. She screamed. The boy reached out and held her down; a cool rag touched her forehead and she saw a smiling girl. The creature moaned again, its icy breath sending a shiver through her body. The boy spoke her name ...
The girl said, 'She's coming out of it ...'

'Elspeth? Are you all right?'

'Darren?'

She woke up abruptly; the darkness, the coldness of her night-mare, fled as rapidly as the wind. The moaning was still there, but distant. It was cold. They were in a small, rocky cavern. A single torch cast an uncertain light on the edges and facets of the rock. Her face was hot and she reached up and touched her cheeks. *Fever*, she thought. And: *Where am I?*

'I thought you were going to die,' said the girl.

'Moir,' cried Elspeth, hugging her. 'Something hit me ... when I was running ...'

'This,' said Darren, holding up the carved rock knife. Tiny crystals in its structure glinted in the torchlight. It was imperfectly fashioned, but he seemed proud of it, now, holding it up before her but not releasing it from his grip when she tried to take it. 'I lost my crystal knife several days ago,' he said. 'Now I have a replacement. You're lucky to be alive, Elspeth.'

'I'm prepared to believe it,' she said. She touched the sore spot on her head, found crusted blood and an intensely painful scalp bruise. 'Where are we, by the way?'

'In a tunnel, some way from the crog. I think we're safe for a while. We've been here two days already.'

'Two days!'

'It seems like more,' said Moir, smiling. 'You've been shouting and thrashing about. A very difficult person to look after.'

'And I'm also starving,' Elspeth said loudly, realizing the fact for the first time. 'Who's the hunter?'

'I'll go,' said Darren. 'But don't expect much. There's a lot of my people looking for us – some of yours too. I'll have to keep low.'

'The crog has closed its gates,' said Moir (Darren had been gone some while and Elspeth was anxious to know the state of affairs outside), 'and the ship has left. It left the day after we rescued you from the Aerani warriors. The Aerani seem full of fear, but are scouring the country for us to kill us. Three of your own people have remained behind too. Two young warriors, and one older man, black-haired. He's the leader. It looks like the three of us are exiles now. I don't think anyone from the crog will chase after us much longer, but we'll have to be careful of those other three. They've started to head into the mountains, but I think they're looking for you. Darren also thinks that two or three older warriors will leave the crog to die honourably in the snowlands, and they'll be looking for us as they go, so I think we should get as far away from here as possible. Darren wants to skirt the marsh and see what sort of lands lie beyond it, forgetting all about the mountains for a while.'

*

'No,' said Elspeth. Darren stopped eating and looked at her sharply.

'You'll do what I say,' he said angrily.

'I'm damned if I will,' said Elspeth. 'And nor will Moir. Will you Moir?'

Moir looked uncomfortable, and wilted when Darren rose and stared down at her. He seemed to be debating whether to strike or not, but Elspeth told him to calm down. He glowered at her and relaxed again. 'We'll do what I say,' he repeated.

'I'm sorry, Darren,' said Elspeth gently, 'But I'm afraid I'm no longer one of you. I'm me, now; Elspeth Mueller, sky stranger. And I take orders from no one, be they man or woman. And Darren … I shan't try to give orders, either. I'm going into the mountains, and if you and Moir want to come, then please do. But on equal terms, that's the only way I'll tolerate you. Equal terms.'

'I'll come with you,' said Moir quickly. She stared at Darren who looked at each woman in turn, then grinned shallowly.

'I'll lead the way, then,' he said.

'Do you know the way?' asked Elspeth.

'Yes, upwards.' His laugh was derisory. Elspeth smiled and after a moment said, 'I want to find the cave of the Earthwind. Do you know the way there?'

Darren looked shocked; Moir stared at Elspeth, wide-eyed. 'What do you want to go there for?' asked the girl.

'You're crazy,' said the boy. 'Nobody but Iondai dares to go there.'

'I dare,' said Elspeth, watching her young friends' horror with a feeling of detachment.

'But it's haunted. The Earthwind haunts the cave. We'd be killed, Elspeth.' Moir looked quite distressed. This puzzled, Elspeth who had earlier thought that Moir was too young to be fully aware of the cultural significance of the symbol.

'If we die, we die,' said Elspeth. 'I'm determined to go there. With or without you both. Now then, Darren. Once again, do you know the way?'

Darren shook his head, slowly, still obviously frightened by the thought of what she was proposing. 'You can see the cave from the high ground a few miles away. It shouldn't be hard to get there. But I still think it's a bad idea. We should head for the clouded valley … cut through there and legend says there's a great lake on the other side that extends round the world ball until it laps at the marshes the other side of the forest.'

'We can go there afterwards,' said Elspeth firmly. 'For the moment, I just want to get to that cave …'

It had been in her grasp for such a fleeting moment – the Earthwind, the meaning behind the complex carving and an understanding of what it had been, what it still was. She vividly recalled the crackling fire and the eerie drift of the songs of earth and wind – she could hear the arguing, and there was a memory of her own body noises: heart and stomach, the whistle of some ghostly sound, filling her head but not the air … and she remembered the moment of under-standing – and then a man dying and Darren fleeing from the crog.

A fragment of those minutes was lost, a fraction only, but *the* fraction. She had forgotten her own insight – it had not had time to imprint on the more permanent chemical recorders of her mind. A flurry of electrical activity and then … the killing, the fleeing, the panic – succeeding the tenuous structure of her intuitive understanding of the symbol that had become so central to her purpose in life.

Brutality and insight, she reflected bitterly, and struggled for a while to contrive some epigram, some sour nutshell that would at once crystallize and catherize her feelings on the relationship between the two things. She failed miserably, angrily, managing to come up with nothing that did not start, *how like life* … and she winced involuntarily as those age-old words crept into her mind, but it was not the cliche that bothered her …

There was no life, no life to remember, no events to add substance and freshness to a routine concept. Life had gone, the past, dark and blank, was a ghost – a void – voices, scenes, faces, echoed and re-echoed, jumbled, crazy, meaningless. It had all gone, all but her visit to Aeran, the events of her life here, the Earthwind, Gorstein and his aggressive sexuality, a vague structure of fact and scenery called Newgrange, an Earth scene (I *remember Earth!*), a tomb – significant yet weakly held in her decaying mind, solely because it contained, the *symbol*, and therefore entered her narrowing field of focus.

As Darren and Moir chewed noisily on the rock-root fungus cakes that were all Darren had been able to gather (Darren watching Elspeth through eyes filled with aggravation, Moir seeming unconcerned again with anything but the satiation of her own hunger) so Elspeth came to terms with the fact that Aeran had caught up with her, had eliminated everything she had held precious and was merely biding its time before it crept in among her neu-rones and rooted out all the traces it had missed over the past few weeks.

How calm she felt. How alone, how dead – and yet, how totally calm. Her life was nearly gone, and yet life was still going on. Filled with ease, lacking totally in anxiety. As if, by the losing of her life, she had eliminated all the causes of anxiety from her system.

By deliberately not thinking about her childhood or the first years of her adulthood, she found that the years of her life were filled with fragments and blurred images of no-places and non-persons, and this served to trick her into thinking that there was nothing wrong. To try to see detail was to come up against the emptiness. Her past was that same sort of indistinct fabrica-tion that existed at the very edge of her vision. Colours and shades, movement and shapes that in no way could be defined or identified, but served to supply a sense of completeness, of reality.

The illusion kept her sane, helped her cope with a situation that should have driven her screaming to the banks of a river whose deep and icy currents offered their own particular end to her darkness.

She drifted into sleep, the food she had eaten lying heavy in her stomach and repeating on her with an almost offensive aftertaste. The distant moaning of some ponderous beast set her skin alive with the bristling fear-reaction of her body hair. She imagined the creature was crawling through the underground caverns towards her, sniffing, scenting, announcing its inexorable approach with its sonorous cries. Opening her eyes in panic she found herself staring at the fully illuminated rock ceiling. Sitting by the torch, Moir was a fragile shape, shivering violently. As Elspeth roused herself, grimacing as pain from her bruised scalp shot through her system, Moir grinned at her.

'Darren's down there.'

'Where?'

Moir looked in the direction of the howling, down a narrow, low-ceilinged passageway. Elspeth, as she shook away the last cloying threads of sleep, recognized the sound as natural, not biological. Wind?

Moir said, 'Down there, near the Earthsong.'

'Is that the Aeran oracle, that sound?' Excitement.

'Earthsong, yes. It blows out of a cave near the crog and Iondai consults it when he wants to learn about the future. We were going to show it to you the day after your first hunt.' Sadness in her voice, memory of happier hours before the beyonders came.

'Iondai consults the wind? How does he do that?'

Moir, obviously puzzled as to why Elspeth was so interested now of all times, shrugged. 'He just stands in it and it speaks to him.'

'And Darren is doing that now?'

'No,' said Moir, surprised that Elspeth had misunderstood. 'No, he's just waiting for it to drop in strength enough for us to walk up the tunnel. He says he's heard there are several tunnels further up and the wind only comes down one. But they all lead up into the mountains and we can use them to get past the hunters.'

Intrigued, Elspeth left the cavern and crept down the passage towards the roaring wind sound. The noise grew deafening as she approached, then abruptly died away; hesitating, wondering what had happened, she saw Darren approaching her. He looked up in the semi-darkness, scrutinized the figure before him for a moment, and then recognized Elspeth.

'Fetch Moir,' he said, 'we may not have very long.'

'I'm right here,' called the girl, and Elspeth realized that Moir had followed her down the passage (perhaps afraid to stay in the cavern alone) and that it was the light from the torch that had followed her down here. Moir passed the torch to Darren who took it and turned away. The leather packs, with some small fragments of food, Moir slung over her shoulders, declining Elspeth's offer of help. When they get heavier, yes, she said. But it isn't necessary yet. Elspeth noticed that Moir still carried her small blackwing pouch around her neck.

They returned to the main wind channel and Darren cautiously stepped out into the wide, low-roofed passageway, stood, for a moment, the torch outstretched, staring into the tunnel's maw. Elspeth could see a glimmer of light in the other direction.

'That's the oracle,' whispered Moir. 'If Iondai is down there he might see the torch.'

'Do you hear that, Darren?' said Elspeth.

'Iondai doesn't concern me,' said Darren, sullenly, but he lowered the torch so that his body screened its light from the other end of the tunnel. 'Come on.'

He led the way across the jagged rock floor. Moir complained about the damp, and her occasional cries of irritation and loud splashing jumps annoyed her brother. Elspeth found the low roof a burden, but she kept quiet, making a conscious effort to stoop at all times. A cold wind, not heavy but ominous, blew against them, cooling sweat, and making bodies shiver violently.

The light behind them vanished. Ahead the single tunnel seemed endless. The wind grew stronger, rising and falling like the disturbed breathing of a nightmare dreamer. If the gale blew now they would be cast back down the passage like flotsam, smashing against the walls and the ceiling until their broken bodies were flung into the outside world …

The image, the sense of broken corpses, flung before violent winds, brought a sense of familiarity back to her, a moment's pang of distress … it passed away rapidly. Just an irrational fear, she guessed.

A sudden gust of bitterly cold wind knocked them all backwards. Moir screamed as the torch went out and the three of them were suddenly in total darkness.

'It's coming back,' cried the girl.

'Shut up!' screamed Darren. 'And run!'

Elspeth, frozen for just a moment by confusion, heard his footfall vanishing away into the distance and she pushed herself away from the wall in pursuit. Stumbling over Moir's crouched and trembling body, she helped the girl to her feet and hauled her along with her.

'Let's go back,' implored Moir. 'This is stupid …'

'Come on!' yelled Darren, already very distant.

'We're coming,' called Elspeth. 'Find that branched tunnel!'

The wind did not increase in force, which surprised Elspeth. It was a strong wind, and they had to fight against its flow in order to run fast, but she expected it to increase in strength steadily; when it held its force constant she was puzzled but immensely relieved.

Minutes passed. Her legs ached with the effort, but slowly Moir became more firm in her own footsteps and eventually, though she hung on to Elspeth's arm, she ran without support.

Ahead of them there was a sudden deep booming sound, a cry as of some angry beast. The voice of the real wind.

Elspeth sensed the passage of a shockwave through her body, chilling her to the bone, making her sick with sudden fear; and yet she kept running, dragging Moir with her, not listening to the girl's terrible cries of pain and fright. The roaring approached, unseen in the total blackness, bearing down on them ...

A moment before it seemed they should be run down by the legs of the giant, trodden to death by the stampede approaching them, strong hands pulled Elspeth out of the tunnel and into a recess. Moir collapsed in a heap and Elspeth felt the girl's body dragged deeper into the hole in the tunnel wall. Darren had found safety with not a second to spare.

In fact, it was some moments before the full force of the gale ripped past them outside, thundering for what seemed like hours, reaching explorative fingers into this sudden nook to try to tease the flimsy humans out of their secure cubby hole ...

And abruptly it passed away, leaving deafening silence, a ringing in their ears, bodies shivering, heads filled with echoing and re-echoing screams and moans, but all imagined ...

Moir sat up and felt for Elspeth in the darkness.

'A close call,' said the beyonder with an unseen grin. 'I don't think I've ever had so much excitement in my life, but I can't quite remember offhand ... that's a joke. Which I really shouldn't expect anyone to get, and even if they did – not funny.'

'Well, Darren,' she said at length, staring into the darkness. 'Where to now?'

There was no sound from where she thought the youth was sitting.

'Darren?'

Moir said, 'There's someone approaching down the tunnel, listen.'

A footfall in the dank rock, the sound of breathing, of pain, reached her ears and she stepped out into the passage, stared into the blackness. 'Who is it?'

'It's me.' Darren's voice. He sounded very hurt.

'Where've you been? Why did you leave the cave?'

'What cave?'

'This cave. What's the matter with you, boy?'

'I've been clinging on to a jutting piece of rock, that's what's the matter with me,' he shouted. A moment later he fell heavily against Elspeth and she had to stagger to keep him upright. She pulled his suddenly limp body into the cave and laid him down, felt for his face and noticed the stickiness of blood coating almost every inch of his body fur. 'For tao's sake, Darren … what have you been up to?'

'There was nowhere to hide,' he gasped. 'When the wind came I was blown backwards against a spur of rock and I just … clung on. I'm tired. I'm really tired.'

'You mean you didn't find this cave?' she asked the invisible face. Her expression, had anyone been able to see it, was totally blank.

'I must have missed it. I'm tired … I want to sleep for a while.'

'Yes … close your eyes and relax.'

Elspeth sat back on her haunches and stared into the nothingness. If not Darren, then who? Whose hand had saved her from extinction? Who had been crouched in this nook in the rock wall, and heard their gasping, screaming, panicking approach, and taken pity on them?

'Moir?'

'I'm here. Elspeth, there's a tunnel at the back of the cave.'

She crawled in the direction of Moir's voice. Sure enough, far from being a shallow hollowing in the wall, this was the start of a low tunnel leading off at an angle from the main passage.

Whoever had saved them had almost certainly left their presence through that tunnel, and obviously knew his way about. It never occurred to Elspeth to debate the point. Instinctively she knew that this was the route to take.

Darren's cuts were extensive, but superficial, and though he was almost certainly bruised over most of his torso, he refused to make any concessions to his obvious agony, as if in some way the admission of pain was an admission of weakness. After an hour or two, during which they finished their scant food supply and watered and washed themselves in the trickle of fluid in the Earthsong tunnel, they began the slow crawl along the coffin-like passage away from danger.

Elspeth could not keep track of time. As they crawled it seemed like hours but when finally, and with joyful cries of relief, they emerged into daylight she had to admit that on reflection they had not been long in the cramped rock tunnel.

They had emerged at the base of a rising cliff, a wall of mossy rock that towered forty or fifty feet above their heads. They were on a slope that ran, uneven and scrub-covered, down to dense vegetation that filled much of the view. But distantly, in its wide clearing, the crog was a brown and green castle, defiant by virtue of its precision in a land otherwise quite disordered. The ship had indeed gone, and Elspeth quietly cheered.

Darren looked far worse than he was, scraped and blood smeared, and it gave Elspeth quite an unpleasant turn to see him. They inspected his wounds more thoroughly, now, and bound up one particularly deep gash on his arm with a strip cut from Elspeth's leggings. She herself was filthy dirty, and her clothes, having been savaged by knife and rock alike, seemed little more than functionless rags. She tied loose ends to make the clothes more secure, but warmth was gone and only a certain sexual privacy remained as a practically unimportant reason for keeping the tatters about her.

'Onwards,' she said at last, and waited for Darren to lead. He looked up the cliff for a moment and Elspeth coughed negatively.

'No way, Darren. We'll take the long route.'

He smiled and shrugged but Elspeth knew that in his present condition the climb would have been beyond his capabilities. She followed him along the base of the cliff and up the steep scramble that took them, gradually and painfully, on to higher ground. Moir scrambled behind them, grunting and complaining, but she kept up well. Always she kept in the background, not contributing to discussion of where to go, or how to do it. Always she stared at her brother as if she saw him in some special way. She never spoke to him and he never spoke to her. They spoke *of* each other, but direct address was a luxury they had mutually forfeited because of the duel that had been fought. At times Elspeth felt sad about the hostility, at other times she felt irritated at its silliness. But as long as she was there the two Aerani were prepared to cooperate with each other.

At no time did they talk about the crog, or their father's death, or their own banishment; they didn't seem sad, but Elspeth felt that the memories of the life they had enjoyed until recently were not far below the surface. They might have been merely numb, at the moment, and the numbness would wear off.

They walked away from the cliff, mile after mile, still on rising ground, but soon the first slopes of the really high hills could be seen. They rose some miles distant, their lower slopes a jumble of colours, mostly greens, their upper slopes becoming almost silver where the dark of rock and the brightness of snow combined to form a brilliant metallic sheen. Elspeth looked at the scattered snow and felt an awful apprehension. She had a feeling that the cave, and the source of the Earthwind, lay beyond those snows. She didn't dare ask for the moment. Her irrational behaviour jarred against her current desperate pragmatism, but she swallowed the inevitable question, put it from her mind. Every dark nook in those fields of white seemed to call to her, to beckon her. Caves and ledges, from this distance they all became gaps in the earth, mysterious pores in the mysterious world.

They slept a night in the shelter of rocks, and woke up frozen but in high spirits. They walked some more, Darren walking easier, now, and Moir herself not lagging too far behind. She had gathered rock-root and some fragments of white-gum, which – she explained – was not food, but by sucking the yellow gum from the porous white rock (it looked like chalk) you could get very happy and very energetic. Save it, said Elspeth, for when we need happy energy.

Darren stopped, after a while, and crouched on the ground. They had come a long way, and yet the distant mountains still seemed as far away. 'I still think we'd do best to head across those foothills towards the valley,' he said, pointing towards the deep cleft between two ranges of snow-capped mountains. 'They say it's good land ...'

Irritated with his insistence that they should do something she didn't want to do, Elspeth said, sharply, 'Who's *they*, Darren? That's twice you've said *they*.'

'Friends,' said the youth. 'Just friends.' What was he hiding? She pressed him for more details.

'And how did you know about the passage in the Earthsong tunnel? *They* again? Your friends? What are you doing, Darren? Taking hugely inspired guesses?'

He shook his head. Moir said, quietly, 'He's been consulting the oracle, I expect,' and laughed, softly, sarcastically.

Darren turned on her furiously, and struck her to the ground. She screamed with pain and shock and when she tried to get up he kicked her. 'I'll kill you,' he shouted, and raised his rock knife.

Moir kicked his legs out from under him and as he tumbled she climbed over him and tried to push out his eyes. His knife hit and slashed her cheek and she rolled over.

'Squatling!' he yelled, abusively. 'Coward! I should have killed you back there. I'll do it now.' Moir looked up at him, completely impassive, ready for the blow he was about to deliver. But Elspeth snatched the knife from his hand and clipped his ear so that he forgot the one fury and turned angrily on her. 'Don't interfere!'

'Don't be foolish,' said Elspeth. 'Help her up.'

Conflict tore Darren's face into a myriad expressions, from fury to doubt to pity. He rose, after a while, and held out his hand for his knife. Elspeth returned the weapon to him silently.

'Iondai told me,' he said bitterly. 'He didn't want to see me killed, so he told me the best place to go.'

Elspeth couldn't understand Darren's apparent need to have these facts known. She said nothing, however, merely smiled and watched the youth as he stormed off to sit on a boulder and look down the mountainside towards the crog. Moir accepted Elspeth's nursing silently, almost with hostility.

'Did you want me to let him kill you, Moir? Should I have left him alone?'

'Maybe.'

'Well, which is it? Let's have it out in the open. We have a long journey ahead of us and a long life together, perhaps. I don't want any festering grudges murmuring away in the background, threatening our relationships at the very moment of success.'

'He'll kill me,' she said sullenly. She touched the pouch round her neck. It contained a hard object, Elspeth noticed, probably a weapon. 'Unless I kill him,' finished the girl.

'Nobody's going to kill anybody, Moir. Understand? I want you two children,' she emphasised the word, 'to come to an understanding with each other and even if you can't find it in your hearts to love again, at least for everybody's sake, *stop hostilities.*'

Darren called out and she turned. He was crouched by a boulder and staring up the hillside into the tree and rock confusion that threatened their easy passage over the next few miles.

'What is it?' she called.

He waved her quiet, irritably. He had obviously heard something, and almost certainly someone. Scanning the ragged landscape herself she finally noticed furtive movement behind some rocks. She went immediately tense; her mouth went dry and she had a sudden vision of Gorstein jumping up before her, grinning malevolently as he wielded an impossibly bright metal sword and shouted, 'Now you'll never find it!'

She darted across to crouch beside Darren. She was praying, urging the unseen forces that shaped destiny, that this would not be Gorstein. She was not yet ready to face him – not yet ready to fight and risk being killed …

Moir shouted warning, quite suddenly, and Darren swung round on his haunches, nearly overbalancing, and then jumped to his feet. From behind a boulder, having skirted round the edge of the natural pathway up the next few hundred yards of slope, Iondai emerged and held up his hands. Darren relaxed, but his relief was not half as great as Elspeth's.

'I'm alone,' called the Seer, and just by his saying it Darren was made suspicious. He jumped on to a rock and scoured the surrounding land. After a minute or so he nodded and climbed down.

'What are you doing up here?' he demanded. The old man smiled nervously.

'Climbing.'

'Where? To the valley?'

Iondai shook his head and glanced at Elspeth. 'The same place as you, I expect.'

'The Earthwind cave? I thought all Aerani were terrified of the place. These two certainly are.'

Iondai sat on the boulder and rubbed his eyes. 'I'm tired. Very tired. I've not stopped since I left the crog. Except when I heard you following me,' he added with a significant look at Elspeth. 'And I lingered long enough to be of some service.'

She had half-thought it might have been Iondai in the tunnel.

'For which we thank you,' she said. 'But why are you going to the cave?'

Iondai stared out across the lowlands. He half-closed his eyes as if sensing more than the wind and the visual beauty of the hundreds of miles of greenness he could see before him. Clouds of blackwing, rising from the edge of the marsh, seemed like smoke particles against the bright grey sky. They all looked at the sudden dark stains in the distance and wondered about the event that was causing the panic. Then Iondai said, almost sadly, 'I'm confused and confounded. It occasionally happens. I have used the oracle for many cycles, but now, for the first time since I visited the cave and heard the source of the Earthsong as a young man, I feel separated from the oracle. I have missed something somewhere. I have drifted, unaware that there was even a current. So I need to return and listen to the song of the Earthwind once again. Perhaps I can discover what has happened, perhaps I can fit the unusual oracle of your beyonder friend, Ashka, into a new understanding.'

Mention of Ashka excited Elspeth, but she noticed a certain sadness in his voice when he spoke the name. Darren went to hunt for a small food animal and Moir chose a different direction to gather edible roots. Elspeth sat by Iondai and shared his view of the world.

'Did Ashka leave with the ship? Or did he stay with Gorstein?'

'He stayed,' said the Seer quietly. 'But on his own.'

A sense of sadness encompassed her. 'Is he dead?'

'Yes.'

The wind dried her eyes, ruffled her hair and seemed to blow away all the warmth of her body. She stared at her hands and at the soil and thought about the old man and how desperately unfair something, either fate or the oracle, had been to him.

'Did Gorstein kill him?' she asked.

'I don't know,' said Iondai.

'He probably did.'

'He had been hit by a fire weapon. His body was very badly burned when we discovered it.'

'Has to have been Gorstein,' she said again. 'What a bastard.'

And he was after her, now, and would have as little – if not less – feeling for her after what she had done. She remembered the look in his eyes that time they had talked, the aggressiveness, the superficiality of the man, but a man driven by forces so near the surface of his personality that he might easily find the jewels in her breast as much a reason to hunt her down as the fact of her murderous dismissal of the monitors. They were all driven by the pressure of desire – desire to understand and to re-assess, desire to kill, and to survive, but Gorstein and Elspeth, perhaps, strove towards more tangible goals, found themselves responding to more symbolic drives within them – earth and stone, she thought. Yes, earth and stone. The voice of earth and the glitter of stone – in the earth symbol in that cave I will find an understanding of something basically very simple, but the achievement will have been the act of discovery, the defiance of natural forces. Gorstein, if he ever exerts his will upon me, will possess the diamonds, and will therefore – in his own eyes – have possessed me. My motivation is desperation – what is his? If a growing need to possess my soul is driving him in pursuit … if he *is* in pursuit … then I have very little chance. I do not feel the need to defend myself against that which he wishes to take. But if he takes my life as well? It might be too late to offer defensive responses when the full thinking behind his action is known.

Her confused thoughts settled back into grey chaos. She felt a passing aggravation with herself. Why am I always unable to think clearly and concisely when I need such thinking the most?

Darren returned with a single catch, a snake-like creature with no obvious head or tail and a line of prickle-edged suckers down its underside. He skinned it and struck fire from his knife and the boulder, and in the shelter of the rocks he began to seal and heat the flesh. Moir came back a bit later with some roots which she cleaned with water from a small pool some yards away. Elspeth, as the preparations for eating were in progress, walked to the edge of the cliff and squatted there for a while, searching the landscape below for a sign of Gorstein.

For all she knew, however, he might have been behind her, further up the mountain … watching.

Having eaten until they could eat no more, and watched the grey skies darken with dusk, they decided to spend the night in the shelter of the rocks, and early in the new day to begin a fast and determined ascent of the mountains by the tougher routes that they could see, reasoning that if Gorstein *was* ahead of them, waiting, he would be waiting along the easier pathways.

Elspeth curled up beneath a slightly overhanging rock and closed her eyes. She welcomed sleep as it came, feeling the peacefulness of total darkness. She dozed for a few minutes, sensing the noises of night, remarking on the dull earth sounds and shrill animal cries that burst across the mountain in rapid exchange, and then fell silent for considerable lengths of time. Iondai was noisily asleep and Moir peacefully so. Darren?

She roused out of her doze and realized that Darren was kneeling by her, staring at her.

'Hello,' she said, and before she could ask what he wanted she felt the warm moistness of his lips against hers. She shuffled round so she lay flat and he lay beside her, the lingering kiss becoming something less than a pleasure as attention became diverted from the touch of their lips to the mutual fumbling with her tunic belt.

Elspeth, aware that she was not in the least aroused (far too cold) wondered isolatedly why she was allowing these movements towards lovemaking. Opening her eyes she saw Darren's own eyes tight closed, heard his muffled sounds and smelled the sweetness of his fur odour. She reached round his neck and touched the sensitive skin of his shoulders, and he responded with a painful caress of his own, which she fought him to ease. Where was the sensuality, the gentleness of the first time?

He tried to force himself over and on to her, but she prevented him and broke the kiss, whispering, 'No – don't be in such a hurry.' Pushing him flat she smiled at him in the darkness and lowered her head to his belly, feeling the first signs of her own arousal as his musty, animal smell filled her senses.

His sudden cry (of pain? pleasure? or perhaps surprise ...) woke Moir who sat up and saw what was happening. Elspeth drew back. In the darkness she couldn't tell if it was bitterness or disappointment that made the girl begin to cry, but the fire-glow glitter of tears on her face was unmistakable.

Predictably, the following morning Moir ignored Elspeth and in no way tried to conceal the underlying hostility that went with her gesture of contempt for the older woman. Elspeth decided that reason would be useless and that the best course of action lay in letting the girl come to her own terms with the fact of the shifted loyalty, for that Moir believed that such a change had occurred was in no question.

Iondai called to them urgently and Elspeth ran to the cliff edge. The old Seer was flat out on his stomach and Darren followed suit. Elspeth dropped to a crouch and followed Iondai's pointing arm. The greyness of rock and the multifarious colour of vegetation greeted her gaze – but resolving itself against this visual confusion ... a man!

He moved slowly through the undergrowth, stopping occasionally to stare up the side of the mountain which, from where he was standing, must have seemed sheer and daunting.

Elspeth recognized the shipMeister and felt a great sense of pleasure: he was below her. He had not located her. She had the edge!

'Destroy all traces of the fire,' she called quickly, and Moir, understanding instantly, buried the ashes beneath a layer of soil. Elspeth and Darren returned the overnight camping place to as near its original condition as possible. With luck Gorstein, probably not trained in techniques of hunting, would fail to see the flattened vegetation behind the rocks.

They moved on up the slope, keeping, as much as possible, to deep gullies, or crouching low in the scrubby bush where they were forced to track across more open faces of the rock. The climb, which they covered at a surprisingly fast rate, was always a mixture of rock scrambling and long walks across mossy turf and sparse 'woodland'. The air grew quite chilly, perhaps not an effect of altitude as yet, but certainly a sign of the cooler environment to come.

They stopped regularly and watched for any sign of Gorstein. Only once did they see him, standing below them, staring up. He made no move to hide, and he seemed to be looking not so much at the whole side of the hill, as at one particular spot. He seemed to be looking directly at them.

'I think he's seen us,' said Elspeth casually.

'I think you're right,' said Darren. 'What do you suggest?'

Moir snickered and Elspeth glanced irritably at her. Then she said, 'We increase our pace, or we attack him.'

'He appears to be alone,' said Iondai. 'I've been watching behind him for some while and have seen no sign of the other two warriors.'

Darren said, 'Three of us should have no trouble killing him.' He fingered the knife that was slung around his neck on its leather cord.

'If he has a gun he'll make short work of us.'

'You mean a fire weapon,' said Moir. Then: 'Not if we attack him from behind. One of us could draw his attention and another kill him from behind. His fire weapon would be useless in that case.'

'There'll be no back-stabbing,' said Elspeth loudly.

'I agree,' said Darren. 'He must be killed in an honourable fashion. I'm not surprised to hear *her* suggest that, though.'

Moir ran away from the group and vanished behind some rocks. Darren laughed but Elspeth reprimanded him. 'Leave her alone, Darren. We'll need her strength and training in the years to come. So please … don't drive her away with your bad feelings for her.'

'She'll never be a warrior, despite what the oracle told her.'

'She might,' said Elspeth thoughtfully, 'if she kills Gorstein.'

'That's true,' said Iondai, and Darren nodded his agreement. They all watched the distant figure, still standing (resting, probably) and staring at them. Iondai went on, 'That's true, but …'

He didn't finish his thought and Elspeth prompted him. Iondai shook his head and smiled. 'Nothing. Nothing that's important. Nothing that can be changed.'

'He's moving, look,' said Darren. Gorstein had vanished by the time Elspeth had relocated the man's original position. 'Let's go. This ledge isn't a good place for an ambush.'

They walked on, covering ground as fast as they could, striving upwards towards the snow line.

Inevitably they found themselves on a low crest, looking downhill into a shallow valley from which the next rocky slopes arose. The sensation, earlier, of being on the mountain itself was such a strong illusion that not even

Iondai – who had come this way years ago – had remembered how easily nature distorted perspective.

They ran down a crumbling rock pathway which had been formed by the gradual erosion of the razor-back crest. Slipping and sliding they covered what seemed like miles, with scratches and bruises and much laughter. Iondai especially made heavy going of the simple descent, and ended the half-mile of slope on his back, screeching for someone to help him as Darren and Moir raced, risking their own necks, to try to grab him. They ended as an exhausted, laughing heap, sprawled across some low, thorny vegetation, unbothered by the welts and lacerations they were receiving. Darren sat up, breathing heavily, and squinted up the slope, watching Elspeth as she slid down the last few yards.

'Are you all right?' she asked the Seer, and the old man grunted something vaguely obscene and stood up. He was bloody, and chips of stone had caught in the tangles of his white hair.

'No,' he suddenly announced as he realized the full extent of his discomfort, but he walked on into the valley with only a slightly noticeable limp.

They reached the thin, shallow stream at the valley bottom shortly before dusk. The time was going by rapidly and it hardly seemed an hour since they had begun the trek this morning, but their bodies ached, and Elspeth longed for a warm bath. As it was, like the other three, she had to content herself with a few seconds splashing in the icy stream; shrieking she emerged and ran on the spot for a few minutes, drying off and warming up. For the fur-covered Aerani drying was more difficult, but Darren and Moir both rolled over and over on the dry vegetation mat and emerged a while later only slightly damp. Darren actually made a gesture towards Moir, a simple smile and a light touch on the arm, but Moir just stared at him, expressionless.

They moved away from the stream as dusk fell across the country, and made a camp in the heart of a small grove of waving plants, each the size of a tree, but comprised of hundreds of thin, white stems that waved and creaked in the darkness, searching for some unknown manna. Iondai assured Elspeth that the plant was quite harmless and Darren also took his word for it, curled up in a tight ball and began to sleep. Moir watched him dispassionately, hugging her knees, then turned her gaze to Elspeth. Elspeth called the girl over to sit with her, but Moir shook her head abruptly and lay down on her side. Iondai again gave Elspeth his leather blanket and scraped together some dead plant material to cover himself with. They were all very cold, but Elspeth herself was almost paralysed by the chill she felt.

Unable to sleep, thankful that Darren's own exhaustion had drained his sexual appetite, she rose from her earth bed and walked up the barren slope a short way, turning to crouch and stare at the crest of the other valley wall. How soon would it be, she wondered, before Karl Gorstein came slipping and sliding down that broken rock pathway? After they reached the cave? No chance. The cave, and her last chance to recapture that fleeting understanding of a few days before, still lay several days journey upwards … across bare rock, and thin ledges … and through snow; deep icy snow.

She shivered uncontrollably as a vision of acres of moving ice filled her head. Why was she so afraid of such a harmless substance? Why did the thought of a feathery snowflake touching her skin make her react with a violent, if repressible, nausea? She couldn't understand it. The answer lay in that blankness that was her past. She could feel no sorrow or bitterness at having lost those years of her life – how could she when she didn't know what had been lost?

Faces … images … a sense of isolation … hour by hour the vacuum on Aeran sucked more and more of the remains away. She found herself using expressions that pulled her up in mid-sentence, wondering what she was saying, what she meant. She could always work it out – the context was usually obvious; but increasingly she found herself on the verge of speaking, only to draw back at the last minute as some apposite metaphor slipped out of her grasp and defeated the sense of what she was saying.

Where was speech, she wondered? Where in the brain? Somewhere at the front, a large area of one hemisphere and a small patch at the back of the brain, or so Ashka had said. That was it, the left hemisphere for speech, the same area of the right hemisphere for geometrical perspective – symbols. It came down to the same thing – an understanding of meaning from various symbols, and these parts of the mind were not – it seemed – of interest to the Aerani psychoparasite that found such pleasure in feeding off the rest of the brain.

And that was not true, really. Only the memory cells were affected. She had not forgotten how to walk, or associate, or write – it was abstract learning that seemed to be sucked away – experiences and recollections, the visual and auditory recordings of her thirty years of life, the pleasure areas, the nostalgia areas, the areas of experience that could be drawn on in an emergency, but which were not *essential* for survival, unlike other acquisitions of life, including communication.

Was it as simple as that? Survival on Aeran! Speech for warning, and all the special motor functions because action, now, might be more effective than introspection. The ancient way, the primitive ethic. Brute force.

Aeran was clearing the redundant material from each mind so that … so that what? So that there would be a nice blank brain ready for new experiences to be recorded? So that the cumbersome memories of another Universe would not be there to confuse the new beast, and influence its chances of survival?

If that was so, it was not Aeran doing the destroying, it was her own mind!

Ashka had said something about that ... what was it?

(Panic, as for a moment there was just whiteness when she tried to recapture that dialogue, but then she remembered the fog. Through the fog she recalled that long and quiet conversation with the rationalist.)

Ashka had been talking about changing relationships with the *ching* – his and her own. It was not the world, he had said, but our own minds. We seem – unconsciously – to be aware of the different time system on Aeran, but like the machines on the ship, the awareness was not – for some reason – linked to any centre that could communicate to the higher cortex. It was in one of the very primitive centres that the response to time-fluctuation existed ...

Centres? she had queried. A cluster of cells, he had explained, which is responsible for a specific job – like keeping body temperature constant, or watching the way chemicals in the body are kept in balance.

This particular centre, this group of cells that was a brain machine set up to detect changes in the flow of time, might have been evolved in primitive animals when such changes were common-place.

But by the time Man had evolved those fluctuations might have ceased, albeit temporarily, because there had been a local change in Ireland in the Stone Age. But for most of his life Man had never experienced anything but a stable space-time system. The tiny centre had become submerged because of disuse, isolated, made redundant and generally pushed into obscurity. Who knew where? Who could know *how* many such tiny centres lay undetected and unappreciated in the human brain? But this one, this *time-sense*, it lay there in each and every human on Aeran and it had detected the change.

Like the earth current in rock, time and energy flowed in precise patterns through the human cortex, and the patterns were a part of our evolutionary heritage, a permanent print, perhaps, on the surface of the brain. When the pattern changed, the cortex – perhaps via the time-sense – knew that time had changed. Perhaps the new pattern itself was recognized by the tiny centre in the more primitive part of the brain, and that centre had then set in motion all the necessary adaptive measures for the mind to follow the body into a smooth relationship with its new environment – it had pushed away the *ching* and its uselessness in a predestined Universe ...

Had it pushed away the memory of the old Universe too? Was she, like all the others, responsible for her own decay? A lost mechanism, lurking quietly among the silent cells of her brain, set there eons before, when the tao imbalances that Ashka believed could cause such upsets in the flow of time had been commonplace and had made necessary an adjustment process?

The shadow in her dream of some days before, the monster that had chased her, took on a new guise, less sinister, but almost more frightening – for the face of the beast was her own face, and she had no control over it.

Ashka had expressed only a single concern, a vague thought ... if the time-centre was so buried, it was possible that it was not functioning correctly, now; it was essential to know that the changes the humans were undergoing were the correct changes, triggered by the time-centre, and not the effects of the time-centre struggling to mobilize changes when the linkages with the higher brain were severed.

The last thing that Ashka had said to her, before her comprehension failed completely, came back to her and refused to go away, now that she was so swept up in her indulgent recollection: sights and sounds, like letters and shapes, they're all symbols (he had said) and can all be used to communicate coded ideas or changes ... and some of the symbols on this world, perhaps on our own world in the distant past, might work on an unconscious level, prompting us to do things without our realizing why we are doing them ... or even *that* we are doing them.

It was a truism, of course, but like so much else that was common sense it had never occurred to Elspeth until she heard it stated. These were the words she had been thinking of in the crog that night when the Earthwind symbol had slipped into her grasp for a moment, only to slip away beneath a wave of sudden panic.

The recollection of his words brought into her mental focus an image of three double spirals, so intricate, so beautiful ... she longed to draw them for herself, longed to scratch them in rock, or in blood, but the darkness was frustration to that desire ...

Tired by the day's exertion she drifted into sleep, still crouched on the hillside and watching the crest of the hill across the valley, outlined starkly against the dark grey sky behind. A shadow moved across the ridge, fleetingly – existing perhaps only in her imagination ...

In the half-sleep where dreams are most vivid she dreamed herself crouched in the narrow passageway of a dark and damp tomb. Flickering torchlight from behind cast her shadow along the uneven floor and highlighted the designs and patterns carved on the walls of the tunnel about her.

Voices, familiar and yet unknown to her, urged her on.

'Who are you?' she asked, frightened, touching the cold stone of the tomb.

'Move on,' said a voice, and she crawled along the passage, beneath sloping orthostats that obliterated all but a narrow pipe of the original approach.

Emerging into the high-roofed tomb she stood and shivered and watched as several men and women followed her from the passage.

'Who are you?' she asked, recognizing the faces but knowing nothing of them.

Everyone was enthralled by the chamber, and flashlight filled the cavern with beams of yellow. 'Look,' said a voice. 'Look at that! Look at this ...'

The excitement peaked.

'Who *are* you?' she asked, looking up at the corbelled roof, slabs of stone overlaying each other in an inverted beehive that was so familiar …

Stone basins on the floor, three small side chambers, all decorated with a profusion of spirals and circles …

'Here it is! Just look at that!'

She looked, along with these strangers, at the complex carving in the middle chamber, facing the entrance passage – double spirals etched in triangular formation … she felt the excitement and the strangeness; the faces grinned at her.

'Who *are* you all?' she asked, but they just laughed and touched the stone. Arms were round her waist, fingers fumbled at her clothes.

'Stop it!' she cried, staring at the smiling face of one of the strange men, and beyond his eyes to the overlapping stones of the roof.

'You're the one who wanted to,' he said. 'You're the one who always talks about the sexuality of these tombs and how much fun it would be to—'

'Stop it!' she cried, and the spirals danced before her eyes, the light of the torches blinded her, the weight of the man, thrusting into her, stifled her breathing, choked her senses – the laughter, the excitement, whirled around her, the cold stone on her naked back—

'*Who are you?*'

Her cry woke her. She was aware of her scream and she smiled as the dream faded. The faces vanished, the whole dream became a blur of strange images, an unimportant fragment of her imagination.

It was almost dawn – in fact, there was sufficient light across the cold countryside for her to decide that dawn might have occurred some while ago. Thick clouds obscured the yellow sun. A breeze set the vegetation bristling and a sense of frost, of snow, suggested that winter was moving down towards them as they moved up towards it.

There was no movement from the camp, the exhaustion of the previous day's trek no doubt drowning the body alarms that would be calling them to attention about now. She herself felt tired, not in her mind but in her body. She was cramped from sleeping in a tight, crouched ball, but she guessed that an agonizing dip in that small river would soon revitalize her.

So she stood up and stretched, searched the gloom for any sign of danger and saw nothing – until she looked down towards the river.

A man was crouched on the opposite bank, splashing his face and holding his hands to his lips to drink.

The shadow in the night, crossing the ridge! Not cloud, not blackwing, but the hunter himself! He had come to within a few hundred yards of them and stopped. If it had not been for the river he might have come among them during the night and left them all cold meat by the following dawn.

fourteen

Elspeth ran into the cover of the grove where the others still slept. She needed a weapon, something effective at a distance, because if Gorstein were armed with a vaze or any other sort of gun, he could not be faced openly. Not yet.

As she wrenched at the tough stem of one of the waving plants, Iondai woke and instantly guessed what had happened. 'How close is he?' he whispered.

'By the river. There's virtually no time. I'll take him on in the stream itself ...' The words 'just like in the old days' rose to her lips but she let them fade away. Another meaningless phrase.

Iondai produced a short bone knife and swiftly cut down the plant. It made an excellent spear and a very good rapier, and he chipped at the base until it was sharp and deadly. Then he worked a few inches in from the point, cutting a notch and shaping the outer edge until he had fashioned the point into a recurving hook.

'One good thrust and you can have his brains out through his eye socket.'

'Lovely,' said Elspeth, fingering the point and feeling tension for the first time. 'Don't wake the others. This is between me and him.'

'Take this too,' said Iondai, giving her the knife. 'That sword won't stand up against bone. Remember that.'

She slipped out of the grove and on to the open hillside.

Gorstein was still crouched by the river, but now he was defecating into the flow, and his back was turned to Elspeth.

She hefted the spear and glanced back at Iondai who was squatting behind a jutting rock, ready to observe the contest from relative safety. With a last concession to fear, allowing her body to grow hot at the thought of a death in the next few minutes, she ran down the slope.

Gorstein heard her coming and rapidly pulled up his trousers, as if modesty still lingered in his otherwise barbaric mind. He was dressed in a therm-stable suit, similar to Elspeth's, but in better condition and probably still functional. She stood at a distance and searched for signs of a vaze. She couldn't see any.

Gorstein grinned at her across the water and from beneath a small ship's blanket, still spread out on the ground, he drew a long, yellow, bone sword, hefted it in his hands, waved it across the stream towards the girl.

'If you're worried that I'm going to shoot you,' he called, 'I haven't got a gun.'

'Why are you following us? Or is this meeting just a pleasant coincidence?'

'Oh, I'm following you, all right. I've been after you for days. I want ...

them, his gaze lowered to her breast, then he looked back at her face. 'And you, of course. I haven't decided what to do with *you* as yet. I may let you live ...'

'Or you may not,' she finished for him. 'What will you do with the diamonds, shipMeister? What will you do with them once you have them?' She hoped he realized she was laughing at him. His brow furrowed, a strange expression formed on his face. Puzzlement, uncertainty. Then he grinned.

'Valuable,' he said. 'Powerful jewels should be for powerful men.'

'I see. Well, let's get down to it.'

Taking a chance that he wasn't lying about the gun, she walked the last few paces to stand ten yards away from him, across the water.

It rushed between them, crystal clear and fresh, a natural barrier, a force in its own right, draining, freezing, an enemy to them both, but a challenge to them both. Elspeth hefted her own rapierlike sword and patted the short knife against her thigh. She knew she looked dishevelled and probably not very warrior-like, but she was bound by no particular code of honour, and needed to match no one's preconception of how a Stone-Age warrior should appear.

'Why didn't you leave with the ship?' she asked, suddenly. It grew lighter around them, and the warm smell of plants began to replace the cool sense of frosty dawn.

'The ship?' He seemed genuinely puzzled. 'Ah,' he said after a moment. 'The ship ... yes ... I don't know ... jewels, this world ... conquest. It's so natural here, Mueller. A man can really ... develop ...' He was still smiling.

'Or die,' she said menacingly.

'I'm a survivor, Mueller. Men like me kill, administer death, administer mercy. We never receive it.'

Arrogant to the last, she thought. But there was something about him, something terribly unsure, uneasy. He looked as bad as she did. She was dirty and unkempt, and he, in masculine equivalence, was unshaven and uncombed. His clothes were filthy, and a makeshift belt around his rotund belly, in which he carried several bone and rock knives, gave him a ferocious appearance, a sense of strength. He would feed on that image, aware of it, pleased by it. Elspeth herself felt too conscious of her weakness. Strategy and care were called for.

'You killed the old man,' she shouted. 'Why did you do that?'

Gorstein stared at her across the water. His face was solemn, confused for a moment. (He had forgotten nearly everything, she realized. Everything: his past, his present, and the future he had visualized. It was nearly gone. Just the stones and a sense of revenge were left. That too would soon be gone. Was it fair to kill him when in just a few days, Time and Decay would kill him for her? Unfortunately she didn't have a few days to spare ...)

383

Gorstein suddenly waved his sword. 'I killed an old man for this,' he said. 'I cut his throat, back a way, over the ridge. An old man, but he put up a good fight. There are several warriors up in these mountains. A man isn't safe. Or a woman ...'

He stepped into the water, grinning, waving the sword in wide side-to-side sweeps. 'I'm going to cut those jewels from you, Mueller. And then I'm going to cut your throat.'

'You're going to try,' she said and raised her weapon in a sword position.

He suspected nothing. When he was half-way across the stream, the water lapping above his knees, she changed her grip on the shaft; holding it as a javelin she drew back her arm, took very careful aim.

He saw what she was about to do and panic fled across his face; roaring with anger he surged towards her, but she threw the spear and it thudded into his right breast, sending him sprawling backwards with a great splash and a scream of agony; blood pumped from around the shaft, staining the crystal waters, diluting to a pinkish haze as it was carried away into the distance.

Gorstein shrieked and tugged at the spear, finally wrenching it free; tatters of flesh and clothing clung to the hook.

To Elspeth's amazement he crawled back to his knees and stared at her, still yelling, but now he cried abuse as well as pain ...

He drew back his arm and flung the spear. Elspeth tried to dodge the weapon but even though he was weakened, his remaining strength sent the javelin back at her too fast for her to avoid completely. It hit her thigh and pierced the skin, hanging from the meat of her leg for a moment before her scrabbling fingers knocked it free.

He was crawling through the water towards her, leaving a wake of brilliant red – where did he get his strength from?

She ran, limping, into the river and fell upon him, raising the knife and bringing it down into his body. He screamed again and knocked her hand from the blade, tore the weapon from his shoulder and thrust it back at her. Slippery with water and blood his grip loosened on the hilt and her last weapon fell into the current. She smashed her fist into his face, but he had upended her and she felt herself flounder in the waist-deep water. Splashing upright, trying to get a grip on the river bed with her numbed feet, she found herself beneath the shipMeister. He straddled her and took her round the throat with his hands, forced her head under the water, right down, until her scalp was grazing against the rock slabs of the bed. She tore at his hands, her eyes closed, her cheeks swollen out with the breath she held. She could not loosen his grip, and slowly his fingers were digging into the sides of her neck, crushing muscle and cartilage. Pain went, and total weakness consumed her. She let go of his hands and floated against the river bed, conscious of the strangulation and her bursting lungs. She could hold no longer. She exhaled slowly, through her constricted neck, and watched the bubbles of air burst on the surface above her, obscuring her picture of the grinning, bloody man who was holding her down.

A moment later his grip relaxed and his body floated above her ...

Icy water filled her lungs and she felt herself dragged upwards by strong hands. She fought against them, fought the agony of fluid in her chest, and found herself lying face down on the river bank, vomiting repeatedly, food and water squeezing itself from her body.

She came back to her senses and sat up. Darren wiped her mouth and face, and Moir rubbed circulation back into her hands.

'What happened?' Her throat hurt and she found talking difficult.

'You're alive, that's what happened.' Darren brushed her damp hair back from her eyes.

'Is he dead?'

Darren shrugged. 'I threw my knife at him. There was no time for anything else. It knocked him out and he floated away, face down. We didn't think to follow his body and make sure ...'

He had retrieved the knife and now cradled it in his hand and smiled at her. She smiled back and after a moment reached out for his hand and kissed it. 'Thank you, Darren. I have a lot to learn – an awful lot.'

She kept remembering those words during the following few hours as they climbed higher towards the snow line. *An awful lot to learn.*

Yes, she thought. A lot to learn about fighting, and about strength and brutality, and dishonour and strategy. A lot to learn about how to use Aeran, now that it's all I have left to use.

She fingered the closed gash on her leg. It was not painful, the juice of some deep root plant having numbed the area (and much of her calf as well) and the edges of the wound were clean and sprinkled with dark spots; some sort of seed that Moir had extracted from the stem of the spear plant she had utilized earlier. The seeds were sticky and kept the wound closed, and she had no inclination to try to discover the tensile strength of the stitches.

Iondai was still annoyed that he had forgotten to poison the spear's tip. 'If he is still alive and following us,' he grumbled as they picked their way through scattered outjuttings of brilliantly crystalline rock, 'I shall blame myself. We ate the leaves of the *nikkals* last night and I should have remembered that the root contains a fearful poison.' He went on and on about it. Elspeth laughed at him, but Darren seemed irritated too. Moir just watched her brother and seemed to be brooding thoughts of her own.

By the middle of the afternoon they were walking across gently sloping earth towards more sheer rock cliffs, whose ledges were snow covered and which seemed, along this route, to be the beginnings of the deeper snow.

Their breath frosted in the crisp air. Iondai loved it and Moir seemed to be enjoying the sensation, but both Darren and Elspeth herself (wrapped in Iondai's blanket, and carrying Gorstein's which none of the others would touch) were uncomfortable with the bitter cold. Dwarf 'woodland' scattered across these final hills: short tree-type plants, several broad, flat trunks rising out of the ground at all angles, richly covered with palmate light-catchers, not really leaves as their structure was indistinguishable from the stems that supported them.

Iondai searched among the forest (most of which was shorter than his own height) and eventually found a disease-smitten specimen. He snapped off the broad extensions of the trunks and piled them up, then showed Darren and Moir how to knit the serrated edges into their own body fur, covering their trunk and thighs and upper arms. Once worked into place the leaves became like armour plating, except not very tough. But warm, they said. Very warm. Iondai spent a long time stripping and shaping the plants to fit snugly to his own shivering form. He even interlocked two of the brown structures into his hair, giving him a bizarre appearance, as if some flattened creature were creeping through his white tresses towards his face.

With Iondai's permission Elspeth took the opportunity to cut the black-wing blanket slightly so that it didn't snag her walking. She tied it around her shoulders and her midriff, and found it made excellent insulation once she could bind it tight to her body. Gorstein's blanket she kept intact. It was big enough to cover them all, and she felt sure the bitter cold to come would change their minds about sharing it with her.

Fingertips suffered most, the answer to which was to keep them flexing, and pulling, and the best way to do that was to keep moving.

Darren slapped his knees after a moment's respite. 'If we're going up – and I still think it's madness, but if we *are* going up – then we'd better get moving. There's a weight of snow on that cliff top and it might just come down on us if the wind gets up.'

Elspeth felt a passing fright as she stared at the cliff and saw the overhangs of ice that suggested Darren was right. She remembered her vivid and terrifying dream of the pursuit towards safety and the sudden surge of white snow out across the ledge and down on to her screaming form ...

Icy fingers clutched her heart and drove cold deep into her blood and bones, despite her double layer of skin. She looked across the stunted growths and imagined she saw a furtive movement in the distance, but it was just the darting of some tiny beast as frightened of her as she was – for the moment – of it. If Gorstein were alive he was still very badly hurt and probably lying, exhausted, on the river bank, gradually recouping his strength. No, there was nothing to fear from the shipMeister any more. Not, at least, for some time to come.

And within a few days his mind would obliterate his motive of revenge and possession.

They crawled up the gully, hauling themselves from foot to handhold of the sheer sections, and scrambling and slipping across the slopes. With walls on each side they made more progress up than non-progress down, simply hanging on, if they slipped, until one of the others could help them find a footing again. Elspeth hardly dared look out across the vast countryside beyond. Because of the gradual slopes they had been walking up for the past two days they felt miles high, rather than yards. To look out during a moment's rest was to see to the distant ocean, across the very marsh itself, an area that no Aerani had ever crossed. The colours of the forest and jungle were jumbled and incoherent, becoming identifiable as individual structures only when the slope of the land cut the middle country off from view, so that the dwarf forest nearest to them seemed to run straight into the jungle that was miles away. There were clouds across some of the lowlands, and the sky, bluer than before, seemed only inches above them.

As she hovered on a ledge in the gully, Elspeth imagined she was on a tower, miles above the ground; her head swam with the idea, and with nothing visual to contradict the fact she reacted violently with paralysing vertigo. Only Darren's irritable shout to move on up snapped her from the daydream and she turned her attention to the remaining part of the gully, where Moir's lithe form was forging ahead of the rest of them.

They reached the ledge towards dusk. A distant light caught their attention and Elspeth realized that it was the crog, setting fire to its rampart torches; the light, which burned as a single beacon, was in fact many lights, merged into one.

They all crouched at the mouth of the gully where the snow was thin enough for it to be brushed away. Breathless and exhausted, they searched below them, as far as the river which could just be seen as a thin, silvery thread, meandering eccentrically across the bottom of the valley. There was no sign of Gorstein, not even his body, but they all decided that it would take an exceptional pair of eyes to be able to spot a motionless human form; a moving shape possibly.

Moir explored the ledge (more a platform, really) and her slim shape soon vanished into the growing darkness. At times she could be seen wading through snow to get to a vantage point a little higher than the platform itself.

Snow was all about them; it covered the flat ground for the half mile or so until the mountain again began to rise towards its summit. It gave a false sense of level ground to what Iondai believed to be a treacherous area of rocks and pits. 'We shall have to cross it with care,' he said. 'This is how I came years ago, and I walked straight across without mishap, so we might be well advised to do the same.'

For the first time Elspeth turned and really looked at the mountain behind her, and at the flooring of white and cold. Her shivering, she knew, was more than chill. Or perhaps her chill was more than just low temperature. She snuggled against Iondai and watched Darren as he tentatively probed a pathway between them and the next (and final) phase of the ascent. Although they had hardly climbed any distance at all, compared to the full height of the mountain, their goal lay beyond the next icy wall of rock; a day, perhaps. A day to reach the cave.

Darren's figure was lost, every few moments, beyond the misting cloud of her breath, coming fast as if she were exhausted, but it was not exhaustion that was driving her body towards excitability. As darkness cut down the glare of the snow she relaxed. The snow became a dull grey mat, cold to the touch, but less threatening. She found herself able to reflect on this strange hatred of such an innocent material. Snow frightened her to death, made her react with panic whenever she touched it – sometimes she could see a face, a familiar face, buried in the snow; a voice seemed to be crying in the distance, but she could not distinguish the words ...

What did it all mean? Where did it all come from?

Huddling deeper in her coat she put the thought from her mind.

Against the wall of rock in front of her a shape etched itself, a shape by now well familiar, a pattern of spirals that was increasingly to the forefront of her consciousness. The hallucination was so vivid that she straightened, wondered how the giant carving had failed to be noticed before. She reached out her hand almost compulsively and traced its shape in the air, following one double spiral out from the centre and into the heart of its neighbour. Iondai saw what she was doing and recognized the symbol.

'The Earthwind,' he said.

'It calls to me, Iondai. It's always in my head, tantalizing me, beckoning me ...'

Slipping out of reach, out of her grasp, dancing away at the last moment while behind her the dark force of obliteration crept closer, reaching for her as she reached in turn for understanding.

'There was a story, now just a fragment of an epic from the first days of the crog ... that in those days the Earthwind called to man and possessed him. None were free of its demands, and all responded, and they reached for the Earthwind just as you seem to be reaching ...'

His gaze was far away, up the mountain, to the top of the cliff where the cave lay, and in the cave ...

'Did it call to you?' she asked. 'Do you see it before your eyes, does it dance in front of you?'

Iondai shook his head. 'It called only the first men,' he said. 'Since then we have lived in its shadow, honouring it. It gives us theEarthsong ...'

Elspeth interrupted him. 'What do you mean, it called only the first men? It called them here? To the cave?'

'The first men were born in the cave,' said Iondai smiling. 'The Earthwind came from beyond the Absolute Darkness and possessed those first men. They carried it with them through the Earthsong passage and survived to reach the place where they built the crog. So legend tells us.' He glanced at Elspeth. 'Now I begin to wonder ...'

He fell silent, and remained so still that only the frosting of the air in front of him testified to his still being alive.

'Why *are* you here, Iondai? Did Ashka confuse you that much?'

'The Earthsong has predicted that in confusion there is death.' He turned to stare at the girl. 'I was consulting it about my own fate.'

'How long ago?'

'Many cycles of the torch, many seasons ... when I was still quite young, and only newly initiated as Seer. Your friend Ashka asked about his fate and the answer he got was not the true answer. He died too soon, and yet in accordance with a prediction by the Earthsong. He must have died in agony, an agony of confusion. I don't understand it myself, and it really shouldn't matter to me. And yet it does. Your *ching* and my Earthsong, they seemed to clash, to fight, to give different answers even though, as I thought at first, the answers appeared to be the same. This *ching*, this ... other oracle ... it has unsettled me. It has confused me.'

'And in confusion lies death,' said Elspeth. 'Do you think, then, that having reached the cave you will never return to the crog?'

Iondai said nothing, remained staring upwards, his face cold in the bitter night, his eyes half-closed against the darkness.

A deep grumbling caught Elspeth's attention after a while; the noise passed as quickly as it had come and she looked about her in surprise. 'That sounded like ...?'

'I told you. We are sitting above the passage of the Earthsong. Deep in the rock, running down the mountainside and under the valley; until eventually it blows through the oracle pit itself.'

The rumbling came again, very deep, very faint, but quite audible despite the cushion of snow.

'And it comes from the cave ...'

'From below the cave,' said Iondai. 'The wind that blows around the mountain is channelled into gullies and the gullies form into a single passageway. As the blast funnels below the cave something happens to it; sometimes it blows through the cave itself, sometimes it continues onwards until it reaches the crog. That's why it comes in such sporadic bursts ...'

'And you think something in the cave, something to do with the Earthwind, affects the flow of the wind?'

Iondai laughed. 'There was a time when yes, yes … that is exactly what I thought. Somehow the Earthsong was filled with the power of far-seeing, and in its after-blow I could read the future of the crog. I was quite happy with that thought, quite content to believe in the natural powers of my world, and my special role in reading the advice for us simple men …'

'And then?'

Iondai looked at her, his eyes searching, as if for a moment he was unconvinced of the wisdom of telling her any more. Then he looked away, stared at the ground. 'And then Ashka. And then his *ching*, his strange ideas, his strangely … disturbing ideas.'

'Confusion.'

'Confusion,' agreed Iondai. 'And death, perhaps. Death of a belief, death of a Watcher. So many Watchers, Elspeth. Our earth singers are the powers of some of them channelled across the crog at night. The wind in the voice of one, the rocks and plants in the voices of others, and the river and clouds … all the Watchers of our tiny crog, guiding our every action, our hunts and duels. But the greatest Watcher …'

Gods, thought Elspeth, determined not to be shy of the word. He's talking about Gods … and I didn't think the crog had such things. How much I missed by not really looking!

'… the greatest Watcher of all, the Earthsong itself, the wind from the earth, the Seer of all times and all destinies.'

'But the Earthsong isn't dead,' said Elspeth. 'We just heard it blowing down the line.' (Strange metaphor! Down the line?)

'Just wind,' said Iondai. 'Ashka's oracle worked not through his *book*, but through his mind. I realized that before he told me. It took me a while to wonder if the Earthsong worked through *my* mind as well. Confusion, doubt, death …'

No oracle at all, then, is what Iondai now believed. Just a man with the power, a man on a world, rationalizing his visionary power by the blowing of wind, and the moaning of earth. And on a world where the body and the mind were at once in the past and future, then surely all of time was in the grasp of all men, and if they were not aware of it, the mind itself might be aware of it (patterns of flow – like earth energy – passing across and through the cortex, exciting, perhaps, the precognitive centres of minds for so long shut away in the moving moment) and in certain men with a special sensitivity, the future might be revealed more easily than to others; not in the crog, or on the open plains, but in the site that had become associated with such power, the oracle cave itself (the place of emergence of the first men to visit Aeran, those colonists of centuries before who seem to have landed high in the mountains rather than on the plains) – henceforth the Seer had responded to a lifetime's conditioning to tune into times-to-come in just that one revered place.

Beneath them the wind moaned deeply, flooded down to the lowlands with a cry that sounded for all the world like despair.

Darren returned after a while, feet frozen through his moks, but looking quite content.

'I've plotted a safe path,' he said, 'But that's a steep climb. Are you sure you went up that way before?'

Iondai affirmed. 'There are many handholds; it's a steep climb, and not an easy one, but it's quite possible.'

'You were younger then,' said Darren with an arrogant grin. 'How about now?'

'I can still manage it,' said the Seer evenly.

Then Moir returned, equally frozen, and she allowed Iondai to massage her feet for a while. There was snow in her hair and Elspeth started to brush it out with her hand, but the girl recoiled and slapped Elspeth's fingers away.

Elspeth was upset and began to try to ease the tension between them, but Moir cut her short.

'There's a gentle pathway up to the top of that cliff,' she said. 'I think it would be better to go that way.'

'The cliff is all right,' said Darren angrily. 'I've worked out our path.'

'It'll take hours to climb that wall of rock,' said Moir staring at her brother through the darkness. 'My way it's just an hour's scramble through some snow.'

Darren looked at Elspeth as if to say, go on, tell her we're taking no notice. Moir, aware of this weakness, laughed bitterly. 'I really don't care which way you go, Darren, but I'm going the easy way. I'll be there before you, so be careful. I might kick you back down.'

With a roar of anger Darren fell upon his sister and might have thrown her over the cliff behind them had Elspeth not intervened. Moir lay on her back laughing, her hair spread out on the snow, blood trickling from the split on her upper lip where Darren's fist had connected.

'Get up, Moir,' said Elspeth. She reached down for her. Again the hand was slapped away and Moir turned over, washing her face in snow and shaking her head to clear her senses.

Darren grumbled and seethed for a while, then said, loudly, irritably, 'Which way, then? Which way do you want to go?'

'The easy way,' said Elspeth. 'How about you, Iondai?'

'Sooner a scramble than a climb,' said the Seer smiling. 'But let the youngsters have some fun on the cliff. Those who want to, anyway.'

Darren shook his head bitterly and cleared more snow from the ledge, scooping it out over the cliff; the streamers of white were lost into the darkness and the distance, falling soundlessly to the bottom of the gully.

'There's something else,' said Moir. 'We could have saved ourselves the climb through the gully. It's an easier climb up from the woodlands over at the edge of this shelf.'

'That no longer concerns us,' snapped Darren.

'Doesn't it? How about your beyonder friend, Elspeth, the man who never seems to die? He can save a lot of time and energy if he searches around a little better than we did.'

'Did you see any sign of him?' asked Elspeth.

'I didn't see very much at all,' said the girl coldly. 'It is night, after all.'

'I heard a sound like the beating of wings,' said Darren, changing the subject. 'There may be some good hunting, even up here.'

'I certainly hope you're right,' said Iondai. He touched his stomach gingerly. 'Very empty.'

They made a wall of snow, curved and high, compacted well enough that it would stand a strong wind, and on the bare rock inside this artificial wall they huddled together and tried to sleep. Sleep came easily to the Aerani, but Elspeth found it difficult to lose herself to her unconscious. A deep-rooted fear kept her awake – perhaps a fear of losing the last remnants of her past, a loss of awareness so total that when she woke she would be just an animal, on a mountain-side, desperate to survive the journey across to the lands beyond.

The Earthwind filled her vision, tantalizing, spinning, hovering, every curve, every aspect of its complex design clearly defined, almost tangible. How she longed to touch it, to run her fingers around it, to seek some release from her agony of slow destruction.

The Earthwind was warmth, satisfaction, a chance to surrender to greater forces with total peace; before she died she *had* to understand; before she became an empty template, ready for refashioning, she had to drive the answer into her brain, where it might get buried, but would always be there. To record her findings, to register her understanding, was all she desired. To resign herself to blankness with a free heart and no single fragment of despair remaining …

Her mind seemed to teeter on the edge of some great abyss; she walked a razor-back ridge between deep chasms, trying to keep her balance, but aware of forces dragging her both ways, trying to suck her down to destruction. Pain darted through her head; visions and faces, images and voices danced and reeled within her skull; in and among them the symbol was a haven of peacefulness towards which she reached and struggled, but it always remained out of touch, slipping backwards into the confusion, becoming lost in the whirlpool of chaotic fragments.

In the morning she woke and climbed to her feet, almost unaware of the ache in her joints and bones, the icy stiffness of her body after its night on the mountainside. She stared up at the cliff and then began to follow the trail of

Moir's footprints, round its base to where a shallower rise would take her upwards.

Darren called to her, and soon all the others, beating their bodies and breathing hard, were trudging through the snow behind her. They said very little, concentrated on keeping warm and placing their feet in the correct positions to take them through this icy hell.

The skies were dark and threatening, a heavy fog obscuring the lowlands and a biting wind sending flurries of snow high into the air and over the cliff beside them. Each time the snow blew up in front of them Elspeth ran around the disturbance, and slowly she began to stoop, her head turning this way and that, as if she searched for something hidden in the air about her, some evil that would emerge from behind and attack her.

By mid-morning their bodies were warmer with the exertion of walking and climbing, but a snowstorm still threatened and drove them onwards at an almost frantic pace. They climbed the path to the top of the final cliff and stopped to rest. It might have been midday but it was impossible to tell. A great sea of snow stretched before them, rising gently for most of its area towards more sheer mountain, and the impossible slopes towards the summit. But their destination took them only across the ocean of white, a mile, perhaps, to the gaping cave that seemed – obscenely – to be vomiting the snow that filled the distance between it and its observers.

'We need food,' said Iondai. 'That's a long walk and we need warmth and food.'

'There are whitewings here,' said Darren. 'I heard them last night and I saw them this morning. With luck I can snare one.'

'With what?' asked Elspeth staring at the cave. She too felt desperately hungry, her stomach contracted and painful, her whole body crying out for food and heat; calmer now than earlier this morning she fought her impulse to surge across the snowfield to the cave, and she settled on to the freezing ground and started to build a simple windbreak.

'I'll use speed,' said the youth. 'The whitewings are unused to man and his tricks. Speed is all it takes.'

'I'll come with you,' ssaid Moir.

'I'll go alone,' snapped her brother, and Elspeth, unwilling to listen to further argument, screamed, 'Go together you silly bastards! Stop rowing!'

Darren raced off through the snow and Moir ran after him. They vanished into the distance, over the gentle rise of the slope.

Iondai and Elspeth waited, arms round each other, eyes closed, trying to will the coldness away, but to no avail.

It seemed like hours had passed, and there was no sign of the youths …

Elspeth, dragging her thoughts away from the Earthwind, suddenly felt a great surge of unease, an awful premonition that all was not well …

When, from a great distance, there came an awful scream, a human scream, a man being cruelly killed ...

She was on her feet in an instant and racing through the snow, smelling blood and death with every pace she took—

(A face staring at her, a mouth opened in soundless agony ... blood on driving snow.)

She came over a ridge and stopped.

A few yards away Moir was wrenching a crystal knife from where it had been driven through Darren's skull, above his eyes. She looked up as Elspeth came into sight and froze for just a moment; the pouch around her neck hung loose and empty ... (Darren's knife? Had she herself stolen the boy's initiation gift?) Then she returned to the weapon and furiously wrenched at it until it came free. Darren's body jerked and twisted for a moment, and then was still. His eyes were staring upwards, his mouth was open.

Moir stood above the body and looked at Elspeth; she clutched the knife to her chest and slowly backed away.

Elspeth screamed, fury and grief combining to give her cry an unearthly sound. She raced through the snow to the dead youth and Moir, thinking she was being attacked, turned and ran, slipping down through the snow and rocks until she was gone from sight.

Elspeth cradled Darren in her arms and wept bitter tears, held him tightly to her own body, trying to drive some of her own warmth into the freezing corpse. She repeated his name over and over, and only when Iondai tugged at her arm did she release her hold on the boy.

His body remained doubled at the waist, the knees rising from the ground as his torso collapsed back into the snow; his skin, beneath his fur, was blue; it felt like ice, cold and hard as bone.

'I could see it coming,' said Iondai. 'I could see that it had to happen.'

'I never thought ... I never ...'

'Come on. We have a long walk to the shelter of the cave.'

'You knew!' she shouted at the Seer. 'You knew she would become a warrior in this way – why didn't you warn him? You knew!'

'What could he have done? Come on, Elspeth. Please ...'

But she shook her head and remained kneeling by the boy she had loved so much.

Time passed. The skies grew more threatening and finally a thick blanket of snow began to fall, covering the corpse, covering Elspeth herself as she knelt beside Darren, tense and frozen, feeling sadness and panic mixing and mingling together, but neither managing to express itself on her face, so cold, so dead were the tissues of her body.

Only when Iondai came running through the snow, crying her name, did she rise stiffly to her feet.

'He's coming!' yelled the Seer, pointing back up the rise. 'He's coming. Quickly!'

'Who …?'

'Gorstein. He's followed us. He's still alive.'

She ran up the ridge and looked back the way they had come. Distantly, blurred through the veil of snow, she could see the man approaching. He was ragged and bloody, and he limped, but the limp did not slow him much; his right arm hung stiffly by his side, and he peered through the snow until he finally saw Elspeth. He began to run. Moments later his cry of triumph reached her ears and she turned and fled towards the distant cave.

Iondai thudded after her, keeping up well; their footsteps and heavy breathing were muffled by the snow that fell around them and beneath them, and no words were exchanged as they covered the distance to the cave. Elspeth's crippling pace did not falter, and she didn't slow even when there was a crack and a crash and Iondai screamed for help; she looked back over her shoulder as she ran and saw him up to his waist in the snow, having fallen into a hole in the rock below; he called to her, in obvious agony, begging for help, but she looked beyond him and saw Gorstein lumbering steadily through the snow, carrying a sword and a spear, his face a mask of effort, but something triumphant about his whole bearing.

She ignored Iondai and raced on. She would never make it, she knew. He was too close, and the cave was still too far; but she kept running, lungs agonized in the bitter softness around her.

Glancing back again she saw Gorstein had stopped. He was stooped over Iondai and working energetically at the struggling shape of the Seer. What he was doing she could imagine all too clearly, and a moment later Iondai's shrill scream penetrated the tumbling snow and set her more determinedly towards the cave.

Suddenly her feet touched bare rock. She hesitated for a moment peering ahead through the white veil that swirled around her, staring at the dark mouth of the cave; then she ran into the womb of the mountain and shouted for joy.

Her voice echoed around the cavern. Water dripped and the wind whined high-pitched through some rock formation high above her head. The roof of the cave dropped rapidly towards the back of the chamber to form a low, almost crushed area, stretching into darkness as far as she could see in the bad light.

But she was here! She was here at last. In the cave where it had all begun, where Iondai had said the Earthwind itself resided!

Hollow, empty sound of her voice. Reverberating dripping of water, snow melting under the pressure of rock and falling to re-crystallise as ice on the slippery cavern floor.

She looked at the walls, at the ceiling, at the floor, at the rock ledges that jutted and twisted out of all these surfaces – she searched for the symbol, she opened her mind to the Earthwind, begged it to possess her, to make her aware—

Nothing!

She cried out in despair (rusted wreckage in one corner of the cave meant nothing to her, now, was just a part of the hole in the earth).

Nothing!

Her mind teetered on the edge of that dual abyss, balancing before its final plunge into darkness. She screamed in agony, dropped to her knees and clapped her hands to her ears as if she could block out the noise and confusion of her crumbling mind ...

A blow from behind sent her sprawling, not unconscious but dazed, and she didn't resist as a rough hand grabbed her arm and turned her over. She stared numbly up at the man, aware of his smell and of his roughly bandaged chest-wound. She made no move to resist as he wielded a sharp bone knife above her and reached down towards her breast, cutting away the material of her thin suit and beginning to laugh as the blade scraped against crystal ...

There was no pain.

She huddled in a corner, deep in the cave, and watched him, crouched at the cavern's mouth, examining his trophies, holding them up against the still-falling snow so that they glittered and sparkled.

If she saw him at all it was only as a shadow among other shadows, for inside her head, now, there was only darkness. The fabric of her past, of her reality, had finally dissolved completely, leaving her void, afloat above the razor sharp ridge that divided the two great chasms. She was poised to plummet into either of them, unable to grip on to any new fabric, unable to lodge securely in one Universe or the other, the one she had left and the one she had so nearly reached in her desperate quest to understand the Earthwind.

(And yet ...)

Now her head was empty – the confusion was gone, crumbled into decay, the fragments absorbed into the earth. She stared blankly ahead of her, seeing all, knowing nothing. In her head there were no questions, no desires, no goals, no aching ignorances that she longed to cure. All these things had passed away.

(And *yet* ...)

It rose before her eyes as it had risen to tease her so often in the past days, the Earthwind, the symbol of ... the pattern that would ...

She straightened (blood had pooled in her lap; it ran on to the rock floor, froze) and reached into the air to try to touch the spirals, feeling a great sense of relief, a momentary light in all the darkness ...

The man in the mouth of the cave sensed something too – perhaps attracted by nothing more than her sudden movement after she had so long crouched motionless, hiding her brutal disfigurement.

In blood, on the rock beside her, she began to draw lines, starting slowly, working steadily, growing more and more excited as each smear added to the overall shape ... the darkness began to clear, her senses opened, there were laughter, cries of pleasure, a sense of well-being as she worked on the rock. The abyss grew distant; she found safety ...

So many times her mind had pushed its forgotten memory forward, the image – the three-spiralled image – of the changed patterns of earth and time, pushed it forward urgently. Earlier, thinking about what Ashka had said, she had understood the importance of the symbol, only to forget it again almost immediately ... but she remembered now, even though that memory meant nothing to her.

Ashka's fear that certain vital connections between the unconscious time-centre and the higher brain had been lost with the span of evolutionary time was almost certainly correct; from deep in the brain the adjustment to the new environment was directed, and though much of the human entity that was Elspeth had been eased across the void between the two Universes, the conscious mind had been isolated from the directing centre, and the triggering pattern had to be implanted manually. So many times in the last few days, when it had finally become critical, so many times her deep unconscious had shown her the symbol and tried to make her draw it, to implant the pattern on her visual cortex in order that it could spread through her conscious mind and trigger the change – but she had only reached for it, reached shaking fingers to the ghostly image, not realizing the importance of the act of design, not realizing how desperately she needed to feed that image directly into her awareness.

... the blackness of death began to retreat in full and a new consciousness crept slowly in among the cells of her brain, and as she drew, as she completed the pattern, so she started to laugh, to feel alive again, felt the pain in her chest, the ache in her thigh, the bruising of her throat ...

As if, too long in a state of despair, she was emerging into contentment.

As if, too long in a state of motionless contemplation of what had passed, she was being shifted into a dynamic state, into a forward-looking mode ...

Shifting – adjusting – easing her intangible mind across the bridge between Universes in pursuit of the animate matter of her body, the flesh and bone, tissues and chemicals that had made the transition in an instant; and now the non-material part of her, the inconstant, elusive mind, was following, a manual operation now that the automatic function had been so effectively severed during evolutionary time. Using feedback from rock to cortex, the design, that bizarre image that all life on Earth could respond to in an unconscious, adaptive way, save Man whose complex mind had buried all but the ghost of the pattern, all but the echo, that image began to take shape.

The man in the cave-mouth watched, then walked closer and closer as if he too felt the effect of the symbol as its image imprinted upon his visual cortex ...

Snow swirled into the cave as the wind grew strong outside. Deep in the earth, in the mountain, a gale funnelled through the rock towards the lowlands, moaning in a frightening parody of the human voice as it began its long journey.

She began the last part of the symbol, touching her breast and then the rock, smearing her warmth against the cold, fashioning their release from a reality past into a reality new.

Beginning at the centre she ran her fingers in tight curves, outwards, outwards, spiralling ...

CODA RENAISSANCE

The first warm breeze of the new season carried the smell of the lowlands high up into the hills, to the cliff where a tall, dark-skinned woman stood, staring thoughtfully into the distance. Behind her a skin-clad hunter cut a small, dead whitewing into joints, scooping the fast-melting snow into ice-packs to preserve the meat for a few days. He grunted while he worked, and occasionally looked up at the woman and snapped at her.

'What're you looking at now? Come and help.'

'I'm looking at the earthworks,' she said. 'I'm thinking about them and how much easier it would be living there than in this hell.'

The man nodded and turned back to the dead animal. The two gleaming diamonds round his neck danced in their leather bindings, scattering light and colour back towards the sun.

The woman turned away from the cliff and stamped her fur-wrapped feet for a while to get them warm. She stared at the man as he worked, watched his muscular frame, listened to the noises he made – the same grunts and groans that he uttered when they loved, or when they killed, or when they ran. A man of few words, but thankfully a strong man.

'They'll kill us if we go back again,' he said, as if it had taken this long to think of an answer.

The woman said nothing. She looked at her left hand, the stumps of two fingers an ugly reminder of the hostility of those who lived in the earth fort.

A sound caught her attention, a furtive movement in the rocks a few yards away. The man heard it too and he slowly rose.

'That girl again,' he said. 'I'll get her this time. She's been haunting us long enough.'

'Stay where you are,' said the woman. 'You keep frightening her away and people are something we need.'

The man turned to look at her, wiping his snow-covered hands across his belly. His body was scarred and gouged, and the lines of battle and defeat showed clearly through the thick black hair that covered his skin. Wearing just his whitewing leather breeches he seemed unaware of the cold. Narrow eyes, framed by lank black hair, pulled into several cords and bound with dried tendons, gave him an angry expression that the woman ignored.

During the bitter winter, during their expeditions into the lowlands, and the skirmishes with the Aerani earth peoples, she had learned to cope with his hysterical anger, and to match it with a fury of her own.

'We don't need *her*,' grumbled the man. More movement in the rocks higher up the slope caught his attention again and he turned to stare up, shading his eyes against the brilliant yellow sun.

'We need warriors,' said the woman, tightening the cord bindings of her loose leather jacket. She wrapped a thick belt of fur around her midriff and slung two thin, stone knives from it. Without taking her eyes from the rocks she reached down and picked up her sling, filled it with a jagged pebble, and hung this too from her belt.

A sudden gusting wind sent snow flurries spiralling out across the cliff, and carried with it the sweaty smell of the girl, confirming their suspicion that she was there, watching them, as she so often watched them.

She had come much closer this time, gaining in confidence, perhaps.

Wetting her hand with snow the woman swept back her growing black hair and smoothed it flat, freeing her vision completely.

'Warriors?' laughed the man, humourlessly. 'She's no warrior.'

'We don't know that.'

'She's one of *them*. A yellowhair.' He grinned. The word had come to mean something vile in their own growing language of slang.

The woman walked towards the rocks, waving the man still with a single, angry gesture. As she reached the beginning of the rise the girl appeared, stepping into the open and whirling her own weighted sling in a threatening, but not dangerous, way. She was a frail-looking girl and not fully mature, patches of her shoulder being hairless and blue-tinged with cold. But there was strength in her eyes, in the way she braced herself for trouble, the sling making rhythmic sounds as it whirled about her hand.

Around her neck she wore a crystal knife, tied in a leather binding, a beautiful and lethal-looking weapon.

The dark-skinned woman smiled and held up both hands. 'Don't run this time. We don't want trouble with you.'

The sling kept moving, but the hostility in the girl's eyes vanished, and she glanced at the man who stood some way off. 'He won't hurt you either. He's just a little bit simple, a little bit violent.'

The sling dropped and the girl unloaded it, flicked the stone away. Still she said nothing, but her breathing grew more relaxed and there was an expression of uncertainty in her eyes.

The woman asked, 'Who are you? Why are you following us like this?'

'Moir … my name's Moir.' Her voice was weak. The woman guessed that hunger, and perhaps fatigue, had at last induced the girl to come into the open. 'You're …' she seemed unsure whether to speak or not, her eyes flickering beyond the woman to where the grinning man was slowly advancing towards her. Then she said, 'Are you still called Elspeth?'

The woman laughed. 'Still called? I've always been called Elspeth. Do you know me then?' She didn't recognize the girl who also, after a moment, shook her head.

'No ... no, not really.'

'Why did you run before?' asked the man angrily. 'We wouldn't have hurt you.'

'This is Karl,' said Elspeth, grinning. 'He's the muscle of the team.'

The girl shrugged, staring at Karl coldly. 'I wasn't sure you wouldn't kill me. I watched you trying to get into the earthworks, in the middle of that blizzard, and I saw what they did to you. I thought you'd be very hostile towards the Aerani. So I wasn't sure what to do. Do you have any food? I haven't eaten for days.'

'We'll feed you,' said Elspeth. 'We have a small fire going further up, in a cave. Will you stay with us?'

The girl smiled, nodded slowly. 'I'd like to.'

'You a warrior?' snapped the man. 'Can you fight?'

'Yes. Yes I am – a warrior; and yes, I *can* fight.'

'Who'd you kill?' asked the man. 'Where's the body? Where's the proof?'

'Karl ...' said Elspeth angrily. 'Not yet. She's weak.'

But Moir said, quickly, 'I killed my brother, who was a great warrior. I buried him a while ago, up on the high plateau, in a snow mound. Perhaps you've seen it.'

Elspeth nodded thoughtfully, staring at the girl. 'We found the grave a few weeks ago. We ate the body. It was the only food there was.'

Moir said nothing, but her eyes fell for just a moment, staring at the white snow of the plateau.

Karl seemed pleased with the girl, now. 'We're going to attack the yellow-hair's earth fort soon. We need good warriors, good fighters. We're going to win this time.'

The girl just smiled. 'Why not go to them peacefully? Have you ever thought of that?'

Karl sniggered loudly. 'And end up with our heads on poles?'

Elspeth was disturbed by the girl. Something was troubling her.

After a moment Moir said, 'May I ask you something?'

'Go ahead.'

'Where have you come from?'

Elspeth laughed, not, for a moment, understanding what the girl meant. Then she said, 'Why, here. We've always been here.'

'For how long? Twenty seasons? Twenty days?'

'Since the Mist,' said Elspeth, uncomfortably. 'All of the winter. Before that the Mist has taken our lives.'

'All you know, then,' said Moir, 'is the winter? And before that, nothing?'

'Nothing we have a right to know,' said Elspeth, and her gaze went up to the high mountain peak. 'The Mist has given us a new life. We were born in a cave, up there, where the Mist lives.' She stared into the girl's eyes. 'That's the way it is. That's the way it has always been.'

'Yes,' said Moir softly. 'That's the way it has always been.'

Were there tears in her eyes?

As Moir tried to walk to the shelter of the small leather cawl nearby, Elspeth stepped in front of her and reached out to touch the crystal knife the girl carried round her neck. For a moment Moir recoiled, but perhaps she recognized something in the other woman's expression, a determination to possess. She unslung the knife and gave it to Elspeth.

Elspeth examined the knife carefully and slowly a smile spread across her face. 'This is beautiful.'

'I took it from my brother. I killed him with it ...'

Elspeth looked at her, then grinned and turned away. 'And now it belongs to me.' She looked at the man. 'This is the beginning, Karl, this is the start. Soon we'll be strong enough and powerful enough to teach those *animals* what it means to try and kill us ...'

She walked to the cliff edge and held the knife out towards the distant forested lowlands. Light flashed from its facets and speared across the land, through the air, bright light, lancing towards the earthworks, unaffected, undeflected by either distance or the wind that sang above the lowlands.

IN THE VALLEY OF THE STATUES
AND OTHER STORIES

CONTENTS

To Eric and Diane (and BJ too!)

I wish to express my thanks to both the Dublin Office of Public Works and to the archives of Trinity College for their patient and interested assistance during my location work on 'Earth and Stone'.

EARTH AND STONE

The sunshine is a glorious birth;
But yet I know, where'er I go,
That there hath past away a glory from the earth.

Wordsworth,
Intimations of Immortality

Carrying loudly across the rolling grasslands the *crack* of transmission was almost indistinguishable from that *crack* which follows the splitting of the great boulders, the megaliths of the tomb-builders who had lived in this land for seven hundred years.

The man, riding on a stocky, black horse, appeared as if out of nowhere. He was well wrapped in skins and fur leggings, and wore his hair in tight, shoulder-length plaits. His beard and moustaches were curled and stiff with some reddish paste. His saddlebags were anachronistic in this third millennium before Christ, but were at least fashioned crudely out of leather; their geometrical bulkiness was unavoidable since the equipment they contained was essential for the man's ultimate return to his own age. Like the horse, the leather bags and what they contained would be destroyed as soon as they had served their purpose. Of that there was no doubt in the man's mind at all; but his conviction was for the wrong reason. He had no intention of ever returning to his own time. He was going to remain here, among the people of the Boyne valley with whom he had become so involved – in an academic sense – during the short span of his life.

His name was John Farrel. He was nearly thirty years old and in this time of earth and stone he expected to be able to live another ten years.

As he came through the transmission field he turned his horse and peered into the blur that was the future. It started to fade and the last air of another time leaked five thousand years into its past, bringing with it a sour smell – the smell of machines, of artificial scent, of synthetic clothes; the odour, the stench, of successful adaptation.

Cold winds, the winter's last voice before the sudden warmth of spring, carried the smell of the future away, dispersed it across a land wider than Farrel had ever known. Machine, perfume, plastic, drained into the earth, were sucked down and away, lost from the grassy crispness of this age of rock and blood.

Farrel rode up the small hillock that lay immediately in front of the transmission field, turned again as he reached the summit, and peered down the valley. The river Boyne wound across the landscape, a silver thread meandering eccentrically between the low hills until it passed out of view. Farrel's mind's eye felt, for a moment, the lack of the sprawl of red brick dwellings that would one day supersede those ragged forestlands of the wider curve. For a moment he thought he saw a car flashing along a main road: sunlight on speeding chrome. The illusion was just the gleam of fragmentary sunlight on the spread wings of a gull, riding the winds above the river, back to the sea.

Where the transmission field was slowly dissolving the river was a blur, the land a green haze that came more and more into focus. Wind caught Farrel's hair, cooled the sweat on his cheeks and made him blink. The grass beneath him seemed to whisper; the wind itself talked an incoherent murmur. It droned, distantly. Grey clouds swept across the pale sun and shadows fled across the valley, were chased away by brightness. The transmission field finally faded and was gone.

For a moment, then, Farrel imagined he saw a woman's face, round and ageing; blonde hair perfectly styled, but eye-shadow blurred and smeared with tears and bitter, bitter anger. *Why you? Why you? Why you?*

Her remembered words were only the gusting winds and the animal sounds of his horse, restless and anxious to be given free rein across this wild land.

How loud the silence after hysteria, he thought. He had not known how haunting another's heartbreak could be. *You'll never come back! Don't lie to me, you'll never come back. I know you too well, John. This is your way out, your means of escape. My God, you must really hate me. You must really hate us all!*

Last words, lost in the roar of street traffic. The stairs had trembled beneath him. The outer door had slammed, an explosion finishing them forever.

I'm here now. I'm here. I got away from them, from all of them, and they think – most of them think – that I'm going back when my job is done. But I'm not! I'm not going back! I'm here and I got away from everything, and I'm not going back!

The ghosts of the future faded, then, following the transmission field forward across the centuries. The land about Farrel came sharply into focus. His mind cleared. He breathed deeply, and though for a second he felt the urge to cry, he stifled that urge and looked around him, stared at the unadulterated landscape.

Small mounds were scattered in clusters down the hillside and concentrated along the river itself (thus being nearer to the river goddess, or so Burton had implied in his last transmission). The oldest tumulus was possibly no more than two hundred years of age. The youngest? Farrel searched among them: four hundred yards away there was a mound, perhaps twice his height, perhaps fifty feet in diameter. It had a kerb of grey stones which separated the dull greenness of the hillside from the dark earth mound, not yet fully covered with its own field of grass. A grave, perhaps no more than half a year old; new, with the cremated remains inside it still heavy with the smell of burning.

He felt dizzy with excitement as he associated this new tomb with the low grassy bump that it would become during the next five thousand years, a tomb so crumbled and weathered that only the discovery of its fractured kerb-stones would identify it. A handful of carbon fragments, preserved in a natural cist between two of the chamber stones and identified as human remains, would raise a thousand questions in the minds of those who were fascinated by this enigmatic neolithic culture. And a year ago those splinters of charred bone might have been alive, walking this very countryside.

A flight of starlings wheeled above his head, spiralling at the mercy of the winds. A lone magpie darted among them until the starlings turned on it, and then the bigger bird dropped away down the hill to vanish against the sheen of the river. The shrill bird song was a brief symphony of panic and Farrel reined his horse around so that he could look towards the distant forest and the rolling downs of what would one day be his home county.

From behind a low, rain-and wind-smoothed boulder, a boy was watching him.

FIRST TRANSMISSION – SECOND DAY

I have arrived in early spring, and as far as I can determine, seven months later than anticipated rather than five months early. I don't blame Burton for not being here to meet me. He must have rapidly become tired of hanging about, especially with something 'fantastic' in the offing. Whatever was about to happen that so excited him, there is no sign, now, of either him or the Tuthanach themselves. Correction: a single Tuthanach ... a boy. This is the strange boy that Burton mentioned in his last transmission, and he is the only human life I have seen in these first few hours, apart from some invisible activity (in the form of smoke) from the direction of the hill of Tara. The boy was not overly curious about the horse, and has shown no interest in its disappearance. He ate some of its meat today and never commented on what must surely have been an unusual flavour. I'm very grateful to everyone who made me bring the horse, by the way. I'd never have caught any of the wild life, and I had to travel a good two miles to find a satisfactory hiding place. The village – I suppose I should say *crog Tutha* – is deserted and shows distinct signs of weathering. I confess that I am somewhat puzzled. The burial mound at Coffey's site K, by the way, is very new, something that Burton failed to report. I had a frightening thought earlier: could Burton be buried there? There is no sign yet of tombs on sites L or B, but there are so many others that are not detectable at all by the twenty-first century that I don't know where to begin. Burton hinted as much, didn't he? I wonder why he didn't go into specifics? The tumulus at site J is already well weathered, which suggests our dating was a little out – say by four hundred years? And as Burton reported, the site of the giant Newgrange mound is still barren. I actually came out of the transmission field on the very spot the great tumulus will occupy. I didn't realize it for quite a while, and then it made me feel very strange. Further details will follow in my second transmission. For the moment, since my fingers are aching: signing off.

For the first two nights Farrel and the boy slept in the spacious shelter afforded by a deep rock overhang and the entwined branches and roots of several stubby elms that surrounded the cave. By the third day Farrel's interest in the unexpectedly deserted crog began to outweigh his reluctance to actually camp in the decaying village. He remained uneasy. What if the Tuthanach returned during the night and took exception to a stranger setting himself down in their tents? Burton's report had not indicated that this particular Boyne people was in any way warlike or violent, but this period of the neolithic was a time of great movement, populations succeeding populations, and axe and spear-head used for drastic and final ends. The megalithic tomb-builders of Brittany, especially, were familiar with this part of the Irish coast. In their massive coracles they hugged the south coast of England until the confused currents around Land's End swept them round the Scillies and up into the warm flow of the Irish Sea. From there they up-oared and the shallow seas carried them automatically to the Irish coast north of Dublin, along just those picturesque beaches that had seen the original settlers putting into shore, seven or eight hundred years before.

In one of his transmissions, Burton had given a single, brief account of a small 'rock-stealing' party that had raided a crog further south, near Fourknocks (crog-Ceinarc). The raiders had killed and been killed, not by the Ceinarc, but by wolves.

Wolves were what Farrel feared most. In his own time wolf packs were quite timid and easily scared. In this age, however, their behaviour was altogether different – they were fierce, persistent and deadly. Better, he thought, to believe in the non-hostility of the Tuthanach than risk the teeth of such wolf packs. Provided he kept clear of the rocks and stones in the territory of crog-Tutha, and in no way 'stole' them by carving his own soul spirit upon them, he imagined he would be safe.

He explained his plan to the boy, whose name was Enniktig-en'cruig (Tignever touch woman-never touch earth). The boy put a hand to his testicles and inclined his head to the right. Uncertainty? Yes, Farrel realized – a shrug, but a shrug overlain with anxiety.

'Would this Tig's people kill us if they returned?' he asked, hoping he had said what he meant to say (Man-woman this Tig and this Farrel on the wind – tomorrow, more tomorrow man-woman close to this Tig this Farrel?)

Tig darted to the entrance of the overhang, peered out across the windy downs, looked up to where the branches of the elms waved and weaved across the drifting clouds. He spat violently upwards, came back to Farrel grinning.

'Death (– wind –) has no room for this Tig. If this Farrel stranger will be my friend (– lover? – earth-turner? –) death will spit at this Farrel too.'

'Did death make room for that Burton?'

Tig sat upright and stared deeply into Farrel's eyes. For two days the boy had declined any knowledge of Burton, pretending (obviously pretending) not to understand. Now Farrel pushed his advantage home.

'Does this Tig want this Farrel stranger as a friend? Then this Tig must tell this Farrel where that Burton lives or dies.'

Tig curled up into a ball, burying his head beneath his arms. He wailed loudly. Farrel was about to ask again when Tig spoke:

'That man-stranger Burton is touching earth. All Tuthanach are touching earth. Not this Tig. Not this Tig. Not this Tig.'

Farrel considered this carefully, not wishing to distress Tig to the point where the boy would leave. He knew that 'touching earth' was something immensely important to the Tuthanach, and he knew that Tig was forbidden his birthright of touching. He could not touch women, he could not touch earth. No love, no involvement with the land. No children for Tig, and no spring harvest as the result of his love for the earth. Poor Tig, denied the two most wonderful consummations of this early agricultural age. But why?

'Where does that Burton touch earth?' he asked.

The boy looked blank.

'Where?' pressed Farrel.

Tig again crawled to the cave entrance and spat into the wind. 'This Tig is just a beast!' he yelled. 'That man-stranger Burton said this Tig is just a beast!'

And with a loud and painful shriek he vanished, running across the downs, a small skin-clad figure, clay-dyed hair sticking stiffly outwards, fat-greased body shimmering in the weak sunlight.

THIRD TRANSMISSION – FIFTH DAY

Still no sign of the boy who ran off three days ago when I questioned him about Burton. I suspect Burton upset him in some way, possibly as simply as calling him names. Burton is 'touching earth' apparently, but I have a suspicion that he is dead and touching it from a few feet under. I hope I'm wrong. But Tig – the boy – has said that *all* his people are touching earth. What can it mean? I see few of the expected signs of agriculture in the area. My hunch is that they are either farming at some distance from the crog, or raiding other neolithic settlements. Time will tell. I confess that I am worried, however. There is no sign of any equipment or any message or record spools of Burton's. I shall continue to search for such things and also for Burton, whether or not he is alive.

I am now encamped in the crog itself. A pack of dogs terrorizes me, but they are sufficiently diffident at times that I suspect they belong to the village. They have one useful function – they help keep the wolves at bay. I have seen wolves prowling through the cemetery, near the river. They seem to scent something and occasionally excavate a shallow trench in the earth, but always they leave in apparent panic. They also prowl around the skin wall of the crog, but the bones and shrivelled carcasses of their own kind that hang suspended from tree limbs have some effect of discouraging their entry. The dogs chase them off which concludes the process, but they always return. I am not myself safe from the obviously starving mongrels that are sometimes my guardians. If only Tig were here, he might be able to control them.

My H.Q. is the largest hut, possibly the headman's house. The inner walls are daubed with eccentric symbols that are identical to the rock carvings in and around the many tumuli. These paintings are absent from other huts, and I may well be in the local shaman's hide-out.

I keep saying 'hut'. I should say tents. The material is deer skin, sewn together with leather thongs. No evidence of weaving, though mats, door edges and light-holes through the tents have been made out of leather threads interlinked in suspiciously familiar ways. Wigwam style, four or five shaped wooden poles hold the tent upright. Each tent has a fence of carved bone points standing around it, and in the centre of the crog is a group of four low tents, skin stretched over bowed wooden frames making four rooms not high enough to stand in. These have been separated from the rest of the community by a deep ditch. Carved boulders, showing circle patterns, stand both sides of a single earth bridge across the ditch. Is it a sacred enclosure? An empty grain store? I don't know. I've explored the tents thoroughly and there is nothing in them save for a few polished stone beads, some maul-shaped pendants, spirally carved, and a skin cloth containing five amphibolite pestle-hammers, unused I think. Maybe you can work it out. (Ironic, isn't it … I'd normally jump to all sorts of conclusions!)

Imagination is the worst enemy still – I'd thought that particular frustration would have stayed behind when I left the future. Ah well. Incidentally – the ditch is probably that small enclosure between the trees at strip-site 20. We're in that sort of area, as I said in my second transmission. Other features along that strip are not in evidence, and may well not be neolithic. I am fairly convinced that this is the Newgrange settlement. There are no other communities in the area, and this one settlement will probably be responsible for all three major tumuli, even though several miles separate them. There's nothing but small burials on the Newgrange site as yet. I wonder when building will begin?

Artifacts? Thousands of drilled stones, pendants; axe and arrow heads; several bows, very short, very limited range; slings, leather of course – two tents used for pottery and some marvellous Carrowkeel pots all lined up ready for firing in small clay and stone kilns. Most of the weapons and stones are clustered inside the skin wall – ready for action? The skin wall itself is two layers of hide, suspended from wooden poles. Human heads have been sewn between the two layers and the outer skins have been drilled with holes so that the dead eyes look out. Although some of the heads are fairly recently severed (both sexes) I can't see Burton's. Hope still flickers.

Head hunting seems to have started even earlier than the pre-Celts, unless these are sacrifices. But no carvings of heads, so perhaps it's just a small part of the culture at the moment.

God, where *are* they all?

It's a marvellous spring. I've never seen so many birds in my life, and the insects!

At dawn of the day following his third transmission, sudden activity among the already noisy lark population of the deserted tents on the western side of the crog brought Farrel running. He recognized the darting grey shape as Tig and called to him. The boy furtively crept out from his hiding place and stared at Farrel, lips slack, eyes dull.

'Glad to see you,' called the man. Tig smiled and slapped his hands together. 'This Tig hungry.'

'This Farrel hungry too. Can this Tig use a sling?' He waved a leather sling he had been practising with. The boy rushed forward, lips wet, eyes wide, snatched the weapon and lovingly caressed the leather. He stared up at Farrel.

'Lark or hare?'

'Which is the tastiest?'

Tig grinned, slapped his stomach, then dropped to his knees and kissed the soil. Jumping to his feet again he ran off out of sight behind the wall of skins, and ultimately out of earshot down a tree-capped slope. He returned after half an hour, blood on his knees, dirt on his face, but carrying two fat white-chested hares. Farrel started a fire in the small outside hearth that seemed to serve as a fire-pit to all the tents in the vicinity. As the wood fire crackled and browned the pungent flesh. Tig threw tiny chips of stone onto the embers. Retrieving one of the fragments Farrel saw it had been scratched with zigzag lines. The patterning, which he recognized as a standard rock-carving of the Boyne Valley area suggested flame and Tig confirmed this. We take fire from the earth, he explained, so we must make the earth complete again with a small soul-carving.

'But this Farrel didn't carve this. Nor did this Tig. Is that the way it is done?'

Tig immediately became worried. He crawled away from the fire and sat distantly, staring at the smoke. Farrel drew out his mock bone knife, scratched a zigzagging line on the same piece of stone, and cast it onto the flames. Tig grinned and came back to the pit.

'This Tig can't carve. This Tig can't touch earth, or carve soul. But this Farrel is a good soul-carver.' He pointed up into the air and Farrel noticed the smoke rising straight up since the wind had suddenly dropped. He didn't understand the significance, but soon forgot to question it as the meat cooked through. The fats sizzled loudly as they fell on the flame and rich odours brought both man and boy crowding to the tiny spit, eyes aglow with anticipation.

'Ee-Tig cranno argak ee-eikBurton en-en na-ig?' *You knew Burton?* (This Tig eye-felt wind-felt that Burton man-stranger?)

Tig spat a small bone onto the dying fire. He eyed Farrel suspiciously for a moment, then rose up on his haunches and passed wind noisily. He seemed to find the offensive action very funny. Farrel laughed too, rose up and repeated the action. Tig opened his mouth wide and shrieked with laughter. Farrel repeated his question and Tig spat onto the fire. The saliva hissed and steamed and Tig laughed. Farrel asked for the third time.

'Kok.' *Yes.*

'Ee-eikBurton 'g-cruig tarn baag?' *Is Burton dead and buried?* (That Burton eats earth, skin cold?)

Tig hesitated. Then his hand touched his genitals, his head inclined. He didn't know, but he was uneasy.

'Ee-eikBurton pa-cruig pronok dag?' *Is he alive?* (That Burton kisses earth, urine warm?)

Tig said he didn't know.

'Ee-Tig ganaag ee-Farrel olo ee-eikBurton ee-Farrel ka'en-kaen?' *Are you afraid of me because you think I was Burton's friend?* (This Tig afraid of this Farrel because that Burton this Farrel were not not-strangers?)

'Kok.'

'Ee-Farrel cranno orgak ee-eikBurton. Ee-Farrel en-Burton, 'n nik Farrel.' *I knew him but I didn't like him. I have a woman.* (This Farrel eye-felt wind-felt that Burton. This Farrel not touch/never touch that Burton. This Farrel close/touch woman Farrel).

What would she think, he wondered, of being used as a sex object to a twelve year-old moron? Joke. How many thousands of years would it be for the joke to be appreciated? To the Tuthanach, to all the Boyne peoples, denial of friendship to a man had to be coupled with a declaration of friendship with a woman. It seemed so unrealistically simple to believe that a man with a woman whose sexual appetite was high would not have a close male friend … (*nik*, woman, implied a sexually aggressive woman; a woman or man without any such desires was called *crum-kii* – stone legs.) It was a bizarre piece of nonsense and yet it appeased. Like the beast that presents its hindquarters to an attacker – submission. The name of the game.

Tig was much happier. He clapped his hands together repeatedly, pausing only to chew a ragged nail on his left index finger.

'Ee-Tig en-Burton. Ee-eikBurton en-Tig. Ee-Tig tarn ee-eikBurton baag na-yit.' *I didn't like Burton either, and he didn't like me. But I killed him some time ago.* (This Tig never touch that Burton. That Burton never touch this Tig. This Tig skin Burton cold several yesterday.)

'A-Tig tarn ee-eikBurton baag?' *You killed him?*

'Ee-Tig …' eyes downcast, voice lowering. 'Ka-kok.' *I hope so/I wish to do so/I think so.* Which was it? Farrel felt infuriated with himself. What *had* Tig said?

'Orga-mak ee-eikBurton m'rog?' *Where is Burton's body?* (In all the wind Burton's head?)

'Ee-Tig-ee-Farrel Tig cranno na'yok.' *I'll show you now.* (This Tig this Farrel Tig eye feel high sun).

FOURTH TRANSMISSION – SIXTH DAY

The simplicity of the language is deceptive, I'm sure. I talk easily with Tig, but have an uncomfortable feeling that he is misunderstanding me in subtle ways. Nevertheless one thing seems sure – Burton is in trouble, and possibly dead, killed at the hands of the backward boy who is now so important to me (while he is in the crog the dogs don't come near). Everyone who should be here is 'touching earth'. You might dispense with that as something unimportant – tilling the ground somewhere? Planting seeds? Nothing of the sort.

Tig led the way across the hills, some miles from the river. The forest is patchy across the downs, never really managing to take a dominant hold on the land – trees in great dense clusters hang to the tops of some hills and the valleys of others so that as one walks across the country there appear to be bald knolls poking through the foliage on all sides. Tig himself is inordinately afraid of the woods and skirts them with such deliberation that I feel some dark memory must be lying within his poor, backward skull.

After about an hour we waded across a small stream and ran swiftly (Tig covering his head with his hands and wailing all the time) through a thinly populated woodland, emerging on the rising slope of one such bald hill that I had seen earlier. Boulders probed through the soil which was perhaps not deep enough to support the tree life. There were shallow carvings on many of the boulders and Tig touched some of these reverently. Most noticeable about this hill, and most puzzling – and indeed, most alarming – was the profusion of small earth mounds, overgrown with a sparse layer of grass and invisible from any substantial distance. Tig ran among these mounds, the highest of which was no more than four or five inches from the ground and vaguely cross-shaped, and eventually found a resting position on one of the least carved boulders. His stiffly crouched figure seemed overwhelmed by fear and regret, his hair sticking out from his head like some bizarre thorn growth, his thin limbs smeared with dirt and crusted with his own faeces. He stared at me with an expression of total confusion and I tried to put him at his ease but he turned half away from me and began to vocalize an imitation of the lark song that echoed around us from the vast early spring population.

I asked him about Burton and he merely clapped his hands together and shrilled all the louder.

You will have the picture – I appeared to be standing in a wide and irregularly laid-out cemetery. Crouching over the nearest mound I excavated a little of the earth away. A few inches below the surface my fingernails raked flesh and came away bloody!

I can't explain it but I panicked completely. Some terrible dread crept into my whole body, some inexplicable fear of what I was witnessing. I left Tig sitting there singing with the larks and starlings and ran back to the crog. I shook for hours and failed to sleep that night. The blood beneath my nails clotted and blackened and when I tried to wash it away it wouldn't come. In my frantic efforts to clean the stain I tore one of my nails right back to the quick and that sudden, appalling pain brought me back to my senses. I can't explain it. My reaction was panic. Something external possessed me for an instant and I was psychologically unready for the power of it. There is something in the ground of that hill, and I don't just mean a body.

I shall return tomorrow and report again.

Farrel left the crog at dawn. The grass was wet underfoot, and across the valley a heavy mist hung silent and sombre. The birds seemed quieter today and what song he heard was often drowned by the murmur of the trees and the disturbing crying of the wind.

Strange, he thought, how mist seems to tangle itself in the forest, hanging in the branches like cotton.

He made his way back towards the strange cemetery on the hill, stopping occasionally to listen to the stillness, hoping to hear Tig crashing towards him, or calling him. When he emerged onto the hillside the mist had lifted and he could see, from the top of the knoll, the river Boyne and the scattered tumuli of the Tuthanach. He could see the hills where, in the next few years, work would begin on the massive sheer-fronted mounds of Newgrange. Who or what, he wondered, would be honoured by that vast structure? And who or what would be honoured by the second and third giant tumuli, built to the east and west of Newgrange at almost the same time (and not centuries earlier as the dating techniques of Farrel's time had suggested).

Of Tig there was no sign. The larks began to sing quite suddenly and sunlight pierced the early morning clouds, setting the forest alive with light and colour. As if – reflected Farrel – some force of night and cold had suddenly gone. Normal service being resumed ...

Where he had dug in the soil of one of the human burial places yesterday, there was now no sign of interference. The earth was smooth and quite firmly packed. Tig, probably, had repaired the damage.

Farrel wasted no time in excavating down to the flesh again. He felt a cold unease as he cleared the soil from the naked back of the Tuthanach male, that same surge of panic, but today he controlled it. He scooped the earth out of the narrow trench until the man's body lay exposed from head to buttocks. Face down in the mud the man looked dead; his skin was cold and pale grey, the pallor of death. His arms were outstretched on either side and Farrel, on impulse, dug the soil away from one limb to discover the fingers, clenched firm into the earth as if gripping.

Turning the man's head over Farrel felt a jolt of disgust, a fleeting nausea. Open mouthed, open eyed, the earth was everywhere. It fell from the pale lips, a huge bolus of soil, dry, wormy. It fell from his nostrils and from his ears – it packed across his eyeballs, under the lids, like some obscene blindness.

Surely the man was dead; but the flesh was firm – cold, yet not in that rigidity associated with recent death, nor the moving liquefaction associated with decay. Easing the body down again Farrel put his ear to the naked back, listened for the heart.

For a long time he heard nothing. Minutes passed and he felt sure the heart was dead. Then ...

A single powerful beat. Unmistakable!

Over the course of half an hour Farrel ascertained that the buried man's heart was beating once every four minutes, a powerful, unnaturally sustained contraction, as if the organ were forcing round some viscous fluid and not the easy liquid blood it was used to ...

An unnerving thought occurred to Farrel and for a second he was ready to cut a vein in the man's hand – but, quite irrationally, fear of what he would find dripping from the body held him back until he recollected the blood under his fingernails and felt a strange relief.

He stood above the body, staring down at the un-dead corpse, then let his gaze wander across the countryside. The spring breeze irritated his scalp by catching the clay-stiffened strands of his hair and bending them at its will. As he stood on the knoll he grew irritated with his make-up and wished he could be clothed in denim shorts and a loose cotton shirt instead of being wrapped in skin that smelled of its previous owner and attracted flies.

Everything, bar this cemetery, was so normal.

The tumuli, the crog, the weapons and pottery, the hunting, the language – it was all just what he had expected, a new stone age colony, conscious of religion, of its ancestry, its future and its agriculture, a colony just a few generations into its life in this green and bountiful land. Further north and south were other communities. Farrel had seen the signs of them, and had read reports about them from previous expeditions to this time. Some were larger than the Tuthanach, some already showing different cultural styles. They all seemed to mix and mingle together (so Tig said) to exchange ideas, to form joint hunting trips during the winter, to compare art forms and techniques of etching them into the rock. They were basically agricultural and peaceful. They feared the Moaning Ones from the earth, and the rock stealers from across the sea, some miles to the east. But for the most part they lived without fear, growing and maturing, becoming ready to accept the new Age of Bronze, still some eight hundred years in their future, at a time when the peacefulness of this country would be shattered by the new sounds of metal clashing with metal.

All those settlements had mixed together and had welcomed Burton – so he had reported – during his first four days in the valley. He had not told them from where he came (his arrival site, like Farrel's) for if the Ceinarc and the Tagda were passively afraid of the Moaning Ones and the Breton raiders, they held a healthy and active hostility for one other thing – crog-Tutha, and the insane settlers from beyond the forest. They would not float their coracles through the wide bend of the Boyne that took them round the foot of the Tuthanach hills, with their scattered mounds and shrieking women. It was a fearsome area, and one where no man could go and return unpossessed.

Reading the reports five thousand years away, Farrel had at first thought this to be a typical piece of forest-fearing, with the settlement on the wrong side of that forest being linked to those same dark forces. He had dismissed them aloud.

Now he realized he shouldn't have dismissed them at all.

There was something wholly unnatural about the people of crog-Tutha. He had travelled more than five thousand years through time and expected surprises – but he had not anticipated being so totally mystified. This was not the simple life of a primitive people – it was something out of the dark corners of the supernatural!

No one up-time would believe him, he was sure of that.

FIFTH TRANSMISSION – SEVENTH DAY (EXTRACT)

... and as I filled the grave back in, Tig appeared at the edge of the wood. He ran up the hill and crouched over the mound, watching fascinated as I covered the body of the Tuthanach. I get the feeling that Tig, when he vanishes, is never far away. I always have an acutely uncomfortable feeling of being watched, and I suspect that wherever I go Tig is never far behind. What do I represent to him, I wonder? He is afraid of me still, and still refuses to show me where Burton is buried (if indeed he *is* buried). There are too many mounds on the knoll to excavate them all on an off-chance, so I really do need the boy to open up a little more.

I sat for an hour or so, on a boulder, looking across the forest to where the great crog on Tara was in evidence as a winding spiral of black smoke. The encampment there. Tig tells me, is surrounded by a wooden post-fence and seems to be more hostile than the other crogs. He says they are raising earth-works behind the wooden walls; does that suggest the first dun is being raised on the site? Fascinating. I have no idea how Tig knows this. Tara lies four days to the south. Would he wander that far?

While I watched Tara Tig sat quietly, chewing moodily on the remnants of one of those hares. I didn't ask him about Burton, or about anything. I hoped he would tell me of his own accord. His eyes suddenly grew wide and the bone dropped from his fingers. He was looking up at the knoll and I turned to see what had scared him. It gave me quite a turn too, and I don't blame Tig for scampering off.

One of the graves was moving, as if the body it contained was trying to force its way out. As if ...? First the man's hands poked through the ground, the fingers bloody and dirty. Then the earth fell away from where his head was raising up and his whole body followed. He stood upright, black with dirt, and earth fell from his ears and mouth. He spat violently and shook more vigorously, brushing soil from his chest and arms. I hid behind the boulder and watched as the strange apparition turned slowly round, looking upwards into the sky through eyes still caked with dirt. He was sexually aroused and the skin of his penis was lacerated and dripping blood profusely. I have the uncomfortable feeling that he had been copulating with the earth.

Several minutes of brushing and shaking exposed his skin again, cleared his eyes and nostrils and he seemed to get his bearings. He swept back his hair, which showed yellow through the mud, and ran off down the knoll, leaping the mounds and entering the woodlands with loud shrieks and pain-ful crashes.

I followed him to a small stream, a tributary of the Boyne, and watched him crouching in the flow, washing and splashing, and emptying his bowels of a phenomenal amount of soil. He warbled bird song and laughed in abrupt, almost humourless bursts. He seemed to wash himself for hours, but finally crawled up onto the bank and sat quietly for a while, obviously sensing and enjoying the scenery around him. Then he rose to his feet, waded the stream, and vanished towards the crog.

That all occurred a few minutes ago and it means I shall not return there myself. I'm too puzzled and too frightened if you must know. I have my transmission equipment with me, but medication and field-link pack are still in the crog, which means I'm trapped here for a while, and must be careful not to injure myself.

When Farrel arrived back at the knoll Tig was crouched over one of the mounds, the only one to show a good grassy overlay, and poking at it. He saw Farrel approaching and ran away, leapt onto a boulder and slapped his hands together.

Farrel stared at him for a moment, then at the grave, and an icy unease crept into his mind. Oh no, he thought. Oh God, this is the moment.

The boy gibbered something incoherent.

Farrel asked, 'Ee-eikBurton 'n cruig pad-cruig?' *Is Burton buried here? …* (Touching earth, feet on earth?)

'Don't know.'

Farrel sensed the lie. He dropped to his knees and scrabbled at the soil and after a moment he found himself staring at black hair, the back of Burton's head. 'Thank God,' cried Farrel, and grinned at the boy.

What should he do though? It might be dangerous to move the man – the best thing would be to leave Burton alone until the strange process had finished and he resurrected himself in the 'natural' way.

But Farrel found he could not resist examining his colleague in the same way as he had examined the Tuthanach earlier. He scraped back the earth from Burton's head and shoulders.

A funny smell.

For a moment his hands hesitated; he stared silently and motionlessly at the body beneath him. The skin was grey, cold – that was, by all accounts, normal. But there was something wrong, something indefinable, something not quite right.

He reached down and turned Burton's head sideways. Earth poured from empty sockets, worms fell from the gaping, toothy mouth. Where skin remained it was taut and shrunken. Putrefaction rose from the rotting brains through the holes in the skull, driving Farrel to his feet with a terrible scream.

Sweeping back the earth from the torso he found the thigh bone fragment that had been driven into Burton's heart as he lay there, thrusting through the rib cage from behind, ripping skin and flesh and cracking bone. The clenched fists of his colleague took on a new significance. He had died in agony.

For a moment Farrel screamed abuse at Tig for what he had done, then his anger drained away. There was something in the boy's eyes, something in his expression … Farrel felt instantly terrified. He reached out towards Tig and shook his head.

'I'm sorry, Tig. Burton called you a beast … I understand…'

'Not once. Many times,' said Tig. 'I hated Burton. I gave Burton everything he had earned.'

Tentatively Farrel touched the boy's shoulder and when Tig did not flinch he secured the grip and smiled. 'Burton was not my friend … but he was known to me and he was important to me. I was upset to see him dead. Forgive me, Tig. I didn't mean what I said.'

'I didn't understand what you said.'

Farrel, guiltily, realized he had shouted in English. He laughed quietly, almost thankfully. He wouldn't have wanted the boy to hear what he had called him. He needed sleep too much and the boy was potentially very lethal.

He walked back to Burton's body and covered it over. A few feet away another mound began to move and Farrel and Tig ran out of sight and watched.

SIXTH TRANSMISSION – EIGHTH DAY

Burton is dead. Tig killed him, perhaps some months ago. I am terrified of Tig now and don't dare question him further about Burton. If only I knew where Burton's equipment was hidden. Tig knows, I'm sure of it. He has hidden it. I pray that in the same way that he indicated Burton's grave to me (uncompromisingly) he will lead me to Burton's records. Burton understood what I have been watching, he must have done – he participated.

Meanwhile I am back in the cave and Tig, now, is in full control. I sleep fitfully and in snatches – terrified of him striking when my defences are down. I woke, last night, to find him crouching over me, peering at my sleeping face. I dare not ask him to refrain from startling me like this. My head hurts and my heart is in pain, as if in anticipation of a long-bone shaft being driven through it.

I can't get my field-link equipment. The crog is active again. Over the last day many Tuthanach have risen from the earth and returned to their homes – men, women, children, they return with bountiful energy and begin to lead a life no different from the Ceinarc or the Tagda – what *were* they doing in the earth? What have they gained? What was the purpose of it all?

SEVENTH TRANSMISSION – TENTH DAY

The trickle of Tuthanach returning to their crog has ceased. They are all home. I remain in the cave, uncertain, insecure. Tig hunts on my behalf, but no longer eats with me. He has become very affectionate, but behind the kindness is a repressed anger that I truly fear. Sometimes he stands in the cave entrance and shrieks with laughter. The garble of words he yells refers to Burton and to me, and I hear 'stone legs' and 'twisting head', two favourite Tuthanach insults. He invariably ends his tirade of abuse by defecating in the cave mouth and elaborately holding his nose and backing away. And a few hours later he brings me a hare or a brace of fat doves, some gift, some appeasement for his show of fury. A bizarre boy and not – I now realize – backward at all, but in some way insane. Listen to me! Do I understand the meaning of my own words any more? What do I mean – insane? Is my behaviour sane? Tig is more than just a boy. I suspect he was chosen for his role – Tig-never-touch-woman-never-touch-earth; the only Tuthanach not to touch earth in the strange way I have described ... why? Why Tig? Or should I ask, why *one Tuthanach?* What was he watching for? What are they asking of him now? What role does he fill?

Tig seems aware of some finality in his role. On his most recent visit he came with a large chunk of meat – deer, I think. Tears filled his eyes as he passed the joint to me and accepted a small portion back. We ate in silence. As he chewed he watched me, and tears flooded down his cheeks. 'Farrel, my friend, my dear friend,' he said, over and over. The warmth was immense. The Tuthanach have no way of expressing magnificent friendship and he struggled to voice his feelings and I eventually had to stop him. I had understood. 'Farrel and Tig are the only ones not to touch earth,' he said. 'Tig can't, but Farrel ...'

Time and time again he began that sentence, staring at me. Each time he said it I was filled with his intensity, and with my own anxiety. The thought is terrifying, truly terrifying.

Then the anger from the boy, the shrieking. He raced out into the dusk and vanished swiftly. I face another night alone, more than half afraid to close my eyes ... not just Tig, though that is certainly a part of it, but the past ... my past. I am haunted by memories and faces; they fill my dreams, and I can sense my own time in everything I smell or see here. It is insecurity that makes me rue the warmth of civilization, and I shall not bend to any great desire to return; but it hurts, sometimes. Sometimes it really hurts.

Three days after the seventh transmission two Tuthanach males came to the cave and crouched in its entrance watching Farrel. They were both middle-aged, dark-haired, and their skin was decorated with green and blue dye: circles around their eyes, lines across their cheeks, elaborate patterns on their breasts and bellies. They looked angry. Farrel remained quite still, trying to hide his fear.

Then Tig came slipping into the cave, boisterous and noisy as ever. Farrel tried to piece together something from the boy's excited gabble, but all he could make out were words for 'woman' and the insult 'stone legs'.

A tension grew in the pit of Farrel's stomach and wild thoughts filled his mind. What was Tig up to?

The next thing he knew he was being chased from the cave by the two men. Tig grinned at him, and winked elaborately. 'Soul curers,' he said, pointing to them. 'Make soul good for this Farrel. Make this Farrel's soul ready for earth.' And he patted his loins.

Farrel felt terrified.

They took him to the crog and led him inside the skin wall, past the fire pit and to a smaller circle of skins around which were grouped several women and children. He was led to a small tent and pushed to the ground. Making no attempt to speak to him, nor demonstrating any puzzlement over him, the men left. After a while one of the younger women got up and walked across to him.

By that time, realizing that his sexual need was far more intense than he had admitted to himself for the last few days, Farrel was lost in thoughts of his past.

He saw the Tuthanach woman through a blur of remembered faces, saturated bodies and irritatingly noisy beds. He smelled her through an imagined veil of perfumes, cigarette smoke and the salty and erotic smell of sweat. He felt pain as he remembered these things, a real pain, unlocalized. The woman had crouched before him, her wool skirt drawn up above her knees so that she displayed her white and grossly fat thighs to Farrel's casual gaze. He tried not to think too hard about what he saw.

Then she extended her hand and cocked her head to one side, smiling broadly, letting him see that only two of her teeth were missing.

Farrel took her hand, pressed the cool, firm fingers and noticed how the woman's palm was sweating like his. The past surged into his mind; agony:

A girl he had known for years as a friend. He had been taking his leave of her small, two-roomed apartment, conscious that his wife would start to worry soon. With his usual calculated shyness he had reached out and shaken her hand again, playing at being nervous. 'I don't like all this hand shaking,' she had said, in a way that made him realize that she had wanted to say it on previous occasions. 'I'd much rather have a cuddle.' So he'd cuddled her, and she hadn't let him draw away. She was tall and lean and felt awkward against his stocky, muscular body. But it had been a long moment, and a good one.

He realized he was excited and the Tuthanach woman was pleased. Her breath was sour as she leaned across him, her left hand gripping him gently between the legs; she kissed each cheek and then the tip of his nose. Then she rose and tugged him to his feet, pulled him into the tent and slipped off her clothes.

She picked up a stone chip, artificially smoothed by all appearances, and made marks on it with a piece of flint. Farrel watched her as he undressed. Her breasts were full and plump at the ends, flat and sac-like where they grew from her body. He hated that. She smelled of animal grease and smoke (as did he) and of something else, something pungent and sexual and offensive. Spitting on the stone she grinned at Farrel and passed it to him, indicating that he should do the same. As he spat he saw the crude phallus she'd drawn on the rock. With her thumb she rubbed the spittle into the sandstone, and laughed as she lay back on the skin-covered floor. She patted her belly with the fragment. She still said nothing.

As Farrel climbed onto her recumbent body and tried to find her he noticed that she popped the stone into her mouth and swallowed it.

They made love for about ten minutes. At the end of it she was obviously disappointed, and Farrel for no reason that he could identify felt like crying.

EIGHTH TRANSMISSION – FIFTEENTH DAY

It has begun. Newgrange, I mean – the building has begun. Yesterday I crept around the crog and went to the hills overlooking the Boyne, where the cemetery is located. There was much activity down by the river, men and women gathering water-rolled granite boulders for the facing of the mound; they carried these, one per person, in a great chain up the hillside and the piles grow large. Earth is being excavated from several sites ready for the tumulus. Several small tombs on the site have been demolished for the earth and rock they can offer. The past no longer matters. Only the great tumulus seems to concern them now. The first massive orthostats have been dragged to the site, and an artist is working on what can only be the small lintel that will lie above the passage entrance. The work, especially the art, will take many months. The air is filled with the sharp sounds of repeated picking blows as symbols and designs are carved on the dressed rocks, ready for incorporation into the tomb. The speed with which they work is fantastic, but the job they face is enormous. Who will be buried here? Who will be honoured?

I walked closer to the activity, managing to remain undetected behind some trees, and watched the artists at work. Imagine my surprise when I discovered Tig directing the symbol-carving operations! Some thirty men, all old, all frail, were crouched beside or above their slabs and each worked on specifications laid down by the darting, probing, shouting form of the boy.

I watched fascinated for a while, until the sun, beating bright and hot upon my naked back, drove me away to a shadier place. Tig must have caught sight of me because, as I crept down the hill towards the slopes rising to the unbuilt mound of Knowth, he came racing after me, calling my name.

'It will be a huge mound,' he said, breathing heavily. 'A great temple.'

'A temple to who, Tig?'

But he just laughed and slapped his hands together. 'They have all forgotten the symbols of the earth, and the wind, and fire and water,' he babbled happily. 'This is why I was left behind, to remember, to teach them...' He was obviously delighted about it. 'Soon this Tig shall no longer be Tig-never-touch-woman.'

'Will this Tig touch earth?' I asked him.

He fell moody, but brightened suddenly and grinned. 'This Tig never touch earth always ... but this Farrel ... this Farrel will touch earth soon ... this Far-rel will understand and learn the symbols.'

'This Tig might kill me,' I said carefully. 'Like he killed that Burton.'

He slapped his genitals repeatedly, not hard, but apparently quite painfully for he winced visibly. 'If this Tig kills this Farrel may legs turn to stone.'

And at that moment ... I felt the compulsion, the fascination to discover, the intrigue, filling me like some uncontrollable ecstasy, like a psychological magnet pulling me down towards the earth. Tig danced happily about ... had he seen my possession? He ran off, then, shouting back over his shoulder, 'This Farrel knows where to go.'

I am torn between desire to know, and fear of knowing. I keep seeing Bur-ton's rotted corpse, lying there, denied that same knowledge by a thin shaft of bone and a vengeful child. But I also remember the pull of the earth, the feel of magic and glory, the glimpse (for glimpse is what it was) of some great power lying beneath the grass ...

I will have to make my choice soon.

Farrel knew where to go all right. He thought about the knoll and its now empty burden of graves, and as the night wore on and a heavy rain began to drum across the countryside, sending icy rivulets across the uneven rock floor of his cave, so the knoll, dark and invisible in the night, seemed to beckon to him. Tig writhed before him, a boy at the mercy, the whim, of forces dying, but still far greater than any that man had ever conceived of, either now or in Farrel's own time, far in the future. And yet, perhaps that was wrong – perhaps the people of this time *had* conceived of the sons and daughters of the earth who somehow, inexplicably, were directing the destiny of the Tuthanach. Perhaps it was only with time and greater self awareness that man came to forget the spirits and guardians of all that he surveyed, the rock and stones, the trees and winds, the earth, the vast earth; mother ...

She called to him and Farrel responded with fear. They had been with him for some time, directing his thoughts, but their touch was tenuous, uneasy. Farrel drew back into his cave and covered his head, blocked his ears and eyes and tried not to see or hear or feel what was coming to him: he tried not to think of it, but he could not empty his mind of their presence.

He screamed, confused and terrified by the strangeness of the contact. Dark-eyed, shivering with cold and terror, he cowered in his cave until morn-ing, and dawnlight, and peace again.

He ran across the storm-threatened land, pacing heavily on the saturated turf, waiting for the next cloudburst. Tig scampered towards him and he felt a great sense of relief.

The boy saw his fear and laughed, jumped high in the air, then clapped his hands together in glee.

'What does it mean?' cried Farrel.

Tig-never-touch-woman-never-touch-earth dropped to his haunches and plunged his fingers between the tightly knotted grass mat.

'This Farrel is being prepared to touch earth,' he said. 'Don't be afraid.'

'But this Farrel *is* afraid. This Farrel is terrified!'

'There is no need to be,' said Tig, suddenly less childish. He watched Farrel through bright, deep brown eyes. Grease and paint were smeared about his cheeks and chin, a meaningless mosaic of colour and half formed design. The wind blew suddenly strong and Tig shivered. He rose to his feet and glanced up, wrapping his thin arms around his naked torso. Farrel too hunched up and followed the boy's gaze into the heavens, where dark clouds and lancing sunlight played confusing chase games across the valley.

'What is going to happen to this Farrel?' asked the man.

Tig smiled, almost patronizingly. 'Wonderful things.'

'What is underneath the grass? What is hidden there?'

'This Farrel will soon know. Fear is unnecessary. This Farrel will lose nothing he has not already lost.'

Farrel stared at him, feeling suddenly old, suddenly alien.

'What has this Farrel lost?'

Tig grinned. 'His past, his people, his dreams, his strange images. This Tig never understood them, never understood the words. This has always been between us. When this Farrel has touched the earth they will be gone. We will build the temple together: we will build our dreams and our people together.'

'It sounds magnificent,' said Farrel. 'But this Farrel is still afraid.'

Tig laughed again. 'Afraid of the earth?' He scuffed the ground with his bare feet. 'Afraid of clouds? Afraid of sun?'

'Afraid of ...' He stopped, unsure. 'This Farrel doesn't know what of.'

Tig slapped his hands together, shook his head. 'This Farrel should go back to the cave. Wait there. When you are called, go to them. Go to them.'

Unquestioningly, resigned to his bizarre fate, Farrel turned and walked back to the overhang.

By dusk it was raining again.

She called to him and again Farrel responded. He was still afraid, but Tig's words, his reassuring attitude, helped him overwhelm that fear and put it from his mind.

He walked through the driving rain, the clay in his hair running into his eyes and mouth, giving him a foretaste of the great oral consummation to come. He swallowed the clay, tasted its texture, wept as he ran through the rain, through the moaning woods. Behind him, high on a hill, torch light burned beneath a skin shelter where an artist worked on stone late into the night, anxious to express the earth symbols that he had relearned from the one boy who had not forgotten. He was an artist who added his soul to the rock and the rock to the temple ... a temple to the earth gods, the Great Ones, the Moaning Ones, those who inhabited the boulders and the wind, the clouds, and the running mud, the grassy turf of uncountable acres of virgin earth.

Through the night and the rain Farrel ran, until he found himself, without thinking, on the knoll that rose above the woods, the great source of earth energy that he had tapped so briefly, so frighteningly, several days before. And here he lay down on the ground, in the trench left by one of the Tutha-nach, and stretched out his arms—

Gripped the mother's flesh—

Penetrated the mother's fertile womb, ejaculated with the ecstasy of contact –

Ate her breast, drank the cold and grainy milk of her glands, felt it flood into his body, through the apertures of his prostrate corpse, driving the substances of his canals before it, replacing his warmth with its own loving cold. Earth closed over his back, the rain filtering through ran down his skin, drained deep into the tissues of the soil below. His lungs filled with mud – he breathed deeply and after a moment his heart stopped, his breathing stopped ... suspended, touching the earth.

Almost immediately they were there, rising out of the deep rock, flowing through the earth and the pores of the soil, entering Farrel's body through the tips of finger and penis, down the earth bridge that extended along the convolutions of his gut. He was consumed by them, consumed them for his own part, welcomed them and heard their dying greeting, the words that had flowed through the minds of the Tuthanach during the weeks previous ...

I am earth, Farrell, I am the earth, I am of earth, the earth is within me and without me, I am soil and rock, diamond and jade, ruby and clay, mica and quartz, I am the litter of the dead who live in crystalline echo in the sediments of sea and lake, I am ground, I am woman who suckles the infant flesh of man and beast, I am womb and anus, mouth and nose and ear of the great world lover, I am cave and tunnel, bridge and haven, I am the sand that sucks, the field that flourishes, I am root and clay, I am man pre-carnate, I am dirt, who has been called Nooma and Shaan, and is Tutha and Cein, and will be Ga-Tum-Dug and Nisaba, I will be Geshtin and Tammuz and my branches will be earth against the sky and all will be one, I will be Faunus and I will be Consus, I will be Pellervoinen and Tapio, I will be Luonnotar who floats on white water and touches the wind, I will be Asia and Asia-Bussu, Lug and

Jesus, I will be coal and ore and I have existed since a time of desolation and of thunder and of sterility – you, Farrel, who know all these things should know also that this is the moment of our great dying, the breath of wind passing out of the body of earth and into the memory of man ...

A second voice: I am wind, who has been called Godsinger by the Kalokki who were the first men, and is called Tag and Feng-po, and Huaillapenyi, I am breath and life, I am death, the rising odour of decay, I am storm and rage, light and dark, I am thunder and fear, I am the changing seasons of time, I am the urger of seas and the calmer of wings, I will be remembered as Taranis and Wotan, Thor and Zephyrus and Ga-oh and Hino and my thunder shall be heard until the final fire, but you, Farrel, who know all these things should know also that this is the moment of our great sorrow, where we abandon our domain and enter the minds of men, for only in the minds of man can we continue to survive ...

And others, then, crowding in, jostling to be heard: I am fire who is Tinedia, who will be Svarogich and Sun and Steropes ... I am water who is Uisceg ... I am sky ... I am serpent ...

All these Farrel heard and consumed, and then they fell away, back into the rock, up into the wind, leaving just a fragment of each god, a morsel of each great being, settling in his crowded mind.

He rose from the earth, shaking his body and feeling the dirt and clay fall from his limbs and his mouth and his eyes. The day was cold; he was conscious of rain, of heavy cloud, of a dullness about the saturated countryside: he loved this. Some greater or lesser part of him was aware that a full two seasons must have passed while he lay in his intimate embrace with the earth. From this same greater or lesser part of him came an alien thought, a last tearful cry from his dead future: *truly a great and noble glory will have gone by my time of glass and steel.*

The new born child turned to regard the virgin land. Rain beat against him, washed him. He opened his mouth to drink it and his laughter joined the gentle sounds of the natural world.

I've found life, at last, at last ...

The great gods were still there, he thought, as he blinked rain away and stared at the greenness all around him. They were dying, now, committing their great suicide, surviving only in the Tuthanach and their children, and their grandchildren, and so on until they were spread everywhere ... this they were doing as a gesture of acquiescence to man, but just by staring through the rain, through the unspoiled distance, the man called Farrel could see those gods, could feel them and smell them and hear them.

As he ran down the knoll he could sense them, too, in the brightness of his mind. They were with him by inheritance when he came here, and now they had come direct and he was ecstatic at the greater awareness they had brought him of so many things … over the centuries their presence would dilute and become weak and perhaps they had not reckoned on that.

There was plenty of time for them to explore him and understand how things would be. As far as Farrel was concerned there were more important things to do than worry over a day and an age when he would be dust and ashes.

He was a part of the earth, now, a man of the earth, a Tuthanach. His people were building a temple to the earth, and he knew how magnificent that temple would be, for he had seen it. He would mark the rocks of the temple with his soul, raise the walls of the temple with his sweat, and fill the temple with his ecstasy. He ran faster across the rain-soaked land until he could hear the sounds of the stone being carved.

The earth went with him.

A SMALL EVENT

There was a great gathering by the banks of the Taim, and we were among the last to arrive.

We had left the gyro spinning silently and happily on the side of a hill, and indulged ourselves in a physical walk across the last few miles of naked moorlands. One of my great pleasures is to feel unfiltered wind on my face, the soft springiness of water-sodden turf beneath my feet; there is no sound quite as mournful and musical as the low moan of wind between hills; no colours can quite match the subtle shades of grey that streak a stormy sky.

And so I had insisted on walking although Harmony, the female of my current triad, soon tiring of this extravagant spending of energy had strapped on her warm-field and gravity belt; she whisked high into the dusk sky, where she bobbed and blew, a small yellow shape, hair and gown streaming in her wake.

I plodded across the low foothills around the Taim valley, examining every brand (no, species! They were natural) of hardy plant I saw.

By early evening we were within sight of the gathering of aesthetes; the MECH's huge machine towered into the sky, breaking the natural skyline with its sharp angles, sparkling with inner light. I too, then, strapped on my gravity belt and rose beside Harmony. She came close and smiled and we held hands so that her power pack was recharged from my own by way of our skin. I tingled when I touched her, and we laughed and flew swiftly down to the river.

We dropped to the ground a short way from the first of the glowing campfires, a small red box from which simulated flames cast light and heat in a circle twenty yards across. The noise of laughter and conversation was inviting and confusing; I imagined I could recognize the voices of old friends, but in the season of alteration it was impossible to say. The nicest, richest voices were never long with a single individual; bought at high prices they passed between two or three persons a year. My own voice had belonged to an actor now seven hundred years dead.

Walking into the area of the gathering I was greeted at once by several acquaintances. By the nearest fire was Helios Ice-Shaper of Polar South who greeted us in that most revolting of south polar ways; he spat in his hand and slapped the palm to my face. I recoiled and he grinned, turning to Harmony, waiting the return of the compliment. Harmony touched a finger to her nose and ran around the man, who turned back to me, surprise and anger in his face.

'Animal!' shouted Harmony. 'Beast!'

I pushed past Ice-Shaper myself, a dramatic gesture received with dramatic silence.

I recognized others, notably Aragos from Isreel and Collector from Old Nor. With both of them we spent long minutes talking and exchanging news. Eventually I found Silver, seated more or less alone by the very edge of the river, his gaze fixed on the moonlit, firelit waves of water. Harmony saw him and ran to him, kissing and fondling the reticent youth while I, the 'older' man, waited my turn with patience.

Silver had lately been the moody member of the triad, and he had left our home some fifteen days before the announcement of the coming event. Harmony had been hysterical at first; myself, approaching the problem practically, I could see no reason why, wherever our silver youth had hidden himself, he would not hear of the forthcoming excitement And he was bound, I had reasoned, to make his way to the site and meet us there.

The accuracy of my prediction earned me much hugging and love from Harmony, who was suddenly as happy and excitable as the mental child she was. I put my arm around her and smiled at Silver, whose face broke into a wide and knowing grin; in the fragmentary moonlight, by the bright light of the fires, his silver skin was alive with glitter and the very act of blinking sent flashes of radiance from his face.

'Why did you flit off like that?' I asked him.

'We were worried,' said Harmony severely. 'You really should tell us when you plan to throw your moods.'

'Yes, I'm sorry,' said Silver, glancing at me with an indefinable expression on his smooth face. 'I was thoughtless.'

'So why go?' needled Harmony, stroking his white hair back from his forehead.

'Oh ... pressure, I suppose ... I don't know ...'

'Love pressure?' I asked. 'Me pressure? Harmony pressure? City pressure? Art pressure? Pressure on its own doesn't tell us anything.'

'Nothing at all,' agreed Harmony. 'What made you go? What *really* made you go?'

Silver shook his head, looked out across the flowing waters of the Taim. 'I don't know. Just ... just a feeling, a depressed feeling. I can't explain it.'

We didn't push him further. We were both too glad to be a threesome again. We erected our tent and consummated the camp site for an hour or so, and if there was something troubling Silver deep down he certainly didn't show it.

Outside, then, for an evening investigation of the MECH.

*

I recognized the human component of the MECH immediately. He was a man in miniature, standing less than half my own height and further testimony to his complete eccentricity was the sparkle of wires across his close-cut hair – a vault-network worn *outside* the cranium. His dwarfdom, however, was a post-nat-tank choice on his part – somewhere in his home city the excess flesh remained, preserved, in case he should decide to return to normal size.

I had last met him seventeen years ago, at the site known locally as Stone-hang, a primitive place of worship which had been long since swallowed into the earth leaving only one or two rounded, weathered boulders as evidence of the site's importance. The MECH, new to me then, with a very small machine component, had impressed us all with his prediction that the site – a focus of time every seventeen hundred years – would give us a five-minute view of the distant past, a shimmering image in the air of sacrifice and seduction, of warring brothers and the bestial feasting of our ancient ancestors. For the Midget's speciality was *time*, and the distortions in time that could be caused by physical effects. I felt an immediate anticipation, a twinge of excitement – time, that most fascinating of dimensions. We would soon witness its disruption, I was sure.

But what purpose was served by the huge bank of machinery?

And huge is no exaggeration. The bank of green-and red-faced screens towered high over the camp site, stretching up for at least twenty feet and lying along the ground fifty feet to the flowing waters themselves. The Midget operated controls along this entire length, concentrating frantically and using the information to send his thoughts racing back along the face of the machine to somewhere else, changing readings, settings, standing back and watching the vector plottings on the great screens above his head – we all looked up to see the glowing white lines, angles, moving dots, pulses, spinning and twisting shapes.

It was all quite unaesthetic, probably substantially meaningless, and yet because of its involvement with time and the consequences of time disruption the MECH probably had to work harder than others to predict the cosmic events that we, the elitist aesthetes, might find amusing. For this reason we were, as we approached, respectful of the man's light show – more than a little of it would be of real importance, and more than a little could go wrong in the event of hostile personal fields tampering with the delicately-tuned interior workings of the machine-man complex.

'Hi, MECH!' I shouted at a moment when the little man relaxed from his involvement with the battery of signals.

He turned, stared through huge blue eyes at his three visitors, looked from one to the other of us, recognized me, smiled, frowned, shouted: 'I'm busy as *sky* and you come *chitterchattering*! Can't you see how delicate everything is, how precise it all has to be? Go away, don't bother me for the moment ...'

Harmony giggled at the little man's strange antics. Silver watched him expressionlessly, failing to observe any humour in the situation. I said, 'But Midget ... what are we to see? What are you predicting?'

The Midget was furious. He shouted something incomprehensible and busied himself with the nearest console of the gigantic machine component. We all watched as certain of the displays went through ugly contortions.

Finally, with an audible screech of frustration, the little man pressed a hand-shaped plate at the very bottom of the machine and came across to us. He had put the whole thing on automatic.

'A human *is* necessary,' he snapped, perhaps detecting my unvoiced thought. 'Imagination for one thing. Check on the machine. Keep a positive life field interlinked with the *son of a bitch*.'

'What sort of language is that?' asked Silver in irritation. His depression was showing at a bad time; it was important to keep the Midget favourably inclined towards us or we might never find ourselves invited by this MECH again.

But the Midget puffed up with pride and began to lecture us on the old languages of earth. That particular expression, he told us, was called *slang*, and it had been spoken by a mighty race who had once lived on a land mass west of Ireland.

It all sounded very improbable, and gently I returned the little man's interest and enthusiasm to the prediction at hand.

'It will hit the Earth at precisely eleven forty-three point three three seven tomorrow morning – we won't notice *that* of course, because it will have already sped through the atmosphere with noticeable and spectacular effect. It will hit the Earth seven feet from the northern shore of the Taim – you can see where the point has been marked with a light focus. I shall, of course, turn that off before the event.'

Still a little confused as to what exactly we were about to see, I tried to keep him in conversation. He grew impatient.

'Look, there are the vectors, you can follow them all night if you wish, just don't bother me. By the time it reaches point 221, that's marked on screen five, I have to exert traction through the machine to alter its course very slightly so that it doesn't miss the Earth. The precise effort on my part will cause it to strike at the co-ordinates I've already given you. Do you see? Will you go now? Will you stop annoying me?'

He bounded away. Silver left our group and went to sit by a camp fire near to our tent. I stood in the chill night, Harmony standing close by and projecting her sympathy for the depressive. She seemed less childish than usual, as if some deeper maturity within her was pushing through the mask she had adopted.

I turned back to the MECH and tried one last time. 'Exactly *what* are we going to see colliding with the Earth?'

His voice, high with anger and excitement, sounded across the campsite, caused heads and bodies to turn. 'A quantum black hole, you fool, a quantum black hole of course!'

What *is* a black hole?

Why, simply (it was explained to us by Robeard of Tunis) a point in time and space where matter has collapsed in upon itself until it is no longer there. A universal node which sucks light from the nether regions thus appearing black since the reverse of light is, of course, dark. A cosmic inaccessibility, a place where the power of a Galaxy is directed, a negative attraction into which whole worlds might easily vanish if the hole had not been properly screened.

At least (added Robeard) that's what I think it is.

Thus enlightened we waited out the night.

Entertainment by the banks of the river Taim:

Silver drew third in the lottery for entertainment during the long night. Harmony drew fourth, but lay just outside the circle around our campfire since her particular artform required some work beforehand. Myself, I drew nothing, which was as well since I had nothing to offer.

The Moon was a pleasant disc, low over the eastern horizon, watching our antics with something less than its full face. The zenith was cloudy, but a sprinkling of stars testified to the ever-present heavens. How, I wondered, as we waited for the entertainment to begin, would one spot a black hole against the black night sky? It seemed to me to be useless to try and distinguish the hole from where we sat, most of us gazing idly heavenwards.

For thirty minutes we watched Jarrol, from the southern land of Isreel, digesting a variety of living creatures; his stomach and belly walls were made of transparent bio-silicone, a closely knit sheet of living connective tissue and silica. He illuminated the proceedings internally, and had treated the animals with special dyes that were released with bizarre effects as Jarrol's ultra-powerful digestive juices stripped layer after layer from the struggling but swiftly motionless beasts.

I had never been convinced of the artistic value of Jarrol's creativity, but my companions applauded wildly. There was a market for anything, I supposed.

More to my taste were the death memories of a strange solitary man called Diabla, from the ancient fortress city of the eastern steppelands that had no name. Diabla had extended his very real telepathic abilities to the watching of the dead as they struggled out of the mortal sphere. We shared what he had seen, a series of edited clips from forty or fifty dying-dead. In the few minutes after life there were voices, shapes, colours, feelings – but they made no sense, and when some sort of familiar pattern did begin to emerge, that was the end of the clip – to have remained linked with a fleeing soul any longer would have been death for Diabla as well.

Then Silver was called into the circle. He was in no mood to be entertaining but he recognized the importance of etiquette at occasions such as this. As I urged him to the centre of the ring he shook me off, roughly, almost angrily, then turned and looked at me with an unvoiced apology in his eyes. He walked away from me to take up his position by the fire; I felt a great sadness, almost despair. Silver was growing away from me, and had been doing so for some weeks. Why he was distancing himself I didn't know, but it made me angry, and the anger was because of my unhappiness. I watched him by the fire, moody, solemn, and I knew that he was thinking of me, and of nothing else, and that I would hate to know what was in his mind.

Silver stripped off his clothes and pushed his silver cells to their full brilliance so that his body gleamed in the firelight like polished alloy. To attune his mind he stared at the nearest visitor to him, and gradually her shape was etched in black and silver upon his torso, the detail becoming sharp after a few seconds.

'How does he do it?' whispered a woman close to me. Her partners had no idea, and after a moment I felt the gentle tingle in my scalp that told of the mind probe she was directing, not only to me but probably to everyone else about the circle (with the exception of Silver, naturally). I allowed my knowledge of Silver's genetic peculiarity to filter three levels toward my conscious mind and felt each fact snipped away by the curious mind that sought enlightenment.

Silver's skin colour was the result of surface melanophores that could, at his will, expand to cover him completely and allow their silver or black pigments to give him his particular colouring. At will he could selectively depigment his body in lines and etchings to show whatever image he wished. Thus: a girl, her hair in artistically portrayed folds, her eyes, large, sparkling in the firelight, her lips moist, parted, ready to engage the sensitive skin of her lovers as soon as the night's enjoyment had become ... tiresome.

Silver, excelling himself, was the focus of attention for nearly half an hour, depicting many of those in the circle engaged in erotic or hilarious activities. His *tour de force* was a scene from history, stretching across his torso from side to side, up to the lower part of his face and down his legs almost as far as his calves. The Great War of antiquity, a war fought between millions of men, with gunpowder and knife, with plane and ship. And what a spectacle Silver made of those events. In the frozen instant of war, in the depiction of a battle as it might have been seen from the air, there were literally thousands of individual shapes, figures, soldiers, engaged in their bloody exchange. Each figure was the controlled expansion of just a few cells!

Silver's final and most dramatic touch was the suffusion of his subcutaneous tissue with blood; through his translucent skin the deeper flesh shone brightly, redly, and the entire montage became awash with rivers of crimson – and there, beneath that wave of gore, those million men died, faded and were lost.

Silver sat quiet, and we were awed. What mental power had been required for that particular feat! What fantastic micro-control! Pride coursed through my body, pride at being the lover of so magnificent an artist. Harmony was almost crying, perhaps for the same reason. We hugged each other while Silver breathed hard, and listened to the resounding applause of his audience. True genius was measured not by the collision of asteroids but in the capability of handling a million body cells all at once.

And yet we all sensed that Harmony's aesthetic display would outshine even Silver's, and as she finally came into the circle, into the firelight, there was an almost tangible sense of anticipation. She kissed Silver, who walked to the edge of the circle and sat solemnly regarding the young woman. Harmony waved quiet the greeting round of chest-slapping and sat down upon the warm turf. She signalled that we should all remain silent for a few minutes, and we fell still. The aura of expectation in the air grew stronger.

Harmony sat with her eyes closed, cross-legged and motionless, concentrating; she had told me, in the past, of the sensations she experienced whilst pushing the biological process in her womb forward at an unnaturally fast rate: some pain, to begin with, then dizziness which had to be controlled (this was the result of wild hormone changes in her blood stream). Then a feeling of peace and a sense of communication – mind filling with the sound of the foetal heart beat, the surge of foetal blood, the multi-levelled waves of foetal awareness unbesmirched by the pollution of sensory input.

After a few minutes Harmony was ready. Distantly, from other fires, came the sound of cheering, of laughter, of singing – the entertainment of the elite took many forms, but our own circle had provided an evening of mainly anatomical amusement.

It was warm in the red light of the fire, with the waters of the Taim splashing gently a few yards away; behind Harmony the slopes of a hill rose to sombre heights, penetrating the lower of the scudding clouds. All was very relaxed.

She disrobed, to the accompaniment of whistles of appreciation; Harmony was slender and graceful, every womanly feature dainty and precise. No angle was too sharp, no curve too round. By looking carefully the slight swelling of her belly could be seen, but it was the only concession to biological deformity discernible by the unpractised eye.

She lay down, right by the fire, drew up her legs and closed her eyes.

'A cyclops!' cried Jarrol.

'With green hair, over all but its face.' This from a girl called Hayzel.

'And a forked tail, threshing wildly!' A man named Helix.

'And a cry like a house-spider …' Jarrol again.

'And—'

'Enough!' I shouted, smiling to let them see I meant no disrespect. 'There may be time for all your tastes.'

We sat back and watched, then. Harmony began to whine as she directed the forces of her mind and imagination to the task at hand; her belly writhed as the life within went through its multifarious changes, and her hands clutched the distorted flesh to ease the pain and pressure.

Finally – only a few minutes had elapsed – she cried aloud and seemed to be exerting great effort. Her womb opened and a single eye regarded us, unblinking, neither hostile nor friendly, a neutral eye, in a pink bare face. The foetus slipped from its watery hiding place, green fur sticky and plastered in bizarre patterns about its eight-inch body. A tail – unforked I noticed – whipped this way, that way, striking the insides of Harmony's legs so that she yelled and sat up.

Stricken with panic the homunculus shrieked high and loud and began to run, ducking under legs and crawling over laps, pleading with cries and strange sounds as if sensing its impending doom. I touched it as it scampered past, and it turned and grasped my finger with two little hands, staring up at me imploringly with its huge single eye. Amused, I poked it away, trying not to hurt it, and it darted towards Silver who – with a flick of his hand – sent it reeling back towards the fire. Finally Harmony snared the tiny being in a neural web and carried it back through the air into her clutches.

It struggled in her grasp for a moment, its plaintive cry bringing sympathetic responses from some of the elite. Then swiftly she dug her thumb and forefinger into its neck, pinching until the soft bones parted. The homunculus kicked and squeaked, scrabbling at Harmony's fingers until its eye glazed over and it fell limp in her grasp; the monstrous head lolled as she tossed the pitiful corpse towards Jarrol, who snatched and scrutinized it, a satisfied expression upon his face.

'Any more?' begged Hayzel. Harmony shook her head apologetically.

'I'm exhausted. That creation was very difficult'

There were murmurs of disappointment, but no argument. Harmony probably had three or four more half-formed embryos in her womb, but would discard them rather than re-incorporate them into her strange germinal tissue. I smiled at her as she sat down beside me, pulling her flimsy robe about her body. Harmony was a true artist! There were no others in the world who could do what she could do, sculpting life itself, moulding the living flesh of her own body. And for that matter, there were few who could compete with Silver. How lucky I was, a non-artist, to be a part of a triad containing two such truly unique artists.

Time passed, minutes only, as the elite contemplated what they had seen, seated in silence, just the breeze and the river sounds drifting across the camp.

I was about to rise and go to our tent when I heard Harmony's unvoiced puzzlement beside me. I looked at her. She was staring beyond me, round the circle, and as I followed her gaze so there came a murmur of query from all the aesthetes around our fire.

I looked to see what was attracting their attention and my heart raced! Silver was standing, his naked form stretched out in a thin, rigid line with toes digging into the soft earth of the river bank and arms high above his head. His skin flashed as it silvered and a moan of anguish left his lips.

'Silver!' I cried, and ran towards him. In an instant his cry became anger as he opened his eyes and stared at me. 'Leave me alone! Leave me alone, Walker! I don't need you! I don't want you! You're always in the way. Walker. Go *away*!'

Shattered, almost sick, I backed away from him and felt Harmony's arms slip around me, comforting.

'What have I done?' I begged.

Tears in her eyes she shook her head. 'I don't know, Walker. I don't understand ...'

We both looked back at Silver, still stretched taut and rigid. On his chest a picture began to form, slowly at first, then more and more explicit as the detail filled in. It was a picture of me, facing a Silver who was armed and angry. In my clutches, looking to Silver for help, was a distressed and dishevelled Harmony.

'No, Silver!' I shouted, shocked at what he was insinuating. 'No ... she's happy! We're all happy!'

Harmony's hold on me became tighter, her small body transmitting her fear to me.

Silver began to shout. 'None of us are happy. Walker! You've stolen her from me ... you've come between us from the start! You're an old man and you've stolen her from me. Why don't you *go away*! GO AWAY!'

'Not old, Silver,' I sobbed, unable to keep back tears. 'Not old, just ... just a passing physical form ... not old; young! In love with you, with Harmony.' I sat down and hugged my body ... not old, just the old form I had adopted at the last season of alteration. Silver should know that ... mature of look, mature of mood. We might reverse everything this coming season. Who knew? I felt a tremendous depression encompass me. Harmony was crying softly, her face in her hands. Depression. Everywhere depression, as if the prevailing mood of one member of the triad could reach out and infect the others.

Then I noticed, on Silver's chest ...

'The figures are moving!'

Jarrol's cry convinced me that I was not seeing things, but even so I could hardly believe it. I could hardly believe the evidence of my own eyes!

A great crowd was moving in to watch the display. On Silver's chest my figure was moving towards the figure of Silver, and suddenly – a knife, produced from Silver's imagination, appeared in his hand, and the figure on his chest sent the blade deep into my body, through the heart, deeply through the heart, and there I watched it, my murder, my assassination. And before my body had crumpled to the ground, becoming a shapeless mass of black and silver shadow and light, there was Silver moving into a love lock with Harmony.

The picture faded, but not the atmosphere. *Body mobiles*, the crowds murmured, naming the artform without hesitation. Silver had invented body mobiles.

And, by finally managing to express something he had, perhaps, been unable to express before, he had destroyed our triad!

A gain and a loss in just a few moments of time.

Silver collapsed to the camp floor and his unconscious form was swiftly carried into the security of our tent. I remained seated, bewildered.

A hand on my shoulder, warm lips on my ear. Harmony, tears in her soft, green eyes; she kissed me, caressed me.

'His last alteration was overdone,' she whispered. 'That's all it is, Walker. He opted for depression and they overdid it. In a few weeks he'll want to forget this as much as I do.'

She was right, of course, and yet the wound had gone deep. Too deep. I shook my head. 'He's envious, Harmony. He's jealous of me, and he's broken us up.'

'Not us ... not you and I, Walker. The three of us, perhaps, but ...' she trailed off, the words catching in her throat. She no more wanted to break with Silver than she would want to break with me. She was comforting me because of my hurt, but I could detect her concern for Silver. As artists they had always had a special affection for each other, nothing unpermissive, but ... special.

I kissed her hand. 'Go and see if he's all right,' I said. She smiled and ran towards the tent.

When I returned to the tent both Silver and Harmony were sleeping. I sat for a long while listening to the sound of their breathing, but the exhaustions of the day overtook me eventually.

I woke late in the morning. Harmony was still curled up, but Silver was gone, perhaps out exploring the terrain before the event hit. The day was still and fairly warm, although ominous grey clouds poured across the sky from the hills, and the air was filled with the signs of an approaching storm. But reassuringly the MECH predicted that the weather would be fine all morning, up until the moment when the tiny black hole caught up with the Earth.

I left the tent and indulged myself with a wash in the icy cold waters of the Taim. This high up in the hills the waters were clear and tasteless; I felt as if I was returning to nature.

Drying myself with a palm-dryer I watched the strange shapes and arrows on the MECH; one display, a summary display, showed me the shape of our Earth and the location of the river Taim, and the approach of the black hole. The singularity would penetrate the Earth almost vertically; at that time the planet would be moving away from the approaching event. The final velocity through the Earth would still be more than twenty miles per second. Yet for the instant the black hole was above the river the MECH would vastly slow our time sense so we would observe the passage of the hole across a time span of several seconds. The effect should be marvellous, I thought, as I made my way to the food mash.

The MECH had instructed us to tune our time-space shields to a very high level. The quantum hole, though only one hundredth the radius of a small atomic nucleus, would nevertheless exert a gravitational pull of over two gravities at a hundred-foot distance, and we would be sitting a little closer than that!

The depression of the previous evening had lifted but I still felt our triad was doomed. Silver's jealousy, I could accept, was the result of a badly tuned construction during the previous season of alteration. But the emotion had been so powerful that I felt there had to be an underlying rationality. Even without his terribly depressive state, he would still have felt jealousy.

Triads often broke up and reformed, two splitting from one, all splitting from each other – it was no new phenomenon. But I had thought this, my third triad, was stable for life. If it broke again I should have to shrug off my chosen façade of age and maturity and adopt a more youthful persona. This was the way things were done in my home city. I was convinced that any split would be between myself and Silver, with Harmony opting to stay with the youth.

I found Harmony as soon as I had eaten, and we sat by the river as the minutes ticked by. She had recovered her full strength after the exertions of the night before, and now she sat and contemplated the spot indicated by the light focus above the river.

'You're very thoughtful, Harmony. Tired?'

'No. Not tired. A little down, that's all. I talked with Silver last night. We talked a lot.'

'About me?'

'Partly. You don't bother him anywhere near as much as he made out last night. That was just anger, and the anger was just … frustration.'

'Frustration over what?'

'Over …' she searched for the words and the silence was long and strained. Her hand found mine, her head shook, her gaze never left the water. 'I suppose it's what I've felt for a long time, and Silver has felt it too. It's a lack of ... of significance!'

'Significant art?' I laughed. 'Art is for enjoyment, for relaxation. It was never meant to be significant!'

'Wasn't it? We play a watching game, Walker. We watch each other creating in different ways, we create for others to watch. But we're idle. We lack compassion, too ... oh we *do*, Walker!'

'We do not!' I cried. 'You're taking the myths of Legend Week too seriously. Those times were primitive, irrational. What is shown during that week are the petty attempts of morons to create art – compassion, yes, they had compassion, but what does that mean? Their art was meaningless, compassion or no. Our art is meaningful – even if not all of us have a conception of compassion.'

'You're wrong. Walker,' she said simply. 'Idleness, self-centredness, indulgence ... they've all perverted art in our hands. I'm sure of it. We've lost that very valuable sense of the primitive that just now you held to be something worthless. Without it our art is totally ... empty!'

I argued no further. If a sense of the past, of the primitive, was really important then it was beyond my ability to see why. But if contact with the past was important then Harmony might find some relevance in the artistic indulgence scheduled for just a few minutes' time – I couldn't believe this particular MECH would advertize a new physical toy unless there was a very real time-contact predicted as well.

Other elite were joining us by the river. I checked the hour and saw no more than ten minutes remained before the arrival of our small event. I ran back to the tent, paged Silver several times without success, and carried the force field generators back to where Harmony was still sitting. Suitably protected in our shells of distorted space-time we were invulnerable to the collision of galaxies.

The MECH was going wild, the Midget frantic.

Where *was* Silver?

We searched the crowds for him, scanned the landscape, the skies. He was nowhere to be seen.

Then:

The wind began to shriek. Above our heads the clouds ceased their graceful flow and became, in an instant, a grey and white confusion of swirling mist ....

Time slowed.

There was grace in the heavenly motion, the clouds forming a spiral as they spun towards the unexpected gravitational upset – the wind growled, the river oozed past us, a viscous, sparkling stream.

'Where's Silver?' shrieked Harmony, her voice in my mind filled with panic and unnatural tone; she was communicating at one hundred times her normal rate.

I scoured the raging skies. There was no sign of him. An instant later the cloud patterns changed and great grey and white streamers poured upwards and out of sight; as we watched so the streams of cloud changed direction, lowering their focus as the black hole dropped through the atmosphere.

Even the waters of the Taim were violent; the surface broke and jumped, great strands of fluid darting upwards, ten, twenty feet from the main flow before shattering and dispersing under the conflicting forces around them.

Harmony screamed, suddenly and loudly, and I looked from the water to the sky and saw Silver, a small, dark shape, totally at the mercy of the gravitational vacuum. His limbs threshed, his body slowly twisted as he rose and fell, fighting ineffectually with his gravity belt but at the mercy of the upward current. He vanished into cloud, re-appeared to plummet down for a second, up for a second, round and round, tossed and flung – plunging towards the event!

Harmony sobbed, but remained motionless, resigning herself to the inevitable death of her lover. I watched in horror as Silver surged along a streamer of cloud towards ...

'THERE!' cried a hundred voices. 'SEE THERE!'

The clouds vanished in the centre of a whirlpool, into an area of distorted imagery and vanishing perspective. And at the very centre flared a brilliant spot of intensely blue-white light.

The quantum black hole itself!

The motionless body of Silver slipped down the gravity gradient followed by a surge of water as the river itself rose in a thrashing sheet and was sucked into the holocaust. Rocks, turf, fragments of mountain followed as the singularity descended toward the dry river bed, sucking water downstream in a miniature *tsunami*.

At the instant of his death Silver had felt at peace. I had felt it and Harmony had felt it. He had wanted to die, and he had died in a fashion that would never be forgotten. Perhaps he had seen death as the only honourable way to apologize to me; perhaps in some peculiar, unfathomable way he had seen it as an answer to his feelings of futility. Perhaps the act of death itself was creative, and he had forever stolen the field for creative death!

We continued to watch, solemnly, numbly, as the area of distortion passed through the wide, bare river bed. A great cascade of rock and coloured fragments rose slowly, beautifully, up into the air, seeming to rise forever until finally turning to tumble back down to the surrounding countryside, here and there spinning harmlessly away from an onlooker's invulnerable force shield.

At that same moment the time distortions began – in the air, thirty feet above the impacting black hole, I saw the first shape struggling into existence: a huge, black-skinned man, dressed in flowing green and yellow robes – he came into our time only to fall slowly and dreamily into the gaping crater below. But even as he fell, others were bursting out of the past.

Men and women, children of all ages – flaxen haired, black haired, naked, clothed in the most diverse of garments – they came tumbling gracefully out of nowhere, some to die instantly as they hit the ground, others recovering to begin running in exaggerated slowness away from the source of the distortion.

The MECH reverted our time sense to normal.

It was bitterly cold as we came from our protective shields, the howl of the wind mingling with the screams of the time relics and the roars and cries of beasts too, for all manner of animals were also pouring from the rent in space-time. One great grey beast towered above everything else, rearing up on hind legs that were huge pillars of flexing muscle; its forearms were tiny and useless, its teeth gleamed in the daylight as the great mouth opened and closed on a fleeing man. After a moment the beast lumbered away from the river, chewing its prey. A large band of the elite set off in hysterical, delighted pursuit.

The time-effect ceased and the outpouring from the past was cut off. Most of the relics were already dead, but a good thirty or forty had survived and were scattering in all directions; men dressed in furs, waving huge metallic weapons (but running just the same), women in brief garments standing and shrieking at the tops of their voices as they were taken by members of the elite ...

The web of a historian reached out from behind me and froze specimen after specimen, and the angry voice of the Collector roared in my ears as he cursed the slaughter of the relics. He managed to secure five of the creatures before they had all dispersed, and set about their examination still grumbling his fury at the waste.

All the rest were in the hills, fleeing, the elite in hot and noisy pursuit.

Harmony ran along the river bank towards a figure that lay writhing and screaming upon a bare rock overhang.

'Walker!' she shouted, by voice and by mind, and I raced after her, attention half on her and half on the scene of confusion and carnage that was spreading in a widening circle around the crater, itself now beginning to fill with the waters of the Taim.

Harmony was crouched over a woman who was, even to my inexperienced eye, obviously in the final stages of a natural childbirth. Her garments were rough and seemed cut straight from the fur of some shaggy beast. She wore metal bracelets and a necklace of polished stone. Her hair was gathered back in a double plait. Her face was unpainted and contorted with pain as she screamed and sobbed, hands clutching at her swollen belly.

Harmony immersed herself and the woman in a warm-field and tore the garments from the threshing body, exploring the distended belly with its network of blue surface-veins. It was the first time either of us had seen such a sight, except on the medigrid, and I thought how rich it was in aesthetic qualities.

'Oh Walker!' cried Harmony, delighted with her find. 'What a beautiful sight.'

She pressed her face to the woman's belly and immediately the woman began to fight her, beating futilely with small clenched fists and whimpering in a language as incomprehensible to my ears as the howling of the wind.

'Hold her, Walker!' cried my mate (had she forgotten Silver so soon? Beneath her delight and enthusiasm did there remain any shred of grief for our lost mate?). I entered the warm field and grasped the arms of the struggling mother-to-be. Again Harmony's head descended to listen to the sound of the unborn child. 'Oh it's so beautiful!' she raved. 'I've never heard anything like it! It's nothing at all like the sounds *I* hear.' She was quiet, then, for a long, long moment, examining with her mind, and then she looked up at me, eyes wide with excited realization.

'Walker … Walker I've got a chance to *really* use my power. Oh Walker what an opportunity, what a moment to be *truly* creative!'

I looked from her to the straining flesh beneath which lay the unborn child, then to the mother's huge blue eyes that looked up at me, not understanding, but … trusting, strangely trusting. Back to Harmony.

'It seems a pity, somehow …'

'Oh Walker, silence! You don't understand. I can – I can *really* put my powers to the test. Help me. *Hold her.* Hold her secure and don't argue with me.'

And I obeyed; I held the woman's arms tightly and watched as Harmony placed her hands on the huge belly and closed her eyes to work her mental magic. After a moment the woman began to scream, but my grip only tightened still further. For now Harmony was possessed totally, and as the minutes passed so the sweat began to drip from her face, and her cheeks lost all their colour.

I wondered what was happening in the womb.

Ten minutes went by and still Harmony had not moved. She broke concentration with startling suddenness, stared down at the unsuspecting woman, then at me. 'I did it, Walker. I did it! Walker – *I did it!*'

And there beneath the threatening skies, by the bank of the river Taim, she induced labour in the woman and delivered her of … perfect twins!

I stared at them – two perfect and identical boy children, each screeching its head off, each head slick with moist black hair, each tiny face a picture of panic, and Harmony soothed them.

'There's not even a mark,' she said, showing me the back of each child's head. 'They were joined halfway down their heads and down to mid-spine. Isn't that fantastic? Such things used to happen a lot in the dark ages.'

'Fantastic,' I said, and took a child into my arms, then passed it to the waiting mother who accepted the sobbing infant with great happiness.

I felt humble, and very proud of Harmony. I had failed to comprehend her disillusionment with art when we had talked earlier, but now fully realized what she had been seeking for. I rose and walked to fetch the gyro, passing the celebrating elite and the broken bodies of the time-relics as I did so. Its function over, the silent mournful shape of the MECH loomed over us and its human operator sullenly regarding the exhibition he had wrought.

IN THE VALLEY OF THE STATUES

one

High clouds and the threat of rain later in the spring day made the arrival of dawn an affair of diffuse light, growing in intensity, rather than that particularly romantic vision of a sudden golden brilliance breaking low across the hills.

Watching from his open window, cool yet comfortable in his night robe, Alexander Arden found that he could not decide with certainty the precise moment at which night had fled and day had come. The land, the valley across which his room gazed, had seemed first to become an area of shadow; those shadows had continuously given way to further shadow, each lighter, each less stark and formidable than that preceding until – without being consciously aware of the subtle process of change – Arden observed that the valley was in colour, and the landscape appreciable in all its remote magnificence.

A thousand statues, each carved from some gleaming white stone, seemed to jut and probe from the sides of the valley; some rested gently upon the flatter land above the winding river; others appeared to move across the higher ground, the legs and arms of the figures given subtle life by the play of light and shade upon their facets. It was, Arden reflected, as if some giant yet sensitive celestial hand had scattered these human artifacts across the valley, and they had lain where they had fallen, untouched by humankind or by the eroding fingers of rain and wind.

Wherever he looked, for as far as he could see down the steep-walled valley, the white faces of stone gleamed between the complex colours of tree and grass and the lichen-covered grey stone of the area, a thousand shades of grey, sheltered by a thousand shades of green.

With dawn came the smell of the unspoiled land, heady, fragrant, something of the wild flower about it, something grassy, something of the pungent odour of woodland and undergrowth; a little something of decay. Arden shrugged off his robe and walked naked through the french windows to stand on the corroding concrete balcony. His hands, on the cold, dark-tinged metal of the safety rail, found the contact of the iron a delight, a sensory extravagance. He turned his back on the deep, rich valley and leaned against the rail, staring up at the sculpted façade of his host's mansion, the ornate and complex designs upon the windows and walls a testimonial to the frantic desire of a single man to outdo nature in the carving of rock into bizarre and beautiful shapes.

At dinner the evening before, the sculptor, Peter Stavanda, had raised his goblet at the conclusion of the simple meal and leaned forward heavily upon the unpolished oak table. 'The beauty, Mr Arden, the magnificence of nature,' he had said, with no hint of the Eastern European accent that Arden had anticipated, 'is its wildness, its irregularity – unpredictable of form, made jagged and free by the disorderly erosion of time.'

He had leaned back, staring at Arden through those intense blue eyes that disturbed the young Englishman so much. Arden guessed that Stavanda was some thirty years older than himself; his thick white hair and crinkled, wind-tanned skin gave him the look of a medieval sorcerer, perhaps of a man of wealth who has hidden within his private cosmos for more years than he can remember.

And yet the woman who dined with them, not his wife, nor even hinted at as being his mistress, was younger even than Arden.

Karina was slender, serene, her black hair tied formally and perfectly into a style that kept her neck free. Her shoulders, bare above her translucent black gown, seemed never to rise with her breathing, or fall when Stavanda's conversation reached its depths of grossness. She smiled only thinly at the Englishman, a cold expression that might have symbolized an English cold-ness of the heart so prevalent among Arden's countrymen. And yet she, this serene woman, knew that Arden was not a man lacking in passion: her eyes, dark, depthless, a Mediterranean warmth about them, an anger, a sexual hunger for the Englishman in every amber corner, her eyes seemed to linger on him, filling him with that same earnest desire to be alone with her that he had felt at their first meeting, in Paris three weeks before.

'And yet,' the sculptor again leaned forward, reaching for the decanter of wine, allowing his goblet to spill over onto the table before he ceased to pour; Arden was uneasy for a second, imagining that he sensed, in Stavanda's half-smile, some awareness of his own passion for Karina. 'And yet Man, most particularly as woman, is beautiful *because* of this contrast with nature!' Sta-vanda punctuated the statement with the edge, then the flat of his hand, pressed against the table, near to the glistening spill of wine. It was his most familiar mannerism, and Arden had found himself adopting it during the long evening and the simple, but drawn out, meal.

Stavanda had talked of his art for hours during the afternoon when they had sat so still, so formal after Arden's arrival, into the evening when they had faced each other across the coarse wood of the table. Arden was anxious to see the statues in the valley, for it was these that had brought him search-ing for Stavanda in Paris: doggedly, the hunter chasing through the reports

447

from paper and magazine, trying to locate the elusive artist, ultimately locating him through the discreet promiscuity of his beautiful companion.

As his eyes lingered on Karina's lips and neck, remembering the taste of them, the smoothness of them, Stavanda was saying, 'Man is smooth, and rounded, he is regular and patterned.

'Man, most particularly as woman, stands apart from nature, arrogant, upright, different in every aspect from the jagged pinnacles of granite and sandstone that time has sculpted. Nature condenses into a myriad forms of life, all ordered and regular, microcosms of pattern in the chaos of the Universe. Man is the greatest of these, and to carve the pattern of man, and of woman, in this cold crystal stone, the primal clay, is to fuse the elements of order and disorder, to bridge the Universe of animate and inanimate.'

He was silent, then, staring moodily, reflectively, at the remains of the roast duck that were such an ugly exception to what he had been saying. Karina politely sipped her wine, watching Stavanda with some embarrassment. Arden had watched her while thinking of the old man's words. Simple, perhaps even narrow, the words expressed that which had driven Stavanda through all the years of his life, fashioning pattern in rock, sculpting from his mind, through his hands, into the – what had he called it? – the primal clay!

'Man thinks and dies,' said Stavanda quietly, glancing up at Arden with suddenly alert eyes, narrowed, penetrating. Was he looking for some response, some furtherance of the philosophy from his youthful guest? 'The stone of the earth exists for all time without consciousness. What must the fusion, then, represent? What occurs when I shape the pattern of life in the crystal rock?'

'I have no idea,' said Arden gently. 'A permanence of form, but not of life ...'

'Not immortality?' said Stavanda with a thin smile. 'Not immortality,' he repeated, almost despondently. 'Perhaps a persistence of memory?'

'The memory of form,' said Arden.

'But not of life; is that what you're saying?'

'Memory of life while those who remember the human who has been depicted in the stone are living.'

Stavanda laughed, then shook his head. 'But what of my life? No memory of that? The artist?'

— Uneasy, Arden met Karina's steady gaze. She was regarding him coolly yet passionately, as she always did. She rarely spoke. In fact, when she spoke it was always in whispers, as if she were afraid for her voice to rise above the barely audible.

'When one carves so realistically,' said Arden, 'it is always easier to see the life represented in the stone, rather than the life that shaped the stone.'

Stavanda shook his head, not in disagreement, but almost fatalistically.

'We still talk of a persistence of memory, an echo, a representation of some energy that has transiently involved itself with the stone. Is there nothing more?' Again he fixed his gaze upon the younger man, and Arden reached for his wine to hide the nervousness he felt. He had wanted to talk to Stavanda, to see his work, to record his thoughts, to profit by them ... Stavanda knew this, and had known it all along. Surely he wasn't in some way trying to punish him for doing his job!

Arden was out of his depth, not because he felt the argument was beyond him, but simply because he did not care as much for the sort of talk that Stavanda wanted as he did for the sort of talk that Karina wanted, the quiet talk of night, of love. He knew the woman would come to him or, at least, that she would make it easy for him to come to her. Stavanda would, surely, be so often in his valley, among his statues, that there would be time in abundance to know this woman's body again, and her mind, and thus certain facets of Stavanda himself that the artist would not supply. In this way, then, in the way he thought, Arden was as much a sculptor as Stavanda himself, planning the manipulation and usage of his material in order to produce something that would be memorable.

'To fuse the animate and the inanimate ...' Stavanda said slowly, almost soberly, staring at the Englishman with an expression Arden thought might have been contempt, 'must be to create something ... something *more* than memory. Surely.'

'Some creature of stone? Of primal clay?' said Arden, and smiled. His face was flushed and he felt hot. 'A golem?'

'Some force of energy, of life,' said the sculptor. 'Something that is neither flesh nor stone, something ... something that is neither, and yet is both ...'

Arden said, 'A golem. You've created a golem, is that what you're saying?'

But Stavanda laughed. 'You speak, my young friend, as if nothing that could emerge from the union could be beautiful. But then, you've not yet seen my statues. You speak of golems, but I always thought such things were forces of evil, without true direction of their own. That you talk of animated life at all amuses me. I speak of something more than just the solid photography of human life. I cannot believe that a sculpture in living rock is no more, no less, than a photograph. One is putting too much into the shaping of the stone. There is a vision there; surely there must be a vision, a creation *beyond* what we think of as creation.'

Arden raised his glass, drained the sweet wine. 'I regret,' he said, 'but I really do not understand what you mean. I feel that I should. I sense that you are aware of something which I, for my ignorant part, cannot grasp. Our perspectives are different. I am sure it will not diminish my pleasure at surveying your work.'

two

The clouds broke towards midday, as Arden walked through the valley of statues some way behind the silent, moody form of Stavanda.

'They are quite magnificent!' called the Englishman, overwhelmed by the power of the sculptures. 'Magnificent,' he repeated, and smiled as Stavanda stopped and turned.

'Is there not a life to them?' said the old man.

'Indeed!' said Arden. 'I begin to understand what you meant.'

He looked about him, cool in the brisk wind which accompanied the sporadic flashes of sun through the high clouds. He wore only his windcheater and jeans but Stavanda himself was in a thin white shirt and loose flannels and must have been quite cool.

The sculptor didn't show it, manifested only a slight irritation with the wind that insisted on blowing his hair about his face. They looked back along the valley to where the house seemed to grow from the rock face of what might have once been a quarry, or a cliff too sheer for any plant to find a perch upon it.

'Yes, a quarry,' said Stavanda when Arden queried the site. 'Very old, very old indeed. Running through the rock is a wide vein of the stone I use for my carvings. White stone, crystal-line; I could have told you the name of it years ago, but names matter less these days. I built the house myself. I carved the façades myself. I *am* the house, Mister Arden; if you like, I am the valley, I am these statues. I am my work, which is why I found it so frightening that you failed to grasp how an artist's life is represented in whatever lifeform he carves.'

He laughed suddenly, staring sideways at Arden, who was agreeing thoughtfully. The Englishman reached out to touch the porcelain-smooth surface of one statue that showed a man, crouching, staring into the distance. The sculptor said, 'Do you see any golems, Mister Arden?'

Arden laughed. 'I apologize for my naïveté.'

'No need to apologize,' said Stavanda as they continued along a winding path. They were several hundred yards from the river, but not hidden from it, for the trees appeared to have been cleared along a stretch of shoreline and Arden watched the cool waters enviously. He loved to swim in rivers, even in cold weather, and this river was as clean and crystal fresh as glass. Stavanda suddenly turned, blocking the pathway so that Arden was forced to stop, thrusting his hands into the pockets of his windcheater. The old man said, 'No need to apologize, because if you think about it … *I* am a golem.'

'Oh yes? You seem very fleshy to me.' Arden laughed nervously. There was something disconcertingly intense about Stavanda's expression and attitude.

'But a golem I nevertheless am, Mister Arden. Look around you. Look at the house, look at the valley, *my* valley. I shaped it, I shaped everything in it. I am an artist. I work in stone, in the fabric of the earth, the floor upon which you stand. I am a shaper, towards an end that instils life into the cold stone. I am in this valley, Mister Arden; I am in the rock that lies beneath your feet, and the white stone that graces your eyes as you look around. And that stone is in me, I am inseparable from my work; it and I are closer than two adjacent drops of water in that river down there. I am stone. Mister Arden; I am the golem that for a second, last night, you feared to see stalking through the valley.'

'Metaphorically,' said Arden, unsure of himself again, nervous beneath Stavanda's intense scrutiny. He felt he was being tested, an appalling sensation. He didn't know what to do or say to impress this old man whose co-operation he needed both in supplying an article and in supplying the time for his interest in Karina.

'Metaphorically what?' said Stavanda. 'Metaphorically stalking?'

'Metaphorically a golem,' said Arden.

'As my statues are metaphorically life?'

'Indeed.'

They walked on, Arden growing restless with thoughts of Karina. He had hoped she would come on this walk with them so that he could at least look at her, smell her, have an excuse – occasionally – to touch her. She had not appeared at breakfast and, though by nature Arden was impolite enough to ask where she might have been, he had not, somehow, found the words to phrase the question without advertising his more subtle intentions.

Wherever he looked in the valley he saw the human shapes of Stavanda's life work. Naked figures, and couples, animals and abstracts, all smooth, all detailed in that precise and irregular way that tells of a truly remarkable eye for accuracy.

Here, a woman bathed her face, leaning above an unseen bowl; the sun on her flanks brought white life to the cold stone, and as Arden watched her so she seemed to move slightly. When he looked at Stavanda the old sculptor was half amused; Arden felt that he understood something of the old man's fixation with the frozen life of his art, a life not human, yet something beyond his own conception of human life. Further along the valley he came across a montage of lovers, legs and arms entwined in the early embrace of potential love; Arden walked about the carving, amazed at the detail, the sensuousness of the white stone as it fashioned the commerce of the unknown couple. Elsewhere a middle-aged man petted a dog, the age depicted upon him as it had hung, loose and awful, upon his living body. The dog was on its hind feet, paws within human hand, mouth open in that anthropomorphic smile that makes a canine such a pleasant companion.

An empty pedestal appeared between high heather; purple-fringed and unnaturally precise, it seemed out of place in the valley and Arden was puzzled to know what might have once stood upon it.

Stavanda, as if in answer to the unspoken question, jumped upon the white stone cube and turned about to face Arden, his arms extended.

'Here stands the artist, alive.'

'A self portrait?' asked Arden, and as he spoke his eyes found the thin markings of the chisel that spelled, in faint relief, the name Stavanda upon the base. 'A self portrait,' he repeated. 'Is it finished?'

'Years ago,' said Stavanda, descending to the earth again. 'I'm polishing the stone, touching it up a little. You shall see it tomorrow.'

'Thank you. I'd like to. Tell me, is there …?'

He caught the flow of words in time, managed to appear distracted by some movement further up the valley.

Stavanda glanced at him, frowning for a second, perhaps angry for a second. 'Is there what? Karina? Is there a statue of Karina?'

Angry with himself, annoyed that his simple question, his simple inability to complete the question, must have sounded intensely suspicious, Arden quickly said, with a surprised smile, 'You've sculpted Karina? That's interesting. No, I was about to ask if there was a possibility of photographing some of your work.'

'Absolutely not!' snapped the old man. 'But believe me,' he added more gently, as he led the way down towards the river, slipping on the fern growth and steadying himself with his hand. 'Believe me, you will never forget my statues. They have an effect upon you. What you remember will remain with you always. Far better than cheap photographs.'

'The persistence of memory,' thought Arden with a smile as he slipped after Stavanda with only slightly more deftness; and, as he walked, so Stavanda sent a chill through him with his next words: 'I wonder, Mr Arden, just what you will make of your article and me. I wonder what a man like you will do with what he learns.'

'A man like me? What sort of man is that?'

Stavanda turned to look back across his shoulder for a moment; there was amusement on his face, mischief in his bright eyes. 'A man who pretends to know so much and comprehends so little.' He looked away from Arden. 'Or perhaps you know the value of my name, if not my art.'

Before Arden could answer they had reached the river. Here they stood and surveyed the statues that were half hidden by low-hanging tree branches and high-growing fronds of fern near the water. 'She is there,' said Stavanda, pointing to the right. 'I know you find her very beautiful. I should be a depressed man if you did not. That, after all, is why I share my love with her.'

For a second Arden was perplexed by the implication of spiritual shallowness in Stavanda's relationship with the woman evinced in his last statement.

Then, his face burning, unable to look back at the old man, he walked towards the nude statue of Karina and stood before it.

She was seated, her legs tucked under her; she was leaning on one hand while her other seemed to brush back stray curls of hair. She looked across the water, serene, cool, as if she watched herself in the distorting ripples of the current. She seemed thoughtful, almost sad. Arden looked at that perfect body, the small breasts, the slender thighs, remembering them, remembering how they had been beneath his fingers, beneath his lips.

Love stirred him, made him redden and he turned away. He stooped and splashed his hand in the cold water, and, when Stavanda came up to him, he apologized.

'It's seeing her like this and knowing I must face her across dinner tonight. It's childish, but I do feel a slight embarrassment.'

The old man laughed. 'What an excellent liar you are,' he said, and when Arden met his gaze he felt as if he himself had been turned to stone.

They returned to the house, Arden quite weary from the extensive walk and frequent scrambling. Almost as soon as they passed up the shallow steps to enter the area of lawned fore-garden, Stavanda excused himself and slipped away, around the side of the house and presumably to his studio, for soon after there came the distant, almost shrill, sound of a chisel working on stone.

Arden amused himself by walking through the shrubbery, past several greenhouses, and through an overgrown and obviously unplanted garden. A scattering of cabbages and potato plants told of previous years of cultivation, but now it was weeds and thistles that dominated the patch of ground behind the house.

He saw no obvious signs of the studio where Stavanda worked, although the sound of chipping continued, apparently coming from within the house itself. After a few minutes Arden arrived back on the front lawn, where he located an easy chair and watched the advance of the afternoon.

After ten minutes or so of quiet contemplation he became suddenly uneasy. He turned on the chair to look back at the house, and for a moment he thought he saw Stavanda watching him from the balcony of his own room. Strangely, the figure moved away abruptly; the sound of stone-working had not ceased; and Arden relaxed slightly, supposing that he had been deceived by the reddening light and the fleetingness of the observation.

But he now found himself thinking almost obsessively about Stavanda, concerned not with the nature of his work but with thoughts of Stavanda's suspicions, or awarenesses, in relation to his guest and Karina. Surely Stavanda had not discovered about the affair in Paris ... the man had spent most of the days walking alone in the streets and along the river, absorbing atmosphere and vision. His invitation to Arden to come to the valley had been warm and enthusiastic, the most noticeable moment of friendliness that Arden had observed from this insular old man.

His thoughts drifted away as the day vanished. Slightly perturbed at being left to his own devices he rose and walked through the french windows into the extensive drawing-room that faced the terrace. He located the drinks cabinet and returned to his chair with a half bottle of scotch and a glass. More relaxed, he consumed several shots of whisky while the lowering sun set the scattered statues to all sorts of fire.

As dusk covered the valley, and the statues became invisible against the universal grey, he became aware that the sounds of work had finished. He rose, slightly unsteadily, and returned to the drawing room. He walked through the hallway to the dining-room, and here found Stavanda already eating. A place was set for him. Karina was not there, nor was the table set for her.

'Forgive me for starting,' said the sculptor, waving a fork by way of greeting, 'but I was reluctant to interrupt your reflections.'

'Not at all. I was quite relaxed.'

'And I was too damned hungry to wait.'

Arden seated himself, reached for the half-full decanter of claret and changed his mind. The scotch was repeating on him, and he felt dizzy and slightly nauseous. Roast beef had been served and he sliced a liberal portion, eating it alone, un-garnished. Stavanda finished his own meal, wiped his mouth and rose from the table.

'Forgive me,' he said, 'but I have work to do.'

And as abruptly and as rudely as that, he was gone.

Arden finished his slight meal and decided on a glass of wine. Eventually he decided on the whole decanter and took this to his room where he lay down on the bed and soon slept.

He woke at a little after midnight and felt quite refreshed. The decanter of wine had spilled onto the counterpane of his bed and he guiltily stripped the covering and piled it in a corner. Combing his hair, removing his jacket in favour of a fresh shirt, he stepped from his room into the dimly lit corridor outside. Pausing at the farther end, by the room he knew to be Stavanda's, he listened hard for breathing. He heard none. Opening the door slightly he peered in, but the bed was made up, unspoiled, and the room had something of a stale, unused air about it.

He closed the door as gently as he had opened it, despite this being rather pointless caution. Walking into the right wing of the sprawling house he paused by Karina's room, listened here as well before gently opening the door and satisfying himself that her room, also, was unoccupied.

'What are you doing, Mr Arden?'

He was startled as Stavanda came up behind him, watching him suspiciously.

Embarrassed, Arden smiled and said, 'I felt like some company. I do apologize ...'

Stavanda smiled thinly. 'I apologize for deserting you,' he said, taking Arden's arm and leading him back to his own room. 'I understand the need for talk in a strange place, and I promise not to abuse your patience again. Karina will be here tomorrow. Goodnight, Mr Arden.'

'Goodnight.'

'Sleep well.'

three

In the morning, after a somewhat restless night, Arden arrived in the breakfast-room quite breathless from running down the stairs; he imagined Karina would be there, waiting for him, but to his disappointment he faced an empty room. The table was set for one.

The food was hot, smoked meats, eggs and toast. He was very hungry – the drink and his small evening meal had seen to that. Thus he soon forgot his irritation at again eating alone and filled himself with eggs, bacon and coffee.

It was only as he finished, and was rising with the intention of seeking someone out, that he saw the small white envelope propped up between two silver serving dishes. Opening the note he found it to be from Karina, asking him to come and find her near the river.

Smiling, he pocketed the paper and left the house.

It was a fine day, still slightly cloudy, but the sun was much more in evidence and there was about the valley that heavy warmth that characterizes summer; perhaps, even during the preceding night, spring had been nudged aside and the new season admitted.

As if to confirm the point he saw a butterfly, huge and speckled with brown and red colouring; it bobbed and weaved above the heather and the gnarled hawthorn until abruptly it stopped, apparently in mid-air, fluttering frantically. Arden walked closer and saw that it was trapped against an immense silvery spider's web spun between the branches of two small thorn trees. The gleaming body of the spider was suspended halfway between its lair and the prey, as if the creature were unsure quite how to approach this immense and violently struggling meal. Arden reached out to rescue the butterfly, but before he could touch it the creature had pulled free by its own efforts. The spider scurried back to its hidey-hole under-neath the branch; Arden could see its trembling shape between the shiny and still life-like husks of its previous insect prey.

Walking on, Arden felt totally relaxed in the warmth. Even the statues seemed more alive, and he reappraised them with an eye far more sympathetic for the honesty of their appearance. They were, he acknowledged, masterpieces of sculpture. It was hard to believe that one man, one mortal pair of hands, had fashioned such beauty from the stone. A god, even two gods, would have been hard put to achieve so much.

As he passed the pedestal which the day before had been empty he found himself gazing at the canny, penetrating stare of Stavanda: perfectly formed in the white marble-like stone, the nude figure was crouched, hands clasped before it, watching him. There, in detail, were the deep lines, the facial sculpture that was the skilled work of time, rather than the chisel, but which was here chiselled in stone in such a perfect copy that Arden stopped and was amazed. He stared at the paunchy figure, the member dangling low between the thighs, the flesh of the legs and arms still firm, but beginning to show signs of deterioration. This was the Stavanda of yesterday, not yesteryear, and now Arden understood why the artist had been so keen to get away, so urgent to be alone. He imagined that this statue, this self portrait, was made to age along with the artist himself. When Arden had arrived, a stranger in the valley, a rare visitor, the ego of the artist had been such that he could not bear for the Englishman to see a sculpture that was not wholly and exactly representative of the lifeform that had inspired it.

While Arden had amused himself with whisky and idle thoughts of the beautiful Spanish girl, Stavanda had been etching into the stone portrait those features of the past few years which time had painted upon his own wind-tanned flesh.

Truly, a magnificent feat, and a wonderful piece of art. Living art. Art that transcended the life implicit in the flesh and the time implicit in the stone, the primal clay that formed the image. Stavanda was right. The stone *did* live, in a way beyond the simple understanding of any man but he who was *in* the stone, and in whom the stone itself resided.

His name was called from a distance – a woman's voice that he recognized as Karina's. He scrambled down the slope to where the land levelled until it reached the river. He saw her; she was sitting on a boulder, in the shade of an old and wind-battered silver ash. She was wearing a wide, knee-length dress with an off-the-shoulder bodice – white of course – that flattered her in every way possible. He walked towards her, glancing, as he passed the spot, at the statue of her nude form that he had scrutinized the day before.

For a second he thought he was looking in the wrong place, for the pedestal he could see there was empty. But Karina called, 'Stavanda has it up at the house, putting a few touches to it. Always the perfectionist.'

Arden laughed. He greeted Karina with a light kiss on the cheek, then took her right hand in both of his and lifted the fingers to his lips. 'Not ageing the statue,' he said. 'There is no need for that.'

'Thank you.'

Unable to prevent the impulsive action, Arden drew the girl to his body and kissed her hard. She melted to him, entwining her arms around him and returning the kiss with all the fierceness of one who has waited, impatient, for too many hours. Breathless, they laughed as they drew apart, and then walked to the river, to sit upon the empty stone pedestal and watch the water.

'Stavanda's talent is quite formidable,' said Arden. 'He must have worked every moment of his life to produce so many beautiful statues. He must produce them with staggering speed.'

Karina squeezed his hand and smiled. 'Stavanda never worked fast. The life of the statues grows slowly, almost agonizingly.'

'But there are so many!' Arden looked about him, seeing little more than tree and undergrowth, but knowing that more than a thousand statues – a figure that Stavanda had himself supplied the day before – were scattered throughout the valley. 'Are you implying that he didn't work alone? He had help?' Suspicious, intrigued, Arden caught the girl's attention, tried to pierce the coolness of her gaze so that he might discern Stavanda's dark secret. But Karina reflected back his suspicion as a millpond reflects sunlight.

'Does any artist work alone? Ever?'

More word games, thought Arden. She's referring to his talent, to that innate energy that drives him and which only he possesses in that particular form.

He said as much aloud.

Karina looked away, looked down. Arden found himself fascinated by the smoothness, the soft tanned skin of her face and neck, the full rise of her breasts, much revealed in the lacy bodice. The love in him stirred angrily, restlessly.

She said, 'When he was still an eternally young man – perhaps no older than you – the stone possessed him, became him, and he it. Since that time he has created almost in concert with the valley itself.' She glanced at him and Arden noticed that she seemed troubled, some dark thought, perhaps, shadowing the brightness of her face. 'It's as if the valley *is* the sculptor, working through his hands, and he is the white stone from the quarry embodied in the dextrous form of the old man.'

'Have you seen him work? Have you watched him?'

Karina shook her head and smiled, her moment of trouble gone as swiftly as it had come. 'Never. Stavanda sculpts from experience, using people he knows or has met as models. Everything he does is part of a design; every action, every movement, every word he speaks, every drop of blood he sheds, all are for the sculpture upon which he is working, upon which the valley is working through him. But I have never watched him in the final work, and I suppose I never shall.'

As if tired of this idle talk, perhaps remembering – as Arden was remembering – their stolen nights in Paris, those several weeks ago, Karina turned and kissed the Englishman, hard and with passion. She reached for his shirt and deftly slipped open the buttons. The sun was hot and summery, the pedestal beneath them warm to the touch, if hard to their flesh.

They slipped off their clothes as quickly and quietly as if they loved in a private house and were behaving with silent discretion. She touched him, gently and expertly, and as his weight came down upon her, easily, feeling with his skin the contours of her body, so they matched and melded, so he sank into her, every part of him, in the warm sex in her where he knew he belonged. Her legs entwined about him, trapping him, and her arms wrapped so tightly about his neck and waist that he thought their bodies would fuse. She allowed him no movement save that of his hips, which he moved quietly, gently, lingering over each deep approach so that they could both feel the power of the other in the drawn-out seconds of pleasure that accompanied each completion of his entry.

They kissed, and when their tongues met her teeth clamped playfully upon him, nipping the soft flesh and trapping him, so that he laughed, caught in this enjoyable fashion, trapped like an insect in a particularly lovely fly trap.

Abruptly she pushed him away, untwined her legs and shifted her body so that he was forced to withdraw.

Arden felt a moment's panic, his heart racing as he glanced about at the trees and river, and at the slopes of the hill. 'Have you heard something? What is it? Stavanda?'

'He's watching us.' Her face was pallid beneath the tan – her eyes wide with fear. She suddenly shivered, drew her blouse about her shoulders. 'I should have told you.'

'Told me what? Where is he?' Arden stared through the shrubs and undergrowth, seeing only statues and the dancing patterns of sun on white stone. 'I can't see him.'

Karina laughed, and Arden thought it sounded almost cruel, almost pitying. 'Of course you can. Didn't I explain to you? He's everywhere, Alexander. He has watched you every moment since you came here. He has been watching patiently, waiting to trap you. Oh God!' She had stopped and suddenly winced with pain, her eyes closed, her hands touching her face. 'It's too late ... too late for you, too late for him ... for me ...' She suddenly laughed again, this time with a tone of irony behind the sound. She looked at Arden and shook her head. 'It had to come to this ... it had to happen that one day I'd love somebody. I'm sorry ...'

Not sure of why he was so afraid, Arden dressed quickly and stood by the pedestal, looking at the semi-naked girl.

'Is he going to kill me?'

She shrugged. 'He's inhuman, Alexander. Quite inhuman. His art is all there is, and the valley is all there is, but the valley *is* his art – it misses only life, real life. He feeds on life, on my life, on your life, on the lives of all who come to the valley. He drinks their souls and shapes the stone perfectly because of it. People leave here as shadows, the shadows of statues. He uses me because of what I am—'

'An insect trap.'

'A life trap. You, more than any man, I think he would like to suck quite dry, to suck your very vitality.'

Arden felt cold sweat break from his skin as he looked anxiously around. 'To suck me dry ... to kill me ... my God, how long has he known about us?'

Karina looked puzzled. 'About us? He's known from the beginning.'

Shocked, Arden found himself staring at her, shaking his head. 'He's always known? Then why – then why has he waited so long to confront me?'

'He doesn't want to kill you because of your affair with me,' said the girl quietly, speaking as if she addressed a child. 'He wants to kill you because you are sordid in his eyes ... and not just sordid, but shallow. Your writing is motivated not by inner turmoil, by some energy of imagination, but by material needs. He will never carve you in stone, but I think he wishes to suck you dry so that he can carve some darkness into the white stone, some imperfection into his perfect creations—' Again she winced with pain, twisted slightly on the stone pedestal, and touched a hand delicately to her naked belly. Her eyes, when she met Arden's concerned gaze, were filled with longing. 'Alex ... kiss me ...' Her body seemed rigid, almost stiff. Slowly she reached for him, her desperation communicating itself through every forced gesture. 'Make love to me, Alex ... love me ... no, *no*! ... swim, swim ... quickly!'

He took a step towards her, drawn to her beauty, desiring her, longing to complete their lovemaking. She cried out, the sound of one dying. Arden turned and ran to the river, plunged in and surfaced out where the flow was fastest. He swam strongly, despite his sodden clothes, and found time to glance back, to the pedestal and that private place among the trees. Karina seemed to be waving to him, her skin quite white at this distance.

The river swept him fast, out of the valley and away from the danger that, in one sense, he had been aware of all along. He smiled to think that perhaps his escape had been a narrow one. He would have found it difficult to comment in depth upon Stavanda's highly personal view of his art and his life, and in all likelihood the article would have been worthless. Facing a cold and wet reality as he struggled against the current, tired now and seeking a place to come ashore, Arden came to terms with the fact that his real interest in Stavanda had always been a part of trying to impress the woman in his life. That brief affair had been worth the wasted effort of coming so far in search of such an unsatisfying art. And he was forewarned, now, against any future recklessness such as pursuing his dream of passion into the very home of the man he was deceiving. He felt pleased with his escape, although it grew bitterly cold in the water and the river swept him faster between the slippery banks.

Ahead of him, then, he saw a place on the shore where he might come aground and strip off his freezing clothes, to warm himself in the bright sun. He swam towards the river bank where it jutted out into the water and was fleetingly aware of the sun reflecting on something white upon the shore.

It was a statue of Karina, her body reclining, her arm out-stretched as if waving, or reaching. The shock of seeing it made Arden lose his rhythm as he swam. He was swept past the place among the trees, and onwards into deeper water, where the river flowed faster, and grew colder, and colder.

And as he swam on, desperate now, struggling to find the strength to keep himself afloat, he heard the unmistakable sound of hammering ... the sound of chisel working stone, with such excitement and energy that the ringing strikes were run together into a single passionate tone.

ASHES

Ash, ash—
You poke and stir.
Flesh, bone, there is nothing there—

Sylvia Plath,
'Lady Lazarus'

I am Joseph Questel: killer. Have you heard of me? I hope so. Not for any satisfaction of my over-rated ego, but because if you *haven't* heard of Joseph Questel you are probably the only person in our wonderful Galaxy who hasn't.

Some people call me 'The Animal'. I prefer Questel. I especially dislike the name 'sadist'. But I have been called 'The Sadist Questel' and it makes me feel a little angry inside.

My name is Kevin Karr. It is a superficial disguise, concealing the killer beneath. I often wear false hair, eye-catching clothes. A flamboyant attire takes the roving eye away from the face.

How many people who catch your eye on a walkway, in a tube, catch your eye because of their facial characteristics? Virtually none? Of course. The human race is a collection of artificial fibres animated by shapeless blobs of pink flesh.

Which is lucky for me.

There are twenty-three Galactic news-sheets. Some are dailies, some are weeklies, some appear but rarely, depending on news content.

And I am news content. I feature on every front page, every day, every month, every year.

Me, Questel, killer of innocent and helpless children. My photograph, my movements, my sadism, my guilt. It's all there in black, red and white; fuzzy photographs, clear-cut caricatures.

So don't tell me you haven't heard of me, don't tell me you haven't seen me. I'm a way of life. And Rainer, he too is a way of life, and Lazlo. And Queron, and Boor-Badalwi. And Jones, and the Galactic nonentity called Major Findik.

Killers all, hated all … running all. News.

We all have a job to do. Mine is to be hated. Never mind me, I'm just a two-dimensional adventure and my screen time is running out.

And I run, and run, and I am hounded and wherever I go I am found. And there is no escape.

May I bask for a moment in self pity? Will you forgive me if I attempt to justify my hatred for everyone and everything? Go ahead, take my words and digest them, feed them to your hate, file them with the pictures and the stories of what I, Questel, did during my war-time career in the 'Eighteen Twenty-Seven' war.

I don't mind. It's my job. Take me or leave me.

Does it surprise you, perhaps, to know that I eat, I sleep, I love … yes, *love*. Is there such a thing?

I love darkness. True love. My truest love was a small attic in a dusty and dingy house on Coneworld. A rat shared that darkness with me. Snug as bugs we lived in our dark corner, sharing our food, sharing our love.

Rats in an attic. When the rat died I moved. The darkness is still there, waiting for me.

If I walk in the street I am rarely recognized. My face has changed, my disguise is effective. I pass unnoticed. And yet always I am found. Explain that!

Women seem to find me fascinating. I believe it is because of a certain youthfulness in my approach.

Forty years ago, when a youth, I fascinated women for a different reason. It was because of a certain maturity in my approach.

The women I fascinated were the same type.

Explain *that*!

I feast on flesh as the films and documents say I feasted on flesh during the war. Only in those days I killed, and now I merely savour. One day it will be taken from me, the right to taste a woman's flesh.

I shan't miss it. Meat is meat. I shall lick my arm and pretend.

Pretence, after all, is my trade. It is what keeps me a free man.

Free in all but mind.

I never married and now I never shall. I shall never do anything that is the right of a man, because I have no rights left. No rights, that is, except the right to run for my life. And I'm good at that, oh yes.

Except I'm always found. Explain it, someone.

To be truthful I don't need it explained and eventually I'll tell you why. In the meantime, pause a moment and think of a sun, a blue-white sun, slowly and gracefully billowing out into space as it begins its journey towards nova. Think of that star, and think of me.

When I was on Timeslow, a small and backward planet in the Dragonfire cluster, I was happier than I have ever been.

I found Joni on Timeslow, and a wonderful sense of isolation. The wind storms that ravished the planet's surface were kin to me, the hail that flung itself through the small city in which I lived was mother and father to me. Fog and sand, they were my most comfortable clothes.

In obscurity I walked, in comfort I lived. On Timeslow I was Kevin Karr, and Joseph Questel was the ghoul who lived within my shadow. And on Timeslow shadows rarely appear.

Once upon a time I slaughtered a billion innocent people. The details aren't necessary. I slaughtered them horribly, many with my own hands. Old men I garrotted. There are pictures of me doing just that. I am not smiling as I wrench the life from their squirming bodies. When it is done I let the bodies slip to the cold ground and I just stand there, and for a moment, before the film is cut, one would almost think I was unaware of what I did.

And I will swear the dead man breathes, but then dead men often do; don't they?

On the news-screen I have my own show.

It is called the 'Search for Joseph Questel'. It occupies the eleven to eleven fifteen pm slot and it has a musical introduction that I recognize as a concerto by Frederick Darzel as interpreted by the contemporary electroharpist David Forbes. I enjoy Forbes's music, his interpretation of early twenty-first century harp music rather than his own compositions. I once heard him play at a concert. He played his interpretation of Minuet in G. That is a piece of music written centuries ago. It was terrible, but then the music of centuries ago is coarse, and vulgar, and tuneless.

When the concert was finished, he was called back for an encore.

'Thank you, ladies and gentlemen,' he said. I smiled from my seat in the back row. I held my hands ready to applaud for I had enjoyed his musical evening. 'Thank you, thank you very much. You have been a wonderful audience. I shall play an encore with the greatest of pleasure. It is a piece of music I have adapted from a concerto by Darzel, and I call it 'The Mind of Questel' because it is hateful and arrogant, superficially beautiful and yet with viciously ugly undertones.'

The news-screen always plays that piece of music before the show starts. Then a wizened little man with sparse grey hair appears on camera and in a racy, excited voice proceeds to outline where the search for me has extended itself in the last twenty-four hours. Then they show film of the bodies on the planet that I used as a dumping ground for the men and women I killed. Then that same bit of film of me dispatching an old man, and looking as if I'm not aware of anything, just before the film cuts off.

The commentary goes like this: 'The hunt for Joseph Questel, the sick man who personally organized and personally helped with the death, by the most gruesome methods, of over one thousand million innocent women and children has today been extended here to Timeslow. This is the first time Timeslow has been the foxhole of Joseph Questel. Throughout the day agents of the

League of Hunters have been infiltrating the major cities and towns of the planet in an attempt to take Questel by surprise, an attempt that failed. Just to remind you of the sort of man the league is hunting, here is some film taken by an agent on Trona, the concentration-planet where the innocents met their grisly demise ...'

By the time the news of the hunters reaching Timeslow was being given its second airing, I was in deep space, light years away from the planet.

I was desperately lonely. Joni was still on Timeslow and I should never see her again.

Within the space of just a few hours my happy seclusion had been broken, and again, with just memories to carry me through the tortuous days and nights, I found myself looking for somewhere to hide.

Even then I was acutely aware of the inconsistencies, of the strange things that repeatedly occurred.

Things like the expression on my face as I killed the old man ...

The way the dead man breathed – or seemed to.

The morning of my hasty departure from Timeslow started badly, and continued as it had started.

First there was the nightmare. I always have nightmares when I awaken before dawn and drift off to sleep again. The nightmare comes then as if it is lingering on the borders between consciousness and unconsciousness, and only in my semi-asleep state can it come through ...

It is a nightmare in which I kill three people. It goes like this: there is a dark and expansive garden and a huge hound running towards me. Its mouth opens and shuts as if it is barking but there is no sound. As it leaps at me, mouth open to tear my throat, I shoot it with a small hand gun and it falls limply to the ground.

The two moons are high and I can see the house, a large, palatial house. There is a single light in one of the upstairs rooms. Tall pines sway and creak in the wind. One pine has recently fallen and it sprawls across the lawn, slowly dying. I run up to the house and my heart is thumping. I push open a window, creep inside, and find my way to the stairs; up the stairs, heart racing, jumping at every shadow, every noise, and then I come to a room where the door is slightly ajar.

I push the door open and creep inside – there are two beds, one has been recently occupied, and in the other a naked woman is sitting bolt upright and staring at me. Then I swing round and there is the man, dressed in pyjamas – he is holding a metal rod with which he lunges at my face. I shoot him through the chest and he gags and vomits a considerable amount of blood. The woman is screaming. As the man falls he strikes again and the rod glances off my forehead and smashes down to break the gun I hold.

The woman is still screaming. I rush across to her and slap her, but she keeps screaming. I panic and I draw my knife and cut her throat quickly. She collapses backwards.

Somebody comes through the door and, in panic, I throw the knife, not really looking to see who is there. As I jump to the window I glance back and there is a small girl slowly collapsing to the floor, the shaft of my knife sticking out of her chest.

I wake up screaming at that point for I fall from the window in the dream and the sensation of falling is the final straw ...

I have that dream many times, but only when I'm in the half sleep of early morning. Usually my nightmares are worse, much worse. I see great lines of people walking slowly towards me and I select one here, one there, and they are taken away to my own house. The rest are herded into execution pits elsewhere and slaughtered according to the whims of the officers in charge. The few I have selected, mostly young women and old men, I kill myself; I feel the bones snap, listen to the gagging cries as their life squeezes desperately past their congested lips.

I have *that* nightmare many times as well. It was no less a nightmare when it was fact, when it was reality.

Why does a man slaughter a thousand million innocent people? You would think that any man capable of such an act would be capable of answering that question. Yet I have no answer. I am unable to supply an answer to that question, even though I have searched my mind for an answer for many long years.

That is another of the inconsistencies.

And Joni ...

My last morning on Timeslow I awoke screaming. Joni was there, holding me, and slowly I became aware that I had been dreaming.

I mouthed an obscenity, climbed out of bed and walked to the window, shaking.

Joni brought me in some coffee and the news-sheet. 'Come back to bed.'

I looked at her. She was very lovely, plump and dark. She was the right height for a woman, and dressed in her black housecoat she looked very homely. That appealed to me more than anything.

I climbed onto the bed and glanced at the paper.

'Oh God ...'

'What is it?' She was sipping her coffee and reading the back page. On the front page was a small headline: 'Hunt for Questel extended to sector fifteen, in particular to Timeslow and Timequick, the two innermost planets of Caprion.'

'Nothing,' I said. And she crawled up the bed and rested her head on my chest.

'There *must* be something. You never blaspheme and you just blasphemed. Now what is it?'

'Timeslow is being invaded by the authorities.'

'But they're not after you!' She sat up and stared at me. 'Kevin, don't *worry* so much. Nobody is after you on Timeslow. They're after that bastard Questel. They have no time for small crims like you.'

Small criminals! If only she knew.

I suppose something of my thoughts expressed itself on my face. She asked. 'Did you have that nightmare again? The one about killing a little girl?'

'Yes,' I said. I had told her about the nightmare and I had convinced her that the reason I was on the run was because I *had* killed a little girl, by accident of course, but that hadn't been the way it had looked.

She understood, but I'm sure it was her instinct to mother me that had drowned out her revulsion.

'But it happened *so* long ago, Kevin. Surely you can't think the police are still after you.'

'I don't know what to think,' I said. She sat up and shook her head, slightly angry.

'I don't know. Anybody would think you were Joseph Questel, instead of Kevin Karr ... hey ...'

I was off the bed in a flash and at the window, clutching the sill as if my life depended on it. I can remember now how my mind was reeling and screaming. Outside, the city was immersed in grey fog. Hovercars zipped across the rooftops, faces peered from windows, blurred pinkness through the fog. And above them all, a hundred feet above the concrete roadway, I stared out across the morning and felt myself slip backwards towards insanity.

It was always the same! As if the expression was a trigger for my relaxing mind to double its efforts at horrifying me. *Anybody would think you were Joseph Questel* ... and when it was said, for a long time I was Joseph Questel again, with memories as vivid as they would have been if they had happened yesterday. An expression that was now almost household, a nasty, sarcastic remark that could bring yesterday in violent and uncompromising visions.

Another strangeness ...

Later, on the ship bound away from Timeslow, I sat in the lounge and watched in confusion as Joni appeared in the hatchway and smiling crossed to sit with me. For a long while I just sat and stared at her, not hearing the words I could see she was speaking.

Beyond her, reflected in the window that peered out across the depthless void of deep space, I could see an old man, a man with hair tinged grey all over, face drawn and haggard. A shadow of a man who had once been very striking to look at. When I turned my head away the man in the window looked away also, and it took a moment for me to realize who it was I regarded with such intensity.

I closed my eyes, then. When on Timeslow I had never seen my shadow. Now I knew why – I had become my own shadow, my body was as dead as if it had never been born.

'Kevin ... listen to me ...'

I was listening to a concerto by Darzel. It was playing in my mind and I could see the eyes of the player. He was stroking the wires of his electroharp and singing. Between the notes that drifted across the audio-chamber I could hear snatches of his song: *the mind of Questel ... an evil mind ... beautiful to regard ... filthy beneath.*

'Why did you follow me?' I asked Joni.

'I knew you would try and get away. But I couldn't let you go.'

I laughed. 'I've gone.'

'From Timeslow, yes. But not from me.' She reached over to hold my right hand. 'I don't ever want you to go from me. I love you, Kevin, don't you even know *that!*'

I nodded, vaguely. The grey haired man in the window watched me impassively. I thought to myself: You've killed whole nations. How do you feel?

The man in the window said: I feel like it never happened.

But it did happen. Because I can remember it.

I can't remember being born. Does that mean it didn't happen?

I don't believe I was born. No man as evil as I could have been born of woman's flesh.

The man in the window seemed to die a little.

Joni said, 'Kevin, tell me why you're so afraid. Nothing is going to stop me staying with you, now, and *I must* know why you are so terrified of everyone. Why do you react so crazily when I say certain things. *Why*, Kevin?'

It might have been an hour later that I let her hand drop from mine and turned away from where she sat on the couch, watching me.

During that hour I had come to a decision. I had decided to destroy everything I had ever cared for. I would tell Joni who I was. I would tell her and thus she would be destroyed. But there was no other way.

I cannot remember anything of that agonizing speech when, for the first time since the war, I admitted to another human being that I was Joseph Questel. I can remember that when I had told Joni as much as I could bring myself to tell her, I sat back and waited.

Joni laughed.

If she had screamed, vomited, died ... that I could have understood, that I could have borne. If she had shot me straight through the head I should have been a happy man.

She laughed.

'You fool, you silly fool.' She was angry. 'Do you think me so stupid that I would accept that ... *story*? Oh Kevin, you annoy me!'

'I don't see what there is to laugh at,' I said angrily. 'I've just told you that I'm the man you most hate in this Galaxy. I expected you to be revolted. At the least I expected you to walk away, quietly. And you laugh!'

She looked at me long and hard. I met her gaze, but I broke first. In the window I imagined I could see Forbes playing an electroharp. The notes formed rain patterns on the glass and trickled downwards to form the shapes of dead people. Behind him a grey-haired man, with sagging shoulders, gazed at nothing. Behind the grey-haired man sat a plump stranger, watching him distractedly.

Joni said to me, 'I believe you really think you *are* Joseph Questel.'

I smiled. 'Keep your voice down – please.'

'Kevin ...' she composed her thoughts. 'Questel, Joseph Questel – let me make this quite clear ... Joseph Questel is not a *real* person. He's imaginary. I swear to you, Kevin. Questel and all the others – Jones, and Lazlo, and Rainer ... they're imaginary people.' She paused a moment to let her words seep into my mind. She finished with: 'There is no such person as Joseph Questel. *Everybody* knows that!'

Once, when I was very young, before I began killing people and hating our wonderful Galaxy, I had a hero. I walked like him, talked like him, dressed like him and behaved like him. I even began to think like him. Thinking with his peculiar logic was what made my passage through the junior grades so easy. I was indebted to that man.

Then someone told me he didn't really exist, that he was a fictional character, and really I had known all along, but I'd been blind through choice.

I felt very bad for weeks.

On a ship speeding away from sector fifteen I had just been told that I didn't exist, that I was an imaginary character. Imaginary characters live, of course, in their own minds, their own imaginary worlds ... but this was reality, and I had just been told I was not a part of that reality.

I felt deeply sick, but inconsistencies came back to me, strangenesses ... things that shouldn't have been strange.

And strangest of all, why should Joni believe so sincerely that Joseph Questel was not a real person? Who was right, she or I?

I said, 'Joni, the man on the half-hour spot on the video – the Hunt *for* Joseph Questel spot. That's me! Look at me, Joni, recognize me!'

Joni laughed. 'Nothing like you. Oh really, Kevin! You're only imagining things – I don't know what has happened but you certainly seem to have flipped a little bit.'

I could hear the Darzel concerto, the soft voice of Forbes: 'The mind of Questel' – arrogant, hideous.

I could hear the concerto reach forte, the strains of the harp multiplying in the cavernous space of the concert hall, ringing their message from the walls, the ceiling.

Allegro – angry!

'Flipped? Christ! I know when I see myself on the video. I know when I see myself being hounded from planet to planet … everywhere I've stopped they've found me …'

'But never caught you …'

'Not yet. But one day the odds are all in favour of them hitting lucky.'

She shook her head. 'You are *not* Joseph Questel. The man on video is nothing like you. Why do you persist that he is?'

'I can recognize myself on the video!' And the man on the video was me.

'The man on the video doesn't look anything like you. Look, Kevin. Let me explain as far as I understand it. Joseph Questel is an imaginary character, invented for the populace of our expanding Galaxy to focus their emotions upon Questel, and all the others – channels for our hate, if you like. It works! That is why it happens. Front pages filled with news of the hated few, video crammed with newsflashes about them – and the billions of intelligent people strung through a hundred billion stars can identify with those creatures and hate them. And they can play the guessing game; where will Questel turn up next? And so on. A profit-making sideline. But mainly, Kevin, mainly a channel for our emotions. Fiction, but through the media of our minds given flesh, given existence.

'But not existence like this …' she patted my hand. 'Not *reality*. Are you saying that you are some hideous not-quite-human that our collective consciousness has brought into being?'

I didn't answer that. I could see the flicker of uncertainty in her eyes, felt her hand pull away momentarily.

The possibility was horrifying.

Horrifying.

There must be times in every man's life when he doubts any sense in his existence. A pointlessness of just *being* gets to us all eventually – with some it stays, a minority who seem to vacuolate and vanish into their own reclusion.

I had never experienced any sense of pointlessness. I went one better.

On a ship bound away from Timeslow and heading … somewhere … in the lounge of that ship I began to doubt my own existence.

Pianissimo. Fade away.

Joni was gone. I could see the plump stranger in the reflection of the lounge, his head hovering above the back of my chair as he, like me, gazed at the blackness of the void. Suddenly he smiled.

'You're Questel,' he called across the empty lounge. 'You don't look like the Questel on the video, but I recognize you. That woman was talking nonsense.'

Fortissimo. Heart beats fast. I could see Forbes as he moved with the increasing volume of his playing, thinking perhaps: This is where Questel's heart beats as he sees the masses of the dead shovelled into a pit somewhere ... Allegro, vivace. Ugly mood.

I said, to the round-faced man, 'I don't know who I am.'

He laughed. I can see him now, throwing back his head and forcing the laugh from his throat. Then he was solemn again. 'Questel. The Killer. I recognize you.'

I crossed the room to where he was sprawled in a couch. He watched me come, his eyes small and narrowed, his face round and moist. His jumpsuit was loosened around his middle.

'Don't worry Questel. I'm no nark. There's something I know about you that I know because I know it about me too. Follow that? Or shall I repeat it? I know *what* you are, because I'm one too. Christ, you must have done something really vicious to be a War Crim.'

'Vicious,' I said, nodding. 'A million vicious things. I killed and loved it.'

'You danced with the Devil!'

I didn't understand. He could see my blankness and explained. 'You no more killed a million people than you danced with Satan ... forget it. Don't you recognize me? Think, Questel. Think. A spot on the vid, about eleven in the evening.'

I didn't recognize him.

'Rainer,' he said. I could see he wasn't – at least, not the Rainer I knew. 'Rainer, himself. That's who I am. We have a lot in common. Questel ...'

'We do,' I said. 'Your crime was as foul as mine but a hundred times more perverted.'

He nodded, still smirking. 'Perverted? Sure. I'm as perverted as they come ... strangely, I don't *feel* perverted any more. Isn't that strange Questel? I was a pervert – they say – for thirty years and suddenly I'm not a pervert any more ... does that ring a bell, Joseph?'

The bell was ringing. I thought again of the question. Why does a man kill a billion innocent people? I remembered my inability to answer that question, my revulsion at the idea of committing the crime I had committed.

My focus returned to Rainer, the fat man with the cheeky grin. He was staring past me through the port. I turned to look. A star was approaching. A beautiful blue-white star, shimmering and gleaming in blue-tinged fire as the ship drew energy from it during a close-pass.

A star at the end of its life, but still to rise as the fabled phoenix in a brief and splendid moments's fire, sending its arms across the void in a sphere of intense radiation and light ... to die in splendour and fade into grey, dead, ash.

I was blue. The phoenix stirred.

Rainer said, 'No nightmares, Questel?'

'Nightmares …? Yes, I have nightmares.' I told him (I don't know why I bothered but I told him) of my day-nightmare.

He shrugged. 'That's it, then. A nasty crime, a very nasty crime. Almost assassination. It happened. Questel. It really happened.'

I shook my head. 'It's just a nightmare. My crime involved the killing of many more than three people.'

Rainer sneered. 'You killed *three*. That's why you're being punished with war crimes.'

I didn't follow. He said, 'You've been caught, Questel. A long time ago … you were caught.'

'I was never caught. That's why I run. That's why I've been running for the past seven years. That's why I'll go *on* running.' *Allegro. Forte.* 'That's why I can never settle, never find peace. That's why my nights are filled with horror, with sights of death, with smells of decay, and the screams of the not-quite-dead-but-being-incinerated-anyway. That's why I left Timeslow, why the video puts out a regular show on me, making people hate me, loathe me, search for me … You say I was caught? Christ – my body would be scattered over the Universe if I'd been caught. What they'd give to *catch* me, Rainer, what they'd *give*.'

'They caught you,' said Rainer disinterestedly. 'Seven years ago. Take my word for it. Look, Questel, I'm only doing this for your own good, only telling you so that at least *one* guy like me can be given a chance not to waste his life being the goose in a wild, wild chase.' He was so calm, so sure. I felt tears in my eyes, my reason spinning, slipping. Just as with Joni, there was an unmistakable ring of truth to his words, and yet I could not, could *not*, accept what he was saying.

'How could I have been caught?'

I was shouting and as I shouted he sat up and shouted back, pointing a pudgy finger at me. 'They caught you, Questel, and erased your past, and made you into Questel, the War Crim. A man with terrible memories – memories to punish you for what you'd done to three people. And now you *are* a War Crim, but little memories creep back through, vague recollections of your previous life, memories that slip through when you least expect them. And me, Joseph … have some pity for me. I'm not a perverted killer. But I think I am – or rather, thought I was up until a few days ago. I believed I was a fugitive, on the run for committing a diabolical crime – as diabolical as yours, in its own way. It's the way, Questel, the way of punishment now. Big bad boys like you and me, committed to an eternity of running. The worse the crime, the worse the crime you *think* you've committed, and have to live with as you run.

'Do you know, Questel, that if a man runs from the law for three years he is as emotionally and physically and psychologically damaged and punished as if he'd served eighty years in the pens on Mars or Trega. Do you know that? And how long have you been running? Seven years? You've been punished, Joseph, punished you have *been*. But there'll be no end, Questel, not yet there won't. Perhaps not until you die! Always you'll think they're after you, and why? Because your name will be in the papers, on the vid, everywhere. And every time you see the unknown face that is Questel you will see your own, because that's the way you have been conditioned. And every time you and the two, three thousand other Questels that exist, all running, each time they come to a planet the bulletins go out. You're all scattered, all of you, like all the Rainers, all the Lazlos, all the Findiks. Scattered across the Universe … but you're observed, and everywhere each one of you goes there are faceless men, with many jobs, one of which is following you and your namesakes; they will see you and the planet you have come to and will then report 'Questel is here'.

'And you'll move on.'

He was quiet for a moment. The ship's engines thrummed into life for a brief moment and died away below perception. 'Time and time again. An eternity of running. For a crime you didn't commit, a crime that is worse than that which you *did* commit and for which you are being punished.'

He sat back suddenly. His eyes glazed over. 'I've been running for thirty years. And suddenly it's as if a veil had been ripped away, and there … I can see how it used to be, and the whole reason for my running I see is just an illusion. It's an accident … this lifting of the veil. It shouldn't have happened, I'm sure. But it has and now I feel sick, Questel, I feel really sick to think that I've been running from nothing for nothing. That's why I'm telling you all this, Joseph. Maybe I can prevent you wasting your life … maybe …' He shook his head. 'But in all likelihood you've been given a conditioned reflex to reject such data as I'm giving you now. But one day you'll feel the same as I feel now because I don't suppose you'll run forever. Some day the veil will be lifted for you, the punishment ended. But by then you will never be the same again.'

He never said another word, just sat back and stared at nothing. I wanted so much to believe him and yet, as he had said, my mind could not accept what he had told me. Even so, a part of my mind was studying his story and one overriding feeling came pouring out of that darkness: surely there was more point to my existence than just being punished? And the longer I thought about it the more I knew that there *had* to be something more, something that Rainer, for all his investigating and snooping, had been unable to come up with. Something … meaningful!

I was right. Looking back on that day when we sat in the lounge, the light from the unstable sun casting flickering shadows about the walls, I can see now how even then things were being framed ready for my final decision.

I didn't tell Joni what I had learned. Not because I was unsure whether or not I believed it but simply because … why should I tell her? I played along with what she had said, and convinced her that I was nervous and cracking, and needed rest, and *that* was why I had said I was Questel. She believed me.

'We will hide at the farthest reach of the Galaxy, on a backward, barren planet, with nothing and nobody but each other,' and she hugged me, ruffling my hair and smiling. 'My grey-haired convict, my beautiful, wonderful middle-aged frightened man. Just remember that I love you.'

Eyes closed, smile so happy, lips full and moist as they pressed against mine, bodies clutched together as we sought for each other and fought against the currents of present time and were lost, out of time, out of the world, lost as only lovers *can* be lost, floating in a dimension as distant from the Universe as that state called Heaven is distant from me.

The next morning, as she slept, I gently pressed a needle into her jugular vein and administered a fatal dose of poison. She jerked in her death sleep, and I kissed her mouth until her body froze and her eyes ran with tears as if she dreamed in death of the life I had prevented her from experiencing.

Now, as my existence slowly comes to an end, there are fires in my mind.

I have immense sympathy for that blue star, somewhere in the void, a star that was visited briefly by a fragmental piece of machinery from another world as it stole an infinitesimally small amount of that dying energy. That sun and I are brothers, on the descending curve of the graph that is life.

Strangely, the descending curve is, at the moment, angled sharply upwards. But the crest is ahead, and beyond the crest there is just darkness.

Ash.

A new 'spot' has appeared on the video.

A smart young man, dressed in the robes of a Senior Galactic Servant, sits before the camera and reads from what are obviously blank sheets. He has memorized already the terrible facts he has to report.

'The mystery assassin has struck at Valliant, a small world in the Yellow Suns cluster. Law officials numbering several hundred were senselessly killed by *tafrin* poisoning and their bodies defiled. This makes over a thousand killings by the man who signs himself 'K.K.'.

'Information is now available on the identity of the killer who is believed to be Joseph Questel, a hunted man, wanted for his crimes of perversion and inhumanity during the Spiral War of "Eighteen Twenty-Seven".'

It went on. And on.

I had to laugh. I didn't mind that they had now revealed my identity. I didn't mind that now I would be snapped into confinement with the ease of an insect caught in a mesh cage.

I had revenged myself for my senseless running, for my broken life. Oh yes, I believed Rainer – with each passing day I believed him more. I had *made* myself believe. And with each passing day the feeling of some deeper, undefined meaning to my life grew stronger.

Fires burning, reaching. Rushing, tearing towards the crest ...

And strangely I no longer thought of a musician with an electroharp, strumming and insulting me with the elegant motions of his sensitive fingers as he rendered music to describe a monster.

I mourned a sun which, from my room, I could see as a glowing healthy sun, years away from the nova that would now be consuming a volume of space greater than the solar system that was my hiding place.

There is an urge within me. I had not noticed it until I embarked upon my spree of killing. And, I might add, the defiling of the bodies was not something I enjoyed, merely something I threw in for the sake of my Galactic viewership.

The hate must be maintained. We all have our jobs to do.

I think of Rainer, sometimes. With his grin, and his tears. A happy man, in the prime of his grief. A soul lost, and wandering. Looking about me at our wonderful Galaxy, at the planets and peoples, and chugging freighters, at the crews and passengers, at the suns and the men who walk upon them (for we walk upon suns in our advanced and wonderful Galaxy) I can see only drawn faces.

It is said that the shape of man is changing. In that ancient era we know of as the Dark Ages a man was tall if he rose above five feet five. In the twenty-first century a tall man was six feet six.

But it is not in physical dimensions that the man of the thirtieth century is changing from his predecessors. I have a photograph of my great-great-great-grandfather. He has a wonderful moustache, and his clothes are nonexistent as was the habit in those days.

He is sitting with his wife. They are both captured on the 3-D gloss in the prime of their life, seventy-six ... they are both smiling.

Looking about me as I walk through moving streets and jump skyscrapers with the hop-over commuters, I cannot find any smiling faces.

Only shadows, dark lines ... and disguised fears.

Perhaps, I think more often than not, perhaps I am a very commonplace specimen. I, Questel, who has been hounded across a Galaxy, without ever having been chased. Perhaps there are many, many like me. Joni, too, would have one day become a haunted figure.

I saved her from that. I hope.

Mankind has lost the forty muscles that enabled him to smile. He still has the sixty that enable him to frown. Once upon a time it was less exhausting on bodily energy to smile than scowl. Now a man has no choice.

The blue sun, yellow seen twenty years in its past, has no choice either. Ash.

The urge within me grows. I try to fight it but I have been conditioned. Knowing this is no weapon to control it. Knowing it is just frustration.

I am ready for the final kill, the final burst of fury (expansion, fires reaching into the coldness) that will encompass a climax, the destructive furies of a nova. And then die ... ash dead, grey dead. Cold and burned out.

Sprawled on a concrete pathway, neck broken. Except in the past.

Isn't it true that the past is the most important part of a man's life? In the past he is always alive. But the further into the future the world moves, the shorter his remembered span becomes, until eventually there remains just his death that is important about him.

A star is dying in the Galaxy and I wish I was out there to die with it. It will die at the same time as I, and yet, from my hideout, it will not appear to die for twenty more years.

From a million light years away that star is immortal. Practically.

Tomorrow night I will accomplish the fulfilment of my conditioned programme, the job that my whole life has been about.

The false memories, the hunting, the desperation ... the revelation, the realization that was inevitable, all were leading to one thing.

The killing.

The killing by Kevin Karr, alias Joseph Questel, the assassination of a family.

The plan of the Programmers has worked almost to the minute. I still cannot believe that Rainer was just the final driving cog, the voice of the Programmer as he set my wheels into motion exactly on cue.

I still cannot understand *why* I was made to believe in Joseph Questel. What purpose did the deception serve, unless, perhaps, to make me totally a pawn in God-like hands, the faceless gamepiece at the edge of the board, unobtrusive, waiting, manipulated with ease, for it is easy to manipulate a mind already comprised of fictional images and false fears.

I have made three visits to the home of my victim. Each time I have tried to go in, to explain that I will kill him soon, but each time I have failed. Until the final time when I shall accomplish the deed.

Will it be as I have dreamed it?

Have I been dreaming the vision of a future-seer, a clairvoyant's picture implanted in my mind so I may read the motions as the lines of a play, or the notes of a musical score?

By Darzel perhaps?

The house is big, the alsatian is fierce. The man within is hard, but his wife and daughter are soft, happy. They alone, perhaps have the forty smiling-muscles in their faces.

For this they will die.

And in our Wonderful Galaxy, faceless men will move a chess piece towards a box at the edge of the board – and drop it in, with the other taken players.

TRAVELLERS

When we finally reached the outskirts of the city the time-node was well advanced. In a sense this meant I had lost valuable hours for searching but as yet, we were told, the visiting forms from the past and future were tenuous and unstable, flitting into vision and out again as fast as they realized they could not find a positive hold in this alien era.

In all likelihood, if Margaretta *was* in the node I would find her again after all these years. But what a frightening number of obstacles stood in the path of that achievement! Had she been alive when this sequence of inconsistency in time reached the fourth millennium? Had she been able to find the node and penetrate it? Was she looking for me as I would be looking for her? And my conscious dreams of her – no, *our* – daughter … were they just imaginative fantasy? Or had she indeed conceived a child, and thus, inexplicably, secured our brief contact across a thousand years?

Too many obstacles, too many uncertainties …

'Wake up, Jaim.'

My travelling companion, Herok, was shaking my arm. I snapped out of my drifting dream and followed him towards the first of the gate-checks. As we walked, burdened by our packs and the necessary implements of survival, he looked round at me and shook his head. 'Still thinking of her? You're going to lose us the chance of a smooth entry.'

'I'm sorry, Herok,' I said. 'I just feel very … anxious.'

'I know.'

'And anxiety is a great distraction.'

'It's all right, Jaim. I'll keep an eye on you.'

Herok was a grand fellow. He was younger than me by ten years. We were both in middle grade, but in two years' time, when I reached forty, I would rise to the next level of the student ladder, the senior grade. My degree would follow within the decade; and a junior lectureship, with luck, within the decade following that. Now, however, we were travelling companions, bronzed and burned by the sun of Southern Asia, and hardened by our adventures in North Africa, where every day had been a test of our fitness to survive.

Over the years I had come to regard Herok as both peer and brother, and if we looked dissimilar – he being tall and thin, and covered with a fine blond down, myself being of shorter, stockier stature, with burnt-umber hair and a fashionable beard – this did not discourage us from pretending a family relationship when it suited us, or when it was convenient.

'I can see the gate up ahead,' said Herok suddenly; I craned to see above the heads of the travelling crowds, and saw it, a primitive barbed and armed barrier to progression, through which a trickle of visitors was being permitted.

We were watched from houses and offices on every side. Here, at the outskirts of the city, the streets were wide, and we joined the queue of travellers, finding ourselves buried in a mass of silken, silky bodies, all pushing and jostling as they waited, impatiently, to try and talk their ways into the time-node. They would fail, of course, but there were always the thousands who believed that persuasion was a powerful weapon.

We jostled, bustled, edged towards the barrier.

'You are approaching the zone of observation,' said a loud and indifferent voice, speaking apparently from mid air. 'Red and green passes only.'

We both had green passes, which would take us through to the node itself. The passes had arrived a few weeks before, shortly after the first signs of the impending node had been spotted. The allocation was based partly on the particular fields of research with which Herok and I were concerned, and partly upon the Psychoscan that had preceded our successful entry into a similar node, ten years before.

We were among the luckiest men on Earth, and I was thankful for the fact.

At the gate we were assigned to one of the many armed guards who took us aside and scrutinized our cards carefully; no doubt he was looking for evidence of forgery, but he found none, naturally, and passed us on.

We were now in the zone of observation and from here much of the node itself could be seen. The whole area appeared normal – if a trifle crowded – and the great mass of human beings that sprawled on walls and rooftops, staring and scanning down the mile or so to the edge of the node, seemed well content with their lot. Looking downhill towards the centre of the city (for the node had risen across most of the city centre and a fraction of the western sector) we saw the tenuous white ghosts of future travellers trying to break through into this time, and failing, although Herok stated positively that he could see the ludicrous garb of men from the next millennium, a time with which we were both well versed, naturally, having secured a great many friends in many future ages.

At the edge of the observation zone a force field of some considerable strength had been erected to prevent any unlawful penetration into the strange time flow beyond, and here we came to the final barrier through which we would have to pass. We were surrounded by men and women of all races and all ages, each and every one of them waving thick wodges of bank notes, or great clusters of sparkling jewellery. Why? The rich, the poor alike were begging us for our entrance passes, and in truth we could have made ourselves among the richest men on Earth that day, for the richest men on Earth were there, begging our favour. Money, wealth, possession, power … these were not the ways to acquire the green passes into the time field. The unseen men who commanded such entry, who imposed the rules upon society during the duration of a node, were interested only in natural attributes, it seemed – perhaps imagination, perhaps intellectual honesty; most of us who found ourselves together beyond this final wall shared something in common – a desire for knowledge for its own sake.

The pitiful creatures who clustered around us during that last walk towards the final gate were wasting their efforts. Communication with other times could far too easily take the form of torment and torture, and the sick and bestial elements of humankind were kept at bay. Even if their bribing succeeded, the passes they would have so obtained would have been useless to them!

A glittering diamond was thrust into my hand by a man who smelled of hyacinth and grinned in his fatty face, plucked nervously at the spun silver cloth he wore. The jewel, I was sure, would have bought me a city, or taken me on an endless cruise of our solar system; a treasure indeed. But beyond the barrier, in the zone of inconsistent time, there was a greater treasure. Margaretta.

I pushed the jewel back and mumbled my apology, but the man followed me, weeping, clutching at my sleeve. I tried to shake him off but his grip moved to my arm, became almost desperate.

Herok was being pestered by two women, both well past their prime, but both splendidly dressed and devastatingly beautiful. They were – I could be certain – offering far more than themselves, and I sympathized with Herok for his predicament.

We were silent and depressed by the time we were facing the armoured guards who stood between the zone of Observation and the huge Examination Hall at the edge of the time node itself. My arms were bruised from the attentions of the beggars; there were tears in Herok's eyes, but I recognized the after-effects of SymPathyn, a drug no doubt worn by many of the women in this zone.

The guards were satisfied with our credentials and passed us on and we walked into the cool, white-walled building, and stood for a moment getting our bearings. There were two queues of people, shuffling slowly forwards. The largest queue was for those with one-day passes, and movement was slow because each person bearing such an entry permit was being fitted with a recall-stud, just below their skin. The other queue was shorter, but the Examiners looked far more intense.

Apprehensive, excited, we joined this queue and within ten minutes were being interrogated as to our purposes and aims for the next few months. As students we had ready answers to most of the questions; Herok, as a trained Security Man, could answer truthfully that he would become such during the stay in the node, and could fit in his study between-times.

Everybody during their stay in the time node was expected to contribute to the maintenance of the enclosed environment.

I, as a trained mental therapist, could truthfully answer that my assistance could be called upon to help badly disoriented travellers from times when security was less stringent than in our own, or in the next few hundred millennia.

The toughest question came last. 'Do you swear that you have no emotional involvement with travellers from any other age?'

'I so swear,' said Herok quietly, and I could almost feel his anxiety. Would the guards notice? They could hardly fail to detect our feelings of worry, but with luck by now their senses would be dulled by repetition.

I could not, I knew, get away with denying my involvement if the minds of the guards were fully tuned, and searching for the tell-tale signs of a lie. Margaretta's importance to me was too great, the love I felt too deep for me to have replied an outright affirmative. I knew this, and Herok knew this, but in the course of our journey across the world from Penang, to Africa, and then to Western Europe, we had rarely discussed either the girl from the next millennium, or the obstacle that she presented to us gaining entrance into this node, the second node we had visited and probably the last that would manifest during our lifetimes.

Now: the crunch.

'No emotional involvement,' I said quickly, and before there was time for any reaction, went on, 'As part of my project I hope to re-contact several people from the next millennium and gain an idea of their time's developments during the intervening years.'

Immediate suspicion. 'Male or female?'

'Both sexes,' I said quickly. I was feeling cooler, now, but the fixed stare from the nearest Examiner, a tall, sour-looking man, with piercing grey eyes, made my heart stutter and the electrical conductivity of my skin seemed to short-circuit all over my face.

'What's your project?' asked this emotionless figure.

'Social dynamism,' I replied obscurely. He frowned briefly, then glanced at his companion, an equally sour man, shorter, possibly an inferior. Behind them four guards stood rigidly to attention, eight eyes fixed upon my face.

'Sounds feasible,' said the shorter Examiner. 'You can hardly re-contact people without *some* anticipation …' He glanced at Herok, then back at me. There was a long tense moment. Then the Examiner nodded, 'Let them pass.'

Herok and I bowed low, and smiled at each other. We gathered up our packs and strode out into the daylight on the time node side of the Examination Hall.

'We've done it,' Herok murmured as we walked through the streets, getting faster with every pace. 'Jaim, we've *done* it! We're in again!'

He began to run, and I followed. He began to laugh, and his laughter was infectious. In the cover of a ramshackle red-brick building we stood, leaning heavily against each other, and yelled our delight, forgetting completely how near we had come to being refused entrance!

We walked through crowded streets and listened to the rising pitch of excitement, the laughing and shouting of men and women hardly able to restrain their enthusiasm for the days to come. Around us ghosts appeared for brief moments and vanished again, some so quickly that there was not even time to turn and look to see from what era of time they had come. I nudged Herok and pointed to where a semi-naked man stood in the shadow of an office block and stared up the glass facing and bulging transparent walls. 'Fifth millennium,' I said, and Herok give it a moment's consideration before nodding. 'Possibly. Margaretta was from the fourth, wasn't she?'

'Late third, early fourth, yes. I wish you had known her, Herok.'

Although ten years ago we had been together in the previous time node we had led separate lives therein and separate adventures. Afterwards I had refused to talk about her for several months, and when I did talk of Margaretta I suppose it had been the ramblings of a lovelorn fool. I had wanted it to be that Herok knew her, had met her, and could therefore appreciate my love for her, but she was a stranger to him, an image created by my inadequate descriptions.

We found lodgings in a huge and draughty hostel and took bunks and meal seats in the wing devoted to men and women from all ages. The wing reserved for third and fourth millennia visitors was already full, and within a couple of weeks visitors would find themselves slotted into any available space, in very mixed company indeed!

The only man already in our wing was a fourth-millennium student-type, a middle-aged man with deep brown eyes who gazed at us nervously as we unpacked and unrolled, and discussed our plans.

'Are you from the third?' he asked abruptly, speaking with the nasal slant to his words that characterizes fourth-millennium interLing. It was the same accent that Margaretta had, and it was instantly warming.

'Yes,' I replied, seating myself by him. I extended my hand after a moment and he gripped it happily, shaking my arm with great gusto. His clothes were sparse and not very warm; a neck and waist band, joined by thin strips of cloth; a pouch to contain and support his genitals, and thick leather bindings down his legs. I felt overdressed in my mock mid-second-millennium kaftan.

'Garri D'rath,' he said. 'My name. Last time I was in a node I found out that I was descended from a family line called Rathbone. Interesting. I'm fascinated by your era ... that's why I've come here. You probably think it's a bit unusual to stay in only one millennium ...' He was smiling, almost selfconsciously. There was a splash of soup on his chin and I wiped it off for him; he tensed, but laughed when I held up my green-stained finger. Slightly embarrassed, he wiped his mouth and chin with a small red tissue.

'Not unusual at all,' I replied. 'I'm Jaim Barron, by the way. This is Herok Vuutgenstein. We're both social dynamism students.'

'There are enough of them about,' laughed Garri. 'But this coincidence makes it a valuable field of study, I suppose.'

'You mean the two nodes so close together?'

He nodded. I grew tense. It was estimated there were just fifty of the node sequences, all spanning the greater part of time and along each of which a lucky few could travel. And for two of these sequences to have stopping points within the space of a man's lifetime was coincidence and gift indeed!

I was worried, however. Just because there had been one thousand and ten years separating the nodes of that first sequence, when I had met Margaretta, didn't mean that in this second, unrelated sequence the time between the nodes had to be the same. If eleven hundred years separated us, Margaretta would be long since dead.

'How long ago was the last node you visited?'

'How long?' He frowned, sought to remember. 'About twelve years. Yes, twelve years.'

She would have aged two years more than I, only two years! It was ten years since we had met, ten years of wandering and remembering. For Margaretta, a twelve-year wait. But was she here? Had she gained entry? Had she even *heard* of this sequence of time nodes?

Garri was saying, 'Myself, I'm a time engineer. That's really all I can tell you at the moment. As you know, there are strict controls about the acquisition of information. Until something is actually discovered, or realized, or worked out, it doesn't become general information to people from earlier times.'

Herok nodded soberly. As a security junior whilst in the node he worked, part of the time, to ensure that that rule was enforced, without knowing what information he was himself restricting. He said, 'Is this node of some importance, then?'

Garri looked thoughtful for a moment, then glanced around, a grossly theatrical concession to secrecy. Looking at us both for a second he nodded slowly. 'You bet,' he said with a wink. 'You just wait and see.'

A loudspeaker blared through the dormitory, summoning all new arrivals to the nearest Control and Allocation Centre. Herok slapped his hands together and called to me. I shook Garri by the hand again. 'We'll see you later. This is where the hard work starts.'

He chuckled. 'Okay. I'll be here.'

As we walked swiftly along the broad streets, through people in amorphous throngs, through seated circles of contemporaries busily discussing what they would do with their three-month liberation in time, so we saw the first signs of more ambitious journeys. A figure, a woman, a beautifully robed woman, shimmered into existence before us, suspended fractionally above the ground; she couldn't see us, of course, as she tried to move into our time, but we watched her for the few seconds that she tried to break across the barrier of years. She was a sixth-millennium visitor and had obviously broken as far back as the fourth millennium, but couldn't summon the mental energy to push back here, to the third. Her limbs waved as she lost control of her body with the pressure of her mind-direction, and for a few seconds she was a silent image of frustrated beauty, threshing in an age a thousand years removed, before finally fading back into future reality, to wait for the node to advance further and facilitate the extra movement required.

Herok laughed as we walked through the space where her image had been, and then a thought struck him and he glanced at me; I caught the unvoiced suggestion and grinned and he shouted, 'Come on!' and gripped me by the hand. He dragged me into a breathtaking run. 'Now!' he yelled, and we directed our minds into the future, and felt the surge of blood as our bodies followed, and the swirling colours of scattering third-millennium denizens left us to be replaced by the sober movement of people a thousand years hence.

We were in a vast square, green and white pavement stones beneath our feet and tall, impossibly tall, sparkling buildings at each of four corners.

As we came into the present, so we turned. She was behind us, watching us (we had arrived still shrieking our excitement) and we stopped, staring at her face and at her body, full and exciting beneath the white translucent material of her robe. Then Herok took the initiative and ran across to her. She seemed startled, and her hands clutched at the folds of her gown as she regarded first the breathless form of Herok, then my own grinning features. Herok said, 'We witnessed your attempts to move into our time, my lady, and when you finally succeed I shall be delighted to act as escort.'

She smiled, then, and bowed to Herok. 'Thank you,' she said. 'I'd like that very much. Your era is my final destination, and if I can return the favour, I have a large apartment in this city – in the sixth millennium – of which you may avail yourself.'

Herok bowed again and behind his back his hand was waving excitedly, the fingers spread wide in a sign of success. She gave him her address on a small blue card, and turned to walk away. Herok and I ran across the square and vaulted back into the past, moving through two walls (strange sense of cold and dark) and returning to the open roadway.

Back in our own time Herok stopped and wiped his face, his hands shaking. 'What a magnificent body,' he said. 'And they say sixth-millennium women are animals … animals!'

'Filthy dog!' I shouted, and he laughed. 'Remember your age, Herok. You're not a child any more.'

'Oh but I feel it, Jaim. I feel – rejuvenated! Excited!' He was grinning all over his face.

'Your exuberance is nauseating,' I pointed out, looking round to see if his noisiness was being observed.

And I saw her!

'Margaretta!' I shouted as she vanished behind a house. Herok grabbed my arm as I started to run. 'The signing on, Jaim. You have to sign on.'

He was right, I shouldn't delay registering but I had seen Margaretta, she was here. And even now was perhaps losing herself in the crowded streets closer to the centre of the city.

I thrust my green identity card into Herok's hand. 'Explain that an important part of my project began prematurely, and that I'll be sure to show my face later.'

I began to run towards the squat, ugly building with its sharply angular corners and gruesome air-vents behind which Margaretta had vanished. Herok called, 'You'll need this in case you're stopped.'

Running, I shouted back, 'I'll take that chance.' Then Herok was out of sight and I was facing a long, narrow street, and there was no sign of Margaretta.

As I ran I prayed to God that I hadn't been mistaken, that the slim girl in the trousers and red blouse who had flitted so briefly through my field of vision had indeed been my fourth-millennium lover.

At the end of the street I faced five ways to go, streets, alleys, entrances. There were people milling about, mostly contemporary with just a smattering of the multifarious types from the next millennium.

For a moment I panicked, and then, again seen from a distance and from behind, I spotted her; she was walking down a roadway beneath a sign that, in many different time languages, said 'City Centre'. As she was about to vanish from sight she looked round, seemed to look right at me …

Margaretta! Without any shadow of doubt, it was Margaretta. I became ecstatic, raced after her, my heart pounding with joy. But when I reached the end of the road there was no sign of her. I jumped to the next millennium, but she was not visible there either. For a moment I felt anxiety, and for a second moment despair, but if I knew Margaretta she would be moving towards the centre of the node, drawn by curiosity and the thought – I hoped – of perhaps finding me in the greater crowds who gathered there.

Back in my own time I pressed on, down side streets and across plazas, pushing through the drifting crowds, avoiding the white and grey forms that filled the air, some successfully breaking through into this time, others fading back into the future (or the past?) to wait a few hours longer.

At length I came to the centre of the node. There was, as I had expected, a huge crowd of sightseers, formed in a vast, excited ring several hundred feet deep. At the centre of the ring was the enigma, and though I had seen it before I felt an urge, a great temptation, to push through the ranks of visitors and natives and view it again ...

A white shape shimmered momentarily before me, but faded quickly when it realized its mistake. Time travel was not permitted this close to the centre. It was too dangerous by far.

I began to push through the crowds; some, inspired by my positive motion, followed in my wake or began to stir up the motionless mob themselves, insinuating their bodies into every crack and gap in the circle of human forms. I kept an eye for Margaretta, and every woman with a babe in arms caused me to stop and stare, even though I had already seen Margaretta without a child, and even though that child, our mutual daughter, would be twelve ... no, eleven years of age and certainly not in her mother's arms.

After a few moments, a smattering of minutes, I reached the innermost ring of the group of humans and found myself pressed against the unseen but impenetrable wall of force that would always protect the enigma from the curious touch of we mortals.

In a small clear space, perhaps eight feet across, surrounded by a wall of silent humanity, was the Traveller. He, she, it ... what was appropriate?

It squatted on the ground and not a fibre, not a muscle moved. It was totally, absolutely black. Not black because of its skin or its clothes, but black because of the total absence of light or shade. The features of the Traveller were distinguishable only by the swelling and rippling of its surface and when one looked closely, when one focused carefully upon those unbroken black surfaces one could see eyes, a nose, organs and organelles upon the body that did not really relate to anything terrestrial. It appeared to be clad in armour plate, and clutched in its two broad hands an all-black machine, a box with black featureless buttons, and it never moved to switch or press a knob, and it never seemed to breathe. Its closed eyes never opened to show us a moment of its black, depthless mind.

It squatted there, the absolute centre of the time node, protected by its force shield, oblivious of its curiosity value. And we stared and did not fully comprehend, except to realize that the figure was a Traveller through space-time moving across our frame of reference for a few brief months.

485

I pulled away from the enigma and bustled out through the crowds, into the clear plaza beyond. There I stood for a moment catching my breath and searching the environs. Margaretta had well and truly vanished.

Sadly I walked back to the hostel. If only ... if only my mind link had remained after the birth of the girl. And what strangeness was contained within that single moment of regret! A *mind* link ... across a thousand years ...

Sounds and sights vanished during those next few minutes, as I walked heavily through streets that could have been paved with burning coals and I'd not have noticed. I was experiencing a vivid reliving of the months following the decline of the previous node, the gathering place of ages when I had first met Margaretta. As the node had faded, as the people around me had faded over the days into ghost forms, as more and more of my contemporaries had arrived back, reluctantly, from far-flung millennia, unable to maintain their space-time distortion, so I had watched Margaretta fade from me, slip into the sea of time, her hand outstretched, her eyes filled with tears. It had been a matter of seconds between the kiss and the loss, and I carried the memory of that last touch for many hours before a biting wind had chafed my lips to numbness and the moisture in my eyes had begun to sparkle and crack.

Sank into depression.

Months. Three months.

Waking during a night, during a dream, during a kiss, a moment's excited touch of Margaretta's body. Awoke and felt heart beat, warm rush of blood, sonorous shift of muscle ...

Room swam. Lay back and stared at ...

Listened to ...

My daughter. My daughter. In fluid womb, floating in warm liquid, basking in Margaretta's awareness.

My *daughter?*

Our daughter, Jaim.

Margaretta, I love you.

Always, Jaim, always. I visit your grave and love you more every moment ...

Shifting, blood runs faster, heart beats harder, across a thousand years.

Fully awake. Vision goes. Dream?

Oh Margaretta ... visiting my grave, cracked gravestone, crumbled bones, but loving me as I live, united through her womb, through the sparkling embryo, the squirming tadpole, the fusion of two ages in the bloody wall of future.

A touch across a thousand years; a vanished hand, holding me close.

Back in the dormitory I found Herok pulling the final piece of his new uniform on to his tall, spare frame. He looked very smart in the green and white outfit of the Security Force, for which he would have to work four hours every day. As I strolled into the long room he turned and smiled.

'When's your first shift?' I asked.

'Right now,' he said ruefully, picking up a sheet of names and jabbing his own name with a gloved finger. 'Right now. But fortunately there are a fair number of faces and figures to memorize ...' He picked up a sheaf of mug shots and flipped through them. 'So shift number one is memory work. Ugly bunch,' he went on. 'Most of them will be making the Big Run, which should mean some action.'

'The *big run*,' I repeated, chuckling. 'I wonder who first called it that?'

Herok shrugged, continued to study one of the faces in his file of illegal node-entrants.

There were two Big Runs: one was into the distant future, and one was into the distant past. The most usual avenue of attempted escape by those criminal types who managed to get into the node in the first place was to move to the distant future and hope to escape the time field that way. The future was more secure than the past, which was a difficult place to survive in and not only because of the flesh-eating Saurians that prevailed at that almost unreachable end of the node sequence. The atmosphere back then was stinkingly rich in toxic gases.

With Herok, the previous time we had ventured into a time node (our first and, so we had thought, our last) we had attempted to move back to the Age of Dinosaurs. We had almost made it, but it had been too difficult. The peak of that node had already passed and there were only a few seconds, a few moments, when the full range of travelling time, which always ended in the mid-Cretaceous, was available for the smallest of mental efforts; it was rumoured that only at that moment, at the peak of the node, could escape from the confines of the pocket of time be effected. Was there truth in such rumours? It was difficult to know, but enough denizens of future ages believed the rumour sufficiently to try and beach themselves at the ends of time, to escape whatever oppression they had been born to.

'Oh by the way,' said Herok suddenly, 'you have to report to Control and Allocation tomorrow, early.'

'Oh.'

Herok grinned and passed me back my identity card. 'Don't worry. I've spun a good yarn on your behalf. I think they fell for it.'

More visitors were arriving and taking bunks in the dormitory. We lingered for a while making their acquaintance and searching for people of specific interest, but found no-one whom we would have wanted to stick with. Most of the arrivals were early fourth millennium; a few were contemporary and there were a few from the second millennium who stood, nervously, watching their confident dormitory mates. Their clothes looked hideously uncomfortable, and their expressions quite moronic, but this was almost certainly due to Time Shock.

Part of my job, whilst in the node, would be to help 'earlier' visitors adjust to later eras, and so we – Herok and I – moved ourselves into conversations with the small band of seconds.

There were the usual questions, the usual anxieties, from those entering their first node, experiencing the strangeness for the first time. We explained, over and over, how it would become easier to move through time as the node advanced, and how they were in no danger of impacting with objects because of the sense of getting frozen and the ease with which one could move away to a safe spot. How time, *in all nodes*, was moving forward, and no-one could ever move to a moment before the moment they had left. Detailed accounts of how paradoxes were impossible because of the Security Force (Herok took a bow), the information embargo, which was imposed on the first four or five millennia after their own (stopping things being known before they were discovered) and the unseen Surveillance Corps, always watching the activities in the nodes. No-one knew who the Surveillance Corps were, but they had absolute authority: yet despite their vigilance the nodes had given rise to all manner of legend and myths, visitations and strange phenomena in times before the second millennium.

Most of the questions concerned the Traveller, and here we had to be careful, remembering that only a certain amount of detail had been ascertained that thousand years past. We told them what we thought was safe to tell, and sent them to their own Control for any extra allowable information. Thus they learned more or less what we ourselves knew, that the enigma was a time traveller, from when to when we didn't know with certainty, or at least, whether travelling forwards or backwards we didn't know; the ends of its run, certainly, were in the middle Cretaceous and at a time in the future nearly five million years removed from the present. The view most often expressed by third-millennium people was that in the distant future, Earth – at that time deserted, we knew – was being used as a Way Station by aliens, exploring the Galaxy (perhaps just the Earth) of the Saurian Age. It was frustrating not knowing, when virtually everyone else in the node *did* know.

Garri arrived back looking thoughtful. He was pleased to see us and we went out into the city for a drink together, Herok deciding to shirk his first shift. Garri's thoughtfulness developed into excitement; he was obviously burning to tell us something, but when we pressed for him to open up he shook his head, looked worried.

'I don't know if I dare, but ...'

'What? Come on, Garri, tell us what you know!'

'The information restriction, though ...'

We huddled closer together. Finally Garri said, 'This node represents a great step forward, anyway, and the information will be declassified before the end, so I suppose it doesn't matter if I tell you.'

We waited. Finally Garri said, 'One of your third-millennium mathematicians is – even now – making observations that permit almost full understanding of the time nodes. What he works out, what he is working out, will lead directly to the establishment of the Surveillance Corps, and to many experiments with time. We are living at a turning point ... history, which most of us have known for all our lives, is being made!'

'Without the sums ... what's he discovered?'

Garri ordered more drinks. We'd drunk too much already and my head was swimming, but we sipped the bitter concoction that he favoured and listened.

'The cause of the nodes,' he said. 'The time traveller theory is right, of course. In the distant future on this world there is an alien installation sending individuals back to the Cretaceous. If the Surveillance Corps know why, they're not telling. Each of the Travellers, though, travels through time in a series of jumps, stopping for infinitely small fractions of his subjective seconds in order to *pull power from the Earth's magnetic field*. They fuel themselves during transit.'

'Wonderful,' murmured Herok. Perhaps he had been expecting something a little more exciting. Myself, I felt quite emotionally moved by what Garri was telling us.

He went on, 'The jumps are very frequent to begin with, which is why there are only half-millennia separating the nodes uptime; they get more and more infrequent as the Traveller builds his time momentum, so that by the Cretaceous there are thousands of years between nodes.'

'Has he worked out – this mathematician – how the nodes get linked?' Herok asked.

'Yes he has, and it's sound maths, too. Practically speaking, each momentary stop by the Traveller distorts the time matrix, and during the few seconds of his time trip those distortions are accumulated and released at the moment of his landing, back in the past. The astronomically small time spans of these distortions and releases actually measure several months – on *our* time scale. The effect is that for several months at the time of each stop for power there is a narrow vein of captured time stretching from the past to the future, and this is what we are riding.'

'Mumbo jumbo,' commented Herok. 'I didn't understand a word.'

Garri laughed. 'I know how you feel. Social science is poles apart from time maths ... but we don't have to let our professional differences spoil a good time, do we?'

Herok, happier, raised his glass and grinned. 'Certainly not, my good fellow.' He knocked the lot back, signalled for more.

For my part I declined a refill but pressed Garri for information about himself. I felt the tingle of static that said a member of the Surveillance Corps had, at some time during the last few minutes, tuned in on our conversation and decided we should be watched, and was now coming close enough to intervene.

Phrasing his words carefully, also aware of our observer, Garri said, 'I'm quite a junior researcher, really, at an Institute for Sub-Quantum Physics. I'm involved with time theory, and am involved with certain practical developments from the maths being turned out at this instant. In fact, there are several tests and experiments being carried out along this node sequence …' he broke off, looking uncomfortable. After a moment the sense of being watched went away. He said, 'I think you'd better steer clear of me, for a while …'

Over the days I searched for Margaretta, between my compulsory service and the necessary work for my project. She had vanished, however, utterly and completely, and I never saw any sign of her. Herok was no help. He had never seen the woman and my description was too sentimental for him to obtain a clear mind's view of her.

I began to feel panic. My excursions through time became thoughtless and reckless; twice in the far future I nearly drowned when I came into a time when the node had opened over the sea; once, in the distant past, when it had opened across the mouth of a volcano, I nearly crisped.

The node advanced, and time flowed easier into the future and the past; other ages arrived and departed, many in groups with a single interpreter; the first of the real aliens showed its face, and all at once a mood of festivity and total excitement burst upon the city, not just in my natural time but in all times. The peak was approaching.

I watched part of the ninth Roman Legion, bedraggled and muddy, pace across rain-logged, marshy European landscape; fifty or sixty men, weary from battle – clattering beneath their equipment, pacing north to join their garrison. They would never arrive. I searched the crowds who watched them, knowing that Margaretta had a fascination for that greatest of European empires, but there was no sign of her. She could not have failed to have heard the Site-watcher's announcement in every time that the legionnaires were passing; she must have declined the temptation to stand, with the hundreds of others behind an Invisibility Seal, and watch their progress.

I went into the distant future and watched the building of huge ships; and further still to see the strange life forms that crawled across the Earth after man had deserted his home world. I talked with a Dhorr, from the Sirian empire that was still, in his time, subservient to the Earth Empire in the Galaxy. He told me, through an interpreter (which itself had nearly as many air-holes as the Dhorr, but which could manifest Earth sound through each one of them rather than speaking different pitches with each set of lips) that he had talked with his own kind of the millennia beyond the extinction of the human race, and they had despatched and received unmanned vessels between the galaxies. There was a great race in Andromeda who were trying to cross the gulf between the star cities, and the Dhorri had a strong feeling that their intentions were not particularly friendly.

We stood, the tubular alien and I, and stared at the black and enigmatic structure of the Traveller, and we wondered ...

'If they had conquered time,' said the Dhorr, 'and crossed the gulf in deep sleep, and thus travelled naturally many millions of years into their own futures, they might use a planet such as this to return, once their journey was finished, to their own time.'

'It's an intriguing thought,' I said.

'And a happy one,' said the Dhorr. 'If they want to conquer the Galaxy of three hundred million years ago, they are very welcome. Neither your race nor mine were around at that time.'

'And if they *did* spread throughout this Galaxy, their conquest has been forgotten. Their leavings dissolved in the natural span of centuries.'

A happy thought indeed!

I searched for Margaretta in her own millennium, stood in the middle of that vast plaza and felt the wind blowing cold against my flesh; shouted her name, searched the crowds.

The beautiful white-robed woman came towards me and remembered me, and asked wistfully after Herok. We talked, and she left.

The node was approaching its peak. Halfway done and I had not found Margaretta. Halfway wasted!

I went back to my own time and found it was night, and I walked through the streets towards the hostel, my soft bunk and a depressed period of sleep. I was nearly home when she called to me from the shadows, and when I stopped she moved into the light and stared at me.

'Jaim?'

'Margaretta!' I cried; ran to her; and for a long time I just hugged her to me and wept with joy.

'I thought I'd never find you, Margaretta.'

'I've been searching for you too,' she said, and stood back to examine me closely. She was still as I remembered her, and age had left little mark; a few more lines around her eyes, a slightly more tired expression; her hair was cut short and her clothes were styled more youthfully. But it was Margaretta in every way, and I thought my heart would burst!

We still had six weeks. Six weeks together until time separated us again, almost certainly for good.

'Where is ...?'

'Jayameeka?'

Jayameeka! She had been called after me! (Well, almost.)

'Yes. Our daughter.'

She looked sad. Her arms unwound from me. 'She's safe, Jaim. But I couldn't bring her. I'm sorry, Jaim, but they ... they wouldn't let me bring her.'

Stunned!

'Who wouldn't let you?'

She shrugged. 'Whoever's in control. The Time Authorities.'

'But why? Why such a restriction?'

'Jaim ... she was conceived in your time – this time; but born in mine, a thousand years hence. She belongs to two times, Jaim, and the authorities are terrified of her ...' She was hiding something; in her voice, in her manner, in her words were the hints of a deception, advanced, perhaps, to protect my feelings.

'Margaretta,' I said, as we stood in the darkened city. 'Tell me.'

When Jayameeka had been born (Margaretta told me) the story, the facts, of our relationship had been made known. Jayameeka had been taken away from her, and brought up in an Institute devoted to obscure scientific studies; Margaretta had had full access to the child, and had spent much time with her, but she had become the object of study; a child of two times might – they had said – give a clue to the nature of time travel. She was too important to waste. And for all those years she had been the centre of interest for a small group of researchers, working in the field of temporal dynamics.

I would never see my daughter!

I had waited eleven years to see the offspring of our love, a desire that had been drowned, certainly, beneath my anxiety, my desire to see Margaretta herself; now that the truth was known, I felt a great emptiness, a substantial and painful sense of loss.

And anger! My daughter, an experimental animal! Why, if they had wanted such children for their studies they could easily have arranged such consummations!

A shiver down my spine; an uneasy glance at Margaretta as we walked through the night streets. Perhaps ...

Had she too thought of the shocking possibility?

Surely, though, such an experiment would not have been undertaken without the awareness of the participating bodies?

Creeping into the dormitory we slipped silently into my bunk and vanished beneath the sheets. She was nervous at first, almost hesitant, a span of so many years causing her desire to be drowned by apprehension; at least, this is what I assumed, since it was happening to me as well.

But after a few minutes of hugging and warming, of gentle touching and featherlight kissing, we became bolder, more confident, and Margaretta returned with passion. If Herok heard, or felt, our joyous reunion he said nothing from the upper bunk.

Strangely the sensation of basking in each other's awarenesses, the slight empathy that had linked us through time (for however brief a span of time) never returned as it had those eleven years back. I didn't comment on it; it would come in a few days, no doubt.

In the morning ...

I opened my eyes and found myself staring at the floor. During the night I had slipped out of the bunk, possibly pushed by Margaretta's sleeping form, and was now draped across the edge of the bed, my right cheek dented and sore from its contact with the rough wooden underfoot.

Margaretta was gone, and for a moment I just sat on the edge of the bunk and rubbed my eyes; then I felt a great panic! If she had left, perhaps too upset by the thought of eventually parting for ever ... how would I ever find her again? It had taken so long, would take too long to repeat the search ...

'Herok!' I shouted and stood up to rouse him out of bed. He too was gone, his night-shift folded neatly across the pillow, the bunk highly presentable. He had been gone some while, probably about his part-time duties as a Security man.

At that moment the door at the end of the dormitory burst open and Herok arrived, running frantically, and breathing like he would burst.

'Where've you been?' I demanded. He waved me quiet.

'Where's that mug file? Ah ...' he found his folder of criminal faces and was leafing through the pages rapidly, excitement in his face, nervousness in his fingers.

'Who are you looking for?'

'I'm sure I've just seen ... ah, yes ... it was! Can't stop, Jaim. I'm about to make my first arrest.' He uttered a little yell of pleasure and raced out of the dormitory, drawing his gun from its pouch on his hip.

I smiled and shook my head at his exuberance, and turned the open folder towards me to see whom he had seen.

Margaretta!

MARGARETTA!

I nearly collapsed, but somehow kept my suddenly useless legs in a straight position and I stared at the picture of Margaretta. He must have seen her as she left ...

My eyes picked out the words below the picture. Wanted ... Time criminal ... illegal entry into node ... Jayameeka Strahn ...

Jayameeka.

*

My world collapsed. I remember hitting the floor with a deafening crash and feeling all sensation leave me.

I came round to the sound of Herok's urgent voice. He was bending over me and looking very anxious. When I recovered consciousness he smiled and helped me up. 'What happened?' he asked. Garri was crouched beside me and holding out a glass of blue liquid; I suspected something very potent and decided that I needed it; sipping the drink I nearly choked, then looked at Herok.

Careful, I thought. Very careful.

'I got out of bed too fast,' I said. 'Fainted.' He grinned; he knew I'd been drinking fairly heavily for the previous few days, and no doubt was imagining pains and uncoordinations in my head that were not, in fact, there. 'Did you get who you were after?' I asked.

They helped me up.

'No,' said Herok, disappointed. 'No, she gave me the slip. But I've alerted the Security forces up and down time. We'll get her.'

Garri said, 'I expect she'll be trying to make the Big Run. It's not long before that will be possible.'

Not long at all, I reflected. It couldn't be pin-pointed with total accuracy, but it would begin sometime this afternoon, the peak of the node, a mere twenty seconds!

If Jayameeka – Jayameeka! My daughter! Where had I miscalculated? – if she could locate that moment and avoid the gathering of Security men, she could slip away into the past or future and, if God was on her side, 'beach' herself on the real world at whichever extreme of the node sequence she was planning on heading for. When – if – time slipped away from her, she would be free of whatever oppression had driven her to such despair. And she would be free of me, lost to me for ever …

Herok left.

'Don't go away,' said Garri, cryptically, and he made to follow Herok. I grabbed his arm.

'Garri … what went wrong?'

He looked blank. 'I don't understand.'

'The nodes … you told me twelve years … twelve years since your last entry into a node sequence!'

He looked uncomfortable, glanced at the dormitory door, then back at me. 'I'm sorry, Jaim. I wasn't thinking at the time. Yes, I see the problem. I was never in the first node-sequence that you visited. My first entry was twelve years ago – a sequence that missed your own time, it arose earlier than you were born, and out over the ocean as well, which is why it was missed. It's thirty years since the first node sequence occurred … thirty years.'

He walked to the door, checked to see if anyone was outside and then called back softly, 'I have a message for you, Jaim, so don't go away. I mean it. If you want to find her again, stay put for a few minutes.'

Before I could do or say a thing, he was gone. I stood slowly and stared after him. I was reluctant to remain in the dormitory, but something about Garri aroused my interest, and my suspicions. That he knew something was too apparent, but that he was more than he seemed to be was a subtle insinuation that I was only now beginning to notice. Who was our fourth-millennium friend, I wondered?

Things were happening just a little too fast for my constitution, I decided. I wanted to be out in the city, shirking my therapist's duties, searching for Jayameeka; but all I would do, I knew, would be to run around aimlessly, and possibly attract the sort of attention I could well do without.

Herok's attention, for example.

Oh Herok! I felt so bitter; not at him, not even at what he represented. He could not have known that my daughter would become one of his prey ... and it would, I had to convince myself, be unfair and unwise to tell him so.

I was not bitter at him, no; but at fate ... at fate I was angry, at the twist, the cruelty of the orderly universe, at that was I furious! They could have spared me the agony ... it was for so few weeks, so insignificant a number of days in the span of the world ... I could have been spared such grief.

I looked at Jayameeka's picture. She was truly beautiful, and looked so like Margaretta that it was almost difficult to believe they were two people. But the differences were there, and I should have seen them. The wider nose, the slightly darker green of her eyes. Her youthfulness. How blind I had been; how susceptible to my dreams, that I should have believed Margaretta would not have aged at all!

If I stood in that fourth-millennium plaza I would be standing in the same time as Margaretta, but she was outside of my grasp, beyond me. Perhaps dead. Perhaps herself locked away. Perhaps hiding behind that wall of twenty years, the difference between us now.

I wept, of course. If I was maudlin, I make no excuses, nor any apology. It was right to weep, and very necessary, and after a few minutes I was calm again.

A chill went through me, then, as I remembered the night. The reconsummation of our love, the virginal tightness of Margaretta/Jayameeka ... the nervousness ... the look in her eyes ...

Oh God. It was not quite an unbearable thought. I dared not look inside the bed ... dared not! The sight of her blood would have driven me to despair.

And yet – for all my worry – she had *permitted* our union – in the full knowledge of who I was, she had permitted it? Was that an act of despair? Or of true love? Or a kiss, passed from Margaretta to me, and communicated through the body of our mutual child?

Where was Garri? I couldn't wait about all day. There were only four hours before the first possible moment of the peak!

He arrived as secretively as he had left. He was carrying a package, concealed half by some black fabric and half by his stooped body. He came up to me and placed the item on my bunk.

Without a word he took off the fabric covering. It was a small heat-set and a copper-coloured belt attached to it by a single cord.

He looked at me. I said, 'Her message. What was her message?'

'She's going down time,' said Garri. 'The main concentration of Security men will be policing the up-time nodes.'

'How do you know all this?'

Garri smiled, said simply, 'She told me.'

'Yes, but why? Why you? Who are you, Garri?'

He stared at me for a long time, and gradually the façade of innocence and naiveté dropped away. His eyes grew dark, his mouth solemn. 'The trouble is,' he said, 'one never knows how much a third-millennium person knows. You're a difficult period in history, the only period, really, where there's any substantial editing of information input. You know she's your daughter, and you know why, although she doesn't know you know. Part of her message to you was to tell you of her true identity. It's a social custom in our era to lose one's virginity to one's father, but I imagine there was a deeper, more inexplicable motivation for her action, don't you?'

I said nothing. Garri was building up to something.

'We knew each other, of course. She was being studied by the Institute where I work. What she represents, a woman born between two times, a woman perhaps free of the full restrictions of space-mind-time, is what myself and many others have been studying, and trying to achieve. There are many like her, though she was unplanned for. She has great strength of mind, is the best subject we have. I say we,' he smiled self-consciously, 'I don't mean we. My own work has been on … this,' he patted the apparatus. 'I became very close to Jayameeka, very close. She was severely restricted in the Institute, and I began to feel it was cruel, heartless – I began to revolt against it. After all, I thought, I'm making more progress than my colleagues …' again he patted the belt. 'So I helped her escape. It's as simple as that. I got her access to this node, but regrettably her illegal presence was discovered, though not my own participation. Her only chance is to beach herself – if it's possible …' again his strange smile: he knew full well whether or not it was possible to escape the node-sequence; it was information denied to my own time. 'Once beached we hope she will demonstrate her ability to move freely through time; for her sake, for our sake ... I hope she has developed that ability. If she ever returns, I shall marry her. But my interest is solely in seeing her out of the criminal clutches of my own Institute.'

He stopped, then, and picked up the strange apparatus. After a moment, he said, 'I really love her, Jaim. I know how you felt, now, leaving Margaretta all that time ago, knowing the wall that would separate you.'

I reached out and gripped his shoulder. 'I love her too, Garri; more than father to daughter, but not as lover to lover. I just need to be with her for a while, need to talk, to know she is safe. Garri, I must stop her making that run. It's selfish, I know. But I must stop her. Or go with her.'

He nodded. 'You can't stop her, Jaim. But go with her? With luck. And this is what will get you back.'

He held the belt towards me. 'What is it?' I asked.

'I imagine something very similar in principle to what is powering the Traveller.'

'A time machine?'

'Mechanical. Effective. Well tested, but it takes some real effort of mind. It will never be released, of course; it is the tool of the authority that guards these nodes and prevents unwarranted passing of information. My era developed it from your era's maths. The fifth millennium will begin to apply it to the policing of these frequent nodes of time.

'I told you, Jaim, that yours is a critical time in history. Before now the nodes have been virtually unknown; after now they are a part of life. This era is at the junction ... denied the results of its own inquisitiveness. But that inquisitiveness will lead to this belt, and to the decision to mate individuals from different times. Until everything was fully tested we ourselves, a millennium hence, didn't know if we *could* develop time travel.'

'And you're giving this to me? Out of *friendship*?'

'Out of a desire to see Jayameeka safe, wherever she is.'

I was incredulous. I took the belt and the headpiece and turned them over in my fingers. Such power! Such potential in so small a fragment of material. 'And no strings ... no catches ...?'

He laughed. 'The age of paranoia was in the second millennium. No strings, Jaim. If you like, you are a final test for the belt; a run through time from the age of the Saurians. Trust me, Jaim. There is a recall mechanism – not well tested, I confess – with which I shall return the belt to my own hands within six subjective months. I'm not making a *gift*, merely a convenience!'

He instructed me on its use, a remarkably facile system of safety buttons, and a great deal of brain power. It would, if my own mind failed, be a boost to my projected brain waves to carry me out of the node and into the prehistoric past ... to 'beach' me, hopefully with Jayameeka safely in my arms.

'You understand,' said Garri finally, 'that you are now no longer a part of your own millennium, that you know too much about the future to live your life without a guardian ...'

I accepted what he said, grimly, unhappily.

I obtained breathing apparatus from the depository on the ground floor of my barracks, and strapped the lightweight system over the head-piece of the time machine. As I ran through the streets towards the centre I saw only a few others who had, in this time at least, opted for the legal excursion down-time to the acrid swamps of an era nearly (not quite) at the end of the Traveller's run. Those going into futurity would not need any special equipment since the air, after man's decline, was rich and sweet.

A Security man halted me as I ran, and warned me about going too close to the centre. I acknowledged the warning and took a moment's respite before walking a few paces further and coming into sight of the central area of the node.

Here the crowds were thick and just as monotonous, most staring at the intergalactic enigma (if that were indeed its nature). I searched for Jayameeka but not surprisingly failed to see her.

I jumped through time.

My passage was swift and remarkably easy. The blur of colour and sensation of roaring were more pronounced. I stopped and found myself in stone ruins, with green and wet countryside all around, and just a few travellers like myself walking and exploring. It was a cold day in the dawn of civilized man; beyond the wall of the node I could see un-domesticated sheep. The ruins, chiselled stone and traces of wattle, were long deserted.

Back further and a strong and biting wind howled across the shrub-covered highland; trees were scattered about, and distantly the land was forest covered and impenetrable.

Five travellers, seated, talking together. As I watched, a sixth, from a very distant future time, slipped into sight and out again.

Back further. Motion through time still very easy and natural.

Sun, baking mudflats, lizard life and prowling mammals. They ran from me as I appeared. The topography of the world was changed, and now I was in a valley, and jagged rock hills rose about me. A river had once passed this way.

A shape flickered in and out of vision, a woman, far older than Jayameeka. As I stood in the heat and watched the shimmering air around me I could see the passage of many travellers. Distantly, hidden almost completely by an overhang of rock, was the black shape of the Traveller himself, unaware of his brief stop at the beginning of the Quaternary.

Back. Water.

And further ... storm clouds and the discharge of lightning. Granitic monoliths rising high above me, shadowy, grey, dimly seen. The heavy movement of animal life, a distant thundering as of water pouring down slopes. White ghosts from the future fading in and out of sight ...

A voice, shouting. Lightning flashes. Thunder, the crumble of rock, the roaring of a great beast, white teeth highlit in the electrically tense atmosphere.

Back. Calm, evening, vegetation of many colours. Moisture dripping from broad leaves.

A figure watching me from the jungle.

'Jayameeka!' I cried.

'Go back, Jaim,' she shrieked, and the tears were in her voice as well as her eyes. I ran towards her. 'You can't follow me,' she sobbed.

'Wait ...'

But she was gone, and I jumped after her, feeling the passage of the centuries measured against the stuttering of my heart. She had seemed surprised, shocked to see me. Had Garri lied to me after all?

Travel became difficult, the passing of the millennia slowed, and I froze, in a time of dinosaurian peak, breathing through my mask and staring into the thick, swampy landscape. The peak of the node had not yet arrived ... Jayameeka was struggling half in and half out of this time, a ghost form split between now and this location as it had been over a million years ago.

I waded through slush towards her, terrified that I might at any moment sink, or be consumed by some huge reptilian swamp dweller, but nothing occurred, save that the peak approached nearer and suddenly we both slipped a million years back in time.

A huge silver platform stood before me, rising out of the swamp, cutting brilliantly through the hazy, leafy air. All around me, half concealed, looking somehow very dead, were the ruins of a gigantic building, perhaps a station, perhaps a city. It was half submerged, but had lost no fragment of glitter, no ounce of sparkle.

Domes and towers, some of them twisted and bent by time and the impact of weather – great glass panels and the remnants of machines. Jayameeka was running along a buckled metal roadway, her feet leaving slimy imprints on the almost flawless ground beneath her. I waded through the mire and heaved myself up on to a ledge of metal, and dragged my soaking body up the steeply sloping surface until I reached level ground. I raced into a large room, where golden snakes hung coiled around tubular rafters, and climbed through the broken window that looked out upon the roadway. I followed Jayameeka as fast as I could, noticing as I ran the dark shape of the Traveller secure and settled in a pit in the middle of the building (idle thought: what was so special about this Traveller that he had his point of arrival marked by such a monument?). Protected against all ravaging agents, this was his last stop, perhaps, before he returned to his own kind, a single jump further into the past, to a moment that no human could reach, a moment beyond us all.

The seconds were racing past. I called for Jayameeka and saw her struggling against the unseen edge of the node. So close, but this far back the confinement of the node was smaller, tighter. There was dry ground above the swamp, and she was struggling to jump towards it from the overhanging metal roadway, but she seemed unable to pass through …

A figure came into view off to my right. I heard a voice shout, 'Stop! Stop or I shoot!'

I could hardly believe what I heard. It was Herok, uniformed and protected, and he was levelling his handgun at the struggling shape of Jayameeka. I could see the tension in his form; the sure sign of a man about to kill …

'NO, HEROK!'

He faltered, glanced at me and realized who I was. 'Jaim! What the hell are you … STOP!' Still shouting at Jayameeka, about to kill at any moment.

'Don't shoot her, Herok,' I begged, and without realizing it my own weapon was in my hands.

'Stay away, Jaim. Stay out of this …'

And without thinking, without bothering to argue any more, I levelled my gun and squeezed the trigger. At the last moment Herok realized what was happening and his mouth opened, his head turned, the gun in his hand fell limply to the roadway and he stared at me …

Too late.

My calm, unhurried shot took his head off at the lower jaw. I shot him as dead as the ruins into which his body tumbled, lost in the darkness of an alien structure and the swamp that was consuming it.

When I looked at Jayameeka she was watching me.

'Come on, Jaim …'

Distantly, all around, other shapes were materializing, some not fading in, some actually coming to rest in this era, anonymous, faceless travellers, each a potential threat.

As I ran towards my daughter she had turned again and was pushing through the wall. There was a tug at my body and my mind, the sensation of being drawn back up time, but I fought it … came closer to Jayameeka when … without a flash, without a scream, she was through the node … she had escaped the confines of distorted time and was free in the age of the giant reptiles. Twenty seconds!

If the helmet failed, I had just twenty seconds to try and force my way out of the node. If any thoughts of *why* I should want to beach myself in the Cretaceous period occurred to me, I pushed them aside. To be with Jayameeka was the only thing of importance now – less than twenty seconds (as I ran three, four strides to the second) – to achieve that which few men had ever succeeded in achieving.

The edge of the node held me back and I began to push, thinking, mentally urging myself through the wall as hard as I could. And behind me – 'Hold it right there! Stop or we shoot!' The air became filled with fire, and from each corner of my eye I saw the shapes of Security men bursting through from the future to try and stop my illegal breakout.

Jayameeka appeared before me, shooting calmly and carefully through the edge of the node. The buzz and roar of blaster charges declined ... Two seconds!

I was not going to make it ... One second!

The pressure in front of me vanished and I sprawled upon the dry hard ground, felt the stillness of the air. Jayameeka stopped shooting and crouched beside me, stroking the hair from my face. She was smiling, but shaking her head. We looked into the node and saw the great wall of red and yellow fire spreading in front of us as the frustrated Security men shot towards us, hoping that a solitary charge might escape the confines of time.

Even through the filters the air was acrid. The ground shook with the passage of some beast. Its bass vocality was frightening.

The node faded, and with it the fire and the frustrated men of future ages. Just the swamp and the great metal ruin remained, and the threat of creatures of this time.

'You shouldn't have followed me,' said Jayameeka. But she was smiling.

'Garri told me you wanted me to ...'

'Garri? He told you?'

'He said you were friends ...'

Jayameeka laughed. 'Friends! He helped me escape for his own rotten ends. He's trapped us both in the past, got rid of me and if I can't travel through time as my ... experimenters, to call them kindly ... would hope I can do, having tuned my mind in ... well, you and me both are doomed to a very early grave, Jaim.'

I couldn't help smiling at her unintentional pun. I hugged her to me and then showed the belt, and explained its principle.

She gasped, looked incredulous, then stared at me. 'You've *really* been suckered, Jaim. That belt has never been tested, not properly.' She laughed, then, almost hysterically. 'Used to the last. Me, you, used to the last. I'll bet, you know, that my whole escape was intricately planned, that every twist and turn I made trying to survive in the node was monitored and planned for.'

The ground shook again, but we took no notice. I fingered the belt controls, feeling dry-mouthed and apprehensive. A test pilot of sorts, I tried to think us three or four days into the future, holding tightly to Jayameeka as I went.

A tingle of electricity on the skin, an abrupt transition from dry day to wet night!

'It works!' I shouted. 'Garri *hasn't* let us down!' Drenched, we hugged. Frozen, we jaunted through the Cretaceous. Laughing, we began the slow journey back to the third millennium after Christ. We would take our time getting there.

THE TOUCH OF A VANISHED HAND

Thank God for Gable's hands.

A blind man once wrote that in the holding of hands there is an awareness of self existence. The blind man's name was André Goriot and he lived in exile on the seventh world of Sirius.

I set down on Sirius 7 in my youth and found the blind man in his self-contained installation, a small, almost featureless construct, set well in at the base of a cliff. He held my hands and talked of what he had learned about perception and isolation. I was bored and tried to keep my murmurings inaudible, but at the time my throat recorder was new to me and an irritating static sent tingling fingers of skin sensation down my chest. Concentration was difficult to maintain. The blind man was just so much boredom, suffered by my adolescent self only because what he told me would be of use in my level one dissertation.

He held my hands for all the time I was with him and I never recovered from the intimacy of the contact. The very touch of a man's hands thereafter made me shiver and recoil. I wore gloves perpetually, and doggedly declined to shake hands in greeting or at an introduction.

It became so unnerving, the physical revulsion to a hand's touch that I underwent corrective psychotherapy. It was not a recourse to which I referred myself willingly. The effect of deep space upon fairly ordinary psychoses has been the subject of thousands of level two and three dissertations, yet still the surface has been no more than scratched. An unexpected linkage in my brain resulted in a simple piece of corrective therapy having an effect on my sexuality. Essentially, my drives reversed.

I had no regrets. Why should I have had? With my new motivations and interests I was content; as content as I had been with my old.

Later there was a man called Christopher Gable who had never heard of Goriot. I met him over dinner at the status-B Eurasian club, of which I was a member on nineteen mapspace worlds. Gable had travelled much. In the lines on his face I read of great loss. In the way he talked I saw a certain lacking of identity. Perhaps the two things were related, but I never found out.

Gable was middle-aged and his blond hair was cut above his ears in a very conservative style. He towered over me in height, and yet his clothes hung loose and creased upon his frame, and when he walked he seemed ill at ease with motion.

When I mentioned Northern Europe he was immediately interested and confirmed that he came from Sweden, although that had been more than a decade in his past. I saw, then, the Scandinavian lilt to his interLing. He had already noticed the unshakeable American accent in my own voice, and I spent a while telling him of my brief and pointless participation in the Chino-American war of '78. I had been made prisoner near the beginning of the fracas and had been interned in a small camp that stretched below the ruins of the Bridge Monument in a part of the prison city that had been San Francisco. My Anglo-French status had been denied me, despite my shouting (they weren't prepared to believe that a European would have volunteered so quickly to come into the war: since we only have to do three months military service I thought to get mine over with as quickly as possible. Surely the first three months of a war is safe enough? I didn't understand war) and I had been branded as a North American and interned with several locals who taught me much of American cynicism. We made gravity nets by the waters edge, and some of them chose to drown, but most of us dreamed of far away worlds, and the freedom of space.

That had been a long time in the past, and the hurt and frustration of those sordid years in confinement had long since passed away.

We turned the conversation towards the arts, and towards the scientific arts, and found a common interest in holospan and mobiloforms. Returning to his apartment that same evening I was astonished at the array of original art forms he possessed. Many had been executed by his own hand. The walls were covered with mobiloforms, mostly reconstructions of his earlier life; I saw people and places that fired my imagination, all moving through their ten second cycles with never tiring repetitiveness.

Over the days our friendship developed and we began to shirk work to be together, to talk over common ground and enjoy the emotions and pleasures of each other's company.

Over the weeks our relationship developed into something more than friendship, and the essential absence of women in the city became an irrelevancy, and Gable wondered why he had ever brooded and pined for female companionship. There was nothing we wanted or desired that we could not both supply for each other.

All this was on Rigel Nine, an oxygen-nitrogen world, so distant from its primary that the sky was never blue in any terran sense, and the surface was always cold. The underground city of Voronezh basked in homeostasis, but shuddered too often for our likings to the cracking and movement of the

Niner's crust as it moved before forces within our comprehension but beyond our capability to control.

The time comes to leave Rigel Nine and we go out onto the surface. The landscape of the planet has been terraformed in as much as it has been flattened. We gaze at miles of flatness, the granite-like rocks ground to sand which has blown away. The deep blue sky is star speckled, as it always is. Immensely tall conoids reach into the sky at regular intervals, black in colour, splitting the wind into confused patterns of flow. These are the power houses of Voronezh and they harness the powers of wind and sun.

The roadways wind between the towers and we walk along one to where another intersects. A hundred yards away, small and opaquely white, is the landing and despatching block; we step upon it and reach out to hold hands.

This is the way of travel and there is nothing particularly intimate in the touch. Our suits coded for our destination, the block transmits us through space in extended seconds. As we move to our goal, the third world of Bianco's Star, we feel the passage of suns and worlds and spread thin to conserve our identity. It is a sensation of disembodiment, time slows, and I know little save the touch of Gable's hands upon my own, and the excitement of our next few months together. The cerebro-tactile linkage keeps us in contact and we travel through the void as a unit. Until.

I come out of space on the third world of Bianco's Star, on the heat-seared equator of the world; I stand upon the cool, white landing block and the gaping maw of a subterranean tunnel opens wide so I might move into the equable temperature of the terran installation below.

I feel Gable's hands clasping my own and turn to him – without thinking that I should be seeing him, without realizing that the grasp should have ceased to be as we landed and separated … as we appear to have done.

Gable holds my hands and he is nowhere to be seen. I have a feeling that I shall never see him again, and as I go below, shocked and weak, I know – because I have heard of these things happening before – that he has been lost and will remain lost forever.

We had come to Bianco's Star to offer our artistic talents to the major art industry of the world – crystal sculpture. I sat in my small apartment for many days, harnessed to the projection headpiece, shattering a seven pound crystal in carefully directed ways, and producing nothing. My thoughts were cloudy, my emotions unpredictable but predominantly blue. The crystal lost weight, the dust filled the air, the shape changed from linear to abstract, to various meaningless forms, to a perfect feather that found some small numbers of admirers and earned me the credit-status to move to Earth.

Gable's touch was on my hands all the time, and I never knew if he was with me in awareness or not.

On Earth I revisited England and found peace of mind, for a while, in the roaring city of London. I hid away in Highgate, in a shack built of red brick and ordinary steel, that stood below the great Northern Flyover. The whole region was a shanty town, a lake of ruins, fire-blackened houses and cracked tarmacadam roadways. The City rose five hundred storeys above the ancient Thames and at night the lights from those roaring megaliths made the shanty town a jungle of harsh concreted walls, and intense shadows.

This was all a vision of San Francisco, a curious reflection and reconstruction of my fears and frustrations in the months following my release from internment. I relived in agonizing dreams and extended periods of unshakeable reminiscence, the exhausting trek across the continent of America, following the straggling columns of Americans all searching their homes and families. And I, with an ocean separating me from my own security, living in dread of death before I could touch the land at Cobh, or Plymouth.

The feeling of wrongness within the city grew, and with each passing day I became more uncomfortable. I talked to virtually no one and lived a hermitic existence, eking out my resources as much as was possible. I became more and more thankful for the continual pressure of Gable's hands upon my own, but attempts to communicate with him failed.

After three weeks in London I could take the isolation no longer, and travelled to Sweden where I found Gable's birthplace. I traced his life through school and three cities, through a broken marriage and a finished career: he had taught emotive art at the University of Uppsala, but his drug commitments and adolescent behaviour (he had created obscene designs out of the vone booths on the university campus) finished him as a lecturer. That had been in the early days of powerthought design, and Uppsala had been the home of many of the earlier models of the projection apparatus that would later become almost a household possession. He had abused his privileged status and he had been sacked.

From the mobiloforms of Gable that I saw there, from the expression on his face, the spring in his step, I decided that the disasters of his early life had not particularly bothered him.

His wife had left him shortly before he would have thrown her out. Their contract was nearly expired anyway, and would not have been renewed because of artistic and culinary incompatibility, the most mundane of reasons for divorce in those days. Gable had moved to Stockholm and opened a breeding contract with a middle-aged Norwegian. I found his seventeen-year-old son living in the lake district of Jutland. He rode an air horse across the marshy ground of his inherited farm and dropped from the seat even before the sleek machine had stopped. He stared at me across a patch of reeds before turning to skim flattened pebbles across the still waters of the lake. I saw Gable in his hair, in his eyes, in the arrogance of his bearing.

'I was not very fond of my father. Nor he of me.'

His voice was Gable's voice. I wanted to listen to him talk for hours, but he fell silent.

'Why did your father leave? Why did he become so depressed?'

'Why?' He laughed. He kicked at some mechanism hidden in the reeds and his lake erupted into turbulence. He stripped off his clothes and walked to the water's edge. Gable in every way. I felt my stomach knot and suppressed the desire I felt. He stepped into the waves and shouted, 'I was greater than him. In every way.' He began to swim and he turned on his back and there was a smile of horrifying coldness upon his face. 'I took his soul. I drained him. I became Him ... and more.'

The pressure on my hands increased. Was Gable listening? I squeezed the unseen hands and felt the despair of the trapped man. I wondered in what hell Gable was existing. Was his son interested in knowing his father's fate? Should I tell him?

Gable's son did not reappear. The turbulence of the lake died quite suddenly and I assumed that the youth had come ashore out of my sight. I sat by the water's edge and after a few hours the lake seemed to shrink and the freshness of the landscape became submerged in an aura of stagnation. I searched for the son and found only ruin ... a ruined farmhouse, an overgrown road, a rusty air horse, unused for many years.

A sudden terrible fear came over me and I ran from the farm, screaming. But when I reached the mainway all was normal again.

In the darkness of the night train to Boulogne, confused and cold, I felt every finger's pressure on my own, imagined I could sense the ooze of sweat in Gable's palms, as he screamed in his emptiness, threshed and struggled to regain his material existence. I sobbed, felt sick.

Under the channel, the red lights hypnotized me as the monorail glided silently through the submarine world. Then Dover, and the smell of the continent I had just left. In Dover, by the hovercraft docks, I knew the pleasures of flesh, immersed myself in the body of a dockside bord, and slept the night dreaming of Gable. His hands clutched desperately at my own and I awoke several times during the night to find my arms outstretched and the fingers clenching and unclenching, the bisexual figure beside me watching in consternation.

There was a moment, some little while later, when I felt my hands touch warm, smooth flesh, and yet I sat alone on the platform of a monorail station, waiting to journey north.

I sat in the lounge of the station and closed my eyes, and it seemed my hands ran across the belly of a small but shapely woman, explored navel and pubis, and stroked the outside of her thighs for an interminable time. I sat in the dimmed light and stared at my palms, and I felt the fullness of a breast, and my finger tips touched the hard button of a nipple and then wandered again in a drunkard's walk towards the feminine apex.

Opening my awareness to the station I found it in ruins, the rails warped and useless, the station tumbledown and filled with the litter of ages, cans and the bodies of air cars. The viscera of a nation, decaying through time.

Leaving Earth, with its frightening transmutations, I jumped to Mars, but found I could not land. I moved on, dispersing through space in the direction of Centaurus. Gable's grip played a bolero on each hand and I squeezed back, reassuring him, always reassuring him. I could not make contact at Centaurus and journeyed on, dispersing even more, and I noticed that the stars were thinning, and as I came in close to Sirius its glowing disc faded and became black, and Gable seemed to hesitate, as if aware of my shock.

The Universe about me was gone in a second and I recalled the events of a moment before, of standing at the platform on Rigel Nine, of holding hands with Gable, of jumping.

And the dream in that drawn-out moment of time between worlds, the events and shock of Gable's loss, in fact, just a sublimation of my own failure to transmit correctly.

And now Gable, on a world somewhere, alive and dreaming every night of his past and his future, and feeling me gripping his hands as I drift through a curious non-existence, wondering whether a day or a million years passes.

Thank God for Gable's touch.

THE GRAVEYARD CROSS

He had been the first to go, but he knew he would not be the first to return. He would not be a hero, but he had no need of that; after twenty years in space he wanted nothing but home.

It would not be his home, either. There would be none of the old gang, the happy group who had watched him leave, nearly three centuries before. But that was not important. There would be greenness beneath his feet and coolness on his face, and his past would be there, inscribed in the very genes of the people whom he would get to know.

He would have lost very little.

He switched on the transceiver with a rising sense of excitement.

'This is Deep Space Probe Orion. Commander Summerson …'

And after a few moments: 'Welcome, Summerson. It's been a long time.'

It was the first human voice he had heard in twenty years. He requested landing permission on Earth, asked for the correct coordinates for touchdown.

'This is Littrow City – on the Moon. You'll have to land at Serenitatis Base, Commander Summerson. You'll have to check in here before anything.'

'No thank you, Littrow – I've waited twenty years for a sight of Earth and I can't wait a second longer. I want to go straight down.'

'Impossible. I repeat, impossible. Commander Summerson, you must *not* attempt to make any such landing. Please bring your ship down at Serenitatis.'

Argument was useless. He complied, reluctantly, complaining all the time that since he had never left the ship in the whole of his mission, there could be no possibility of his having acquired a strange disease. Why did he need quarantine?

'It isn't quarantine, Commander. But you've been gone three centuries and things have changed on Earth. You may not want to go …'

'Oh I'll want to go! And nothing is going to stop me.'

He snapped off the transceiver, and swallowed his disappointment, but he landed at the huge unmanned base in the Mare Serenitatis, and waited to be picked up.

Decontamination. Then de-robing.

Summerson was small, less than five feet five inches, and his body was thin. To look at him was to think: emaciation. But he was very fit. And something within him drove him towards Earth, something irrational, perhaps, but something strong.

Debriefing, and an account of stars and worlds that set alight the minds of those who listened. Those sessions were quiet indeed save for the voice of Summerson as he told of *Cyberon* and *Vax Sinester*, of worlds passing silently below, searched and then ignored as he went deeper into the deep, watching for a second Earth that he would never find.

When the sessions were finished Summerson packed his belongings together and went to Base Commander Wolfe to say goodbye. His job was done; now at last he could go back to Earth.

Wolfe said No, and Summerson sat quietly and watched the younger man.

'Explain that.' Icy.

'Earth has changed.'

'Of course. I'm expecting to be the alone-est man on Earth for a while. But the things I want most of all won't have changed.'

'Everything has changed,' said Wolfe. 'Everything down to the smallest leaf. Summerson, that isn't Earth any more. Earth died a long time ago; after you left, before I was born. It died of a cancer that had begun hundreds of years ago. Small and unnoticed in those days, it eventually took hold and Earth died. It's a different planet, Summerson. Totally.'

Summerson shook his head and his fists clenched. 'War? Are you telling me that there was—'

Wolfe laughed. 'Not war, never war. War maims – it never destroys. Let me rephrase what I said. Earth *evolved.*'

'Let me ask some questions,' said Summerson, and inside he was breaking up because there was something wrong, something very wrong, and it was going to stop him; he knew it and he could not face it.

'Are there humans on Earth?' Wolfe smiled, nodded his head. 'Are there two sexes of humans? Do they have arms and legs, a single head and a heart on the left side of their chest cavities?' All affirmative.

'Is there air on Earth? Is there water? Is there food? Life? Cities?'

'Certainly there are.'

'Can I live on Earth?'

'You can. You can live there like any of us could live there. It wouldn't be much of a life – at the outside probably a day. Long enough to see a few sights before you choke up so much blood you drown, and find yourself being consumed before you've fully died.'

Summerson stared at Wolfe and shook his head.

'Your Earth is dead, Summerson. Face the facts.'

'Not dead,' cried Summerson. 'Only hidden. It's there, beneath, disguised, distorted perhaps, but there just the same. I must see it.'

'Fine. We'll fly you across it. As many times as you like.'

'I must *stand* on it.'

'Wear a suit and we'll take you to the desert areas.'

'Oh Christ, Wolfe, don't you understand? I must *be* there, I must feel it in my body like it was in my body twenty years ago!'

'Three hundred years ago!' shouted Wolfe, and they glared at each other, softened and fell back into sullen silence.

'You can't go back,' said Wolfe.

'I'm going back,' said Summerson.

'You won't survive.'

'I'm going back at any cost. You can't stop me, Wolfe, not you, not anyone. I'm going back at any cost.'

'The cost will be very great.'

'I'm a rich man. My investments at the time I left were—'

'Not the money cost. You'll never need money at Littrow, or Tycho, or Clavius, or Mars ... you are a lifelong guest if you care to stay.'

'I don't. I don't care to stay, I care to go. What cost?'

Lafayette, in white, with deep-set brown eyes that never seemed capable of meeting Summerson's gaze, fixed him down on a bed of steel, and began to push electrodes. He worked with an intensity that negated conversation and Summerson was glad because he was thinking of Oxford Street and a park (with a lake) that was called Hyde Park and had vanished a long time ago, Wolfe had said.

The electrodes aggravated and there were so many of them, and a computer burbled self-indulgently and planned and plotted Summerson's body and designed the frame that could be built upon the frame he already had.

Lafayette, talking with a slightly French accent (he was from French Imbrium where the French tradition was maintained) told Summerson that he was to sleep now, and he would wake in twenty hours. Nothing would have changed, but over the weeks he would grow.

Summerson grew, and from five feet five he reached six six, and that was where he stopped because the computer said to stop. His long bones had lengthened and widened, his ribs had expanded, his shoulders broadened, the overall calcium content of his frame was increased (with no noticeable effect on his increased weight) and a para-parathyroid stopped his body correcting the fault. He was skeletal to look at and his head was small, but only because his body was so large.

He looked at himself in the mirror and felt sick. But it would get him back to earth.

He was fed, and nourished, and the skeletal display vanished and thick muscle appeared at a noticeable rate and eventually he was heavy set and a monstrous-looking man, and only two months had passed since he had insisted on the treatment.

Wolfe came to see him.

'How does it feel to be tall?'

'Why did they do it? Why is it necessary?'

They sat facing each other and Wolfe grinned. 'It gives you a competitive advantage. Or put it this way, it deletes the competitive disadvantage of your short height.'

'And there's more? Yes, I can see there's more.'

'It was your choice.'

It had been his choice and there was no denying it. To get back to Earth he would have to adapt to Earth. So Summerson tried to forget about being six foot six when he had lived a lifetime as a short man among men, and he tried to think of Earth, which was easy to do.

Wolfe sent him a woman and when he didn't express absolute delight, he sent a second, and a third. Summerson rejected them all.

Wolfe was upset and made the fact plain in no uncertain terms. Summerson accepted the anger and when Wolfe was calm again he pointed out that blind dates went out with the Ark.

'We could make your life on the Moon – or Mars – one long, lingering holiday. Summerson, I appeal to you. Don't risk your life, don't waste your experience by going down to Earth. If you want work, there is masses of it. Anywhere in the System, Summerson, anywhere. Name it and you'll go there and you'll never want, never need.'

Summerson clenched his fists. 'You don't – you won't – understand. Sure, in a year, maybe two, I'll come back, I might *beg* you to take me back. But only after I've been Home, Wolfe. I must go home first. I must survive and I must feel Earth again. *Then* send me beautiful women and the keys to the Solar System ...'

Wolf sighed. 'Earth will chew you up and spit you out, even with the changes we can make in you. Once down you'll never find peace, you'll never be able to return. Think, Summerson, think man. The Solar System is buzzing with life. It's all new, it's all fresh, clean. It's frontier work, the sort of work a man like you would find second nature. You're a leader, Summerson, a man to place on a pedestal. Think about it.'

'I've thought all I need. Earth, Wolfe, Earth is where I'm going, and *then* I'll think about your offers.'

He was a frantic scrambling shape, sending up clouds of dust as he flailed across the crater bed beneath bigger and heavier loads: Earth watched.

In time he could move as fluently as a sprinter in track gear, and he could dodge and duck, and reverse direction on a thin and unexpected line. All this on Luna, and when they placed him in the IG simulator he did as well. He became fast and powerful; he could run. He could escape.

Lafayette began to thicken his skin.

'Why?' said Summerson. And Lafayette just smiled. 'Your choice,' he said.

'You sound like Wolfe. Why? Why thicken my skin?'

'Radiation,' said Lafayette. 'There's less oxygen on Earth, now, but more supersonic air vessels. The ozone layer has been reduced to an ozone smear. The UV reaching the surface would fry you in a week.'

'My God,' said Summerson as his skin thickened across the days. 'The effect on evolution!' He sat up. Already his brain was learning to cope with new surface sensations. Heat he never felt. He could blister himself before he felt the pain. But his body was aware of heat and his reflexes remained fast. Pain came slowly. Damage was less likely because of his almost chitinous pelt.

'Exactly,' said Lafayette, 'what exactly will happen is anybody's guess. Over the next few generations we should start to see an effect.'

They tanned him then, and he emerged as brown as oak. 'Is everybody this colour?'

'Getting that way,' said Lafayette.

There was a day when they took out his lungs and placed them in a machine. The machine cycled its strange body fluids through the veins and arteries of Summerson's gas-bags, and the walls, the linings of the air sacs, thickened. They became more resistant as the chemicals in the machine blood stimulated them and coaxed them. The mucous glands multiplied and spread about, and the cilia tracts in the bronchi became as dense as forests.

For several days the lungs wheezed on the machine and Summerson breathed not at all, his blood cycling through the body of a volunteer who lay, with Summerson, in a coma, breathing high oxy atmosphere and keeping their resting bodies alive and nourished.

The lungs found their way back to the body, and then there was his heart, which they removed and enlarged, made it into a three times as powerful squeeze-bag of muscle and sinew, and the bundle of *His* was removed and replaced with an artificial cable that was ten times as fast and twenty times as efficient, and would remain so for a thousand years thanks to the way that Lafayette had designed it.

One day Summerson awoke after sleeping for twenty days and found himself hung like Goliath. 'Why? For whose benefit?'

'Sexual prowess is very important. It can save your neck.'

'To impress women?'

'To quiesce dominant males.'

'How bloody stupid.'

'Earth has changed,' said Wolfe simply.

'Oh my God,' said Summerson, and crept away to hide.

They strengthened his fingers and thickened his nails until he carried five spears at the end of each arm, and could dent hard-board with a single prod.

They toughened the edge of each hand until the nerve endings had gone and the horny layer was thick and strong as iron.

As Summerson slept Lafayette removed the scalp and the skin around his eyes; down to his mouth the living bone was exposed and for twenty days a grinning skull watched as Lafayette softened the bone, and then thickened it, and as the calcium and phosphate lay down in crystal lattices so he inserted a criss-cross of non-irritating steel rods, and Summerson's skull became as strong as a helmet, and the brain below it was not the least affected.

Lafayette built a new cornea and fixed it to Summerson's so that the join could not be seen. The new cornea was a biological material that joined at the edge of the eye with the old cornea and formed a tough and deflective barrier against a normally blinding stab.

When Summerson looked into a mirror he could no longer see himself. But since he knew he was there he could take the shock and sublimate it into mere uneasiness.

If Summerson ever had doubts he walked to the edge of the enclosed city; there, standing dark and unreal, he would stare at the planet Earth. When the planet was in full bloom he felt something inside him stir and cry, and he knew that whatever was happening to him, he was right to go through with it, for it meant survival on that beautiful world.

When the Earth was in quarter phase then, as the months went by, he would feel uncertainty. He would look at himself and remember how he had been, and only the knowledge that no one down there was going to recognize him anyway kept him from screaming to Lafayette to 'take it all off'.

Monitoring his frustration, Wolfe arranged for a visit by Roz Steele.

There was a time when Summerson would have gasped. Women as large as Roz were circus exhibits, not lovers. And yet, standing inches taller than her, he found her magnificent.

She was black skinned and when he touched her she hardly felt the touch, and when he kissed her she hardly felt the kiss, and when he took her hand he found the callouses and stiffened fingers and he knew, then, that ...

Roz said, 'Don't look so surprised. You knew that other starmen had been arriving back before you.'

'And you wanted to go to Earth ... and this is what they did to you.'

Roz nodded. 'I'm a damn sight better looking than I was when I left.'

'And you went back to Earth.'

'No. I never made it. I gave up wanting to go down towards the end of my adaptation. I've lived the fullest life possible since then.'

For a moment Summerson found himself nodding, then he realized. 'Wolfe sent you to work on me.'

'He sent me to lie with you. As simple as that. You will work on yourself. I hope you *do* go down to Earth. You'll be the first one that did.'

'And the others?'

'Scattered through the solar system, mostly on Mars. That's a world and a half. I spent ten years there. I'm going back soon. Why don't you come with me?'

Summerson smiled. 'How do you know we'll get along?'

She reached over and unbuttoned his tunic. Summerson stood motionless with his heart hammering and the excitement of the moment causing him to rise to his full gargantuan extent. When he was naked she unbuttoned her own robe and let it slip from her shoulders.

It was a passion that Summerson might never have known, for he was not, in his original form, a passionate man. An attitude to love depends largely on confidence in one's physical appearance, and now Summerson felt powerful, and he was a powerful lover.

Lafayette, seeming to relish his task, called for Summerson for one last time and while Summerson slept he made him into a high-tension man. He altered the threshold level of the feedback loop that governed the adrenalin flow into Summerson's vascular system, and when Summerson emerged he found that the slightest sensation of unease precipitated him into a state of complete mental and physical alertness. He began to bristle, he began to twist and turn as he walked as if some shadow haunted him and, should it creep up on him, would overcome him.

Likewise his temper suffered and he snapped and jumped, and his eyes became the eyes of a searching man, never still, always restive.

Except when they gazed at Earth.

Roz took her leave and Summerson watched her go with regret. She shipped for Mars and inside him Summerson knew that should he ever leave Earth he would head after her.

He had lost his taste for food and Lafayette explained that his stomach was changed. It would now break down alcohol in a matter of seconds. No hangovers for Summerson. At the slightest sign of poison or infected food the stomach would void its contents and flush the chamber with acid which would also be voided. Much of the food on Earth was unfit to eat because of high phosphorous and chlorine contamination. It would be poison to Summerson. A tiny bio-sensor in the wall of his stomach was his guardian.

'Food is not so important to you now,' said Lafayette. 'You're a walking storehouse of all the vital amino-acids, vitamins and elements you need. Only a few weeks' supply, of course, but no doubt you *will* eat and these are just backups.

There are bio-monitors in the hepatic portal and right brachial veins and they're reading your blood composition all the time. Any ingredient falling below the necessary level you can rectify at once. Prolonged deficit will be made known to you by a skin itch over your right arm. A timing mechanism – a unit of monkey liver cells actually, designed to accumulate whatever your stores are secreting; critical level reached – reflex loop to histamine-loaded cells in your skin, and you are warned.'

'Monkey cells,' said Summerson, almost in disbelief.

'Your body thinks they're you. We tagged them with your identity factor. Settling in nicely I should imagine.

'We've done much the same thing to some highly educated lymphocytes – they've been exposed to every disease organism we know about. They'll be your watch-dogs. Instead of the delay to produce primary immunity, during which time you'd die of many of these diseases, you can now react with secondary immunity which appears very fast.'

'And I won't reject the cells?'

'Not if I've done my job properly. Those, by the way, are human lymphocytes, but like the monkey cells they've been tagged with your own identity-factor. You'll greet them like friends. They're also very long-lived cells – just a lysosome stabilizing gimmick that was developed about a hundred years ago.'

'When I die my white cells will live on, is that it? Roaming the wastelands of Earth searching for a host.'

For a few hours, as Summerson basked in Earthlight on the rim of a small crater, south-west of the colony at Littrow, he imagined that the preparations were finished. His body had been rebuilt and he could no longer call himself Summerson with quite the same meaning as before.

But now it seemed worthwhile, the waiting, the delaying, the endless sleeps while Lafayette had probed and changed and strengthened and destroyed.

Lafayette had enjoyed his task. He was the Base surgeon but the few travellers who returned and who needed the engineering job for their return to Earth were his real interest.

And yet, when it was finished, none ever returned. It was as if their changed bodies caused their minds to change, made them find Earth as repulsive as Wolfe found it.

Summerson felt no such repulsion. He was a hideous being by his own standards, and if he reflected the needs of Earth, then Earth was probably a hideous world. But beauty, as the saying went, is only skin deep. Summerson was interested in a deeper level of Earth. And the longing was still with him; the desire to return, whilst not now voiced as often as it had been voiced by his newly returned (shorter, whiter, less perfect) self, was just as strong.

He returned to Littrow and to his solex, and though Roz was gone and the room was cold and empty, he found comfort there.

And D'Quiss.

'I'm Felix D'Quiss,' he said, rising from the couch. A tall, thin man; sparse blond hair over a nordic head; eyes blue, quite intense. A firm shake of ugly hands, the big meeting the grotesquely big. Smart, in a white protex suit, the telltale signs of medical status scattered across the pockets – a watch, a pen, a probe, a contact unit unobtrusively lodged behind his ear.

'Summerson,' said Summerson. 'Mark II.'

'I know. You have taken the changes with remarkable complacency.'

'I want to get down to Earth. I'd change anything for that.'

'I'm glad to hear it.'

Summerson shivered and crossed to the ice-box. He fetched out two mash cans and proffered one to D'Quiss who declined it. Summerson opened his own and sipped the drink. 'Let me guess,' he said, crossing to the wall window and watching as Earth seemed to twist away again, just out of reach. 'My mind.'

'Yes.'

'You're going to change it. You're going to remove Summerson from my head like you removed him from my body.'

'Part of the sacrifice,' said D'Quiss, smiling. 'You said when they started on you that no cost was too great. You will have to have meant it if you want to get to Earth.'

'I certainly want to do that!' Summerson said loudly. 'With the emphasis on the *I*. If you alter my mind out of all proportion, if you take the little Summerson in my skull and change him into a para-Summerson, then it isn't *me* any longer. The man who goes down to Earth might not give a damn about the planet … Is that what you want? Is that what happened to Roz and the others? After all this anatomical change you then "make" us not want to return? Because in fact you've been adapting us to conditions on Mars …? Well, I'm sorry to disappoint you, Mr D'Quiss, but I've taken all the change I intend to take. And I *still* intend to go down to Earth.'

D'Quiss nodded, smiling in a self-assured way. 'Is this the rational and calm Summerson that came to Littrow?'

'I'm losing my identity, D'Quiss. That's enough to make any man jumpy.'

'You're not losing your identity, merely your appearance, your inadequacies.'

'I've lost all the inadequacies I intend to lose. Tell Wolfe I'm leaving right now.'

D'Quiss sat quietly and stared at Summerson. He told him, then, that there would be no more change. That the adaptation by engineering was over, finished. The mind, however, was a delicate organ, dependent for its function on environment, both social and physical, and Summerson's mind could not tolerate the environment, both social and physical, of Earth.

'So you want to change it. Like I said, chop here, replace there, Mark III Summerson, grinning idiot, oblivious, nonexistent.'

Nothing of the sort, said D'Quiss. A few emplacements to help Summerson fight the mental pressures.

'Look at it this way. You've already manifested several neuroses.'

'For example?'

'Your shame, embarrassment when Lafayette expanded your sex organ.'

'Oh ... that.'

'Yes, that. A small enough point on its own, but on Earth do you realize how destructive any sort of sexual embarrassment is? You would not survive to walk down the street. But we can mask, condition, certain facets of your personality that might be embarrassing to you.'

'No. Positively no.'

'Or we can place artificial connections between several areas of your brain that will allow you to see exactly when a dangerous mood, feeling, response is approaching, and you can then say to yourself, *careful, Summerson, pretend* ... you see? It will give you the ability to conquer your mental inadequacies without losing the power of choice. Well?'

Summerson was silent.

D'Quiss went on. 'Let me put it this way. Earth is totally hostile. Not hostile by its own standards – it has the same range from extreme to extreme within the population with the bulk of the population filling the centre of the curve. But in the three hundred years you have been away that curve has shifted towards the hostile extreme. What was extreme in your day is now matter of fact. Violence, death, attitude to privacy, of body and home, all these things are set within different parameters. You wouldn't last five minutes.'

'So you keep telling me. So Wolfe and Lafayette keep telling me.'

'All right, so it's a figurative expression. You might survive a week, a month, a year, but it would be fighting all the time, a terrible struggle for survival.'

D'Quiss was watching him very intently, but his face showed complete calm, unlike Wolfe who had seemed almost exasperated by Summerson's doggedness. 'And with a few electrodes in my head I would find it easier to survive. Is that what you're saying?'

D'Quiss nodded. 'The most essential thing is that you keep your wits about you, that you remain even-tempered. Stable. When your heart breaks your mind has got to be oblivious to it; when your heart sings, the same thing goes. When your temper flares you can calm at a moment's thought, but the cause of your anger will not be obliterated so you can still act on it.'

'A few electrodes ... no invisible conditioning, no twisting of a paranoia here and moving it slightly so I can't feel persecuted?'

'Not unless you want it.'

'I don't want it! I want Summerson – me! – to see Earth as he saw it when he left. I want to see the change, feel the difference, seek out the unchanged elements. I want to feel the sadness or the horror as Summerson, *this* Summerson, would have felt it three hundred years ago.' He turned to stare up at the Crescent Earth. 'When I was twenty years younger,' he said softly.

D'Quiss watched him impassively. After a while Summerson moved from the window and sprawled out in an armchair, staring at the other man.

D'Quiss showed no discomfiture. 'Why do you want to go back? What's the real reason?'

Summerson laughed. 'Does there have to be a *real* reason? Isn't it possible that I was telling the truth?' D'Quiss said nothing. After a moment Summerson went on, his eyes focused nowhere in particular. 'It's funny you know. I can remember standing on the ramp at Southend, looking at the shuttle. Such a tiny ship. I wanted nothing else but to get away from Earth. Since I was a kid I wanted to be a probepilot. My parents did everything they could to discourage me, but I was too determined. They came to Southend when I was launched and watched me leave, and I didn't even say goodbye to them. Twenty years in space and I couldn't stop thinking about them. I really came to understand them, to love them. Can you imagine that? Twenty years, and no way back ...'

'It must be an intolerable thought.'

'Thanks,' said Summerson dully. 'But no, nothing is intolerable. It's just ... the emptiness.'

'The emptiness of space?'

'Of everything. A man is much more than just a mind in a body. That's just a small part of him. He's everything that relates to him and which he relates to in turn, and that part of me has gone and I feel just ... just a shard. There's only one place I know where I can come to terms with that emptiness.'

'Earth?'

'Earth.'

'What do you plan on doing once you get there?'

'Oh, explore. Remember. Write. Talk to people.'

'What if they regard you as a freak?'

'Why should they?'

'Why shouldn't they? An off-worlder, *the* off-worlder to many of them. You will be the first to set foot on Earth for more than two generations. They will react to you, I'm sure of that, but that reaction could well be hostile; and if not hostile to begin with, then later certainly. When the novelty wears off ...'

'Will they leave me alone? Will they let me search for the things I want to search for?'

'I don't know,' said D'Quiss. 'You'll have to find yourself employment which could be difficult. And if you feel that you might want to leave for the Moon, then we'll have to arrange a method of communication so we can come and pick you up.'

'You'd do that? After I've declined your every offer for help whilst I was here?'
'We're not barbarians,' said D'Quiss.

Summerson slept.

After five days he awoke looking the same, (feeling the same, but weighing slightly more – the weight of the bio-lam electrodes and miniature power pack embedded partly in his skull and partly in the substance of his brain.

They tried a simple test involving the arousal of his anger and he became angry. They explained that he had merely to think about *not* getting angry and it would pass. They tried the test again and he felt anger rise in him, and then he thought it away and he saw the test for what it was. He tried to think away the remorse at losing Roz, but he couldn't.

It only worked for the future. And when he eventually left Earth he would be able to lose the electrodes, the power pack and the influence of D'Quiss.

He packed his bags and, almost fatalistically, walked towards Wolfe's office. Wolfe was there, and Lafayette. And D'Quiss sitting relaxedly in a corner and smoking a non-inhalant cigarette.

'Are you ready to go?'
'You mean no more changes? I can hardly believe it.'
Wolfe smiled. 'You'll survive unless there's something we've overlooked, something important.'
'Which we don't know about,' said Lafayette, almost as if he were justifying a certain failure.
'But which we will know about after your decline,' said D'Quiss from the side of the room.

Now at last Summerson took his grateful leave and went to the base airlock. A bus took him to Serenitatis, to a small ship, now long disused, that would take him down to Earth.

He had been on the Moon for over a year. And as he walked across the metal ramp to the waiting ship he suddenly felt all the excitement at going home he had felt as he had arrived in the Solar System, all those months before.

With a yell and a laugh he jumped high in the vacuum and bounded to the ship, to take his place (the only passenger) in the small cabin. Wolfe was a black shape in the brightly lit bus, parked half a mile from the ramp.

The sea, the ocean, heaving, white flecked (but somehow ... duller than he remembered), Summerson's eyes trying to leave his head to see down to the Earth. Asia, drifting below, and China, and the China Sea, scattered islands, the buzz of highflying planes, eyes peering at the ship as it glided slowly round the world.

The coast of California sliding below like some huge projection – more buzzing, a swarm of high-flying sightseers, klaxon blasts rending the high atmosphere, the swarms dropping away in front to reassemble behind.

The Atlantic, darker, more sombre than the Pacific, and England, then, and down.

Home.

He was an island. There was dust and shadows. There was no moon. The sun shone through clouds. There was movement, and the cries of the dying. There was dying, and the roar of movement. There was the barking of dogs and the straying of cats.

He was an island and he stopped in the middle of the world and there was nothing to see but the shadows that moved by, and the walls that enclosed him, brick fingers pointing to the sky. He went to where he had once lived.

It was now a slag tip, the waste of centuries poured across an area of several square miles. Bomb waste, desolation, with driverless machines calmly chewing their way through the sea of junk.

There was a girder twisted into the shape of a cross, a single cross, a graveyard cross. He walked through ghosts and filth and picked up a handful of ash and stared at it for a long time.

He saw no people, just dark, hard faces. He heard them, he touched them physically, but they moved so fast, they lived so distant. He tried to move fast to match velocities, but they changed direction and he could never keep up. He drifted through streets, cities, towns, breathing the dust, choking up his food, waking up with his face a bloody mess, registering the attack of screaming gangs, feeling the delayed pain, conscious of his own ferocity ... everything moved around him, never with him. Everything seemed so fast. He spoke words and the words were heard, and he heard words back, but there was never any ...

Communication.

There was no communication. He was a perfectly adapted man, but they could not have known about communication. They had prepared him for poison, fumes, attack and flight, but they had not prepared him for the indifference.

He died a hundred times – hit, spin, shattered – left naked to die and he crept away and found himself and ...

Hit, spin, slugged, and woman's laughter, and an insane and blind achievement of sexual satisfaction and ...

Crawled away.

There was the filth of alleyways, the smell of faeces, the pain of broken bones that healed so quickly ...

The fierceness of dogs, the fastness of movement, the stench of air, the burning of sun, the coldness of children, the emptiness of thought. Confusion, starvation of emotion.

No communication.

He could not identify. He was planes apart, worlds away, points out of focus, miles off target. He was so alien that he hardly registered, and his body was a fragment of litter and it blew away ...

Something went wrong and his anger became uncontrollable. He was hit on the head and something dislodged, and he lost control. And there were armed men and he was hustled away at right angles to the human flow, and he found himself:

In peace. There was peace. A small room, a barred window, the distant grating of metal locks. A filthy pit in the floor, a hard bed. Rats, roaches, sweat, tears ... Light from the window – sounds so distant they were almost familiar. Peace – and Earth.

He had found Earth again.

Sitting in the stillness he knew he was home at last.

MYTHAGO WOOD

When, in 1944, I was called away to the war, I felt so resentful of my father's barely expressed disappointment that, on the eve of my departure, I walked quietly to his desk and tore a page out of his notebook, the diary in which his silent, obsessive work was recorded. The fragment was dated simply 'August 34', and I read it many times, appalled at its incomprehensibility, but content that I had stolen at least a tiny part of his life with which to support myself through those painful, lonely times.

Following a short, and very bitter comment on the distractions in his life – the running of Oak Lodge, our family home, the demands of his two sons, and of his wife (by then, I remember, desperately ill and close to the end of her life) – was a passage quite memorable for its incoherence:

A letter from Watkins – agrees with me that at certain times of the year the aura around the woodland could reach as far as the house. Must think through the implications of this. He is keen to know the power of the oak vortex that I have measured. What to tell him? Certainly not of the first mythago. Have noticed too that the enrichment of the pre-mythago zone is more persistent, but concomitant with this, am distinctly losing my sense of time.

I treasured this piece of paper for many reasons, for the moment or two of my father's passionate interest that it represented – and for the way it locked me out of its understanding, as he had locked me out at home. Everything he loved, everything I hated.

I was wounded in early 1945, and in a military hospital met a young Frenchman, and became close friends with him. I managed to avoid evacuation to England, and when the war finished I stayed in France, travelling south to convalesce in the hills behind Marseilles; it was a hot, dry place, very still, very slow; I lived with my young friend's parents, and quickly became a part of the tiny community.

Letters from my brother Christian, who had returned to Oak Lodge after the war, arrived every month throughout the long year of 1946. They were chatty, informative letters, but there was an increasing note of tension in them, and it was clear that Christian's relationship with his father was deteriorating rapidly. I never heard a word from the old man himself, but then I never expected to; I had long since resigned myself to the fact that, even at best, he regarded me with total indifference. All his family had been an intrusion in his work, and his guilt at neglecting us, and especially at driving his wife to taking her own life, had blossomed rapidly, during the early years of the war, into an hysterical madness that could be truly frightening. Which is not to say that he was perpetually shouting; on the contrary, most of his life was spent in silent, absorbed contemplation of the oak woodland that bordered our home. At first infuriating, because of the distance it put between him and his family, soon those long periods of quiet became blessed, earnestly welcomed.

He died in November 1946, of the illness that had afflicted him for years. When I heard the news I was torn between my unwillingness to return to Oak Lodge, at the edge of the Knaresthorpe estate in Herefordshire, and Christian's obvious distress. He was alone, now, in the house where we had lived through our childhood together; I could imagine him prowling through the empty rooms, perhaps sitting in father's dank and unwholesome study and remembering the hours of denial, the smell of wood and compost that the old man had trudged in through the glass-panelled doors after his week-long sorties into the deep woodlands. The forest had spread into that room as if my father could not bear to be away from the rank undergrowth, and cool, moist oak-glades even when making token acknowledgement of his family. He made that acknowledgement in the only way he knew: by telling us – and mainly telling my brother – stories of the ancient forestlands beyond the house, the primary woodland of oak and ash in whose dark interior (he once said) wild boar could still be heard, and smelled, and tracked by their spoor.

I doubt if he had ever seen such a creature, but I vividly recalled (in that evening as I sat in my room, overlooking the tiny village in the hills, Christian's letter a crushed ball still held in my hand) how I had listened to the muffled grunting of some woodland animal, and heard the heavy, unhurried crashing of something bulky moving inwards, towards the winding pathway that we called Deep Track, a route that led spirally towards the very heart-woods of the forest.

I knew I would have to go home, and yet I delayed my departure for nearly another year. During that time Christian's letters ceased abruptly. In his last letter, dated April 10th, he wrote of Guiwenneth, of his unusual marriage, and hinted that I would be surprised by the lovely girl to whom he had lost his 'heart, mind, soul, reason, cooking ability and just about everything else, old boy'. I wrote to congratulate him, of course, but there was no further communication between us for months.

Eventually I wrote to say I was coming home, that I would stay at Oak Lodge for a few weeks, and then find accommodation in one of the nearby towns. I said goodbye to France, and to the community that had become so much a part of my life, and travelled to England by bus and train, by ferry, and then by train again. And on August 20th, hardly able to believe what was happening to me, I arrived by pony and trap at the disused railway line that skirted the edge of the extensive Knaresthorpe estate. Oak Lodge lay on the far side of the grounds, four miles further round the road, but accessible via the right of way through the estate's fields and woodlands. I intended to take an intermediate route and so, lugging my single, crammed suitcase as best I could, I began to walk along the grass-covered railway track, peering, on occasion, over the high, red-brick wall that marked the limit of the estate, trying to see through the gloom of the pungent pine-woods. Soon this woodland, and the wall, vanished, and the land opened into tight, tree-bordered fields, to which I gained access across a rickety wooden stile, almost lost beneath briar and full-fruited blackberry bushes. I had to trample my way out of the public domain and so onto the south trackway that wound, skirting patchy woodland and the stream called 'sticklebrook', up to the ivy-covered house that was my home.

It was late morning, and very hot, as I came in distant sight of Oak Lodge. Somewhere off to my left I could hear the drone of a tractor. I thought of old Alphonse Jeffries, the estate's farm supervisor, and with memory of his weather-tanned, smiling face came images of the mill-pond, and fishing for pike from his tiny rowing boat.

Memory of the mill-pond was as tranquil as its surface, and I moved away from the south track, through waist high nettles and a tangle of ash and hawthorn scrub until I came out close to the bank of the wide, shadowy pool, its full size hidden by the gloom of the dense stand of oak woodland that began on its far side. Almost hidden among the rushes that crowded the nearer edge of the pond was the shallow boat from which we had fished, years before; its white paint was flaked away almost entirely now, and although the craft looked watertight, I doubted if it would take the weight of a full grown man. I didn't disturb it but walked around the bank and sat down on the rough concrete steps of the crumbling boat-house; from here I watched the surface of the pool rippling with the darting motions of insects, and the occasional passage of a fish, just below.

'A couple of sticks and a bit of string ... that's all it takes.'

Christian's voice startled me. He must have walked along a beaten track from the lodge, hidden from my view by the shed. Delighted, I jumped to my feet and turned to face him. The shock of his appearance was like a physical blow to me, and I think he noticed the fact, even though I threw my arms about him and gave him a powerful brotherly bear-hug.

'I had to see this place again,' I said.

'I know what you mean,' he said, as we broke our embrace. 'I often walk here myself.' There was a moment's awkward silence as we stared at each other. I felt, distinctly, that he was not particularly pleased to see me. 'You're looking brown and drawn, old boy,' he said. 'Healthy and ill together ...'

'Mediterranean sun, grape-picking, and shrapnel. I'm still not one hundred percent.' I smiled. 'But it *is* good to be back, to see you again.'

'Yes,' he said dully. 'I'm glad you've come, Steve. Very glad. Really. I'm afraid the place ... well, a bit of a mess. I only got your letter yesterday and I haven't had a chance to do anything. Things have changed quite a bit, you'll find.'

And he more than anything. I could hardly believe that this was the chipper, perky young man who had left with his army unit in 1944. He had aged incredibly, his hair quite streaked with grey, more noticeable for his having allowed it to grow long and untidy at the back and sides. He reminded me very much of father, the same distant, distracted look, the same hollow cheeks and deeply wrinkled face. But it was his whole demeanour that had shocked me. He had always been a stocky, muscular chap; now he was like the proverbial scarecrow, wiry, ungainly, on edge all the time. His eyes darted about, but never seemed to focus upon me. And he smelled. Of mothballs, as if the crisp white shirt and grey flannels that he wore had been dragged out of storage; and another smell beyond the naptha ... the hint of woodland and grass. There was dirt under his fingernails, and in his hair, and his teeth were yellowing.

He seemed to relax slightly as the minutes ticked by. We sparred a bit, laughed a bit, and walked around the pond, whacking at the rushes with sticks. I could not shake off the feeling that I had arrived home at a bad time.

'Was it difficult ... with the old man, I mean? The last days.'

He shook his head. 'There was a nurse here for the final two weeks or so. I can't exactly say that he went peacefully, but she managed to stop him damaging himself ... or me, for that matter.'

'Your letters certainly suggested a growing hostility. To understate the case.'

Christian smiled quite grimly, and glanced at me with a curious expression, somewhere between agreement and suspicion. 'You got that from my letters, did you? Well, yes. He became quite crazed soon after I came back from the war. You should have seen the place, Steve. You should have seen him. I don't think he'd washed for months. I wondered what he'd been eating ... certainly nothing as simple as eggs and meat. In all honesty I think, for a few months at any rate, he'd been eating wood and leaves. He was in a wretched state. Although he let me help him with his work, he quickly began to resent me. He tried to kill me on several occasions, Steve. And I mean that, really desperate attempts on my life. There was a reason for it, I suppose ...'

I was astonished by what Christian was telling me. The image of my father had changed from that of a cold, resentful man into a crazed figure, ranting at Christian and beating at him with his fists.

'I always thought that, for you at least, he had a touch of affection; he always told *you* the stories of the wood; I listened, but it was you who sat on his knee. Why would he try to kill you?'

'I became too involved,' was all Christian said. He was keeping something back, something of critical importance. I could tell from his tone, from his sullen, almost resentful expression. Did I push the point or not? It was hard to make the decision. I had never before felt so distant from my own brother. I wondered if his behaviour was having an effect on Guiwenneth, the girl he had married. I wondered what sort of atmosphere she was living in up at Oak Lodge.

Tentatively, I broached the subject of the girl.

Christian struck angrily at the rushes by the pond. 'Guiwenneth's gone,' he said simply, and I stopped, startled.

'What does that mean, Chris? Gone where?'

'She's just gone, Steve,' he snapped, angry and cornered. 'She was father's girl, and she's gone, and that's all there is to it.'

'I don't understand what you mean. Where's she gone *to*? In your letter you sounded so happy ...'

'I shouldn't have written about her. That was a mistake. Now let it drop, will you?'

After that outburst, my unease with Christian grew stronger by the minute. There was something very wrong with him indeed, and clearly Guiwenneth's leaving had contributed greatly to the terrible change I could see; but I sensed there was something more. Unless he spoke about it, however, there was no way through to him. I could find only the words, 'I'm sorry.'

'Don't be.'

We walked on, almost to the woods, where the ground became marshy and unsafe for a few yards before vanishing into a musty deepness of stone and root and rotting wood. It was cool, here, the sun being behind us now, and beyond the thickly foliaged trees. The dense stands of rush moved in the breeze and I watched the rotting boat as it shifted slightly on its mooring.

Christian followed my gaze, but he was not looking at the boat or the pond; he was lost, somewhere in his own thoughts. For a brief moment I experienced a jarring sadness at the sight of so fine a young man so ruined in appearance and attitude. I wanted desperately to touch his arm, to hug him, and I could hardly bear the knowledge that I was afraid to do so.

Quite quietly I asked him, 'What on earth has happened to you, Chris? Are you ill?'

He didn't answer for a moment, then said, 'I'm not ill,' and struck hard at a puffball, which shattered and spread on the breeze. He looked at me, something of resignation in his haunted face. 'I've been going through a few changes, that's all. I've been picking up on the old man's work. Perhaps a bit of his reclusiveness is rubbing off on me, a bit of his detachment.'

'If that's true, then perhaps you should give up for a while. The old man's obsession with the oak forest eventually killed him, and from the look of you, you're going the same way.'

Christian smiled thinly and chucked his reedwhacker out into the pond, where it made a dull splash and floated in a patch of scummy green algae. 'It might even be worth dying to achieve what he tried to achieve ... and failed.'

I didn't understand the dramatic overtone in Christian's statement. The work that had so obsessed our father had been concerned with mapping the woodland, and searching for evidence of old forest settlements. He had clearly invented a whole new jargon for himself, and effectively isolated me from any deeper understanding of his work. I said this to Christian, and added, 'Which is all very interesting, but hardly *that* interesting.'

'He was doing much more than that, much more than just mapping. But do you remember those maps, Steve? Incredibly detailed ...'

I could remember one quite clearly, the largest map, showing carefully marked trackways and easy routes through the tangle of trees and stony outcrops; it showed clearings drawn with almost obsessive precision, each glade numbered and identified, and the whole forest divided into zones, and given names. We had made a camp in one of the clearings close to the woodland edge. 'We often tried to get deeper into the heart-woods, remember those expeditions, Chris? But the deep track just ends, and we always managed to get lost, I seem to recall, and very scared.'

'That's true,' Christian said quietly, looking at me quizzically; and added, 'What if I told you the forest had *stopped* us entering? Would you believe me?'

I peered into the tangle of brush, tree and gloom, to where a sunlit clearing was visible. 'In a way I suppose it did,' I said. 'It stopped us penetrating very deeply because it made us scared, because there are few trackways through, and the ground is choked with stone and briar ... very difficult walking. Is that what you meant? Or did you mean something a little more sinister?'

'Sinister isn't the word I'd use,' said Christian, but added nothing more for a moment; he reached up to pluck a leaf from a small, immature oak, and rubbed it between thumb and forefinger before crushing it in his palm. All the time he stared into the deep woods. 'This is primary oak woodland, Steve, untouched forest from when all of the country was covered with deciduous forests of oak and ash and elder and rowan and hawthorn ...'

'And all the rest,' I said with a smile. 'I remember the old man listing them for us.'

'That's right, he did. And there's more than eight square miles of such forest stretching from here to well beyond Grimley, eight square miles of original, post-Ice Age forestland. Untouched, uninvaded for thousands of years.' He broke off and looked at me hard, before adding, 'Resistant to change.'

I said, 'He always thought there were boars alive in there. I remember hearing something one night, and he convinced me that it was a great big old bull boar, skirting the edge of the woods, looking for a mate.'

Christian led the way back towards the boathouse. 'He was probably right. If boars *had* survived from mediaeval times, this is just the sort of woodland they'd be found in.'

With my mind opened to those events of years ago, memory inched back, images of childhood – the burning touch of sun on bramble-grazed skin; fishing trips to the mill-pond; tree camps, games, explorations ... and instantly I recalled the Twigling.

As we walked back to the beaten pathway that led up to the lodge, we discussed the sighting. I had been about nine or ten years old. On our way to the sticklebrook to fish we had decided to test out our stick and string rods on the mill-pond, in the vain hope of snaring one of the predatory fish that lived there. As we crouched by the water (we only ever dared go out in the boat with Alphonse) we saw movement in the trees, across on the other bank. It was a bewildering vision that held us enthralled for the next few moments, and not a little terrified: standing watching us was a man in brown, leathery clothes, with a wide, gleaming belt around his waist, and a spiky, orange beard that reached to his chest; on his head he wore twigs, held to his crown by a leather band. He watched us for a moment only, before slipping back into the darkness. We heard nothing in all this time, no sound of approach, no sound of departure.

Running back to the house we had soon calmed down. Christian decided, eventually, that it must have been old Alphonse, playing tricks on us. But when I mentioned what we'd seen to my father he reacted almost angrily (although Christian recalls him as having been excited, and bellowing for that reason, and not because he was angry with our having been near the forbidden pool). It was father who referred to the vision as 'the Twigling', and soon after we had spoken to him he vanished into the woodland for nearly two weeks.

'That was when he came back hurt, remember?' We had reached the grounds of Oak Lodge, and Christian held the gate open for me as he spoke.

'The arrow wound. The gypsy arrow. My God, that was a bad day.'

'The first of many.'

I noticed that most of the ivy had been cleared from the walls of the house; it was a grey place now, small, curtainless windows set in the dark brick, the slate roof, with its three tall chimney stacks, partially hidden behind the branches of a big old beech tree. The yard and gardens were untidy and unkempt, the empty chicken coops and animal shelters ramshackle and decaying. Christian had really let the place slip. But when I stepped across the threshold, it was as if I had never been away. The house smelled of stale food and chlorine, and I could almost see the thin figure of my mother, working away at the immense pinewood table in the kitchen, cats stretched out around her on the red-brick floor.

Christian had grown tense again, staring at me in that fidgety way that marked his unease. I imagined he was still unsure whether to be glad or angry that I had come home like this. For a moment I felt like an intruder. He said, 'Why don't you unpack and freshen up. You can use your old room. It's a bit stuffy, I expect, but it'll soon air. Then come down and we'll have some late lunch. We've got all the time in the world to chat, as long as we're finished by tea.' He smiled, and I thought this was some slight attempt at humour. But he went on quickly, staring at me in a cold, hard way, 'Because if you're going to stay at home for a while, then you'd better know what's going on here. I don't want you interfering with it, Steve, or with what I'm doing.'

'I wouldn't interfere with your life, Chris—'

'Wouldn't you? We'll see. I'm not going to deny that I'm nervous of you being here. But since you are ...' he trailed off, and for a second looked almost embarrassed. 'Well, we'll have a chat later on.'

Intrigued by what Christian had said, and worried by his apprehension of me, I nonetheless restrained my curiosity and spent an hour exploring the house again, from top to bottom, inside and out, everywhere save father's study, the contemplation of which chilled me more than Christian's behaviour had done. Nothing had changed, except that it was untidy, and untenanted. Christian had employed a part-time cleaner and cook, a good soul from a nearby village who cycled to the Lodge every week and prepared a pie or stew that would last the man three days. Christian did not go short of farm produce, so much so that he rarely bothered to use his ration book. He seemed to get all he needed, including sugar and tea, from the Knaresthorpe estate, which had always been good to my family.

My own room was dust free, but quite stale. I opened the window wide and lay down on the bed for a few minutes, staring out and up into the hazy, late summer sky, past the waving branches of the gigantic beech that grew so close to the Lodge. Several times, in the years before my teens, I had climbed from window to tree, and made a secret camp among the thick branches; by moonlight I had shivered in my underpants, crouched in that private place, imagining the dark doings of night creatures below.

Lunch, in mid-afternoon, was a substantial feast of cold pork, chicken and hard-boiled eggs, in quantities that, after two years in France on strict rations, I had never thought to see again. We were, of course, eating his food supply for several days, but the fact seemed irrelevant to Christian, who at any rate only picked at his meal.

Afterwards we talked for a couple of hours, and Christian relaxed quite noticeably, although he never referred to Guiwenneth, or to father's work, and I never broached either subject. We were sprawled in the uncomfortable armchairs that had belonged to my grandparents, surrounded by the time-faded mementoes of our family … photographs, a noisy rosewood clock, horrible pictures of exotic Spain, all framed in cracked mock-gilded wood, and all pressed hard against the same floral wallpaper that had hugged the walls of the sittingroom since a time before my birth. But it was home, and Christian was home, and the smell, and the faded surrounds, all were home to me. I knew, within two hours of arriving, that I would have to stay. It was not so much that I belonged here – although I certainly felt that – but simply that the place belonged to me, not in any mercenary sense of ownership, more in the way that the house and the land around the house shared a common life with me; we were part of the same evolution; even in France, even as far as Greece, where I had been in action, I had not been separated from that evolution, merely stretched to an extreme.

As the heavy old rosewood clock began to whirr and click, preceding its laboured chiming of the hour of five, Christian abruptly rose from his chair and tossed his half-smoked cigarette into the empty fire grate.

'Let's go to the study,' he said, and I rose without speaking and followed him through the house to the small room where our father had worked. 'You're scared of this room, aren't you?' he said as he opened the door and walked inside, crossing to the heavy oak desk and pulling out a large leather-bound book from one of the drawers.

I hesitated outside the study, watching Christian, almost unable to move my legs to carry myself into the room. I recognized the book he held, my father's notebook. I touched my back pocket, the wallet I carried there, and thought of the fragment of that notebook that was hidden inside the thin leather. I wondered if anyone, my father or Christian, had ever noticed that a page was missing. Christian was watching me, his eyes bright with excitement now, his hands trembling as he placed the book on the desk top.

'He's dead, Steve. He's gone from this room, from the house. There's no need to be afraid any more.'

'Isn't there?'

But I found the sudden strength to move, and stepped across the threshold. The moment I entered the musty room I felt totally subdued, deeply affected by the coolness of the place, the stark, haunted atmosphere that hugged the walls and carpets and windows. It smelled slightly of leather, here, and dust too, with just a distant hint of polish, as if Christian made a token effort to keep this stifling room clean. It was not a crowded room, not a library as my father would have perhaps liked it to be. There were books on zoology and botany, on history and archaeology, but these were not rare copies, merely the cheapest copies he could find at the time. There were more paperbacks than stiff-covered books, and the exquisite binding of his notes, and the deeply varnished desk, had an air of Victorian elegance about them that belied the otherwise shabby studio.

On the walls, between the cases of books, were his glass-framed specimens, pieces of wood, collections of leaves, crude sketches of animal and plant life made during the first years of his fascination with the forest. And almost hidden away among the cases and the shelves was the patterned shaft of the arrow that had struck him fifteen years before, its flights twisted and useless, the broken shaft glued together, the iron head dulled with corrosion, but a lethal-looking weapon nonetheless.

I stared at that arrow for several seconds, reliving the man's agony, and the tears that Christian and I had wept for him as we had helped him back from the woodlands, that cold autumn afternoon, convinced that he would die.

How quickly things had changed after that strange, and never fully explained incident. If the arrow linked me with an earlier day, when some semblance of concern and love had remained in my father's mind, the rest of the study radiated only coldness.

I could still see the greying figure, bent over his desk writing furiously. I could hear the troubled breathing, the lung disorder that finally killed him; I could hear his caught breath, the vocalized sound of irritation as he grew aware of my presence, and waved me away with a half-irritated gesture, as if he begrudged even that split second of acknowledgement.

How like him Christian looked, now, standing there all dishevelled and sickly looking, and yet with the mark of absolute confidence about him, his hands in the pockets of his flannels, shoulders drooped, his whole body visibly shaking.

He had waited quietly as I adjusted to the room, and let the memories and atmosphere play through me. As I stepped up to the desk, my mind back on the moment at hand, he said, 'Steve, you should read the notes. They'll make a lot of things clear to you, and help you understand what it is I'm doing as well.'

I turned the notebook towards me, scanning the sprawling, untidy handwriting, picking out words and phrases, reading through the years of my father's life in a few scant seconds. The words were as meaningless, on the whole, as those on my purloined sheet. To read them brought back a memory of anger and of danger, and of fear. The life in the notes had sustained me through nearly a year of war and had come to mean something outside of their proper context. I felt reluctant to dispel that powerful association with the past.

'I intend to read them, Chris. From beginning to end, and that's a promise. But not for the moment.'

I closed the book, noticing as I did that my hands were clammy and trembling. I was not yet ready to be so close to my father again, and Christian saw this, and accepted it.

Conversation died quite early that night, as my energy expired, and the tensions of the long journey finally made themselves known to me. Christian came up with me and stood in the doorway of my room, watching as I turned back the sheets and pottered about, picking up bits and pieces of my past life, laughing, shaking my head and trying to evoke a last moment's tired nostalgia. 'Remember making camp out in the beech?' I said, watching the grey of branch and leaf against the still bright evening sky. 'Yes,' said Christian with a smile. 'Yes, I remember very clearly.'

But it was as fatigued as that, and Christian took the hint and said, 'Sleep well, old chap. I'll see you in the morning.'

If I slept at all, it was for the first two or three hours after putting head to pillow. I woke sharply, and brightly, in the dead of night, one or two o'clock, perhaps; the sky was very dark now, and it was quite windy outside. I lay and stared at the window, wondering how my body could feel so fresh, so alert. There was movement downstairs, and I guessed that Christian was doing some tidying, restlessly walking through the house, trying to adjust to the idea of me moving in.

The sheets smelled of mothballs and old cotton; the bed creaked in a metallic way when I shifted on it, and when I lay still the whole room clicked and shuffled, as if adapting itself to its first company in so many years. I lay awake for ages, but must have drifted to sleep again before first light, because suddenly Christian was bending over me, shaking my shoulder gently.

I started with surprise, awake at once, and propped up on my elbows, looking around. It was dawn. 'What is it, Chris?'

'I've got to go, old boy. I'm sorry, but I have to.'

I realized he was wearing a heavy oilskin cape, and had thick-soled walking boots on his feet. 'Go? What d'you mean, go?'

'I'm sorry, Steve. There's nothing I can do about it.' He spoke softly, as if there were someone else in the house who might be woken by raised voices. He looked more drawn than ever in this pale light, and his eyes were narrowed, I thought with pain, or anxiety. 'I have to go away for a few days.

You'll be all right. I've left a list of instructions downstairs, where to get bread, eggs, all that sort of thing. I'm sure you'll be able to use my ration book until yours comes. I shan't be long, just a few days. That's a promise ...'

He rose from his crouch and walked out of the door. 'For God's sake Chris, where are you going?'

'Inwards,' was all he said, before I heard him clump heavily down the stairs. I remained motionless for a moment or two, trying to clear my thoughts, then rose, put on my dressing-gown and followed him down to the kitchen. He had already left the house. I went back up to the landing window and saw him skirting the edge of the yard and walking swiftly down towards the south track. He was wearing a wide-brimmed hat, and carrying a long, black staff; on his back he had a small rucksack, slung uncomfortably over one shoulder.

'Where's inwards, Chris?' I said to his vanishing figure, and watched long after he had disappeared from view. 'What's going on inside your head?' I asked of his empty bedroom as I wandered restlessly through the house; Guiwenneth, I decided in my wisdom, her loss, her leaving ... how little one could interpret from the words 'she's gone'. And in all our chat of the evening before he had never alluded to the girl again. I had come home to England expecting to find a cheerful young couple, and instead had found a haunted, wasting brother living in the derelict shadow of our family home.

By the afternoon I had resigned myself to a period of solitary living, for wherever Christian had gone (and I had a fairly good idea) he had hinted clearly that he would be gone for some time. There was a lot to do about the house, and the yard, and there seemed no better way to spend my time than in beginning to rebuild the personality of the house. I made a list of essential repairs, and the following day walked into the nearest town to order what materials I could, mostly wood and paint, which I found in reasonable supply.

I renewed my acquaintance with the Knaresthorpe family, and with many of the local families with whom I had once been friendly. I terminated the services of the part-time cook; I could look after myself quite well enough. And I visited the cemetery; a single, brief visit, coldly accomplished.

The month of August turned to September, and I noticed a definite crispness in the air by evening, and early in the morning. It was a season I loved, the turn from summer to autumn, although it bore with it association of return to school after the long vacation, and that was a memory I didn't cherish. I soon grew used to being on my own in the house, and although I took long walks around the deep woodlands, watching the road and the railway track for Christian's return, I had ceased to feel anxious about him by the end of my first week home, and had settled comfortably into a daily routine of building in the yard, painting the exterior woodwork of the house ready for the onslaught of winter, and digging over the large, untended garden.

It was during the evening of my eleventh day at home that this domestic routine was disturbed by a circumstance of such peculiarity that afterwards I could not sleep for thinking about it.

I had been in the town of Hobbhurst for most of the afternoon, and after a light evening meal was sitting reading the newspaper; towards nine o'clock, as I began to feel ready for an evening stroll, I thought I heard a dog, not so much barking as howling. My first thought was that Christian was coming back, my second that there were no dogs in this immediate area at all.

I went out into the yard; it was after dusk, but still quite bright, although the oakwoods were melded together into a grey-green blur. I called for Christian, but there was no response. I was about to return to my paper when a man stepped out of the distant woodland, and began to trot towards me; on a short, leather leash he was holding the most enormous hound I have ever seen.

At the gate to our private grounds he stopped, and the dog began to growl; it placed its forepaws on the fence, and in so doing rose almost to the height of its master. I felt nervous at once, keeping my attention balanced between the gaping, panting mouth of that dark beast, and the strange man who held it in check.

It was difficult to make him out clearly, for his face was painted with dark patterns and his moustaches drooped to well below his chin; his hair was plastered thickly about his scalp; he wore a dark woolen shirt, with a leather jerkin over the top, and tight, check-patterned breeches that reached to just below his knees. When he stepped cautiously through the gate I could see his rough and ready sandals. Across his shoulder he carried a crude-looking bow, and a bundle of arrows, held together with a simple thong and tied to his belt. He, like Christian, carried a staff.

Inside the gate he hesitated, watching me. The hound was restless beside him, licking its mouth and growling softly. I had never seen a dog such as this, shaggy and dark-furred, with the narrow pointed face of an Alsatian, but the body, it seemed to me, of a bear; except that its legs were long and thin, an animal made for chasing, for hunting.

The man spoke to me, and although I felt familiar with the words, they meant nothing. I didn't know what to do, so I shook my head and said that I didn't understand. The man hesitated just a moment before repeating what he had said, this time with a distinct edge of anger in his voice. And he started to walk towards me, tugging at the hound to prevent it straining at the leash. The light was draining from the sky, and he seemed to grow in stature in the greyness as he approached. The beast watched me, hungrily.

'What do you want?' I called, and tried to sound firm when I would rather

535

have run inside the house. The man was ten paces away from me. He stopped, spoke again and this time made eating motions with the hand that held his staff. *Now* I understood. I nodded vigorously. 'Wait here,' I said, and went back to the house to fetch the cold joint of pork that was to last me four more days. It was not large, but it seemed an hospitable thing to do. I took this, half a granary loaf, and a jug of bottled beer out into the yard. The stranger was crouched, now, the hound lying down beside him, rather reluctantly, it seemed to me. As I tried to approach them, the dog roared in a way that set my heart racing, and nearly made me drop my gifts. The man shouted at the beast, and said something to me. I placed the food where I stood and backed away. The gruesome pair approached and again squatted down to eat.

As he picked up the joint I saw the scars on his arm, running down and across the bunched muscles. I also smelled him, a raw, rancid odour, sweat and urine mixed with the fetid aroma of rotting meat. I nearly gagged but held my ground watching as the stranger tore at the pork with his teeth, swallowing hard and fast. The hound watched me.

After a few minutes the man stopped eating, looked at me, and with his gaze fixed on mine, almost challenging me to react, passed the rest of the meat to the dog, which growled loudly and snapped at the joint. The hound chewed, cracked and gulped the entire piece of pork in less than four minutes, while the stranger cautiously – and without much apparent pleasure – drank beer, and chewed on a large mouthful of bread.

Finally this bizarre feast was over. The man rose to his feet and jerked the hound away from where it was licking the ground noisily. He said a word I intuitively recognized as 'thank you'. He was about to turn when the hound scented something; it uttered a high-pitched keen, followed by a raucous bark, and snatched itself away from its master's restraining grip, racing across the yard to a spot between the ramshackle chicken houses. Here it sniffed and scratched until its master reached it, grabbed the leather leash, and shouted angrily and lengthily at his charge. The hound moved with him, padding silently and monstrously into the gloom beyond the yard. The last I saw of them they were running at full speed, around the edge of the woodland, towards the farmlands around the village of Grimley.

In the morning the place where man and beast had rested *still* smelled rank. I skirted the area quickly as I walked to the woods and found the place where my strange visitors had exited from the trees; it was trampled and broken, and I followed the line of their passage for some yards into the shade before stopping and turning back.

Where on earth had they come from? Had the war had such an effect on men in England that some had returned to the wild, using bow and arrow and hunting dog for survival?

Not until midday did I think to look between the chicken huts, at the ground so deeply scored by that brief moment's digging. What had the beast scented, I wondered, and a sudden chill clawed at my heart. I left the place at a run, unwilling, for the moment, to confirm my worst fears.

How I knew I cannot say; intuition, or perhaps something that my subconscious had detected in Christian's words and mannerisms the week or so before, during our brief encounter. In any event, late in the afternoon that same day I took a spade to the chicken huts, and within a few minutes of digging had proved my instinct right.

It took me half an hour of sitting on the back doorstep of the house, staring across the yard at the grave, to find the courage to uncover the woman's body totally. I was dizzy, slightly sick, but most of all I was shaking; an uncontrollable, unwelcome shaking of arms and legs, so pronounced that I could hardly pull on a pair of gloves. But eventually I knelt by the hole and brushed the rest of the dirt from the girl's body.

Christian had buried her three feet deep, face down; her hair was long and red; her body was still clad in a strange green garment, a patterned tunic that was laced at the sides and, though it was crushed up almost to her waist now, would have reached to her calves. A staff was buried with her. I turned the head, holding my breath against the almost intolerable smell of putrefaction, and with a little effort could gaze upon the withering face. I saw then how she had died, for the head and stump of the arrow were still embedded in her eye. Had Christian tried to withdraw the weapon and succeeded only in breaking it? There was enough of the shaft left for me to notice that it had the same carved markings as the arrow in my father's study.

Poor Guiwenneth, I thought, and let the corpse drop back to its resting place. I filled in the dirt again. When I reached the house I was cold with sweat, and in no doubt that I was about to be violently sick.

Two days later, when I came down in the morning, I found the kitchen littered with Christian's clothes and effects, the floor covered with mud and leaf litter, the whole place smelling unpleasant. I crept upstairs to his room and stared at his semi-naked body; he was belly down on the bed, face turned towards me, sleeping soundly and noisily, and I imagined that he was sleeping enough for a week. The state of his body, though, gave me cause for concern. He was scratched and scarred from neck to ankle, and filthy, and malodorous to an extreme. His hair was matted with dirt. And yet, about him there was something hardened and strong, a tangible physical change from the hollow-faced, rather skeletal young man who had greeted me nearly two weeks before.

He slept for most of the day, emerging at six in the evening wearing a loose-fitting grey shirt and flannels, torn off just above the knee. He had half-heartedly washed his face, but still reeked of sweat and vegetation, as if he had spent the days away buried in compost.

I fed him, and he drank the entire contents of a pot of tea as I sat watching him; he kept darting glances at me, suspicious little looks as if he were nervous of some sudden move or surprise attack upon him. The muscles of his arms and wrists were pronounced. This was almost a different man.

'Where have you been, Chris?' I asked after a while, and was not at all surprised when he answered, 'In the woods, old boy. Deep in the woods.' He stuffed more meat into his mouth and chewed noisily. As he swallowed he found a moment to say, 'I'm quite fit. Bruised and scratched by the damned brambles, but quite fit.'

In the woods. Deep in the woods. What in heaven's name could he have been doing there? As I watched him wolf down his food I saw again the stranger, crouching like an animal in my yard, chewing on meat as if he were some wild beast. Christian reminded me of that man. There was the same air of the primitive about him.

'You need a bath rather badly,' I said, and he grinned and made a sound of affirmation. 'What have you been doing, Chris? In the woods. Have you been camping?'

He swallowed noisily, and drank half a cup of tea before shaking his head. 'I have a camp there, but I've been searching, walking as deep as I could get. But I still can't get beyond ...' he broke off, and glanced at me, a questioning look in his eyes. 'Did you read the old man's notebook?'

I said that I hadn't. In truth, I had been so surprised by his abrupt departure, and so committed to getting the house back into some sort of shape, that I had forgotten all about father's notes on his work. And even as I said this I wondered if the truth of the matter was that I had put father, his work and his notes, as far from my mind as possible, as if they were spectres whose haunting would reduce my resolve to go forward.

Christian wiped his hand across his mouth and stared at his empty plate. He suddenly sniffed himself and laughed. 'By the Gods, I do stink. You'd better boil me up some water, Steve. I'll wash right now.'

But I didn't move. Instead I stared across the wooden table at him; he caught my gaze and frowned. 'What is it? What's on your mind?'

'I found her, Chris. I found her body. Guiwenneth. I found where you buried her.'

I don't know what reaction I expected from Christian. Anger, perhaps, or panic, or a sudden babbling burst of explanation. I half hoped he would react with puzzlement, that the corpse in the yard would turn out not to be the remains of his wife, and that he had no involvement with its burial. But Christian knew about the body. He stared at me blankly, and a heavy, sweaty silence made me grow uncomfortable.

Suddenly I realized that Christian was crying, his gaze unwavering from my own, but moistened, now, by the great flood of tears through the remaining grime on his face. And yet he made no sound, and his face never changed its expression from that of bland, almost blind contemplation.

'Who shot her, Chris?' I asked quietly. 'Did you?'

'Not me,' he said, and with the words his tears stopped, and his gaze dropped to the table. 'She was shot by a mythago. There was nothing I could do about it.'

Mythago? The meaning was alien to me, although I recognized the word from the scrap of my father's notebook that I carried. I queried it and Chris rose from the table, but rested his hands upon it as he watched me. 'A mythago,' he repeated. 'It's still in the woods ... they all are. That's where I've been, seeking among them. I tried to save her, Steve. She was alive when I found her, and she might have stayed alive, but I brought her out of the woods ... in a way, I did kill her. I took her away from the vortex, and she died quite quickly. I panicked, then. I didn't know what to do. I buried her because it seemed the easiest way out ...'

'Did you tell the police? Did you report her death?'

Christian grinned, but it was not with any morbid humour. It was a knowing grin, a response to some secret that he had not yet shared; and yet the grin was merely a defence, for it faded rapidly. 'Not necessary Steve ... the police would not have been interested.'

I rose angrily from the table. It seemed to me that Christian was behaving, and had behaved, with appalling irresponsibility. 'Her family, Chris ... her parents! They have a right to know.'

And Christian laughed.

I felt the blood rise in my face. 'I don't see anything to laugh at.'

He sobered instantly, looked at me almost abashed. 'You're right. I'm sorry. You don't understand, and it's time you did. Steve, she had no parents because she had no life, no real life. She's lived a thousand times, and she's never lived at all. But I still fell in love with her ... and I shall find her again in the woods; she's in there somewhere ...'

Had he gone mad? His words were the unreasoned babblings of one insane, and yet something about his eyes, something about his demeanour, told me that it was not so much insanity as obsession. But obsession with what?

'You *must* read the old man's notes, Steve. Don't put it off any longer. They will tell you about the wood, about what's going on in there. I mean it. I'm neither mad nor callous. I'm just trapped, and before I go away again, I'd like you to know why, and how, and where I'm going. Perhaps you'll be able to help me. Who knows? Read the book. And then we'll talk. And when you know what our dear departed father managed to do, then I'm afraid I have to take my leave of you again.'

There is one entry in my father's notebook that seems to mark a turning point in his research, and in his life. It is a longer entry than the rest of that particular time, and follows an absence of seven months from the pages. While his entries are detailed, he could not be described as having been a dedicated diarist, and the style varies from clipped notes to fluent description. (I discovered, too, that he himself had torn many pages from the thick book, thus concealing my minor crime quite effectively. Christian had never noticed the missing page.) On the whole, he seems to have used the notebook, and the quiet hours of recording, as a way of conversing with himself – a means of clarification of his own thoughts.

The entry in question is dated September 1933, and was written shortly after our encounter with the Twigling. After reading the entry for the first time I thought back to that year and realized I had been just nine years old.

Wynne-Jones arrived after dawn. Walked together along the south track, checking the flux-drains for signs of mythago activity. Back to the house quite shortly after – no-one about, which suited my mood. A crisp, dry autumn day. Like last year, images of the Urscumug are strongest as the season changes. Perhaps he senses autumn, the dying of the green. He comes forward, and the oakwoods whisper to him. He must be close to genesis. Wynne-Jones thinks a further time of isolation needed, and it must be done. Jennifer already concerned and distraught by my absences. I feel helpless – can't speak to her. Must do what is needed.

Yesterday the boys glimpsed the Twigling. I had thought him resorbed – clearly the resonance stronger than we had believed. He seems to frequent woodland edge, which is to be expected. I have seen him along the track several times, but not for a year or so. The persistence is worrying. Both boys clearly disturbed by the sighting; Christian less emotional. I suspect it meant little to him, a poacher perhaps, or local man taking short cut to Grimley. Wynne-Jones suggests we go back into woods and call the Twigling deep, perhaps to the hogback glade where he might remain in strong oak-vortex and eventually fade. But I know that penetrating into deep woodland will involve more than a week's absence, and poor Jennifer already deeply depressed by my behaviour. Cannot explain it to her, though I dearly want to. Do not want the children involved in this, and it worries me that they have now twice seen a mythago. I have invented magic forest creatures – stories for them. Hope they will associate what they see with products of their own imaginations. But must be careful. Until it is resolved, until the Urscumug mythago forms, must not let any but Wynne-Jones know of what I have discovered. The completeness of the resurrection essential. The Urscumug is the most powerful because he is the primary. I know for certain that the oakwoods will contain him, but others might be frightened of the power they would certainly be able to feel, and end it for everyone. Dread to think what would happen if these forests were destroyed, and yet they cannot survive for ever.

Today's training with Wynne-Jones: test pattern 26: iii, shallow hypno-
sis, green light environment. As the frontal bridge reached sixty volts,
despite the pain, the flow across my skull was the most powerful I have ever
known. Am now totally convinced that each half of the brain functions in a
slightly different way, and that the hidden awareness is located on the right
hand side. It has been lost for so long! The Wynne-Jones bridge enables a
superficial communion between the fields around each hemisphere, and the
zone of the pre-mythago is excited accordingly. If only there were some way
of exploring the living brain to find exactly where the site of this occult presence lies.

The forms of the mythagos cluster in my peripheral vision, still. Why never
in fore-vision? These unreal images are mere reflections, after all. The form of
Hood was subtly different – more brown than green, the face less friendly,
more haunted, drawn. This is certainly because earlier images (even the Hood
mythago that actually formed in the woodland, two years ago) were affected
by my own confused childhood images of the greenwood, and the merry
band. But now, evocation of the pre-mythago is more powerful, reaches to the
basic form, without interference. The Arthur form was more real as well, and
I glimpsed the various marshland forms from the latter part of the first millennium AD. Wynne-Jones would love me to explore these folk heroes,
unrecorded and unknown, but I am anxious to find the primary image.

The Urscumug formed in my mind in the clearest form I have ever seen
him. Hints of the Twigling in shape, but he is much more ancient, far bigger.
Decks himself with wood and leaves, on top of animal hides. Face seems
smeared with white clay, forming a mask upon the exaggerated features
below; but it is hard to see the face clearly. A mask upon a mask? The hair a
mass of stiff and spiky points; gnarled hawthorn branches are driven up
through the matted hair, giving a most bizarre appearance. I believe he carries
a spear, with a wide, stone blade ... an angry-looking weapon, but again, hard
to see, always just out of focus. He is so old, this primary image, that he is fading from the human mind, and in any event is touched with confusion, the
over-assertion of later cultural interpretation of his appearance ... a hint of
bronze particularly, mostly about the arms (torques). I suspect that the legend
of the Urscumug was powerful enough to carry through all the neolithic and
on into the second millennium BC, perhaps even later. Wynne-Jones thinks
the Urscumug may pre-date even the neolithic.

Essential, now, to spend time in the forest, to allow the vortex to interact
with me and form the mythago. I intend to leave the house within the next
week.

Without commenting on the strange, confusing passage that I had read, I
turned the pages of the diary and read entries here and there. I could clearly

recall that autumn in 1933, the time when my father had packed a large ruck-sack and wandered into the woods, walking swiftly away from my mother's hysterical shouting, flanked by his diminutive scientist friend (a sour-faced man who never acknowledged anyone but my father, and who seemed embarrassed to be in the house when he came to visit). Mother had not spoken for the rest of the day, and she did nothing but sit in her bedroom and occasionally weep. Christian and I had become so distraught by her behav-iour that in the late afternoon we had penetrated the oakwoods as deeply as we dared, calling for our father, and finally panicking at the gloomy silence, and the loud, sudden sounds that disturbed it. He had returned weeks later, dishevelled and stinking like a tramp. The entry in his notebook, a few days later, is a short and bitter account of failure. Nothing had happened. A single, rather rambling paragraph caught my attention.

The mythogenetic process is not only complex, it is reluctant. My mind is not at rest and as Wynne-Jones has explained, it is likely that my human consideration, my worries, form an effective barrier between the two mytho-poetic energy flows in my cortex – the *form* from the right brain, the *reality* from the left. The pre-mythago zone is not sufficiently enriched by my own life force for it to interact in the oak vortex. I fear too that the natural disappearance of so much life from the forest is affecting the interface. The boars are there, I'm sure. But perhaps the life number is critical. I estimate no more than forty, moving within the spiral vortex bounded by the ashwood intrusions into the oak circle. There are no deer, no wolves, although the most important animal, the hare, frequents the woodland edge in profusion. But perhaps the absence of so much that had once lived here has thrown the balance of the formula. And yet, through the primary existence of these woods, life was changing. By the thirteenth century there was much botanical life that was alien to the *ley matrix* in places where the mythagos still formed. The form of the myth men changes, adapts, and it is the later forms that generate easiest. Hood is back – like all the Jack-in-the-Greens, is a nuisance, and several times moved into the ridge-zone around the hogback glade. He shot at me, and this is becoming a cause of great concern! But I can-not enrich the oak vortex sufficiently with the pre-mythago of the Urscumug. What is the answer? Perhaps the memory is too far gone, too deep in the silent zones of the brain, now, to touch the trees.

Christian saw me frown as I read through this tumble of words and images. Hood? Robin Hood? And someone – this Hood – shooting at my father in the woods? I glanced around the study and saw the iron-tipped arrow in its long, narrow glass case, mounted above the display of woodland butterflies. Chris-tian was turning the pages of the notebook, having watched me read in silence for the better part of an hour. He was perched on the desk; I sat in father's chair.

'What's all this about, Chris? It reads as if he were actually trying to create copies of storybook heroes.'

'Not copies, Steve. The real thing. There. Last bit of reading for the moment, then I'll go through it with you in layman's terms.'

It was an earlier entry, not dated by year, only by day and month, although it was clearly from some years before the 1933 recording.

I call those particular times 'cultural interfaces'; they form zones, bounded in space, of course, by the limits of the country, but bounded also in time, a few years, a decade or so, when the two cultures – that of the invaded and the invader – are in a highly anguished state. The mythagos grow from the power of hate, and fear, and form in the natural woodlands from which they can either emerge – such as the Arthur, or Artorius form, the bear-like man with his charismatic leadership – or remain in the natural landscape, establishing a hidden focus of hope – the Robin Hood form, perhaps Hereward, and of course the hero-form I call the Twigling, harassing the Romans in so many parts of the country. I imagine that it is the combined emotion of the two races that draws out the mythago, but it clearly sides with that culture whose roots are longest established in what I agree could be a sort of *ley matrix*; thus, Arthur forms and helps the Britons against the Saxons, but later Hood is created to help the Saxons against the Norman invader.

I drew back from the book, shaking my head. The expressions were confusing, bemusing. Christian grinned as he took the notebook and weighed it in his hands. 'Years of his life, Steve, but his concern with keeping detailed records was not everything it might have been. He records nothing for years, then writes every day for a month.'

'I need a drink of something. And a few definitions.'

We walked from the study, Christian carrying the note-book. As we passed the framed arrow I peered closely at it. 'Is he saying that the real Robin Hood shot that into him? And killed Guiwenneth too?'

'It depends,' said Christian thoughtfully, 'on what you mean by real. Hood came to that oak forest, and may still be there. I think he is. As you have obviously noticed, he was there four months ago when he shot Guiwenneth. But there were many Robin Hoods, and all were as real or unreal as each other, created by the Saxon peasants during their time of repression by the Norman invader.'

'I don't comprehend this at all, Chris – but what's a "ley matrix"? What's an "oak vortex"? Does it mean anything?'

As we sipped scotch and water in the sitting room, watching the dusk draw closer, the yard beyond the window greying into a place of featureless shapes, Christian explained how a man called Alfred Watkins had visited our father on several occasions and shown him on a map of the country how straight lines connected places of spiritual or ancient power – the barrows, stones and churches of three different cultures. These lines he called leys, and believed that they existed as a form of earth energy running below the ground, but influencing that which stood upon it. My father had thought about leys, and apparently tried to measure the energy in the ground below the forest, but without success. And yet he had measured *something* in the oakwoods – an energy associated with all the life that grew there. He had found a spiral vortex around each tree, a sort of aura, and those spirals bounded not just trees, but whole stands of trees, and glades. Over the years he had mapped the forest. Christian brought out that map of the woodland area, and I looked at it, again, but from a different point of view, beginning to understand the marks made upon it by the man who had spent so much time within the territories it depicted. Circles within circles were marked, crossed and skirted by straight lines, some of which were associated with the two pathways we called south and deep track. The letters H B in the middle of the vast acreage of forest were clearly meant to refer to the 'hogback' glade that existed there, a clearing that neither Christian nor I had ever been able to find. There were zones marked out as 'spiral oak', 'dead ash zone' and 'oscillating traverse'.

'The old man believed that all life is surrounded by an energetic aura – you can see the human aura as a faint glow in certain light. In these ancient woodlands, *primary* woodlands, the combined aura forms something far more powerful, a sort of creative field that can interact with our unconscious. And it's in that unconscious that we carry what he calls the premythago – that's *myth imago*, the image of the idealized form of a myth creature. This takes on substance in a natural environment, solid flesh, blood, clothing, and – as you saw – weaponry. The form of the idealized myth, the hero figure, alters with cultural changes, assuming the identity and technology of the time. When one culture invades another – according to father's theory – the heroes are made manifest, and not just in one location! Historians and legend seekers argue about where Arthur of the Britons, and Robin Hood *really* lived and fought, and don't realize that they lived in *many* sites. And another important fact to remember is that when the premythago forms it forms in the *whole* population ... and when it is no longer needed, it remains in our collective unconscious, and is transmitted through the generations.'

'And the changing forms of the mythago,' I said, to see if I had understood my sketchy reading of father's notes, 'is based on an archetype, an archaic primary image which father called the Urscumug, and from which all later forms come. And he tried to raise the Urscumug from his own unconscious mind ...'

'And failed to do so,' said Christian, 'although not for want of trying. The effort killed him. It weakened him so much that his body couldn't take the pace. But he certainly seems to have created several of the more recent adaptations of the Urscumug.'

There were so many questions, so many areas that begged for clarification. One above all: 'But a thousand years ago, if I understand the notes correctly, there was a country-wide *need* of the hero, the legendary figure, acting for the side of Right. How can one man capture such a passionate mood?

'How did he *power* the interaction? Surely not from the simple family anguish he caused among us, and in his own head. As he said, that created an unsettled mind and he couldn't function properly.'

'If there's an answer,' said Christian calmly, 'it's to be found in the wood-land area, perhaps in the hogback glade. The old man wrote in his notes of the need for a period of solitary existence, a period of meditation. For a year, now, I've been following his example directly. He invented a sort of electrical bridge which seems to *fuse* elements from each half of the brain. I've used his equipment a great deal, with and without him. But I already find images – the pre-mythagos – forming in my peripheral vision *without* the complicated programme that he used. He was the pioneer; his own inter-action with the wood has made it easier for those who come after. He achieved a certain suc-cess; I intend to complete his work, eventually. I shall raise the Urscumug, this hero of the first men.'

'To what end, Chris?' I asked quietly, and in all truth could not see a rea-son for so tampering with the ancient forces that inhabited both woodland and human spirit. Christian was clearly obsessed with the idea of raising these dead forms, of finishing something the old man had begun. But in my reading of his notebook, and in my conversation with Christian, I had not heard a single word that explained *why* so bizarre a state of nature should be so important to the ones who studied it.

Christian had an answer. And as he spoke to me his voice was hollow, the mark of his uncertainty, the stigma of his lacking conviction in the truth of what he said. 'Why, to study the earliest times of man, Steve. From these mythagos we can learn so much of how it was, and how it was hoped to be. The aspirations, the visions, the cultural identity of a time so far gone that even its stone monuments are incomprehensible to us. To learn. To commu-nicate through those persistent images of our past that are locked in each and every one of us.'

He stopped speaking, and there was the briefest of silences, interrupted only by the heavy rhythmic sound of the clock. I said, 'I'm not convinced, Chris.' For a moment I thought he would shout his anger; his face flushed, his whole body tensed up, furious with my calm dismissal of his script. But the fire softened, and he frowned, staring at me almost helplessly. 'What does that mean?'

'Nice-sounding words; no conviction.'

After a second he seemed to acknowledge some truth in what I said. 'Per-haps my conviction has gone, then, buried beneath … beneath the other thing. Guiwenneth. She's become my main reason for going back now.'

I remembered his callous words of a while ago, about how she had no life yet a thousand lives. I understood instantly, and wondered how so obvious a fact could have remained so doggedly elusive to me. 'She was a mythago herself,' I said. 'I understand now.'

'She was my father's mythago, a girl from Roman times, a manifestation of the Earth Goddess, the young warrior princess who can unite the tribes. I can find no recorded legends about her, but she is associated with the oral tradition, with the Celtic tradition of keeping a name silent. She was a powerful woman, and led – in all her appearances – a powerful resistance to the Romans ...'

'Like Queen Boadicea.'

'Before and after that uprising. Legends of Guiwenneth inspired many tribes to take offensive action against the invader.' His gaze became distant for a moment. 'And then she was formed in this wood, and I found her and came to love her. She was not violent, perhaps because the old man himself could not think of a woman being violent. He imposed a structure on her, disarming her, leaving her quite helpless in the forest.'

'How long did you know her?' I asked, and he shrugged.

'I can't tell, Steve. How long have I been away?'

'Twelve days or so.'

'As long as that?' He seemed surprised. 'I thought no more than three. Perhaps I knew her for many months, then, but it seems no time at all. I lived in the forest with her, trying to understand her language, trying to teach her mine, speaking with signs and yet always able to talk quite deeply. But the old man pursued us right to the heartwoods, right to the end. He wouldn't let up – she was *his* girl, and he had been as struck by her as had I. I found him, one day, exhausted and terrified, half buried by leaves at the forest edge. I took him home and he was dead within the month. That's what I meant by his having had a reason for attacking me. I took Guiwenneth from him.'

'And then she was taken from you. Shot dead.'

'A few months later, yes. I became a little too happy, a little too content. I wrote to you because I had to tell *someone* about her ... clearly that was too much for fate. Two days later I found her in a glade, dying. She might have lived if I could have got help to her in the forest, and left her there. I carried her out of the wood, though, and she died.' He stared at me and the expression of sadness hardened to one of resolve. 'But when I'm back in the wood, her myth image in my own subconscious has a chance of being formed ... she might be a little tougher than my father's version, but I can find her again, Steve, if I look hard, if I can find that energy you asked about, if I can get into the deepest part of the wood, to that central vortex ...'

I looked at the map again, at the spiral field around the hog-back glade. 'What's the problem? Can't you find it?'

'It's well defended. I get near it, but I can't ever get beyond the field that's about two hundred yards around it. I find myself walking in elaborate circles even though I'm convinced I've walked straight. I can't get in, and whatever's in there can't get out. All the mythagos are tied to their genesis zones, although the Twigling, and Guiwenneth too, could get to the very edge of the forest, down by the pool.'

But that wasn't true! And I'd spent a shaky night to prove it. I said, 'One of the mythagos has come out of the wood … a tall man with the most unbelievably terrifying hound. He came into the yard and ate a leg of pork.'

Christian looked stunned. 'A mythago? Are you sure?'

'Well, no. I had no idea at all what he was until now. But he stank, was filthy, had obviously lived in the woods for months, spoke a strange language, carried a bow and arrows …'

'And ran with a hunting dog. Yes, of course. It's a late bronze age, early iron age image, very wide-spread. The Irish have taken him to their own with Cuchulainn, made a big hero out of him, but he's one of the most powerful of the myth images, recognizable all across Europe.' Christian frowned, then. 'I don't understand … a year ago I saw him, and avoided him, but he was fading fast, decaying … it happens to them after a while. Something must have fed the mythago, strengthened it …'

'Some *one*, Chris.'

'But who?' It dawned on him, then, and his eyes widened slightly. 'My God. Me. From my own mind. It took the old man years, and I thought it would take me a lot longer, many more months in the woodlands, much more isolation. But it's started already, my own interaction with the vortex …'

He had gone quite pale, and he walked to where his staff was propped against the wall, picked it up and weighed it in his hands. He stared at it, touched the markings upon it.

'You know what this means,' he said quietly, and before I could answer went on, 'She'll form. She'll come back, my Guiwenneth. She may be back already.'

'Don't go rushing off again, Chris. Wait a while; rest.'

He placed his staff against the wall again. 'I don't dare. If she has formed by now, she's in danger. I have to go back.' He looked at me and smiled thinly, apologetically. 'Sorry brother. Not much of a homecoming for you.'

As quickly as this, after the briefest of reunions, I had lost Christian again. He was in no mood to talk, too distracted by the thought of Guiwenneth alone and trapped in the forest to allow me much of an insight into his plans, and into his hopes and fears for some resolution to their impossible love affair.

I wandered through the kitchen and the rest of the house as he gathered his provisions together. Again and again he assured me that he would be gone for no more than a week, perhaps two. If she was in the wood he would have found her by that time; if not, then he would return and wait a while before going back to the deep zones and trying to form her mythago. In a year, he said, many of the more hostile mythagos would have faded into non-existence, and she would be safer. His thoughts were confused, his plan that he would strengthen her to allow her the same freedom as the man and the hound did not seem supportable on the evidence from our father's notes; but Christian was a determined man. If one mythago could escape, then so could the one he loved.

One idea that appealed to him was that I should come with him as far as the glade where we had made camp as children, and pitch a tent there. This could be a regular rendezvous for us, he said, and it would keep his time sense on the right track. And if I spent time in the forest I might encounter other mythagos, and could report on their state. The glade he had in mind was at the edge of the wood, and quite safe.

When I expressed concern that my own mind would begin to produce mythagos, he assured me that it would take months for the first pre-mythago activity to show up as a haunting presence at the edge of my vision. He was equally blunt in saying that, if I stayed in the area for too long, I would certainly start to relate to the woodland, whose aura – he thought – had spread more towards the house in the last few years.

Late the following morning we set off along the south track. A pale yellow sun hung high above the forest. It was a cool, bright day, the air full of the scent of smoke, drifting from the distant farm where the stubbly remains of the summer harvest were being burned. We walked in silence until we came to the mill-pond; I had assumed Christian would enter the oak woodland here, but wisely he decided against it; not so much because of the strange movements we had seen there as children, but because of the marshy conditions. Instead, we walked on until the woodland bordering the track thinned. Here Christian turned off the path.

I followed him inwards, seeking the easiest route between tangles of bracken and nettles, enjoying the heavy stillness. The trees were small, here at the edge, but within a hundred yards they began to show their real age, great gnarled oak-wood trunks, hollow and half-dead, twisting up from the ground, almost groaning beneath the weight of their branches. The ground rose slightly, and the tangled undergrowth was broken by weathered, lichen-covered stubs of grey limestone; we passed over the crest and the earth dipped sharply down, and a subtle change came over the woodland; it seemed darker, somehow, more alive, and I noticed that the shrill September bird-sound of the forest edge was replaced, here, by a more sporadic, mournful song.

Christian beat his way through bramble thickets, and I trudged wearily after, and we soon came to the large glade where, years before, we had made our camp. One particularly large oak tree dominated the surrounds, and we laughed as we traced the faded initials we had once carved there. In its branches we had made out look-out tower, but we had seen very little from that leafy vantage point.

'Do I look the part?' asked Christian, holding his arms out, and I grinned as I surveyed his caped figure, the rune-inscribed staff looking less odd, now, more functional.

'You look like something. Quite what I don't know.'

He glanced around the clearing. 'I'll do my best to get back here as often as I can. If anything goes wrong, I'll try and leave a message if I can't find you, some mark to let you know ...'

'Nothing's going to go wrong,' I said with a smile. It was clear that he didn't wish me to accompany him beyond this glade, and that suited me. I felt a chill, an odd tingle, a sense of being watched. Christian noticed my discomfort and admitted that he felt it too, the presence of the wood, the gentle breathing of the trees.

We shook hands, then embraced awkwardly, and he turned on his heels and paced off into the gloom. I watched him go, then listened, and only when all sound had gone did I set about pitching the small tent.

For most of September the weather remained cool and dry, a dull sort of month, that enabled me to drift through the days in a very low-key state. I worked on the house, read some more of father's notebook (but quickly tired of the repetitive images and thoughts) and with decreasing frequency walked into the woodlands and sat near, or in the tent, listening for Christian, cursing the midges that haunted the place, and watching for any hint of movement.

With October came rain and the abrupt, almost startling realization that Christian had been gone for nearly a month. The time had slipped by, and instead of feeling concerned for him I had merely assumed that he knew what he was doing, and would return when he was quite ready. But he had been absent for weeks without even the slightest sign. He could surely have come back to the glade once, and left some mark of his passing.

Now I began to feel more concern for his safety than perhaps was warranted. As soon as the rain stopped I trudged back through the forest and waited out the rest of the day in the miserable, leaking canvas shelter. I saw hares, and a wood owl, and heard distant movements that did not respond to my cries of 'Christian? Is that you?'

It got colder. I spent more time in the tent, creating a sleeping bag out of blankets and some tattered oilskins I found in the cellar of Oak Lodge. I repaired the splits in the tent, and stocked it with food and beer, and dry wood for fires. By the middle of October I noticed that I could not spend more than an hour at the house before becoming restless, an unease that could only be dispelled by returning to the glade and taking up my watching post, seated cross-legged just inside the tent, watching the gloom a few yards away. On several occasions I took long, rather nervous sorties further into the forest, but I disliked the sensation of stillness and the tingling of my skin that seemed to repeatedly say that I was being watched. All imagination, of course, or an extremely sensitive response to woodland animals, for on one occasion, when I ran screaming and yelling at the thicket wherein I imagined the voyeur was crouched, I saw nothing but a red squirrel go scampering in panic up into the crossed and confused branches of its home oak.

Where *was* Christian? I tacked paper messages as deep in the wood, and in as many locations, as I could. But I found that wherever I walked too far into the great dip that seemed to be swallowing the forest down, I would, at some point within the span of a few hours, find myself approaching the glade, and the tent again. Uncanny yes, and infuriating too; but I began to get an idea of Christian's own frustration at not being able to maintain a straight line in the dense oak-wood. Perhaps, after all, there *was* some sort of field of force, complex and convoluted, that channelled intruders back onto an outward track.

And November came, and it was very cold indeed. The rain was sporadic and icy, but the wind reached down through the dense, browning foliage of the forest and seemed to find its way through clothes and oilskin and flesh to the cooling bones beneath. I was miserable, and my searches for Christian grew more angry, more frustrated. My voice was often hoarse with shouting, my skin blistered and scratched from climbing trees. I lost track of time, realizing on more than one occasion, and with some shock, that I had been two, or perhaps three days in the forest without returning to the house. Oak Lodge grew stale and deserted. I used it to wash, to feed, to rest, but as soon as the worst ravages to my body were corrected, thoughts of Christian, anxiety about him, grew in my mind and pulled me back to the glade, as surely as if I were a metal filing tugged to a magnet.

I began to suspect that something terrible had happened to him; or perhaps not terrible, just natural: if there really were boars in the wood, he might have been gored by one, and be either dead or dragging himself from the heartwoods to the edge, unable to cry for help. Or perhaps he had fallen from a tree, or quite simply gone to sleep in the cold and wet and failed to revive in the morning.

I searched for any sign of his body, or his having passed by, and I found absolutely nothing, although I discovered the spoor of some large beast, and marks on the lower trunks of several oaks that looked like nothing else than the scratchings of a tusked animal.

But my mood of depression passed, and by mid-November I was quite confident again that Christian was alive. My feelings, now, were that he had somehow become trapped in this autumnal forest.

For the first time in two weeks I went into the village, and after obtaining food supplies, I picked up the papers that had been accumulating at the tiny newsagents. Skimming the front pages of the weekly local, I noticed an item concerning the decaying bodies of a man and an Irish wolfhound, discovered in a ditch on farmland near Grimley. Foul play was not suspected. I felt no emotion, apart from a curious coldness, a sense of sympathy for Christian, whose dream of freedom for Guiwenneth was surely no more than that, a fervent hope, a desire doomed to frustration.

As for mythagos, I had only two encounters, neither of them of much note; the first was with a shadowy man-form that skirted the clearing, watching me, and finally ran into the darkness, striking at the trunks of trees with a short, wooden stick. The second meeting was with the Twigling, whose shape I followed stealthily as he walked to the mill-pond and stood in the trees, staring across at the boat-house. I felt no real fear of these manifestations, merely a slight apprehension. But it was only after the second meeting that I began to realize how alien was the wood to the mythagos, and how alien were the mythagos to the wood. These were creatures created far away from their natural age, echoes of the past given substance, equipped with a life, a language and a certain ferocity that was quite inappropriate to the war-scarred world of 1947. No wonder the aura of the woodland was so charged with a sense of solitude, an infectious loneliness that had come to inhabit the body of my father, and then Christian, and which was even now crawling through my own tissues, and would trap me if I allowed it.

It was at this time, too, that I began to hallucinate. Notably at dusk, as I stared into the woodlands, I saw movement at the edge of my vision. As first I put this down to tiredness, or imagination, but I remembered clearly the passage from my father's notebook in which he described how the pre-mythagos, the initial images, always appeared at his peripheral vision. I was frightened at first, unwilling to acknowledge that such creatures could be resident in my own mind, and that my own interaction with the woodland had begun far earlier than Christian had thought; but after a while I sat and tried to see details of them. I failed to do so. I could sense movement, and the occasional manlike shape, but whatever field was inducing their appearance was not yet strong enough to pull them into full view; either that, or my mind could not yet control their emergence.

On the 24th of November I went back to the house and spent a few hours resting and listening to the radio. A thunderstorm passed overhead and I watched the rain and the darkness, feeling quite wretched and cold. But as soon as the air cleared, and the clouds brightened, I draped my oilskin about my shoulders and headed back to the glade. I had not expected to find anything different, and so what should have been a surprise was more of a shock.

The tent had been demolished, its contents strewn and trampled into the sodden turf of the clearing. Part of the guy rope dangled from the higher branches of the large oak, and the ground hereabouts was churned as if there had been a fight. As I walked into the space I noticed that the ground was pitted by strange footprints, round and cleft, like hooves, I thought. Whatever the beast had been it had quite effectively torn the canvas shelter to tatters.

I noticed then how silent the forest was, as if holding its breath and watching. Every hair on my body stood on end, and my heartbeat was so powerful that I thought my chest would burst. I stood by the ruined tent for just a second or two and the panic hit me, making my head spin and the forest seem to lean towards me. I fled from the glade, crashing into the sopping undergrowth between two thick oak trunks. I ran through the gloom for several yards before realizing I was running *away* from the woodland edge. I think I cried out, and turned and began to run back.

A spear thudded heavily into the tree beside me and I had run into the black wood shaft before I could stop; a hand gripped my shoulder and flung me against the tree. I shouted out in fear, staring into the mud-smeared, gnarled face of my attacker. He shouted back at me:

'Shut up, Steve! For God's sake, shut up!'

My panic quietened, my voice dropped to a whimper and I peered hard at the angry man who held me. It was Christian, I realized, and my relief was so intense that I laughed, and for long moments failed to notice what a total change had come about him.

He was looking back towards the glade. 'You've got to get out of here,' he said, and before I could respond he had wrenched me into a run, and was practically dragging me back to the tent.

In the clearing he hesitated and looked at me. There was no smile from behind the mask of mud and browning leaves. His eyes shone, but they were narrowed and lined. His hair was slick and spiky. He was naked but for a breechclout and a ragged skin jacket that could not have supplied much warmth.

He carried three viciously pointed spears. Gone was the skeletal thinness of summer. He was muscular and hard, deep-chested and heavy-limbed. He was a man made for fighting.

'You've got to get out of the wood, Steve; and for God's sake don't come back.'

'What's happened to you, Chris …?' I stuttered, but he shook his head and pulled me across the clearing and into the woods again, towards the south track.

Immediately he stopped, staring into gloom, holding me back. 'What is it, Chris?' And then I heard it too, a heavy crashing sound, something picking its way through the bracken and the trees towards us. Following Christian's gaze I saw a monstrous shape, twice as high as a man, but man-shaped and stooped, black as night save for the great white splash of its face, still indistinct in the distance and greyness.

'God, it's broken out!' said Chris. 'It's got between us and the edge.'

'What is it? A mythago?'

'*The* mythago,' said Chris quickly, and turned and fled back across the clearing. I followed, all tiredness suddenly gone from my body.

'The Urscumug? That's *it*? But it's not human ... it's animal. No human was ever that tall.'

Looking back as I ran, I saw it enter the glade and move across the open space so fast I thought I was watching a speeded up film. It plunged into the wood behind us and was lost in darkness again, but it was running now, weaving between trees as it pursued us, closing the distance with incredible speed.

Quite suddenly the ground went out from under me. I fell heavily into a depression in the ground, to be steadied, as I tumbled, by Christian, who moved a bramble covering across us and put a finger to his lips. I could barely make him out in this dark hidey hole, but I heard the sound of the Urscumug die away, and queried what was happening.

'Has it moved off?'

'Almost certainly not,' said Christian. 'It's waiting, listening. It's been pursuing me for two days, out of the deep zones of the forest. It won't let up until I'm gone.'

'But why, Chris? Why is it trying to kill you?'

'It's the old man's mythago,' he said. 'He brought it into being in the heart-woods, but it was weak and trapped until I came along and gave it more power to draw on. But it was the old man's mythago, and he shaped it slightly from his own mind, his own ego. Oh God, Steve, how he must have hated, and hated *us*, to have imposed such terror onto the thing.'

'And Guiwenneth ...' I said.

'Yes ... Guiwenneth ...' Christian echoed, speaking softly now. 'He'll revenge himself on me for that. If I give him half a chance.'

He stretched up to peer through the bramble covering. I could hear a distant, restless movement, and thought I caught the sound of some animal grumbling deep in its throat.

'I thought he'd failed to create the primary mythago.'

Christian said, 'He died believing that. What would he have done, I wonder, if he'd seen how successful he'd been.' He crouched back down in the ditch. 'It's like a boar. Half boar, half man; it walks upright, but can run like the wind. It paints its face white in the semblance of a human face. Whatever age it lived in, one thing's for sure, it lived a long time before man as *we* understand "man" existed; this thing comes from a time when man and nature were so close that they were indistinguishable.'

He touched me, then, on the arm, a hesitant touch, as if he were half afraid to make this contact with one from whom he had grown so distant.

'When you run,' he said, 'run for the edge. Don't stop. And when you get out of the wood, don't come back. There is no way out for me, now. I'm trapped in this wood by something in my own mind as surely as if I were a mythago myself. Don't come back here, Steve. Not for a long, long time.'

'Chris—' I began, but too late. He had thrown back the covering of the hole and was running from me. Moments later the most enormous shape passed over-head, one huge, black foot landing just inches from my frozen body. It passed by in a split second, but as I scrambled from the hole and began to run I glanced back and the creature, hearing me, glanced back too, and for that instant of mutual contemplation, as we both moved apart in the forest, I saw the face that had been painted across the blackened features of the boar.

The Urscumug opened its mouth to roar, and my father seemed to leer at me.

CODA

One morning, in early spring, I found a brace of hare hanging from one of the pot-hooks in the kitchen; below them, scratched in the yellow paintwork on the wall, was the letter C. The gift was repeated about two months later, but then nothing, and a year has passed.

I have not been back to the wood.

I have read my father's diary ten times if I have read it once, steeping myself in the mystery of his life as much as he had steeped himself in the mystery of his own unconscious links with the primeval woodland. I find, in his erratic recordings, much that tells of his sense of danger, of what – just once – he calls 'ego's mythological ideal', the involvement of the creator's mind which he feared would influence the shape and behaviour of the mythago forms. He had known of the danger, then, but I wonder if Christian had fully comprehended this most subtle of the occult processes occurring in the forest. From the darkness and pain of my father's mind a single thread of gentleness and love had emerged in the fashioning of a girl in a green tunic, dooming her to a helplessness in the forest that was contrary to her natural form. But if she were to emerge again it would be with Christian's mind controlling her, and Christian had no such pre-conceived ideas about a woman's strength or weakness. It would not be the same encounter.

It is summer now. The trees are full-leaved, the forest at its most impenetrable. I stay in the house, out of range, although I've noticed that, at dusk especially, shapes and figures begin to cluster in my peripheral vision. The aura of the woodland has reached the front of the house. Only in the back room, among the books and specimens, can I find a temporary escape from the encroaching dark.

If you've enjoyed these books and would like to read more, you'll find literally thousands of classic Science Fiction & Fantasy titles through the **SF Gateway**

✳

For the new home of
Science Fiction & Fantasy . . .

✳

For the most comprehensive collection
of classic SF on the internet . . .

✳

Visit the SF Gateway

www.sfgateway.com

Robert Holdstock (1948–2009)

Robert Paul Holdstock was born in a remote corner of Kent, sharing his childhood years between the bleak Romney Marsh and the dense woodlands of the Kentish heartlands. He received an MSc in medical zoology and spent several years in the early 1970s in medical research before becoming a full-time writer in 1976. His first published story appeared in the *New Worlds* magazine in 1968 and for the early part of his career he wrote science fiction. However, it is with fantasy that he is most closely associated.

1984 saw the publication of *Mythago Wood*, winner of the BSFA and World Fantasy Awards for Best Novel, and widely regarded as one of the key texts of modern fantasy. It and the subsequent 'mythago' novels (including *Lavondyss*, which won the BSFA Award for Best Novel in 1988) cemented his reputation as the definitive portrayer of the wild wood. His interest in Celtic and Nordic mythology was a consistent theme throughout his fantasy and is most prominently reflected in the acclaimed Merlin Codex trilogy, consisting of *Celtika*, *The Iron Grail* and *The Broken Kings*, published between 2001 and 2007.

Among many other works, Holdstock co-wrote *Tour of the Universe* with Malcolm Edwards, for which rights were sold for a space shuttle simulation ride at the CN Tower in Toronto, and *The Emerald Forest*, based on John Boorman's film of the same name. His story, 'The Ragthorn', written with friend and fellow author Garry Kilworth, won the World Fantasy Award for Best Novella and the BSFA Award for Short Fiction.

Robert Holdstock died in November 2009, just four months after the publication of *Avilion*, the long-awaited, and sadly final, return to Ryhope Wood.

www.robertholdstock.com